VLSI DESIGN
&
TECHNOLOGY

For
**Final Year (BE) Degree Courses in
Electronics/Electronics and Telecommunication Engineering**

**According to New Revised Syllabus of University of Pune
(Effective From July 2011)**

**Also Useful For
Dr. Babasaheb Ambedkar Marathwada University Aurangabad,
Shivaji University, Kolhapur.**

Dr. D. S. BORMANE
M.E. (Electronics), Ph.D.
Principal, Rajarshi Shahu College of Engg.,
Tathwade, PUNE
(Formerly Principal B.V's Women's College of Engg., PUNE.)

DR. M. S. NAGMODE
M.E. (Electronics), Ph. D.
Assistant Professor in E & TC. Deptt.
MIT College of Engineering,
PUNE

V. M. SARDAR
M.E. (Electronics)
Assistance Professor in E & TC Dept.
Jaywantrao Sawant College of Engineering,
Hadapsar, PUNE.

R. N. CHAVAN
M.E. (Electronics)
Assistance Professor, Electronics Dept.
Walchand College of Technologies,
SOLAPUR

NIRALI PRAKASHAN

N1362

VLSI DESIGN & TECHNOLOGY   **ISBN 978-93-81595-15-2**

Fifth Edition   :   **August 2014**

©   :   **Authors**

Published By :
NIRALI PRAKASHAN
Abhyudaya Pragati, 1312, Shivaji Nagar,
Off J.M. Road, PUNE – 411005
Tel - (020) 25512336/37/39, Fax - (020) 25511379
Email : niralipune@pragationline.com

DISTRIBUTION CENTRES

PUNE

Nirali Prakashan
119, Budhwar Peth, Jogeshwari Mandir Lane
Pune 411002, Maharashtra
Tel : (020) 2445 2044, 66022708, Fax : (020) 2445 1538
Email : bookorder@pragationline.com

Nirali Prakashan
S. No. 28/25, Dhyari,
Near Pari Company, Pune 411041
Tel : (020) 24690204 Fax : (020) 24690316
Email : dhyari@pragationline.com
bookorder@pragationline.com

MUMBAI

Nirali Prakashan
385, S.V.P. Road, Rasdhara Co-op. Hsg. Society Ltd.,
Girgaum, Mumbai 400004, Maharashtra
Tel : (022) 2385 6339 / 2386 9976, Fax : (022) 2386 9976
Email : niralimumbai@pragationline.com

DISTRIBUTION BRANCHES

NAGPUR
Pratibha Book Distributors
Above Maratha Mandir, Shop No. 3, First Floor,
Rani Jhanshi Square, Sitabuldi, Nagpur 440012,
Maharashtra, Tel : (0712) 254 7129

BENGALURU
Pragati Book House
House No. 1, Sanjeevappa Lane, Avenue Road Cross,
Opp. Rice Church, Bengaluru – 560002.
Tel : (080) 64513344, 64513355,
Mob : 9880582331, 9845021552
Email:bharatsavla@yahoo.com

JALGAON
Nirali Prakashan
34, V. V. Golani Market, Navi Peth, Jalgaon 425001,
Maharashtra, Tel : (0257) 222 0395
Mob : 94234 91860

KOLHAPUR
Nirali Prakashan
New Mahadvar Road,
Kedar Plaza, 1st Floor Opp. IDBI Bank
Kolhapur 416 012, Maharashtra. Mob : 9855046155

CHENNAI
Pragati Books
9/1, Montieth Road, Behind Taas Mahal, Egmore,
Chennai 600008 Tamil Nadu, Tel : (044) 6518 3535,
Mob : 94440 01782 / 98450 21552 / 98805 82331, Email : bharatsavla@yahoo.com

RETAIL OUTLETS

PUNE

Pragati Book Centre
157, Budhwar Peth, Opp. Ratan Talkies,
Pune 411002, Maharashtra
Tel : (020) 2445 8887 / 6602 2707, Fax : (020) 2445 8887

Pragati Book Centre
Amber Chamber, 28/A, Budhwar Peth,
Appa Balwant Chowk, Pune : 411002, Maharashtra,
Tel : (020) 20240335 / 66281669
Email : pbcpune@pragationline.com

Pragati Book Centre
676/B, Budhwar Peth, Opp. Jogeshwari Mandir,
Pune 411002, Maharashtra
Tel : (020) 6601 7784 / 6602 0855

PBC Book Sellers & Stationers
152, Budhwar Peth, Pune 411002, Maharashtra
Tel : (020) 2445 2254 / 6609 2463

MUMBAI
Pragati Book Corner
Indira Niwas, 111 - A, Bhavani Shankar Road, Dadar (W), Mumbai 400028, Maharashtra
Tel : (022) 2422 3526 / 6662 5254, Email : pbcmumbai@pragationline.com

www.pragationline.com   info@pragationline.com

SYLLABUS

UNIT-I

VHDL Modeling and Design Flow :

Introduction to VLSI : Complete VLSI design flow (with reference to an EDA tool), Sequential Data flow, and Structural Modeling. Functions, Procedures, Attributes, Test benches, Synthesizable, and Non-synthesizable statements; Packages and configurations, Modeling in VHDL with examples of circuits such as counters, shift registers, bi-directional bus, etc.

UNIT-II

FSM and Sequential Logic Principles :

Sequential Circuits, Meta-stability Synchronization, Design of Finite State Machines, and State minimization, FSM CASE STUDIES - Traffic Light control, Lift Control and UART STA and DTA.

UNIT-III

Programmable Logic Devices :

Introduction to CPLDs, Study of architecture of CPLD, and Study of the architecture of FPGA.

UNIT IV

System-On-Chip :

One, two phase clock, Clock distribution, Power distribution, Power optimization, SRC and DRC, Design validation, Global routing, Switch-box routing, Off chip connections, I/O Architectures, Wire parasitics, EMI immune design. Study of memory-Basics of memory include Types of Memory cells and Memory architectures, Types of memory, based on architecture specific and application specific viz. SRAM, DRAM, SDRAM, FLASH, FIFO.

UNIT V

CMOS VLSI :

CMOS parasitics, equivalent circuit, body effect, Technology Scaling, λ parameter, Detail study of Inverter Characteristics, Power dissipation, Power delay product, CMOS combinational logic design and W/L calculations, Transmission gates, Introduction to CMOS layout.

UNIT VI

Testability :

Need of Design for testability, Introduction to Fault Coverage, Testability, Design-for-Testability, Controllability and Observability, Stuck-at Fault Model, Stuck-Open and Stuck-Short faults, Boundary Scan check, JTAG technology; TAP Controller and TAP Controller State Diagram. Scan path, Full and Partial scan, BIST.

◇◇◇

CONTENTS

UNIT 1

CHAPTER 1: ANALOG CMOS DESIGN   **1.1 – 1.38**

1.1	Introduction	1.1
1.2	MOS Transistor – Small Signal Model	1.4
	1.2.1 MOS Switch	1.7
	1.2.2 MOS Diode	1.9
	1.2.3 MOS Diode as a Voltage Divider	1.10
	1.2.4 MOS Switch as a Resistor	1.11
1.3	Current Sink and Source using MOS	1.11
	1.3.1 Current Sink	1.11
	1.3.2 Current Source	1.12
	1.3.3 Current Mirror	1.13
	1.3.4 Inverters using CMOS Transistors	1.14
	1.3.5 Small Signal Model for the Active Load Inverter	1.15
	1.3.6 Parasitic Capacitance in Active Load Inverter	1.17
	1.3.7 Current Source Inverter	1.17
	1.3.8 Push-Pull Inverter	1.19
1.4	Differential Amplifiers	1.21
	1.4.1 CMOS Differential Amplifier using NMOS Transistors	1.23
	1.4.2 CMOS Differential Amplifier using a Current Mirror Load	1.25
	1.4.3 CMOS Differential Amplifier using p-channel Input MOSFETs	1.26
	1.4.4 Small Signal Model of the CMOS Differential Amplifier	1.27
1.5	Cascode Amplifier	1.27
1.6	CMOS Operational Amplifiers	1.29
	1.6.1 Two-stage Op-amp	1.29
	1.6.2 Ideal Op-amp	1.30
	1.6.3 Non-ideal Op-amp	1.31
1.7	Classification of Op-amps	1.33
	1.7.1 Classical Two-stage CMOS Op-amp	1.34
1.8	Folded Cascode Op-amp	1.35
1.9	Design of Op-amps	1.36
	Questions	1.38

UNIT 2

CHAPTER 2 : DIGITAL CMOS DESIGN	**2.1 – 2.70**
2.1 Introduction	2.1
2.2 MOS Structure	2.2
2.3 MOS Transistor	2.3
2.3.1 MOSFET Structure	2.3
2.3.2 The Enhancement mode MOSFET	2.4
2.3.3 Calculation of Threshold Voltage	2.6
2.3.4 Depletion Type MOSFETs	2.8
2.4 Logic Levels	2.14
2.5 Implementation of Gates using NMOS	2.16
2.5.1 NMOS Inverter	2.16
2.5.2 NMOS NAND	2.17
2.5.3 NMOS NOR	2.18
2.6 Implementation of Gates using CMOS	2.19
2.6.1 CMOS NAND	2.19
2.6.2 CMOS NOR	2.20
2.6.3 Complex Gate Design	2.20
2.6.4 Multiplexer using CMOS	2.21
2.7 CMOS Inverter	2.22
2.8 Noise Margin	2.44
2.9 Fan-out and Fan-in	2.45
2.10 Transmission Gate (TG)	2.46
2.11 Power Dissipation	2.50
2.11.1 Static Dissipation	2.51
2.11.2 Dynamic Dissipation	2.51
2.11.3 Short Circuit Dissipation	2.52
2.11.4 Total Power Dissipation	2.53
2.12 β_n/β_p Ratio	2.54
2.13 Design Considerations	2.55
2.13.1 Layer Representations	2.55
2.13.2 Design Style – Stick Diagrams	2.56
2.13.3 Design Rules	2.61
2.13.4 Layout Diagrams	2.62
2.14 MOSFET Fabrication	2.63
Questions	2.68

CHAPTER 3 : INTRODUCTION TO VLSI DESIGN	3.1 – 3.10

3.1	Introduction	3.1
3.2	Computer Aided Design (CAD) Process	3.1
	3.2.1 Design Entry	3.1
	3.2.2 Initial Synthesis	3.3
	3.2.3 Functional Simulation	3.3
	3.2.4 Logic Synthesis and Optimization	3.3
	3.2.5 Physical Design	3.3
	3.2.6 Timing Simulation	3.4
	3.2.7 Chip Implementation	3.4
3.3	Introduction To VLSI Design	3.4
	3.3.1 Classification of IC Technology	3.4
	3.3.2 What is VLSI ?	3.4
3.4	Programmable Logic Devices (PLDs)	3.5
3.5	EDA Tools	3.5
3.6	VLSI Design Flow	3.6
3.7	Comparison between VHDL and VERILOG	3.9
3.8	Top-Down and Bottom-Up Design Approach	3.9
	Questions	3.10

UNIT 3

CHAPTER 4 : DESIGN USING VHDL	4.1 – 4.138

4.1	Introduction to VHDL	4.1
4.2	Features of VHDL	4.3
4.3	Levels of Abstraction	4.4
4.4	Elements of VHDL	4.6
4.5	Language Elements	4.6
	4.5.1 Identifier	4.6
	4.5.2 Object Types	4.7
	4.5.3 Data Types	4.7
	4.5.4 Predefined VHDL Data Types	4.16
	4.5.5 Operators	4.17
4.6	Entity	4.20
4.7	Architecture	4.23
4.8	Concurrent Statements	4.26
	4.8.1 Concurrent Signal Assignment	4.26
	4.8.2 Block Statement	4.30
	4.8.3 Component Instantiation Statement	4.32
	4.8.4 Generate Statement	4.38
	4.8.5 Process Statement	4.40

4.9	Sequential Statements	4.44
	4.9.1 If Statement	4.44
	4.9.2 Case Statement	4.45
	4.9.3 Null Statement	4.47
	4.9.4 Loop Statement	4.47
	4.9.5 Next Statement	4.48
	4.9.6 exit Statement	4.49
	4.9.7 report statement	4.50
4.10	Styles of Modeling	4.55
	4.10.1 Data Flow Modeling	4.55
	4.10.2 Behavioral Modeling	4.55
	4.10.3 Structural Modeling	4.56
4.11	Package and Library	4.58
	4.11.1 Package	4.58
	4.11.2 Design Libraries	4.60
	4.11.3 Std_Logic_1164 [Multivalued Logic]	4.63
4.12	Generic	4.64
4.13	Configuration	4.65
	4.13.1 Configuration Declaration	4.65
	4.13.2 Configuration Specification	4.67
4.14	Subprogram	4.69
	4.14.1 Function	4.69
	4.14.2 Procedure	4.71
4.15	Attributes	4.74
	4.15.1 Value Kind Attributes	4.74
	4.15.2 Function Kind Attributes	4.76
	4.15.3 Signal Kind Attributes	4.78
	4.15.4 Type Kind Attributes	4.78
	4.15.5 Range Kind Attributes	4.78
4.16	Alias	4.79
4.17	Operator Overloading	4.79
4.18	Subprogram Overloading	4.81
4.19	Multiple Drivers and Resolution Function	4.83
4.20	Delays in VHDL	4.86
4.21	Test Bench	4.116
	4.21.1 Waveform Generation	4.119
	Questions	4.135

CHAPTER 5 : SIMULATION — 5.1 – 5.18

5.1	What is Simulation ?	5.1
5.2	Simulation at Different Levels	5.1
5.3	Types of Simulation	5.4
5.4	Software Languages Vs HDLs (Why is Concurrency Required ?)	5.6
5.5	How is Concurrency Achieved ?	5.7
5.6	How Logic Simulator Works ?	5.9
	5.6.1 Steps in Simulation	5.9
	5.6.2 Simulation Process	5.11
5.7	Difference in Execution of Sequential and Concurrent Statements	5.15
5.8	Types of Simulator	5.16
	Questions	5.18

CHAPTER 6 : SYNTHESIS — 6.1 – 6.24

6.1	What is Synthesis ?	6.1
6.2	Synthesis Process	6.1
6.3	Synthesis Flow (Steps in Synthesis Process)	6.7
6.4	Advantages of Using Synthesis	6.10
6.5	Expectations from Synthesis Tools	6.10
6.6	Hardware Modeling Examples	6.11
6.7	Synthesis Guidelines	6.16
6.8	Place and Route	6.21
	Questions	6.24

CHAPTER 7 : SEQUENTIAL MACHINE DESIGN — 7.1 – 7.56

7.1	Introduction	7.1
7.2	Block Diagram of a Sequential Circuit	7.1
7.3	Types of Sequential Circuits	7.2
7.4	Timing Considerations in Sequential Circuits	7.4
7.5	Finite State Machines (FSM)	7.5
	7.5.1 General Model of a Sequential or Finite State Machine	7.5
	7.5.2 Classification of FSM	7.7
7.6	Design of Sequential Circuit	7.9
	7.6.1 State Description and State Diagram	7.9
	7.6.2 Analysis and Design of Sequential Circuits	7.27
7.7	FSM Modeling using VHDL	7.28
7.8	Lift Controller	7.48
	7.8.1 Operation of the Lift Controller	7.48
7.9	Traffic Light Controller	7.51
	Questions	7.55

UNIT 4

CHAPTER 8 : PROGRAMMABLE LOGIC DEVICES   8.1 – 8.112

8.1	Introduction	8.1
8.2	Programming Technologies	8.2
	8.2.1 Fusible Link Technologies	8.2
	8.2.2 Antifuse Technologies	8.2
	8.2.3 PROM-based Technologies	8.3
	8.2.4 EPROM-based Technologies	8.3
	8.2.5 EEPROM-based Technologies	8.4
	8.2.6 Flash Technology	8.5
8.3	ASIC	8.7
	8.3.1 Full Custom ASICs	8.7
	8.3.2 Semi-Custom ASICs	8.7
	8.3.2.1 Standard Cell-based ASICs	8.8
	8.3.2.2 Gate Array-based ASICs	8.9
	8.3.2.3 Mixed Mode and Analogue ASICs	8.10
8.4	Programmable Logic Devices	8.10
8.5	Read Only Memory (ROM) as a PLD	8.11
	8.5.1 ROM Organization	8.12
	8.5.2 Circuit Realization using ROM	8.14
8.6	Programmable Logic Arrays (PLAs)	8.17
	8.8.1 Architecture of PLA	8.18
	8.8.2 Circuit Realization using PLA	8.23
8.7	Programmable Array Logic (PAL)	8.26
8.8	Complex Programmable Logic Devices (CPLDs)	8.29
	8.8.1 Block Diagram of CPLD	8.29
	8.8.2 CPLD Programming	8.31
	8.8.3 CPLD Packaging	8.32
	8.8.4 Xilinx's XC9500XV CPLD	8.32
8.9	Field Programmable Gate Array (FPGA)	8.52
	8.9.1 FPGA	8.52
	8.9.2 Comparison of SRAM and Antifuse FPGA	8.53
	8.9.3 Example-FPGA Families	8.56
	8.9.4 Details of FPGA Architecture	8.57
	8.9.5 Configurable I/O Blocks	8.57
	8.9.6 Clock Circuitry	8.59
	8.9.7 Small versus Large Granularity	8.59
8.10	Xilinx, XC5200 Series FPGA	8.60

8.11	XC5200	8.61
	8.11.1 GRM	8.61
	8.11.2 VersaBlock	8.61
	8.11.3 Logic Cell of XC5200	8.63
	8.11.4 VersaRing I/O Interface	8.63
	8.11.5 IOB	8.63
	8.11.6 Pin Descriptions	8.64
	8.11.7 Configuration	8.64
8.12	Spartan – II 2.5 V FPGA Family	8.65
8.13	Spartan – 3 FPGA Family	8.67
	8.13.1 Spartan-3 Family Architecture	8.68
	8.13.2 Configuration	8.69
	8.13.3 Pin Out Description of Spartan-3 Family	8.70
8.14	ProASIC Plus Flash Family FPGAs	8.71
	8.14.1 ProASIC^{PLUS} Architecture	8.72
	8.14.2 Flash Switch	8.73
	8.14.3 Logic Tile	8.74
	8.14.4 Routing Resources	8.74
	8.14.5 Clock Resources	8.75
	8.14.6 Input/Output Blocks	8.75
	8.14.7 Boundary Scan (JTAG)	8.76
	8.14.8 ProASIC^{PLUS} Clock Management System	8.77
	8.14.9 User Security	8.78
	8.14.10 Embedded Memory	8.78
	8.14.11 Pin Description	8.79
8.15	Comparison of CPLD and FPGA	8.80
8.16	Comparison of PLDs, ASICs and FPGAs	8.80
8.17	Functions of FPGAs Today	8.81
8.18	XC4000 Series FPGA	8.81
	8.18.1 Designing with FPGAs	8.109
8.19	Comparison of CPLDs and FPGAs	8.110
	Questions	8.111

UNIT 5

CHAPTER 9 : FAULT TOLERANCE AND TESTABILITY 9.1 – 9.34

9.1	Testability	9.1
9.2	Need of Design for Testability	9.2
9.3	Defects or Faults on a Chip	9.3
9.4	Delay Faults	9.4

9.5	Controllability and Observability	9.5
	9.5.1 Controllability	9.8
	9.5.2 Observability	9.8
9.6	Fault Coverage	9.9
9.7	Comparison of Verification and Testability	9.10
9.8	Test Methodology	9.10
9.9	Testing Combinational Logic	9.11
	9.9.1 Testing AND-OR Network	9.12
9.10	Boundary Scan	9.16
9.11	Test Access Port (TAP)	9.17
	9.11.1 Test Access Port Architecture	9.17
	9.11.1.1 TAP Controller	9.18
	9.11.1.2 Instruction Register (IR)	9.18
	9.11.1.3 Test Data Registers (DRs)	9.19
	9.11.1.4 Boundary Scan Registers	9.19
9.12	Testing Sequential Logic	9.21
9.13	Scan Testing	9.22
9.14	Boundary Scan Test (BST)	9.24
9.15	Built-In-Self-Test	9.28
9.16	Joint Test Access Group (JTAG)	9.31
9.17	Full scan and Partial scan	9.33
9.18	Fault Simulation	9.33
	Questions	9.34

UNIT 6

CHAPTER 10 : SIGNAL INTEGRITY AND SYSTEM-ON-CHIP   10.1 – 10.50

10.1	Introduction	10.1
10.2	What is SoC ?	10.1
10.3	Important Issues in SoC Design	10.3
10.4	Clocked Systems and Clocking Strategies	10.4
	10.4.1 Single Phase Clock	10.5
	10.4.2 Two Phase System	10.6
	10.4.3 System Timing	10.9
	10.4.4 Clock Distribution	10.9
10.5	Power Optimization	10.13
10.6	Power Distribution	10.15

10.7   Wire and Vias   10.17
       10.10.1 Wire Parasitics   10.18
       10.10.2 Wire Resistance   10.21
10.8   Design Validation   10.21
10.9   Floorplanning   10.23
       10.9.1   Global Routing   10.26
       10.9.2   Switchbox Routing   10.28
       10.9.3   Off-chip-Connections   10.30
10.10 I/O Architecture   10.32
       10.10.1 Pad Design in a Chip   10.33
                10.10.1.1 Input pad Design   10.34
                10.10.1.2 Output pad Design   10.35
                10.10.1.3 Three State pad Design   10.35
10.11 Layout Design Rules and Analysis Tools in CMOS   10.36
       10.11.1 A Layout Editor   10.36
       10.11.2 Design Rule Checker (DRC) Program   10.36
       10.11.3 Circuit Extraction   10.37
10.12 Memory Elements   10.37
       10.12.1 High Density Memories   10.38
       10.12.2 RAM   10.39
       10.12.3 Memory-Chip Architecture   10.40
       10.12.4 Static RAM   10.41
                10.12.4.1 TTL RAM Cell   10.41
                10.12.4.2 MOS RAM Cell   10.42
       10.12.5 Dynamic RAM   10.43
       10.12.6 Non-Volatile RAM (NVRAM)   10.45
       10.12.7 Row Decoders in RAM Cells   10.45
       10.12.8 Sense Amplifiers   10.48
       10.12.9 First In First Out Memory (FIFO)   10.48
       10.12.10 Read Only Memory (ROM)   10.49
       Questions   10.50
Appendix – A   **A.1 – A.6**
Appendix – B   **B.1 – B.12**
Appendix – C   **C.1 – C.6**
University Question Papers : May 2008 to May 2011   **P.1 – P.10**

◊◊◊

PREFACE TO THE FIRST EDITION

It gives us great pleasure to bring out the book on **"VLSI Design"**. VLSI Design is one of the dominated technologies of the century used to design and manufacture integrated circuits at very complex level.

This book is useful for the students of final year degree courses in Electronics / Electronics and Telecommunication Engineering of Pune university. It is also useful for the students of Babasaheb Ambedkar Marathawada University, Aurangabad and Shivaji University, Kolhapur and also for other Universities from Maharashtra.

This book gives the theoretical and practical knowledge of the VLSI Design using VHDL language.

This book is organized in 6 Units.

UNIT I : Unit I covers the VLSI design flow and introduces different EDA tools. It also describes the Hardware description language, VHDL in detail and throughout the rest of the book VHDL is used to design digital systems.

UNIT II : Unit II covers finite state machine and sequential circuits. Also the design of Traffic light control, Lift control and UART is described.

UNIT III : Unit III gives details of different programmable logic devices such as CPLDs and FPGAs. It describes the details of CPLD XC9500 family, FPGA 5200, Spartan 2 and Spartan 3 details. It also gives the details of ProASIC PLUS family of Actel.

UNIT IV : Unit IV covers the topics related to the system-on-chip design. It gives the clock and power distribution schemes. Different routing methods, different parasitics associated with the design are covered. Different types of memories and their architecture are also described.

UNIT V : Unit V covers CMOS technology and basics of CMOS manufacturing. CMOS Inverter design and its characteristics is given in detail. W/L calculations, Transmission Gates are also given.

Unit VI : Unit VI covers the Testability in detail. It covers need of Design for Testability, Controllability and Observability. Different fault modes, Scan methods such as Boundary Scan check, JTAG technology are discussed.

Finally, there are appendices. Appendix A summarizes VHDL language, Appendix B gives design implementation using Xilinx ISE 6.3i and modelism tools and Appendix C provides sample synthesis report. It has been tried to put forward best in this book. The authors will welcome reader's doubt and suggestions to improve the text and contents of this book.

*** Dassara**
2nd October 2006.
Pune.   **Authors**

ACKNOWLEDGEMENT

We take this opportunity to thank Management JSPM's Pune, Terana College of Engineering, Osmanabad and Pune Vidyarthi Griha's College of Engineering and Technology, Pune for the encouragement and support to write this book.

Also we thank to Principal, Head of Department and colleagues of our relative colleges for giving inspiration and moral support.

Nirali Prakashan put the book what we thought into reality. Our sincere thanks to **Shri. Dineshbhai Furia, Shri. Jignesh Furia** and **Shri M.P. Munde**. The book could be completed in time due to sincere and hard work of Nirali Prakashan's staff namely Mrs. Prachi Sawant and Mr. Kiran Velankar.

We will be missing if we don't thank our family and wives whose moral support and wishes have gone a long way in making of this book.

Thanks to all those whose names are not mentioned here, but were directly or indirectly associated with this task.

Constructive criticisms for improvement of this book are welcome.

*** Dassara**
2nd October 2006.
Pune.   **Authors**

Chapter 1: ANALOG CMOS DESIGN

1.1 Introduction

CMOS technology has become the most commonly used technology for analog circuit design in a mixed signal environment. This unit presents the material necessary to introduce CMOS analog circuit design. It gives the introduction and concepts related to the Enhancement MOSFET, its parasitics such as resistors, diodes, etc.

VLSI technology has developed to the point where millions of transistors can be integrated on a single die or chip. They now integrate complete systems on a chip by combining both analog and digital functions. Complementary metal oxide semiconductor (CMOS) technology has been mainly used semiconductor technology for the mixed signal implementations. CMOS provides density and power savings on the digital side. It also provides a good mix of components for analog side. Therefore, the **CMOS technology is widely used**.

CAD (computer aided design) methodologies have been very successful in automating the design of **digital systems** given a behavioral description of the function desired. But that is not the case for Analog Circuit design. Analog circuit design still requires a **"hands on"** design approach in general. It is necessary to understand and examine the design process of analog circuits and to identify those principles that will increase design productivity. This unit deals with the CMOS analog circuit design.

IC (Integrated Circuit) design is separated into two major categories: analog and digital. The term **"mixed signal"** is widely used term describing circuits with both analog and digital circuitry on the **same silicon substrate**.

Circuit design in the process of developing a circuit from the given properties or specifications. Analog integrated circuit design includes following steps.

    (1) Design definition or Specification.

    (2) Implementation or Synthesis.

    (3) Simulation or Modeling.

(4) Geometrical (layout) description.

(5) Parasitic extraction.

(6) Simulation using the geometrical parasitics.

(7) Fabrication of the IC.

(8) Testing and verification.

Fig. 1.1 shows the approach of the design of analog integrated circuit.

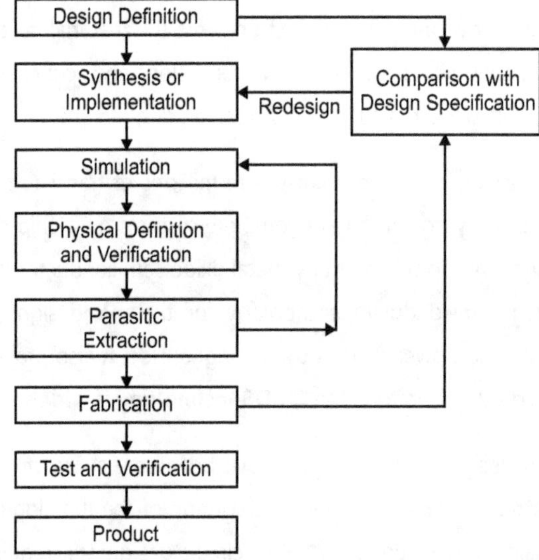

Fig. 1.1: Analog integrated circuit design process

The step is to define the design using specifications, then synthesize the function. These steps are crucial since they determine the performance capability of the design. The next step is the simulation of the circuit i.e. to predict the performance of the circuit. The designer makes approximations about the physical design of the circuit initially. After the completion of the layout, simulations are checked using parasitic information derived from the layout. At this step, the designer may redesign the circuit using the simulation results of the parasitic components, to improve the circuit's performance.

After that, the designer can address the next step i.e. the geometrical description (layout) of the circuit. The layout design should be checked with the electrical performance of the circuit. After the layout, it is necessary to include the geometrical effects in additional simulations. After that, the circuit is ready for fabrication.

Symbols used in the design:

Fig. 1.2: n-channel enhancement mode MOSFET

Fig. 1.3: p-channel enhancement mode MOSFET

Fig. 1.4: Independent voltage and current sources

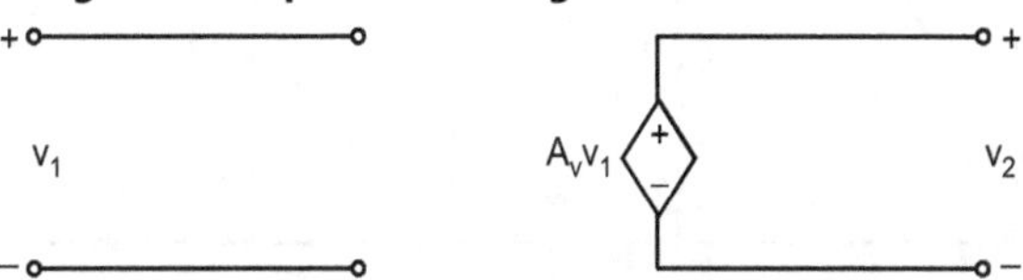

Fig. 1.5: Voltage controlled voltage source (VCVS)

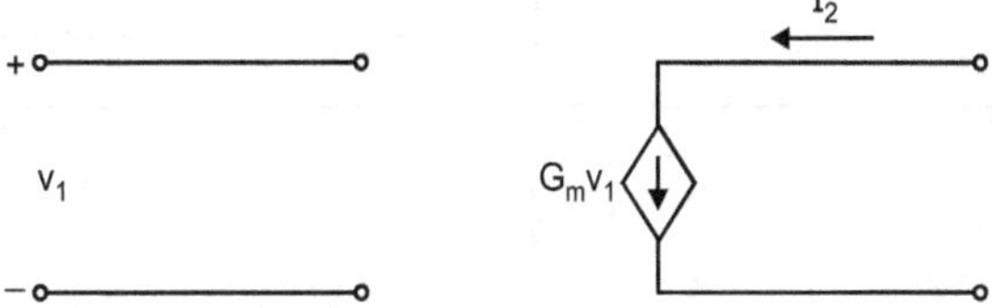

Fig. 1.6: Voltage controlled current source (VCCS)

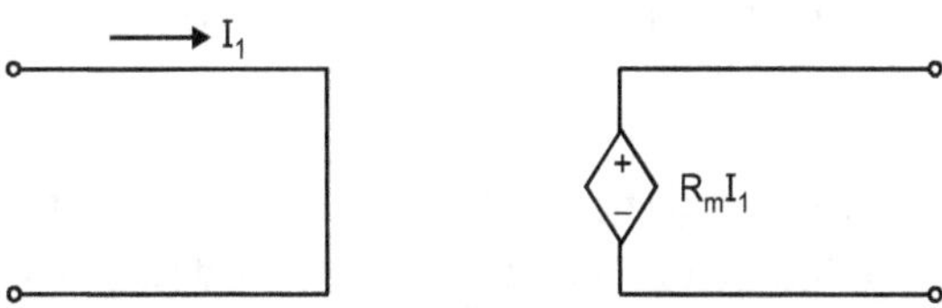

Fig. 1.7: Current controlled voltage source (CCVS)

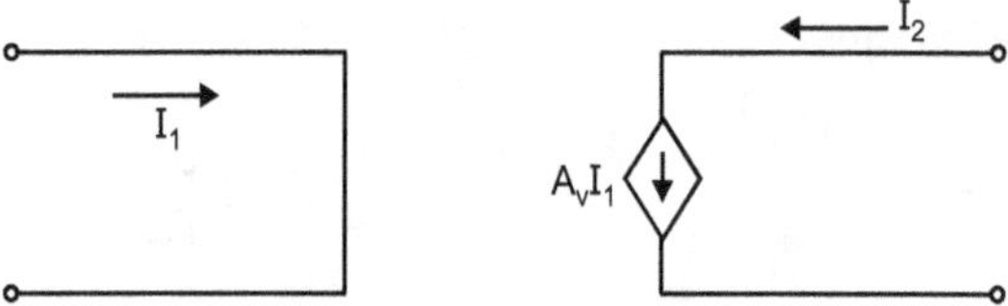

Fig. 1.8: Current controlled current source (CCCS)

1.2 MOS Transistor - Small Signal Model

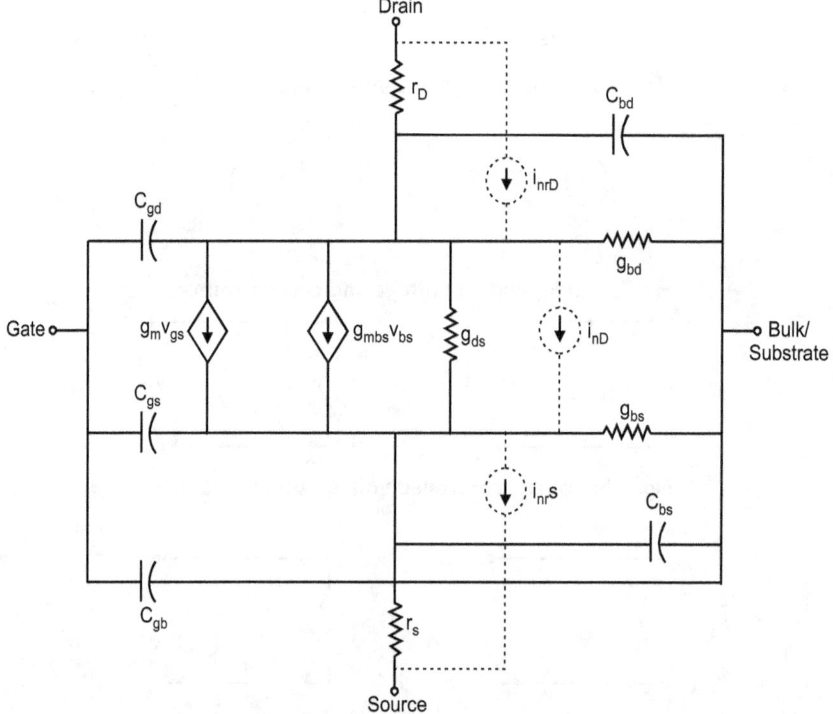

Fig. 1.9: MOS transistor-Small signal model

In small signal model, the parameters of the small signal model will be designated by lower case subscripts.

g_{bd} and g_{bs} are the equivalent conductances of the bulk to drain and bulk to source junctions. These junctions are normally reverse biased, therefore the conductances are very small. These are defined as,

$$g_{bd} = \frac{\partial i_{BD}}{\partial v_{BD}}$$

and
$$g_{bs} = \frac{\partial i_{BS}}{\partial v_{BS}}$$

These conductances are calculated at the quiescent point $\cong 0$.

The channel conductances are g_m, g_{mbs} and g_{ds}. They are defined as,

$$g_m = \frac{\partial i_D}{\partial v_{GS}}$$

$$g_{mbs} = \frac{\partial i_D}{\partial v_{BS}}$$

and
$$g_{ds} = \frac{\partial i_D}{\partial v_{DS}}$$

All these are evaluated at the quiescent point.

The values of these small signal parameters depend on which region the quiescent point occurs in.

In the saturated region, g_m can be found as,

$$g_m = \sqrt{(2k'\ W/L)\ |I_D|\ (1 + \lambda\ v_{DS})}$$

$$g_m \approx \sqrt{(2k'\ W/L)\ |I_D|} \qquad\qquad \dots (1)$$

Above equation indicates the dependence of the small-signal parameters on the large signal operating conditions.

The small signal **channel transconductance (g_{mbs})** due to v_{SB} is found by

$$g_{mbs} = \frac{-\partial i_D}{\partial v_{SB}} = -\left(\frac{\partial i_D}{\partial v_T}\right)\left(\frac{\partial v_T}{\partial v_{SB}}\right) \qquad\qquad \dots (2)$$

By using $\left(\dfrac{\partial i_D}{\partial v_T}\right) = -\left(\dfrac{\partial i_D}{\partial v_{GS}}\right)$, we get,

$$g_{mbs} = g_m \frac{\gamma}{2\ (2\ |\phi_F| + |\ v_{SB}|)^{1/2}} = \eta g_m \qquad\qquad \dots (3)$$

where 'v' indicates the **body factor**.

This transductance will become important in small signal analysis of the MOS transitor when the ac value of the source-bulk potential v_{SB} is not zero.

The small signal **channel conductance, g_{ds} (g_o)** is given as,

$$g_{ds} \;=\; g_o \;=\; \frac{I_D\lambda}{1 + \lambda V_{DS}} \approx I_D\lambda \qquad \text{... (4)}$$

The channel conductance will be dependent on L through λ. It is inversely proportional to L.

Some model parameters for a typical CMOS n-well process:

(1) v_{TO} : Threshold voltage ($v_{BS} = 0$).

(2) k': Transconductance parameter (in saturation).

(3) γ : Bulk threshold parameter.

(4) λ: Channel length modulation parameter.

(5) $2 \mid \phi_F \mid$: Surface potential at strong inversion.

Typical values of these parameters are:

Parameter	n-channel	p-channel	Unit
v_{TO}	0.7 ± 0.15	-0.7 ± 0.15	V
k'	$110.0 \pm 10\%$	$50.0 \pm 10\%$	$\mu A/V^2$
γ	0.4	0.57	$V^{1/2}$
λ	0.04 (L = 1 μm)	0.05 (L = 1 μm)	V^{-1}
$2 \mid \phi_F \mid$	0.7	0.8	V

The transconductance parameter β is given in terms of physical parameters as,

$$\boxed{\beta \;=\; k'\frac{W}{L} \cong \mu_o\, C_{ox} \cdot \frac{W}{L}} \quad (A/V^2)$$

When devices are characterized in the non-saturated region with low gate and drain voltages, the value for k' is approximately equal to $\mu_o\, C_{ox}$.

where $\qquad\qquad\qquad \mu_o$ = Surface mobility of the channel for the n-channel or p-channel device (cm^2/V-s)

$$C_{ox} \;=\; \frac{\varepsilon_{ox}}{t_{ox}} \;=\; \text{Capacitance per unit area of the gate oxide (F/cm}^2)$$

1.2.1 MOS Switch

The main advantage of MOS technology is that it provides a good switching characteristics.

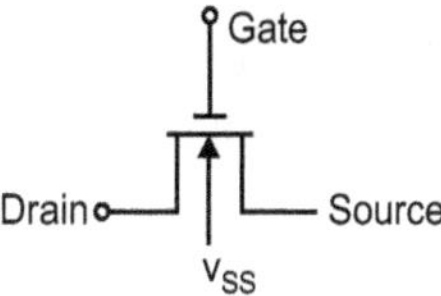

Fig. 1.10: An n-channel transistor as a switch

The MOS switch finds many applications in IC design. The switch can be used to implement some useful functions such as

    (1) Simulation of a resistor.

    (2) Multiplexing and modulation.

    (3) Transmission gate in digital circuits.

Fig. 1.11 shows the n-channel MOS used as a switch. Now, we begin with the characteristics of a **voltage-controlled switch**. Fig. 1.11 shows a model for the device.

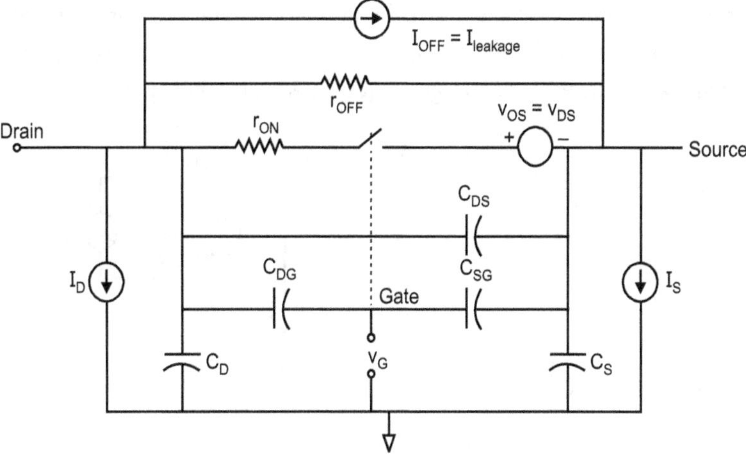

Fig. 1.11: Model for a non-ideal switch

The voltage v_G controls the state of the switch i.e. ON or OFF. The most important characteristics of a switch are its ON resistance, r_{ON} and its OFF resistance, r_{OFF}. In ideal case r_{ON} is zero and r_{OFF} is infinite. But, in practical case, r_{ON} is never zero and r_{OFF} is never infinite.

V_{DS} represents the small voltage that may exist between the terminal drain and source, when the swtich is in the ON state.

I_{OFF} represents the leakage current that may flow in the OFF state of the switch.

Currents I_D and I_S represent leakage currents from the switch terminals to ground.

The parasitic capacitors are an important consideration in IC technology. Capacitors C_D and C_S are the parasitic capacitors between the switch terminals-drain and source.

C_{DS}: parasitic capacitor between the switch terminals-drain and source.

C_{DG}: parasitic capacitor between drain and gate.

C_{GS}: parasitic capacitor between gate and source.

The ON resistance of the MOS transistor consists of the series combination of r_D, r_S and whatever channel resistance exists. By the design of the MOS device, the values of r_D and r_S are small, therefore the channel resistance is considered as the ON resistance.

The small signal channel resistance is given as,

$$r_{ON} = \left.\frac{1}{\partial i_D/\partial v_{DS}}\right|_Q = \frac{L}{k'W\,(v_{GS} - v_T - v_{DS})}$$

where Q designates the quiescent point of the transistor.

Fig. 1.12 shows the graph of drain current of an n-channel transistor as a function of the voltage across the drain and source terminals, plotted for the equal increasing steps of v_{GS} (v_G). Note that, as the value of voltage v_{GS} (v_G) goes on increasing, the drain current also increases.

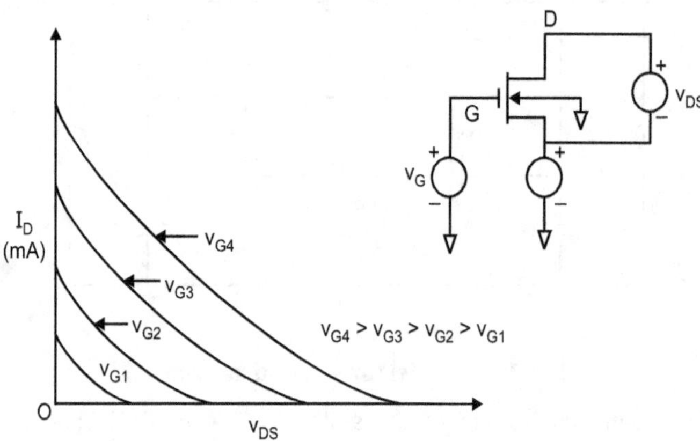

Fig. 1.12: I-V characteristics of an n-channel transistor operating as a switch

The limitation of this switch is the **clock feedthrough effect**. Clock feedthrough effect is also called as the charge injection and charge feedthrough. This effect is due to the coupling capacitance from the gate to both source and drain. This coupling allows charge to be transferred from the gate signal to the source and drain nodes. It is an undesirable effect. But, we cannot avoid it.

Advantages of MOS transistors:

    (1) They require small area.

    (2) They dissipate very little power.

    (3) They provide reasonable values of r_{ON} and r_{OFF} for most applications.

1.2.2 MOS Diode

N-channel MOS diode is formed by shorting drain and gate of the MOS transistor as shown in Fig. 1.13. The I-V characteristics are similar to a pn-junction diode. The MOS diode is used as a component of a current mirror and for level translation.

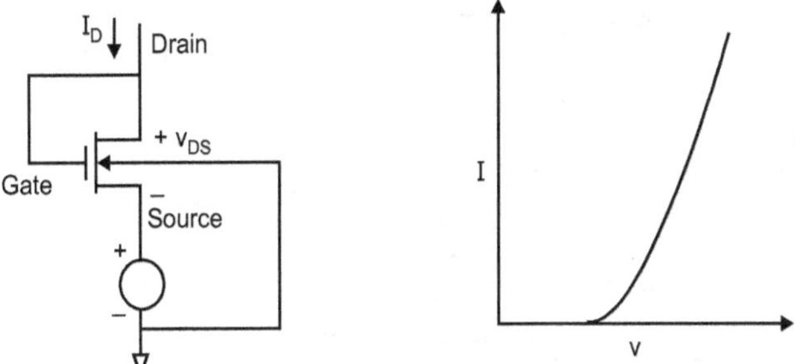

Fig. 1.13: N-channel MOS diode and I-V characteristics

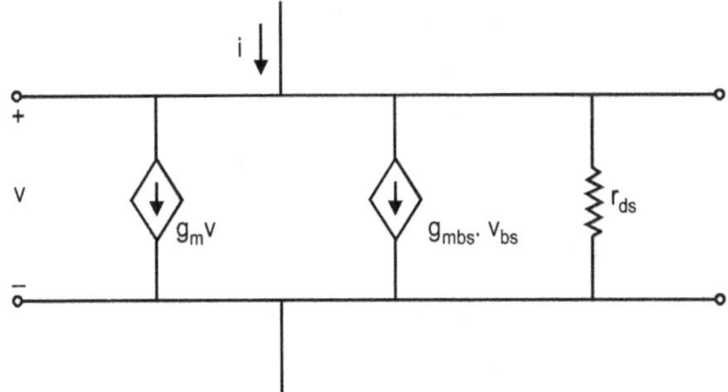

Fig. 1.14: Small signal model

The drain current in saturation is given by,

$$I = I_D = \left(\frac{k'W}{L}\right)[(v_{GS} - v_T)^2]$$

$$\boxed{I_D = \frac{\beta}{2}(v_{GS} - v_T)^2} \qquad \dots (1)$$

or $$\boxed{V = v_{GS} = v_{DS} = v_T + \sqrt{2I_D/\beta}} \qquad \dots (2)$$

If V and I are given then the remaining variables can be designed by using equations (1) and (2) and solving for the value of β.

For diode, gate is connected to the drain, it means that v_{DS} controls I_D. Therefore, the channel transconductance becomes a channel conductance. The small signal model of a MOS diode (excluding capacitors) is shown in Fig. 1.14.

The small signal resistance of a MOS diode is,

$$r_{out} = \frac{1}{g_m + g_{mbs} + g_{ds}} \approx \frac{1}{g_m} \qquad \dots (3)$$

where g_m is greater than g_{mbs} or g_{ds}.

1.2.3 MOS Diode as a Voltage Divider

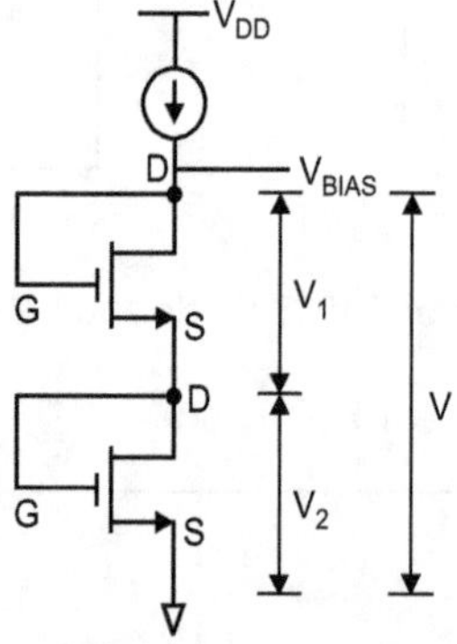

Fig. 1.15: Voltage division using MOS diode

As shown in Fig. 1.15, the bias voltage is generated with respect to ground (V_{BIAS}). Noting that $v_{DS} = v_{GS}$ for both devices,

$$v_{DS} = \sqrt{2I\beta} + v_T = v_{ON} + v_T$$
$$v_{BIAS} = v_{DS_1} + v_{DS_2} = 2v_{ON} + 2v_T$$

As shown in Fig. 1.15,

$$v = v_1 + v_2$$

Therefore, the voltage division takes place in the above circuit.

MOS diode is also called as the active resistor.

1.2.4 MOS Switch as a Resistor

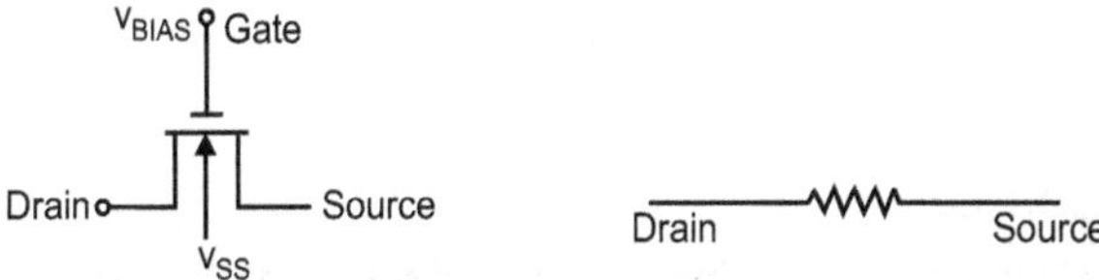

Fig. 1.16: Floating active resistor using a single MOS transistor

The MOS switch shown in Fig. 1.16 is also called as a resistor. The transistor's drain and source form the two ends of a floating resistor. The range of resistance values is large but nonlinear. When the transistor is operated in the non-saturation region, the resistance can be calculated as

$$r_{ds} = \frac{L}{k'W\,(v_{GS} - v_T)} \qquad \ldots (1.4)$$

where v_{DS} is assumed to be small.

1.3 Current Sink and Source using MOS

The MOS device is used as a current sink and current source. Current sink and current source are actually two terminal components. The current at any instant of time is independent of the voltage across their terminals.

1.3.1 Current Sink

Fig. 1.17 shows the current sink using MOS device. The gate voltage is applied to whatever voltage is necessary to create the desired value of current. In the non-saturated region, the MOS device is not a good current source.

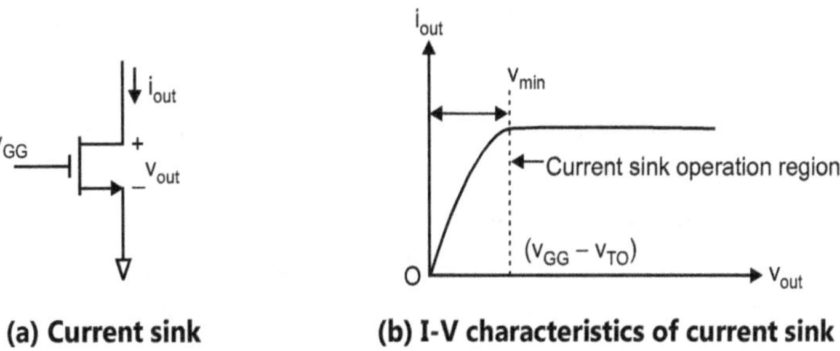

(a) Current sink   **(b) I-V characteristics of current sink**

Fig. 1.17

The voltage across the current sink must be larger than v_{min} in order for the current sink to perform properly.

$$V_{OUT} \geq V_{GG} - V_{TO}$$

If the source and bulk are both connected to ground, then the small signal output resistance is given by,

$$r_{out} = \frac{1 + \lambda V_{DS}}{\lambda I_D} \approx \frac{1}{\lambda \cdot I_D}$$

1.3.2 Current Source

Fig. 1.18 shows the current source using a p-channel transistor. The gate is applied with the constant potential. This current source works for values of v_{out} given by

$$V_{out} \leq V_{GG} + |V_{TO}|$$

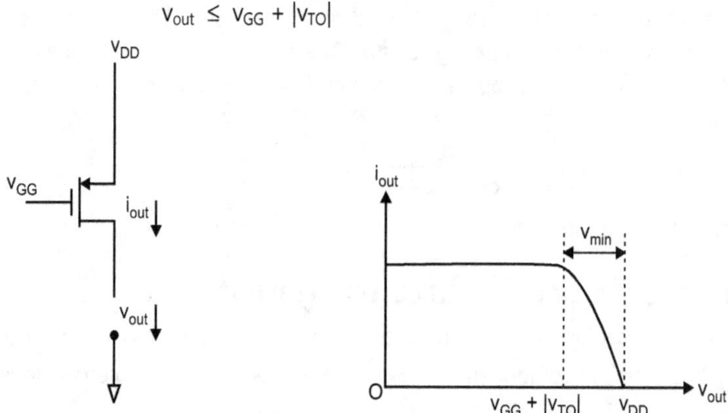

(a) Current source	**(b) Current-voltage characteristics of current source**

Fig. 1.18

The small signal output resistance of the current source is given by,

$$r_{out} = \frac{1 + \lambda V_{DS}}{\lambda \cdot I_D} \approx \frac{1}{\lambda \cdot I_D}$$

Advantage of current sink and current source is their simplicity. But, we need to increase the performance of the current sink.

(1) One improvement is to increase the small signal output resistance. It results in a more constant current over the range of v_{out} values.

(2) The second improvement is to reduce the value of v_{min}, thus allowing a larger range of v_{out} over which the current sink/source works properly.

To improve small signal output resistance by using the circuit shown below in Fig. 1.19.

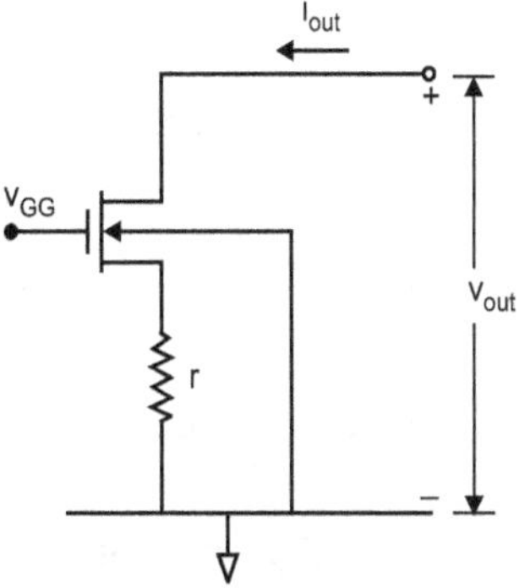

Fig. 1.19: The output resistance of a resistor 'r' increasing technique

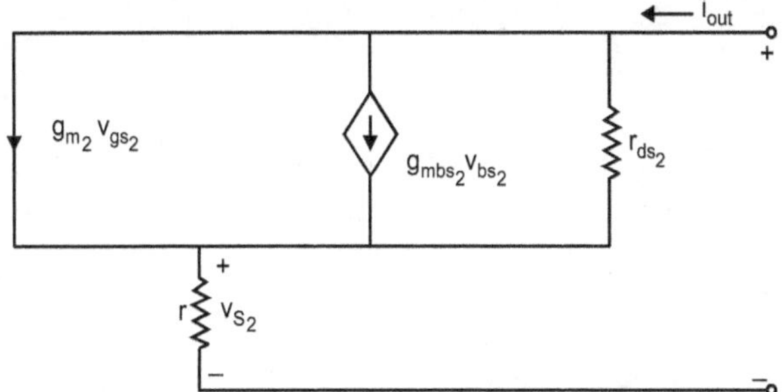

Fig. 1.20: Small signal model of circuit in Fig. 1.19

It uses the common gate configuration to multiply the source resistance r by the approximate voltage gain of the common gate configuration with an infinite load resistance. The value of output resistance r_{out} can be calculated from the small signal model of Fig. 1.20, as

$$r_{out} = \frac{V_{out}}{i_{out}} = r + r_{ds_2} + [(g_{m2} + g_{mbs2})\, r_{ds_2}]\, r$$

$$\approx (g_{m2}\, r_{ds_2})\, r$$

where $g_{m\ rds_2} \gg 1$ and $g_{m2} > g_{mbs2}$.

1.3.3 Current Mirror

The n-channel current mirror is shown in Fig. 1.21. The current mirror uses the principle that, if the gate-source potentials of two identical MOS transistors are equal, the channel currents should be equal. The current i_1 is assumed to be defined by a current source, i_o is the output or mirrored current.

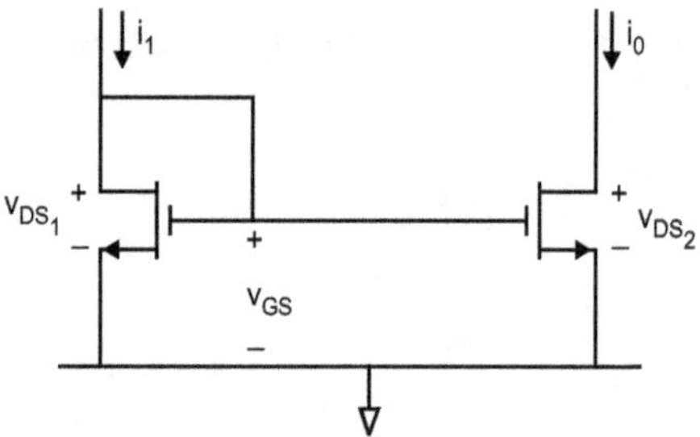

Fig. 1.21: n-channel current mirror

Transistor M_1 is in saturation because $v_{DS_1} = v_{GS_1}$. The ratio of i_0 to i_1 is

$$\frac{i_0}{i_1} = \left(\frac{L_1 W_2}{W_1 L_2}\right)\left(\frac{v_{GS} - v_{T_2}}{v_{GS} - v_{T_1}}\right)^2\left[\frac{1 + \lambda v_{DS_2}}{1 + \lambda v_{DS_1}}\left(\frac{k_2'}{k_1'}\right)\right] \qquad \dots (1)$$

The components of the current mirror are processed on the same integrated circuit. Therefore, all the physical parameters such as v_T and k' are identical for both devices (M_1 and M_2). Therefore, the equation (1) simplifies to

$$\frac{i_0}{i_1} = \left(\frac{L_1 W_2}{W_1 L_2}\right)\left(\frac{1 + \lambda v_{DS_2}}{1 + \lambda v_{DS_1}}\right) \qquad \dots (2)$$

If $v_{DS_1} = v_{DS_2}$, then equation (2) becomes

$$\frac{i_0}{i_1} = \left(\frac{L_1 W_2}{W_1 L_2}\right) \qquad \dots (3)$$

From equation (3), the i_0/i_1 is a function of the aspect ratios, which is under the control of the designer.

1.3.4 Inverters using CMOS Transistors

There are three types of inverting CMOS amplifiers using active load. These are

- (i)   Active PMOS load inverter.

- (ii) Current source load inverter.

- (iii) Push-pull inverter.

Active PMOS load inverter:

Fig. 1.22 shows the diagram of active PMOS load inverter. It is a low gain inverting stage. It has highly predictable small and large signal characteristics.

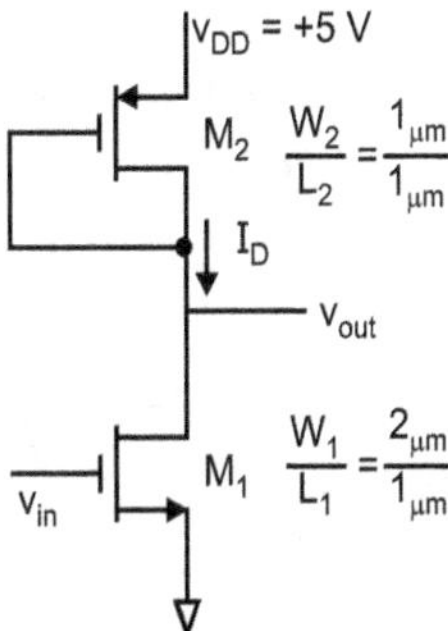

Fig. 1.22: Active PMOS load inverter

The characteristics of active PMOS load inverter is shown in Fig. 1.23.

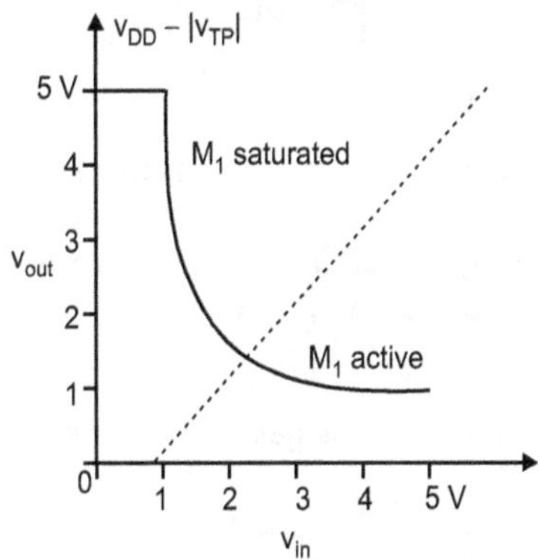

Fig. 1.23: v_{in} versus v_{out} characteristics of the PMOS active load inverter

The maximum output voltage $v_{out\,(max)}$ is equal to $v_{DD} - |v_{TP}|$.

$$v_{out\,(max)} \approx v_{DD} - |v_{TP}|$$

1.3.5 Small Signal Model for the Active Load Inverter

Small signal model of the active load inverter is given above.

The small signal voltage gain of the inverter with an active resistor load is given from Fig. 1.24.

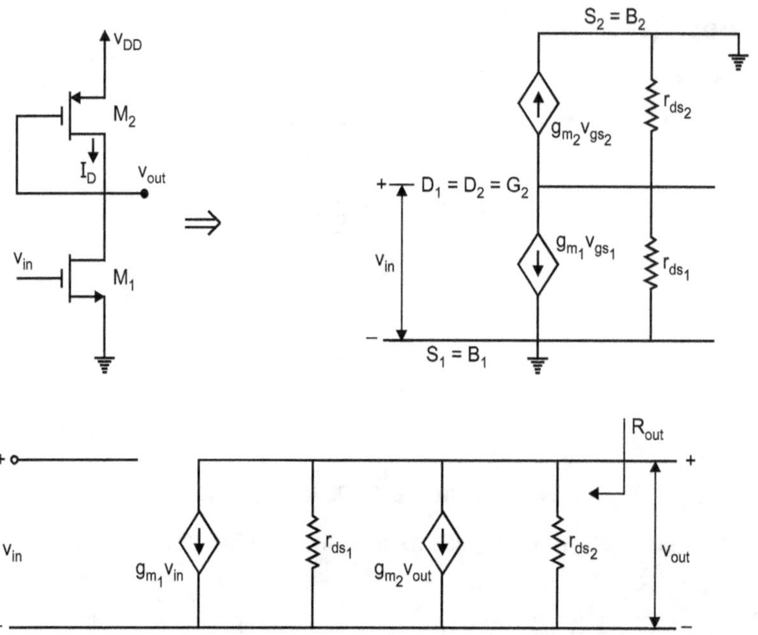

Fig. 1.24: Small signal model of active load inverter

The gain is expressed by summing the currents at the outputs to get

$$g_{m_1} v_{in} + g_{ds_1}\, v_{out} + g_{m_2}\, v_{out} + g_{ds_2}\, v_{out} = 0 \qquad \ldots (1)$$

Now, solving above equation for the voltage gain v_{out}/v_{in}, gives

$$\frac{v_{out}}{v_{in}} = \frac{-g_{m_1}}{g_{ds_1} + g_{ds_2} + g_{m_2}} \cong -\frac{g_{m_1}}{g_{m_2}} = -\left(\frac{k_N' W_1 L_2}{k_P' L_1 W_2}\right)^{1/2} \qquad \ldots (2)$$

The small signal output resistance of the small signal model is given by,

$$R_{out} = \frac{1}{g_{ds_1} + g_{ds_2} + g_{m_2}} \cong \frac{1}{g_{m_2}} \qquad \ldots (3)$$

From equation (3), the output resistance of the active-resistive load inverter will be low because of the low resistance of the diode connected to transistor M_2. This low output resistance is very useful in situations, when a large bandwidth is required from an inverting gain stage.

1.3.6 Parasitic Capacitance in Active Load Inverter

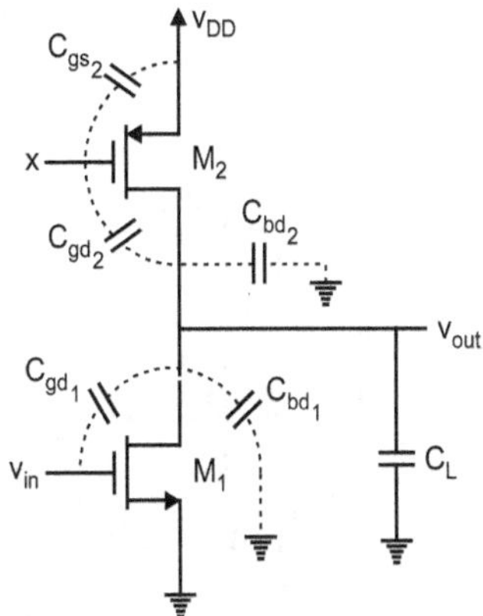

Fig.1.25: Inverter and its parasitic capacitances

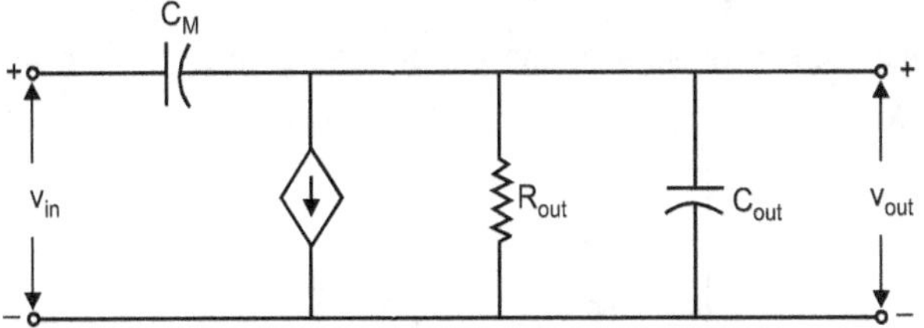

Fig. 1.26: Small signal model

Fig. 1.26 shows the different parasitic capacitances associated with the inverter.

C_{bd_1} and C_{bd_2} represent the bulk capacitances, C_{dd_1} and C_{gd_2} represent the gate to drain capacitances. These are also called as overlap capacitances.

C_L is the load capacitance seen by the inverter.

In Fig. 1.26,

$$R_{out} = (g_{ds_1} + g_{ds_2} + g_{m_2})^{-1} \cong g_{m_2}^{-1}$$
$$C_M = C_{gd_1}$$
$$C_{out} = C_{bd_1} + C_{bd_2} + C_{gs_2} + C_L$$

1.3.7 Current Source Inverter

We need higher gain for the inverter. Therefore, current source inverter is used. Current source inverter has higher gain than the active load inverting amplifier. It is shown in

Fig. 1.27. In this, instead of a PMOS diode as a load, a current source load is used. The current source is a common-gate configuration using a p-channel transistor with the gate connected to a dc bias voltage v_{G_2}.

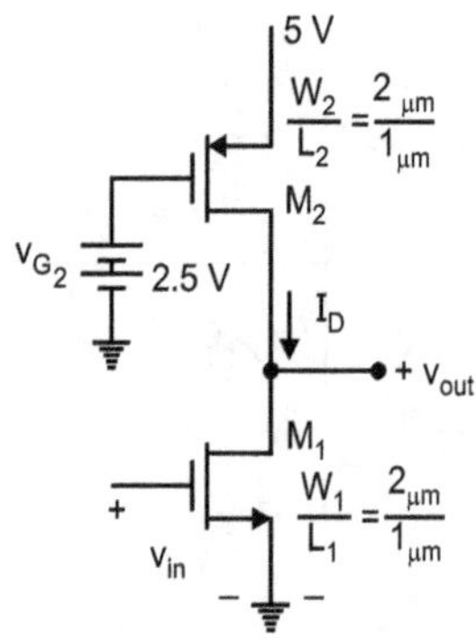

Fig. 1.27: Current source load inverter

The voltage transfer characteristics of the current source inverter is given graphically as shown in Fig. 1.28.

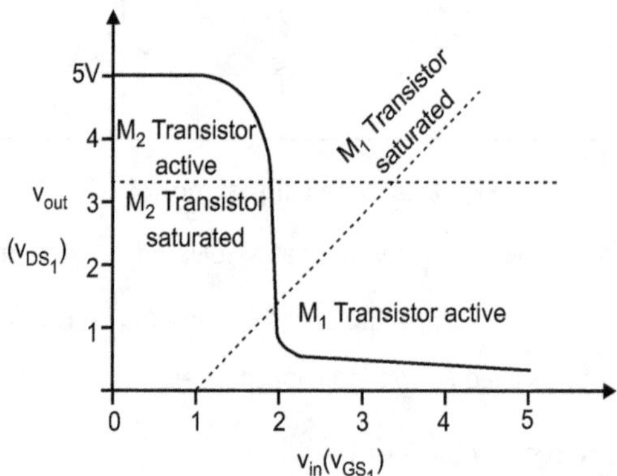

Fig. 1.28

As seen from the graph, the maximum positive output voltage is

$$\boxed{V_{out\,(max)} \cong V_{DD}} \qquad \ldots (1)$$

whereas, in case of active PMOS load inverter, $v_{out\,(max)}$ is less than current source load inverter.

The small signal voltage gain is given as

$$\frac{V_{out}}{V_{in}} \propto \frac{1}{\sqrt{I_D}} \qquad \ldots (2)$$

From equation (2), it is observed that as the drain current decreases, the gain increases.

The small signal output resistance of the CMOS inverter with a current source load is given by

$$R_{out} = \frac{1}{g_{ds_1} + g_{ds_2}} \qquad \text{... (3)}$$

$$C_M = C_{gd_1} \qquad \text{... (4)}$$

$$C_{out} = C_{gd_2} + C_{bd_1} + C_{bd_2} + C_L \qquad \text{... (5)}$$

1.3.8 Push-Pull Inverter

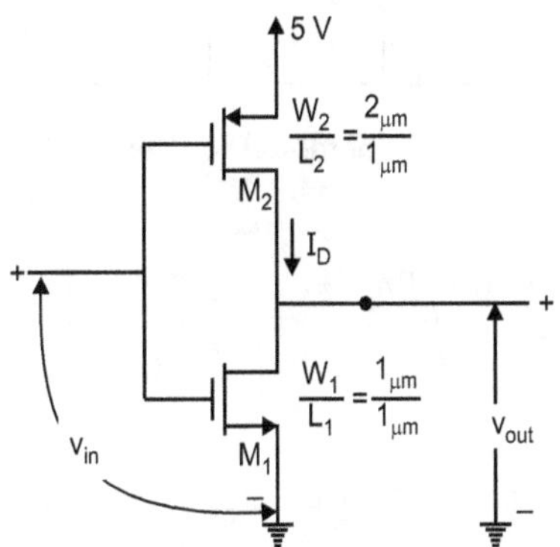

Fig. 1.29: Push-pull inverter

In push-pull inverter, the gates of transistors M_1 and M_2 are connected together. The voltage transfer function characteristics are shown in Fig. 1.30.

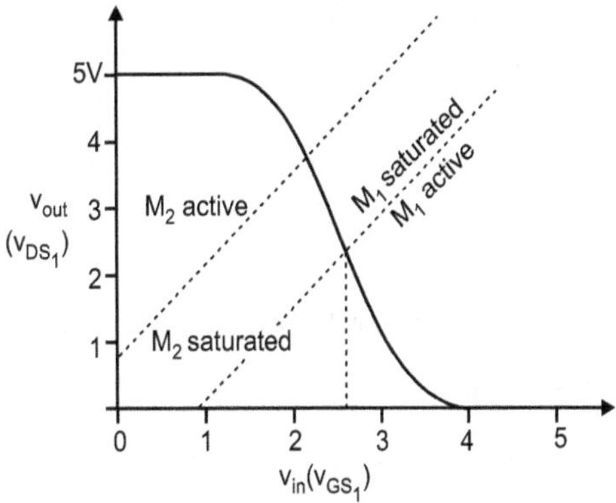

Fig. 1.30

After comparing the characteristics between the current-source and push-pull inverter, it is observed that the push-pull inverter has a higher gain assuming identical transistors. Both the transistors are being driven by v_{in}.

Small signal model for the CMOS inverter is shown in Fig. 1.31.

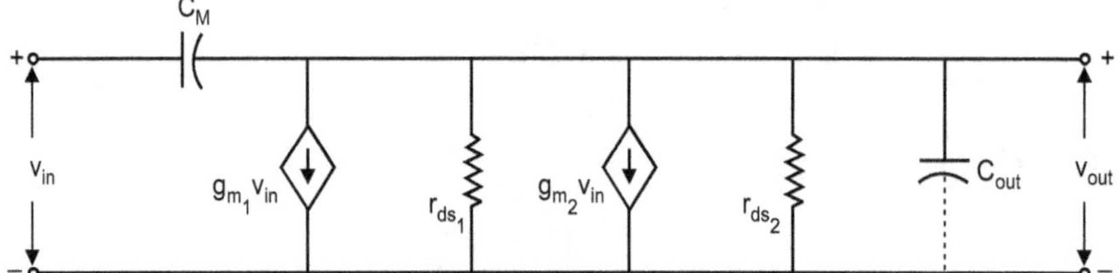

Fig. 1.31: Small signal model for the CMOS inverter

The small signal voltage gain is given by,

$$\frac{V_{out}}{V_{in}} \propto \sqrt{\frac{2}{I_D}}$$

In this case also, the voltage gain is inversely proportional to the drain current. The noise model for the push-pull CMOS inverter is shown in Fig. 1.32.

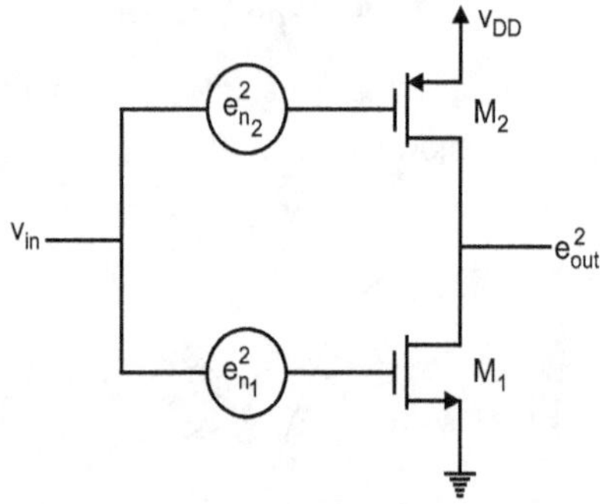

Fig. 1.32: Noise model of the push-pull CMOS inverter

M_1 and M_2 are the noise-free MOSFETs.

$e_{n_1}^2$ and $e_{n_2}^2$ are the mean square-voltage noise spectral density.

e_{out}^2 indicates the output voltage noise spectral density.

The output voltage noise spectral density of this inverter is given as,

$$e_{out}^2 = (g_{m_1} R_{out})^2\, e_{n_1}^2 + (g_{m_2} R_{out})^2\, e_{n_2}^2 \qquad \text{... (1)}$$

The equivalent input voltage noise spectral density of the push-pull inverter (e_{eq}) is obtained by dividing e_{out}^2 by square of the gain.

$$e_{eq} = \sqrt{\left(\frac{g_{m_1}\, e_{n_1}}{g_{m_1} + g_{m_2}}\right)^2 + \left(\frac{g_{m_2}\, e_{n_2}}{g_{m_1} + g_{m_2}}\right)^2} \qquad \text{... (2)}$$

If the transconductances are balanced i.e. $g_{m_1} = g_{m_2}$, then the noise contribution of each device is divided by 2.

1.4 Differential Amplifiers

Differential amplifier is very compatible with the integrated-circuit technology. It serves as the input stage to most op-amps.

The symbol of differential amplifier is shown in Fig. 1.33.

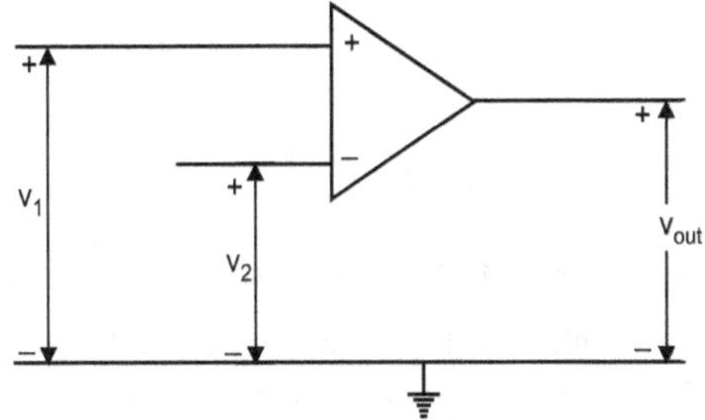

Fig. 1.33: Differential amplifier symbol

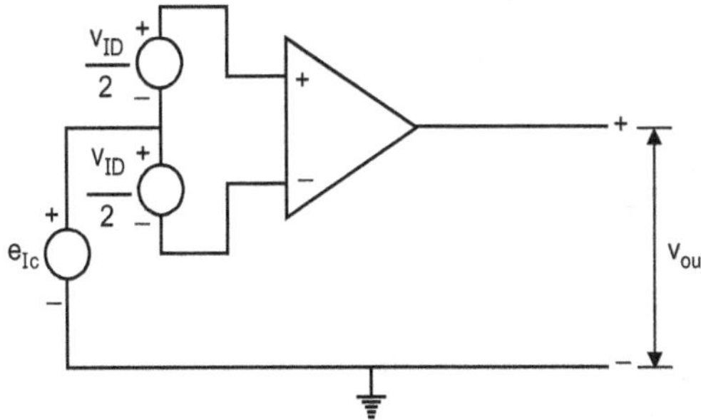

Fig. 1.34: Differential mode (v$_{ID}$) and common mode (v$_{IC}$) input voltages

The voltages v_1, v_2 and v_{out} are called as the single-ended voltages. It means that, they are defined with respect to ground. The differential mode input voltage v_{ID}, is defined with respect to ground.

$$v_{ID} = |v_1 - v_2|$$

... (1)

v_{ID} is the difference between v_1 and v_2 voltages.

The common mode input voltage v_{IC} is given by the average values of v_1 and v_2.

$$v_{IC} = \frac{v_1 + v_2}{2}$$

... (2)

v_1 and v_2 can also be given as,

$$v_1 = v_{IC} + \frac{v_{ID}}{2}$$

... (3)

and

$$v_2 = v_{IC} - \frac{v_{ID}}{2}$$

... (4)

The output voltage for the differential amplifier is given by

$$v_{out} = A_{VD}\, v_{ID} \pm A_{VC}\, v_{IC}$$

$$= A_{VD}\, (v_1 - v_2) \pm A_{VC} \left(\frac{v_1 + v_2}{2} \right)$$

where A_{VD} is the differential mode voltage gain and A_{VC} is the common-mode voltage gain.

The differential amplifier is mainly used to amplify only the difference between two different potentials regardless of the common mode value. The important characteristic of the differential amplifier is the common mode rejection ratio (CMRR). CMRR is the ratio of the magnitude of the differential gain to the common mode gain.

$$CMRR = \left| \frac{A_{VD}}{A_{VC}} \right|$$

In ideal case, the A_{VC} is zero and therefore CMRR is infinite.

Offset voltage also affects the performance of the differential amplifier. Ideally, when the input terminals of the differential amplifier are connected together, the output voltage is at a desired quiescent point. In a practical differential amplifier, the output offset voltage is the difference between the actual output voltage and the ideal output voltage when the input terminals are connected together.

If the output offset voltage is divided by the differential voltage gain of the differential amplifier, then it is called as the input offset voltage. Typically, the input offset voltage of a CMOS differential amplifier is 5-20 mV.

1.4.1 CMOS Differential Amplifier using NMOS Transistors

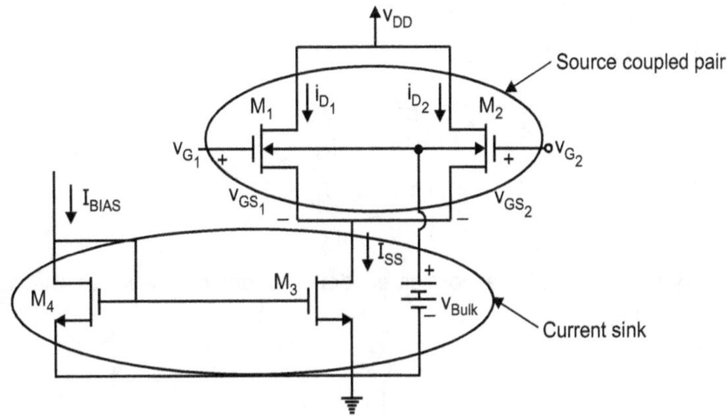

Fig. 1.35: Differential amplifier using NMOS transistor

As shown in Fig. 1.35, the CMOS differential amplifier that uses n-channel MOSFET's, M_1 and M_2 to form a differential amplifier.

M_1 and M_2 transistors are biased with a current sink I_{SS} connected to the sources of M_1 and M_2. M_1 and M_2 form the source coupled pair. M_3 and M_4 are used to implement current sink I_{SS}. Source terminals of M_1 and M_2 are connected to the bulk voltage v_{bulk}.

The n-channels are fabricated in p-well CMOS technology, as shown in Fig. 1.36.

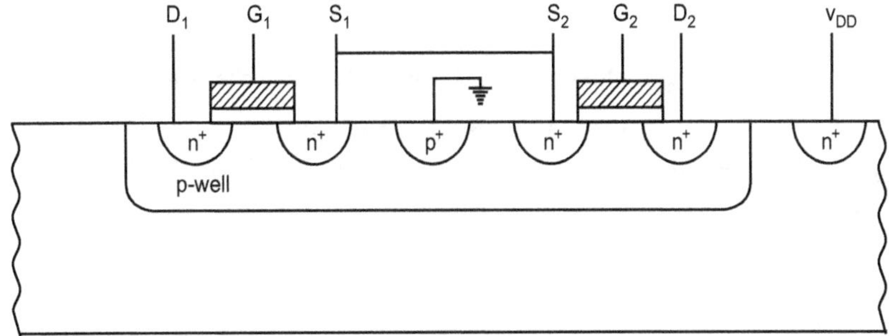

Fig. 1.36: Cross-section of M_1 and M_2 in a p-well CMOS technology

The large signal analysis study begins by assuming that M_1 and M_2 are perfectly matched and they are always in saturation.

The large signal behavior is given as,

$$v_{ID} = v_{GS_1} - v_{GS_2} = \left(\frac{2i_{D_1}}{\beta}\right)^{1/2} - \left(\frac{2i_{D_2}}{\beta}\right)^{1/2} \qquad \ldots (1)$$

and $\qquad I_{SS} = i_{D_1} + i_{D_2} \qquad \ldots (2)$

Solving above equations for i_{D_1} and i_{D_2},

$$i_{D_1} = \frac{I_{SS}}{2} + \frac{I_{SS}}{2}\left(\frac{\beta v_{ID}^2}{I_{SS}} - \frac{\beta^2 v_{ID}^4}{4I_{SS}^2}\right)^{1/2} \qquad \ldots (3)$$

and $\qquad i_{D_2} = \frac{I_{SS}}{2} - \frac{I_{SS}}{2}\left(\frac{\beta v_{ID}^2}{I_{SS}} - \frac{\beta^2 v_{ID}^4}{4I_{SS}^2}\right)^{1/2} \qquad \ldots (4)$

Fig. 1.37 shows the graph of the normalized drain current of M_1 versus the normalized differential input voltage.

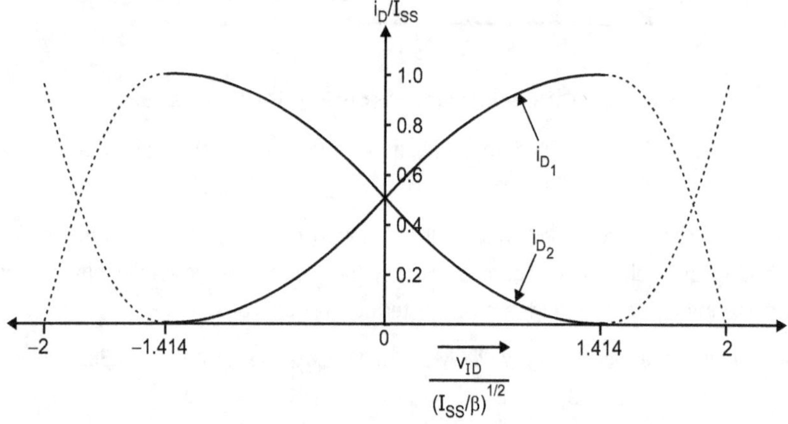

Fig. 1.37: Graph of large signal transconductance characteristics

of a CMOS differential amplifier

The differential transconductance of the differential amplifier is given by differentiating i_{D_1} with respect to v_{ID} and setting $v_{ID} = 0$,

$$g_m = \frac{\partial i_{D_1}}{\partial v_{ID}}(v_{ID} = 0) = (\beta I_{SS}/4)^{1/2}$$

$$g_m = \left(\frac{k_1' I_{SS} W_1}{4L_1}\right)^{1/2} \qquad \ldots (5)$$

From above equation, it is important to note that as I_{SS} increases, the transconductance also increases.

1.4.2 CMOS Differential Amplifier using a Current Mirror Load

In this, a p-channel current mirror is inserted between the drains of M_1, M_2 and v_{DD} as shown in Fig. 1.38.

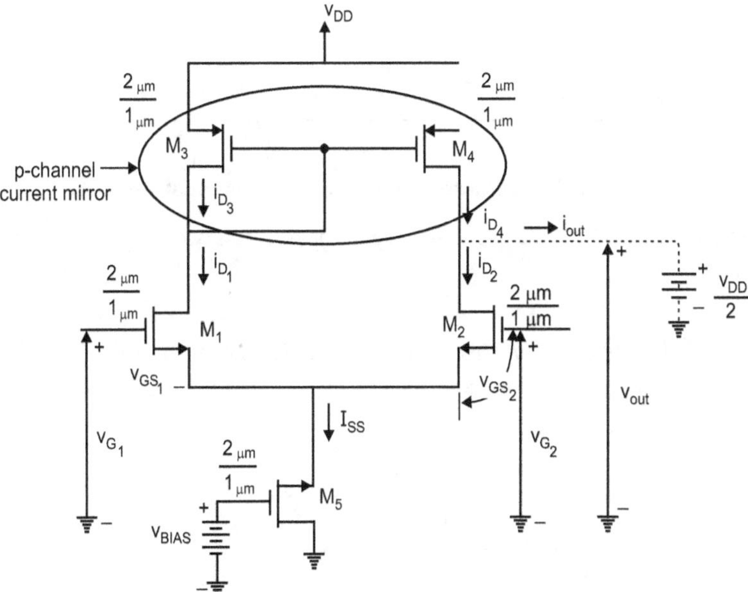

Fig. 1.38: CMOS differential amplifier using current mirror load

Under quiescent condition (no applied differential signal i.e. v_{ID} = 0 V), the two currents in M_1 and M_2 are equal and sum to I_{SS}, the current in the current sink M_5.

The current in M_1 will determine the current in M_3. Ideally, this current is same as the current in M_4. If v_{GS_1} = v_{GS_2} and M_1 and M_2 are matched, then the currents in M_1 and M_2 are equal.

The current that M_4 sources to M_2 should be equal to the current that M_2 requires, which causes i_{out} to be zero. (i.e. external load resistance is infinite). In above analysis, all transistors are assumed to be saturated.

The differential in, differential out transconductance is twice g_m and can be written as,

$$g_{md} = \frac{\partial i_{out}}{\partial v_{ID}} \cdot (v_{ID} = 0) = \left(\frac{k_1' I_{SS} W_1}{L_1} \right)^{1/2} \quad \ldots (1)$$

which is equal to the transconductance of the common source MOSFET, if $I_D = I_{SS}/2$.

Voltage transfer curve for the above differential amplifier is shown in Fig. 1.39.

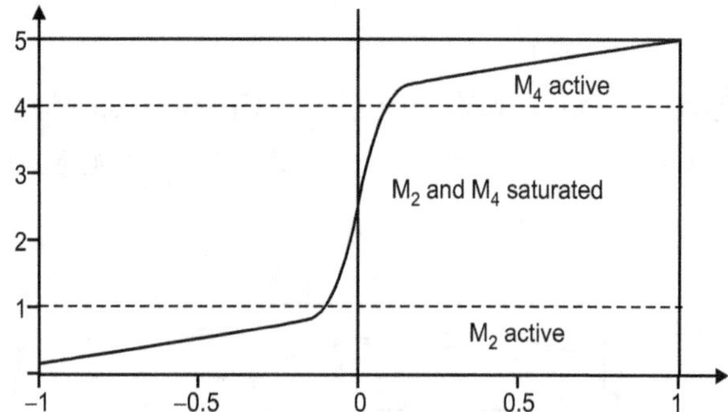

Fig. 1.39: Voltage transfer curve for the differential amplifier

As seen from Fig. 1.39, the largest small signal gain occurs when both M_2 and M_4 are saturated.

1.4.3 CMOS Differential Amplifier using p-Channel Input MOSFETs

The CMOS differential amplifier which uses the p-channel MOSFET devices, M_1 and M_2, as the differential pair is shown in Fig. 1.40.

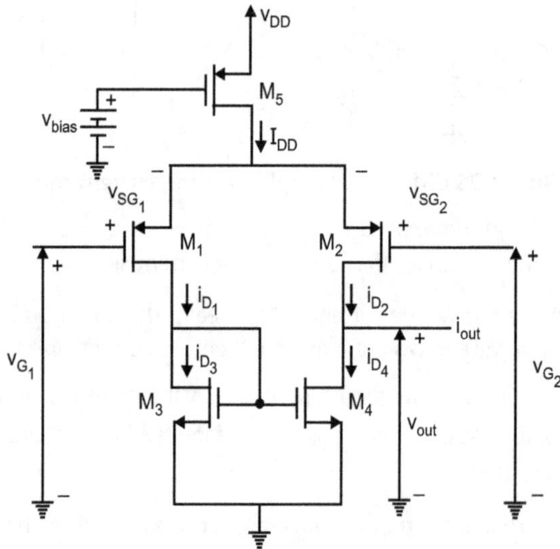

Fig. 1.40: CMOS differential amplifier using p-channel input MOSFETs

The operation of the circuit is identical to that of Fig. 1.39.

1.4.4 Small Signal Model of the CMOS Differential Amplifier

The small signal analysis of the differential amplifier is given by the model shown in Fig. 1.41.

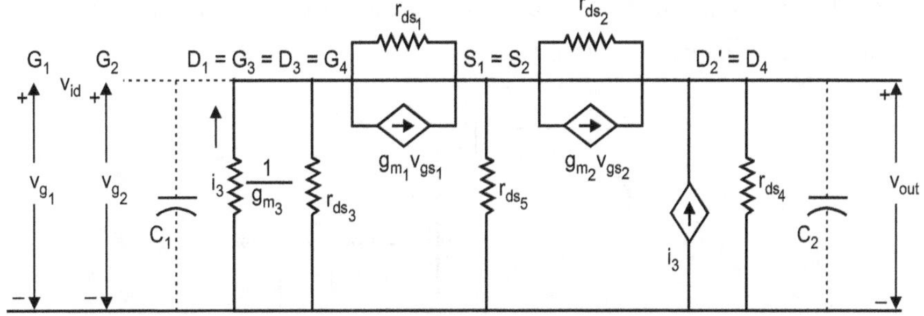

Fig. 1.41: Exact small signal model of the CMOS differential amplifier

The simplified model of above is shown in Fig. 1.42.

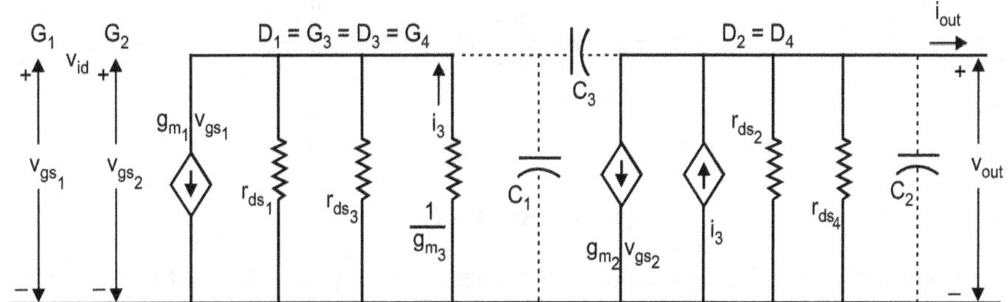

Fig. 1.42: Simplified equivalent model

In this both sides of the differential amplifier are assumed to be perfectly matched. The small signal output resistance is given by

$$r_{out} = \frac{1}{g_{ds_2} + g_{ds_4}} \qquad \ldots (1)$$

The voltage gain is given as the product of g_{md} and r_{out}.

$$A_v = \frac{V_{out}}{V_{id}} = \frac{g_m d}{g_{ds_2} + g_{ds_4}}$$

1.5 Cascode Amplifier

Advantages of cascode amplifier compared to inverting amplifier.

(1) It provides a higher output impedance.

(2) It reduces the effect of the Miller capacitance on the input of the amplifier, which will be very important in designing the frequency of the op-amp.

Fig. 1.43 shows the cascode amplifier. It consists of transistors M_1, M_2 and M_3. The transistor M_2 is used to keep the small signal resistance at the drain of M_1 low. The small signal resistance looking back into the drain of M_2 is approximately $r_{ds_1}\, g_{m_2}\, r_{ds_2}$. It is much larger than that seen looking into M_3 which is r_{ds_3}.

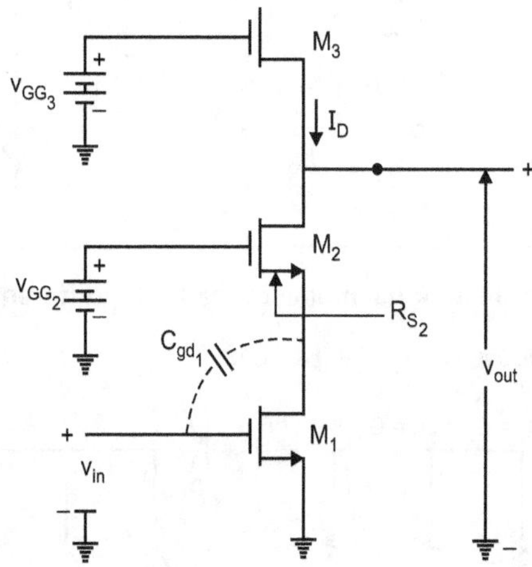

Fig. 1.43: Cascode amplifier

The small signal gain of the cascode amplifier is approximately twice that of the inverter. It is because R_{out} has increased by roughly a factor of 2.

The voltage transfer curve of cascode amplifier is shown in Fig. 1.44.

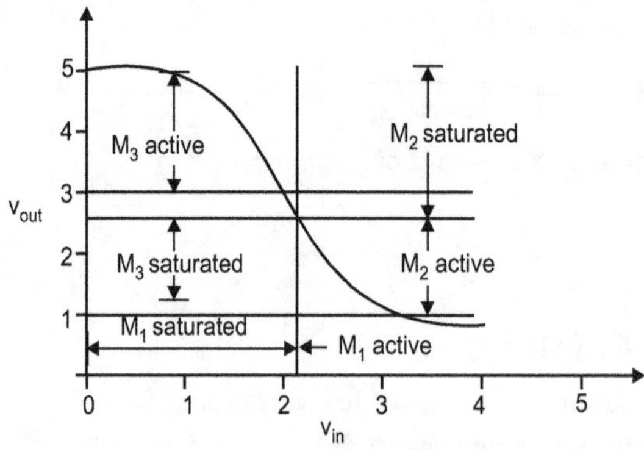

Fig. 1.44: Voltage transfer curve of cascode amplifier

The largest output voltage for which all transistors of the cascode amplifier are in saturation is given as

$$V_{out\,(max)} = V_{DD} - V_{SD_3\,(sat)}$$

and the minimum output voltage is,

$$V_{out\,(min)} = V_{DS_1\,(sat)} + V_{DS_2\,(sat)}$$

1.6 CMOS Operational Amplifiers

Operational amplifier has become one of the most versatile and important building blocks in analog circuit design. There are basically two terms used to describe the operational amplifiers:

 (1) Operational transconductance amplifiers (OTAs).

 (2) Voltage operational amplifier.

Operational transconductance amplifier has a high output resistance and voltage operational amplifiers has low output reisstance. OTAs are also called as unbuffered amplifiers and voltage operational amplifiers are also called as buffered opamps.

The main requirement of opamp is to have sufficiently large gain open-loop gain to implement the negative feedback concept. The two stage opamp is used to implement the important concept of compensation. The goal of compensation is to maintain stability when negative feedback is applied around the opamp.

1.6.1 Two-stage Op-amp

Fig. 1.45 shows a block diagram that represents the important aspects of an op-amp. The first stage is the differential transconductance stage.

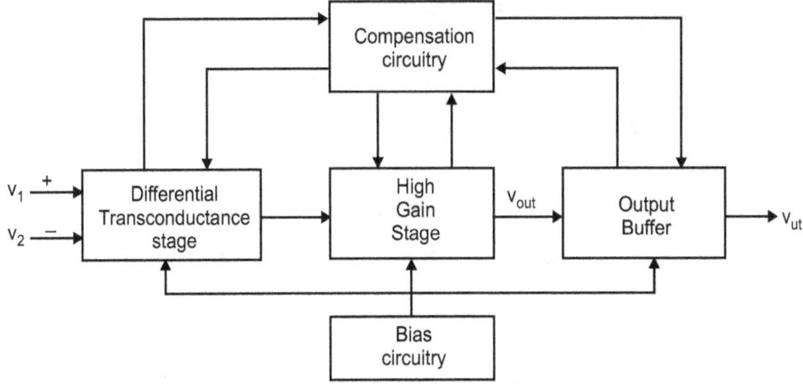

Fig. 1.45: General two-stage op-amp block diagram

This stage provides the differential to single-ended conversion. It improves the noise and offset performance of the op-amp. It also provides sufficient gain. The second stage is the inverter, which is used to provide high gain. Output buffer stage is used to lower the output resistance and to maintain a large signal swing. Bias circuits are provided to establish the proper operating point for each transistor in its quiescent state. Compensation circuitry is used to achieve stable closed-loop performance.

1.6.2 Ideal Op-amp

In ideal case, an op-amp has

    (1) Infinite differential voltage gain.

    (2) Infinite input resistance.

    (3) Zero output resistance.

But, in practical case, we are not getting ideal values.

The output voltage of op-amp in practical case is given as

$$\boxed{V_{out} = A_v (v_1 - v_2)}$$

where, A_v is the open-loop differential voltage gain. v_1 and v_2 are the input voltages applied to the noninverting and inverting input terminals, respectively. The symbol of the op-amp is shown in Fig. 1.46.

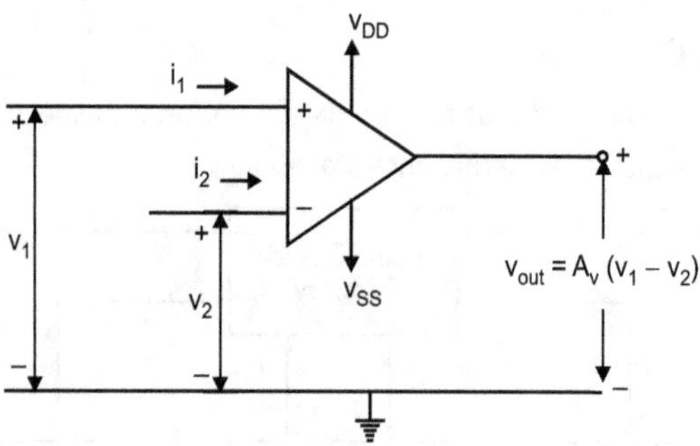

Fig. 1.46: Symbol of an op-amp

V_{DD} and v_{SS} are the integral part of an op-amp. It is very important while designing the op-amp on an IC.

Op-amp as a voltage amplifier:

The output is connected through R_2 to the inverting input, to provide the negative feedback path. The input can be applied to the positive or negative inputs. If only input is applied to the positive input, then it is called a noninverting amplifier. If the input is applied to the negative input, then it is called as inverting amplifier.

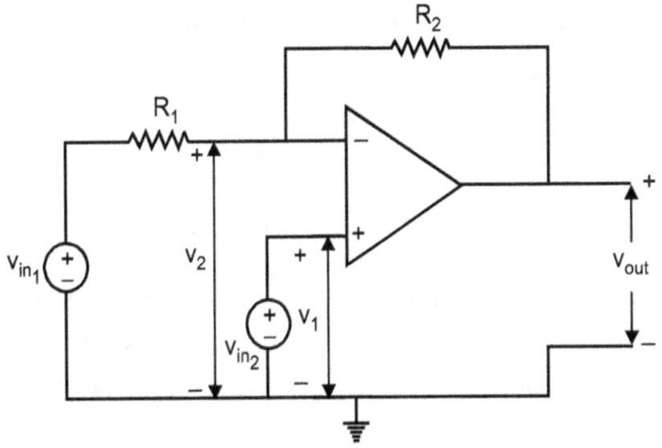

Fig. 1.47: Op-amp as a voltage amplifier

1.6.3 Non-ideal Op-amp

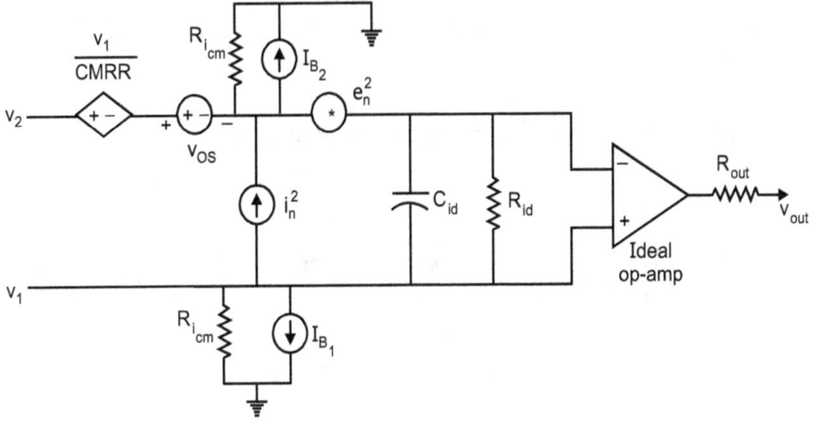

Fig. 1.48: Non-ideal op-amp model

In Fig. 1.48, the notations are

R_{id} and C_{id}: Finite differential input impedance.

R_{out}: Output resistance.

R_{icm}: Common mode input resistance.

v_{os}: Input offset voltage.

I_{os}: Input offset current.

I_{B_1} and I_{B_2}: Input bias currents.

The common mode rejection ratio CMRR is modeled by the voltage controlled voltage source indicated as v_1/CMRR.

$\overline{i_n^2}$ and $\overline{e_n^2}$ indicates the op-amp noise. These are rms current and voltage noise sources with units of mean square volts and mean square amperes respectively. These noise sources have no polarity and are always assumed to be added.

The output voltage of operational amplifier is defined as

$$V_{out}(s) = A_v(s)\,[v_1(s) - v_2(s)] \pm A_c(s)\left(\frac{v_1(s) + v_2(s)}{2}\right)$$

Differential part   Common mode part
of $v_{out}(s)$ of $v_{out}(s)$

The differential frequency response is given as $A_v(s)$ and the common mode frequency response is given as $A_c(s)$.

A typical differential frequency response of an op-amp is given as

$$A_v(s) = \frac{A_{vo}}{\left(\dfrac{s}{p_1} - 1\right)\left(\dfrac{s}{p_2} - 1\right)\left(\dfrac{s}{p_3} - 1\right)\ldots}$$

where p_1, p_2 ... are poles of the operational amplifier open-loop transfer function. The pole p_i is expressed as,

$$p_i = -\omega_i$$

$A_v(0)$ is the gain of the op-amp as the frequency approaches zero.

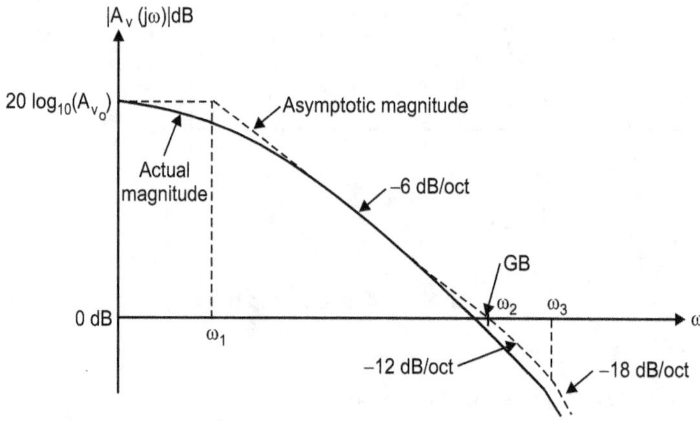

Fig. 1.49: Frequency response of the magnitude of $A_v(j\omega)$ for an op-amp

In above frequency response, ω_1 is much lower than the rest of the break frequencies.

GB: The frequency where the − 6 dB/oct slope from the dominant pole intersects with the 0 dB axis is designated as the unity gain bandwidth.

PSRR (Power supply rejection ratio): It is defined as the product of the ratio of the change in supply voltage to the change in output voltage of the opamp caused by the change in the power supply and the open-loop gain of the op-amp. Thus,

$$PSRR = \frac{\Delta V_{DD}}{\Delta V_{out}} A_v(s)$$

$$= \frac{V_o/V_{in} \quad (V_{dd} = 0)}{V_o/V_{dd} \quad (V_{in} = 0)}$$

Settling time: The important characteristics of opamp is the settling time. This is the time needed for the output of the op-amp to reach a final value when excited by a small signal.

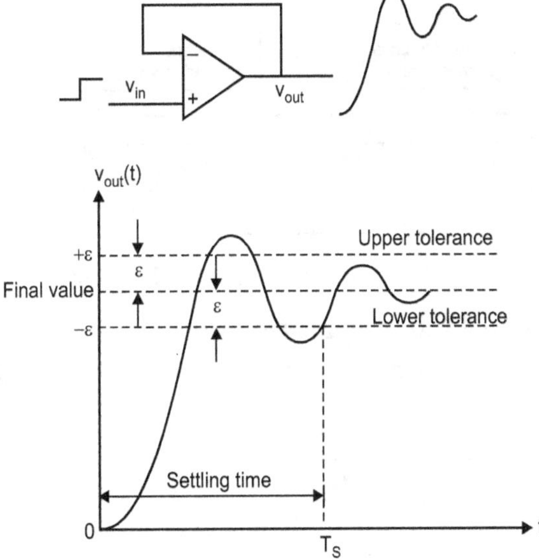

Fig. 1.50: Transient response of op-amp with negative feedback, illustrating settling time T$_s$, ε is the tolerance to the final value used to define the settling time

A longer settling time implies that the rate of processing analog signals must be reduced.

1.7 Classification of Op-amps

To understand the design of CMOS op-amp, it is necessary to examine their classification and categorization. Table 1.1 gives a hierarchy of CMOS op-amps that is applicable to nearly all CMOS op-amps. Amplifiers generally consist of cascade of voltage to current or current to voltage converting stages.

A voltage to current stage is called a transconductance stage and current to voltage stage is called a load stage.

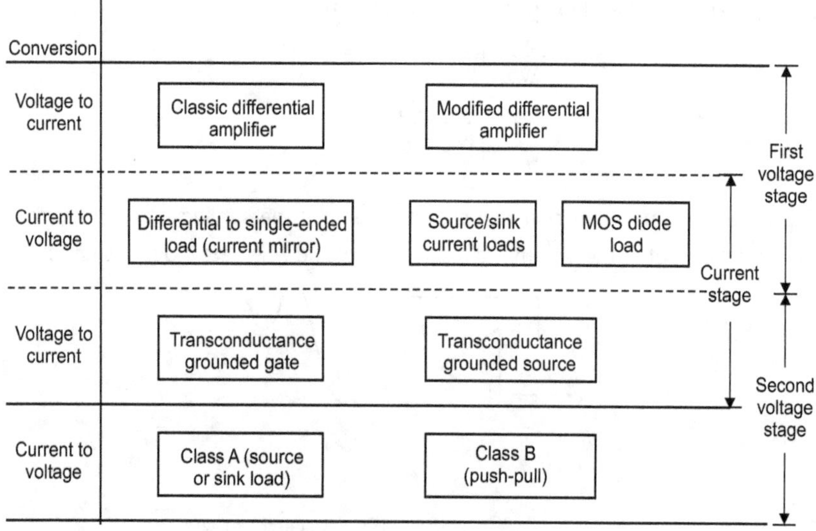

Table 1.1: Categorization of MOS op-amps

1.7.1 Classical Two-stage CMOS Op-amp

It is a two-stage op-amp. It consists of a cascade of V $\rightarrow$ I and I $\rightarrow$ V stages and is shown in Fig. 1.51.

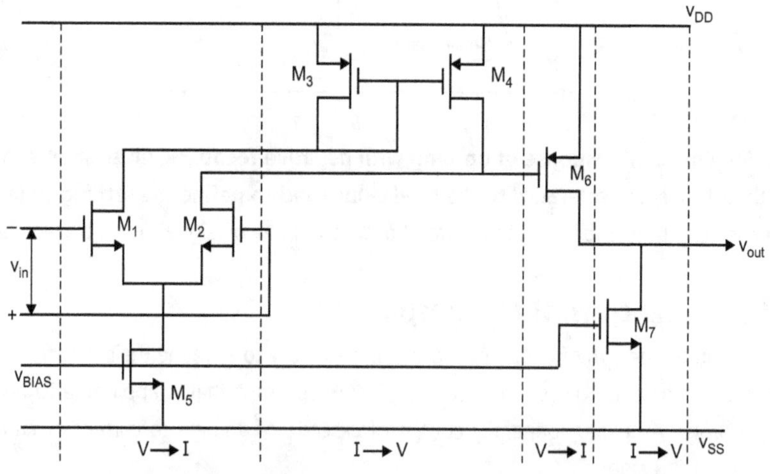

Fig. 1.51: Classical two-stage CMOS op-amp

The first stage consists of a differential amplifier which converts differential voltage to differential currents. These differential currents are applied to a current mirror load recovering the differential voltage. The second stage is a common-source MOSFET converting the second stage input voltage to current. This transistor is loaded by a current-sink load, which converts the current to voltage at the output.

1.8 Folded Cascode Op-amp

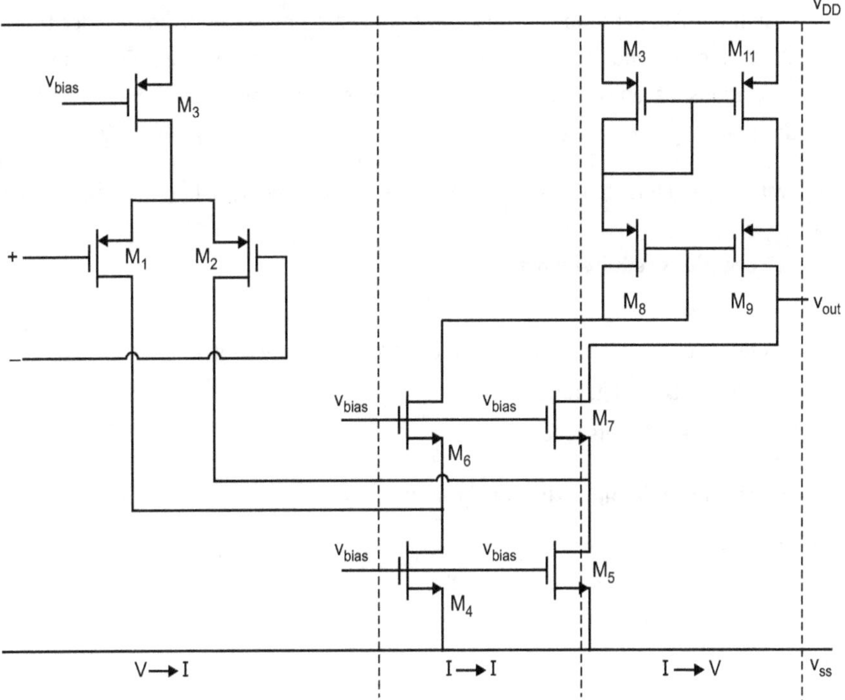

Fig. 1.52: Diagram of folded cascode op-amp

This architecture is developed to the input, common-mode range and the power supply rejection of the two-stage op-amp. In this a differential transconductance stage is cascaded with a current stage followed by a cascode current mirror load. It has a push-pull output. The op-amp can actively sink or source current from the load.

1.9 Design of Op-amps

The design of op-amp is divided into two parts:

    (a) The first stage involves choosing or creating the basic structure of the op-amp. It creates the diagram that describes the interconnection of all of the transistors. This structure does not change throughout the remaining portion of the design. But, in some cases, certain characteristics of the chosen design must be changed by modifying the structure.

    (b) The second stage involves selecting the dc currents and to size the transistors and design the compensation circuits. Devices must be properly scaled in order to meet all of the ac and dc requirements imposed on the op-amp. Computer-based simulations, based on hand calculations are used extensively to help the designer in this phase.

The following parameters/items must be considered before the actual design of the op-amp begins.

Boundary conditions requirements:

    (1) Process specifications (i.e. v_T, k', C_{ox}).

    (2) Operating temperature and range of the circuit to be designed.

    (3) Supply voltage and its range.

    (4) Supply current and its range.

Requirements of the op-amp while designing:

    (1) Settling time.

    (2) Gain

    (3) Gain bandwidth.

    (4) Slew rate.

    (5) Input common mode range, ICMR.

    (6) Common mode rejection ratio, CMRR.

    (7) Power supply rejection ratio, PSRR.

    (8) Output resistance.

    (9) Offset.

    (10) Output voltage swing.

    (11) Layout area.

    (12) Noise.

For unbuffered CMOS op-amp, the important specifications are listed below:

(1)	Gain	$\geq$	70 dB
(2)	Settling time	$\leq$	1 μs
(3)	Gain bandwidth	$\geq$	5 MHz
(4)	Slew rate	$\geq$	5 V/μs
(5)	ICMR	$\geq$	$\pm$ 1.5 V
(6)	CMRR	$\geq$	60 dB
(7)	PSRR	$\geq$	60 dB
(8)	Output swing	$\geq$	$\pm$ 1.5 V
(9)	Offset	$\leq$	$\pm$ 10 mV
(10)	Noise	$\leq$	100 nV/$\sqrt{Hz}$ at 1 kHz
(11)	Layout area	$\leq$	5000 $\times$ (minimum channel length)^2
(12)	Supply voltage	$\pm$	2.5 V $\pm$ 10%
(13)	Supply current		100 μA
(14)	Temperature range		0 – 70°C

The design procedure of the op-amp must be **iterative**, since it is almost impossible to relate all specifications simultaneously. For a typical CMOS op-amp design, the following steps are used:

(1) Decide suitable configuration: After examining the specifications in detail, determine the type of configuration required. For example: for low power requirement, a class AB type of output stage is necessary. Also, for low offset and noise, a high gain input stage is required. Also, depending on the application, a configuration is used.

(2) The type of compensation needed to meet the specifications: There are various ways for the compensation of op-amp. For example, an op-amp that drive very large capacitances might be compensated at the output. Also, compensation depends on the type of input and output stages needed.

(3) Sizes of the device for proper dc, ac and transient performance: Hand calculations are required in this case. Compensation components are also sized in this step of the procedure. A circuit simulator is used to fine tune the design, after each device is sized by hand.

Hand calculations can achieve about 80% of the complete job. But sometimes, the hand calculations can be misleading due to their approximate nature. But, the hand calculations are necessary to give the designer a feel for the sensitivity of the design to parameter variation. Iteration by computer simulation gives the designer very little feeling for the design.

In short, the design process has two major steps. The first is the conception of the design and the second is the optimization of the design. The first step is accomplished by proposing an architecture to meet the given specifications. The second step is to take the first cut design and verify and optimize it. It is done by using computer simulation and can include such influences as environmental or process variations.

QUESTIONS

1. Explain the necessity of the analog CMOS design.
2. Draw the small signal model of MOS transistor and explain.
3. Explain analog integrated circuit design process.
4. Explain MOS transistor as a switch.
5. What is the difference between ideal and non-ideal CMOS switch. Explain with model of a non-ideal switch?
6. Draw and explain the I-V characteristics of an n-channel transistor operating as a switch.
7. How the diode is formed using MOSFET? Explain.
8. Explain MOS diode as a voltage divider.
9. Explain MOSFET as a resistor.
10. Draw and explain current source and current sink with its I-V characteristics.
11. Draw and explain current mirror.
12. Draw and explain active PMOS load inverter, also draw the small signal model.
13. Explain current source inverter with diagram.
14. Draw push-pull inverter and explain.
15. Explain the noise model of the push-pull CMOS inverter.
16. Draw and explain differential amplifier and its characteristics.
17. Explain CMOS differential amplifier using NMOS transistor, also draw its characteristics.
18. Draw and explain CMOS differential amplifier using current mirror load.
19. Draw and explain small signal model of the CMOS differential amplifier.
20. Explain cascode amplifier. What are its advantages?
21. Explain general two-stage op-amp block diagram.
22. Draw and explain nonideal op-amp model.
23. Explain the design of op-amp using CMOS technology.
24. What are the requirements of the op-amp while designing?

Chapter 2: DIGITAL CMOS DESIGN

Topics discussed: MOS structure, Logic levels, Implementation of gates using CMOS, Theory of CMOS inverter, Noise margin, Fan-out and Fan-in, Power dissipation, Design consideration, Fabrication process.

2.1 Introduction

A CMOS transistor has four terminals gate, source, drain and substrate. It acts as a switch. When switch is on (transistor is on), it allows current to flow between the source and drain terminals. The transistors can turn on or off using the gate terminal.

There are two kinds of CMOS transistors: n-channel and p-channel transistors. An n-channel transistor requires logic '1' on the gate terminal to make the switch conducting (transistor on). A p-channel transistor requires logic '0' on the gate terminal to make the switch conducting (transistor on). The p-channel transistor symbol has a bubble on a gate terminal to specify that the gate has to be a '0' to turn the transistor on. The symbols of CMOS transistors are shown in Fig. 2.1 (a) and (b).

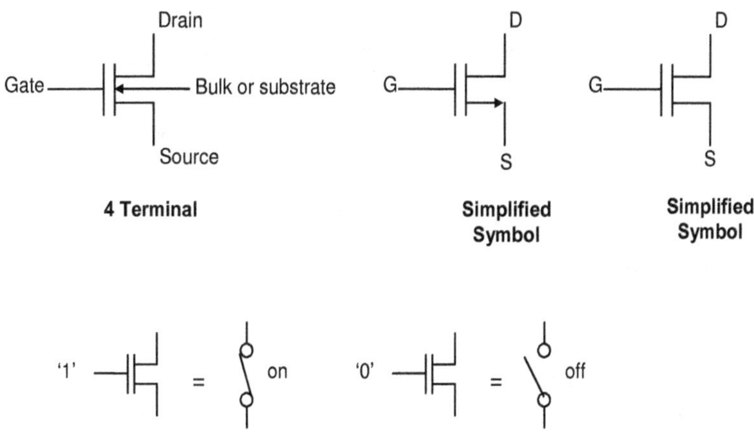

Fig. 2.1 (a): An n-channel transistor

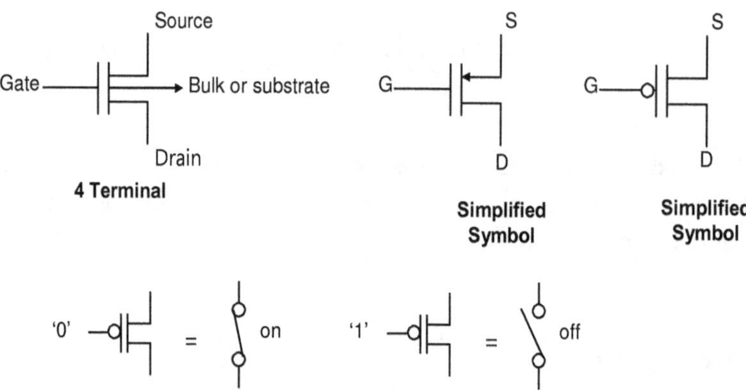

Fig. 2.1 (b): p-channel MOS transistor

2.2 MOS Structure

The metal oxide semiconductor structure is shown in Fig. 2.2.

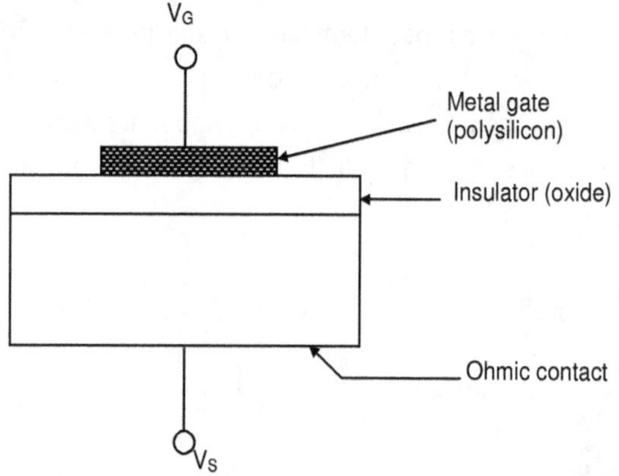

Fig. 2.2: MOS Structure

The structure consists of three layers:

- The metal gate electrode of polysilicon or aluminium
- The insulating oxide SiO_2
- Substrate semiconductor p-type Si

V_G is the applied gate voltage and V_S is the substrate voltage. This substrate acts as a capacitor with gate and semiconductor as two plates and SiO_2 as the dielectric of the capacitor.

2.3 MOS Transistor

2.3.1 MOSFET Structure

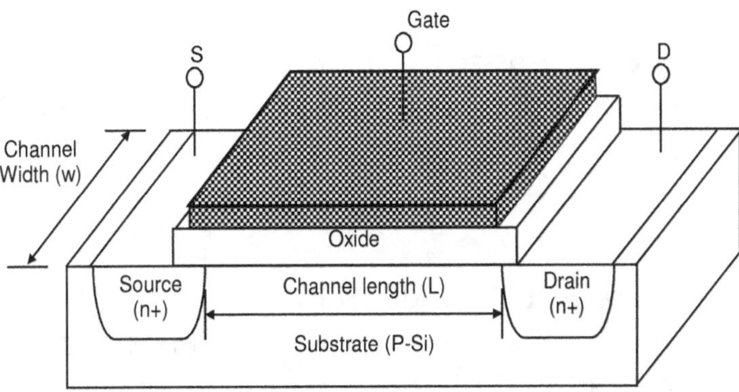

Fig. 2.3: Schematic of MOSFET

A MOSFET consists of a MOS capacitor and two diffused regions. These diffused regions serve as ohmic contacts to an inversion layer of free charge carriers at the surface of the semiconductor, i.e., at the semiconductor oxide interface. Depending on the type of substrate used, MOSFETs are classified as n-channel MOSFET or p-channel MOSFET. In an n-channel MOSFET, the substrate is p-type silicon and the inversion charge consists of electrons, hence the name is n-channel. This conducting channel is formed between the two n+ ohmic contacts called the source and drain. The depletion regions formed between the two n-regions and the p-type substrate, provide isolation between the devices fabricated on the same substrate. The device structure is completely symmetrical with respect to the drain and source regions. A schematic view of the n-channel MOSFET is shown in Fig. 2.3. The electric field is established by applying a voltage between the gate and the substrate. This electric field is transmitted through the oxide layer. The source and drain regions are heavily doped. The distance between the source and drain diffusion region is called the channel length L. The lateral extent of the channel (inside the semiconductor) is known as channel width W. The thickness of the oxide layer is taken as t_{ox}. L, W and t_{ox} determine the electrical behavior of MOSFETs. The gate material is usually polysilicon or aluminium and the length of the gate is almost equal to the channel length L.

There are two types of MOSFET

1) **The depletion MOSFET:** At zero gate voltage and a fixed drain voltage, the current is maximum and then decreases with applied gate potential.

2) **The enhancement MOSFET:** It exhibits no current at zero gate voltage and the magnitude of the output current increases with the increase in the magnitude of gate potentials.

Both types of MOSFETs exist in either p or n-channel variety.

2.3.2 The Enhancement Mode MOSFET

The structure of a p-channel MOSFET (PMOS) and n-channel MOSFET (NMOS) of enhancement type are shown in Fig. 2.4.

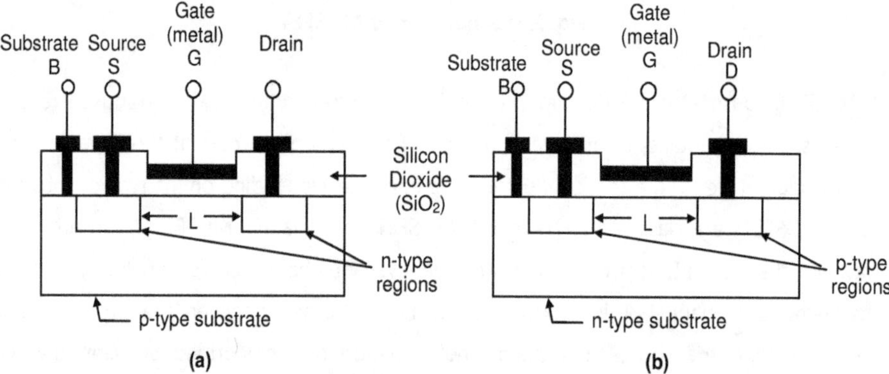

Fig. 2.4: (a) n-channel MOSFET, (b) p-channel MOSFET

In Fig. 2.4 (a), the two n-type regions are embedded in the p-type substrate. The n-type regions are the source and drain electrodes. The region between the source and drain is the channel region which is covered by a thin silicon dioxide layer. The gate is placed at the top of oxide layer. Because of the presence of insulating silicon dioxide layer, the device is also known as Insulated Gate Field Effect Transistor (IGFET). It is because of this layer the MOSFETs have a high input resistance.

To study the electrical behavior of the NMOS device, external bias is applied as shown in Fig. 2.5.

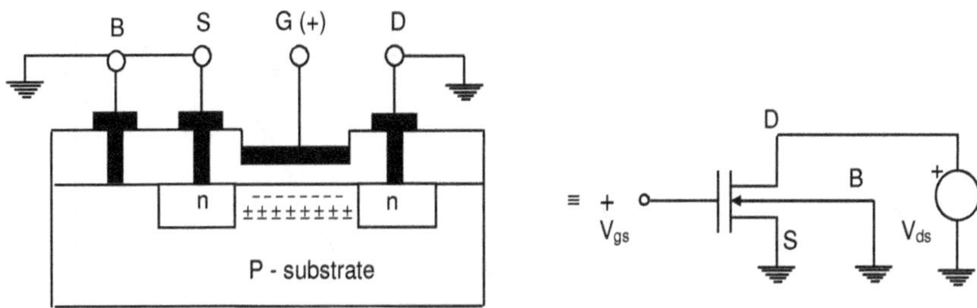

Fig. 2.5: n-channel MOSFET with source and drain grounded

The source and substrate are at ground potential. The drain to source voltage is initially zero. If a positive voltage is applied to the gate, an electric field is established. This field will induce negative charges near the semiconductor surface. These surface charges are the electrons obtained from the source and drain and thus inversion layer is formed, when certain gate voltage is applied. This value of gate voltage at which inversion of semiconductor surface takes place is known as threshold voltage. The threshold voltage V_t, for a MOS transistor is defined as the voltage applied between the gate and the source of a MOS device below which the drain to source current I_{ds} effectively drops to zero. As gate voltage (V_{gs}) increases beyond V_t, the charges in the inversion layer increase and the channel conductivity increases (transistor ON). When a positive potential is applied between the drain and source (V_{ds}), a current is produced in the channel between source and drain. Thus the drain current is enhanced by the positive gate voltage and so the device is known as enhancement type MOSFET.

When the drain-source voltage is increased, keeping the gate source voltage ($V_{gs} > V_t$) constant, three cases occur depending on the value of V_{ds}.

- At $V_{ds} < V_{gs} - V_t$: As V_{ds} increases, the drain current increases linearly and the MOSFET behaves as a resistance.
- At $V_{ds} = V_{gs} - V_t$: The drop across the channel increases in magnitude and hence the voltage across the oxide at the drain side of channel decreases. As the potential difference is lowered, the field across the drain end of the oxide is reduced. So the number of inversion charges in this region is also reduced and at a point where $V_{ds} = V_{gs} - V_t$, the channel is said to be pinched off. This results in a slow increase of drain current with increase in V_{ds}.
- At $V_{ds} > V_{gs} - V_t$, a further increase in V_{ds} produces no change in drain currant and the current saturation occur. This is the saturation region of device operation.

Fig. 2.6 shows transfer characteristics of enhancement type MOSFET.

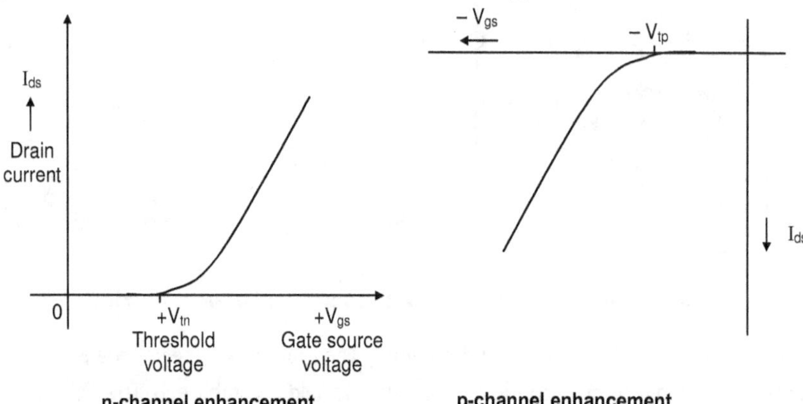

Fig. 2.6: Transfer characteristics of enhancement type MOSFET

2.3.3 Calculation of Threshold Voltage

When zero voltage is applied at gate and source, drain, substrate (bulk) are grounded, the MOSFET offers very high resistance and no current flows from source to drain.

When a positive voltage is applied to gate, the holes from the p-substrate are repelled, a depletion region is formed and the minority carriers, electrons accumulate at the semiconductor surface forming an inversion layer. The width of the depletion region is given by equation (1) and the depletion region charge density is given by equation (2).

$$x_d = \sqrt{\frac{2\in_{si} |\phi_s - \phi_F|}{q\,N_A}} \qquad \text{... (1)}$$

$$\phi = -q\,N_A\,x_d = -\sqrt{2qN_A \in_{si} |\phi_s - \phi_F|} \qquad \text{... (2)}$$

When an inversion layer is formed, the fixed charge stored in the depletion region is given by

$$Q_{BO} = -\sqrt{2qN_A \in_{si} |-2\phi_F|} \qquad \text{... (3)}$$

Equation (3) is valid only when bias $V_{SB} = 0$, where

    N_A -   density of carriers in the doped semiconductor substrate.

    q -   electron charge = 1.602×10^{-9} coulomb

    $\in_{si}$ -   permittivity of silicon = 1.06×10^{-2} farads/cm

    $\phi_s - \phi_F$ - difference between the Fermi energy level of the intrinsic semiconductor. This is bulk potential.

When a positive substrate bias is applied, the surface potential required for strong inversion increases to $|-2\phi_f + V_{SB}|$ and the charge stored in the depletion region modifies to

$$Q_{BO} = -\sqrt{2qN_A \in_{si} \left|-2\phi_F + V_{SB}\right|}$$

... (4)

Threshold voltage is defined as the gate voltage for which strong inversion of the semiconductor surface occurs.

Flat band voltage

This is the built-in voltage offset across the MOS structure. Flat-band voltage V_{FB} consists of work function difference ϕ_{ms} (between polysilicon gate and silicon), oxide fixed charge Q_{OX} and threshold adjusting implantation impurities Q_t.

$$V_{FB} = \phi_{ms} - \frac{Q_{ox}}{C_{ox}} - \frac{Q_1}{C_{ox}}$$

... (5)

where C_{ox} is the gate oxide capacitance per unit area given by

$$C_{ox} = \frac{\in_{ox}}{t_{ox}}$$

... (6)

$\in_{ox}$ = 3.97 × $\in_0$ = 3.5 × 10^{-13} F/cm is the oxide permittivity, $\in_0$ is the free space permittivity and t_{ox} is the oxide thickness.

Voltage drop across the depletion region at inversion is equal to $-2\phi_F$.

Voltage drop across the gate oxide is given by Q_B/C_{OX}.

So, the threshold voltage is expressed as:

$$V_t = V_{FB} - 2\phi_F - \frac{Q_B}{C_{ox}}$$

$$= \phi_{ms} - \frac{Q_{ox}}{C_{ox}} - \frac{Q_1}{C_{ox}} - 2\phi_F - Q_F - \frac{Q_B}{C_{ox}}$$

... (7)

By substituting the value of Q_B from equation (4) and rearranging the terms, we have

$$V_t = V_{to} + \gamma\left(\sqrt{\left|-2\phi_F + V_{SB}\right|} - \sqrt{\left|-2\phi_F\right|}\right)$$

... (8)

where, $V_{to} = \phi_{ms} - 2\phi_F - \dfrac{Q_{Bo}}{C_{ox}} - \dfrac{Q_{ox}}{C_{ox}} - \dfrac{Q_1}{C_{ox}}$

... (9)

and $\gamma = \dfrac{\sqrt{2q\in_{si} N_A}}{C_{ox}}$

γ is known as **body effect co-efficient** or **body factor**.

From the expression of threshold voltage, one can see that the threshold voltage is affected by the material parameters and the substrate voltage. The expression for threshold voltage is applicable to PMOS and NMOS transistors by writing the correct polarities for Fermi potential (negative in NMOS, positive in PMOS), depletion region charge densities (negative in NMOS and positive in PMOS) body effect co-efficient (positive in NMOS, negative in PMOS). The threshold voltage of an n-channel enhancement type MOSFET is positive and p-channel enhancement type MOSFET is negative.

2.3.4 Depletion Type MOSFETs

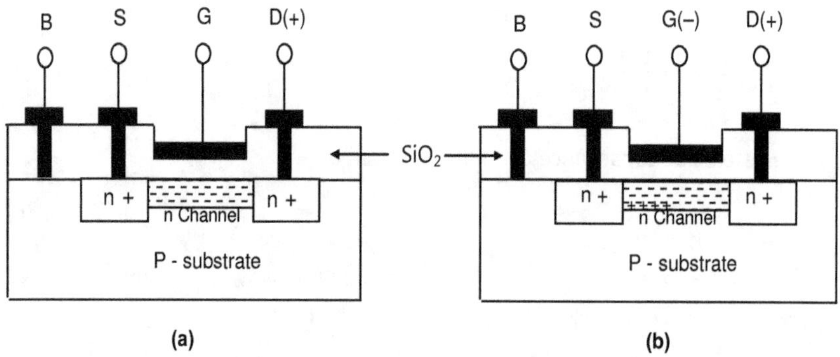

Fig. 2.7: n-channel depletion layer MOSFET for different biases at gate

If a narrow n-channel is embedded into the substrate between the source and drain at the time of fabrication, the structure is known as depletion type MOSFET. Fig. 2.7 shows the structure of an n-channel depletion mode MOSFET, with the applied drain to source voltage kept at zero potential and a negative gate voltage induces positive charge into the channel. The recombination of induced positive charge with the existing negative charge in the channel causes a depletion of majority carriers. Thus the name depletion MOSFET has been assigned to them. If the gate voltage is made more negative, majority carriers can be depleted and thus the channel is removed and the drain current reduces to zero. Threshold voltage is that value of gate voltages for which the channel is depleted of majority carriers. If V_{gs} = 0 and positive drain source voltage is applied, drain current increases and then saturates. This is because of the voltage drop along the channel due to I_D. The region of the channel at the drain side is depleted more and this is the so called pinch-off. The electrical behavior is same as the enhancement type n-channel MOSFET.

Fig. 2.8 shows an n-channel depletion type MOSFET with V_{gs} = 0 V and drain source voltages V_{ds} applied.

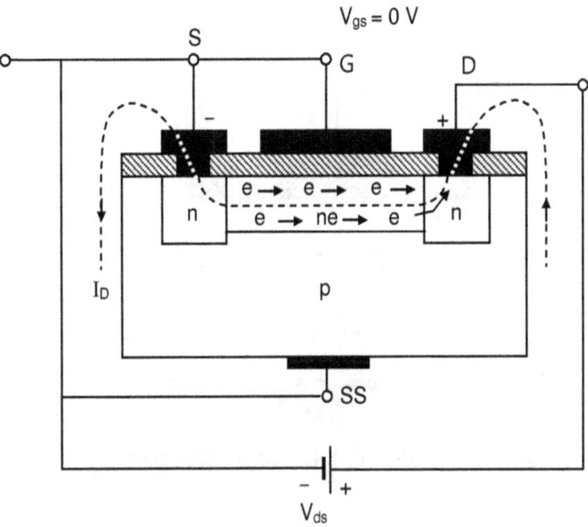

Fig. 2.8: Depletion MOSFET with V_{gs} = 0 V and V_{ds} applied

Since the gate and source are tied together to ground potential, there is an attraction for the positive potential at the drain by the free elections of n-channel and a current is established in the channel. The resulting current with V_{gs} = 0 V is termed as I_{dss}. If a negative voltage is applied to the gate terminal, then the negative potential at the gate will force the electrons in the channel towards the p-type substrate and attract the holes from the p-type substrate. The magnitude of the negative bias applied at gate (V_{gs}) will cause recombination between electrons and holes. This will reduce the number of free electrons in the n-channel available for conduction. For large negative biases, more recombination will take place and hence the drain current will reduce.

For positive values of gate source voltage, additional electrons from the p-type substrate will be attracted towards the gate and the drain current will increase. Thus the application of a positive gate to source voltage has enhanced the level of free carriers in the channel.

In p-channel depletion type MOSFET, the substrate is of n-type and the channel is of p-type. The voltage polarities and current directions are reverse of that in the case of n-channel depletion type MOSFETs. The drain source voltages have negative values. Fig. 2.9 shows p-channel depletion MOSFET. The drain current here will increase from cut-off at $V_{gs} = V_p$ the pinch-off voltage in the positive V_{gs} region to I_{dss} and then continuously increases for negative values of V_{gs}.

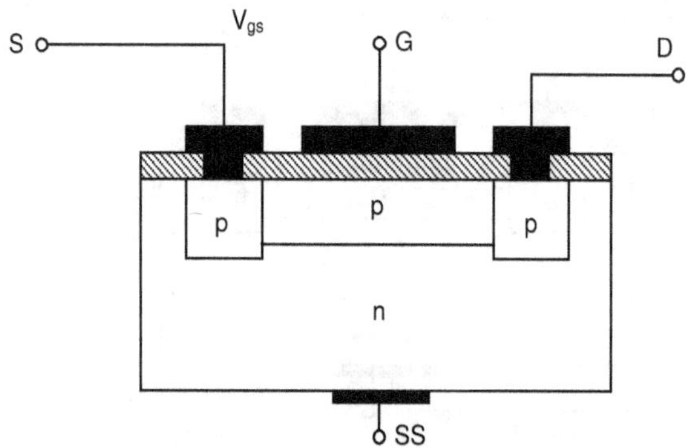

Fig. 2.9: p-channel depletion MOSFET

Fig. 2.10 shows transfer characteristics of depletion type MOSFET.

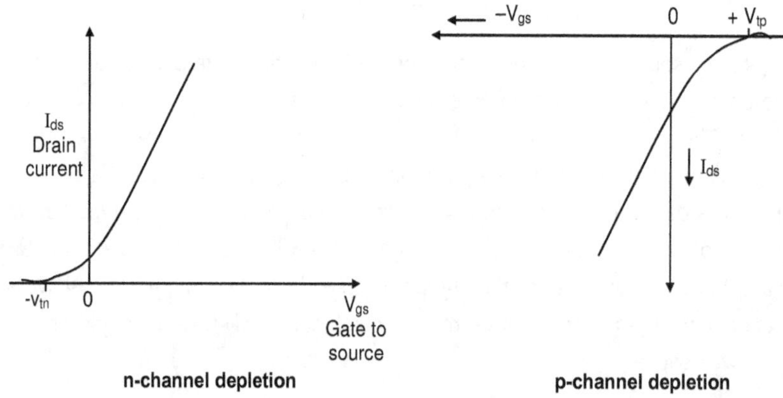

Fig. 2.10: Transfer characteristics of depletion type MOSFET

Comparison of CMOS and Bipolar Technologies

CMOS devices have the disadvantage of limited load driving capability. It is due to the limited current sourcing and sinking abilities associated with both p and n channel MOS. Comparison points of CMOS and Bipolar Technologies are as follows:

CMOS Technology	Bipolar Technology
1. Static power dissipation is low.	1. High power dissipation.
2. Low drive current means high input impedance.	2. High drive current means low input impedance.
3. High noise margin.	3. Low noise margin.
4. Packing density is very high.	4. Low packing density.
5. Fan out limitations. High delay sensitivity to load.	5. Low delay sensitivity to load.
6. Low output drive current.	6. High output drive current.
7. Drain and source can be interchangeable means bidirectional capability.	7. Essentially unidirectional.
8. Ideal switching device.	8. Not ideal switching device as that of CMOS.

Body Effect in CMOS devices: All devices, which consist of MOS device, are made of a common substrate. Due to this, the substrate voltage of all devices is normally equal. But, when we arrange the devices to perform the required gate function, for example, the circuit is shown in Fig. 2.11. Two NMOS transistors are connected in series. As we proceed vertically along the series chain of NMOS transistors, there is an increase in source to substrate voltage V_{sb}. As shown in Fig. 2.11, V_{sb2} and V_{sb1} are not same.

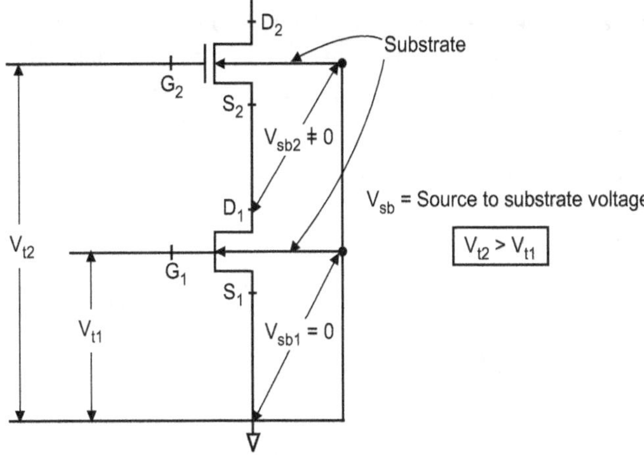

Fig. 2.11: Body effect, the effect of substrate bias

The variation in the source to substrate voltage (V_{sb}) results in variation in threshold voltage. As a result, threshold voltage V_{t2} is greater than V_{t1}.

The variation of threshold voltage with source to substrate voltage is called as the **body effect**. This body effect can significantly affect the speed of complex logic gates.

The amount by which the threshold voltage is increased is given by

$$\Delta V_t = \gamma_n \left(\sqrt{\phi_s + V_{sb}} - \sqrt{\phi_s} \right)$$

The term γ_n is called as the body effect factor, which depends on the gate oxide thickness and the substrate doping.

$$\gamma_n = \sqrt{\frac{2q\varepsilon_{si}N_A}{C_{ox}}}$$

Hot Electron Effect and Impact Ionization

The modern MOS transistor is more complex than the basic transistor. A number of improvements to the basic MOS structure have been introduced, to increase performance and permit the construction of efficient, short channel devices. As the gate length of the MOS transistor is reduced, the electric field at the drain of a transistor in saturation increases, keeping fixed drain voltage.

For the gate length in submicron, the electric field at the drain can become so high that electrons are imparted enough energy to become "hot". These hot electrons impact the drain, dislodging holes that are then swept towards the negatively charged substrate. Due to this there is a substrate current. This effect is known as impact ionization. Also, these hot electrons can penetrate the gate oxide, causing a gate current. This leads to degradation of the MOS device parameters such as threshold voltage, sub threshold current and transconductance, which in turn can cause the failure of the circuit. This effect is called as the hot electron effect.

Hot holes have lower mobility; therefore they do not normally present a problem.

Latch up in CMOS

It is a condition in which the parasitic components give rise to the establishment of low resistance conducting paths between V_{DD} and V_{SS}. Due to the low resistance path between supply and ground; it may give some disastrous results. Therefore, careful control during manufacturing is necessary to avoid this problem.

CMOS Parasitics

Wires, vias and transistors all introduce parasitic elements into the circuit. Two main parasitic components of interest are resistance and capacitance.

Fig. 2.12 shows the parasitic capacitances associated with a MOS transistor.

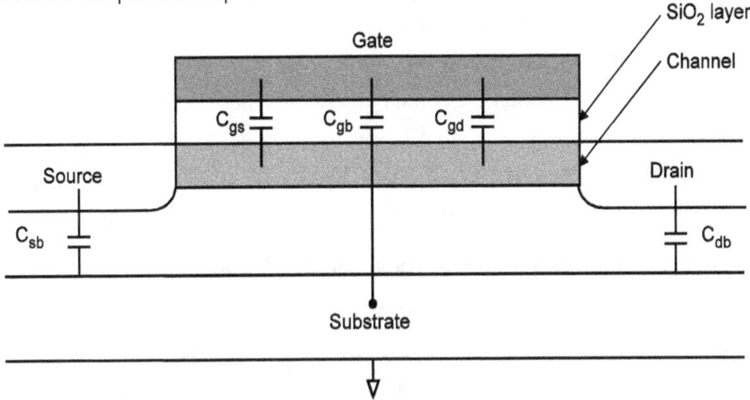

Fig. 2.12: Parasitic capacitance of a MOS transistor

As shown in Fig 2.12, the following parasitic capacitances are present:

$C_{gs} \rightarrow$ gate to source capacitance
$C_{gb} \rightarrow$ gate to substrate capacitance
$C_{gd} \rightarrow$ gate to drain capacitance
$C_{sb} \rightarrow$ source to substrate capacitance
$C_{db} \rightarrow$ drain to substrate capacitance.

It is also possible to view this model in circuit symbols as shown in Fig. 2.13.

The total gate capacitance of a MOS transistor is given by,

$$C_g = C_{gs} + C_{gb} + C_{gd}$$

C_g i.e., total gate capacitance behaviour depends upon the three regions of operation of the MOS device.

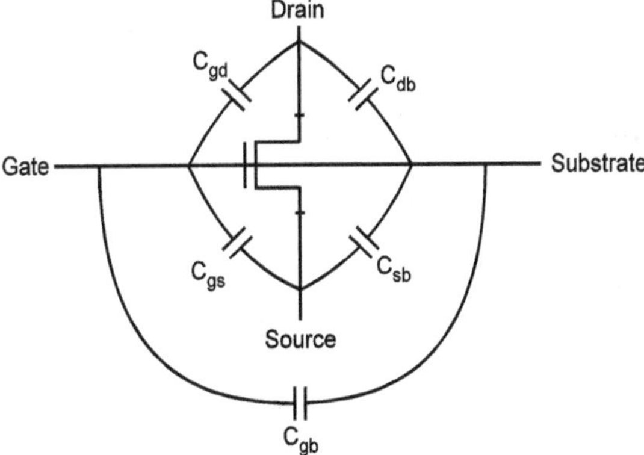

Fig. 2.13: Parasitic capacitance in circuit symbols

(1) **When $V_{gs} < V_t$ i.e. OFF region:** In this region, there is no channel, therefore $C_{gs} = C_{gd} = 0$ and total gate capacitance is C_{gb}.

(2) **Non-saturated region, when $(V_{gs} - V_t) > V_{ds}$:** Due to the channel formation, the gate to channel capacitances come into picture. These capacitances are dependent on gate voltage.

(3) **Saturated region, when $(V_{gs} - V_t) < V_{ds}$:** In this mode, the drain region of the channel is pinched off, causing C_{gd} to be zero.

Equivalent circuit of MOS transistor for small signal model

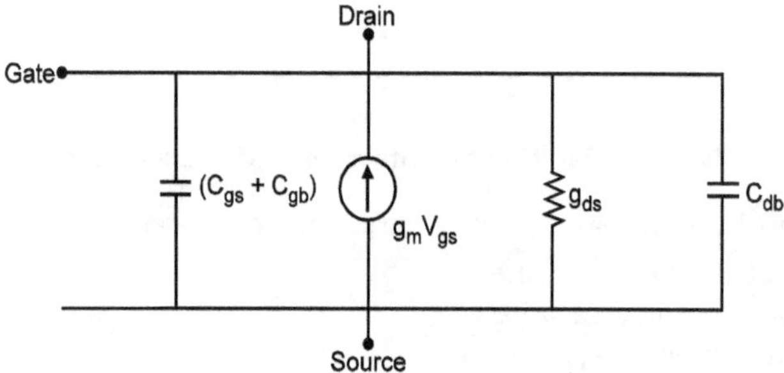

Fig. 2.14: MOS transistor, small signal mode

As shown in Fig. 2.14, the MOS transistor is modeled as a voltage controlled current source (g_m). The equivalent circuit is drawn by assuming $V_{sb} = 0$. g_{ds} represents output conductance and C_{db} gives the capacitance between drain and source. The input capacitance is offered by the gate terminal and its value is ($C_{gs} + C_{gb}$). The output conductance can be decreased by lengthening the channel (i.e. L). The transconductance g_m gives the relationship between output current I_{ds} and input voltage V_{gs} and it is given by:

$$g_m = \frac{\Delta I_{ds}}{\Delta V_{gs}}\bigg| = V_{ds = constant}$$

2.4 Logic Levels

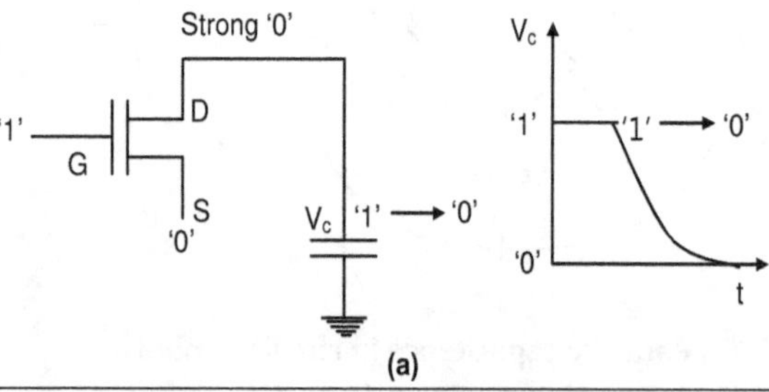

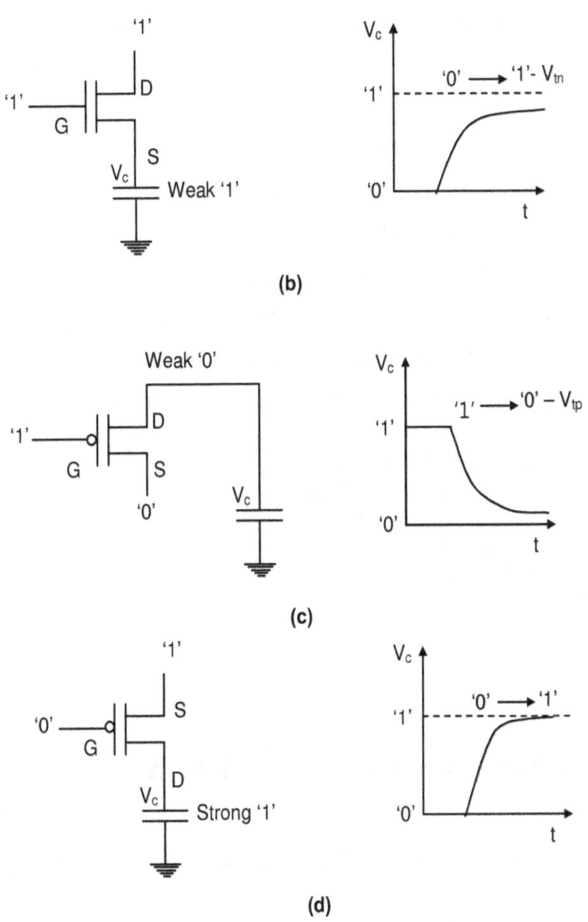

Fig. 2.15: CMOS Logic levels
(a) Strong '0', (b) A weak '1', (c) A weak '0', (d) A strong '1'
(V_{tn} is positive and V_{tp} is negative)

Fig. 2.15 shows how to use transistor as logic switches. In Fig. 2.15 (a), logic '1' (or V_{DD}) and logic '0' (V_{SS}) is applied to the gate and to the source respectively. The application of these voltages makes the n-channel transistor conduct current (ON), and electrons flow from source to drain. Suppose the drain is initially at logic '1', then the n-channel transistor will begin to discharge any capacitance that is conducted to its drain. This will continue until the drain terminal reach a logic '0', and at that time V_{GD} and V_{GS} both are equal to V_{DD}, a full logic

'1'. The transistor is strongly conducting now. The transistor will strongly object to attempt to change its drain terminal from logic '0'. We say that the logic level at the drain is a strong '0'.

In Fig. 2.15 (b), logic '1' is applied to the drain. The transistor is on but V_{GS} is decreasing as the source voltage approaches its final value. In fact, the source terminal never gets to logic '1'. The source will stop increasing in voltage when V_{GS} reaches V_{tn}. At this point transistor is nearly off and source voltage reaches slowly up to $V_{DD} - V_{tn}$. Because the transistor is nearly off, it would be easy for a logic cell connected to the source to change the potential there, since there is so little channel charge. The logic level at the source is a weak '1'. Fig. 2.15 (c) and (d) show the state for a p-channel transistor is the exact reverse or complementary of n-channel transistor situation.

An n-channel transistor provides a strong '0', but a weak '1'.

A p-channel transistor provides a strong '1', but a weak '0'.

In CMOS technology, both types of transistors are used together to produce strong '0' as well as strong '1' logic levels.

2.5 Implementation of Gates Using NMOS

2.5.1 NMOS Inverter

Fig. 2.16 shows the NMOS inverter and truth table of the inverter (NOT gate).

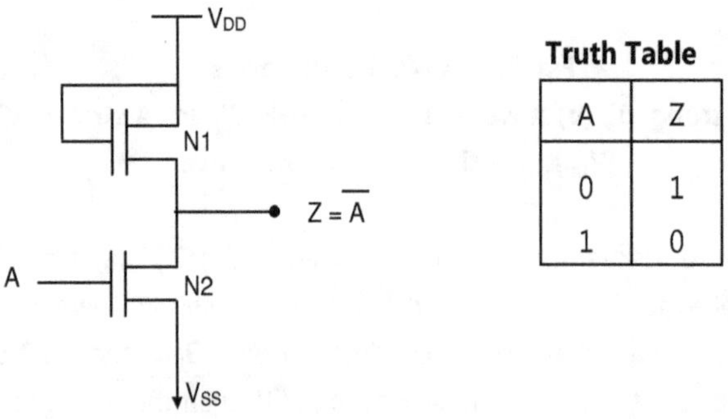

Fig. 2.16: MNOS inverter

Two NMOS transistors N1 and N2 are connected in series. Gate of transistor N1 is connected to V_{DD}; therefore, it is always on. When input A is at logic '1', the transistor N2 is turned on, hence the output Z is shorted to V_{SS}. Therefore output Z is at logic '0'. When input A is at logic '0', transistor N2 is turned off, and output Z is pulled up to level V_{DD} i.e. logic '1'. Thus, the circuit behaves as an inverter.

2.5.2 NMOS NAND

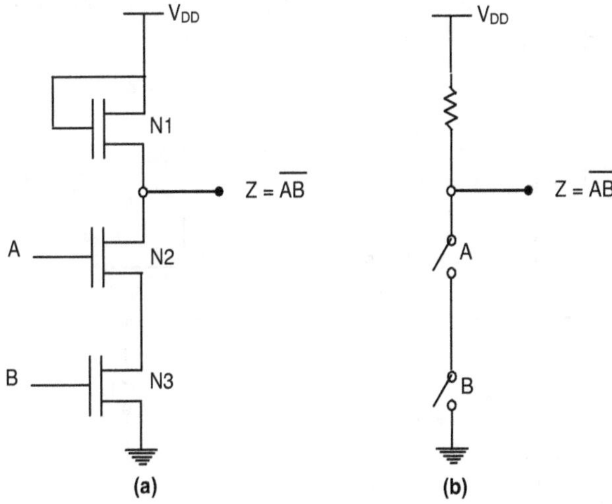

Fig. 2.17: (a) Circuit of 2 input NAND gate

(b) Switch representation

The two input NAND gate is constructed by connecting three transistors in series as shown in Fig. 2.17 (a). Transistor N1 is load and transistors N2, N3 are drivers. The truth table of NAND gate is as shown below:

A	B	Z
0	0	1
0	1	1
1	0	1
1	1	0

Current path exists only if both the switches are closed, i.e. A and B are at logic '1' and the output Z is at logic '0' state. The drivers are the enhancement type and load is of depletion type. When any one of the driver is off (A or B is at logic '0'), one of the switch is open, then no current path exists and the load transistor keeps the output at logic '1'. The high and low output levels can be computed by equating the current equation:

$$I_{DN1} = I_{DN2} = I_{DN3}$$

2.5.3 NMOS NOR

Fig. 2.18 shows the circuit of two input NOR gate and its switch representation.

NMOS NOR gate consists of two identical enhancement type NMOS drivers (transistors N2 and N3) and one depletion type load (transistor N1).

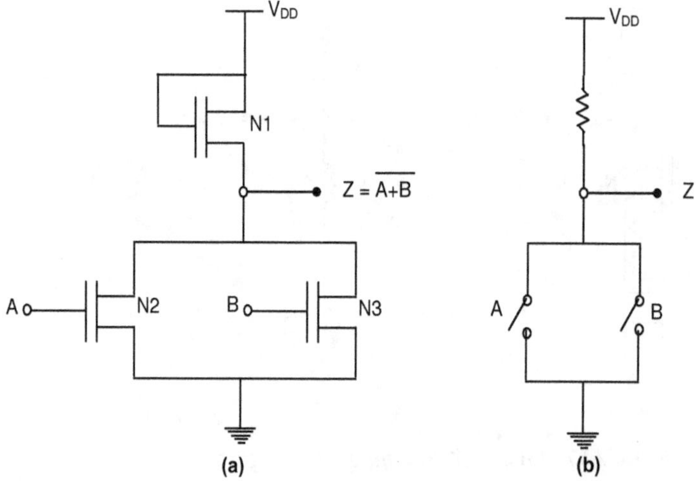

Fig. 2.18: (a) Circuit diagram of two input NOR gate
(b) Switch representation

The truth table of two input NOR gate is as shown below:

A	B	Z
0	0	1
0	1	0
1	0	0
1	1	0

If the input A or B are at logic '1', the corresponding transistor turns on and provides a conducting path from output to the ground and so the voltage at the output node decreases (logic '0'). When both inputs are high, the output is again pulled down to logic '0'. When inputs A and B are at logic '0' (less than the threshold voltage), then the transistors N2 and N3 are in cut-off region and the load transistor pulls the output to a high logic level.

The output low and output high (V_{OL} and V_{OH}) can be found by equating drain current equation of load to the drivers

$$I_{DN1} = I_{DN2} + I_{DN3}.$$

2.6 Implementation of Gates using CMOS

2.6.1 CMOS NAND

Fig. 2.19 shows a two input CMOS NAND gate.

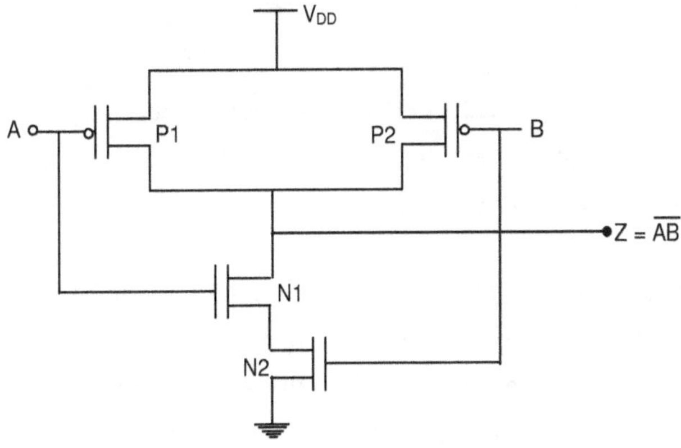

Fig. 2.19: CMOS two input NAND gate

The NMOS transistors of the CMOS are connected in series and they provide a conducting path between the output node and the ground, if both input voltages are at logic '1'.

When both the inputs A and B are at logic '1', transistors P1 and P2 turn off and transistors N1 and N2 turn on. Hence output Z is pulled down to ground (Z at logic '0').

When one of the inputs A and B or both inputs A and B are at logic '0', either N1 or N2 or both are off. Transistors P1 or P2 or both are on. Therefore output Z is at logic '1'.

The N input NAND gate can be constructed by connecting N NMOS transistors in series and N PMOS transistors in parallel.

2.6.2 CMOS NOR

The circuit diagram of two input CMOS NOR gate is as shown in Fig. 2.20.

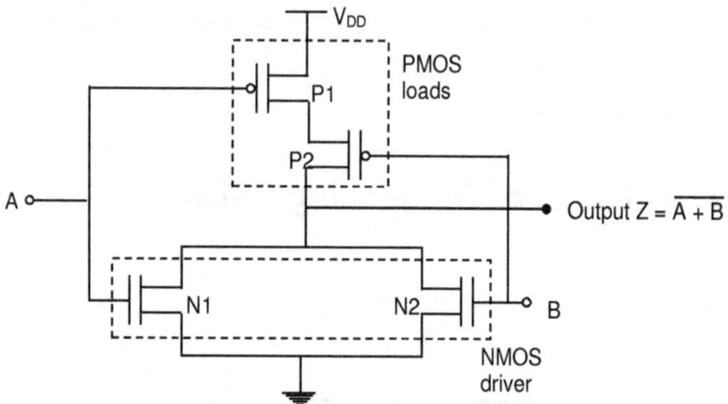

Fig. 2.20: CMOS two input NOR gate

The NMOS drivers are connected in parallel and the PMOS loads are connected in series. When either A or B or both are at logic '1', the output Z is grounded (i.e. Z at logic '0').

When both the inputs A and B are at logic '0', both PMOS transistors P1 and P2 turn on and both NMOS transistors turn off. Hence output is connected to V_{DD} and Z is at logic '1'.

The complementary nature of the circuit is explained below in details.

- When one or both input are high, the NMOS transistors are on and create a conducting path between output and ground. At the same time, PMOS transistor is cut off. So output is at logic '0'.

- When both input voltages are low, then the NMOS transistors are cut off, but their PMOS counterparts are on and they create a conducting path between the output and the power supply voltage. So output is at logic '1'.

- Thus the complementary action of the circuit allows that for any given input combination, the output is connected either to V_{DD} or to the ground.

2.6.3 Complex Gate Design

In complex gate design in CMOS, we have to design the NMOS network and the PMOS network for a given circuit. The NMOS network is the pull-down network and PMOS network is the pull-up network that must be the dual network of the n-net. That is the parallel connections in the NMOS pull-down network will correspond to a series connection in the PMOS pull-up network and the series connections in the pull-down network correspond a parallel connection in the pull-up network.

Fig. 2.21 shows realization of function $Z = \overline{AB + CD}$.

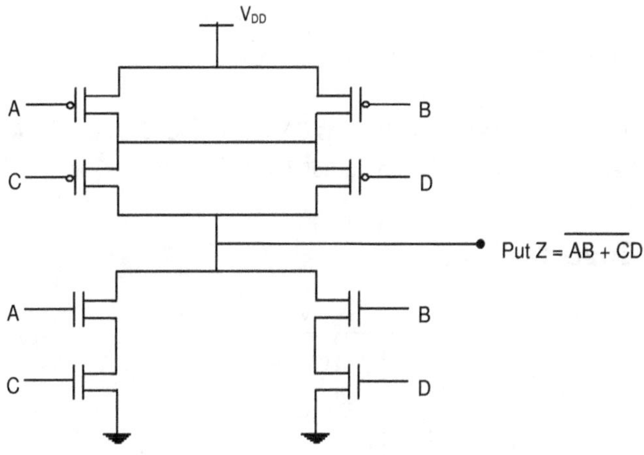

Fig. 2.21: Construction of function Z = $\overline{AB + CD}$

2.6.4 Multiplexer using CMOS

Fig. 2.22 shows 2:1 multiplexer.

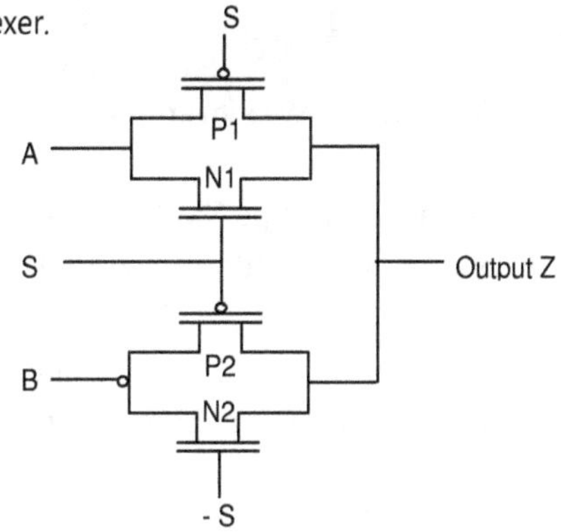

Fig. 2.22: Circuit of 2:1 multiplexer

Truth Table

A	B	S	–S	Output Z
X	0	0	1	0 (B)
X	1	0	1	1 (B)
0	X	1	0	0 (A)
1	X	1	0	1 (A)

The above circuit implements the function $Z = A.S + B.\overline{S}$

When S is at logic '1', NMOS transistor N1 turns ON and output Z is equal to A. When S is at logic '0', PMOS transistor P2 turns ON and output Z = B.

2.7 CMOS Inverter

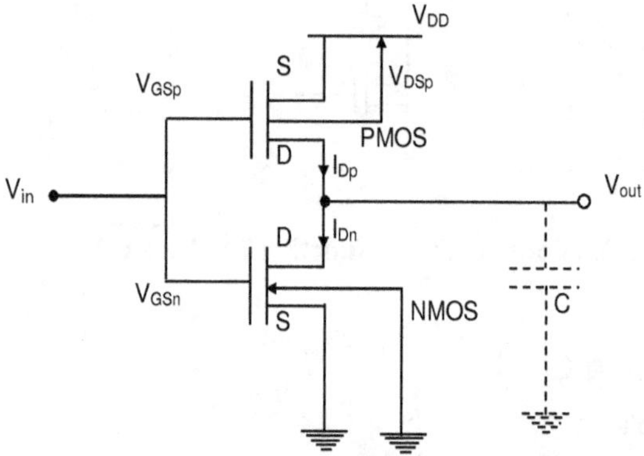

Fig. 2.23: A CMOS inverter circuit

CMOS inverter consists of an enhancement type NMOS transistor and an enhancement type PMOS transistor working in complementary mode as shown in Fig. 2.23.

For high input, NMOS transistor is on and it pulls down the output to ground and the PMOS acts as the load. For low input voltages, NMOS transistor is cut off and PMOS transistor is on and it pulls up the output and NMOS acts as a load.

The main advantages of CMOS inverter are:
- Low power dissipation
- Full swing of output voltage from 0 to V_{DD}.
- Sharp transition between states, which increases the noise margin.

From Fig. 2.23, we observe that the input voltage is connected to the gate of NMOS and PMOS transistors. The substrate of NMOS is connected to ground and the substrate of PMOS is connected to V_{DD}. The effective source substrate bias $V_{SB} = 0$ for both the transistors. It is also observed that,

$$\left.\begin{aligned} V_{GSn} &= V_{in} \\ V_{DSn} &= V_{out} \end{aligned}\right\} \qquad \qquad \text{... (1)}$$

and

$$\left.\begin{aligned} V_{GSp} &= -(V_{DD} - V_{in}) \\ V_{DSp} &= V_{DD} - V_{out} \end{aligned}\right\} \qquad \qquad \text{... (2)}$$

CMOS Inverter

The operation of the CMOS inverter can be divided into five different regions as shown in Fig. 2.24 (a). The switching point is designed at the supply voltage = $V_{DD}/2$. During transition both the transistors in the CMOS inverter are momentarily ON resulting in a short pulse of current as shown in Fig. 2.24 (b).

Operation of CMOS inverter in five regions is as discussed below:

Region 1:

In this region V_{in} is given as $0 \le V_{in} \le V_{tn}$, in which NMOS is cut off and PMOS is in linear region. In this case, the output voltage is,

$$V_{out} = V_{DD}$$

Region 2:

V_{in} in this region is given by,

$V_{tn} \le V_{in} \le V_{DD}/2$, in which PMOS is in non-saturated region, while NMOS is in saturation. The output voltage in this region is given by,

$$V_{out} = (V_{in} - V_{tp}) + \sqrt{(V_{in} - V_{tp})^2 - 2\left(V_{in} - \frac{V_{DD}}{2} - V_{tp}\right)V_{DD} - \frac{\beta_n}{\beta_p}(V_{in} - V_{tn})^2}$$

where, β_n and β_p are the gain factors for NMOS and PMOS respectively. **β_n and β_p are also indicated by k_n and k_p.**

Region 3:

In this region, both NMOS and PMOS devices are in saturation. In this region, V_{in} is $V_{DD}/2$.

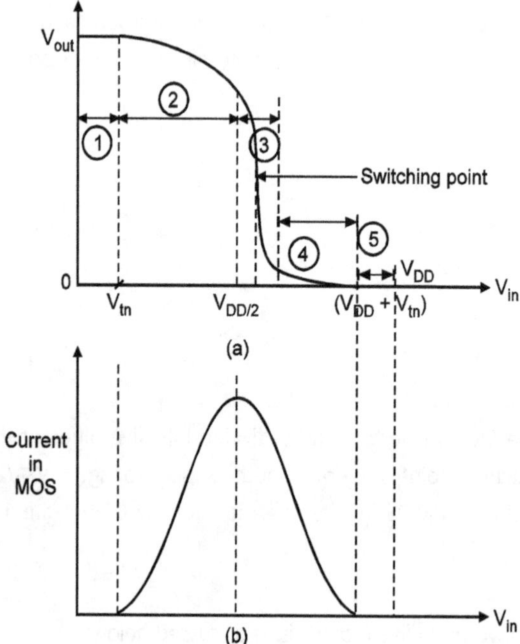

Fig. 2.24: Transfer characteristics and current in CMOS inverter

Region 4:

V$_{in}$ in this region is given by,

$V_{DD}/2 < V_{in} \le (V_{DD} + V_{tp})$

The PMOS is in saturation and the NMOS is in its non-saturated region. The output voltage is given by:

$$V_{out} = (V_{in} - V_{tn}) - \sqrt{(V_{in} - V_{tn})^2 \frac{\beta_p}{\beta_n}(V_{in} - V_{DD} - V_{tp})^2}$$

Region 5:

When $V_{in} \ge V_{DD} + V_{tp}$, in which PMOS is cut off and the NMOS is in linear mode. The output voltage in this region is given by,

$$V_{out} = 0$$

β_n/β_p Ratio in CMOS inverter

β means the MOS transistor gain factor which is given by:

$$\beta \;=\; K\frac{W}{L} \qquad\qquad \text{... (1)}$$

where the factor K is a technology dependent parameter, K given by:

$$K \;=\; \frac{\varepsilon_{ins} \cdot \varepsilon_0 \cdot \mu}{D} \qquad\qquad \text{... (2)}$$

where,

D　　$=$　thickness of gate insulator also called as t_{ox}.

ε_{ins}　$=$　relative permittivity of insulation between gate and channel

ε_0　　$=$　permittivity of free space

μ　　$=$　mobility of holes or electrons

The W/L is contributed by the geometry

W = Width of the channel

L = Length of the channel

The transfer curves for different values of β_n/β_p of CMOS inverter are plotted as shown in Fig. 2.25.

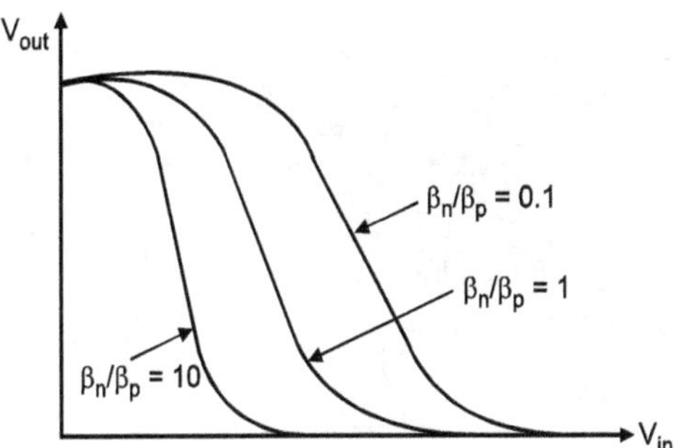

Fig. 2.25: Transfer characteristics of CMOS inverter for different values of β_n/β_p

From equation (1), β of the transistor depends on W/L ratio. Thus, for a given process, if we want to change β_n/β_p ratio, we need to change the channel dimensions i.e. channel width W and channel length L. From Fig. 2.25, we can observe that as β_n/β_p ratio decreases, the transition region shifts from left to right, however the output voltage transition remains sharp.

For the CMOS inverter, the best value for β_n/β_p ratio is 1.

$$\boxed{\dfrac{\beta_n}{\beta_p} = 1 \text{ is the desirable value}}$$

When $\beta_n/\beta_p = 1$, it allows a capacitive load to charge and discharge in equal times by providing equal amount of current source and sink capabilities.

Table 2.1 refers to the various input voltages and corresponding output voltages and the operating region of the NMOS and PMOS transistors.

Table 2.1

	V_{in}	V_{out}	NMOS	PMOS
Case 1	$< V_{TOn}$	V_{OH}	Cut-off	Linear
Case 2	V_{IL}	$\cong V_{OH}$	Saturation	Linear
Case 3	V_{th}	V_{th}	Saturation	Saturation
Case 4	V_{IH}	$\cong V_{OL}$	Linear	Saturation
Case 5	$> V_{DD} + V_{TOp}$	V_{OL}	Linear	Cut-off

The voltage transfer curve of CMOS inverter is shown in Fig. 2.26.

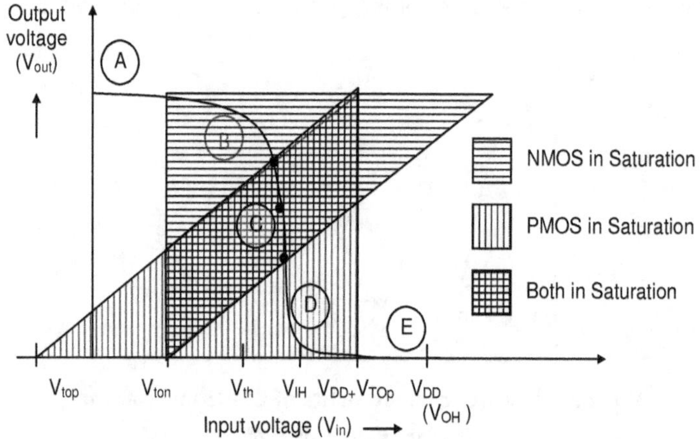

Fig. 2.26: Voltage transfer curve of CMOS inverter

From voltage transfer curve, we define five voltage points.

- V_{OH} is defined as the maximum output voltage when output level is at logic 1 ($V_{OH} = V_{DD}$).
- V_{OL} is the minimum output voltage when the output level is logic 0 ($V_{OL} = 0$).
- V_{IL} is the maximum input voltage which can be read as logic 0.

- V_{IH} is the minimum input voltage which can be read as logic 1.
- V_{th} is the input voltage at input voltage = output voltage.
- V_{top} = threshold voltage of PMOS
- V_{ton} = threshold voltage of NMOS.

Now for a range of input voltages, the characteristic of the circuit will be studied.

Calculation of V_{OH}

When $V_{in} < V_{ton}$, the NMOS transistor is cut off and PMOS is in linear region. The drain current of NMOS transistor $I_{Dn} = 0$, so $I_{Dp} = 0$.

$$I_{Dn} = I_{Dp} = 0 \qquad \text{... (3)}$$

So drain source voltage of PMOS is also zero.

$$V_{DSp} = V_{DD} - V_{out}, \text{ but } V_{DSp} = 0$$
$$V_{out} = V_{DD} = V_{OH} \qquad \text{... (4)}$$

Calculation of V_{OL}

When the input voltage exceeds $V_{DD} + V_{top}$, the PMOS transistor is cut off and NMOS transistor is on. So $I_{Dp} = I_{Dn} = 0$ and $V_{DSn} = 0$

$$\text{Hence,} \qquad V_{out} = V_{DSn} = 0 = V_{OL} \qquad \text{... (5)}$$

Calculation of V_{IL}

V_{IL} is the smaller of two input voltages for which slope of voltage transfer curve is −1. When input is low, the NMOS transistor is in saturation and the PMOS transistor is in linear region.

The saturation current for the NMOS transistor is given by,

$$I_{DSn} = \frac{k_n}{2}\left[V_{GSn} - V_{To_n}\right]^2 \qquad \text{... (6)}$$

where k_n = NMOS gain factor

$$= \frac{\mu_n \in}{t_{ox}}\left(\frac{W_n}{L_n}\right)$$

where,

μ_n = mobility of electrons

W_n = channel width of n device

L_n = channel length of n device.

The current for the p device is obtained by

$$I_{DSP} = -\frac{k_p}{2}\left[2(V_{GSP} - V_{To_P})V_{DSp} - V^2{}_{DSp}\right] \qquad \text{... (7)}$$

Equating equations (6) and (7) and substituting equations (1) and (2) we have

$$\frac{k_n}{2}(V_{in} - V_{Ton})^2 = \frac{k_p}{2}\left[2(V_{in} - V_{DD} - V_{Top})(V_{OUT} - V_{DD}) - (V_{out} - V_{DD})^2\right]$$

Differentiating with respect to V_{in}, we obtain

$$k_n(V_{in} - V_{Ton}) = k_p\left[(V_{in} - V_{DD} - V_{Top})\frac{dV_{out}}{dV_{in}} + (V_{OUT} - V_{DD}) - (V_{out} - V_{DD})\frac{dV_{out}}{dV_{in}}\right]$$

Now $\qquad V_{in} = V_{IL} \quad$ and $\quad \dfrac{dV_{out}}{dV_{in}} = -1$

So,

$$k_n(V_{IL} - V_{Ton}) = k_p(2V_{out} - V_{IL} + V_{Top} - V_{DD})$$

Rearranging the terms to obtain V_{IL},

$$V_{IL} = \frac{2V_{out} + V_{Top} - V_{DD} - \dfrac{k_n}{k_p}V_{Ton}}{1 + \dfrac{k_n}{k_p}} \qquad \text{... (8)}$$

Output voltage can be obtained by arranging equation (8) and substituting $V_{IL} = V_{in}$.

$$V_{out} = (V_{in} - V_{Top}) + \sqrt{(V_{in} - V_{Top})^2 - 2\left(V_{in} - \frac{V_{DD}}{2} - V_{Top}\right)V_{DD} - \frac{k_n}{k_p}(V_{in} - V_{Ton})} \qquad \text{... (9)}$$

Calculation of V_{IH}

Since V_{IH} is the higher value of input voltage for which the slope of the voltage transfer curve is equal to zero. Also the NMOS transistor is in linear region and the PMOS transistor operates in saturation.

So equating the current equation, we have

$$\frac{k_n}{2}\left[2(V_{GSn} - V_{Ton})V_{DSn} - V^2{}_{DSn}\right] = \frac{k_p}{2}(V_{GSp} - V_{Top})^2$$

Substituting equations (1) and (2), we have

$$\frac{k_n}{2}\left[2\left(V_{in}-V_{Ton}\right)V_{out}-V^2_{out}\right]=\frac{k_p}{2}\left(V_{in}-V_{DD}-V_{Top}\right)^2 \qquad \text{... (10)}$$

Differentiating with respect to V_{in},

$$k_n\left[\left(V_{in}-V_{Ton}\right)\frac{dV_{out}}{dV_{in}}+V_{out}-V_{out}\frac{dV_{out}}{dV_{in}}\right]=k_p\left(V_{in}-V_{DD}-V_{Top}\right)$$

Now $\qquad \dfrac{dV_{out}}{dV_{in}}=-1$ and $V_{in}=V_{IH}$

$$k_n\left(-V_{IH}+V_{Ton}+2V_{out}\right)=k_p\left(V_{IH}-V_{DD}-V_{Top}\right)$$

Rearranging the equations

$$V_{IH}=\frac{V_{DD}+V_{Top}+\dfrac{k_n}{k_p}\left(2V_{out}+V_{Ton}\right)}{1+\dfrac{k_n}{k_p}} \qquad \text{... (11)}$$

Now V_{out} is an unknown quantity and so equations (10) and (11) have to be solved simultaneously to obtain the values of V_{IH} and the corresponding output voltage.

Calculation of V_{th}

The inverter threshold voltage V_{th} is defined as that voltage for which V_{in} = V_{out}. When input and output are same, the PMOS and NMOS transistors are in saturation. So equating the current equation, we have

$$\frac{k_n}{2}\left(V_{GSn}-V_{Ton}\right)^2=\frac{k_p}{2}\left(V_{GSp}-V_{Top}\right)^2$$

Substituting for V_{GSn} and V_{GSp} from equations (1) and (2),

$$\frac{k_n}{2}\left(V_{in}-V_{Ton}\right)^2=\frac{k_p}{2}\left(V_{in}-V_{DD}-V_{Top}\right)^2$$

Substituting V_{in} = V_{th}

$$V_{th}=\frac{V_{Ton}+\sqrt{\dfrac{k_p}{k_n}}\left(V_{DD}-V_{Top}\right)}{1+\sqrt{\dfrac{k_p}{k_n}}} \qquad \text{... (12)}$$

Inverter threshold characterizes the dc performance of the circuit. Threshold voltage of the inverter lies between V_{IL} and V_{IH}.

CMOS Switching Characteristics

The switching speed of CMOS inverter is limited by the load capacitance C_L. The load capacitance C_L takes time to charge and discharge. When there is an input transition, it results in an output transition that either charges C_L towards V_{DD} or discharges C_L towards V_{SS}.

Speed of Operation in CMOS Inverter

Speed of operation or **propagation delay** of a gate is the average transition delay time for the signal to propagate from input to output when the signal changes its value. The signals passing through a gate take certain time to propagate through it to give a valid output. This time interval is defined as the propagation delay. The signal travels through a number of gates and the total delay is calculated by the delay times of individual gates. The speed of operation depends on the propagation delay of each gate. The smaller the delay, the faster is the speed of operation.

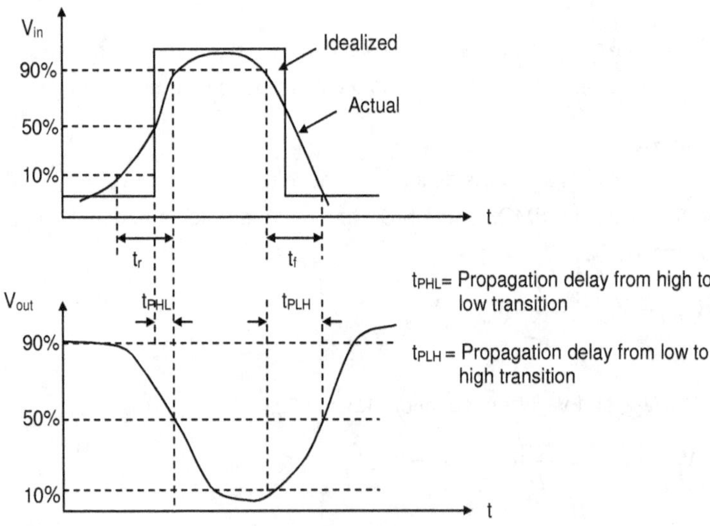

Fig. 2.27: Propagation delay

The average propagation delay time of a gate is calculated from the input and output voltage waveforms as shown in Fig. 2.27. The **rise time** t_r for a given signal is defined as the time required for the signal to make the transition from 10% point to 90% point on the waveform. The **fall time** t_f is defined as the time required to fall from 90% to 10% of its steady state value. The voltages at 10% and 90% points are defined in terms of V_{OL} and V_{OH}.

The propagation delay t_p is the difference between the times for which the input and output voltages are at their 50% values.

$$V_{50\%} = \frac{V_{OH} + V_{OL}}{2}$$

The average propagation delay t_p is defined as,

$$t_p = \frac{t_{PLH} + t_{PHL}}{2}$$

Typically, propagation delay is measured in nanoseconds.

Delay Models in CMOS Inverter

The switching speed of CMOS inverter is limited by the load capacitance C_L. The load capacitance C_L takes time to charge and discharge. When there is an input transition, it results in the output transition that either charges C_L towards V_{DD} or discharges C_L towards V_{SS}.

Now, we will see the effect of load capacitance C_L on rise and fall time in CMOS inverter.

Rise Time Estimation

Fig. 2.28 shows the CMOS inverter and the equivalent circuit when the input changes from high to low.

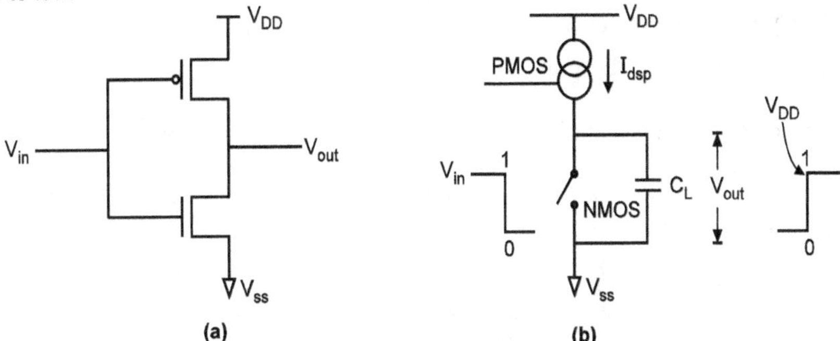

Fig. 2.28: Rise-time model of CMOS inverter

Fig. 2.28 (a) shows CMOS inverter and Fig. 2.28 (b) shows the rise-time model when input changes from high to low. In this, we assume that PMOS stays in saturation for the entire charging period.

The saturation current in PMOS transistor is given by,

$$I_{dsp} = \frac{\beta_p(V_{gs} - |V_{tp}|)^2}{2}$$

where I_{dsp} = Drain to source current in PMOS

     V_{tp} = Threshold voltage of PMOS.

As shown, I_{dsp} charges capacitor C_L and since its magnitude is approximately constant, we have,

$$V_{out} = \frac{I_{dsp}.\,t}{C_L}$$

Substituting the value of I_{dsp}, we get

$$V_{out} = \frac{\beta_p(V_{gs} - |V_{tp}|)^2}{2} \cdot \frac{t}{C_L}$$

Rearranging for time 't' i.e. t_r (t = t_r)

$$\therefore \quad t = t_r = \frac{2\,C_L.\,V_{out}}{\beta_p\,(V_{gs} - |V_{tp}|)^2}$$

Now V_{out} = +V_{DD} and solving above equation, we will get rise time t_r as

$$t_r = \frac{kC_L}{\beta_p.V_{DD}}$$

where k is from 3 to 4.

Similarly, we can derive the equation for fall time t_f, and it is given by

$$t_f = k \times \frac{C_L}{\beta_n\,V_{DD}}$$

where k = 3 to 4 for values of V_{DD} = 3 to 5 volts and V_{tn} = 0.5 to 1 volts.

From the rise and fall time equations, we can see that, the delay is directly proportional to the load capacitance C_L. Therefore, to design high speed circuits, one has to minimize the load capacitance (C_L) seen by a gate. Also t_r and t_f are inversely proportional to supply voltage V_{DD}. It means, as the V_{DD} supply is raised, the delay time reduces. If we lower the supply voltage, it reduces the speed of the gates.

The t_r and t_f delays are inversely proportional to the β of driving transistor. As β is directly proportional to width (W), lowering width decreases β and increases delay time. Also length of the transistor is inversely proportional to β, i.e., lowering the length increases β and decreases delay time.

So, the CMOS logic gate's speed is basically decided by these three factors:

1) $C_L \rightarrow$ Load capacitance
2) $V_{DD} \rightarrow$ Supply voltage
3) $\beta = W/L \rightarrow$ gain factor of MOS.

For equal sized PMOS and NMOS transistors,

$$\beta_n \;=\; 2 \text{ to } 3\beta_p$$

It means β_n and β_p are different for NMOS and PMOS transistors, when they are manufactured with the same width and length. It is because of the mobility of holes and electrons, mobility of electrons is more as compared to the mobility of holes ($\mu_n = 2\mu_p$).

Therefore, the rise time and fall time is different for the same sized PMOS and NMOS transistors.

$$t_f \;=\; \frac{t_r}{2 \text{ to } 3}$$

Fall time is faster than the rise time. Therefore, if we require approximately the same rise and fall time for an inverter, we need to make

$$\frac{\beta_n}{\beta_p} \;=\; 1$$

It means that, the channel width for the PMOS must be increased to approximately two to three times that of the NMOS device, so,

$$W_p \;=\; (2 \text{ to } 3)\, W_n$$

where,

W_p = channel width of PMOS

W_n = channel width of NMOS

The input and the output voltage waveforms for high to low transition are shown in Fig. 2.29. The switching speed of CMOS gate is limited by the time taken to charge and discharge the load capacitance C_L. For 0 to V_{DD} input transition, capacitor C discharges towards ground (0V) and for V_{DD} to 0V input transition, C_L charges towards V_{DD}.

Initially, the NMOS transistor is in saturation. When the output voltage decreases to $V_{DD}-V_{tn}$, the NMOS transistor conducts in linear region.

In the first case, when NMOS transistor is in saturation,

$$I_{Dn} = \frac{k_n}{2}\left(V_{in} - V_{Tn}\right)^2$$

$$= \frac{k_n}{2}\left(V_{OH} - V_{T_1 n}\right)^2 \qquad\qquad \ldots (13)$$

when $V_{OH} - V_{Tn} < V_{out} \leq V_{OH}$

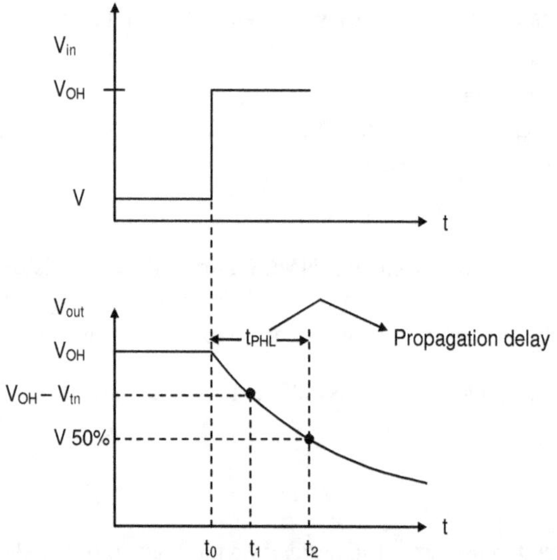

Fig. 2.29: Input-output waveforms for calculation of fall time

Equation (13) can also be written as

$$\int_{t_0}^{t_1} dt = -C \int_{V_0}^{V_1} \left(\frac{1}{I_{Dn}} \right) dV_{out}$$

where, $V_0 = V_{OH}$

$V_1 = V_{OH} - V_{tn}$

Substituting value of I_{Dn} from equation (13) and integrating we have,

$$t_1 - t_0 = \frac{2CV_{Tn}}{k_n(V_{OH} - V_{Tn})^2}$$

At $t = t_1$ the output voltage is $V_{DD} - V_{t1n}$ and the transistor is at the boundary of saturation linear region.

In the linear region

$$I_{Dn} = \frac{k_n}{2} \left[2(V_{in} - V_{Tn})V_{out} - V^2_{out} \right]$$

$$= \frac{k_n}{2} \left[2(V_{OH} - V_{Tn})V_{out} - V^2_{out} \right] \text{ when } V_{out} \leq V_{OH} - V_{Tn}$$

This equation can be written in terms of capacitor current as

$$\int_{t_1}^{t_2} dt = -C \int_{V_1}^{V_2} \left(\frac{1}{I_{Dn}} \right) dV_{out}$$

where $V_1 = V_{OH} - V_{tn}$

$\qquad V_2 = V_{50\%}$

Solving above equation yields

$$t_2 - t_1 = -\frac{2C}{k_n} \frac{1}{2(V_{OH} - V_{Tn})} ln \left[\frac{V_{out}}{2(V_{OH} - V_{Tn}) - V_{out}} \right]_{V_1}^{V_2}$$

Or

$$t_2 - t_1 = \frac{C}{k_n(V_{OH} - V_{Tn})} ln \left[\frac{2(V_{OH} - V_{Tn}) - V_{50\%}}{V_{50\%}} \right]$$

Now $t_{PHL} = t_2 - t_0 = (t_2 - t_1) + (t_1 - t_0)$

$$= \frac{C}{k_n(V_{OH} - V_{Tn})} \left[\frac{2V_{Tn}}{V_{OH} - V_{Tn}} + ln \frac{4(V_{OH} - V_{Tn})}{V_{OH} + V_{OL}} - 1 \right]$$

Since $V_{OH} = V_{DD}$ and $V_{OL} = 0V$ for CMOS inverter, we have

$$t_{PHL} = \frac{C}{k_n(V_{DD} - V_{Tn})} \left[\frac{2V_{Tn}}{V_{DD} - V_{Tn}} + ln \left[\frac{4(V_{DD} - V_{Tn})}{V_{DD}} - 1 \right] - 1 \right] \qquad \text{... (14)}$$

When the input switches from high to low, the driver NMOS transistor is cut off and the capacitor charges up through the load PMOS transistor. The propagation delay time t_{PLH} can be obtained by following the similar steps followed above and can be written as

$$t_{PLH} = \frac{C}{k_p\left(V_{OH} - V_{OL} - |-V_{Tp}|\right)} \left[\frac{2|V_{Tp}|}{V_{OH} - V_{OL} - |V_{Tp}|} + ln \left[\frac{2(V_{OH} - V_{OL} - |V_{Tp}|)}{V_{OH} - V_{50\%}} - 1 \right] \right]$$

Since $V_{OH} = V_{DD}$ and $V_{OL} = 0\ V$

$$t_{PLH} = \frac{C}{k_p\left(V_{DD} - |V_{Tp}|\right)} \left[\frac{2|V_{Tp}|}{V_{DD} - |V_{Tp}|} + ln \left[\frac{4(V_{DD} - |V_{Tp}|)}{V_{DD}} - 1 \right] \right] \qquad \text{... (15)}$$

Substituting $R_{onp} = \dfrac{1}{k_p\left(V_{DD} - |V_{Tp}|\right)}$ and $V_{tp} = -1$ V, $V_{DD} = 5$ V

we have

$$t_{PLH} = 1.3 R_{onp}, \; C \cong \frac{0.325}{k_p} \qquad \text{... (16)}$$

We know that $\beta_n > \beta_p$ (generally $\beta_n \approx 2$ to $3\,\beta_p$).

For NMOS transistor

$$R_n \; \propto \; \frac{L_n}{W_n \beta_n}$$

where R_n is the resistance of NMOS.

Similarly, for PMOS transistor,

$$R_p \; \propto \; \frac{L_p}{W_p \beta_p}$$

where R_p is the resistance of PMOS.

As $\beta_n > \beta_p$, R_n has the low value compared to R_p ($R_n < R_p$). But for equal current in NMOS and PMOS, we need equal value of resistance, i.e. we need $R_n = R_p$ for designing.

Hence, we need $\qquad R_n = R_p$

$$\therefore \qquad \frac{L_n}{W_n \beta_n} = \frac{L_p}{W_p \beta_p}$$

(Assume $L_n = L_p = 2$) means same length.

$$\therefore \qquad \frac{W_p}{W_n} = \frac{\beta_n}{\beta_p}$$

But $\qquad \beta_n \approx 2.5\,\beta_p$

$$\therefore \qquad \frac{W_p}{W_n} \approx \frac{2.5\,\beta_p}{\beta_p}$$

$$\therefore \qquad W_p \approx 2.5\, W_n$$

$\therefore$ For equal drive, take width of PMOS, 2.5 times width of NMOS (assuming length for PMOS and NMOS same).

NAND Gate Device Sizing

The circuit for NAND gate is as shown in Fig. 2.30.

Now, consider the worst case, for the NMOS (pull down) section, i.e. when both NMOS transistors are ON. R_n is given by,

$$R_n = \left(\frac{L}{W}\right)_{neff} \cdot \frac{1}{\beta_n}$$

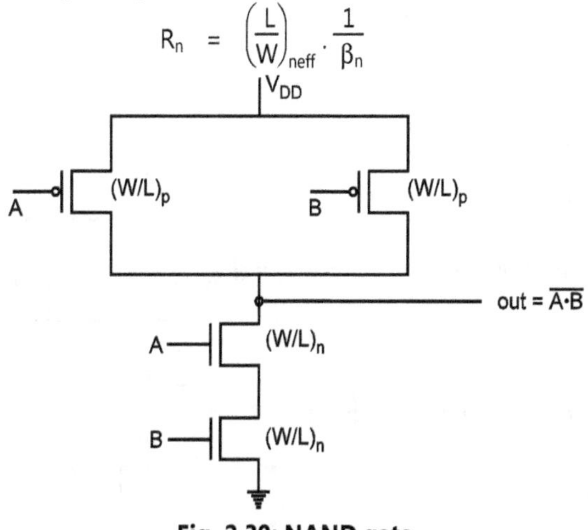

Fig. 2.30: NAND gate

As two NMOS are in series, n_{eff} is given by,

$$\left(\frac{L}{W}\right)_{neff} = \frac{L_n}{W_n} + \frac{L_n}{W_n} = \frac{2L_n}{W_n}$$

Now, for PMOS, two PMOS are in parallel. So, for the worst case, we need to consider only one PMOS. Therefore R_p is given by,

$$R_p = \frac{L_p}{W_p \beta_p}$$

Now, we will consider the total path for the current. i.e. the path with the maximum value of resistance R (maximum number of transistors in series with ON state).

∴ For the worst case, we need same values of R_n and R_p.

$$\therefore \qquad R_n = R_p$$

Substituting values of R_n and R_p

$$\therefore \qquad \left(\frac{2L_n}{W_n}\right) \cdot \frac{1}{\beta_n} = \frac{L_p}{W_p \beta_p}$$

Now, assuming

$$\left(\frac{W_n}{L_n}\right) = \frac{6}{2}$$

we will keep same length i.e. $L_n = L_p = 2$

$$\therefore \qquad \left(\frac{2 \times 2}{6}\right) \cdot \frac{1}{\beta_n} = \frac{2}{W_p \beta_p}$$

(Now taking $\beta_n \approx 3\,\beta_p$)

$$\therefore \qquad \frac{2 \times 2}{6} \times \frac{1}{3.\beta_p} \;=\; \frac{2}{W_p\,\beta_p}$$

$$\therefore \qquad\qquad W_p \;=\; 9$$

$\therefore$ We can design NAND gate with

$W_n = 6, \qquad L_n = 2$

$W_p = 9, \qquad L_p = 2$ for $\beta_n \approx 2\beta_p$

Design of Complex Circuits

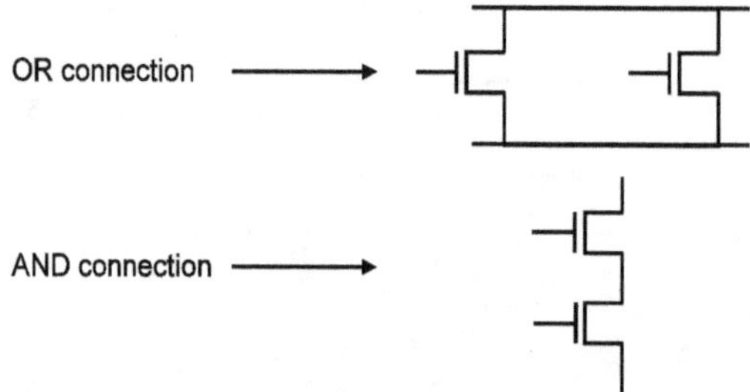

Fig. 2.31

Example 1: $\qquad Z = \overline{ab + c(d + e)}$

For pull up $\quad Z = \overline{ab} \cdot \overline{c(d + e)}$

$$= (\bar{a} + \bar{b}) \cdot (\bar{c} + \overline{d + e})$$

$$= (\bar{a} + \bar{b}) \cdot (\bar{c} + \bar{d} \cdot \bar{e})$$

The diagram for pull up part is as shown in Fig. 2.32.

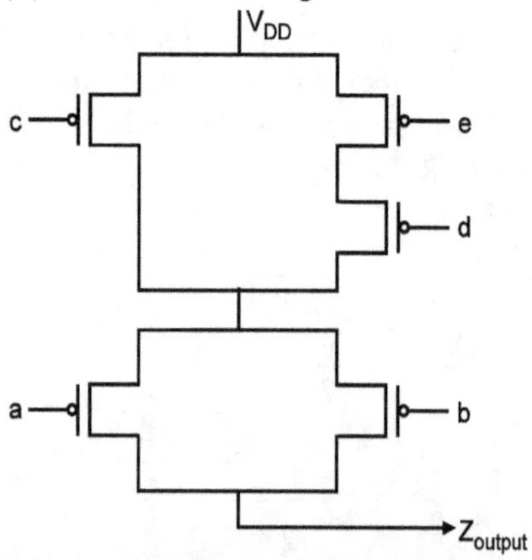

Fig. 2.32: Pull up part using PMOS

Now, to find the pull down part,

$$Z = \overline{ab + c(d + e)}$$

Taking $\overline{Z}$ $\therefore$ $\overline{Z} = \overline{ab + c(d + e)} = ab + c(d + e)$

Therefore the circuit for pull down part using NMOS is,

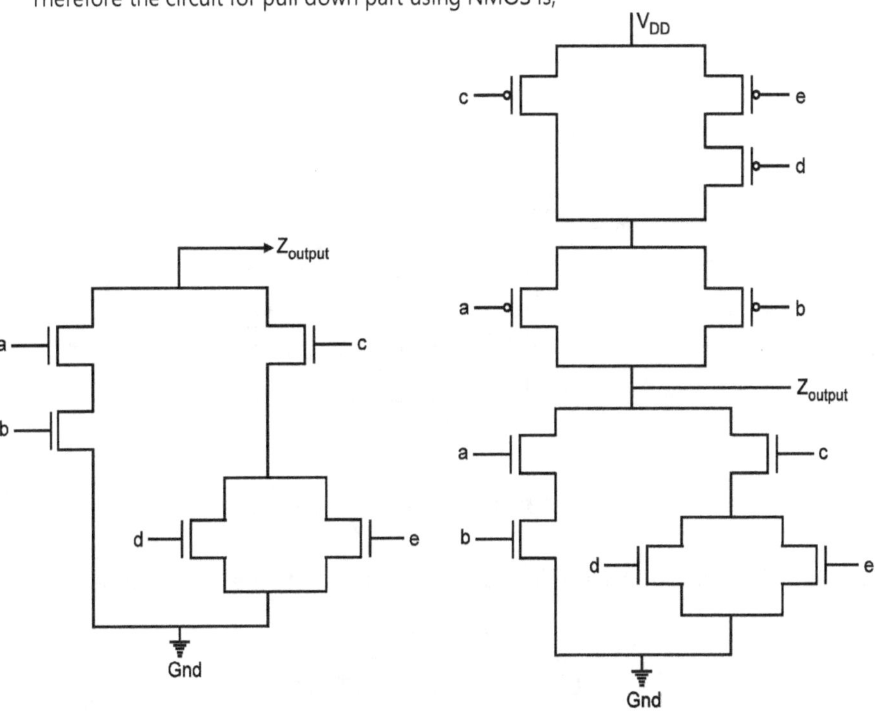

Fig. 2.33 : Pull down part using NMOS   **Fig. 2.34 : Circuit for $Z = \overline{ab + c(d + e)}$**

Therefore, the total circuit for

$$Z = \overline{ab + c(d + e)} \text{ is given in Fig. 2.34.}$$

Example 2: $Z = \overline{a + (b + c).d}$

For pull up part,

$$Z = \overline{a + (b + c).d} = \overline{a}\,(\overline{b}.\overline{c} + \overline{d})$$

For pull down part,

$$\overline{Z} = a + (b + c)\,d$$

Circuit is shown in Fig. 2.35.

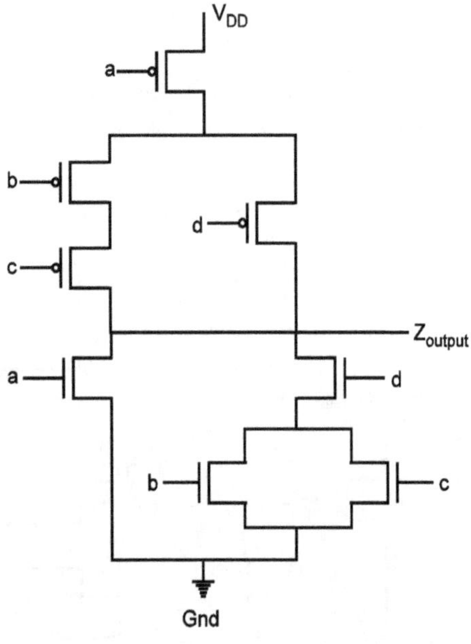

Fig. 2.35: Circuit for Z = $\overline{a + (b + c).d}$

Example 3: What should be the device sizing for equal drive of the circuit shown in Fig. 2.36?

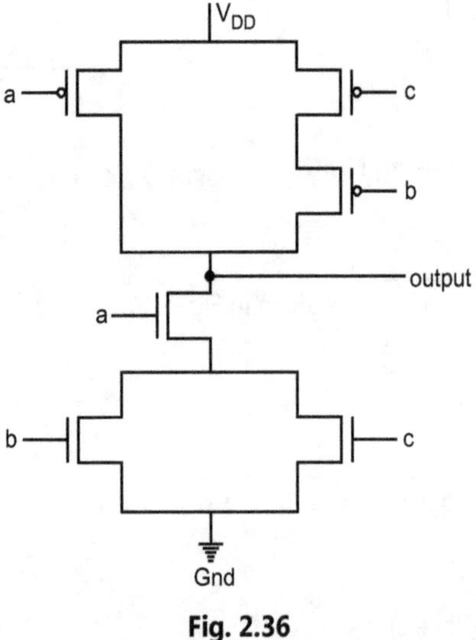

Fig. 2.36

Solution: Considering the worst case i.e. the paths with maximum R (maximum number of transistors in series with ON state).

For equal current drive, we need

$$R_n \approx R_p$$

Considering the worst case

N type ON Drivers	Out to Gnd path
a – b	$R_{na} + R_{nb}$
a – c	$R_{na} + R_{nc}$

For worst case, both n devices are in series, doubling the effective L_n.

$$\therefore \qquad R_n = \left(\frac{L}{W}\right)_{neff} \cdot \frac{1}{\beta_n}$$

$$\text{where,} \qquad \left(\frac{L}{W}\right)_{n_{eff}} = \frac{L_n}{W_n} + \frac{L_n}{W_n} = \frac{2\,L_n}{W_n}$$

$$\therefore \qquad \boxed{R_n = \left(\frac{2L_n}{W_n}\right) \cdot \frac{1}{\beta_n}}$$

In pull up region, considering the worst case,

P type ON Drivers	Out to V_{dd} path
a	R_{pa}
c – b	$R_{pc} + R_{pb}$

For worst case, both p devices are in series, doubling the effective L_p.

$$R_p = \left(\frac{L}{W}\right)_{P_{eff}} \cdot \frac{1}{\beta_p}$$

$$\text{where,} \qquad \left(\frac{L}{W}\right)_{P_{eff}} = \frac{L_p}{W_p} + \frac{L_p}{W_p} = \frac{2\,L_p}{W_p}$$

$$\therefore \qquad R_p = \left(\frac{2L_p}{W_p}\right) \cdot \frac{1}{\beta_p}$$

Now, for equal current drive, we need $R_n \approx R_p$.

$$\text{where,} \qquad R_n = \left(\frac{2L_n}{W_n}\right) \cdot \frac{1}{\beta_n}$$

$$R_p = \left(\frac{2L_p}{W_p}\right) \cdot \frac{1}{\beta_p}$$

$\therefore$ For $\qquad R_n \approx R_p$

$$\left(\frac{2L_n}{W_n}\right) \cdot \frac{1}{\beta_n} = \left(\frac{2L_p}{W_p}\right) \cdot \frac{1}{\beta_p}$$

Assuming $L_n = L_p = L$, $W_n = W$, $\beta_n = 3\,\beta_p$.

$$\therefore \quad \left(\frac{2L}{W}\right) \cdot \frac{1}{3\beta_p} = \left(\frac{2L}{W_p}\right) \cdot \frac{1}{\beta_p}$$

$$\therefore \quad \left(\frac{1}{W}\right) \cdot \frac{1}{3} = \left(\frac{1}{W_p}\right)$$

$$\therefore \quad \boxed{W_p = 3W} \quad \text{for worst case (c − b)}$$

Size of $(W/L)_{pa}$ can be found as,

$$\left(\frac{L}{3W} + \frac{L}{3W}\right) = \frac{3W}{2L}$$

$$\therefore \quad \boxed{W_{pa} = \frac{3}{2} \cdot W}$$

Example 4: Design the circuit described by the function,

$y = \overline{a\,(b + c)\,(d + e)}$ using CMOS logic. Also find the equivalent CMOS inverter for simultaneous switching of the inputs, assuming that $(W/L)_p = 5$ for all PMOS transistors and $(W/L)_n = 2$ for all NMOS transistors.

Solution: The equivalent (W/L) ratio of NMOS and PMOS network are determined by using the series and parallel equivalent rules. The circuit for $y = \overline{a\,(b + c)\,(d + e)}$ can be drawn as,

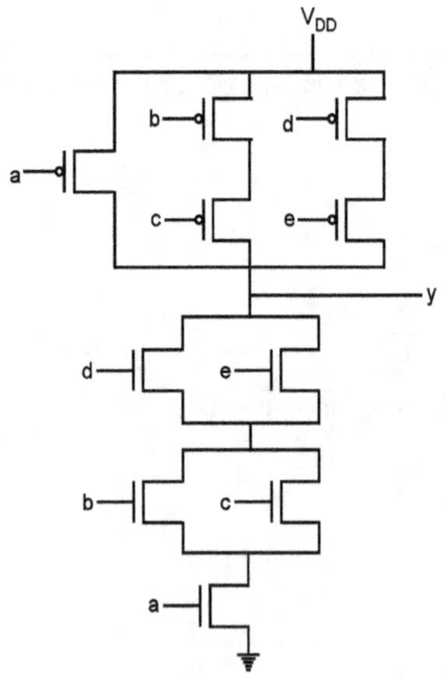

Fig. 2.37

For the above circuit, $\left(\dfrac{W}{L}\right)_{nequ}$ is given by

$$\left(\frac{W}{L}\right)_{nequ} = \cfrac{1}{\cfrac{1}{\left(\frac{W}{L}\right)_d + \left(\frac{W}{L}\right)_e} + \cfrac{1}{\left(\frac{W}{L}\right)_b + \left(\frac{W}{L}\right)_c} + \cfrac{1}{\left(\frac{W}{L}\right)_a}}$$

$$= \cfrac{1}{\cfrac{1}{2+2} + \cfrac{1}{2+2} + \cfrac{1}{2}} = 1$$

Similarly for $\left(\dfrac{W}{L}\right)_{pequ}$

$$\left(\frac{W}{L}\right)_{pequ} = \cfrac{1}{\cfrac{1}{\left(\frac{W}{L}\right)_d} + \cfrac{1}{\left(\frac{W}{L}\right)_e}} + \cfrac{1}{\cfrac{1}{\left(\frac{W}{L}\right)_b} + \cfrac{1}{\left(\frac{W}{L}\right)_c}} + \cfrac{1}{\cfrac{1}{\left(\frac{W}{L}\right)_a}}$$

$$= \cfrac{1}{\cfrac{1}{5} + \cfrac{1}{5}} + \cfrac{1}{\cfrac{1}{5} + \cfrac{1}{5}} + \cfrac{1}{\cfrac{1}{5}} = 5.8$$

Example 5: Design CMOS logic for $y = \overline{ab + c(d + e)}$

Calculate total area in terms of width of MOSFET.

Solution:

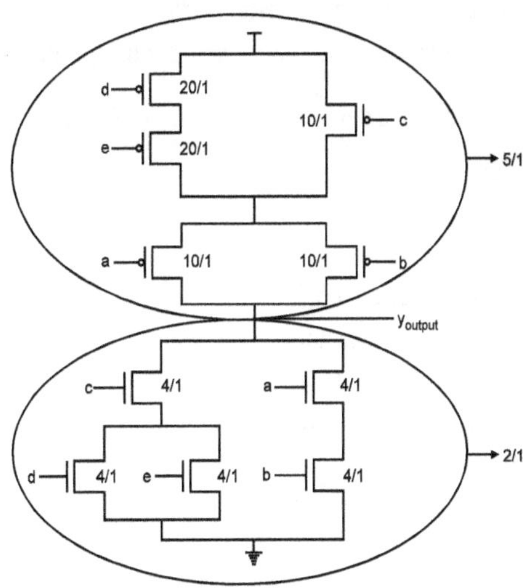

Fig. 2.38: Circuit for $y = \overline{ab + c(d + e)}$

2.8 Noise Margin

Noise in an electronic circuit is the presence of any unwanted signal which may be from power supply ripple or electromagnetic radiation. It is essential for all logic gates that they do not respond to noise present.

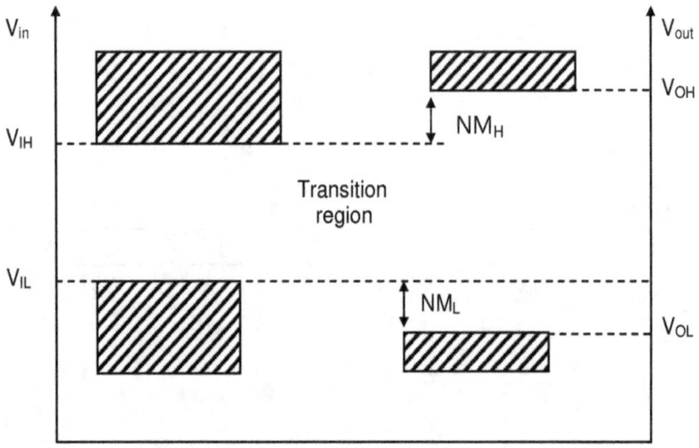

Fig. 2.39: Noise margin

Noise margin is defined as the allowable noise voltage on the input of a gate so that the output will not be affected. There are two noise margins depending on logic 0 and logic 1.

The low noise margin (NM_L) and high noise margin (NM_H) are defined as

$$NM_L = |V_{IL}\,max - V_{OL}\,max|$$
$$NM_H = |V_{OH}\,max - V_{IH}\,max|$$

where,

V_{IL} = maximum allowable LOW input voltage.

V_{OL} = maximum allowable LOW output voltage.

V_{IH} = maximum allowable HIGH input voltage.

V_{OH} = maximum allowable HIGH output voltage.

NM_L is defined as the difference in magnitude between the maximum LOW output voltage of the driving gate and the maximum LOW input voltage recognized by the driven gate.

NM_H is defined as the difference in magnitude between the maximum HIGH output voltage of the driving gate and the maximum HIGH voltage recognized by the receiving gate.

In an ideal inverter, $NM_H = NM_L = V_{DD}/2$. The significance of the noise margin is that an unwanted signal of amplitude less than NM (Noise Margin) will not alter the logic state. The definition of noise margin is shown in Fig. 2.39. The shaded regions in Fig. 2.39 show the valid range of input and output voltages. Thus, the noise margins are the amount of variation in the signal levels that can be allowed when the signal is transmitted.

2.9 Fan-out and Fan-in

Fan-out is the number of circuits a gate can drive. A logic gate must be capable of providing inputs to a number of similar circuits without degrading its normal operation. A limited number of gates can be connected to the output of gate, because the output of gate is connected to input of other gates and each input consumes a certain amount of current from the gate output that means each additional connection adds to the load of the gate. A load is the amount of current needed by the input of another gate of the same family.

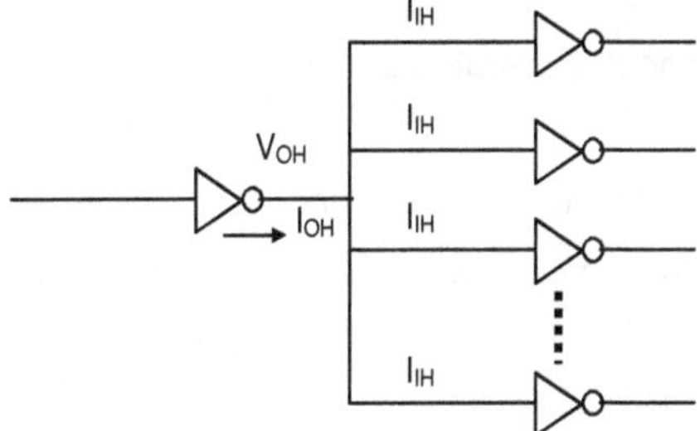

Fig. 2.40: Example of fan-in and fan-out

The fan-out is calculated from the amount of current available in the output of a gate and the amount of current needed to drive each gate input. For example, from Fig. 2.40, we observe that the output of first gate has a logic high output equal to V_{OH} and corresponding to it a current I_{OH} is supplied to the inputs of other gates. Input of each gate requires a current I_H for its operation. So fan-out of a gate is calculated from the ratio of current output to current input i.e.

$$\text{Fan-out} = \frac{I_{OH}}{I_{IH}}$$

Thus the number of inputs that can be connected to the output depends on the current ratios. Increase in number of loads may affect the functioning of the device.

Similarly fan-in is the number of inputs a logic circuit can accept. Exceeding the number of fan-in may result in an undefined output to excessive loading.

2.10 Transmission Gate (TG)

Transmission Gate (TG) is also called as the pass gate. Fig. 2.41 shows the transmission gate and its symbol.

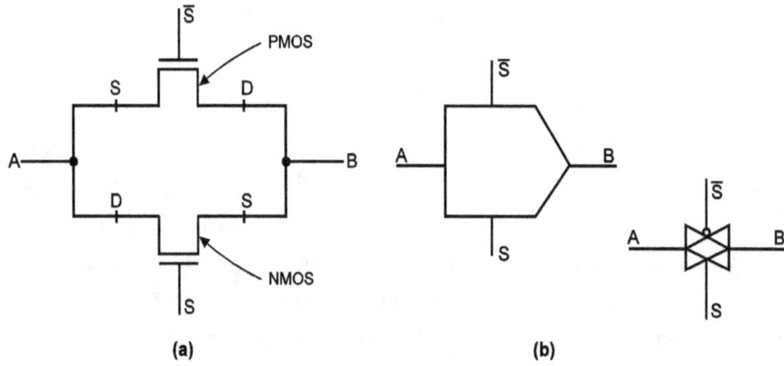

Fig. 2.41: CMOS transmission gate

It consists of NMOS and PMOS transistors, with separate gate connections, and common source and drain connections. The control signal 'S' is applied to the gate of the NMOS and its complement is applied to the PMOS. The CMOS TG operates as a bidirectional switch between nodes A and B, which is controlled by signal S.

If the control signal S is logic-high, then both transistors are turned ON and provide a low-resistance current path between the nodes A and B. On the other hand, if the control signal is low, then both transistors will be OFF and the path between A and B will be open circuit. This condition is also called as the high impedance state.

We need to consider the substrate bias effect for both the transistors. The substrate terminal of the NMOS is connected to ground and the substrate terminal of the PMOS is connected to V_{DD}.

DC Analysis of CMOS TG

For DC analysis, the input node A is connected to a constant logic high voltage $V_{in} = V_{DD}$. The control signal is also at logic high level; therefore both the transistors are turned ON as shown in Fig. 2.42.

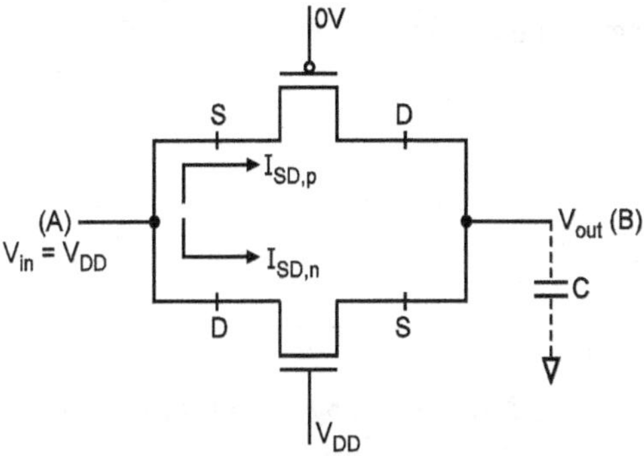

Fig. 2.42: Bias conditions of the CMOS TG

The output node can be connected to the capacitor C, which represents capacitive loading of the subsequent logic stages driven by TG.

For NMOS transistor, the drain to source and gate to source voltages are given by,

$$V_{DS,\,n} \quad = \quad V_{DD} - V_{out}$$
$$V_{GS,\,n} \quad = \quad V_{DD} - V_{out}$$

From above equations, we can observe that the NMOS transistor will be turned OFF for,

$$V_{out} \quad > \quad (V_{DD} - V_{T,\,n})$$

and it will operate in the saturation region for,

$$V_{out} \quad < \quad (V_{DD} - V_{T,\,n})$$

Similarly for PMOS transistor, the V_{DS} and V_{GS} voltages are given by,

$$V_{DS,\,p} \quad = \quad V_{out} - V_{DD}$$
$$V_{GS,\,p} \quad = \quad V_{DD}$$

Therefore, the PMOS transistor is in saturation for,

$$V_{out} \quad < \quad |V_{T,\,p}|$$

and it operates in the linear region for,

$$V_{out} \quad > \quad |V_{T,\,p}|$$

Therefore PMOS transistor remains turned ON, regardless of the output voltage V_{out}.

From above analysis, there are three regions of operation for CMOS TG as shown in Fig. 2.43.

Region 1	Region 2	Region 3
NMOS = Saturation	NMOS = Saturation	NMOS = cut off
PMOS = Saturation	PMOS = linear region	PMOS = linear region
Both ON		

0V $\qquad$ $|V_{T,p}|$ $\qquad$ $(V_{DD} - V_{T,n})$ $\qquad$ V_{DD} $\quad$ V_{out} (V)

Fig. 2.43: Operating regions of the CMOS TG

The total current flowing through the TG is given by,

$$I_D = I_{DS,n} + I_{SD,p}$$

Now, we will find the equivalent resistance for each transistor, as follows:

$$\frac{R_{eq.\,n}}{(NMOS)} = \frac{V_{DD} - V_{out}}{I_{DS\,n}}$$

$$\frac{R_{eq.\,p}}{(PMOS)} = \frac{V_{DD} - V_{out}}{I_{SD\,p}}$$

The total equivalent resistance of the CMOS TG is the parallel combination of these two resistances.

$$R_{eq} = R_{eq,n} \,//\, R_{eq,p}$$

Region 1: In this region, the output voltage is smaller than absolute value of PMOS transistor voltage i.e. $V_{out} < |V_{T,p}|$

In this region both the transistors are in saturation.

Region 2: In this region, PMOS transistor is operating in the linear region and NMOS transistor continue to operate in saturation.

Region 3: In this, the output voltage is $V_{out} > (V_{DD} - V_{T,n})$.
Due to this the NMOS transistor will be turned OFF and PMOS transistor is continued to operate in the linear region.

Now, we will plot the total equivalent resistance found in the three operating regions, as a function of output voltages.

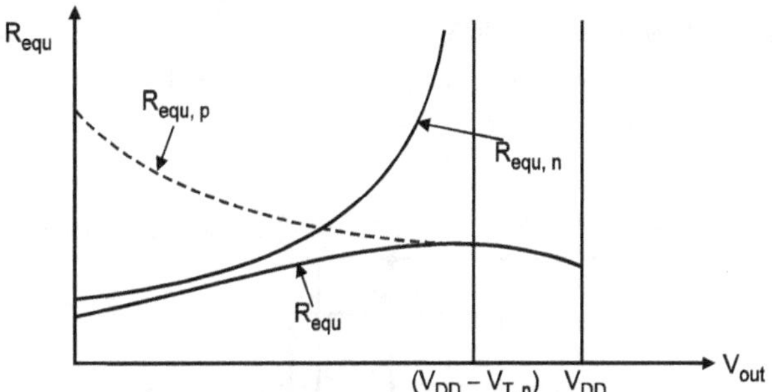

Fig. 2.44: R_{equ} as a function of V_{out}

The total equivalent resistance remains relatively constant, its value is almost independent of the output voltage, but the individual equivalent resistances of both NMOS and PMOS are strongly dependent on V_{out}. Therefore, we can replace the CMOS TG which is turned ON by a logic-high control signal by its simple equivalent resistance for dynamic analysis as shown in Fig. 2.45.

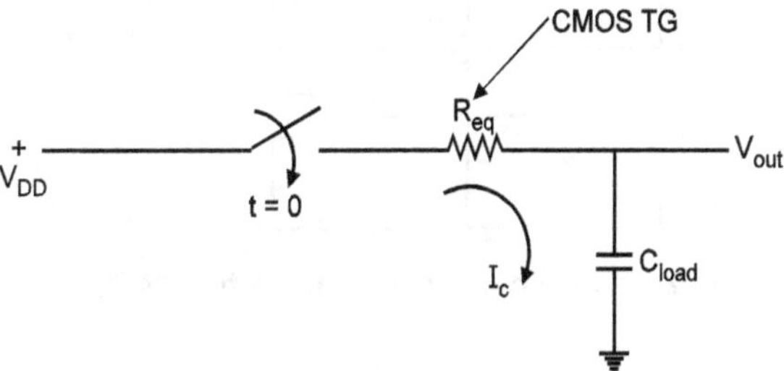

Fig. 2.45: Replacing CMOS TG with R_{equ}

The advantage of using CMOS TG is that it results in **compact circuit structures** which may even require a smaller number of transistors than their standard CMOS counterparts.

Two input multiplexer circuit using two CMOS Transmission Gates

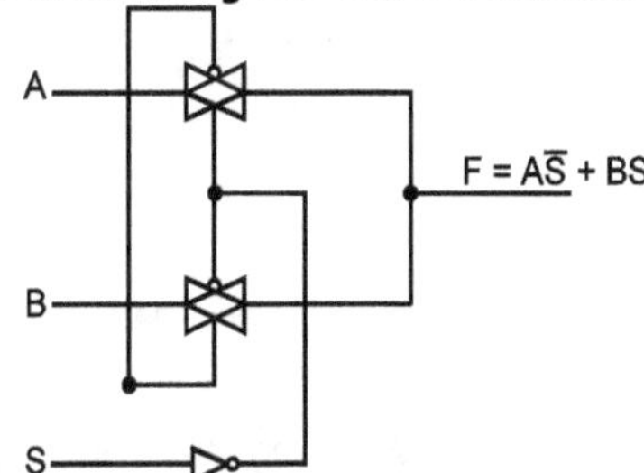

Fig. 2.46: Two input MUX using CMOS TG

Fig. 2.46 shows 2 input MUX using CMOS TG. If the control input S = 1, then the bottom TG will conduct and the output will be equal to the input B. If the control input S = 0, then bottom TG will turn OFF and the top TG will connect the input A to the output node.

Similarly, we can implement the XOR functions by using CMOS TG as shown in Fig. 2.47.

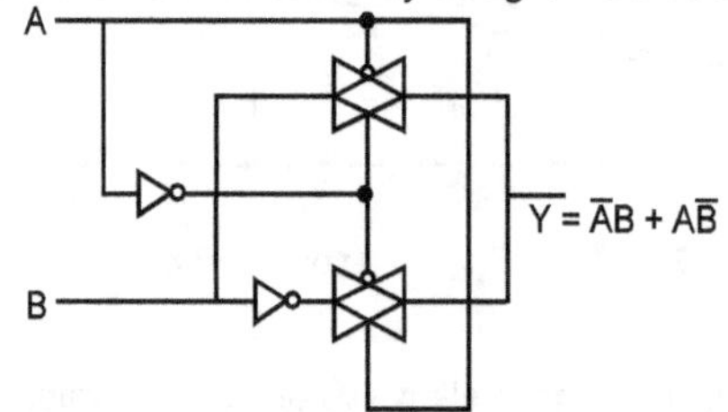

Fig. 2.47: XOR gate using 8 transistor CMOS TG

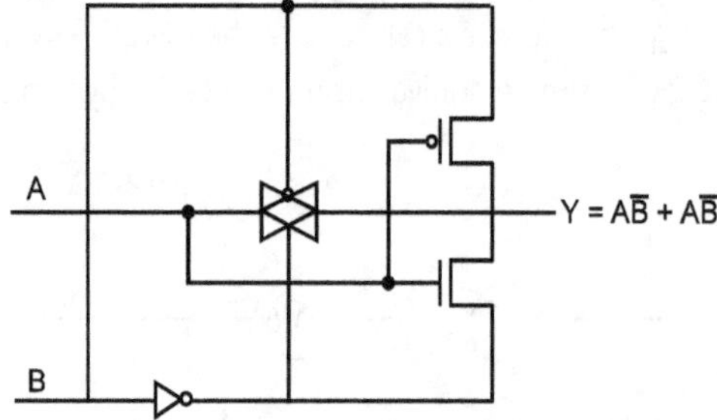

Fig. 2.48: XOR gate using 6 transistor CMOS TG

2.11 Power Dissipation

Power dissipation represents the power delivered to the gate from the power supply. Power dissipation is a non-zero quantity.

The dc power dissipation of an inverter circuit is calculated as the product of its power supply voltage and the amount of current drawn from the power supply in steady state i.e. $P_{DC} = V_{DD} * I_{DC}$

Power dissipation in CMOS circuits are,

- **Static dissipation:** Due to leakage current or other current drawn continuously from the supply.
- **Dynamic dissipation:** Due to switching transient current and charging and discharging of load capacitance.

2.11.1 Static Dissipation

In CMOS inverter, one of the transistors is always OFF. Since no current flows into the gate terminal and there is no DC current path from V_{DD} to V_{SS} (ground), the resultant steady state current and hence static power dissipation P_s is zero.

However, there is small static power dissipation due to reverse bias leakage between diffusion regions and substrate. The leakage current per unit drain area typically ranges between 10-100 pA /μm^2 at room temperature. For a die with 1 million gates, each with a drain area of 0.5 mm^2 and operated at a supply voltage of 2.5 V, the worst-case power consumption due to diode leakage equals 0.125 mW, which can be ignored.

However, the value of junction leakage currents increases with increasing junction temperature.

The total static power dissipation P_s is,

$$P_s = \sum_1^n \text{ Leakage current * supply voltage}$$

where n is the number of devices.

2.11.2 Dynamic Dissipation

Both the transistors are ON for a short period of time, during transition from either '0' to '1' or '1' to '0'. This results in a short current pulse from V_{DD} to V_{SS} (ground). There is also current to charge and discharge load capacitance C.

The capacitor C gets charged through the PMOS transistor, its voltage rises from 0 to V_{DD} and certain amount of energy is drawn from the power supply.

As the capacitive load increases, the charge or discharge current starts to dominate the current drawn from the power supplies.

For a square wave input V_{in}, having repetition frequency $f_p = 1/t_p$, dynamic power P_d during switching is given by,

$$P_d = \frac{1}{t_p} \int_0^{t_{p/2}} i_n(t) V_{out} dt + \int_{t_{p/2}}^{t_p} i_p(t)(V_{DD} - V_{out}) dt$$

where, i_n = n device transient current

i_p = p device transient current.

For a step input and with $i_n(t) = C\, dV_{out}/dt$, C is load capacitance.

$$P_d = \frac{C}{t_p}\int_0^{V_{DD}} V_{out}\, dV_{out} + \frac{C}{t_p}\int_{V_{DD}}^{0}(V_{DD}-V_{out})\, d(V_{DD}-V_{out})$$

$$P_d = \frac{CV^2{}_{DD}}{t_p}\ \text{with}\ f_p = \frac{1}{t_p}$$

$$P_d = C\,V^2{}_{DD}\,f_p$$

P_d is proportional to the switching frequency and independent of the device parameters.

2.11.3 Short Circuit Dissipation

Short circuit power dissipation is given by $P_{SC} = I_{mean} * V_{DD}$

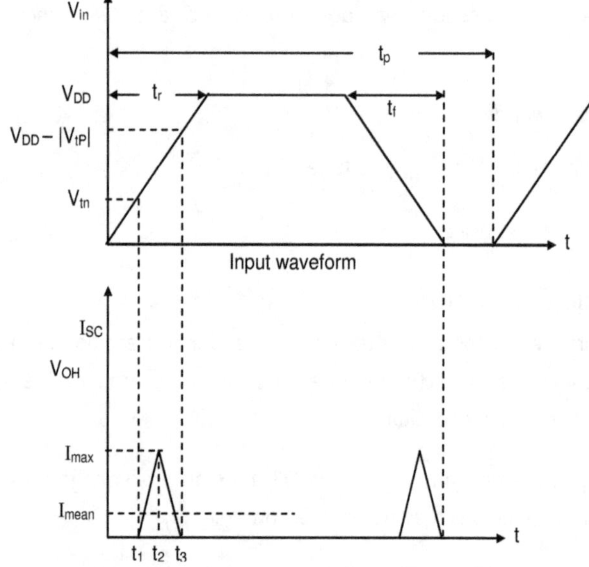

Fig. 2.49

For the input waveform in Fig. 2.49, the short-circuit current in an unloaded inverter is

$$I_{mean} = 2\times\left[\frac{1}{T}\int_{t_1}^{t_2} I(t)\,dt + \frac{1}{T}\int_{t_2}^{t_3} I(t)\,dt\right]$$

Assume, $V_{tn} = -V_{tp}$ and $k_n = k_p = K$ and behavior is symmetrical about t_2.
Then,

$$I_{mean} = 2\times\frac{2}{T}\int_{t_1}^{t_2}\frac{K}{2}\left[V_{in}(t)-V_t\right]^2 dt$$

with $V_{in}(t) = \dfrac{V_{DD}}{t_r} \cdot t$

$$t_1 = \frac{V_t}{V_{DD}} t_r$$

$$t_2 = \frac{t_r}{2}$$

Assume, $t_r = t_f = t_{rf}$

Then,

$$P_{SC} = \frac{K}{12}(V_{DD} - 2V_t)\frac{3t_{rf}}{t_P}$$

where, t_p = period of input waveform

The short-circuit current is dependent on K and input waveform rise and fall times. Slow rise times can result in significant short-circuit dissipation.

2.11.4 Total Power Dissipation

The total power dissipation can be obtained from the sum of the three dissipation components: $P_{total} = P_S + P_d + P_{SC}$

To calculate the power dissipation, add all capacitances operating at a particular frequency and calculate the power. Then the power from other groups operating at different frequencies may be summed.

Power Dissipation

Example 6:

A CMOS logic is operating at 10 MHz and 3 volt with the load of 100 pF. The static power dissipation is 100 μW. Calculate the total power dissipation if the frequency is increased to 100 MHz.   **(Dec. 2005, 8 Marks)**

Solution:

C_L = 100 pF

P_s = 100 μW.

V = 3 volts

f = 100 MHz.

We need to calculate dynamic power dissipation.

$$P_d = C_L \cdot V_{DD}^2 \cdot f_p$$
$$= (100 \times 10^{-12}) \cdot (9) \cdot (100 \times 10^6)$$
$$P_d = 90 \text{ mW}.$$

∴ Total power dissipation,

$$P_T = P_s + P_d = 100 \ \mu W + 90 \text{ mW}$$

∴ $\boxed{P_T = 90.1 \text{ mW}}$

2.12 β_n/β_p Ratio

$$\beta = \text{MOS gain factor}$$
$$= \frac{\mu \in}{t_{ox}} \left(\frac{W}{L} \right)$$

where,

μ = mobility of electrons

t_{ox} = thickness of oxide layer

W = channel width

L = channel length

$\in$ = silicon permittivity

The transfer characteristics of CMOS inverter is a function of β_n/β_p, shown in Fig. 2.50. The gate threshold voltage V_{th} depends on β_n/β_p. To change β_n/β_p, the channel dimensions i.e. channel width W and channel length L has to change. As the ratio β_n/β_p is decreased, the transition region shifts from left to right.

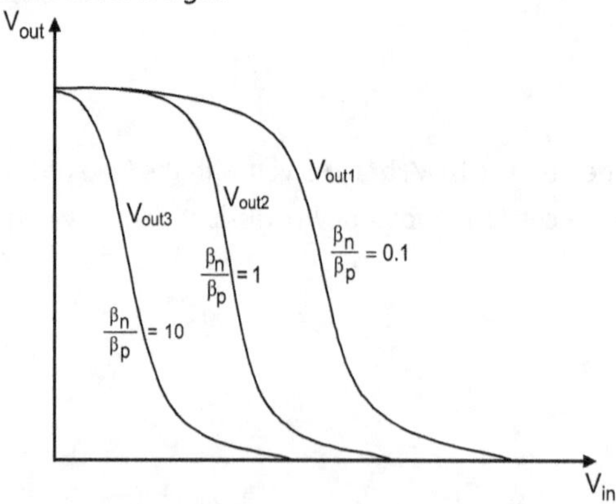

Fig. 2.50: Effect of β_n/β_p ratio on CMOS inverter characteristics

For the CMOS inverter, a ratio β_n/β_p should be equal to 1. It allows a capacitive load to charge and discharge in equal times. This provides equal current source and sink capabilities.

The transfer characteristic of an inverter is also affected by temperature. As the temperature increases, the effective carrier mobility μ decreases. This results in decrease in β.

The voltage transfer characteristic is dependent on the ratio of β_n/β_p and the mobility of both holes and electrons are similarly affected. Hence this ratio is independent of temperature. Both V_{tn} and V_{tp} decrease slightly as temperature increases.

2.13 Design Considerations

In MOS designing, a mask is made and this mask is then used to process the silicon according to the requirement. Usually four basic layers are used, n-diffusion, p-diffusion, polysilicon and metal. These layers are isolated from each other by thin or thick oxide layers.

2.13.1 Layer Representations

Layout levels represent the physical features observed in the final silicon wafer. A typical CMOS process has the following features:
- Two different substrate (for n transistor and p transistor)
- Doped regions for both n and p transistors
- Forming material
- Transistor gate electrodes
- Interconnection paths and inter layer contacts.

The layers are represented in various figures by a colour scheme, varying stipple patterns and varying line styles. Layer representation for the n-well CMOS process is shown in table.

Layer	Colour	Symbolic	
N-well	Brown		
Thin oxide	Green	n-transistor	
Polysilicon	Red	Polysilicon	
P+	Yellow	p-transistor	
Metal1	Light blue	Metal1	Connection between
Metal2	Tan	Metal2	Metal1 and Metal2
Contact cut, Via	Black	Contact	can be made using
Metal3 over glass	Gray	Metal3	metal vias, cuts or just vias

2.13.2 Design Style – Stick Diagrams

Stick diagrams are used to convey layer information through the use of a colour code.

Fig. 2.51 shows some of the stick encoding.

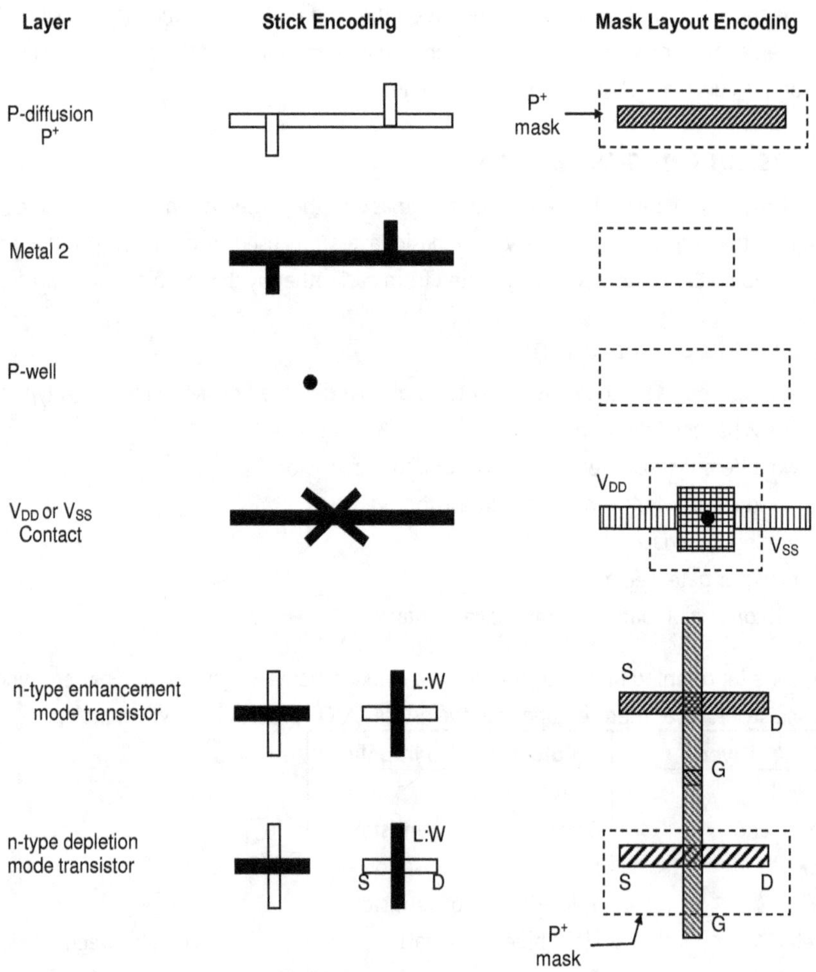

Fig. 2.51: Stick encoding examples

The layout of the stick diagrams accurately reflects the topology of the actual layout in silicon.

The stick diagram of p-well CMOS inverter is shown in Fig. 2.52.

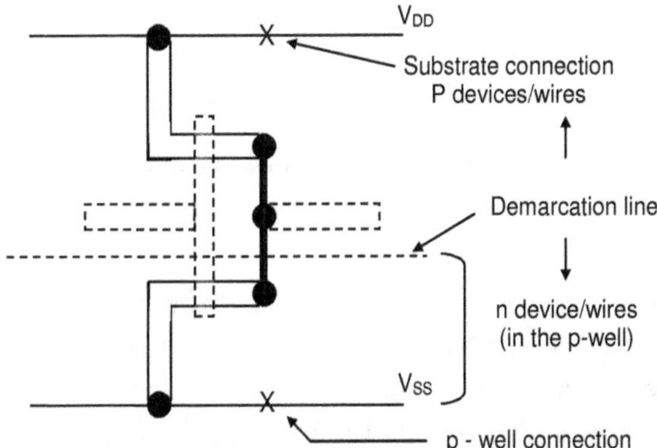

Fig. 2.52: Stick diagram of p-well CMOS inverter

The stick diagram represents only a small section of circuit which can be replicated many times. The power rails and buses run in parallel in metal. The two types of transistors used in CMOS are separated by a demarcation line. p-transistors are placed above the demarcation line and n-transistors are placed below it as shown in Fig. 2.52.

For CMOS design style, remember the following points:

- Diffusion paths must not cross the demarcation line and n-diffusion and p-diffusion wires must not join.
- The n and p transistors are joined by metal where a connection is required.
- Crosses are put on the V_{DD} and V_{SS} (GND) rails to represent the substrate and p-well connection respectively.
- Only metal and polysilicon can cross the demarcation line.

Technology Scaling

The ability to make ever smaller devices is the driving force behind Moore's law. Manufacturing processes are constantly being improved. But many characteristics of the fabrication process do not change as devices shrink. There is no need to redesign the layout, but simply shrunk in size.

The design rules are expressed in terms of λ, the size of the smallest feature in a layout. All features can be measured in integer multiples of λ. Chips actually get faster as layouts shrink. If we are taking proper care while scaling layouts, then there is no need to redesign the circuits for each new process. After scaling, if the circuit became slower with smaller transistors, then we need to redesign the circuits and layouts for each process.

The total delay of the logic circuit depends on:
1) The capacitance to be charged.
2) The voltage through which the capacitance must be charged.
3) The current available. So, we will use $\dfrac{CV}{I}$ as a measure of the speed of a circuit over scaling.

Assume all the basic physical parameters of the chip are shrunk by a factor $1/x$, such as:
1) Doping concentrations: $N_d = N_d/x$
2) Lengths and widths: $W = W/x$, $L = L/x$
3) Vertical dimensions, i.e. SiO_2 oxide thickness $t_{ox} = t_{ox}/x$
4) Supply voltages : $(V_{DD} - V_{SS}) = (V_{DD} - V_{SS})/x$

Now, we will compute the values of scaled physical parameters, which are denoted by variables with hat ($\wedge$) symbols.

The scaling of gate capacitance is given by:
$$\hat{C_g}/C_g = 1/x$$
where,
$$C_g = \frac{\varepsilon_{ox}\, W/L}{t_{ox}}$$

Similarly, the power supply voltage scales by factor $1/x$. Also the current scaling $\hat{I_d}/I_d = 1/x$. So as the layout is scaled from λ to $\hat{\lambda} = \lambda/x$, the circuit is actually speeded up by a factor x.

Basically, there are three ways of scaling:
1) Constant field scaling (E remains constant)
2) Constant voltage scaling (V_{DD} constant)
3) Lateral scaling.

Constant field scaling indicates that the characteristics of an MOS device can be maintained and the basic operational characteristics preserved if the critical parameters of a device are scaled in accordance to a given criterion. In constant field scaling, the scaled device is obtained by applying a dimensionless factor x to,

- All dimensions, i.e. W, L, also dimensions those are vertical to the surface.
- Device voltages
- The concentration densities.

When the above mentioned device dimensions are scaled by the constant parameter x, then the depletion layer thickness d, the threshold voltage V_t, and the drain to source current I_{ds} are also scaled. One important factor is that, since the voltage is scaled, electric field E, in the device remains constant. This has the desirable effect that many non-linear factors essentially remain unaffected.

In constant voltage scaling, the V_{DD} voltage is kept constant, while the process is scaled. But, in this, electric field E increases. To reduce the effects of high electric field, we need to develop some process.

Another way of scaling is the lateral scaling. In lateral scaling only the gate length is scaled. This is also called a "gate shrink", because it can be easily done to an existing mask database for a design.

The depletion regions associated with the pn junctions of the source and drain determines the channel length between source and drain. The source to drain distance must be greater than the sum of the widths of the depletion layers. This ensures that the gate is able to exercise control over the conductance of the channel. Thus, in order to reduce the length of the channel, we need to reduce the width of the depletion layers. This can be done by increasing the doping level of the substrate silicon.

In constant field scaling, when we scale the device dimensions by 1/x, the drain to source current, I_{ds} per transistor decreases to 1/x, the circuit density (number of transistors per unit area) scales up by x^2, which results in current density scaling linearly by x.

In case of constant voltage scaling, when we scale the device dimensions by 1/x, the current density increases by a factor x^3 while a gate shrink increases the current density by x^2. Therefore, we need proportionately wider metal power conductors for more densely packed structures. This is solved by adding metal layers that are used solely for power and ground.

Another advantage of constant field scaling, is that even though the number of devices per unit area increases, the power density remains constant. For constant field scaling, both, static power dissipation and dynamic power dissipation decreases by $1/x^2$, due to this even though number of devices increases, power density remains constant.

While in case of constant voltage scaling the power density increases by x^3, and in lateral scaling the power density increases by x^2. The increase in power density for constant voltage scaling and lateral scaling has forced manufacturers to develop new package solutions.

As the temperature increases, the mobility of carriers fall, which reduces the gain of devices. This may reduce the speed of circuits. The effect of scaling on MOS device characteristics are given in Table 2.2.

Therefore, if we need to design high temperature and high speed circuits, we need to take special considerations. We need better metalization, usually more layers, to deal with metal migration problems.

Interconnect Layer Scaling

As seen, the scaling gives a number of advantages. But of circuit parameters, which exhibit significant degradation with scaling. These parameters are voltage drop, line propagation delay, current density and contact resistance.

Table 2.2: Effect of scaling on MOS device characteristics

Parameter	Scaling Model		
	Constant Field	**Constant Voltage**	**Lateral**
Length (L)	$1/x$	$1/x$	$1/x$
Width (W)	$1/x$	$1/x$	1
Supply Voltage (V)	$1/x$	1	1
Gate-oxide thickness (t_{ox})	$1/x$	$1/x$	1
Current ($I = (W/L\,(1/t_{ox})\,V^2$)	$1/x$	x	x
Trans-conductance g_m	1	x	x
Junction Depth (X_j)	$1/x$	$1/x$	1
Substrate doping (N_A)	x	x	1
Electric field across gate oxide (E)	1	x	1
Depletion layer thickness	$1/x$	$1/x$	1
Load capacitance ($C = WL/t_{ox}$)	$1/x$	$1/x$	$1/x$
Gate Delay (VC/I)	$1/x$	$1/x^2$	$1/x^2$
	Resultant influence		
DC power dissipation (P_s)	$1/x^2$	x	x
Dynamic power dissipation (P_d)	$1/x^2$	x	x
Power delay product	$1/x^3$	$1/x$	$1/x$
Gate area ($A = WL$)	$1/x^2$	$1/x^2$	$1/x$
Power density (VI/A)	1	x^3	x^2
Current density	x	x^3	x^2

Scaling the thickness and width of a conductor by x reduces the cross-sectional area by x^2. The scaled line resistance R' is given by

$$R' = \frac{\rho}{(t/x)} \left(\frac{(L/x)}{(W/x)} \right) = xR$$

where ρ is the conductivity and t is the conductor thickness.

Limitations for Scaling

- When signals are required to propagate over long paths, the actual RC delays and voltage drops that are seen are greater than those predicted which limits the switching speed.
- Therefore, the distribution and organization of clocking signals becomes a major problem as geometrics are scaled.
- Also, the metal lines must carry a higher current with respect to cross-sectional area. So we need to consider the metal migration factor. Therefore, as processes are developed, more metal layers have been added before scaling the gate dimensions drastically.
- As the density increases, the average line length on a chip also increases, which in turn increases the capacitance. Also the resistance of wires increases and becomes more important relative transistor resistance.
- Also, the power dissipation per gate decreases. In such cases, the average gate delay is determined by the interconnection rather than the gate itself.

2.13.3 Design Rules

Once the layer information and topology is conveyed by using stick diagram, the mask layouts can be made.

The physical mask layout of any circuit to be fabricated using any process (NMOS, PMOS, CMOS) must satisfy a set of geometric constraints or rules known as design rules. The objective of these design rules is to allow a ready translation of circuit design concepts-instick diagram or symbolic form-into actual geometry in silicon. The design rules are interface between the circuit designer and the fabrication engineer.

These design rules specify the minimum allowable line widths for physical objects on-chip like metal-polysilicon interconnects or diffusion areas, small feature sizes and small separation between the features.

The layout design rules represent a reasonable optimum point in terms of yield, reliability and density. The layout design rules significantly increases the probability of fabricating a successful product with high yield. There are usually two kinds of design rules.

- **Macron rule:** In micro rules the layer constraints like minimum feature size and minimum allowable feature separation are stated in terms of absolute dimensions in micron meters.
- **Lambda rules:** In lambda rules the constraints in terms of signal parameter (λ) are specified and thus allow linear, proportional scaling of all geometrical constraints.

  The layout rules provide strict guidelines for preparing the geometrical layouts that will be used to configure the actual masks during fabrication.

2.13.4 Layout Diagrams

Mask layout diagrams can be hand drawn on squared paper when λ-based design rules are considered, the side of each square is taken to represent λ and for μ-based (micron) rules, it will be taken to represent the least common factor associated with the rules.

Fig. 2.53 shows layout examples of CMOS inverter circuit. The circuit is fabricated on a p-type wafer which acts as a substrate for NMOS transistor. The PMOS transistor is fabricated in n-well which acts as substrate for it.

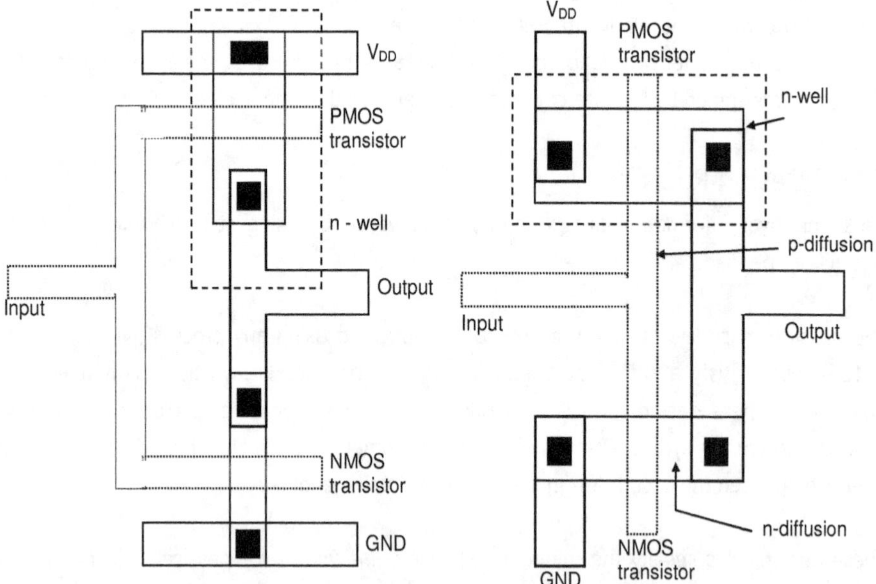

Fig. 2.53: Layout examples of CMOS inverter circuits

The layout steps are

- Run V_{DD} and V_{SS} in metal at the top and bottom of all.
- Run a vertical polysilicon line for each gate input.
- Order the polysilicon gate signals to allow the maximum connection between transistors. Thus, form gate segments.
- Place n-gate segments close to V_{SS} and p-gate segments close to V_{DD}.
- Connections to complete the logic gate should be made in polysilicon, metal etc. In diffusion keep capacitance on internal nodes low.

2.14 MOSFET Fabrication

Each processing step requires that certain area be defined on chip by masks. The integrated circuit is viewed as a set of patterned layers of doped silicon, polysilicon, metal and silicon dioxide. Using lithography each layer is patterned. The following steps show how MOSFETs are fabricated and illustrated in Fig. 2.54.

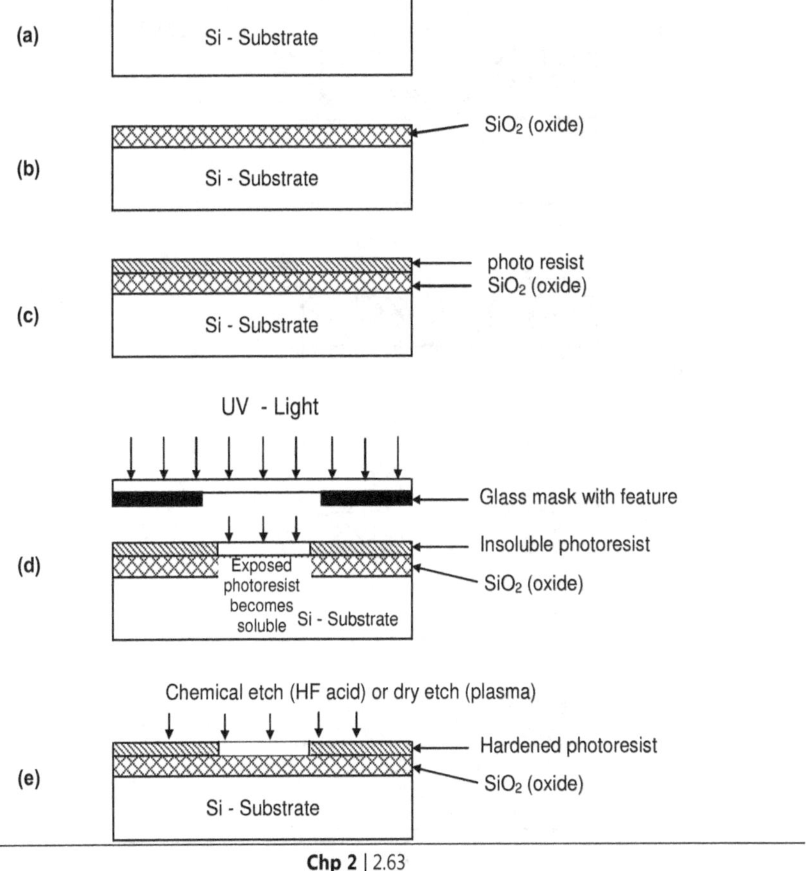

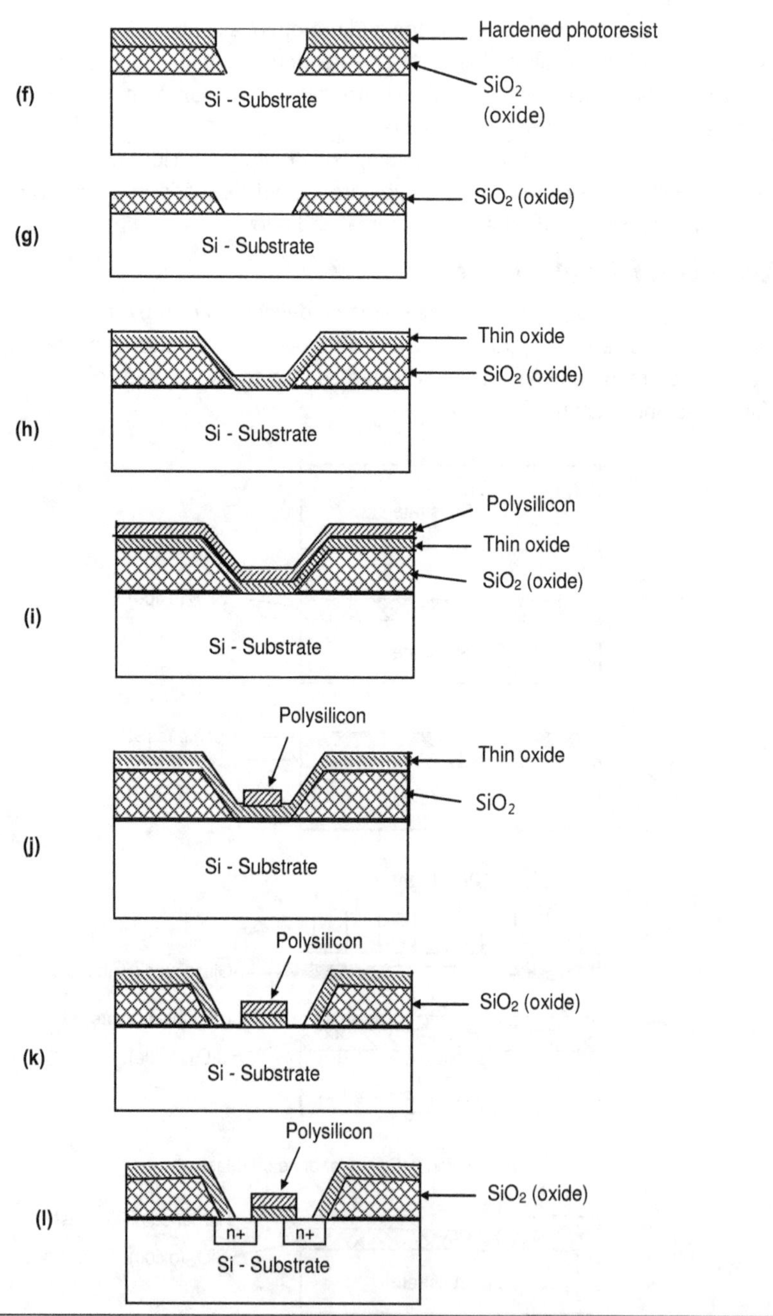
Hardened photoresist
SiO2 (oxide)
Si - Substrate
(f)
SiO2 (oxide)
Si - Substrate
(g)
Thin oxide
SiO2 (oxide)
Si - Substrate
(h)
Polysilicon
Thin oxide
SiO2 (oxide)
Si - Substrate
(i)
Polysilicon
Thin oxide
SiO2
Si - Substrate
(j)
Polysilicon
SiO2 (oxide)
Si - Substrate
(k)
Polysilicon
SiO2 (oxide)
n+
n+
Si - Substrate
(l)

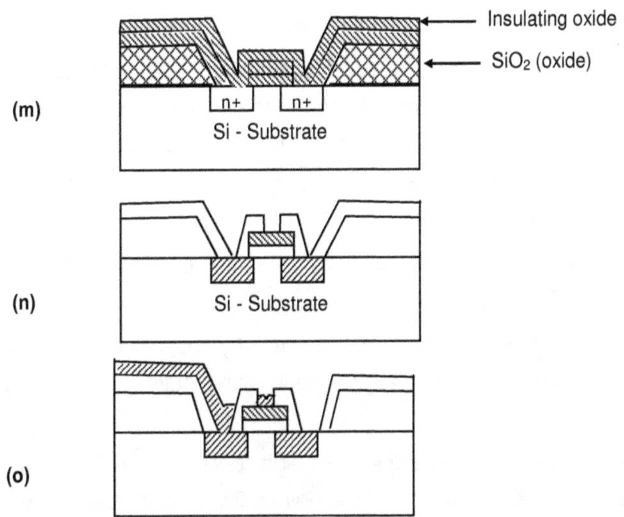

Fig. 2.54: Steps in fabrication of MOSFET

- Processing is carried out on a thin silicon wafer, cut from a single crystal of high purity and p-type impurities are introduced at the time of crystal growth. [Fig. 2.54 (a)]
- A layer of silicon dioxide is grown all over the surface of the wafer by thermal oxidation. The thickness of the oxide layer is about 1 μm. [Fig. 2.54 (b)]
- The surface is covered with a photo resist which is deposited on to the wafer and spin to achieve an even distribution of required thickness. This photoresist is light sensitive, acid-resistant organic polymer, initially insoluble in the developing solution. [Fig. 2.54 (c)]
- The photoresist layer is then exposed to ultraviolet light through a mask which defines those regions into which diffusion takes place together with transistor channels. Areas exposed to ultraviolet radiation are polymerized and the areas required for diffusion are shielded by the mask and remain unaffected [Fig. 2.54 (d)]
- The unexposed portions of the photoresist are removed by a solvent. The silicon dioxide regions which are not covered by the hardened photoresist can be etched away either by using a chemical solvent or by using a dry etch. [Fig. 2.54 (e)]
- An oxide window is now opened and it reaches down the silicon surface [Fig. 2.54 (f)]
- The remaining photoresist is now stripped from the silicon dioxide layer by another solvent, leaving the patterned silicon dioxide feature on the surface. [Fig. 2.54 (g)]

- A thin, high quality oxide layer of 0.1 μm thickness is grown over the entire chip surface which later forms the gate oxide of MOS transistor [Fig. 2.54 (h)]

- On the top of thin oxide layer, a layer of polysilicon is deposited to form the gate structure later. This also acts as an interconnect medium in integrated circuits. The polysilicon layer consists of heavily doped polysilicon deposited by chemical vapor deposition. In fabrication of fine pattern devices, precise control of thickness, impurity concentration and resistivity is needed. [Fig. 2.54 (i)]

- After deposition the polysilicon layer is patterned and etched to form the interconnects and the gate of MOSFET. [Fig. 2.54 (j)]

- The region where thin gate oxide is not covered by the polysilicon is etched away and silicon is exposed. It is in this region, source and drain regions will be formed. [Fig. 2.54 (k)]

- The exposed area of silicon is now doped with high concentration of impurities either by diffusion or by the ion implantation. Diffusion is achieved by heating the wafer to high temperature and passing a gas containing the desired n-type impurity over the surface. In this step the polysilicon with underlying thin oxide and thick oxide act as mask during diffusion. This is the process of self-aligning. The dopant penetrates through the exposed areas and forms the source and drain regions. [Fig. 2.54 (l)]

- Thick oxide is grown over the entire surface. [Fig. 2.54 (m)]

- The oxide layer is then masked with photoresist and patterned to expose selected areas of the source, drain regions and of the polysilicon gate. Connections are to be made from these cuts. [Fig. 2.54 (n)]

- The whole chip has then metal deposited over its surface to a thickness of around 1 μm. This metal layer is then masked and etched to form the required interconnection pattern. [Fig. 2.54 (o)]

A second layer of metallic interconnect can also be added on top of this structure by creating another insulating layer, cutting contacts depositing and patterning the metal.

CMOS Fabrication:

There are basically three approaches for CMOS fabrication.

1) p-well
2) n-well
3) twin-tub.

The p-well process is widely used in practice and n-well process is also popular. The steps involved in n-well process for CMOS fabrication are discussed below:

1) Start with the lightly doped p-type substrate (wafer). In this p-type substrate, we need to create n-type well, for the p-channel devices.

2) The first mask defines the n-well as shown in Fig. 2.55 (a). P-channel transistors will be fabricated in this well.

3) Ion implantation or deposition and diffusion are used to produce the n-well.

4) This diffusion of n-well must be carried out with special care since the n-well doping concentration and depth will affect the threshold voltages as well as the breakdown voltages of n transistors.

5) Then SiO_2 layer is deposited as shown in Fig. 2.55 (a).

6) Polysilicon layer is used to form the gate as shown in Fig. 2.55 (b).

7) Then p-substrate is diffused with the n-diffusion, which is used to form NMOS transistor as shown in Fig. 2.55 (c).

8) The n-well is used to form the PMOS transistor after the p-diffusion.

n-well CMOS circuits are superior to p-well because of the lower substrate bias effects on the transistor threshold voltage and lower parasitic capacitances associated with source and drain regions.

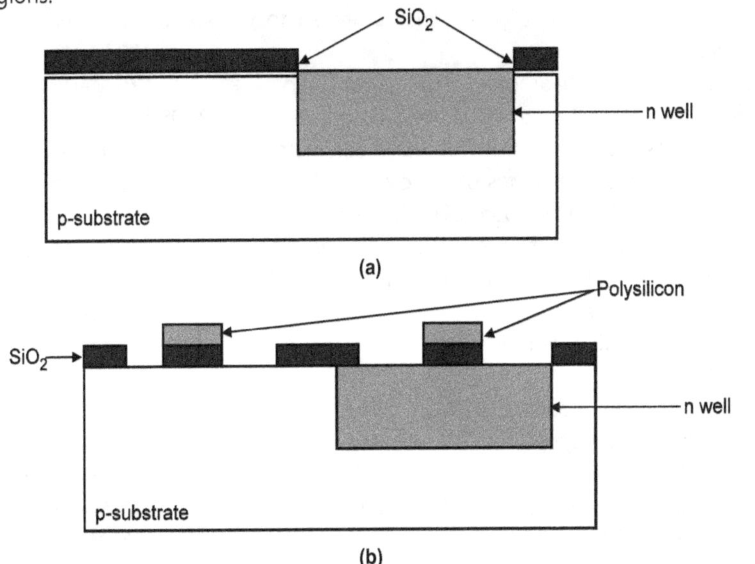

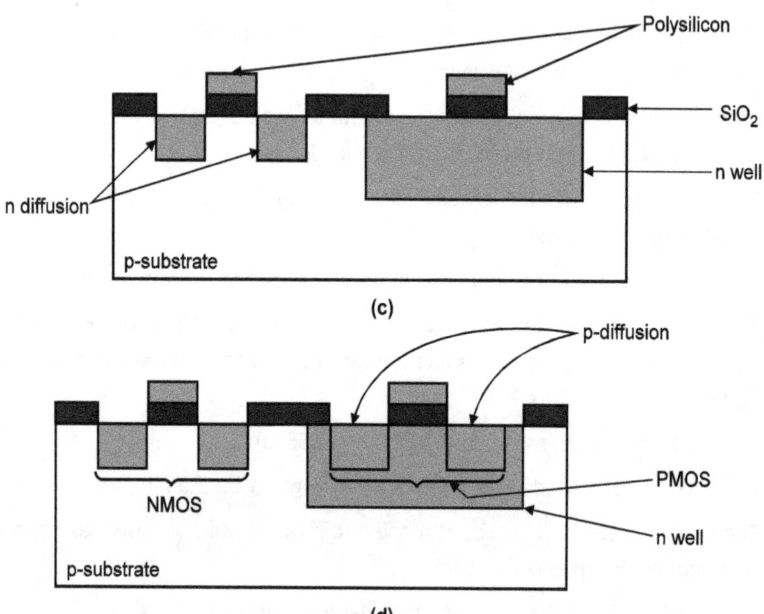

Fig. 2.55: CMOS n-well process steps

QUESTIONS

1. With the help of circuit diagram, explain the operation of CMOS inverter. Develop the inverter static transfer characteristics with all its regions well labelled. How is the slope of transition region in these characteristics related to various family features, based on CMOS inverter?   **(10 Marks, Nov. 2000)**

2. Write a note on n-well process for CMOS fabrication.   **(6 Marks, Nov. 2000)**

3. Define rise time, fall time and propagation delay for a CMOS inverter with capacitive load. Discuss the factors on which these parameters depend. Explain the role of β_n/β_p ratio in adjusting dimensions of devices in CMOS structure to have equal rise and fall times. What are the advantages of having these times equal?   **(10 Marks, Nov. 2000)**

4. Why does CMOS structure offer least power dissipation under static and dynamic condition? Why BJT based structures are not feasible for achieving very large scale integration silicon chip?   **(6 Marks, Nov. 2000)**

5. Explain the following terms in brief:
   i) MOSFET
   ii) Enhancement mode MOSFET.
   iii) Threshold voltage (V_T)
   iv) CMOS.   **(8 Marks, May 2001)**

6. Draw the diagram for CMOS NAND process in detail.   **(12 Marks, Nov. 2001)**

7. Write note on: TTL Vs. CMOS.   **(6 Marks, May 2001)**

8. Explain n-well CMOS fabrication process in detail.   **(12 Marks, Nov. 2001)**
9. Explain noise margin NM_L and NM_H with respect to CMOS.   **(4 Marks, Nov. 2001)**
10. Explain CMOS inverter dc transfer characteristics in detail. What is desirable β_n/β_p ratio?
11. Write a note on methods of reduction of V_T in enhancement MOSFET.
                                                                          (6 Marks, Nov. 2001)
12. Comparison of p with n-channel MOS.   **(6 Marks, Nov. 2001)**
13. Static, dynamic and short-circuit power dissipation in MOS.   **(6 Marks, Nov. 2001)**
14. Explain n-well process for CMOS fabrication.   **(12 Marks, May 2002)**
15. Draw, NAND, NOR gates using CMOS.   **(4 Marks, May 2002)**
16. Draw the static transfer characteristics of CMOS inverter. Explain different regions with expressions. What are improvement techniques?   **(12 Marks, May 2002)**
17. Explain the static and dynamic power dissipations.   **(4 Marks, May 2002)**
18. Write note on: Enhancement mode MOSFET.   **(6 Marks, May 2002)**
19. Why NAND gate is preferred over NOR gate? Design CMOS logic gates for the following functions:
    a) Z = A (buffer)
    b) Z = ABCD
    c) Z = A + B + C + D   **(16 Marks, Dec. 2003)**
20. Draw the schematic for the following equation using CMOS. Derive W/L ratio for each MOSFET.
          Y = A + B (C + D)   **(9 Marks, Dec. 2004)**
21. How the above equation is implemented in FPGA?   **(2 Marks, Dec. 2004)**
22. Assume that above circuit consumes 20 mW when idle and 320 mW when operated at f = 1 MHz and V_{CC} = 5.0 V.
    (i)   How much power does it use at f = 500 kHz and V_{cc} = 5.0 V?
    (ii) How much power does it use at f = 100 kHz and V_{cc} = 2.5 V?   **(5 Marks, Dec. 2004)**
23. Design CMOS logic for

    $$Y = \overline{AB + C (D + E)}$$

    Calculate total area in terms of width required for MOSFETs on chip.
                                                                          (8 Marks, Dec. 2005)
24. A CMOS logic is operating at 10 MHz and 3 volts with the load of 100 pF. The static power dissipation is 100 µW. Calculate the total power dissipation if the frequency is increased to 100 MHz.   **(8 Marks, Dec. 2005)**
25. Prove that (W/L) ratio of PMOS to NMOS banks in CMOS is nearly 2.
                                                                          (8 Marks, Dec. 2005)
26. Draw CMOS inverter and explain electrical transfer curve.   **(8 Marks, Dec. 2005)**
27. What do you mean by technology scaling?   **(2 Marks, May 2005)**
28. What are the effects of technology scaling on chip level design?   **(2 Marks, May 2005)**
29. What is current features size?   **(2 Marks, May 2005)**
30 Draw the spice model of MOSFET.   **(4 Marks, May 2005)**

31 Derive the expressions for static and dynamic power dissipations in CMOS inverter.

(8 Marks, May 2005)

32. Explain parasitic capacitances in CMOS.
33. Write a note on technology scaling.
34. What is a CMOS Transmission gate? Explain.
35. What are the lambda rules for CMOS layout?
36. Explain body effect and hot electron effect.   **(4 Marks, May 2005)**
37. What do you mean by technology scaling? What are the effects of technology scaling on chip level design?   **(4 Marks, May 2005)**
38. Write a note on enhancement mode MOSFET.   **(6 Marks, May 2002)**
39. Draw the diagram for CMOS NAND gate and CMOS NOR gate.   **(8 Marks, May 2001)**
40. Explain CMOS Inverter DC transfer characteristics in detail. What is desirable β_n/β_p ratio? How to achieve this?   **(8 Marks, Nov. 2001)**
41. Draw static transfer characteristics of CMOS inverter. Explain different regions with expressions. What are improvement techniques?   **(12 Marks, May 2002)**
42. Define rise time, fall time, and propagation delay for a CMOS inverter with capacitive load. Discuss the factors on which these parameters depend. Explain the role of β_n/β_p ratio in adjusting dimensions of devices in CMOS structure to have equal rise and fall times.   **(10 Marks, Nov. 2000)**
43. Explain noise margin NM_L and NM_H with respect to CMOS.   **(4 Marks, Nov. 2001)**
44. Why does CMOS structure offer least power dissipation under static and dynamic condition? Why BJT-based structures not feasible for achieving very large scale integration silicon chip?   **(6 Marks, Nov. 2000)**
45. Write a note on: Static, Dynamic and short circuit power dissipation in CMOS.

(6 Marks, Nov. 2001)

46. Explain static and dynamic power dissipation.   **(4 Marks, May 2002)**
47. Derive the expressions for static and dynamic power dissipations in CMOS inverter.

(8 Marks, May 2005)

48. Design CMOS logic for Y = A + BC + DE. Calculate the area in terms of W.

(8 Marks, May 2007)

49. What do you mean by λ parameter ? What is technology scaling ? How does it affect the power dissipation, parasitics and speed ?   **(8 Marks, May 2007)**
50. Design 4 : 1 MUX using Transmission Gates. Compare this schematic with conventional design.   **(8 Marks, May 2007)**
51. "The logic circuit consumes more power if operated at higher CLK frequency". Justify. What is power delay product? Explain the significance.   **(8 Marks, May 2007)**

◊◊◊

Unit 3

Chapter 3: INTRODUCTION TO VLSI DESIGN

Topics discussed: CAD process, EDA tools, VLSI design flow, Comparison between VHDL and VERILOG.

3.1 Introduction

We know that, any digital circuit consists of few basic circuits; AND, OR, and NOT gates, a memory element FLIP-FLOP, irrespective of the size and complexity of the circuit. The digital circuits can be designed using manual methods, such as, simplification of Boolean expressions using Boolean algebraic theorems, graphical methods, tabular methods, using available SSI and MSI devices (mux/demux, registers, counters etc) etc. These design (synthesis) methods or tools are well for design of systems which are small in size and are not complex enough in today's context.

However, the increasing size and the complexity of digital systems require design methods with use of computers. These methods are known as Computer Aided Design (CAD) methods. Number of CAD tools have been developed for this purpose.

CAD tools has made it possible to design modern complex logic circuits, and also made the design work much easier. Many tasks in the design process are performed automatically by the CAD tools resulting in faster and efficient design.

A number of Hardware Description Languages (HDLs) have been developed for describing the structure and behavior of complex digital circuits and number of HDL based CAD tools have been developed for the design of digital systems. The common HDLs are VHDL and VERILOG.

3.2 Computer Aided Design (CAD) Process

Fig. 3.1 illustrates a process to design a digital system.

3.2.1 Design Entry

Design entry is the process of entering the functionality of the design using a software tool. The system to be designed may be described by one of the following three methods.

i. Design Entry using Truth Table

The Truth Table of a logic function or a timing waveform diagram may be specified for designing the necessary hardware. The CAD tools used for drawing timing diagram and transforming it into a network of logic gates is known as the **waveform editor**. This method of design entry can be used only for a small number of variables.

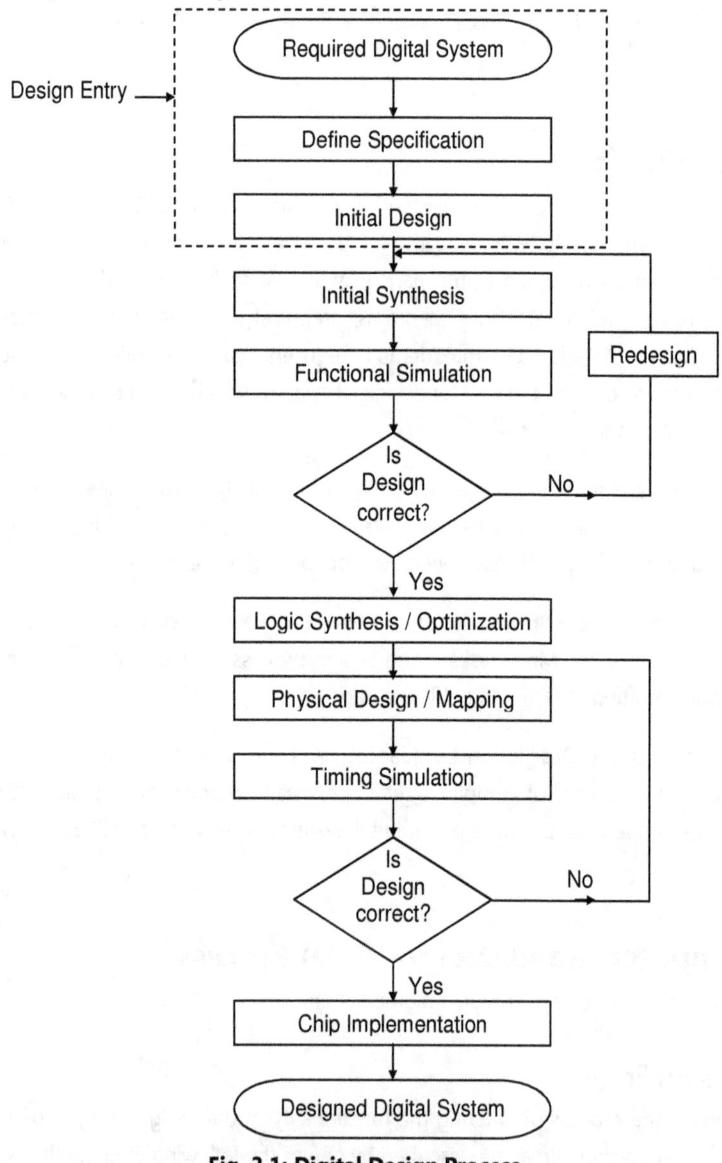

Fig. 3.1: Digital Design Process

ii. Design Entry using Schematic

The hardware to be designed is described by drawing the circuit diagram. Circuit elements are represented by their graphical symbols and the connections between circuit elements are drawn as lines. The tool known as **graphic editor** in a CAD system can be used to draw a schematic diagram.

iii. Design Entry using Hardware Description Languages (HDLs)

Similar to programming languages, a number of languages have been developed to describe hardware. The two most commonly used hardware description languages (HDLs) in industry are: **VHDL** (**V**ery High-speed Integrated circuit **H**ardware **D**escription **L**anguage) and **VERILOG**. Both these HDLs are IEEE standards. Using a HDL, logic circuit is represented in its code which is used for design entry. This method can be used for efficiently designing small as well as large system.

3.2.2 Initial Synthesis

Synthesis is the process of transforming design entry information of the circuit into a set of logic equations. By using synthesis tools, logic equations that describe the logic function needed to realize the circuits are generated automatically. The logic equations produced by the initial synthesis tools are not in the optimal form, since these equations are generated on the basis to designer's input to the CAD tools.

3.2.3 Functional Simulation

Functional simulation is the process of verification of the circuit function of designed circuit using a CAD tool known as **Functional Simulator**. Functional simulator simulates the circuit function from the logic equations obtained from the synthesis and the inputs which are applied. The output of simulator, which is obtained either in the truth table form or as the timing diagram is examined to verify whether the designed circuit meets the required function. If the output from the simulation process is not correct then the design is to be modified.

3.2.4 Logic Synthesis and Optimization

Logic synthesis and optimization tools are used to obtain optimized design to achieve design goals such as cost, speed, or the technology of implementation.

3.2.5 Physical Design

After the logic expressions are optimized, the next step is to design the circuit using the available logic resources in the target chip. This step is known as **physical design** or **layout synthesis**. The physical design consists of two operations: placement of logic functions in the optimized circuit in the target chip (CPLD or FPGA) and interconnecting the components in the chip, called as **routing**. The placement and routing tools are used for this purpose.

3.2.6 Timing Simulation
Timing simulation is the verification of design considering the propagation delays of logic gates and delays through the interconnection wires. Timing simulation tools are used for this.

3.2.7 Chip Implementation
Chip implementation is the process of downloading of designed circuit in the target chip (CPLD or FPGA).

3.3 Introduction to VLSI Design
The first IC was introduced in 1961 i.e. 14 years after the transistor. The first IC was of flip-flop which consists of two transistors and resistors.

Then silicon technology is growing as per Moore's law who has stated that silicon technologies will double the number of transistors per chip every 18 months and it is happening. Now on the same amount of slice, 10 million transistors can be fabricated.

3.3.1 Classification of IC Technology

Type	Device	Year	Function
SSI	1-100	1960	Gates, Op_amps
MSI	100-1k	1965	Filters
LSI	1k-10k	1970	Microprocessor, A/D
VLSI	>10k	1975	Memory, DSP

3.3.2 What is VLSI?
VLSI stands for Very Large Scale Integration. It is the process of integrating million of transistors on tiny silicon chips. VLSI circuit technology is one of the basic components of today's high technology. VLSI devices are found in all varieties of applications, from simple home appliances to complex spacecrafts. The main benefit of VLSI circuits is complex functionality in very small packages.

VLSI field has opened up a big opportunity to do things that were not possible before. Now-a-days, VLSI circuits are used almost everywhere, cell phones, computer, car, digital camera, etc. But, all this involves a lot of expertise on many fronts within the same field, which will be discussed in later sections.

Programmable Logic Devices (PLDs) and EDA (Electronic Design Automation) tools have changed the VLSI design scenario.

3.4 Programmable Logic Devices (PLDs)

PLDs are standard ICs that are available in standard configurations, and are sold in very high volume to many different customers. PLDs are prefabricated ICs i.e. all the basic digital elements (gates, mux, demux, registers, counters, etc.) are already fabricated on silicon chip. Hence, PLDs are configured/programmed to create a part customized to a specific application. PLDs use different technologies to allow programming of the device. PLDs are available as erasable or mask-programmed. Commonly used PLDs are CPLD (Complex Programmable Logic Device) and FPGA (Field Programmable Gate Arrays). The vendors of PLDs are Xilinx, Altera, Lattice, Vantis, and Actel.

3.5 EDA Tools

EDA tools are Design software available for designing programmable logic. Using EDA tools, PLDs can be configured/ programmed. EDA tools are used for design entry, logic synthesis and optimization, and design simulation.

EDA tools available for:

i. **Design Entry:**
   - Viewlogic (ViewDraw - a hierarchical schematic capture and block diagram tool).
   - Mentor Graphics (Renoir).
   - Cadence Design Systems.
   - OrCAD.
   - ALDEC (Active-HDL).
   - Simucad (Silos-3).

ii. **Design Simulation:**
   - Model Technology (Modelsim)
   - Synopsys
     VCS (High performance VERILOG simulation)
     VSS (High performance VHDL simulation)
   - Cadence
     VERILOG XL simulator
     DRACULA - the physical verification standard.
   - Quickturn Design Systems (Powersuite)
   - VIVElogic (Fusion/ Speedwave - a VHDL Simulator)

iii. Logic Synthesis and Optimization:

- Synopsys.
    - FPGA Express, FPGA Compiler
- Synplicity – Synplity
- Exemplar logic - Leonardo Spectrum
- VIVElogic – Intelliflow
- Cadence Design System
- ALDEC – Aldec. (Active - HDL)

3.6 VLSI Design Flow

Fig 3.2 illustrates a process of programming/configuring of PLDs using EDA tools. This process is also used to design model of an IC. The following flow is economical for a very few quantity of an IC for same design. For a mass production of an IC, we have to go for foundry process.

Writing a Specification

The importance of a specification cannot be overstated. This is an absolute must, especially as a guide for choosing the right technology and for making your needs known to the vendor. As specification allows each engineer to understand the entire design and his or her piece of it. It allows the engineer to design the correct interface to the rest of the pieces of the chip. It also saves time and misunderstanding. There is no excuse for not having a specification.

A specification should include the following information:

- An external block diagram showing how the chip fits into the system.
- An internal block diagram showing each major functional section.
- Description of the I/O pins including
    - Output drive capability
    - Input threshold level
- Timing estimates including
    - Setup and hold times for input pins
    - Propagation times for output pins
    - Clock cycle time
- Estimated gate count
- Package type
- Target power consumption
- Target price
- Test procedures including in-system test requirements.

It is also very important to understand that this is a living document. Many sections will have best guesses in them, but these will change as the chip is being designed.

Design Entry

It is the process of entering the functionality of the design using a software tool using either a Hardware Description Language (VHDL or VERILOG) or schematic entry. Schematic entry is constructing a netlist of predefined components.

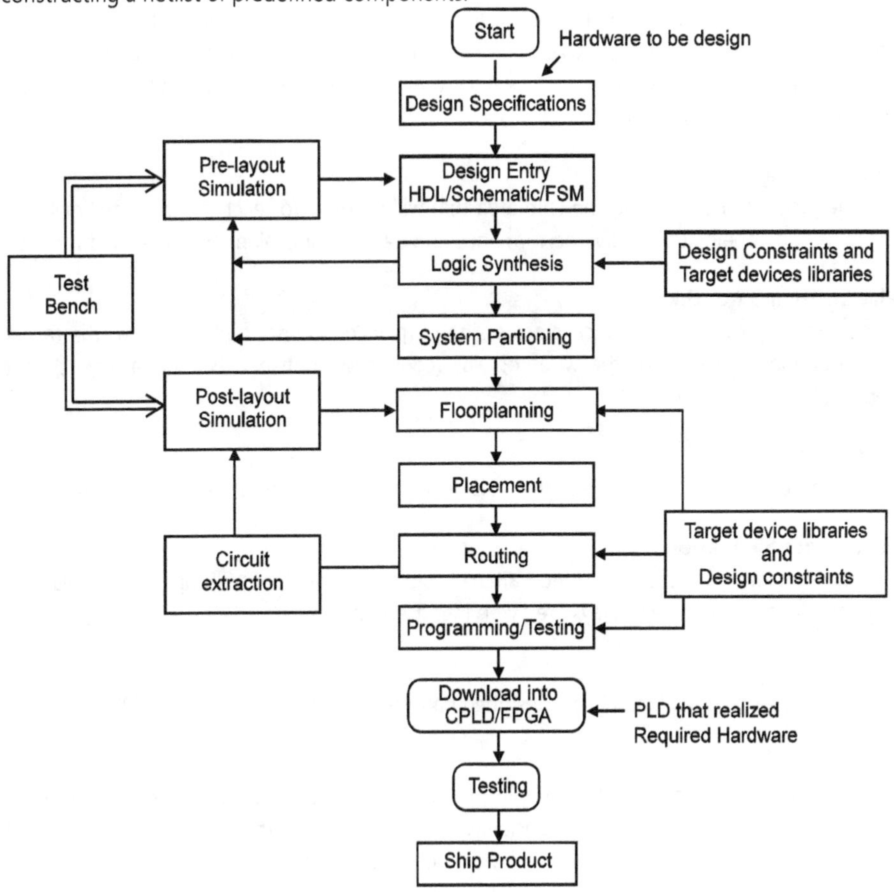

Fig. 3.2: VLSI Design Flow

Logic Synthesis

It is the process of creating representation of a system at a lower level of design abstraction from a higher level representation - Synthesized representation should have the same function as the higher level representation. For this logic, synthesis tool is used. Netlist (textual information) is produced from synthesis process. A netlist is a description of the logic cells and their interconnections. **Netlist is an EDIF (Electronic Data Interchange Format) file**. Logic cell is a basic architecture block or element of a target PLD.

System Partitioning

It is the process of dividing a large system into smaller and standard modules.

Pre-layout Simulation

It is a functional verification of a circuit design through software programs. It is a process of applying stimuli to a design over time and producing, recording and analyzing the corresponding responses from the model. It eliminates the time consuming need for constant physical prototyping.

Floorplanning

It is the process of estimating the chip area that will be used for each standard cell or block in the design. It helps to improve performance and density. Floorplanner tool is used for this.

Placement and Routing

In placement process, all logic cells are assigned (placed) to specific locations in the target chip. Routing is laying out the wires or vias (connection between two metal layers) that connect the circuits or cells.

Extraction

It is the process of determination of the resistance and capacitance of interconnections.

Post-layout Simulation

It is the simulation process performed after physical place and route. Propagation delays of logic cells and interconnect delays are taken into account.

Programming

It is the process of downloading the designed hardware into target device like CPLD or FPGA.

Testing

For a programmable device, you simply program the device and immediately have your prototypes. You then have the responsibility to place these prototypes in your system and determine that the entire system actually works correctly. If you have followed the procedure upto this point, chances are very good that your system will perform correctly with only minor problems. These problems can often be worked around by modifying the system or changing the system software. These problems need to be tested and documented so that they can be fixed on the next revision of the chip. System integration and system testing is necessary at this point to ensure that all parts of the system work correctly together.

When the chips are put into production, it is necessary to have some sort of burn-in test of your system that continually tests your system over some long amount of time. If a chip has been designed correctly, it will only fail because of electrical or mechanical problems that will usually show up with this kind of stress testing.

3.7 Comparison Between VHDL and VERILOG

VHDL	VERILOG
• VHDL is somewhat difficult and complex than VERILOG.	• VERILOG is relatively simple especially for 'C' language users.
• It results in slower simulation.	• Results in fast simulation.
• It is superior in higher system level designs.	• It has very good acceptance in ASIC (Application-Specific Integrated Circuit).
• Procedures and functions may be placed in a package so that they can be used for any design.	• There is no concept of packages in VERILOG.
• A library is a store for compiled VHDL code.	• No concept of a library.
• VHDL allows concurrent procedure calls.	• VERILOG does not allow concurrent task calls.

3.8 Top-Down and Bottom-Up Design Approach

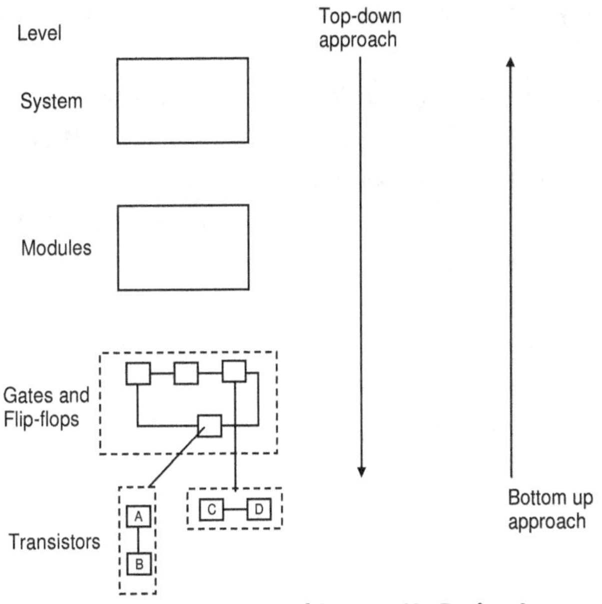

Fig. 3.3: Top-Down and Bottom-Up Design Approach

The study of system deals in its specification and implementation. Specification means description of its function and of other characteristics required for its use like speed, technology and power consumption. Implementation means how the system is constructed from simpler components. Implementation is a digital network consisting of interconnections of digital modules like simple gates to complex processors. The hierarchical implementation using top-down and bottom-up approach is shown in Fig. 3.3.

Implementation of a system is described in following different level(s).
- Module level: The system is divided into many modules that can do a specific function like registers, counters, multiplexers, etc.
- Logical (level: The modules are divided into many logic gates and basic combinational and sequential components that work with binary input values.
- Physical levels: The gates are realized in some technology like bipolar or CMOS at transistor level.

QUESTIONS

1. List the different advance tools being used for:
   (i) Simulation (ii) Synthesis (iii) Floor planning.   **(6 Marks, Dec. 2003)**
                                                                       (3 Marks, Dec. 2004)

2. What are different industry standard tools for simulation and synthesis?
                                                                       (4 Marks, Nov. 2001)

3. Explain design flow for a typical EDA tool for VLSI design.
                                                            (6 Marks, Nov. 2000, May 2002)

4. Explain in detail ASIC design flow.   **(8 Marks, Nov. 2001)**

5. Explain the VLSI design flow.

6. Compare VHDL and VERILOG.

7. List out the tools used for Simulation and Synthesis.

8. Explain Top-down and Bottom-up approach in VLSI design.

9. What is the necessity of test benches? State types of test benches and explain any one with suitable example.   **(8 Marks, May 2009)**

◊ ◊ ◊

Topics discussed: VHDL in detail, Levels of abstraction, Elements of VHDL, Test bench, Designing with VHDL.

4.1 Introduction to VHDL

VHDL is a Hardware Description Language used for modeling digital system made of interconnection of components. VHDL is an acronym for VHSIC Hardware Description Language and VHSIC is an acronym for Very High Speed Integrated Circuit. VHDL is an industry standard language used to describe the hardware from abstract to the concrete level and has become the communication medium of design and for specifying input and output from various design tools.

Digital electronics designing using VHDL means the designer writes code in VHDL language and then verifies the function by using a simulator, after that the code is synthesized into a netlist. Synthesis means the code is translated into schematic with gates and flip-flops.

Need of VHDL:
Every electronics design engineer should learn and use a HDL language to keep pace with the productivity of competitors. Using VHDL, we can quickly describe and synthesize circuit of 20 thousands or more gates on a single chip. VHDL provides the capabilities (advantages) described below:

VHDL provides capabilities as described below:

    (1) VHDL provides Device Independent/Technology Independent Design: VHDL makes it possible to design or verify electronic designs or models without knowing the implementation device/technology (CPLD/FPGA etc.). With one electronic design, we can target many device architectures.

    (2) VHDL is a standardized language: This makes it possible to change development tools. The language can also be used as an exchange medium between chip vendors and CAD tool users. We can verify the functionality of the same VHDL code by using different software tools such as Xilinx, Actel, etc.

    (3) VHDL has powerful language constructs and flexible: VHDL has powerful language constructs due to which we can write code descriptions of complex control logic. VHDL supports both top-down and bottom-up or mix methodology. The language supports modifiability, as the language is easy to read, hierarchical and structured.

(4) VHDL is portable language: Because VHDL is a standard; your design description can be simulated on different tools, one platform to another. The source code of VHDL for a design can be used with any synthesis tool and the design can be implemented in any device, which is supported by a synthesis tool.

(5) Application Specific Integrated Circuit (ASIC) migration: If we implement the VHDL code on a CPLD or FPGA, it increases the efficiency of the product to hit the market quickly. When the production volumes reach above appropriate level, VHDL facilitates the development of an ASIC. As the VHDL is a well defined language, we can be assured that ASIC vendor will deliver a device with the expected functionality.

(6) Lower cost and quick time to market: PLDs and VHDL together facilitate a speedy design process. VHDL makes it possible to describe out design quickly and correctly, and along with programmable logic devices we can shorten the Non-Recurring Engineering (NRE) expenses. Therefore, VHDL and PLDs combine together, acts as a powerful vehicle to bring the product to the market in record time.

Shortcomings or Disadvantages of VHDL:

Synthesis results of same VHDL code vary from one tool to another. Most systhesis (synthesis) tools allow the designer to use synthesis directives to obtain some level of control over implementation; to make area efficient versus speed-efficient implementation choices.

VHDL compilers do not produce optimal implantations. The optimal solution depends on the design objectives. Poor implementation is also due to the result of inefficient code. For example - inefficient C or C++ code, results in slow execution times or poor memory utilization. Also inefficient VHDL code results in repetitive, unneeded and non-optimal logic.

The purpose of VHDL language is to free the design engineer from having to specify gate-level implementation. Most synthesis tools allow designers to specify technology specific, gate-level implementations, but descriptions of these types are neither high-level nor device independent.

For Analog Electronics, the VHDL is not yet standardized. The standardization work is in progress on VHDL with an analog extension (AHDL) to allow analog systems to be described.

History :

In 1981, the Institute for Defense Analysis (IDA) had arranged a workshop to study
- Various Hardware Description methods
- Need for a standard language
- Features required by such a standard.

A team of three companies IBM, Texas Instrument, and Intermetrics were awarded contract by DOD to develop a language. Version 7.2 of VHDL was released along with language Reference manual in 1985.

In 1987, VHDL is standardized by IEEE known as the IEEE standard 1076-1987. Revised standard named IEEE standard 1164 extends the VHDL language with multi-value logic that is needed for describing real-time systems.

4.2 Features of VHDL

i.　Concurrent Language:

Concurrent statements execute at the same time in parallel, as in hardware.

$Z <= C+X;$

$X <= A+B;$

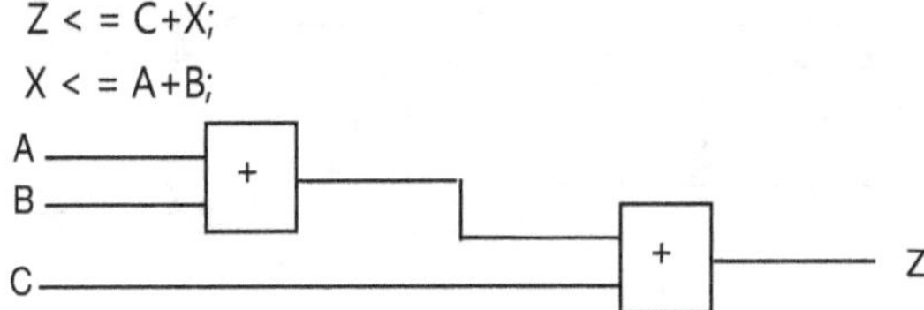

Fig. 4.1

Here sequence of statements is not important.

ii.　Sequential Language:

Sequential statements execute one at a time in sequence as in any conventional language. Sequence of statement is important. VHDL is the amalgamation of concurrent and sequential language.

iii.　Net-List Language:

Net-List is produced after synthesizing VHDL code. Net-List is textual information of logic cells and their interconnections. It is in industry standard format named EDIF (Electronic Design Interchange Format). Net-List is used to exchange graphical and electronic data between EDA tools from various vendors.

iv.　Timing Specifications:

Clocks of different frequencies can be generated by using VHDL. Time Specification can be assigned to the signals. VHDL supports both synchronous and asynchronous timing models.

v.   Test Bench:

Test Benches can be written using VHDL to test other VHDL models. Test bench is VHDL model that generates a set of test vectors and sends them to the module being tested. Test Benches are needed to ensure that design is correct or not.

vi.   Design Hierarchy:

Hierarchy can be represented using VHDL. Consider example of a full adder which is the top-level module, being composed by three lower level modules i.e. half adder and OR gate.

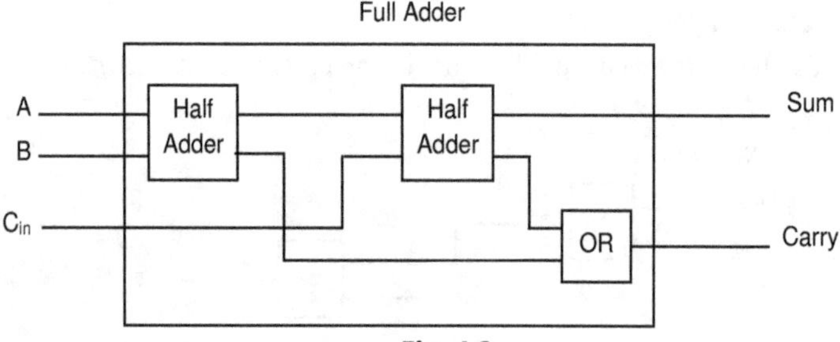

Fig. 4.2

It means VHDL is a structural language.

vii.   Supports Design Libraries:

The analyzed VHDL code can be inserted into a design library. Design library is a storage facility in which analyzed VHDL descriptions are stored. These design units can be used for any other design.

viii.   VHDL has **powerful language constructs** such as if-else, with-select, case-when etc.

ix.   VHDL has a **9 value package std_logic_1164**, so we can assign one of value from 9 values to the system.

x.   The VHDL supports flexible design methodologies top down, bottom up or mixed.

4.3 Levels of Abstraction

Different styles are adopted for writing VHDL code. Abstraction defines how much detail about the design is specified in a particular description. There are four main levels of abstraction.

i. Layout level:

It is the lowest level of abstraction. It specifies actual layout of design on silicon. Detailed timing information, analog effects are specified.

ii. Logic level:

A model is described by the logic gates and the connection between logic gates. This design has information about function, architecture, technology, detailed timing. Layout information and analog effects are ignored.

iii. Register transfer level:

This model describes the flow of data between registers and how a design processes the data. The design is specified using register and the logic in between.

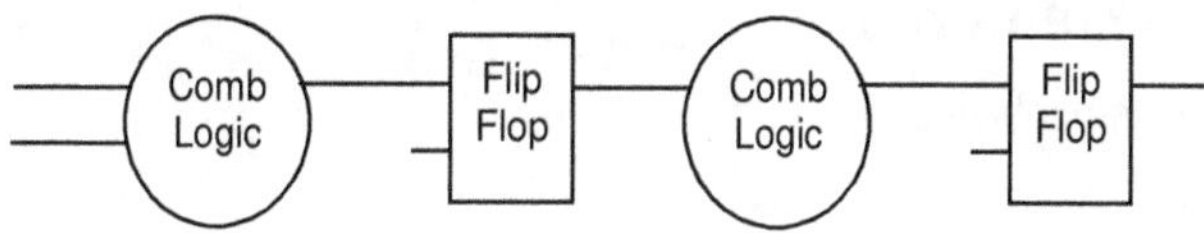

Fig. 4.3

Design contains architecture information, no details of technology, no specification of absolute timing delays.

Entire code is partitioned between clocked and combinational processes.

iv. Behavioral level:

The model is specified by describing functionality of the design using HDL without specifying the architecture of registers.

It contains timing information required to represent a function.

e.g., Behavioral model of an AND gate with A and B inputs, and C as output.

process (A, B)

    begin

  if (A = '1' *and* B = '1') *then*

      C <= '1';

    else

      C <= '0';

    end if;

end process;

4.4 Elements of VHDL

- Language Elements
- Entity
- Architecture
- Concurrent Statement
- Component Instantiation
- Sequential Statement
- Package and Library
- Configuration and Generics
- Attributes

4.5 Language Elements

VHDL language elements are

1. Identifier
2. Object Types
3. Data Types
4. Operators

4.5.1 Identifier

An identifier in VHDL is a user-defined name for constant, variable, signal, function, entity, subprogram, etc.

Rules for defining identifier are listed as below:

- Basic Identifier can only contain letters, numbers and underscore.
- Identifier must begin with a letter.
- Lower case and upper case letters are considered to be identical i.e. VHDL is not case sensitive.
- First character must be a letter and the last character should not be an underscore.
- Reserved words (Keywords) can not be used as identifiers.
- No spaces are allowed inside an identifier.
- They can be of any length but there is size limitation on some tools - it should not exceed 16 characters.

Example:

Legal identifiers:
> encoder_1,   DFT,   size_N,   NO_ACK

Illegal identifiers:
> _encoder_1,   1DFT,   size # N,   NO-ACK.

4.5.2 Object Types

A VHDL object consists of one of the following:

- Constant
- Variable
- Signal

• Constant

Constant objects are names assigned to specific values of a type. Constant is an object whose value can not be changed once defined for the design. By use of constant, model becomes more readable and easy to update.

The syntax is

constant constant_name : type_name: = value;

The value specification is optional

e.g.   *constant* PI: *real*: = 3.1414;
> *constant* WIDTH: *integer*. = 8;
> *constant* delay: *time*:= 10 *ns*;

• Variable

A Variable is an object with single current value. The value of variable may change. Variables are used for local storage in process statements and subprograms. All value assignments to variable occur immediately.

The variable declaration syntax is,

variable variable_name: type_name:= initial value;

e.g. *variable* P, Q: *bit*;
> *variable* DELAY: *time*;
> *variable* WIDTH: *std_logic_vector (7 downto 0)*;

- **Signal**

Signal objects are used to connect entities together to form models. Signals are communication media between entities. Signals are nothing but the wires (which connect two or more components) lying inside an IC.

Signals can be declared in entity declaration section, architecture declaration section, and package declarations. Signals declared in packages can be shared among entities and called global signals.

The syntax is

       signal signal_name: signal _type: = initial value;
       The value specification is optional.

e.g.   *signal* VCC: *bit.* = '1';
       signal GROUND: *std_logic:* = '0';
       signal INT_BUS: *bit_vector (7 downto 0);*
       signal CONTROL: *std_logic_vector (15 downto 0);*

Signals declared in entity declaration section are global to any architecture for that entity. Signals declared in architecture can only be referenced in that architecture only.

- **Comparison between Variable and Signal**

Variable	Signal
1) The value of variable is updated immediately, after the execution of variable assignment statement.	The value of signal is updated after an amount of time or after a delta delay, after the execution of signal assignment statement.
2) Variables are declared under the process.	Signals are declared in architecture before begin statement.
3) A variable has only two properties attached to it: Type and Value.	A signal has three properties attached to it: Type, Value, and Time.
4) During simulation, variables occupy less storage than signal.	During simulation, signals occupy more storage than variables.

4.5.3 Data Types

Data objects are declared using type specification to specify the characteristic of the object. VHDL contains a wide range of types that can be used to create simple or complex objects.

To define a new type, a type declaration is used. A type declaration defines the name of type and range of the type. Type declarations are allowed in package, entity, architecture, subprogram declaration sections.

The syntax is:

    type type_name *is* type_mark;

type_mark specifies a wide range of methods for specifying a type

Fig. 4.4 shows the data types available in VHDL.

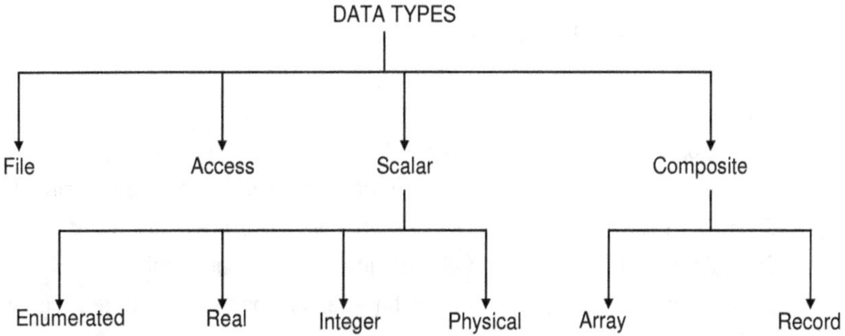

Fig. 4.4: VHDL data types diagram

i. Scalar Types

Scalar types describe the object which holds one value at a time. The type can contain multiple values, but an object that is defined to be a scalar type can hold, at most, one of the scalar values at any point in time. Scalar types encompass following classes of types:

- Integer types
- Real types
- Enumerated types
- Physical types

Integer types are same as mathematical integers. Add, subtract, multiply, and divide operations can apply to integer types. The integer range is from − 2, 147, 483, 647 to + 2, 147, 483, 647.

    e.g.   *process* (Z)

          variable A: *integer;*

          begin

          A: = 1;   -- OK   1

          A: = −1; -- OK   2

          A: = 1.0; -- Error 3

          end process;

The statements 1 and 2 show examples of a positive integer assignment and negative integer assignment respectively. Statement 3 shows a non-integer assignment to an integer variable, which causes the compiler to issue an error message.

Real types are used to declare objects with mathematical real numbers. The range of real numbers is from 1.0E + 38 to + 1.0E + 38.

    e.g. *architecture* TEST_ARCH *of* TEST *is*

      Signal D: *real;*

        begin

        D <= 2.0;   -- OK

        D <= 2;   -- Error - integer value is assigned to real signal

        D <= -2.0 e12;   -- OK - assigned very large negative number

        D <= 2.5 e – 20;   -- OK - assigned a very small number

        D <= 4.3 *ns;*   -- Error-time can not be assigned to real signal.

      end TEST;

Enumerated types are a very powerful tool for abstract modeling. Enumerated types represent the values required to a specific operation. The values of an enumerated type are user defined. The values can be identifiers or single character literals. Character literals are single character enclosed in quotes such as 'x', '1' and '0'.

e.g., **type** COLOUR **is** (red, yellow, blue, green, orange); values to identifier are defined in ascending order.

Physical types are used to represent physical quantities such as distance, current, time and so on. A physical type provides a base unit and successive units are then defined in terms of base unit. Base unit represents the smallest unit.

    e.g.   *type* CURRENT *range* from 0 *to* 1000000000

          units

             na;   -- Base unit nano amps

             µa = 1000 na;   -- Micro amps

             ma = 1000 µa;   -- Milli amps

              a = 1000 ma   -- Amps.

        end units;

   units section is used to define successive units. The range limits the minimum and maximum value that the physical type can represent in base units.

In VHDL physical type *time* is predefined. Base unit is fs (femta second). Successive units are:

ps = 1000 fs; ns = 1000 ps; µs = 1000 ns; ms = 1000 µs; sec = 1000 ms; min = 60 sec; hr = 60 min.

ii. Composite Types

It represents a collection of values. There are two composite types: array types and record types.

1) Array Types

It consists of multiple elements of the same type.

The predefined types are

type bit_vector is array (natural range < >) of bit;
type std_ulogic_vector is array (natural range < >) of std_ulogic;
type std_logic_vector is array (natural range < >) of std_logic;

These are unconstrained arrays, means the number of bits, std_ulogics and std_logics in them are not specified (range <>), rather the arrays are bounded only by natural. These types are commonly used for buses.

For example,

signal a: std_logic_vector (7 down to 0);

We can also define our own types

For example:

type addr_bus is array (0 to 31) of bit;
object declaration for addr_bus is
signal a: addr_bus;
type Data_bus is array (0 to 15) of std_logic;
signal a: Data_bus;

Two-dimensional arrays used to create a look up table are as follows:
type LUTable is array (0 to 3, 0 to 3) of bit;
constant square: LUTable: = (
        "0000",
        "0001",
        "0100",
        "1001");

Similarly look up table for cube of the number is
    type LUTcube is array (0 to 7, 0 to 5) of bit;
    constant cube: LUTcube: = (
            X "00",
            X "01",
            X "08",
            X "1B",
            X "40",
            X "7D");

In above example, 'X' indicates hexadecimal number, it means X "7D" is equal to "0111 1101".

The base specifier for hexadecimal is X, the base specifier for octal is 0, the base specifier for binary is B.

Some more examples:
    type ROM is array (0 to 125) of std_logic;
    variable ROM_addr: ROM;

String is also a **predefined array** of characters. We can create signals or variables to the string array as follows:

Variable message: string (1 to 21): = "Welcome, to VLSI Design";

String is an unconstrained array type. **Unconstrained** array means number of elements in the array is **not specified explicitly**.

Constrained array means elements in the array are specified explicitly.

Array of arrays
            type Data_word is array (7 down to 0) of std_logic;
            type RAM is array (0 to 120) of Data word;
            -- now declare a variable for RAM.
            variable RAM_addr: RAM;
            RAM_addr is a one-dimensional array object that consists of 121 elements, each
element being another array object consisting of eight elements of type std_logic;

We have thus created an array of arrays.

Assignment can be made to an entire array or to an element of an array, or to a slice of an array, for example:

```
RAM_addr (5): = "0111 1110";
        -- assign to an element of an array.
RAM_addr (0 to 5): = X "FF";
        -- assign to a slice of an array.
```

Other ways to assign to an array object.

```
variable data_bus: std_logic_vector (0 to 7);
data_bus: = "0100 0000"
        -- A string literal is assigned.
data_bus : = ('0', '1', '0', '0', '0', '0', '0', '0');
        -- positional association is used, First value
        -- is assigned to data_bus (0) = '0'
        -- data_bus (1) = '1' etc.
data_bus: = 1 => '1', 5 => '0', other => '0');
        -- Named association, data_bus(1) = '1'
        -- and data_bus(5) = '0' and the rest
        -- of the values are '0'.
data_bus : = (others => '0');
        -- all values set to '0'.
```

Others is a keyword (reserved word). By using (others => '0') assignment, the entire vector regardless of the vector length, will be assigned the value '0'. This method is very effective and makes the code easier to maintain.

Advantages of others: If the length of the vector is to be changed, only the declaration for the vectors has to be modified and not the code in the architecture.

2) Record Types

A Record Type contains elements of different data types:

Syntax:

```
type <name_of_record> is record
        record definition
              ↓
        end record;
```

Example: The following is the example for student's record.

```
    architecture behavior of example is
    type students is record
    Roll_no: integer range 1 to 60;
    name: string ;
    Marks: integer 1 to 100;
    Passed: Boolean;
    end record;
signal S1, S2, S3, S4, S5: students;
    begin
        S1.Roll_no <= 10;
        S1.name <= "xyz";
        S1.marks <= 60;
        S1.passed <= TRUE;
    end;
```

Actually, record in VHDL is almost similar to the structure in C language. '•' operator is used to access the record elements. In above example, five signals S1, S2, S3, S4 and S5 are declared for record students. To access elements of record students for S1, we are using the statements such as S1.Roll_no. <= 10 are used.

Alternatively, the above record of students for S1 can be assigned with aggregate assignment, for example:

```
        S1 <= (10, "xyz", 60, TRUE);
```

Records are very powerful in certain types of design.

We will see one more example of memory record.

```
    type memory is record
        addr_bus: std_logic_vector (15 downto 0);
        data_bus: std_logic_vector (7 downto 0);
        enable: bit;
        write: std_logic;
        read: std_logic;
    end record;
    signal m1, m2, m3: memory;
    signal data1: std_logic_vector (7 downto 0);
```

```
m1.data_bus <= data1;
m2.data_bus <= m1. data_bus;      -- assigning one field
m2.enable <= '1';
m3 <= m2;                         -- assigning entire object.
```

iii. Access Types

An access type in VHDL is very similar to a pointer in a language 'C'. It is an address, or a handle, to a specific object.

Access type allows the designer to model objects of dynamic nature. Dynamic queues, FIFO and so it can be modeled easily using access types.

Only variables can be declared as access types. Access types can only be used in sequential processing. It is not synthesizable. For access type object, two predefined functions are available for manipulation of the object. Their functions are:

new -- allocates memory of the size of the object in bytes and returns the access value and **deallocate** takes in the access value and returns the memory back to the system.

```
process (X)
    type    FIFO_ELEMENT_T is array (0 to 3) of std_logic ;      --line 1
    type    FIFO_EL_ACCESS is access TITO_ELEMENT_T;             --line 2
    variable FIFO_PTR: FIFO_EL_ACCESS: = null;                   --line 3
    variable TEMP_PTR: FIFO_EL_ACCESS: = null;                   --line 4
begin
        TEMP_PTR: = new FILE_ELEMENT_T                            --line 5
        TEMP_PTE: all: = ('0', '1', '0', '1');                   --line 6
     FIFO_PTR: = TEMP_PTR;                                        --line 7
 end process;
```

Line 2, an access type is declared using the type declared in line 1.

Line 3 and 4 declares two access type variables of type from line 2.

Line 5 call the predefined function *new*, which allocates memory for a variable of type FIFO_ELEMENT_T and returns an access value to the memory allocated. The access value returned is then assigned to variable TEMP_PTR, which is now pointing to an object of type FIFO_ELEMENT_T.

In line 6, a value is assigned to the object pointed to by TEMP_PTR. *'all'* specifies that the entire object is being accessed.

In line 7, access value of TEMP_PTR is assigned to FIFO_PTR.

iv. File Types

A file type allows declarations of file object, which is subtype of variable object type. File object can not be assigned with assignment state. A file object can be read from, written to, and checked for end of file only with special procedures and functions. Every file ends with an end_of_file mark.

read (file, data) procedure allows read from file.

write (file, data) procedure allows write to file.

endfile (file) function returns true when the file is currently at the end_of_file mark.

Following is an example of a file type declaration.

type INT_FILE   *is file of integer;*

It specifies a file type INT_FILE of type integer.

file MEM: INTEGER_FILE *is in* "/temp/problems/prob_file";

It declares a file object MEM that is an input file of type INTEGER_FILE. The last argument is the path on the physical disk where the file is located.

Subtypes

Subtype declarations are used to define subsets of a type.

e.g.

type NUMBERS *is* (00 *to* 99);

subtype MID_NUM *is* NUMBERS *range* 13 *to* 17;

MID_NUM is Subtype of NUMBERS type.

Subtype is useful for range checking and for imposing additional constraints on types.

4.5.4 Predefined VHDL Data Types

IEEE VHDL consists of two packages STANDARD and TEXTIO

The STANDARD package of data type is included in all VHDL source files. TEXTIO package defines types and operations for communication with a standard programming environment (terminal and file I/O).

bit type is predefined in the standard package as an enumerated data type with only two values '0' and '1' ;

bit is used for single line signal

bit_vector type is predefined in the standard package as a one-dimensional array type with each element being of the BIT type. *bit_vector* is used for multi-line signal 4.

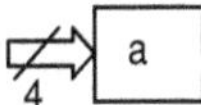

Boolean type is defined in the STANDARD package as an enumerated data type with two possible values: false and true.

Boolean type is used for conditional operations.

4.5.5 Operators

Operators specify operation to be performed. VHDL operators are classified as

i.   Logical   Lowest priority except "not"
ii. Relational
iii. Shift
iv. Adding
v.   Multiplying
vi. Miscellaneous   Highest priority

Expressions are evaluated from left to right. Operations with higher priority are evaluated first.

i. Logical Operators

The Logical operators defined in VHDL are

    and   **or**   **nand**   **nor**   **xor**   **xnor**   **not**

Logical operators are defined for type *bit* and *Boolean*, one-dimensional array of *bit* and *Boolean* type.

    e.g.   c <= a *and* b;

ii. Relational Operators

These are used to check condition.

=   Equality
/= Inequality
<   Less than
<= Less than or equal
>   Greater than
>= Greater than or equal

"=" and "/=" are predefined for all types except file type.

"<", "<=", ">", ">=" are predefined for integer, enumerated, one-dimensional arrays of enumeration and integer types.

For array types, operands are aligned to the left and compared to the right. These operators return the TRUE logic value when the condition in the given relation is met.

iii. Shift Operators

The shift operators are defined for one-dimensional array with elements of the type *bit* and *Boolean*.

sll	shift left logical
srl	shift right logical
sla	shift left arithmetic
sra	shift right arithmetic
rol	rotate left logical
ror	rotate right logical.

An array to be shift is the left operand and integer value is the right operand.

e.g.

Assume 'A' is a bit_vector equal to "10010101" and then

A *sll* 2 is "01010100" (shift lift logical, filled with '0' at LSB side).

A *srl* 3 is "00001010" (shift right logical, filled with '0' at MSB side).

A *sla* 3 is "10101111" (shift lift arithmetic, filled with MSB at LSB side).

A *sra* 2 is "11100101" (shift right arithmetic, filled with LSB at MSB side).

A *rol* 3 is "10101100" (rotate left, MSBs are placed at LSBs).

A *ror* 2 is "01100101" (rotate right, LSBs are placed at MSBs).

iv. Adding Operators

'+' is used for addition operation

'-' is used for subtraction operation

'+' and '−' are predefined for all integer operands.

'&' is the concatenation operator. '&' operator works on vector only, i.e. operands can be one-dimensional array type or an element of an array. '&' is used to add a single element to the beginning or end of an array, to combine two arrays.

e.g.   *signal A: bit _vector (3 downto 0);*

signal B: bit _vector (3 downto 0);

signal C: bit _vector (7 downto 0);

C <= not A & not B

Now, C will be having element of complements of A & B array element.

v. Unary Operators

These are sign operators

'+' positive,   '-' negative

vi. Multiplying Operators

Multiplying operators are predefined for all integer types.

'*' is used for integer multiplication

'/' is used for integer division

'*' and '/' are also used for floating point numbers.

mod is same as '*'

rem is same as '/'

'*' and '/' are defined only for integers

vii. Miscellaneous Operators

abs

The *abs* operator has only one operand. It allows defining the operand's absolute value. The result is of the same type as the operand.

'**' is Exponential operator defined for any integer or floating point number.

Example:

2**8 = 256

3.8 **3 = 54.871

abs (-1) = 1

Aggregates

Assign values to the elements of an array

e.g.   a <= (*others* => '0'); is identical to a <= "00000".

We can assign values to some bits in a vector and use "*others*" clause to assign the remaining bits.

e.g.

A <= (1 => '1', 3 =>'1', *others* => '0'); is identical to A<= "01010".

signal D_BUS: *bit_vector* (15 *downto* 0);

D_BUS <= (14 *downto* 8 => '0', *others* => '1');

is identical to D_BUS <= "1000000011111111"

'--' is used for writing comments.

'<=' is used for signal assignment.

':=' is used for variable assignment.

VHDL Component

A component is a very important concept in VHDL. A component can be a complete design or a small part of a system.

VHDL component has two parts:
1) Entity
2) Architecture

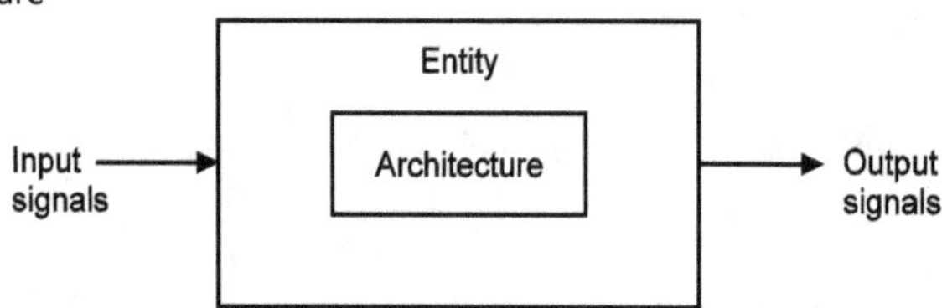

Fig. 4.5: A VHDL component

Entity: It is actually used for port declaration for inputs and outputs. An entity is the most basic building block in VHDL. So, entity acts as a black box, which gives the external view of the design. Entity does not know about the internal behaviour of the component.

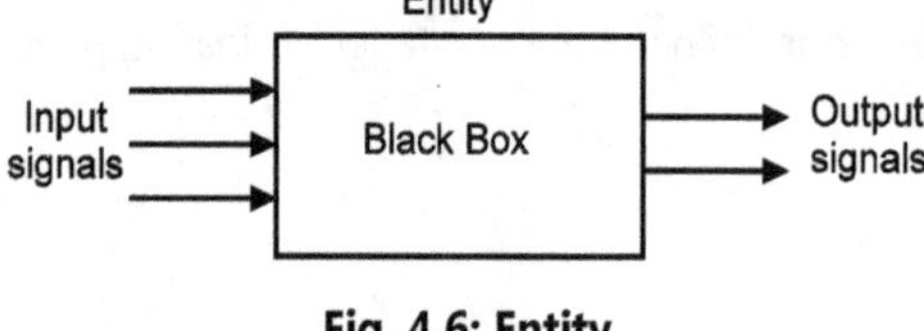

Fig. 4.6: Entity

Entity name is the same as the component name.

For example, the entity of full adder looks like as shown in Fig. 4.7.

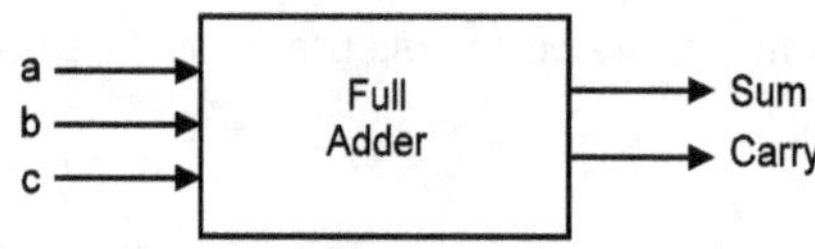

Fig. 4.7: Entity for full adder

4.6 Entity

The entity describes the design's interface to the external circuit. It is equivalent to pin configuration of an IC. Entity declaration defines the input and output ports of the design. Each port in the port list must be given a name, data flow direction and a type. Entity can be used as a component in other entities after being compiled into a library.

The syntax for entity declaration is:

> *entity* ENTITY_NAME is
> *port* (Port list);
> *end* ENTITY_NAME;

e.g.   *entity* OR_ GATE *is*
> port (A1, A2, A3, A4: *in bit;*
> B1, B2, B3, B4: *in bit;*
> Y1, Y2, Y3, Y4: *out bit*);
> end OR_GATE;

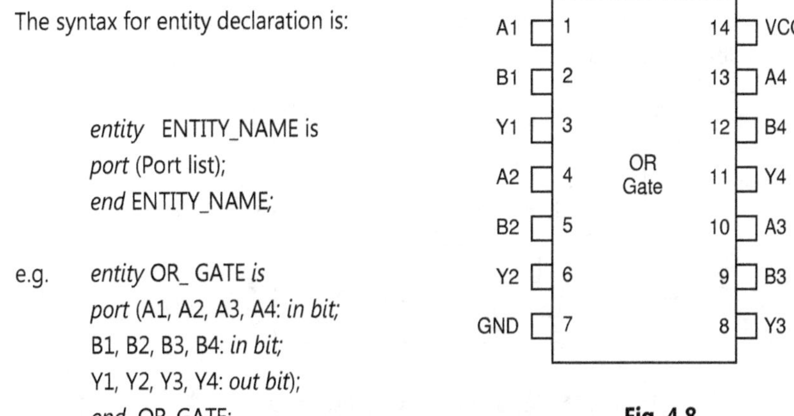

Fig. 4.8

Entity declaration starts from keyword *entity* and ends with keyword *end*. Between this ports are defined with keyword *port*. Ports are declared with their name, mode and type.

Mode specifies the direction of ports. Four types of modes are defined in VHDL.

Mode   *in*   – value can be read but not assigned. i.e. input port.

Mode   *out*   – value can be assigned but not read. i.e. output port.

Mode   *inout* – value can be read and assigned. i.e. input/output port.

(bidirectional signals)

Mode *buffer* – output port with internal read capability.

In above example, entity OR_GATE is declared for an IC of OR gate as shown. Ports A1, A2, A3, A4, B1, B2, B3, B4 are defined as an input port of bit type.

Y1, Y2, Y3, Y4 are declared as output ports. There is no semicolon after last line in port list.

Every VHDL code must start with entity. VHDL design description must include only one entity and at least one corresponding architecture.

Buffer:
Once a port is declared as mode buffer, it is similar to a port which is declared as mode out, but out mode does not allow for internal feedback.

Mode buffer is used for ports, which are readable within the entity, such as for counter outputs. In counter, present state used to determine the next state, so the value of counter must be in the feedback loop, therefore counter outputs are declared as buffer.

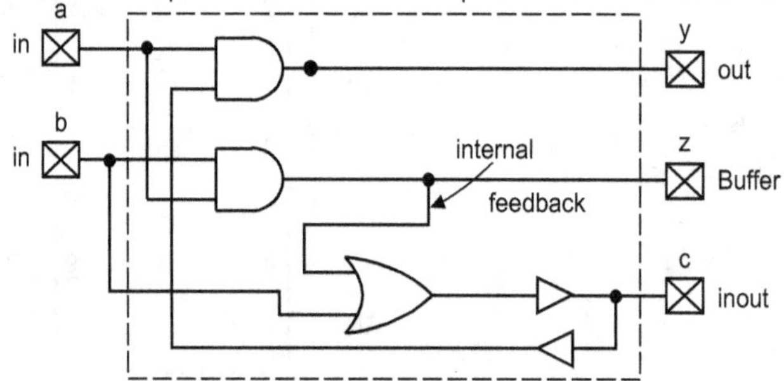

Fig. 4.9: Modes and their signal sources

As shown in Fig. 4.9, signals a and b act only as the input, signal y acts only as output. Signal z is declared as buffer; therefore, it can be reread internally. Signal c acts as the bidirectional signal; i.e. input or output.

Example 1:

Write entity for an IC shown in Fig. 4.10.

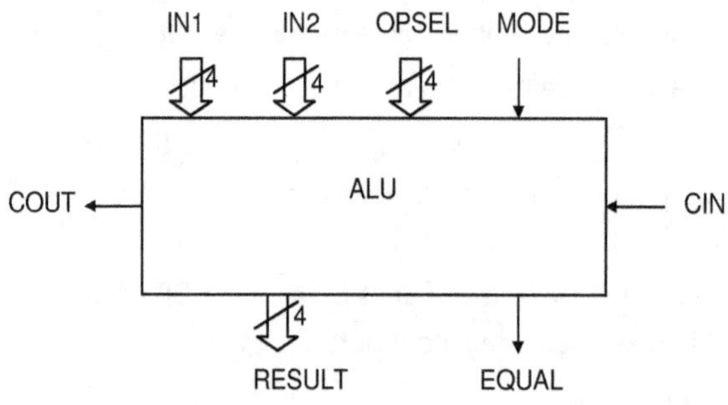

Fig. 4.10

Solution:

```
entity ALU is
    port (IN1, IN2, OPSEL: in bit_ vector (3 downto 0);
       MODE, CIN: in bit;
       COUT, EQUAL: out bit;
        RESULT: out bit _vector (3 downto 0));
    end ALU;
```

Example 2:

Write the entity construct for the R-S flip flop circuit as shown below.

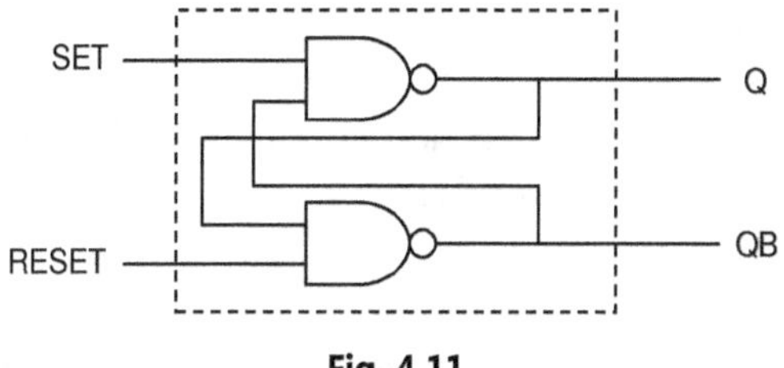

Fig. 4.11

Solution:

Let the name of the entity be RSFF. It has two input ports SET and RESET and two bidirectional ports Q and QB. Then entity construct will be

entity RSFF *is*

    port (SET, RESET: *in bit;*

      Q, QB: *inout bit*);

  end RSFF;

4.7 Architecture

Architecture describes a design's behavior and functionality (internal behaviour of entity). Architecture specifies behavior, function, interconnections, relationship between inputs and output of an entity.

Architecture can contain only concurrent statement. An entity can have more than one architecture. There can be no architecture without an entity.

The syntax of architecture body is

architecture ARCHITECTURE_NAME *of* ENTITY_NAME *is*

    [declarative part]

begin

[Statement part]

end ARCHITECTURE_NAME ;

The words *architecture, of, is, begin* and *end* are keywords in VHDL.

ARCHITECTURE_NAME

Architecture must be given a name consisting of a text string which should be assigned by a designer in a way meaningful to the design.

ENTITY_NAME

Must write the name of entity for which the architecture is to be written.

Declarative part

It appears before the keyword *begin*. It can be used to declare signals, user_defined types, constants, components, subprogram etc.

Statement part

It is contained between the keywords *begin* and *end*. All the statements are executed concurrently (simultaneously).

The functionality of the design can be expressed in terms of following styles which are called styles of modeling.

1. **Data flow**
2. **Behavioral**
3. **Structural**

These different styles of modeling are explained in section 4.10

Example 3:

Write the VHDL code for the circuit shown in Fig. 4.12.

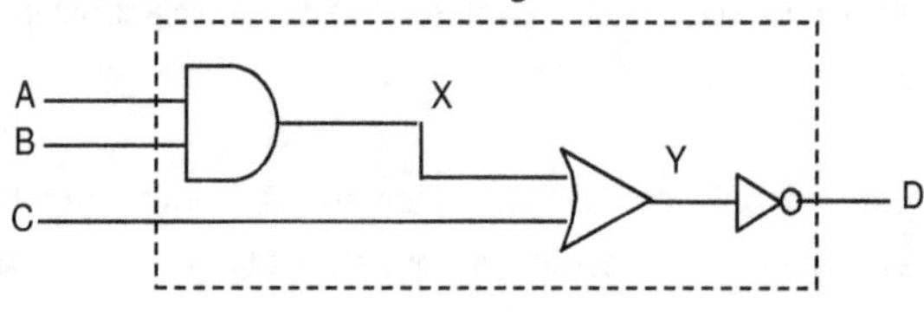

Fig. 4.12

Solution:

This circuit is having three inputs A, B, C and one output D. To express D in terms of A, B, C, we have to consider intermediate wires X and Y. Inputs A, B, C and output D must be defined in entity declaration.

The intermediate wires (wires running inside an IC) X, Y should be declared as signal in declarative part of architecture body.

```
entity ANDORNOT is
  port (A, B, C: in bit;
          D: out bit);
end ANDORNOT;
```

architecture ANDORNOT_ARCH *of* ANDORNOT *is*
signal X,Y: *bit;*
begin
      X <= A *and* B;
      Y <= X *or* C;
      D <= *not* Y;
end ANDORNOT_ARCH;

The sequence of statement is not important.

Example 4:

Write the VHDL code to design half adder.

Solution:

The truth table and circuit of half adder is as shown.

Input		Output	
IN1	IN1	Sum	Carry
0	0	0	0
0	1	1	0
1	0	1	0
1	1	0	1

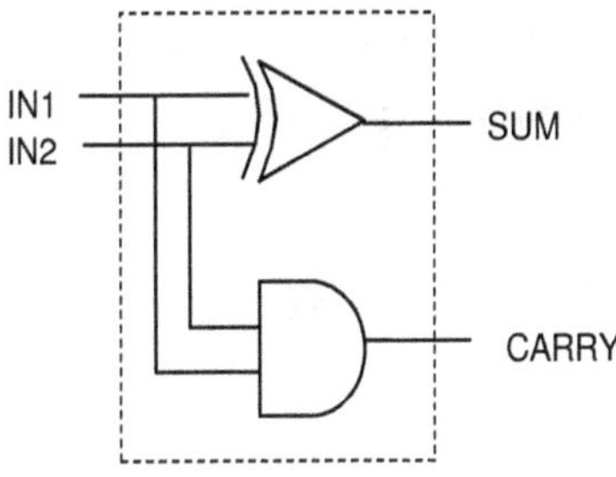

Fig. 4.13: Half adder

Half adder is having two inputs IN1, IN2 and two outputs SUM, CARRY.
No need of signal declaration.

entity HALFADDR *is*
port (IN1, IN2: *in bit;*
        SUM, CARRY: *out bit*);
end HALFADDR;

```
architecture HALFADDR_ARCH  of HALFADDR  is
begin
        SUM < = IN1 xor IN2;
        CARRY < = IN1 and IN2;
end HALFADDR_ARCH;
```

4.8 Concurrent Statements

A VHDL architecture body consists of a set of interconnected concurrent statements. Concurrent statement in a design executes simultaneously. All concurrent statements describe the functionality of multiplexer structure. It is not possible to design storage elements like flip-flop using concurrent statements only.

The concurrent statements defined in VHDL are:

- Concurrent signal assignment
- Block statement
- Component Instantiation statement
- Generate statement
- Process statement

4.8.1 Concurrent Signal Assignment

i.   Simple Concurrent Signal Assignment

The syntax is

        Target <= expressions;

i.e. Target signal receives the value of an expression. A signal assignment is defined by '<='

        e.g.   Z <= A and B;

The logical AND of A and B is assigned to Z. This statement is executed whenever either A or B has an event occurred on it. An event on a signal is a change in the value of that signal. [Whenever value of A or B changes, statement will execute].

A signal assignment statement is said to be sensitive to changes on any signal that are to the right of the <= symbol. The above statement is sensitive to A and B.

Signal assignment statement creates the driver. Z <= A and B statement will create one AND gate with A and B inputs and Z as output.

i.e. It has created driver for Z.

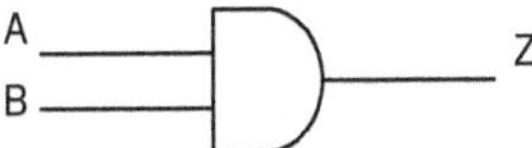

Let, X <= Y; It will connect nodes X and Y. Driver for X will be created like

In concurrent statements, there are no implied registers.

ii. Conditional Concurrent Signal Assignment

The syntax is

> target <= Boolean expression1 when condition
>> else
>> Expression2;
> *when* statement can also be nested.

While executing *when* statement,

1. Each condition is tested in the order in which it is written.
2. The value of that expression whose associated condition is true will be assigned to the target.
3. If none of the conditions are true, the value of expression associated with last *else* is assigned to the target.

> e.g.   Z <= A *when* ASSIGN_A = '1'
>> *else*
>> B *when* ASSIGN_B = '1'
>> *else*
>> C;

ASSIGN_A is tested; if it is '1', then the value of A will be assigned to Z.

If ASSIGN_A is not equal to '1', then condition ASSIGN_B is tested, if it is '1' then Z will be equal to B.

If ASSIGN_B is not equal to '1' then the value of C will be assigned to Z.

iii. Selected Concurrent Signal Assignment

The syntax is

> *with* choice_ expression *select*
> > target <=   expression 1 *when* choice 1,
> > expression 2 *when* choice 2,
> > expression N *when* choice N,
> > expression *when others* ;

'*with_select*' statement evaluates choice_expression and compares that value to each choice value in the order in which they are written. The value of that expression where match is found is assigned to the target. If no match is found, expression associated with *others* will be assigned to target.

- No two choices can overlap.
- All possible choices must be enumerated.
- Each choice can be either a static expression (such as 3) or a static range (such as 1 to 3).
- Each value in the range of the choice expression type must be covered by one choice.
- "*others*" clause is optional.
- All choices for the expression must be included, **otherwise "*others*" clause must be the last choice**.

Example 5:

Write VHDL code for 2 bit comparator.

Solution:

For 2 bit comparator, there are two 2 bit inputs A, B and three outputs Y0, Y1, Y2.

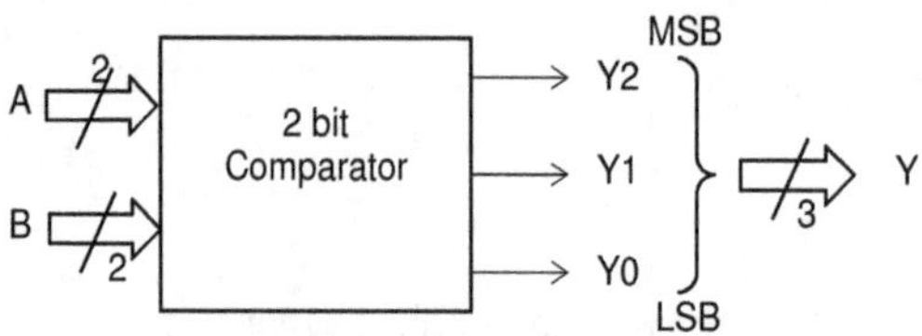

Fig. 4.14: 2 bit comparator

Truth table:

If A = B	then	Y2 = 0, Y1 = 0, Y0 = 1	i.e. Y = 001
If A > B	then	Y2 = 0, Y1 = 1, Y0 = 0	i.e. Y = 010
If A < B	then	Y2 = 1, Y1 = 0, Y0 = 0	i.e. Y = 100

From truth table itself, we can describe the relationship between input and output and hence no need of gate circuitry for this design.

entity COMP1 *is*
    port (A, B: *in bit_vector* (1 *downto* 0);
     Y: *out bit_vector* (2 *downto* 0);
end COMP1;

    architecture COMP1_ARCH *of* COMP1 *is*
    begin
   Y <= "001" *when* A = B
     else
     "010" *when* A > B
     else
     "100" *when* A < B;
    end COMP1_ARCH;

- Single bit value must be specified in single quotes i.e. '1', '0'.
  Multi bit value must be specified in double quotes i.e. "100", "1010".
- Let Y = Y2 Y1 Y0
  If declared as Y: *out bit_vector* (2 *downto* 0); then Y0 is considered as LSB and Y2 as MSB.
  If declared as Y: *out bit_vector* (0 *to* 2); then Y2 is considered as LSB and Y0 as MSB.

Example 6:
Design 4:1 multiplexer using VHDL.

Solution:
4:1 multiplexer and its functionality is as shown in Fig. 4.15.

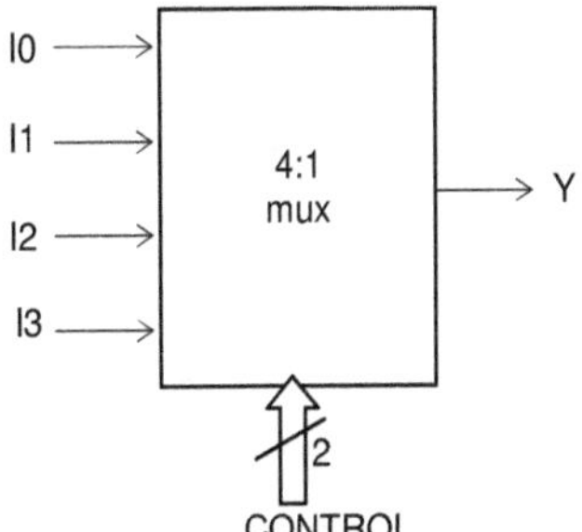

S		Y
S1	S0	
0	0	I0
0	1	I1
1	0	I2
1	1	I3

Fig. 4.15

```
entity MUX4 is
        port (I0, I1, I2, I3: in bit;
           CONTROL: in bit_vector (1 downto 0);
           Y: out bit);
end MUX4;
architecture MUX4_ARCH of MUX4 is
   begin
   with CONTROL select
     Y <= I0 when "00",
           I1 when "01",
           I2 when "10",
           I3 when "11",
           '0' when others;
end MUX4_ARCH ;
```

4.8.2 Block Statement

Main purpose of block statement is organizational only. It constructs only separate part of the code without adding any functionality. It allows the designer to logically group areas of the model.

Each block represents a self-contained area of the model. Signals, types, constants etc. declared in the block are local to that block and can not be referenced outside of that block.

The syntax is

```
        label: block
        [block declarative item]
        begin
        concurrent statements
        end block [label] ;
```

                                              optional

   label → is required to name the block.

```
e.g.    ALU: block
   signal QBUS: bit_vector (31 downto 0);
   begin
       C <= A add B;
       C <= A sub B;
   end block;
```
Block can also be nested.

e.g.   BLK1: *block*

      signal QBUS: *bit_ vector* (31 *downto* 0);

      begin

        BLK2: *block*

        signal QBUS: *bit_ vector* (31 *downto* 0);

        begin

         -- BLK2 statements

        end block BLK2 ;

          -- BLK1 statements

      end block BLK1;

In this example, signal QBUS is declared in two blocks. One block is contained in the other. BLK1 is the parent block of BLK2. The QBUS signal from BLK1 has been overridden by a declaration of the same name in BLK2.

Guarded block contains a guard expression which can enable and disable drivers inside the block. The guard expression is a Boolean expression. When guard expression is true, drivers contained in the block are enabled, and when false, the drivers are disabled.

    e.g.

      BLK: *block* (CLK = '1')

      begin

        Z <= *guarded not* X;

      end *block* BLK ;

      The guard expression is CLK = '1'.

When CLK is equal to '1' then guarded signal assignment statement (Z <= *guarded not* X) is enable i.e. compliment of X will be assigned to Z.

When CLK is not equal to '1' then the statement Z <= *guarded not* X is disabled.

Keyword *guarded* is used to specify guarded signal assignment statement.

Example 7:

    Write VHDL code to design D-latch.

Solution:

    The pin configuration of D-latch is as shown in Fig. 4.16.

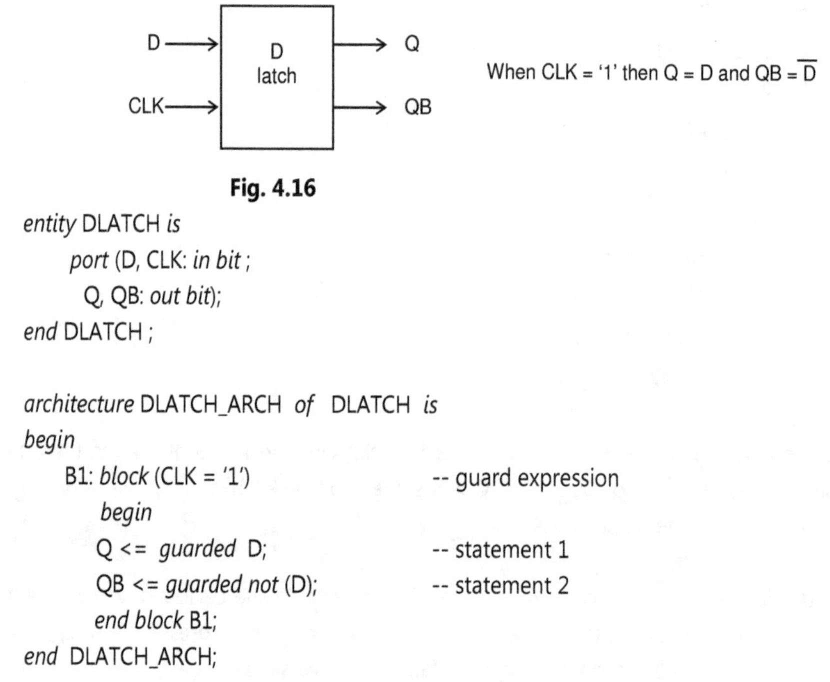

Fig. 4.16

entity DLATCH *is*
    port (D, CLK: *in bit* ;
     Q, QB: *out bit*);
end DLATCH ;

architecture DLATCH_ARCH *of* DLATCH *is*
begin
    B1: *block* (CLK = '1')   -- guard expression
     begin
      Q <= *guarded* D;   -- statement 1
      QB <= *guarded not* (D);   -- statement 2
     end block B1;
end DLATCH_ARCH;

When CLK is equal to '1' then value of D and its complement will be assigned to Q and QB respectively.

When CLK is not equal to '1' then statement 1 and statement 2 (guarded statement) will disable or turned off (does not execute).

4.8.3 Component Instantiation Statement

Component is predesigned, preanalyzed, precompiled entity_architecture pair (VHDL model). Components are normally placed in design library. Component specifies a subsystem, which can be instantiated in another architecture leading to a hierarchical specification.

The component can be defined in package, design entity, architecture, or block declarations. Components must be declared before *begin* statement of architecture, if it is declared in architecture. A component must be declared before it is instantiated. e.g. Suppose VHDL code for half adder is written, compiled and verified, and placed either in design library or in working directory, then for full adder design, we can use half adder as component because full adder can be designed using two half adders and one OR gate.

The syntax for component declaration is:

> *component*   component_name
> > *port* (port_list);
>
> *end component;*

e.g.   *component* HALFADDR
port (IN1, IN2: *in bit* ;
> SUM, CARRY: *out bit*);
end component ;

Component_name should be same as entity name of VHDL code which is using as component. In port list copy the port list of entity (entity of VHDL code which is using as component).

Component Instantiation:

It is selecting a compiled specification of component in the library and linking it with the architecture where it will be used.

Component Instantiation statement is used to build a net list in VHDL by referencing a previously defined hardware component in current design.

It introduces a subsystem declared elsewhere as a component in current design.

The syntax for component instantiation is:

> Instance_name: component_name
> > *port map* ([port_name =>] expression
> > > [port_name =>] expression.);

Instance_name is name of the instance of the component.

Component_name is name of the component to be instantiated.

Port map connects each port of this instance of component_name to a signal valued expression in the current entity.

Ports can be mapped to signals by 'named' or 'positional' notation.

Ports of the component are called formal ports. Ports of top_level entity (entity of main design) are called actual ports. Named association is port maps by names are preferred because it makes the code more readable and pins can be specified in any order.

All positional port mapping should be placed before any named port mapping.

Example 8:

Write VHDL code for NAND gate and write VHDL code for the logic circuit shown in Fig. 4.17 by using NAND gate design as component.

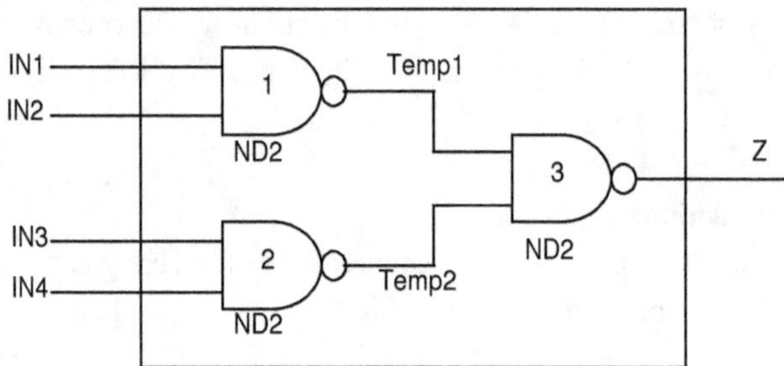

Fig. 4.17

Solution:

(a) Design of NAND gate

Let

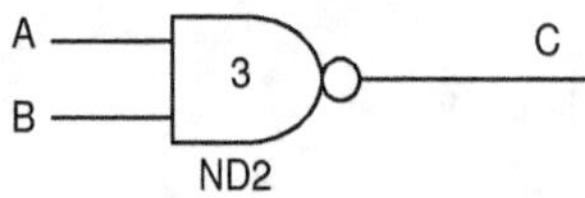


```
entity ND2 is
     port (A, B: in bit;
         C: out bit);
end ND2;


architecture ND2_ARCH of ND2 is
begin
    C <= A nand B;
end  ND2_ARCH;
```

If we save the VHDL file, it will save with its entity name.

i.e. This file will save as ND2.VHDL. Now if this file is compiled, verified and placed either in design library or in working directory, then this VHDL code can be used as component in design of any other circuit.

(b) Design of given circuit (Structural Model)

```
entity COMPND2  is
  port ( IN1, IN2, IN3, IN4 :  in bit;
              Z: out bit );
end  COMPND2 ;


architecture  COMPND2_ARCH  of  COMPND2  is
          component ND2
              port ( A, B: in  bit;
              C: out bit );
          end component;
        signal TEMP1, TEMP2: bit;
begin
I1: ND2 port  map ( IN1, IN2, TEMP1 );                --Positioned port mapping
I2: ND2 port  map ( A => IN3, B => IN4, C => TEMP2 );   -- Named port mapping
I3: ND2 port map (TEMP1, TEMP2, C=> Z);                -- Mixed port mapping
end COMPND2_ARCH;
```

ND2 design is declared as component in architecture before *begin* statement. Signals TEMP1 and TEMP2 are declared. Three component instantiation statements I1, I2, and I3 are written.

I1 instance creates one copy of ND2 design i.e. NAND gate1 with two inputs mapped IN1, IN2 and one output named TEMP1.

Similarly, I2 instance creates NAND gate2 with input named IN3, IN4 and an output TEMP2.

I3 instance creates NAND gate3 with input TEMP1 which gets connected to the output of NAND gate1 and TEMP2 connected to the output of NAND gate2 and output Z.

Example 9:

Design one bit full adder using half adder (see Example 4) as component.

Solution:

Full adder can be designed using half adder as shown in Fig. 4.18.

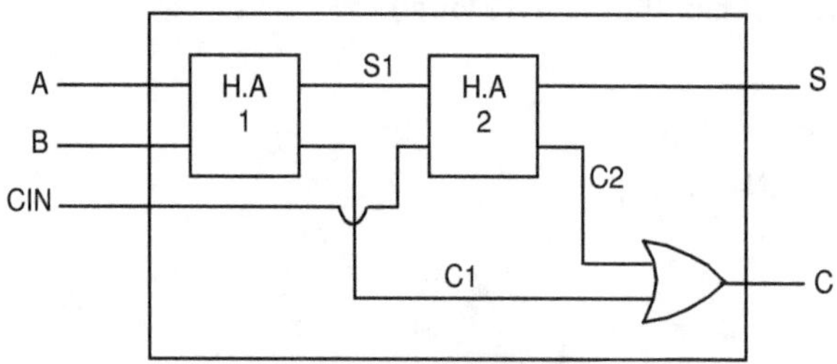

Fig. 4.18: Full adder

In above circuit, there are two instances of half adder.

```
entity FULLADDR is
     port ( A, B, CIN: bit;
       S, C: out bit );
end FULLADDR;


architecture FULLADDR_ARCH of FULLADDR is
    component HALFADDR       -- half adder design declared as component
        port ( IN1, IN2 : in bit;
          SUM, CARRY: out bit);
     end component;
     signal S1, C1, C2: bit;
begin
HA1:  HALFADDR port map ( A, B, S1, C1 );
HA2:  HALFADDR port map ( S1, CIN, S, C2 );
        C <= C1 or C2;
end FULLADDR_ARCH;
```

HA1 creates a copy of half adder design i.e. half adder1 shown in Fig. 4.18.

HA2 creates half adder2.

In both the instances, ports are mapped by their position. Hence sequence of signals/ports is important.

We can also map the ports by their name, as follows.

HA1: half adder *port map* (IN1 =>A, IN2 =>B, SUM => S1, CARRY => C1);

HA2: half adder *port map* (IN1 =>S1, IN2 =>CIN, SUM => S, CARRY => C2);

While mapping the ports by name, first write formal port then after '=>' write actual port.

Example 10:

Write VHDL code for 4 bit full adder using 1 bit full adder.

Solution:

4 bit full adder can be designed using four 1 bit full adders as shown in Fig. 4.19.

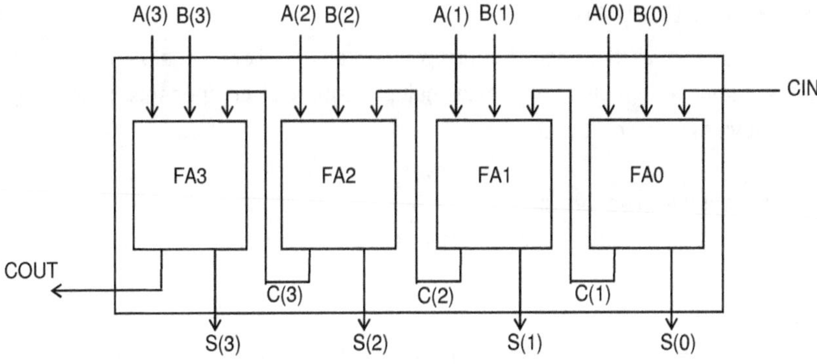

Fig. 4.19

```
entity ADDR4  is
        port (A, B: in  bit_vector (3 downto 0);
            CIN: in bit;
                S: out bit_vector (3 downto 0);
            COUT: out bit);
end ADDR4;


architecture ADDR4_ARCH  of  ADDR4  is
        component FULLADDR
            port (A, B, CIN: in  bit;
                    S, C: out bit);
        end component;
        signal TEMP: bit_vector (4  downto  0);      -- is used for CIN, C(1), C(2), C(3) and
                                                     -- COUT
```

begin
    TEMP (0) <= CIN;
   FA0: FULLADDR   *port map* (A(0), B(0), TEMP(0), S(0), TEMP(1));
   FA1: FULLADDR   *port map* (A(1), B(1), TEMP(1), S(1), TEMP(2));
   FA2: FULLADDR   *port map* (A(2), B(2), TEMP(2), S(2), TEMP(3));
   FA3: FULLADDR   *port map* (A(3), B(3), TEMP(3), S(3), TEMP(4));
       COUT <= TEMP (4);
end ADDR4_ARCH;

4.8.4 Generate Statement

Generate statement is used to select concurrent statements conditionally or to replicate concurrent statements. It is used to create multiple copies of components, processes, or blocks i.e. it provides a compact description.

Generate statement have two forms:
  (i) *for...generate*　　　　　　　(ii) *if...generate*

(i) *for...generate*

It creates multiple copies of components, processes, or block i.e., it executes concurrent statements number of times.

The syntax is :
    label: *for* identifier *in* range *generate*
       {concurrent statements}
     end generate [label] ;

Number of copies is determined by a discrete range. Range must be computable integer, in either of following forms:
- integer_expression to integer_expression
- integer_expression downto integer_expression
- Each integer_expression evaluates to an integer

for_generate statement declares a new local integer variable with the name identifier. Identifier is assigned the first value of range, and each concurrent statement is executed once. Identifier is then assigned next value in range, and each concurrent statement is executed once more. This is repeated until identifier is assigned the last value in range. Each concurrent statement is then executed for the last time and execution continues with the statement following *end generate* statement. The loop identifier is then deleted.

(ii) *if...generate*

It creates zero or one copy, conditionally.

The syntax is
    label: *if* expression *generate*
            {concurrent statement}
        end generate [label] ;

If expression is true, then concurrent statements are executed once, otherwise no execution of concurrent statements.

e.g.   CKO: *if* K=0 *generate*
            DFF: D_FLIP *port map* (COUNT, CLOCK, QCK);
        end generate CKO;

Example 11:

Design 4-bit full adder with 1-bit full adder as a component using ***generate*** statement.

Solution:

Refer Example 10.

Where four copies of one bit full adder are created by instantiating component full adder four times. For this four instances, (FA0, FA1, FA2, FA3) are written.

Same can be done by writing one instance and using for-generate statement as follows:

```
entity ADDRGEN  is
    port ( A, B: in  bit_ vector (3 downto 0);
         CIN: in bit;
          S: out bit_vector (3 downto 0);
         COUNT: out bit);
end ADDRGEN;

architecture ADDRGEN_ARCH of ADDRGEN is
    component FULLADDR
        port (A, B, CIN: in  bit;
                 S, C:  out bit);
    end component;
      signal TEMP: bit_vector (4  downto  0 );
```

```
begin
        TEMP(0) <= CIN;
        GK: for K in 0 to 3 generate
              FA: FULLADDR port map (A(K), B(K), TEMP(K), S(K), C(K+1) );
            end generate GK;
        COUT <= TEMP(4);
end ADDRGEN_ARCH;
```

4.8.5 Process Statement

In architecture, all statements are concurrent. So where do sequential statement exist in VHDL ?

In VHDL, *process* statement contains only sequential statement.

Process is the primary concurrent VHDL statement used to describe sequential behavior (i.e. sequential statements). All the statements in the process are executed sequentially, hence order of statements is important. All the processes in an architecture execute concurrently.

Signals to which some value is assigned within a process are not updated with their new values until the process suspends.

The syntax for process declaration is:

```
process (sensitivity list)
        Declaration part
begin
    Sequential statements
end process;
```

In declaration part, types, variables, constants, subprograms can be declared. Statement part contains only sequential statement.

Process never stops, it repeats forever, unless suspended.

To suspend the process, either sensitivity list or *wait* statements are used.

Sensitivity list

Sensitivity list is a list of signals to which process is sensitive. Sensitivity list defines the signals that cause the statements inside the process statement to execute whenever one or more elements of the list changes its value.

Process executes when any one of the signals in the sensitivity list changes. A process with a sensitivity clause must not contain an explicit *wait* statement. Process should either have a sensitivity list or *wait* statement at the end. Only static signal names are allowed in the sensitivity list.

Wait Statement

Wait statement is only used in the process statement. This statement provides an alternate way to suspend the execution of a process.

A process can be suspended by means of a sensitivity list, i.e. when a process has a sensitivity list it always suspends after executing the last sequential statement in the process. For example, given in listing. This process executes, when there is an event on a or c and suspends after executing the last statement.

```
process (a, c)
begin
    if a > c then
        y <= '1';
    else
        y <= '0';
    end if;
end process;
```

listing ------ process statement with sensitivity list.

The alternate way to suspend the process is by using a wait statement.

```
process
begin
        if a > c then
            y <= '1';
        else
            y <= '0';
        end if;
    wait on a, c;
end process;
```

listing ----- process statement with wait statement.

The wait statement is placed at the end of a process. If wait statement is the last statement in the process, the process resumes execution from the first statement in the process.

There are basically **three types** of wait statements:

1) wait on sensitivity_list;
2) wait until Boolean_expression;
3) wait for time_expression;

We can also combine these statements into a single statement as,

wait on sensitivity_list until boolean_expression for time_expression;

Examples of wait statements are discussed below:

1) Wait until Clk = '1'

It means that for the wait condition to be satisfied and execution of the code to continue, there must be an event on signal Clk, i.e. change in value and that value of Clk must be equal to '1' i.e. a rising edge for Clk.

2) Wait on x, y, z

In this the execution of wait statement causes the enclosing process to suspend and then wait for an event to occur on signals x, y or z. When there is an event on x, y or z, the process resumes execution from the next statement onwards after the wait statement. If the wait statement is the last statement in the process, the process resumes execution from the first statement.

3) Wait for 12 ns

This wait statement causes the enclosing process to suspend for 12 ns, and when the simulation time advances to T + 12 ns, the enclosing process resumes execution from the statement following the wait statement. We can also use the command as

constant period : time := 12 ns;
wait for 3 period;

4) Wait on clock for 15 ns

The execution of wait causes the enclosing process to suspend and then wait for an event to occur on clock for a time_out interval of 15 ns. If there is no event on clock within 15 ns, the process resumes execution with the statement following the wait.

5) Wait until answer > 80 for 10 ns

When wait statement executes, it suspends the process. The Boolean condition (answer > 80) is evaluated every time there is an event on answer. If the answer > 80, (after the event on answer) then it will resume the execution of the next statement.

If there is no event on answer or if the Boolean condition is false, then it will wait for maximum 10 ns and resumes the execution of the next statement.

6) Wait on clock until answer > 80

When this wait statement executes, it suspends the execution of process. It checks the Boolean condition only after there is an event on clock, if the Boolean condition is true, then only go to the next statement, otherwise continue to wait.

7) Wait for 0 ns

It means to wait for one delta time. This statement is useful when we want the process to be delayed so that delta-delayed signal assignments within a process can take effect. For example,

```
process
begin
    wait on a;
    y <= a;
    wait for 0 ns;
    z < = y;
end process;
```

Process takes very less time to execute (less than delta delay). If signal a changes at 20 ns, y is scheduled to get the new value of a at 20 ns + 1 delta. The wait statement (wait for 0 ns) causes the process to suspend for one delta. Signal y gets updated with it's new value. Process resumes at 20 ns + 1Δ, z gets the new value of y at 20 ns + 2Δ.

If the "wait for 0 ns" statement was not present, then both the statements (y <= a and z <= y) get executed sequentially at time 20 ns and in that case, y gets the new value of a, but z gets the old value of y i.e. logic '0'.

It is an error if both a sensitivity list and a wait statement are present within a process.

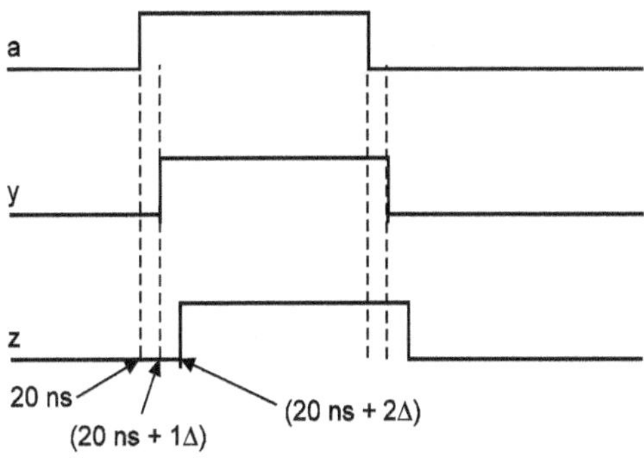

Fig. 4.20: Effect of 'wait for 0 ns'

It is permissible to have several wait statements, inside the same process.

Example:

```
process
begin
    --
    wait until clock = '0';
    --
    wait until clock = '0';
    --
    wait until clock = '0';
end process;
```

The wait is actually a sequential command. The wait command can not be used in functions, but wait can be used in procedures and processes.

4.9 Sequential Statements

Sequential statements are executed one after the another, in the order in which they are written. Sequential statements can appear only in process or subprograms. Only sequential statements can use variables.

4.9.1 if statement

The syntax is:

```
if condition then
    sequential statements
end if;
```

If condition is true then statements will execute.

if _else statement

The syntax is

```
if condition then
        statements1;
else
    statements2;
end if;
```

If condition is true then statements1 will execute, otherwise statements 2 will execute.

Nested if_else

The syntax is

```
        if condition1 then
            statements1;
        elseif condition2  then
            statements2;
        else
            statements3;
        end if ;
```

If condition1 is true then statements1 will execute. Then it checks condition2, if it is true, statements2 will execute. Otherwise statements3 will execute.

if statement evaluates each condition in order. It generates a priority structure. It is same as concurrent statement *when_else.*

Use of *if* statement is suitable or easy up to three or four levels (conditions).

```
    e.g.
        process ( A,B,C,X )
        begin
        if ( X = "0000") then
            Z <= A;
        elsif ( X <= "0101") then
            Z <= B;
        else
          Z <= C;
        end if ;
    end process;
```

4.9.2 case statement

The syntax is:

```
    case expression is
        when choice1 =>  statement1 ;
        when choice2 =>  statement2 ;
        when choice N=>  statementN;
        when others  => statements;
    end case ;
```

e.g.

```
process ( A,B,C,X )
begin
   case X is
            when   0 to 4  => Z <= B ;
            when     5     => Z <= C ;
            when   6 to 9  => Z <= A ;
            when   others  => Z <= '0' ;
   end case;
end process;
```

case statement selects for execution, one of the number of alternative sequence of statements. Statements following each *when* clause is executed, only if the choice value matches the expression value. Each choice can be either a static expression (such as 4) or a static range (such as 1 to 5).

Every possible value of the case expression must be covered in one and only one *when* clause i.e. no choices can overlap.

It corresponds to *"with_select "* in concurrent statement.

case statement produces parallel logic whereas *"if"* statement produces priority encoded logic.

Example 12:

Design 8:1 multiplexer using *case* statement.

Solution:

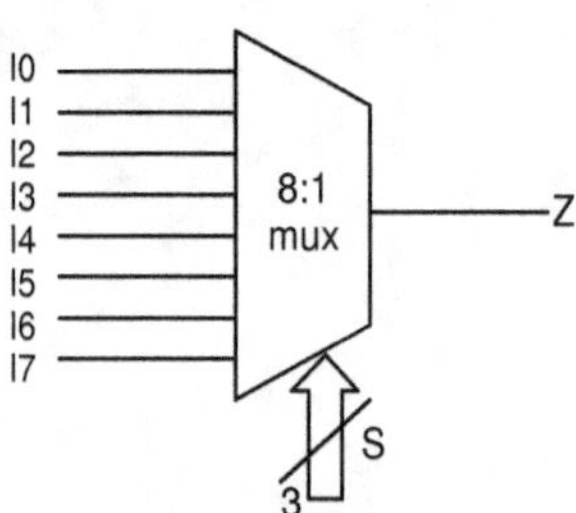

Fig. 4.21: Multiplexer

```
entity   MUX81 is
    port (I0, I1, I2, I3, I4, I5, I6, I7: : in bit;
             S: in bit_vector (2 downto 0);
             Z: out bit);
end MUX81;

architecture MUX81_ARCH of MUX81 is
begin
    process (I0, I1, I2, I3, I4, I5, I6, I7, S)
    begin
    case S is
             when "000"  =>  Z<= I0;
             when "001"  =>  Z<= I1;
             when "010"  =>  Z<= I2;
             when "011"  =>  Z<= I3;
             when "100"  =>  Z<= I4;
             when "101"  =>  Z<= I5;
             when "110"  =>  Z<= I6;
             when "111"  =>  Z<= I7;
             when  others =>  Z<= '0';
    end case;
    end process;
  end MUX81_ARCH;
```

4.9.3 null statement

null statement does not perform any action. It can be used to indicate that when some condition is met, no action is to be performed.

```
e.g. case S is
             when "00"   => Z<= '1';
             when "01"   =>  Z<= '0';
             when others => Z<= null
    end case ;
```

4.9.4 loop statement

loop statement is used to execute sequence of sequential statements repetitively.

while loop statement

The syntax is:

```
loop_label: while condition loop
    Sequence_of_statements
    end loop loop_label;
```

Sequence of statement will execute till condition is true.

e.g.   *process* (A)
               begin
                  L1 : *while* P < = 4 *loop*
                   Z (I) <= A(I+4);
                       I = I +1;
                  end loop L1;
               end process;

It has a Boolean iteration scheme. Condition is evaluated before execution.

for loop statement

The syntax is:
loop_label: *for* loop_parameter *in* range *loop*
                    sequence_of_statements
                    end loop loop_label;

The loop is executed once for each value in the range. Range determines number of execution of loops. The range is tested at the beginning of loop execution.

The loop parameter is a constant, which may be used but not altered. Loop counter only exists within the loop.

e.g.   FACTORIAL: = 1;
        L1: *for* NUMBER *in* 2 *to*10 *loop*
                FACTORIAL: = FACTORIAL * NUMBER;
        end loop L1;

4.9.5 next statement

The syntax are:
    i.   *next;*

    ii. *next* loop_label *when* condition;

"*next*" statement is used only inside a loop. "*next*" statement skips the remaining statement in the current iteration of the loop and execution starts from the first statement of the next iteration of the loop.

e.g.   *for* X *in* 1 *to* 10 *loop*
        SUM: = SUM +5;
        if (SUM =100) *then*
            next;
        else
            null;
        end if;
        Y: = Y + 1;
    end loop;

The *next* statement also causes an inner loop to be existed.

    L1: *for* X *in* 10 *down*to 1 *loop*
        Statement group 1;
    L2: *loop*
      Statement group 2;
      next loop L1 *when* flag = '1';
      Statement group 3;
      end loop L2;
      Statement group 4;
      end loop L1;

When flag = '1', statement group 3 and 4 are skipped and execution starts from the first statement of loop L1 and L2 was terminated.

4.9.6 exit statement

exit statement entirely terminates the execution of the loop in which it is located.

The syntax are:
    i.   *exit;*
    ii. *exit* loop_ label *when* condition;

e.g. 1
    exit L1_LOOP *when* (I < 5);
This statement completes the execution of the loop labelled L1_LOOP when the expression (I < 5) is true.

The *exit* statement provides a quick and easy method of exiting a loop statement when all processing is finished or an error or warning condition occurs.

e.g. 2

```
SUM: =1;   J: = 0;
    L3: loop
        J: = J + 21;
        SUM: = SUM * 10;
        If (SUM > 100) then
                exit L3;
        end if;
    end loop L3;
```

Loop L3 will execute till condition SUM > 100 is false. When SUM >100 becomes true, execution of loop L3 will completely terminate.

4.9.7 report statement

The syntax is:

```
report string_expression;
    [severity expression];
```

"report" statement is used to print or display the specified string and the severity level to be reported to the simulator for appropriate action.

The severity is specified in the STANDARD package and contains following values:

       note,   warning,   error,   failure

Default value is *note*.

Normally, report statement is used with **assertion statement**.

Assert Statement:

It is basically used for Error Management in VHDL. With Assert statement, it is possible to test function and time constraints on a model inside a VHDL component.

If the condition for an **assert** is not met (false) during simulation of a VHDL code, a **message** of a certain **severity** is sent to the user (to the simulator).

Syntax:

```
Assert <condition>
Report <message>
Severity <error_level>
```

If the condition is not met (condition is false), the report statement is executed and gives the message to the simulator. Also there are four different severity levels for the message (error_levels). These are:

*   Note-- Note is the Default severity level.
*   Warning
*   Error
*   Failure

The message and severity level are displayed in the VHDL simulator's command window.

An Assert is both a **sequential** and a **concurrent** command.

We will see an example of a concurrent assertion statement used in SR flip-flop model. The code is written to ensure that the input signals R and S are never simultaneously zero. The VHDL code is given below. As shown, in the assert command, when both S and R are '0', at that time, Assert command becomes false. As "not (S='0' and R='0')", is false when both S and R are '0' simultaneously, then the message is given as "R and S are both low, not valid inputs".

```
library ieee;
use ieee.std_logic_1164.all;

entity SRFlip_Flop is
    port (S, R : in std_logic; Q, Qbar: out std_logic);
end SRFlip_Flop;

architecture SR-arch of SRFlip_Flop is
begin
    assert not (S = '0' and R = '0')
Report "S and R are both low, not valid input";
severity ERROR;
end SR_arch;
```

Similarly, the equivalent process statement for above example is given below:

```
process
begin
    assert not (S = '0' and R = '0')
    report "S and R are both low, not valid inputs";
    severity ERROR;
    wait on S, R;
end process.
```

Next, we will see a program, to check that the simulator time does not exceed 1000 ns. The code is given below.

Now is a predefined function that returns the current simulation time.

```vhdl
process (clk)
begin
    assert now < 1000 ns
    report "simulator time exceeds 1000 ns";
    severity Failure;
end process;
```

Next, we will see a program of rising edge triggered D-flip-flop. It uses assertion statement to check for setup and hold times.

```vhdl
library ieee;
use ieee.std_logic_1164.all;

entity D-Flipflop is
    port (D, clk: in Bit ; Q, Qbar: out Bit);
end D-Flipflop;

architecture DFF_arch of D-Flipflop is
constant Hold_Time: TIME: = 4 ns;
constant Setup_Time: TIME: = 3 ns;
begin
process (D, clk)
    variable LastEventonD, LastEventonclk: TIME;
begin
    -- check for hold time
    if D'Event then
        assert Now = 0 ns or (Now – LastEventonD) > = Hold_Time;
        report "Hold Time is too short";
        severity ERROR;
        LastEventonD: = Now;
    end if;
    -- check for setup time
    if clk = '1' and clk'Event then
```

```
            assert Now = 0 ns or (Now – Last EventonD) >= Setup_Time.
            report "Setup time is too short"
            severity Error;
            LastEventonclk := Now;
        end if;
                    -- Behavior of FF
        if clk = '1' and clk event then
                Q <= D;
                Qbar <= not D;
        end if;
        end process;
    end DFF_arch;
```

The hold time is the minimum time the data must remain stable **after** the clock changes.

The setup time is the minimum time the data input must be stable **before** the clock changes as shown in Fig. 4.22.

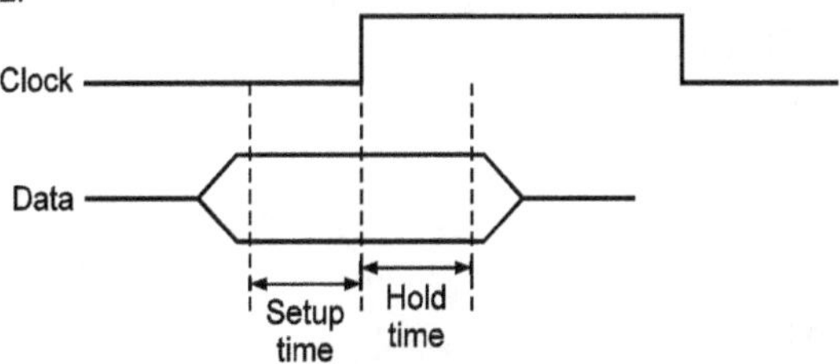

Fig. 4.22: Set up and Hold time

As already discussed, **Now** is a function which returns the current simulation time. All processes are executed until they suspend during the **initialization phase**. To prevent misleading message appearing during initialization phase of simulation, the expression "Now = 0 ns" is used in the assertion statement. In the DFF example, as shown already when there is an event on signal D or clk, the process executes. The first if statement is executed when there is an event on D. The assertion statement

    (Now = LastEventonclk) >= Hold_time

checks for the Hold_time. The difference between the current simulation time and the last time an event occurred on signal clk is greater than a constant Hold_time. If this statement is false, it means the Hold_time is short and it prints the message.

Similarly, the setup time is checked. The last if statement describes the latch behavior of the D type flip-flop.

We will see one more example to check spikes at the input of a buffer.

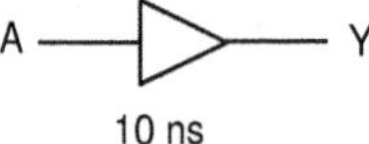

The buffer has 10 ns propagation delay. If the spike has width of 5 ns or less, then print the message as "spike is detected".

```
library ieee;
use ieee.std_logic_1164.all;

package PACK is --- package to store propagation delay and min-pulse
    constant min_pulse : TIME := 5 ns;
    constant propagation_delay : TIME : = 10 ns;
end PACK;

library ieee;
use ieee.std_logic_1164.all;
use work. PACK. all;

entity buffer is
    port (A: in bit;
          Y: out bit);
    end buffer;

    architecture buffer_arch of buffer is
begin
    process (A)
        variable LastEventonA : TIME := 0 ns;
    begin
        assert Now = 0 ns or (Now–LastEventonA) >= min_pulse;
        report "spike detected on input of buffer";
        severity WARNING;
        LastEventonA := Now;
        Y <= A after propagation_delay;
    end process;
end buffer_arch;
```

4.10 Styles of Modeling

The styles or ways in which functionality of design is described are called styles of modeling. Three modeling styles are

        (i) Data flow, (ii) Behavior, (iii) Structural

4.10.1 Data Flow Modeling

In this modeling, the flow of data through the entity is expressed using concurrent signal assignment statements, i.e. it has a set of concurrent assignment statements. Each statement is executed when any of its input signal changes its value. This modeling needs Boolean equations as design specification.

e.g.   Design of AND gate

```
entity AND1D is
    port ( A, B: in  bit ;
                C: out  bit );
    end AND1D;

    architecture AND1D_ARCH  of  AND1D  is
    begin
                C <= A and B;
    end AND1D_ARCH;
```

4.10.2 Behavioral Modeling

In this modeling, the behavior of entity (relation between input and output) is expressed using statements which are executed sequentially. It is also known as High-level description. In this modeling, there is no need to focus on the gate level implementation of a design. A behavioral design method defines a circuit in terms of a textual language rather than a schematic of interconnected symbols.

The functionality of design is described in an algorithmic representation in *process* statement. This modeling needs truth table as design specification.

e.g.   Consider entity AND1D

```
    architecture AND1B_ARCH  of  AND1D  is
begin
                process (A, B)
                begin
```

if (A= '1' *and* B= '1') *then*
        C <= '1';
else
        C <= '0';
end if;
end process;
end AND1B_ARCH ;

4.10.3 Structural Modeling

In structural modeling, an entity is described as a set of interconnected components in the architecture body. In this modeling, components from libraries or from working directory are connected together. This design method is hierarchical.

Each component can be individually simulated. A structural design method is used to split a design into manageable units.

This modeling needs logical diagram as design specification.

e.g.   Design of full adder using half adder (Refer Example 9).

If the two or more modeling styles are mixed in a single architecture body, then it is called **mixed style modeling.**

Example 13:

Write down VHDL code for the given AND-OR network shown in Fig. 4.23 using structural modeling.

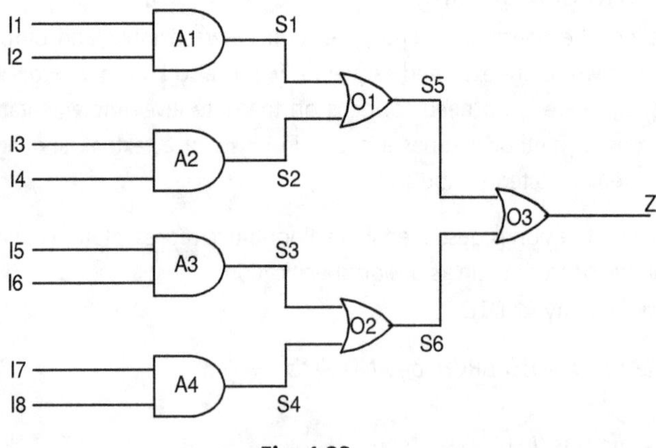

Fig. 4.23

Solution:

Assume AND1 and OR1 entity_architecture pair is precompiled, verified and are available in working directory.

```
entity  STRUCT  is
     port (I1, I2, I3, I4, I5, I6, I7, I8: in bit;
               Z: out bit);
end  STRUCT;

architecture  STRUCT_ARCH  of  STRUCT  is
    component AND1
        port ( A, B: in  bit;
                  C: out  bit );
     end component;
     component  OR1
        port ( P, Q: in  bit;
                  R: out bit );
     end component;
       signal S1, S2, S3, S4, S5, S6: bit;
     begin
        A1: AND1          port  map ( I1, I2, S1 );
        A2:  AND1         port  map ( I3, I4, S2 );
        A3:  AND1         port  map ( I5, I6, S3 );
        A4:  AND1         port  map ( I7, I8, S4 );
        O1:  OR1          port  map ( S1, S2, S5 );
        O2:  OR1          port  map ( S3, S4, S6 );
        O3:  OR1          port  map ( S5, S6, Z );
     end STRUCT_ARCH;
```

Example 14:

Write a VHDL code for the logic shown in Fig. 4.24 using mixed style modeling.

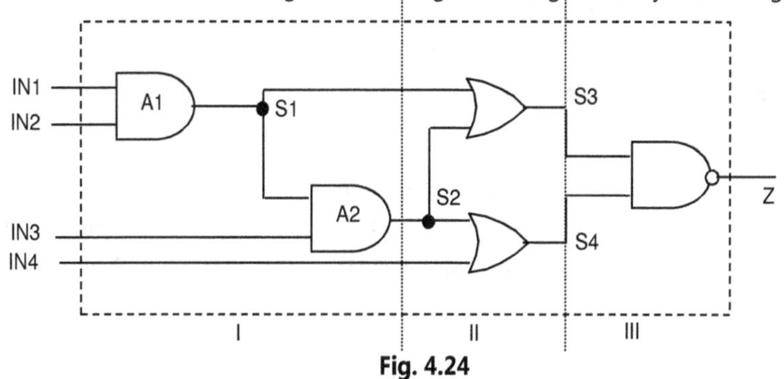

Fig. 4.24

Solution:

```
entity STRUCT1  is
        port (IN1, IN2, IN3, IN4: in  bit;
                Z: out bit);
end STRUCT1;


    architecture STRUCT1_ARCH  of  STRUCT1  is
        component AND1
            port ( A, B: in  bit;
                    C: out bit);
        end component ;
    signal S1, S2, S3, S4, S5, S6: bit;
begin
    A1: AND1 port map (IN1, IN2, S1);
    A2: AND1 port map (S1, IN3, S2);
    process ( S1, S2, IN4 )
    begin
        S3 <= S1 or S2;
        S4 <= S2 or IN4;
    end  process;
        Z <= S3 nand  S4;
end STRUCT1_ARCH;
```

AND gates are specified by structural modeling, OR gates by behavioral style and NAND gate is specified by data flow modeling.

4.11 Package and Library

4.11.1 Package

Package is a collection of commonly used subprograms, data types, constants etc. A package is common storage area. Packages are used to hold the data to be shared among a number of entities. The data declared inside a package can be referenced by other entities.

A package consists of two parts:

      (i) Package declaration   (ii) Package body

(i) Package declaration

It defines the interface for the package (similar to entity).

The package declaration section can contain the following declarations:
- Subprogram declaration
- Type subtype declaration
- Constant, deferred constant declaration
- Signal declaration creates a global signal
- File declaration
- Alias declaration
- Component, attribute declaration
- Use clause.

All the items declared in the package declaration section are visible to any design unit that uses the package with a *use* clause.

The constants whose names and types are declared in the package declaration section, but actual values specified in the package body section are called as **deferred constant**.

The syntax for package declaration is

> *package* package_name is
>   declarations;
> *end* [*package*] package_name;

e.g.   *package* P1 is
        constant RISE, FALL: *time*;
          end P1;

… RISE and FALL are deferred constants.

(ii) Package body

Package body is used to define the values for deferred constants, to specify the subprograms bodies for subprogram declared in package declaration.
Package body also contains
- Subprogram declaration
- Subprogram body
- Type, subtype declaration
- Constant, file, alias declaration
- Use clause.

It specifies the actual behavior of the package (similar to architecture).

A package declaration can have only one package body, both having the same name (contrast to entity_architecture).

Writing of package body is optioned.

It contains the hidden details of a package (i.e. package body is not visible).

The syntax for package body is

> *package body* Package_name *is*
>> Declarations;
>> subprograms body;
> *end* Package_name;

> e.g.   *package body* P1 *is*
>> RISE: = 5 *ns*;
>> FALL: =10 *ns*;
> *end* P1 ;

Packages are stored in libraries for convenience purposes. User-created packages by default stored in work library.

"*use*" statement is used to access a package from a library and "*library*" keyword is used to access particular library.

The syntax is
> *library* Library_name;
> *use* Library_name. package_name. particular_name;

> e.g.   *library* BLIB ;   -- allows your design to access library BLIB
> *use* BLIB .P1.*all* ;   -- allows your design to use entire P1 package from library BLIB.
> *use* BLIB .P1.NAND2;   -- allows your design to use only component NAND2 from package P1 which is kept in library BLIB.

4.11.2 Design Libraries

A **design library** is an area of storage in the file system of the host environment. The management of the design libraries is not defined by the language and is tool - implementation - specific.

Generally, there are three types of libraries in VHDL:
1) Library IEEE
2) Library WORK
3) Library STD

When a VHDL component is compiled, it is saved in the **work library as default**. The work library is not the name of a directory on the PC, on which the compilation is being done, but a **logical name**.

VHDL tools usually define the work library **automatically** when the tool is started up. This means that different work libraries will be obtained depending on where the VHDL compiler is started. All compiled components are stored in a library. Packages too are usually stored in a library. The VHDL standard is defined in such a way that the **WORK and STD** libraries are always **visible**. These two libraries do not, have to be specified in the VHDL code. The following **invisible lines are always included** in every VHDL code.

> Library work;
> Library std;
> use std.standard.all;

The STD library has the package named standard. In standard package itself, data types such as bit, bit_vector, character, time and integer are defined.

STD library has two packages predefined, these are **standard** and TEXTIO.

Package standard is a predefined package that contains the definitions for the predefined types and functions of the language. This package contains the following types – BOOLEAN, BIT, CHARACTER, SEVERITY_LEVEL, INTEGER, REAL, TIME, STRING, FILE_OPEN_KIND AND FILE_OPEN_STATUS.

Standard package also contains the following subtypes such as: DELAY_LENGTH (from type TIME), NATURAL (from type Integer), POSITIVE (from type Integer). Standard package also contains the function *Now*.

Package TEXTIO

It contains declarations of types and subprograms that support formatted I/O operations on text files.

TEXTIO package contains types such as LINE, TEXT, SIDE, WIDTH. It has standard text files such as INPUT and OUTPUT. It has input procedures such as Readline and Read, and output procedure write.

Library IEEE

It contains the package STD_LOGIC_1164, which defines a nine value logic type and its associated overloaded functions and other utilities.

Package STD_LOGIC_1164:

This package shall be compiled into a design library. It contains the following:

```
type STD_ULOGIC is      (     'U' – Uninitialized
                              'X' – Forcing unknown
                              '0' – Forcing '0'
                              '1' – Forcing '1'
                              'Z' – High impedance
                              'W' – Weak unknown
                              'L' – Weak 0
                              'H' – Weak 1
                              '–' – don't care
                        );
```

It also contains STD_ULOGIC_VECTOR as type,

function RESOLVED, subtype STD_LOGIC.

subtype STD_LOGIC is Resolved STD_ULOGIC,

　　-- STD_LOGIC is Resolved from STD_ULOGIC

type STD_LOGIC_VECTOR is array (Natural range < >)

　　of STD_LOGIC;

This package also contains subtypes such as, X01, X01Z, UX01, UX01Z etc.

There are also functions available. These functions are and, nand, or, nor, xor, xnor, not.

The conversion functions are To_BIT, To_BITVECTOR, To_STDULOGIC, To_STDLOGICVECTOR, To_STDULOGICVECTOR.

Edge detection functions such as RISING_EDGE, FALLING_EDGE etc.

Library Clause:

The library clause makes visible the logical names of design libraries. The format is

　　library TTL, CMOS;

Above statement makes the logical names TTL and CMOS visible in the design unit.

The library clause

　　library STD, work;

　　is implicitly declared for every design unit.

Use Clause:

Two forms of use clause

  use library_name . primary_unit_name;

  use library_name . primary_unit_name.item;

If all items within a primary unit are to be made visible, the keyword **all** can be used. For example,

  use IEEE.STD_LOGIC_1164.all;

 If we need to use TEXTIO package, then it must be declared in the VHDL code,

  use STD.TEXTIO.all;

4.11.3 Std_logic_1164 [Multivalued logic]

So far we have used bit type signals. To bit type signal, only two values i.e. '0', '1' can be specified. Bit type is a default type of VHDL.

The IEEE-1164 standard specifies a 9 valued logic system for use with VHDL. The nine logic values defined in this standard are;

  'U' - Uninitialized

  'X' - Forcing unknown

  '0' - Forcing 0

  '1' - Forcing 1

  'Z' - High impedance

  'W' - Weak unknown

  'L' - Weak 0

  'H' - Weak 1

  '_' - Don't care.

The unknown '0' and '1' values come in two strengths – forcing and weak. If a forcing signal and a weak signal are tied together, the forcing signal dominates. For example, if '0' and 'H' are tied together, the result is '0'.

The nine valued logic is useful in modeling the internal operation of certain types of ICs.

Now onwards, to design digital system, we will use package std_logic_1164 from IEEE library by adding following two lines before entity.

  library IEEE ;

  use IEEE.STD_LOGIC_1164.*all* ;

 In this package, type STD_LOGIC and STD_LOGIC_VECTOR are defined for single bit and multi-bit signals respectively.

4.12 Generic

Generic is used to pass certain types of information into a description from its environment. Generics of an entity are declared along with its ports in the entity declaration. Generic declares a constant object whose value can be specified in one of the following:

- Entity declaration
- Component declaration
- Component instantiation
- Configuration specification
- Configuration declaration

A value for a generic must be specified at least once using any of the methods mentioned above.

Here is an example, where value of generic is specified in the entity declaration. This is the default value for the generic. This value can be overridden by others.

```
entity AND1 is
    generic ( X: integer : =  4 );
    port ( A: in bit_vector ( X downto 0 );
            B: out bit);
end AND1;
```

Following example gives specification of generic value in a component declaration and component instantiation statement.

```
entity ABC is
    :
end ABC ;

architecture ABC_ARCH  of  ABC  is
  component AND1
      generic ( X: integer );
      port (A:  in  bit_vector (X downto 0);
            B: out bit);
  end component;
  component OR1
      generic ( Y: integer. = 5 );
      port ( A: in  bit_vector ( Y downto 0 );
            B: out bit);
```

```
    end component;
        signal S1, S2, S3: bit;
        signal S4: bit_vector ( 0 to 3 );
        signal S5: bit_vector ( 0 to 4 );
        signal S6: bit_vector ( 0 to 3 );
        signal S7:  bit_vector  ( 0 to 4 );
    begin
        A1: AND1 generic map (5);
        O1: OR1    generic map (4);
        A2: AND1 port map (S6, S3);
        O2: OR1 port map (S7, S4);
    end ABC_ARCH;
```

When first component instantiation is executed, the value of the generic specified in the instance A1 5 is assigned to generic X. Generic Y is declared in the component declaration OR1 as 5. The last instance assigns this value 5, to the generic Y. For instance O1, value of generic Y(5) is overridden by the value specified by the generic map of O1 i.e. 4. Instance A2 is illegal, since the generic value is not specified either by the component declaration or by the component instance.

4.13 Configuration

Configurations are used for the following:
1. To bind desired architecture to the entity – As multiple architectures can be written for the same entity. But for simulation, only one architecture has to be chosen.
2. To bind specific component to an entity – Suppose, if component A is declared in architecture, then by default it will bind to entity A. But to bind component A to any other entity in library than entity A, configuration is used.
3. To bind generic to one of the entity to that component.
    VHDL provides following two ways of performing architecture to entity and entity to component binding.
    - By using configuration declaration.
    - By using configuration specification.

4.13.1 Configuration Declaration

A configuration declaration is a separate design unit. It allows for late binding of components i.e. the binding can be performed after the architecture body has been written.

The syntax is:

    configuration configuration_name *of* entity_name *is*

      for architecture_name

        for instance_name: component_name

          use library_name. entity_name (architecture_name)

        end for;

      end for;

    end configuration_name;

e.g.   Let

    entity COMP *is*

        port (--);

    end COMP;

    architecture COMP1_ARCH *of* COMP *is*

      component A

        port (--);

      end component;

    begin

      I1: A *port map* (   );

      I2: A *port map* (   );

    end COMP1_ ARCH ;

    architecture COMP2_ ARCH *of comp is*

    begin

      -----

    end COMP2_ ARCH;

In above example, two architectures are written for same entity. Now to bind COMP1_ ARCH architecture, configuration should be declared as follows:

    configuration COMP1_CONFIG *of* COMP *is*

      for COMP1_ARCH

      end for;

    end COMP1_CONFIG.

COMP1_ARCH architecture will get binded with entity COMP. Component A will bind to entity A.

Now, to bind Component A to entity B (kept in work library and architecture name is B_ ARCH) for instance I2, configuration should be written as follows.

```
configuration COMP1_CONFIG. of COMP is
        for COMP1_ARCH
            for I2: A
                    use WORK. B (B_ARCH)
                end for;
            end for;
        end COMP2_CONFIG.
```

In COMP2_CONFIG configuration, architecture COMP1_ARCH is binded with entity COMP and component A is binded with entity B from library WORK for the instance I2 of component A. For the instance I1, component A will bind with entity A only.

4.13.2 Configuration Specification

Configuration Specification appears in the declaration part of the architecture or block in which the components are instantiated.

Here is an example:
```
        architecture ABC_ARCH of ABC is
        component  AND1
                port (A, B: in bit ;
                        C: out bit);
            end component ;
            component OR1
            port (A, B: in bit ;
                        C: out bit);
            end component;
        -- configuration specification.
            for A1: AND1
                use entity HS_LIB. AND2 (AND2_ ARCH)
                    port map (HS_A⇒A, HS_B⇒B, HS_C⇒C);
            for others : AND1
                use entity WORK. AND1 (AND1_ARCH);
            for all: OR1
                use entity CMOS_LIB. OR2 (OR2_ ARCH);
            signal S1, S2, S3, S4, S5, S6, S7 S8: bit ;
```

```
begin
    A1: AND1 port map        (S1, S2, S3);
    A2: AND1 port map        (S3, S4, S5);
    A3: AND1 port map        (S1, S3, S6);
    O1: OR1   port map       (S3, S5, S7);
    O2: OR1   port map       (S1, S3, S8);
end ABC_ARCH;
```

First configuration specification indicates that component instance A1 uses component AND1, which is associated with entity AND2, which is present in the design library HS_LIB, and AND2 is associated with architecture AND2_ARCH from the same design library.

The second configuration specification indicates that all unbound instances of component AND1. That is instances A2, A3 are associated with entity AND1 and architecture AND1_ARCH from library work.

The third configuration specification indicates that component instances of component OR1 are associated with entity OR2 and architecture OR2_ARCH specified in library CMOS_LIB.

Configuration specification can be used to specify value of a generic. Consider the following example:

```
architecture ABC_ARCH of ABC is
        component AND1
                generic ( RISE, FALL: time );
                port ( A, B: in bit;
                        C: out bit);
        end component ;
for A1, A2 : AND1
        use entity WORK. AND1 (AND1_arch);
        generic map (THE⟹ FALL, TLH⟹ RISE )
        port map (A,B,C) ;
for others: AND1
        use entity work. AND2 (AND2_ARCH)
        generic map (1 ns, 3 ns)
        port map ( A => S0, B => S1, C => S2 );
signal S0, S1, S2, S3, S4, S5, S6 : bit;
```

begin

      A1: AND1 *generic map (3 ns, 4 ns) port map (S0, S1, S2);*
      A2: AND1 *generic map (4 ns, 5 ns) port map (S2, S3, S4);*
      A3: AND1 *port map (S4, S5, S6);*
      A4: AND1 *generic map (4 ns, 4 ns) port map (S0, S1, S2);*
  end ABC_ARCH ;

Port map used in configuration specification gives association between ports of the component and the ports of the associated entity.

For instance A1 and A2 value of generic is not specified by configuration specification, but value is assigned to generics RISE and FALL by the instantiation statements A1 and A2.

For instance A3, value of generic is not specified by instantiation statement, so value assigned to the generic in this case is the value specified by the configuration specification for instance A3 (for others).

The component instance A4, overrides the value of generics RISE and FALL mentioned in the last configuration specification statement.

4.14 Subprogram

Subprogram consists of procedures and functions. A function always returns just one argument. A procedure can return more than one argument. In function all parameters are input parameters; a procedure can have input, output, inout parameters.

There are two versions of procedures and function; a concurrent procedure and concurrent function exist outside of a process statement or another subprogram; the sequential procedure and sequential function exist only in a process statement or other subprogram statements.

All statements inside a subprogram are sequential.

A function is usually used in an assignment statement or expression; a procedure exists as a separate statement in an architecture or process.

4.14.1 Function

A function executes a sequential algorithm and returns a single value to the calling program.

The general form of a function declaration is:

function function_name (formal parameter_list)

  return return_type *is*

  [declarations] ;

begin

  sequential statements;

  return return_value;

end function_name;

The general form of a function call is:

function_name (actual parameter_ list);

e.g., *function* ROTATE (REG : *std_logic_vector*)

   return std_logic_vector is

  begin

   return REG *ror* 1;

  end ROTATE;

When the above function is called, it returns a std_logic_vector equal to the input std_logic_vector (REG) rotated one position to the right.

A function call can be used anywhere that an expression can be used. For example if A= "10010101", the statement

  B <= ROTATE (A) would set B equal to "11001010", and leaves A unchanged.

Example 15:

Write a VHDL function which adds two 4-bit vectors and a carry, and returns a 5-bit sum.

Solution:

  function ADD4 (A, B: *bit_vector* (3 *downto* 0);

    CARRY: *bit*)

  return bit_vector is

  variable COUT: *bit;*

  variable CIN: *bit.* = CARRY;

  variable SUM: *bit_vector* (4 *downto* 0): = "00000";

```
begin
LOOP1: for I in 0 to 3  loop
        COUT: = (A( I )  and B( I ))  or  (A( I ) and C( I )) or (B( I )  and CIN);
        SUM( I ): = A( I )  xor B( I ) xor CIN;
        CIN: = COUT;
      end loop  LOOP1;
      SUM(4): = COUT;
  return  SUM;
  end  ADD4;
```

In above example, function name is ADD4, the formal parameters are A, B and CARRY, and return_type is bit_vector. Variables COUT and CIN are defined to hold intermediate values during calculation. The variable SUM is used to store the value to be returned.

When function is called, the value of CARRY will be assigned to CIN.

The *for* loop adds the bits of A and B serially as follows.

$$
\begin{array}{rcl}
A & = & 1\,0\,1\,0 \\
 & & + \\
B & = & 1\,0\,1\,1 \\
carry & = & 0 \longleftarrow \\
\hline
 & =^1 & 1\,0\,1\,1 \\
\end{array}
$$

5 bit sum

The first time through the loop, COUT and SUM(0) are computed using A(0), B(0), and CIN. Then the CIN value is updated to the new COUT value and execution of the loop is repeated. After four times through the loop, all values of SUM(I) have been computed and SUM is returned.

The function call is of the form:

ADD4 (A, B, CARRY);

e.g.   Z <= (X, *not* Y, '1');

This statement calls the function ADD4. Parameters A, B, and CARRY are set equal to the values of X, *not* Y, and '1' respectively. X and Y must be bit_vector dimensioned 3 *downto* 0. The function computes,

SUM = A + B + CARRY =X + not Y + '1'

and return the value of SUM.

4.14.2 Procedure

Procedure can be used to decompose VHDL code into modules. Procedure can return any number of values using output parameters.

The form of procedure declaration is:

> *procedure* Procedure_name (formal parameter list) *is*
>   [Declaration]
> *begin*
>   sequential statements
> *end* procedure_name;

The formal parameter list specifies the inputs and outputs to the procedure and their types.

A procedure call is a sequential or concurrent statement of the form:

> procedure_name (actual parameter_list);

As an example, the following procedure is written to add two N-bit vectors and a carry, and return an N-bit sum and a carry.

```
procedure VECTADD
            (IN1, IN2        : in bit_vector,
             CIN             : in bit;
              signal SUM    : out bit_vector,
              signal COUT  : out bit,
              N               : in position) is
variable C: bit,
begin
   C: = CIN;
   LOOP1: for I  in 0 to N-1 loop
       SUM( I ) <= IN1( I ) xor IN2( I ) xor C ;
          C: = ( IN1( I ) and IN2( I )) or (IN1( I ) and C) or (IN2( I ) and C ) ;
          end loop LOOP1;
      COUT < = C;
end VECTADD;
```

In above example, IN1, IN2 and CIN are input parameters. SUM and COUT are output parameters. N is a positive integer used to specify the number of bits in the bit_vector.

The addition in algorithm is the same as the one used in the ADD4 function. C must be a variable, since the new value of C is needed each time through the loop. After N times through the loop, all the values of the signal SUM have been computed.

The procedure call is of the form:

> VECTADD (IN1, IN2, CIN, SUM, COUT, N);

Within the procedure declaration, the class (i.e. signal, variable or constant), mode (in or out or inout) and type (bit, bit_vector, std_logic or std_logic_vector) of each parameter must be specified in the formal parameter list.

If class is not specified, constant is used as the default. The formal and actual parameter must be of the same type. The parameter of mode "in" can not be changed in the procedure, but parameters of mode "in" and "inout" can be changed in the procedure, so they are used to return values to the caller.

Following table summarizes the mode and classes that may be used for procedure and function parameters.

Mode	Class	Procedure call	Function call
in *	Constant**	Expression	Expression
	Signal	Signal	Signal
	Variable	Variable	Not Allowed
out/inout	Signal	Signal	Not Allowed
	Variable***	Variable	Not Allowed

* default mode for function

** default for mode in

*** default for mode out/inout.

Comparison of Function and Procedure

Function	Procedure
1) Function can return only one value.	1) Procedure can return more than one value.
2) It has only input parameters (mode : IN).	2) It has IN, OUT and INOUT mode parameters.
3) Functions execute in zero simulation time, wait statement cannot be used in functions.	3) Procedures may not execute in zero simulation time, depending on wait statement.
4) Functions are called as part of expression.	4) Procedure call is considered as separate statement.
5) Functions are used to perform computation on data available immediately.	5) Procedure may wait on some input data.
6) Functions represent frequently used block of code.	6) Procedures are used to partition large code.

4.15 Attributes

An attribute is data attached to VHDL objects or predefined data about VHDL objects. Examples are the current drive capability of a buffer or the maximum operating temperature of the device.

Attributes can be used for modeling hardware characteristics. An attribute provides additional information about signals, array and types.

Attributes can be classified as:
- Value kind
- Function kind
- Signal kind
- Type kind
- Range kind.

4.15.1 Value Kind Attributes

Value attributes are used to return a particular value about an array of a type, a block, or a type in general.

Value attributes are broken into three subclasses.

- Value type attributes_Return the bounds of a type
- Value array attributes_Return the length of an array
- Value block attributes_Return block information

Value Type Attributes:

There are *four* predefined attributes of *value type category*:

- *T'left* → Returns the left bound of a type or subtype
- T'*right* → Returns the right bound of a type or subtype
- T'*high* → Returns the upper bound of a type or subtype
- T'*low* → Returns the lower bound of a type or subtype

Attributes are specified by the character " ' " and then the attribute name. The object preceding the " ' " is the object that the attribute is attached to.

The " ' " character is pronounced as "tick".

For example,

1) Type smallint is –32767 to 32767 lower and left bound is –32767 and right and upper bound is 32767.

2) *process* (X)

    type BIT_LENGTH *is array* (15 *downto* 0) *of bit;*

    variable L_RANGE, R_RANGE, UP_RANGE;

    LOW_RANGE: *integer;*

    begin

    L_RANGE:= BIT_LENGTH'*left;*   -- returns bit 15

    R_RANGE:= BIT_LENGTH'*right;*   -- returns bit 0

    UP_RANGE:= BIT_LENGTH'*high;*   -- returns bit 15

    LOW_RANGE:= BIT_LENGTH'*low;*   -- returns bit 0

   end process ;

3) *type* DAY *is* (MON, TUE, WED, THUR, FRI, SAT, SUN)

    left bound   right bound

    low bound   high bound

Value Array Attributes:

'length is a value array attribute. It returns total length of the array range specified.

e.g.   *process*

    type BIT8 *is array* (0 *to* 7) *of bit;*

    variable LEN1: *integer* ;

    begin

    LEN:= BIT8' *length;*   -- returns 8

   end process;

Value Block Attributes:

There are two attributes working with blocks and architectures. Attributes *'structure* and *'behavior* return information about how a block in a design is modeled. Attribute *'behavior* return true if the block specified by the block label, or architecture specified by architecture name, contains no component instantiation statement. Attribute *'structure* returns true if the block or architecture contains only component instantiation statement and/or passive process.

e.g.   *entity* X is

|

          end   X;
          architecture X_ARCH *of* X *is*
          component DF

|

          end component;
          begin
             U1: DF *port map* (   );
             U2:
       end X _ARCH;

          X_ARCH*'behavior,* -- returns false
          X_ARCH*'structure;* -- returns true

4.15.2 Function Kind Attributes

Function attributes return information about types, arrays and signals.

Function attributes can be subdivided into three categories.

- Function type attributes.
- Function array attributes.
- Function signal attributes.

Function Type Attributes:

Function type attributes return type value.

Function type attributes are:

- *'pos* (value) which returns position number of value passed in.
- *'val* (value)   which returns value from position number passed in.
- *'succ* (value) which returns next value in type after input value.
- *'pred* (value) which returns previous value in type before input value.
- *'leftof* (value) which returns value immediately to the left of the input value.
- *'rightof* (value) which returns value immediately to the right of the input value.

e.g.   *type* COLOUR *is* (RED, YELLOW, GREEN, BLUE, PURPLE, ORANGE);

          COLOUR*'succ* (BLUE)   -- returns purple.
          COLOUR*'pred* (GREEN)   -- returns yellow.
          COLOUR*'rightof* (BLUE)   -- returns purple.
          COLOUR*'leftof* (GREEN)   -- returns yellow.

Function Array Attributes:

Function array attributes return the bounds of array types.

The four types of function array attributes are:

- array'*left*(N),   which returns the left bounds of index range N.
- array'*right*(N),   which returns the right bounds of index range N.
- array'*high*(N),   which returns the upper bounds of index range N.
- array'*low*(N),   which returns the lower bounds of index range N.

These attributes are same as value type attributes, except that these attributes work with arrays.

For ascending range (0 *to* 3)

array'*left* = array'*low*

array'*right* = array'*high*

For descending range (3 *downto* 0)

array'*left* = array'*high*

array' *right* = array'*low*

Function Signal Attributes:

Function signal attributes return information about the behavior of the signals.

There are five Function signal attributes:

'*event* --	returns true if an event occurred during current delta; otherwise, return false.
'*active* --	returns true if a transaction occurred during the current delta; otherwise, return false.
'*last_event* --	returns time elapsed since the previous event transition of signal.
S'*last_value* --	returns previous value of S before the last event
'*last_active* --	returns time elapsed since the previous transition of signals.

e.g.   '*event* attribute is very useful to determine clock edges

if (CLK = '1') *and* (CLK'*event*) *then*

   Q <= D;

Q is equal to D, if CLK is changing from its value 0 to 1 (positive/rising edge).

if (CLK= '0' *and* CLK'*event*) *then*

   Q <= D;

Q is equal to D when CLK is changing from its value 1 to 0 (negative/trailing edge).

4.15.3 Signal Kind Attributes

Signal kind attributes create special signals. Signal kind attributes return information such as whether a signal has been stable for a specified amount of time, when a transaction has occurred on a signal, and a delayed version of the signal can be created. These attributes cannot be used within a subprogram.

There are four Signal kind attributes.

'delayed [(time)] –	creates a signal, delayed by the time of the optional time expression.
'stable [(time)] --	creates a Boolean signal that is true whenever the reference signal has no events for the time specified.
'quiet [(time)] --	creates a Boolean signal that is true whenever the reference signal has no transaction or events for the time specified.
S*'transaction* --	creates a signal of type bit that toggles its value for every transaction or event that occurs on S.

e.g.　　1)　C <= A*'delayed* (5 *ns*)　　-- signal A is delayed by 5 ns and assigned to C.

　　　　2)　C<= A*'stable* (10 *ns*)　　-- True ('1') will be assigned to C, if signal A is stable (not changing its value) for 10 ns.

4.15.4 Type Kind Attributes

Type attributes return a value of kind type. There is only one type attribute. It must be used with another value or function type attribute. The type attribute available in VHDL is *tbase*. This attribute returns the base type of a type or subtype.

e.g.　　*process* (X)

　　　　Type COLOUR is (RED, BLUE, GREEN, YELLOW, BROWN, BLACK);
　　　　subtype COLOUR_GUN *is* COLOUR *range* RED *to* GREEN;
　　　　variable　A: COLOUR;
　　　　begin
　　　　A:= COLOUR_GUN*'base'right* ;　-- A= black
　　　　A:= COLOUR'_base*'left;　　-- A= red
　　　　A:= COLOUR_ GUN*'base'succ*(GREEN);　-- A= yellow
　　　end process;

4.15.5 Range Kind Attributes

Range kind attributes return a value kind of range. These attributes work only with constrained array types and return the index range specified by the optional input parameter.

There are two range kind attributes:
- A'*range* [(N)]
- A'*reverse_ range* [(N)]

Attribute '*range* returns the Nth range denoted by the value of parameter N. Attribute '*range* returns the range in the order specified, and *reverse_range* returns the range in the reverse order.

These attributes can be used to control the number of times that loop statement loops.

e.g.　　1)　*for* I *in* ARR'*range loop*

　　　　　　　　-- -- --

　　　　　　　end loop;

The number of times that the loop needs to be executed is determined by the number of bits in the input argument ARR.

　　2)　*type* ARRAY8 *is array* (0 *to* 15) *of bit;*

　'*range* attribute returns 0 to 15, and the '*reverse_range* attribute returns 15 to 0.

4.16 Alias

An alias creates a new name for all or part of the range of an array type. It is very useful for naming parts of a range.

The syntax is,

　　　alias alias_name: type *is* item_name;

　item_name can be a constant signal, variable, file, function name, type name, etc.

　e.g. *signal* INSTRN: *std_logic_vector* (15 *downto* 0);

　　　alias OPC: *std_logic_vector* (3 *downto* 0) *is* INSTRN (15 *downto* 12);

　　　alias SRC: *std_logic_vector* (3 *downto* 0) *is* INSTRN (11 *downto* 8);

　　　alias DEST: *std_logic_vector* (3 *downto* 0) *is* INSTRN (7 *downto* 4);

In architecture, we can use following signals,

　　OPC for INSTRN(12) to INSTRN(15),

　　SRC for INSTRN(8) to INSTRN(11),

　　DEST for INSTRN(4) to INSTRN(7).

4.17 Operator Overloading

As in VHDL, arithmetic operators + and − are defined to operate on integers, but not on bit_vectors. By using operator overloading function, the definition of + and − can extend, so that + and − operators can be operated on bit_vectors.

For example, if the designer wants to add two bit_vector objects, + operator do not work. So the designer must write a function that overloads the operator to accomplish this operation.

The following package shows an overloaded function for the operator + that allows addition of two objects of bit_vector type.

```
package MATH is
    function "+" ( L, R: bit_vector ) return integer;
end MATH;

package body MATH is
function VECTOR_TO_INT (S : bit_vector) return integer is
    variable RESULT: integer: = 0;
    variable PROD:  integer: = 1;
begin
    for I in S'range loop
      if (S( I ) = '1') then
              RESULT: = RESULT + PROD;
      end if;
      PROD: = PROD + 2;
    end loop;
    return RESULT;
end VECTOR_TO_INT;

function "+"(L, R : bit_vector) return integer is
  begin
      return (VECTOR _TO_INT(L) + VECTOR _TO_INT(R));
  end ;
  end MATH;
```

Whenever the + operator is used in an expression, the compiler calls the + operator function that matches the types of operands. When the operands are of type integer, the built-in + operator function is called. If the operands are of type bit_vector, then the function from package MATH is called.

The following example shows uses for both functions:

```
library WORK;
use WORK.MATH. all;

entity ADDER is
    port (A, B: in bit_vector (0 downto 7);
            C: in integer;
            DOUT: out integer);
end ADDER;

architecture ADDER_ARCH  of  ADDER  is
signal INTERNAL:  integer;
begin
        INTERNAL <= A + B;
        DOUT <= C + INTERNAL;
end ADDER_ARCH;
```

For the statement internal <= A +B, the overloaded operator function defined in package MATH is called because A and B are of bit_vector. This function adds the values of A and B together and returns an integer value to be assigned to signal internal.

For the statement internal DOUT <= C + INTERNAL, the built-in addition function is called because both operands C and INTERNAL are of same type.

4.18 Subprogram Overloading

Overloading allows the designer to write much more readable code. An object is overloaded when the same object name exists for multiple subprograms or type values. The VHDL compiler selects the appropriate object to use in each instance.

Subprogram overloading allows the designer to write multiple subprograms with the same name, but the number of arguments, the type of arguments, and return value can be different. The VHDL compiler selects the subprogram that matches the subprogram call. If no subprogram matches the call, an error is generated.

The following example illustrates how a subprogram can be overloaded by the argument type:

```
library IEEE;
use IEEE. STD_LOGIC_1164. all;

package P_SHIFT  is
    type S_INT is range 0 to 255;
    type S_ARRAY is array ( 0 to 7 ) of std_logic;

    function SHIFTER ( A: S_ARRAY ) return S_ARRAY;
    function SHIFTER ( A: S_INT ) return S_INT;
end P_SHIFT;

package body P_SHIFT  is
    function SHIFTER ( A: S_ARRAY ) return S_ARRAY is
        variable RESULT: S_ARRAY;
    begin
        for I in A'range loop
            if I = A'high then
                RESULT (I):= '0;
            else
                RESULT (I):= A (I + 1);
            end if ;
        end loop;

        return RESULT;
    end SHIFTER;

    function SHIFTER ( A : S_INT ) return S_INT is
    begin
        return ( A / 2 );
    end SHIFTER;
end P_SHIFT;
```

The package P_SHIFT contains two functions both named SHIFTER. Both functions provide a right-shift capability, but each function operates on a specific type. One function works only with type S_INT, and the other works only with type S_ARRAY. The compiler picks the appropriate function based on the calling argument(s) and return argument.

Overloading Subprogram Argument Types:

To overload argument types, the base type of the subprogram parameters or return value must differ. For example, base types do not differ when two subtypes are of the same type. Two functions that try to overload these subtypes produce compile error. Following is an example:

package TYPE_ERROR *is*
  subtype LOG4 *is* *bit_vector* (0 *to* 3);
  subtype LOG8 *is* *bit_vector* (0 *to* 7);

    -- this function is OK
   function NOT (A: LOG4) *return integer* ;

   -- this function declaration will cause an error
   function NOT (A: LOG8) *return integer*,

  end TYPE_ERROR;

This package declares two subtypes LOG4 and LOG8 of the bit_vector type. The two functions named NOT are then declared using these subtypes. The first function declaration is legal, but the second function declaration causes an error. The error is that two functions have been declared for the same base type. The two types LOG4 and LOG8 are not distinct, because they both belong to the same base type.

Subprogram Parameter Overloading:

Two or more subprograms with the same name have a different number of parameters. The types of parameters can be the same, but the number of parameters can be different.

4.19 Multiple Drivers and Resolution Function

Suppose, if a signal has multiple drivers as shown below:

    Z <= A *and* B;
    Z <= C *and* D;

Then what should be the value of Z?

VHDL has unique way of handling **multiple driven signals.** A multiply driven signal has many drivers. In above case, Z is multiple driven signal because it has two drivers (A *and* B) and (C *and* D). Signals with multiple sources can be found in numerous applications. Multiple driven signals are very useful for modeling a data bus, a bidirectional bus, and so on. Such multiple source signals require a method for determining the resulting value when several sources are concurrently feeding the same signal line. VHDL uses a **Resolution Function** to determine the actual value. For a multiple driven signal, values of all drivers are resolved together to create a single value for the signal. Resolution Function examines the values of all the drivers and returns a single value called resolved value of the signal.

Resolution function consists of a function that is called whenever one of the drivers for the signal has an event occurred on it. In typical simulators, resolution functions are built in, or fixed. With VHDL, the designer has the ability to define any type of resolution function desired, wired-or, wired-and, average signal value, and so on.

A resolution function has a single-argument input and returns a single value. The single-input argument consists of an unconstrained array of driver values for the signal that the resolution function is attached to. If the signal has two drivers, the unconstrained array is two elements long; if the signal has three drivers, the unconstrained array is three elements long.

Fig. 4.25 shows two tristate buffers with their outputs tied together, and the VHDL representation. All the signals in this example are of type 'X 0 1 Z' and can assume the four values: 'X', '0', '1', and 'Z'. The tristate buffers have an active-high output enable, so that when B=1 and D=0, F=A; when B=0 and D=1, F=C; and when B=D=0, the output F assumes the high-Z state. If B=D=1, an output conflict can occur.

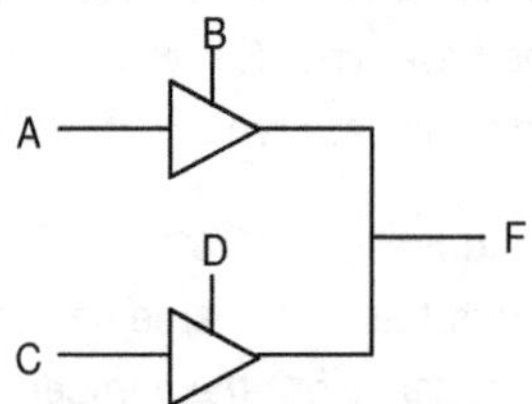

Fig. 4.25: Tristate buffers

use WORK.FOURPACK.*all*; -- values for type X 0 1 Z are defined in package fourpack

entity TBUFF *is*
     port (A, B, C, D: *in* X01Z;
                   F: *out* X01Z);
end TBUFF;

architecture TBUFF_ARCH of TBUFF *is*
begin
     F <= A *when* B = '1' *else* 'Z'; -- statement 1
     F <= C *when* D = '1' *else* 'Z'; -- statement 2
end TBUFF_ARCH;

VHDL uses a resolution function to determine the actual output. For example, if A=C=D=1 and B=0, F is driven to 'Z' by statement 1 and F is driven to '1' by statement 2. The resolution function is automatically called to determine that the proper value of F is '1'. The resolution function will supply a value of 'X' (unknown) if F is driven to both '0' and '1' at the same time.

The resolution function, which is based on the operation of a tristate bus, is specified by the following table:

	X	0	1	Z
X	X	X	X	X
0	X	0	X	0
1	X	X	1	1
Z	X	0	1	Z

This table gives the resolved value of a signal for each pair of input values: Z resolved with any value returns that value, X resolved with any value returns X, and 0 resolved with 1 returns X. The resolution function for X01Z logic is shown below. The function RESOLVE4 has an argument, S, which represents a vector of one or more signal values to be resolved.

Resolution Function for X01Z Logic:

```
package FOURPACK  is
  type U_X01Z  is  ( 'X', '0', '1', 'Z', );    -- U_X01Z is unresolved
    type U_X01Z_VECTOR  is  array ( natural range <> ) of   U_X01Z;
    function RESOLVE4 (S: U_X01Z_VECTOR ) return U_X01Z;
    subtype X01Z  is  RESOLVE4 U_X01Z;
    -- X01Z is resolved subtype which uses the resolution function RESOLVE4
    type X01Z_VECTOR  is array ( natural  range <> ) of  X01Z;
end FOURPACK;

package body  FOURPACK  is
    type X01Z_TABLE  is array ( U_X01Z, U_X01Z )  of  U_X01Z;
    constant RES_TABLE : X01Z_TABLE: = (
                                        ( 'X', 'X', 'X', 'X' )
                                        ( 'X', '0', 'X', '0' )
                                        ( 'X', 'X', '1', '1' )
                                        ( 'X', '0', '1', 'Z' ) );
```

```
      function RESOLVE4 ( S: U_X01Z_VECTOR ) return U_X01Z  is ;
        variable RESULT: U_X01Z: = 'Z' ;
      begin
         if ( S'length = 1 )  then
                 return S ( S'low );
          else
             for I in S'range loop
               RESULT: = RES_TABLE ( RESULT, S ( I ) );
             end loop ;
           end if ;
         return RESULT;
       end RESOLVE4;
     end FOURPACK;
```

In order to write VHDL code using X01Z logic, we need to define the required operations for this type of logic.

4.20 Delays in VHDL

Delta Delay/Delta Time:

The time between two sequential events is called a delta delay. It is infinitesimally very small delay. Delta delay has no equivalence in real time but it exists when the simulation clock is standing still.

In signal assignment statement, the delta delay is present. For example,

        y <= a; -- signal y assigns value of signal a after one delta delay.

The Delta delay mechanism provides for ordering of events on signals that occur at the same simulation time.

Example:

```
x <= y;          -- y assigned to x after delta delay
z <= x;          -- x assigned to z after delta delay.
```

When an event occurs on signal y, say at 10 ns, the statement x <= y gets executed, which causes signal x to change after 1 delta delay, at (10 ns + 1Δ), when time advances to (10 ns + 1Δ), signal x changes. This triggers the second statement z <= x, causing signal z to get the new value after another delta delay, that is at (10 ns + 2Δ). This sequence of waveforms is shown in Fig. 4.26.

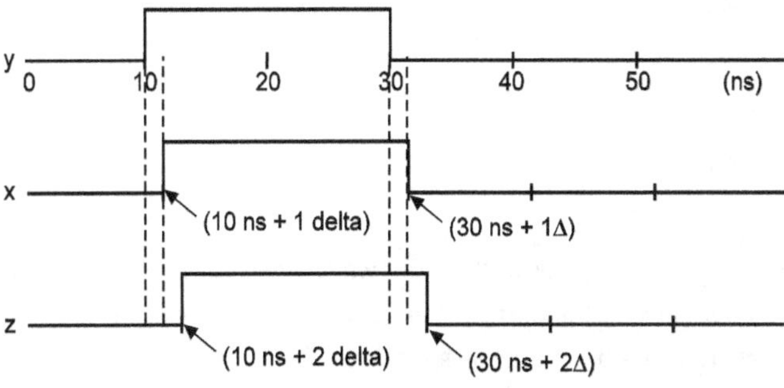

Fig. 4.26: Delta delay

Advantage of Delta Delay:
To prevent VHDL simulator's jamming, most simulators stop after 1000 delta times. The number can usually be set.

For example,

$$q <= not\ q;$$

This is a correct VHDL code, but generates a design which oscillates for infinite number of times. It causes the same line to be executed again and q will be updated after another delta time.

The VHDL simulator will count up the number of delta times until all signals are stable.

This problem is easy to solve by inserting a delay.

$$q < = not\ q\ after\ 10\ ns;$$

Transport and Inertial Delay:
There are basically two types of propagation delay models:
  (1) Inertial delay
  (2) Transport delay

(1) Inertial Delay Model:
Inertial delay models the delays found in switching circuits. This is the default delay in VHDL. They are generally used to specify component delays.

Syntax:

signalobject <= [reject pulse_rejection_limit] inertial expression after
inertial_delay_value;

For example,

     y <= reject 4 ns inertial q after 12 ns;

In above, delay will ignore all spikes at the input which are less than 4 ns. Pulses which are 4 ns or larger will be visible at the output after 12 ns. In inertial delay, reject is optional, but if reject command is used, inertial has to be specified.

If no pulse rejection limit is specified, then the default pulse rejection limit is the inertial delay value itself.

Example:

y <= reject 5 ns inertial q after 8 ns;

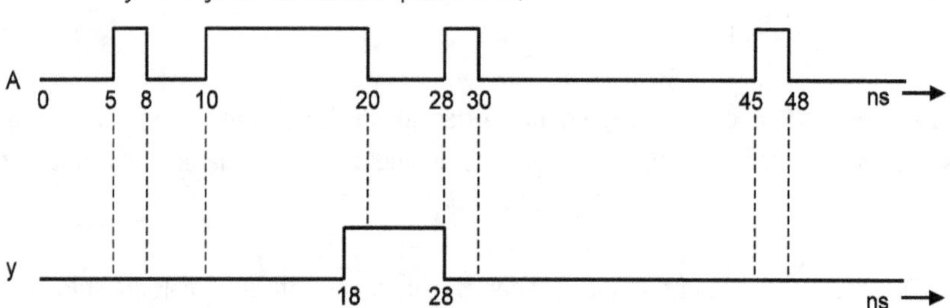

Fig. 4.27

In above example, y signal rejects the pulses which are less than 5 ns duration.

The inertial delay model is often used to filter out unwanted spikes and transients on signals.

Transport Delay Model:

This delay represents pure **propagation delay**, means any changes on an input are transported to the output, no matter how small, after the specified delay.

They generally represent **Routing / interconnect** delays. To use transport delay model, the keyword "transport" must be used in a signal assignment statement.

Fig. 4.28 shows an example of transport delay of 10 ns.

   y < = transport B after 10 ns;

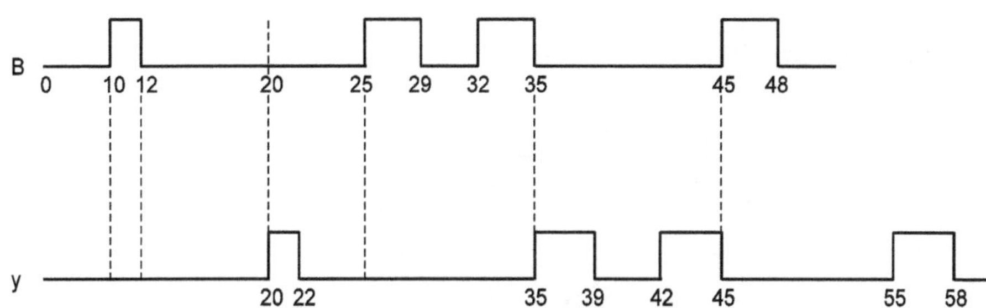

Fig. 4.28: Transport delay example

In this case, spikes can be propagated.

We will see one more example to get better understanding of Inertial and Transport Delay.

Suppose signal A is

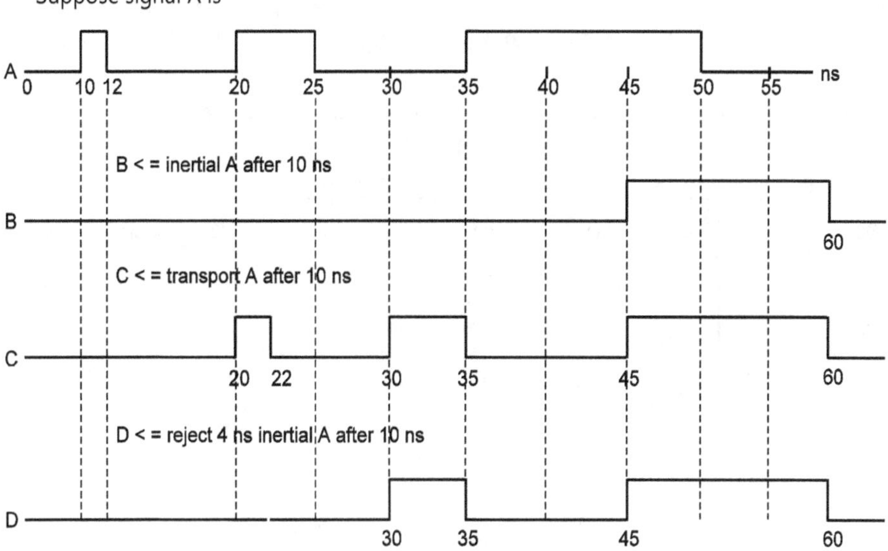

Fig. 4.29: Transport and Inertial Delay models

As shown in Fig. 4.29, signal B rejects pulses which are less than 10 ns, signal C represents transport delay model, which provides the propagation delay of 10 ns. Signal D represents inertial delay model, which rejects pulses less than 4 ns.

The **synthesis** tool **does not** support any of these delay models. These delay models are best used when making VHDL models for simulation.

SOLVED EXAMPLES

Example 16:

Write a VHDL code for 1:8 demultiplexer.

Solution:

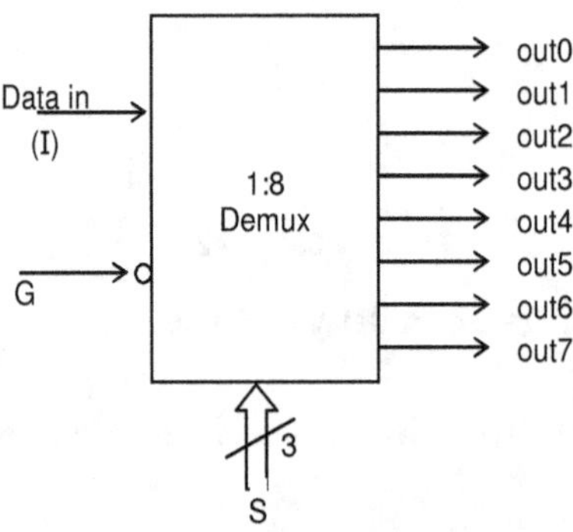

Fig. 4.30: 1:8 Demultiplexer

G is active /enable pin. G must be equal to zero to enable demultiplexer.

Truth table

S2	S1	S0	Out7	Out6	Out5	Out4	Out3	Out2	Out1	Out0
0	0	0	0	0	0	0	0	0	0	I
0	0	1	0	0	0	0	0	0	I	0
0	1	0	0	0	0	0	0	I	0	0
0	1	1	0	0	0	0	I	0	0	0
1	0	0	0	0	0	I	0	0	0	0
1	0	1	0	0	I	0	0	0	0	0
1	1	0	0	I	0	0	0	0	0	0
1	1	1	I	0	0	0	0	0	0	0

library IEEE;

use IEEE. STD_LOGIC_1164. *all*;

```
entity DMUX18  is
     port ( I, G: in  std_logic;
         S: in std_logic_vector (2  downto  0);
         OUT0, OUT1, OUT2, OUT3, OUT4, OUT5, OUT6, OUT7: out std_logic);
end DMUX18;
architecture DMUX18_ARCH  of  DMUX18  is
begin
   process ( S, I )
   begin
       if ( G = '0' )  then
          case  S  is
               when  "000" =>  OUT0 <= I;
               when  "001" =>  OUT1 <= I;
               when "010" =>   OUT2 <= I;
               when  "011" =>  OUT3 <= I;
               when  "100" =>  OUT4 <= I;
               when  "101" =>  OUT5 <= I;
               when  "110" =>  OUT6 <= I;
               when  "111" =>  OUT7 <= I;
            end case;
          end if ;
     end process;
   end DMUX18_ARCH;
```

Example 17:

Write a VHDL code to design 3:8 decoder.

Solution:

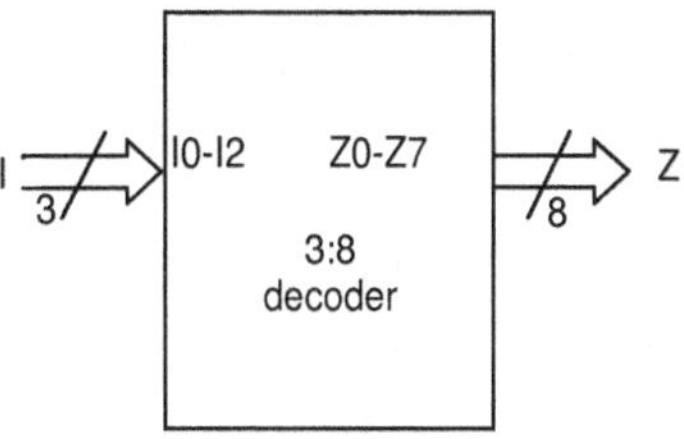

Fig. 4.31: 3:8 Decoder

Truth Table

I(2)	I(1)	I(0)	Z(7)	Z(6)	Z(5)	Z(4)	Z(3)	Z(2)	Z(1)	Z(0)
0	0	0	0	0	0	0	0	0	0	1
0	0	1	0	0	0	0	0	0	1	0
0	1	0	0	0	0	0	0	1	0	0
0	1	1	0	0	0	0	1	0	0	0
1	0	0	0	0	0	1	0	0	0	0
1	0	1	0	0	1	0	0	0	0	0
1	1	0	0	1	0	0	0	0	0	0
1	1	1	1	0	0	0	0	0	0	0

```
library IEEE;
use IEEE. STD_LOGIC_1164. all;

entity DECODER38 is
        port ( I: in std_logic_vector (2 downto 0);
         Z: out std_logic_vector (7 downto 0));
end DECODER38;

architecture DECODER38_ARCH of DECODER38 is
begin
    process (I)
    begin
    case I is
                when "000" => Z <= "00000001" ;
                when "001" => Z <= "00000010" ;
                when "010" => Z <= "00000100" ;
                when "011" => Z <= "00001000" ;
                when "100" => Z  <= "00010000";
                when "101" => Z <= "00100000" ;
                when "110" => Z <= "01000000" ;
                when "111" => Z <= "10000000" ;
                when  others => Z <= "zzzzzzzz";
    end case;
    end process;
    end DECODER38_ARCH;
```

Example 18:

Write a VHDL code to design a BCD to seven-segment decoder for a single digit LED display.

Solution:

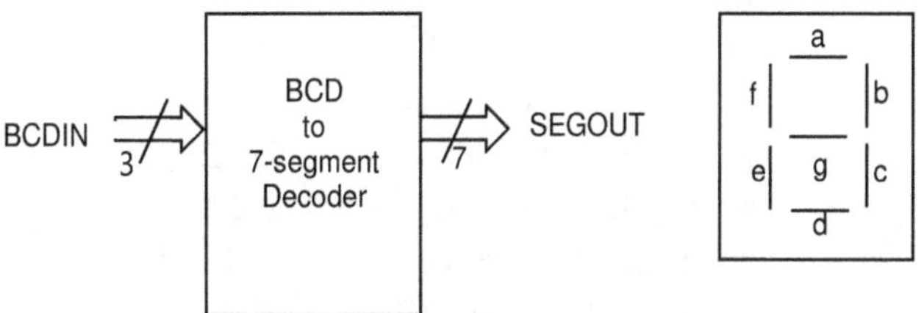

Fig. 4.32: BCD to 7-segment decoder

Look-up Table

Decimal Digit	BCDIN	SEGOUT						
		a	b	c	D	e	f	g
0	0 0 0 0	1	1	1	1	1	1	0
1	0 0 0 1	0	1	1	0	0	0	0
2	0 0 1 0	1	1	0	1	1	0	1
3	0 0 1 1	1	1	1	1	0	0	1
4	0 1 0 0	0	1	1	0	0	1	1
5	0 1 0 1	1	0	1	1	0	1	1
6	0 1 1 0	1	0	1	1	1	1	1
7	0 1 1 1	1	1	1	0	0	0	0
8	1 0 0 0	1	1	1	1	1	1	1
9	1 0 0 1	1	1	1	1	0	1	1

```
library IEEE;
use IEEE.STD_LOGIC_1164.all;

entity BCD_SEG is
    port ( BCDIN : in  std_logic_vector ( 3 downto 0 );
         SEGOUT :  out std_logic_vector ( 6 downto 0 ) );
end BCD_SEG;

architecture BCD_SEG_ARCH of BCD_SEG is
begin
   process (BCDIN)
       begin
```

```
            case BCDIN  is
        when "0000" => SEGOUT <= "1111110";
                    when "0001" => SEGOUT <= "0110000" ;
                    when "0010" => SEGOUT <= "1101101" ;
                    when "0011" => SEGOUT <= "1111001" ;
                    when "0100" => SEGOUT <= "0110010" ;
                    when "0101" => SEGOUT <= "1011011" ;
                    when "0110" => SEGOUT <= "1011111" ;
                    when "0111" => SEGOUT <= "1110000" ;
                    when "1000" => SEGOUT < = "1111111" ;
                    when "1001" => SEGOUT <= "1111011" ;
                    when  others => SEGOUT <= "0000000" ;
            end case;
        end process;
    end BCD_SEG_ARCH;
```

Example 19:

Write a VHDL code for Synchronous and asynchronous reset 'd' flip-flop.

Solution:

Synchronous reset D flip-flop: flip-flop is reset on active edge (positive or negative edge) of the clock when reset is held active.

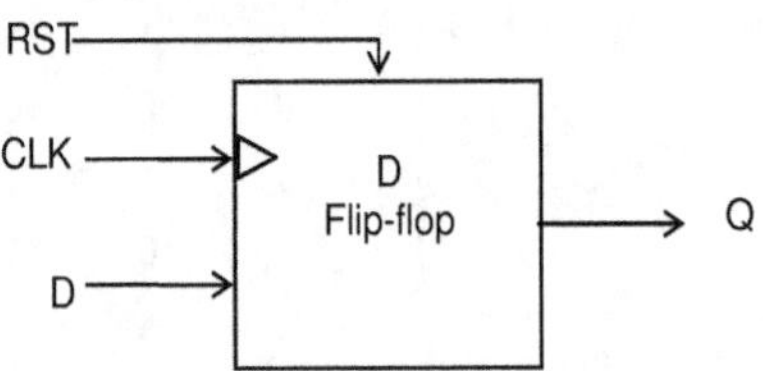

Fig. 4.33: D flip-flop

```
library  IEEE;
use IEEE.STD_LOGIC_1164 . all;

entity DFF is
        port ( CLK, RST, D : in  std_logic;
                Q : out  std_logic );
end DFF;
```

```vhdl
architecture DFFSYN of DFF is
begin
   process (CLK)
   begin
      if (CLK'event and CLK = '1' ) then   -- if positive edge then
         if (RST = '1') then
               Q <= '0';
         else
               Q <= D;
         end if ;
      end if,
   end process;
end DFFSYN;
```

Asynchronous reset D flip-flop: Flip-flop is cleared as soon as reset is asserted.

```vhdl
library IEEE;
use IEEE .STD_LOGIC_1164. all;

entity DFF is
    port ( CLK, RST, D : in std_logic;
                         Q: out std_logic );
end DFF;

architecture DFFASYN of DFF is
begin
    process ( CLK, RST )
     begin
         if ( RST = '1' ) then
                 Q <= '0';
             elseif ( CLK'event and CLK = '1' ) then
                 Q <= D;
             end if ;
         end process;
end DFFASYN;
```

Example 20:

Write a VHDL code for J-K flip-flop.

Solution:

J-K flip-flop:

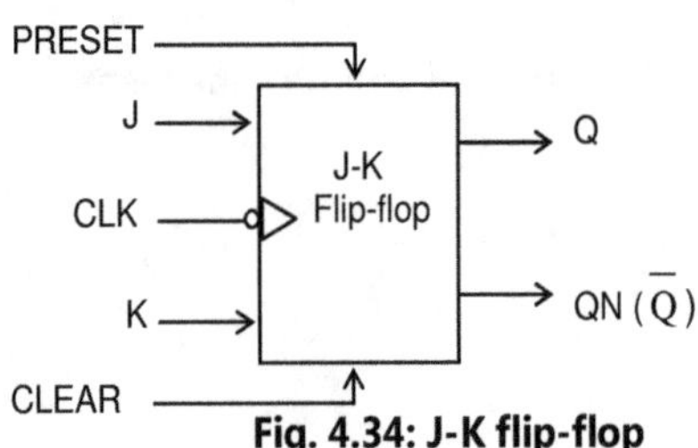

Fig. 4.34: J-K flip-flop

PRESET and CLEAR inputs are clear inputs which are used to set (Q=1) and reset (Q=0) the flip-flop respectively.

The flip-flop shown in Fig. 4.34 is negative edge triggered i.e. Q will change when CLK changes from logic '1' to '0'.

The truth table is as shown:

J	K	Q	Q+
0	0	0	0
0	0	1	1
0	1	0	0
0	1	1	0
1	0	0	1
1	0	1	1
1	1	0	1
1	1	1	0

The characteristic equation derived from the truth table using K-map is

$$Q = J\overline{Q} + \overline{K}Q$$

library IEEE;
use IEEE .STD_LOGIC_1164. all;

entity JKFF is
port (PRESET, CLEAR, CLK, J, K: in std_logic;
                    Q: inout std_logic;
                    QN: out std_logic);
end JKFF;

```
architecture JKFF_ARCH  of  JKFF  is
begin
    process ( PRESET, CLEAR, CLK )
    begin
        if ( CLEAR= '1')  then
                Q <= '0' after 10 ns;
        elseif ( PRESET = '1')  then
                Q <= '1' after 10 ns;
        elseif ( CLK= '0' and CLK'event ) then
                Q <= ( J and ( not Q ) )  or  ( ( not K )  and  Q ) after 10 ns;
        end if;
    end process ;
    QN <= not Q;
end JKFF_ARCH;
```

Q is declared as inout because it appears on both the left and right sides of an assignment statement within the architecture.

The flip flop can change the state in response to change in PRESET, CLEAR and CLK, so these three signals are included in the sensitivity list.

The condition (CLK=0 and CLK'event) is true only if CLK has just changed from '1'to '0.'

Example 21:

Write a VHDL code for 00 to 99 up-down counter.

Solution:

```
library IEEE;
use  IEEE .STD_LOGIC_1164 . all;

entity COUNT99  is
    port ( CLK, UP_DOWN :  in std_logic;
        COUNT: out integer range 0 to 127);
end COUNT99;
```

```
architecture COUNT99_ARCH of COUNT99  is
begin
    process (CLK)
      variable CNT:  integer  range 0 to 127;
      constant MAX: integer. = 99;
      begin
        if ( CLK'event  and  CLK= '1' )  then
          if ( UP_DOWN = '1' )  then
          if ( CNT = MAX )  then
            CNT: = 0;
              else
              CNT: = CNT +1;
                end if,
            else
              if ( CNT = 0 )  then
            CNT: = MAX;
              else
             CNT: = CNT - 1;
               end if ;
              end if ;
          end if,
     COUNT <= CNT;
       end process;
end COUNT99_ARCH;
```

Example 22:

Write a VHDL code for following counter shown in Fig. 4.35.

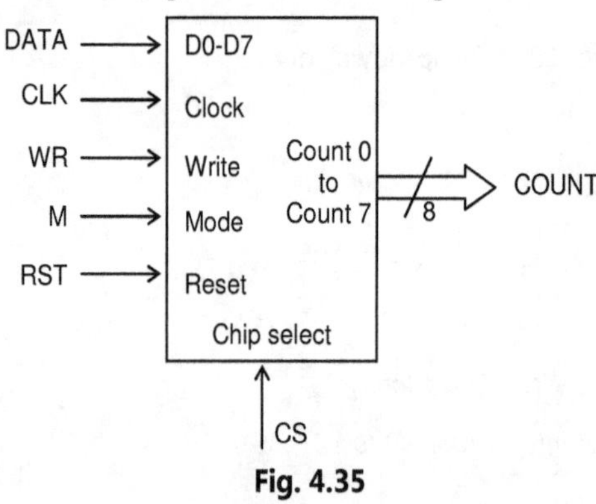

Fig. 4.35

Truth Table

CS	RST	M	WR	CLK	Operation
1	1	X	X	X	Count = 00 H (Reset)
1	0	X	1	X	Count = data (Loading)
1	0	1	0	⌐	Up count
1	0	0	0	⌐	Down count
0	X	X	X	X	Latch the count

Solution:

```vhdl
library IEEE;
use IEEE. STD_LOGIC_1164. all;
use IEEE. STD_LOGIC_UNSIGNED. all;
use IEEE. STD_LOGIC_ARITH. all;

entity COUNTER is
    generic ( BUS: integer. = 8 );
    port ( DATA: in std_logic_vector (BUS downto 0);
            CLK, WR, M, RST,CS : in std_logic;
            COUNT: out std_logic_vector (BUS downto 0));
end COUNTER;

architecture COUNTER_ARCH of COUNTER is
        signal TEMP: std_logic_vector (BUS downto 0);
begin
    process (CLK, RST,WR)
    begin
        if ( RST= '1') then
        TEMP <= (others => '0');
        elseif (WR = '1') then
        TEMP <= DATA;
```

elseif (CLK = '1' *and* CLK'*event*) *then*

if ((CS = '1') *and* (WR = '0')) *then*

if (M = '1') *then*

TEMP <= DATA + 1;

else

TEMP <= DATA - 1;

end if;

end if ;

end if;

end process;

COUNT <= TEMP;

end COUNTER_ARCH;

Example 23:

Write a VHDL code for parallel in parallel out shift register (e.g., SN74174).

Solution:

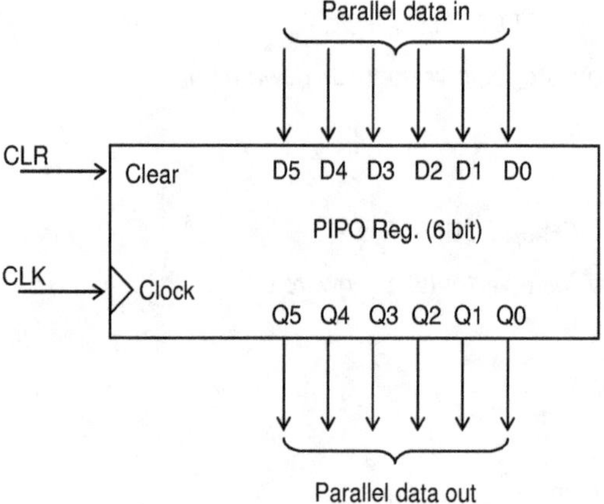

Fig. 4.36 (a): PIPO shift register

Functional block diagram

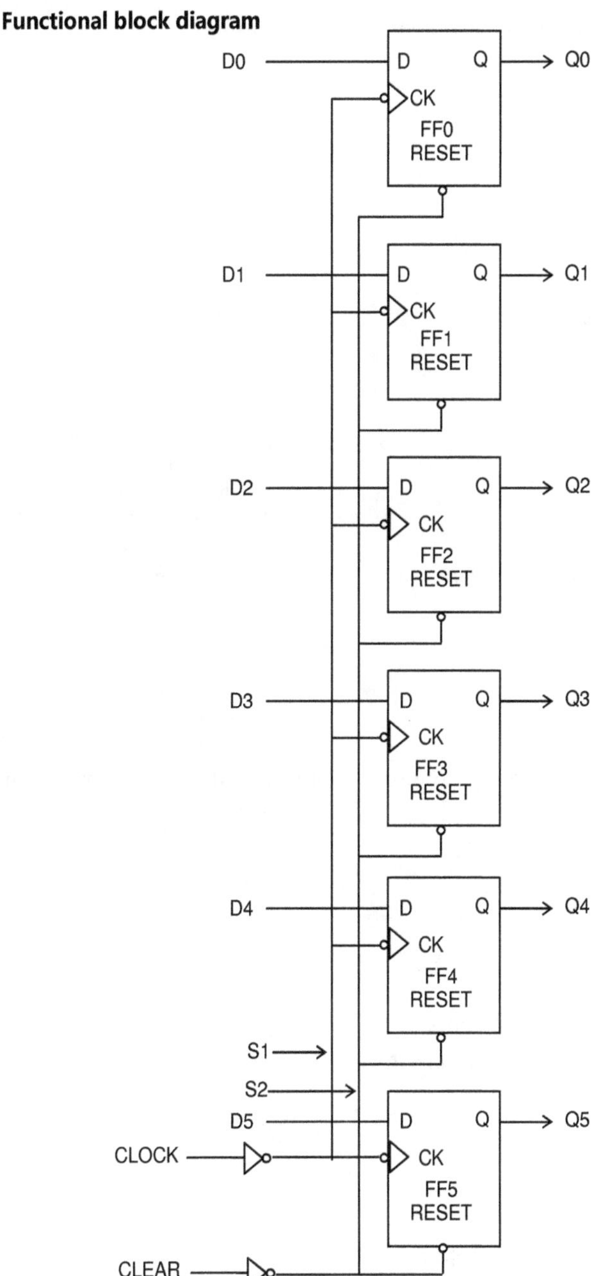

Fig. 4.36 (b): Functional block diagram of PIPO shift register

First VHDL code for required D flip-flop is written.

```vhdl
library IEEE;
use IEEE.STD_LOGIC_1164. all;

entity DFF  is
    port ( D, CK, RST: in  std_logic;
                        Q:  out std_logic );
end DFF;

architecture DFF_arch  of  DFF  is
begin
    process (CK)
    begin
        if (RST = '1') then
        Q <= '0';
      else
          elseif (CK= '1' and CK'event)  then
                Q <= D;
      end if;
      end process;
end DFF_ARCH ;
```

Now save this VHDL file in working directory so that, it can be used as component in design of shift register as shown below:

```vhdl
library  IEEE;
use  IEEE. STD_LOGIC_1164. all;

entity RSHIFT is
    port (CLK, CLR: in  std_logic;
              D: in  std_logic_vector (5  downto 0 );
              Q: out  std_logic_vector (5  downto 0 );
end  RSHIFT;

architecture  RSHIFT_ARCH of  RSHIFT is
    component DFF
        port (D, CK, RST: in  std_logic;
                        Q: out std_logic);
    end component;
    signal S1, S2: std_logic;
```

```
begin
        S1 <= not CLK;
        S2 <= not CLR;
        ff0: DFF    port map (D(0),  S1,  S2,  Q(0));
        ff1: DFF    port map (D(1),  S1,  S2,  Q(1));
        ff2: DFF    port map (D(2),  S1,  S2,  Q(2));
        ff3: DFF    port map (D(3),  S1,  S2,  Q(3));
        ff4: DFF    port map (D(4),  S1,  S2,  Q(4));
        ff5: DFF    port map (D(5),  S1,  S2, Q(5));
end RSHIFT_ARCH;
```

Example 24:

Design a 10-bit shift register as shown in Fig. 4.37.

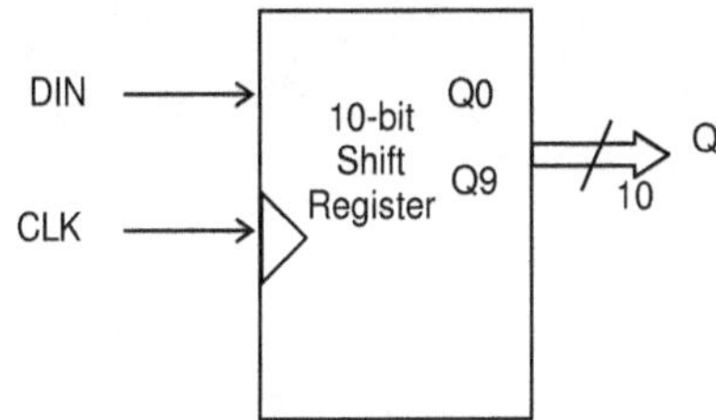

Fig. 4.37: 10 bit shift register

At first rising edge of clock, Q(0)=DIN. On second rising edge of clock, Q(1)=Q(0), Q(0)=DIN and so on.

Solution:

```
library IEEE
use IEEE. STD_LOGIC_1164.all;

entity SHIFT10  is
    port ( DIN, CLK: in  std_logic;
             Q: out std_logic_vector (9 downto 0));
end SHIFT10;

architecture SHIFT10_ARCH  of  SHIFT10  is
begin
    process (CLK)
    begin
            if (CLK = '1'  and  CLK'event)  then
```

```
                QIN ( 0 ) <=  DIN ;
                QIN ( 1 ) <=  QIN( 0 );
                QIN ( 2 ) <=  QIN( 1 );
                QIN ( 3 ) <=  QIN( 2 );
                QIN ( 4 ) <=  QIN( 3 );
                QIN ( 5 ) <=  QIN( 4 );
                QIN ( 6 ) <=  QIN( 5 );
                QIN ( 7 ) <=  QIN( 6 );
                QIN ( 8 ) <=  QIN( 7 );
                QIN ( 9 ) <=  QIN( 8 );
        end if ;
      end process;
       Q <= QIN;
  end SHIFT10_ARCH;
```

Example 25:

Design an 8-bit latch register.

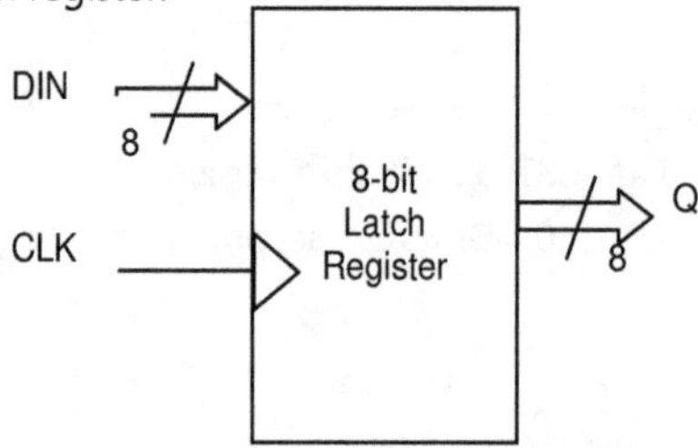

Fig. 4.38: 8-bit latch register

Solution:

```
     library IEEE;
     use  IEEE. STD_LOGIC_1164. all;

        entity  LATCHRG is
            port DIN: in  std_logic_vector ( 7  downto 0 );
                 CLK: in  std_logic;
                   Q: out  std_logic_vector ( 7 downto 0 ) );
            end  LATCHRG;
```

```
    architecture  LATCHRG_ARCH  of  LATCHRG  is
    begin
        process (CLK)
        begin
            if ( CLK = '1'  and  CLK'event )  then
        Q <= DIN;
        end if ;
    end process;
end LATCHRG_ARCH;
```

Example 26:

Design an 8:3 encoder.

Solution:

```
    library IEEE;
    use IEEE. STD_LOGIC_1164. all;

    entity ENCOD  is
        port (DIN :  in  std_logic (7 downto 0);
              Q   :  out std_logic_vector (2 downto 0);
              ERR  : out std_ logic);
    end  ENCOD;

    architecture ENCOD_ARCH  of  ENCOD  is
    begin
        process ( DIN )
        begin
      case DIN  is
            when "00000001"  =>  Q <=  "000";
            when "00000010"  =>  Q <=  "001";
            when "00000100"  =>  Q <=  "010";
            when "00001000"  =>  Q <=  "011";
            when "00010000"  =>  Q <=  "100";
            when "00100000"  =>  Q <=  "101";
            when "01000000"  =>  Q <=  "110";
            when "10000000"  =>  Q <=  "111";
            when  others       =>  ERR <=  '1';
        end case;
      end process;
end ENCOD_ARCH;
```

Example 27:

Write a VHDL code for Hamming Encoder.

Solution:

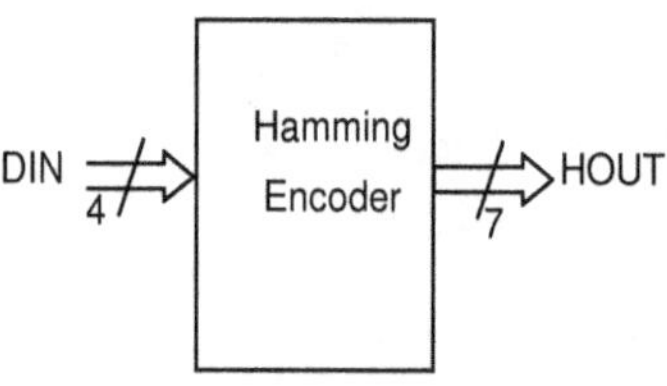

Fig. 4.39: Hamming encoder

If DIN = d3d2d1d0, then HOUT will equal to d3d2d1d0p2p1p0 where (,)

PO = d3 ⊕ d2 ⊕ d0

P1 = d3 ⊕ d1 ⊕ d0

P2 = d2 ⊕ d1 ⊕ d0

```vhdl
library IEEE;
use IEEE.STD_LOGIC_1164. all;


entity HAMEN  is
        port ( DIN: in  std_logic_vector (3  downto 0 );
                HOUT: out std_logic_vector ( 6 downto 0 ) );
        end HAMEN;


architecture HAMEN_ARCH  of  HAMEN  is
        signal P0, P1, P2: std_logic;
begin
    P0  <=  DIN( 3 )  xor  DIN( 2 )  xor  DIN( 0 );
P1 <=  DIN( 3 )  xor  DIN( 1 )  xor  DIN( 0 );
P2 <=  DIN( 2 )  xor  DIN( 1 )  xor  DIN( 0 );
    HOUT (6 downto 3) <= DIN (3 downto 0);
    HOUT (2 downto 0) <= (P2, P1, P0);
end HAMEN_ARCH ;
```

Example 28:

Write a VHDL code for Hamming Decoder.

Solution:

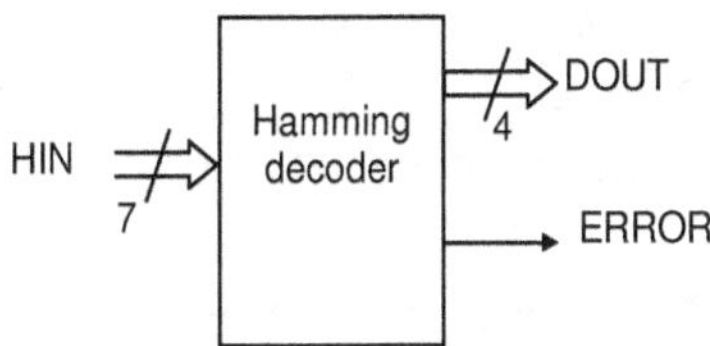

Fig. 4.40: Hamming decoder

Let HIN = d3d2d1d0p2p1p0

Hamming decoder generates syndrome bits as follows.

$$S0 = P0 \oplus d3 \oplus d2 \oplus d0$$

$$S1 = P1 \oplus d3 \oplus d1 \oplus d0$$

$$S2 = P2 \oplus d2 \oplus d1 \oplus d0$$

S0, S1, S2 must be equal to zero, for error-free data.

If S2S1S0 =110, then error in bit d1, so decoder will invert bit d1 (not d1).

If S2S1S0 = 101 then error in bit d2

If S2S1S0 = 011 then error in bit d3

If S2S1S0 = 111 then error in bit d0

For other values of S2S1S0, error output goes high.

```vhdl
library IEEE;
use  IEEE. STD_LOGIC_1164.all;

entity HAMDE  is
    port ( HIN:  in  std_logic_vector (6 downto 0);
            DOUT:  out std_logic_vector (3 downto 0);
            ERROR:  out std_logic);
end HAMDE;

architecture HAMDE_ARCH  of  HAMDE  is
begin
    process ( HIN )
    variable S: std_logic_vector ( 2  downto  0 );
    begin
        S( 0 ) <=  HIN( 0 )  xor  HIN( 6 )  xor  HIN( 5 )  xor  HIN( 3 );
        S( 1 ) <=  HIN( 1 )  xor  HIN( 6 )  xor  HIN( 4 )  xor  HIN( 3 );
        S( 2 ) <=  HIN( 2 )  xor  HIN( 5 )  xor  HIN( 4 )  xor  HIN( 3 );
```

```
        case S  is
            when "111" =>  DOUT( 0 ) <=  not HIN( 3 );
                    DOUT (3 downto 1 ) <=  HIN( 6 downto 4 );
                        ERROR <= '0';
        when "110" =>      DOUT( 1 ) <=  not HIN( 4 );
                    DOUT( 0 ) <=  HIN( 3 );
                        DOUT( 3  downto 2 )  <=  HIN( 6 downto 5 );
                        ERROR <= '0';
        when "101" =>    DOUT( 2 ) <=  not HIN( 5 );
                        DOUT( 3 ) <=  HIN( 6 );
                        DOUT (1 downto 0 )  <=  HIN( 4 downto 3 );
                        ERROR <= '0';
        when "011" =>    DOUT( 3 )  <=  not HIN( 6 );
                        DOUT( 2  downto 0 ) <= HIN ( 5  downto  3 );
                        ERROR <= '0';
        when "000" =>    ERROR <= '0';
                        DOUT( 3 downto  0)  <= HIN( 6  downto  3 );
        when others =>   ERROR <= '1';
                        DOUT ( 3 downto 0 )  <=  HIN( 6  downto 3 );
    end case;
  end process;
end HAMDE_ARCH;
```

Example 29:

Write a VHDL code for ALU which can perform following operation.

Solution:

The symbol for ALU is as shown in Fig. 4.41.

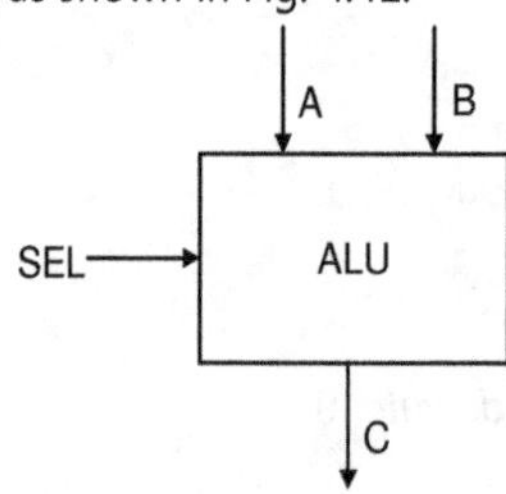

Fig. 4.41: ALU

A and B are the two input buses upon which ALU operations are performed. Output C returns the result of the ALU operation. Input SEL determines operations to be performed.

ALU Function Table:

SEL Input	Operation
0000	C = A
0001	C = A AND B
0010	C = A OR B
0011	C = NOT A
0100	C = A XOR B
0101	C = A + B
0110	C = A - B
0111	C = A + 1
1000	C = A - 1
1001	C = 0

```
library  IEEE;
use IEEE. STD_LOGIC_1164. all;
use IEEE. STD_LOGIC_ARITH. all;


Package  ALU_LIB  is
        constant  ALUPAS  : unsigned ( 3  downto 0 )  :=  "0000";
        constant  ANDOP   : unsigned ( 3  downto 0 )  :=  "0001";
        constant  OROP    : unsigned ( 3  downto 0 )  :=  "0010";
        constant  NOTOP   : unsigned ( 3  downto 0 )  :=  "0011";
        constant  XOROP   : unsigned ( 3  downto 0 )  :=  "0100";
        constant  PLUS    : unsigned ( 3  downto 0 )  :=  "0101";
        constant  ALUSUB  : unsigned ( 3  downto 0 )  :=  "0110";
        constant  INC     : unsigned ( 3  downto 0 )  :=  "0111";
        constant  DEC     : unsigned ( 3  downto 0 )  :=  "1000";
        constant  ZERO    : unsigned ( 3  downto 0 )  :=  "1001";

        type T_COMP  is  ( EQ, NEQ, GT, GTE, LT, LTE );
        subtype BIT8  is std_logic_vector ( 7  downto 0 );
        subtype ALU_T  is  unsigned ( 3  downto 0 );
end ALU_LIB;
```

This package describes the subtype BIT8 of std_logic_vector (7 downto 0) type and ALU_T of unsigned (3 downto 0) type. Constants are declared with their values to specify the ALU functionality.

Using ALU_LIB package, the code for ALU is written

```vhdl
library IEEE;
use IEEE. STD_LOGIC_1164. all;
use IEEE. STD_LOGIC_UNSIGNED all;
library WORK;
use WORK. ALU_LIB. all;

entity ALU  is
          port ( A, B: in  BIT8;
                  SEL: in ALU_T;
                    C: out BIT8);
end ALU;

architecture ALU_ARCH  of  ALU  is
begin
    process ( A, B, SEL )
    begin
      case  SEL  is
              when ALUPAS      => C <=  A   after 1 ns;
              when ANDOP       => C <=  A  and  B  after 1 ns;
              when OROP        => C <=  A  or  B  after 1 ns;
              when XOROP       => C <=  A  xor B  after 1 ns;
              when PLUS        => C <=  not  A  after  1 ns;
              when ALUSUB      => C <=  A + B  after 1 ns;
              when INC         => C <=  A  + "00000001"  after 1 ns;
              when DEC         => C <=  A - "00000001"  after 1 ns;
              when ZERO        => C <=  "00000000"  after 1 ns;
              end case;
        end process;
   end ALU_ARCH;
```

Example 30:

Write a VHDL code for comparator.

Solution:

The symbol of comparator is shown in Fig. 4.42.

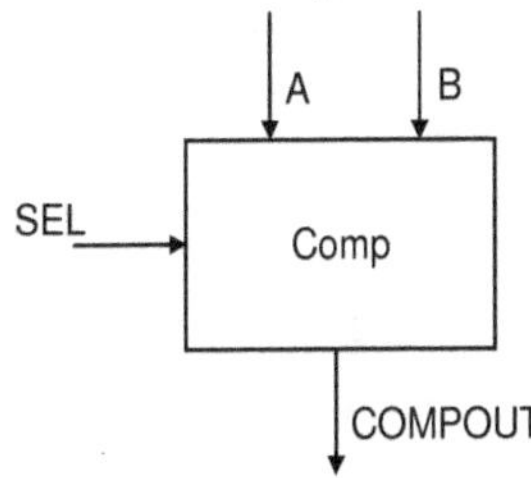

Fig. 4.42: Comparator

This comparator compares two values (A, B) and return either a '1' or '0' depending on the type of comparison requested and the values being compared. The type of comparison is determined by the value of SEL input. e.g., to compare if inputs A and B are equal, apply the value EQ (value of equal) to input port SEL. If input ports A and B have the same value, output port COMPOUT returns '1'. If the values are not equal, '0' is returned.

The comparator operation table is as shown in the table:

SEL input value	Comparison
EQ (000)	COMPOUT = 1 when A equal B
NEQ (001)	COMPOUT = 1 when A is not equal B
GT (010)	COMPOUT = 1 when A is greater than B
GTE (011)	COMPOUT = 1 when A is greater than or equal to B
LT(100)	COMPOUT = 1 when A is less than B
LTE(101)	COMPOUT = 1 when A is less than or equal to B

T_COMP type is declared in package ALU_LIB (see Example 29) for SEL input value.

library IEEE;

use IEEE. STD_LOGIC_1164. *all;*

use IEEE. STD_LOGIC_ARITH. *all;*

library WORK;

use WORK. ALU_LIB. *all;*

```vhdl
entity COMP is
    port ( A, B: in  BIT8;
          SEL:  in T_COMP;          -- T_COMP type is declared in package
          COMPOUT:  out  std_logic); -- ALU_LIB (see Example 29) for SEL input
                                     value
end COMP;

architecture COMP_ARCH  of  COMP  is
begin
    process ( A, B, SEL )
    begin
            case SEL  is
                when EQ =>
                    if ( a =  b ) then
                        COMPOUT <= '1' after 1 ns;
                    else
                        COMPOUT <= '0' after 1 ns;
                    end if ;
                when  NEQ =>
                    if ( A  /=  B ) then
                        COMPOUT <= '1' after 1 ns;
                    else
                        COMPOUT <= '0'after 1 ns;
                    end if ;
                When GT =>
                    if ( A  > B ) then
                        COMPOUT <= '1' after 1 ns;
                    else
                        COMPOUT <= '0' after 1 ns;
                    end if ;
                When GTE =>
                    if ( a >=  b ) then
                        COMPOUT <= '1' after 1 ns;
                    else
                        COMPOUT <= '0' after 1 ns;
                    end if ;
```

```
                When LT =>
                        if ( A < B )  then
                            COMPOUT <= '1' after 1 ns;
                        else
                            COMPOUT <= '0' after 1 ns;
                        end if ;
                When LTE =>
                        if ( A <= B )  then
                            COMPOUT <= '1' after 1 ns;
                        else
                            COMPOUT <= '0' after 1 ns;
                        end if,
            end case;
            end process;
        end COMP_ARCH;
```

Example 31:

Write a VHDL code for static RAM.

Solution:

The block diagram of static RAM is as shown in Fig. 4.43.

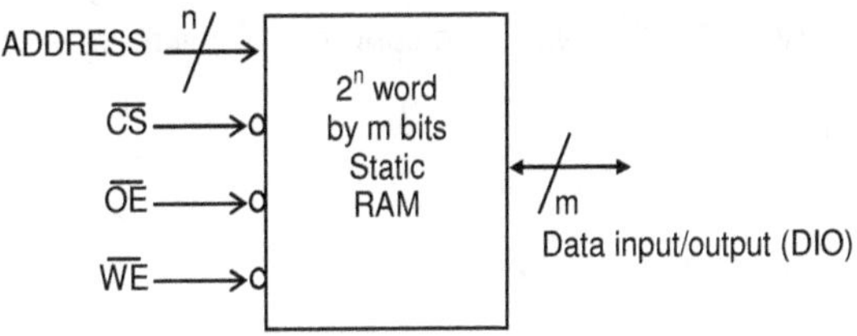

Fig. 4.43: Static RAM

Truth Table for Static RAM

$\overline{CS}$	$\overline{OE}$	$\overline{WE}$	Operation	I/O Pins
H	X	X	not selected	High-Z
L	H	H	Output disabled	High-Z
L	L	H	read	Data out
L	X	L	Write	Data in

```vhdl
package MEM_LIB is
    function VECTOINT ( VECT1: bit_vector )  return  integer ;
end  MEM_LIB;


package body  MEM_LIB  is
        function VECTOINT ( VECT1: bit_vector )  return integer is;
        variable RETVALUE: integer : = 0;
        alias VECT: bit_vector ( VECT1'length -1 downto 0) is VECT1;
begin
    for I in  VECT high downto 1  loop
        if ( VECT ( I )  = '1')  then
            RETVALUE: = (RETVALUE +1) * 2;
              else
                  RETVALUE: = RETVALUE * 2;
              end if ;
        end loop;
        if ( VECT( 0 ) = '1') then
         RETVALUE: = RETVALUE +1;
         end if ;
     return RETVALUE;
   end VECTOINT;
end MEM_LIB;
```
The above function (VECTOINT) is written to convert a bit vector to an integer.

Memory model:
```vhdl
library   IEEE;
use IEEE. STD_LOGIC_1164. all;


library WORK;
use WORK. MEM_LIB. all;


entity SRAM is
    port (CS, OE, WE: in bit;
        ADDRESS:  in bit_vector (7 downto 0);
                DIO: inout  std_logic_vector (7 downto 0));
    end SRAM;
```

```vhdl
architecture SRAM_ARCH  of  SRAM  is
type  RAMT is array ( 0 to  225) of  std_logic_vector ( 7 downto  0 );
signal RAM1: RAMT: = (others => (others =>'0'); -- initialize RAM1 with all bits to '0'
begin
     process
     begin
            if (CS= '1') then
                DIO <= "zzzzzzzz" -- chip disabled
            else
            if (WE = '0' and WE' event) then
                RAM1 (VECTOINT (ADDRESS'delayed)) <= DIO; --write operation
                wait for 0 ns; --wait for RAM update
            end if;
            if (WE = '1') then
                    DIO <= RAM1 (VECTOINT (ADDRESS)); -- read operation
            else
                    DIO <= "zzzzzzzz"; -- I/O lines in high-Z
            end if ;
            end if ;
                wait on WE, CS, ADDRESS;
        end process;
    end SRAM_ARCH;
```

RAM memory array is represented by an array of standard logic vectors (RAM1). ADDRESS is typed as bit_vector, so it must be converted to an integer to index the memory. Data input/output (DIO) lines set to high-Z, if chip is not selected. Otherwise, the data on the I/O lines is stored in RAM1 on the rising edge of WE.

If ADDRESS and WE change simultaneously, the old value of address should be used. ADDRESS' delayed is used to delay address by one delta to make sure that the old address is used. To store data in the RAM before it is read back out, wait for 0 ns is written. If WE= '1' the RAM is in the read mode and I/O is the data read from memory array. If WE= '0' the memory is in write mode, and the I/O lines are driven to high-Z, so external data can be supplied to the RAM.

4.21 Test Bench

A test bench is used to verify the functionality of a design. The test bench allows input test vectors to be applied to a design (DUT / UUT) and output test vectors to be observed by waveform, recorded in an output vector file or compared within the test bench against the expected values.

Advantages of test bench over interactive simulation are:
1) It allows the input and output test vectors to be easily documented.
2) The same functional tests can be repeated during iterations of design changes; therefore, little time is required after a design change to return tests.
3) The same test bench can be used to verify the functionality and timing described by a postfit model.

Fig. 4.44 shows the structure of a test bench.

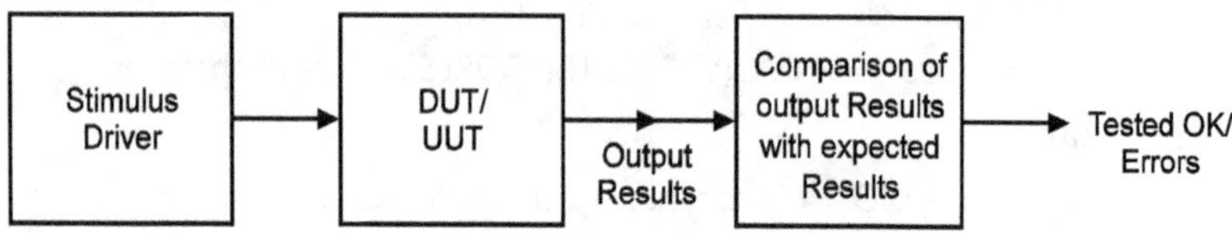

Fig. 4.44: The structure of a test bench

The stimulus Driver applies the stimulus/waveforms to the design under test. The output results from the DUT are collected and compared with the expected values. If the output results and expected values match, then it means that the test is OK, otherwise there is an error in DUT.

The purposes of test bench are:
1. To generate stimuli for simulation. Stimuli is a set of signals that are declared internally in the test bench architecture and assigned to unit under tests (UUT) ports in its instantiation.
2. To apply the stimuli to the unit under test and collect the output responses.
3. To compare output responses with expected values.

Disadvantage of Test bench:
The designer can make errors while writing the test bench, i.e., designer thinks the test is correct, when it is in fact incorrect.

A typical test bench format is:

> *entity* TEST_BENCH
> *end* TEST_BENCH; -- empty entity
>
> *architecture* TEST_ARCH *of* TEST_BENCH *is*
> *component* ENTITY_TEST -- entity to be verified
> *port* (list of ports);
> *end component*;
> *signal* declarations   -- signals required for verification (I/O) signals
> *begin*
>> Generate waveforms;
>> Apply to entity under test by writing instance as
> I1: ENTITY_TEST *port map* (port association);
>> Monitor values and compare with expected values;
> *end* TEST_ARCH;

The following are the most common test bench types:

1. **Stimulus only:** contains only the stimulus driver and the design under test. It does not contain any result verification.
2. **Full test bench:** contains stimulus driver, known good results, and result comparison.
3. **Simulator specific:** test bench is written in a simulator specific format.
4. **Hybrid test bench:** combines techniques from more than one test bench style.
5. **Fast test bench:** written to get ultimate speed from simulation.

The following table shows advantages of above test bench types:

	Speed	**Flexibility**	**Portability**
Stimulus only	Slow	High	High
Full test bench	Slow	High	High
Simulator specific	Medium	High	Low
Hybrid test bench	Medium	Medium	High
Fast test bench	Extremely Fast	Low	High

Example 32:

Write a test bench to verify design of AND gate.

Solution:

Design of AND gate:

library IEEE;
use IEEE. STD_LOGIC_1164 . *all*;

```vhdl
entity AND1  is
     port ( A, B:  in std_logic;
          C:  out std_logic);
end AND1;


architecture AND1_ARCH  of  AND1  is
begin
        C <= A   and   B;
end AND1_ARCH;
```

Test bench for AND1 design:

```vhdl
library IEEE;
use IEEE. STD_LOGIC_1164. all;

entity  AND1_TEST  is --   As test bench does not include interface ports, empty
                          entity is declared.
entity AND1_TEST;

architecture AND1_TEST_ARCH  of  AND1_TEST is
   Component AND1            -- Declared design under test as component.
       port (A, B: in  std_ logic;
                    C: out std_ logic);
   end component;
   signal A, B, Y: std_logic ;   -- declared the signals required for verification.

begin
   I1: AND1 port map (A=>A, B=>B, C=>Y)
   process                              -- process is defined to apply stimulus.
   constant PERIOD: time: = 40 ns;
   begin
       A <= '1';
       B <= '1';
       wait for PERIOD;
       assert (Y= '1')
           report "Test failed" severity error;
       A <= '1';
       B <= '0';
       wait for PERIOD;
```

```
        assert (Y = '0')
            report "Test failed" severity error;
        A <= '0';
        B <= '1';
        wait for PERIOD;
        assert (Y = '0')
            report "Test failed" severity error;
        A <= '0';
        B <= '0';
        wait for PERIOD;
        assert (Y = '0')
            report "Test failed" severity error;
    end process;
  end AND1_TEST_ARCH;
```

4.21.1 Waveform Generation

Concurrent signal assignment statement with a constant on-off delay can be used to generate repetitive pattern.

```
        CLK I <= not CLK after 20 ns;
```

This creates a waveform as shown in Fig. 4.45.

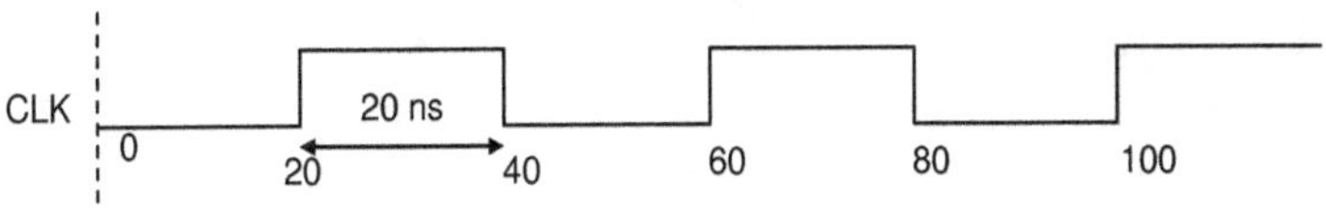

Fig. 4.45

A process statement can be used to generate a clock with varying on-off period.

```
    process
        constant TON: time: = 20 ns;
        constant TOFF: time: = 10 ns;
    begin
        wait for TOFF;
                CLK <= '1';
        wait for TON;
                CLK <= '0';
    end process;
```

This creates a waveform as shown in Fig. 4.46.

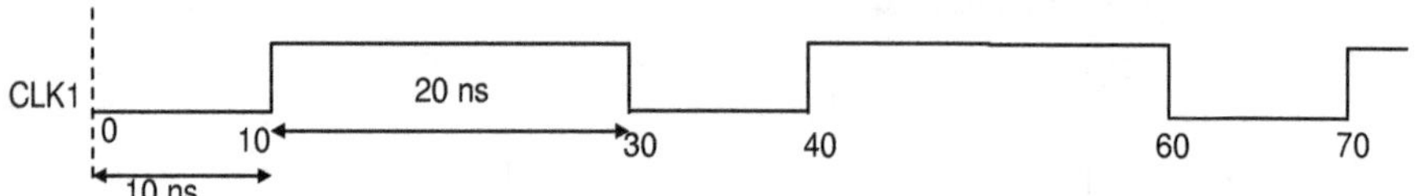

Fig. 4.46

Example 33:

Write a VHDL code for 8-bit up-down counter.

Solution:

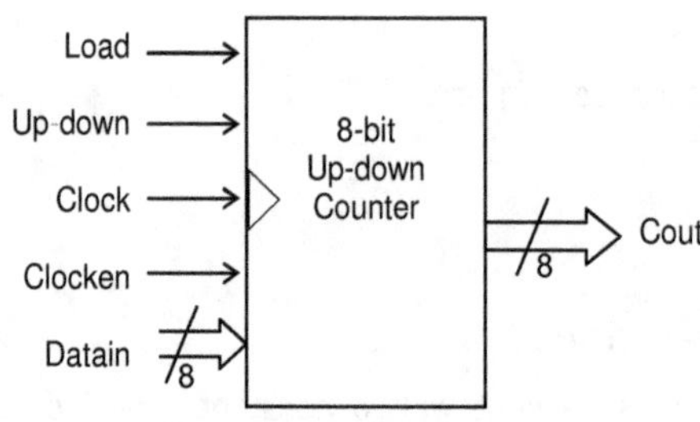

Fig. 4.47: 8-bit up-down counter

When up-down = '1' it will work as up counter.

```
library IEEE;
use IEEE. STD_LOGIC_1164. all;

entity COUNT8 is
        port (CLOCK, UPDOWN, LOAD, CLOCKEN: in std_logic;
                DATAIN: in integer range 0 to 255;
                COUT:  inout integer range 0 to 255);
end COUNT8;

architecture COUNT8_ARCH of COUNT8 is
    signal COUNT_VAL: integer range 0 to 255;
begin
        process ( LOAD, UPDOWN, DATAIN, COUT )
        begin
        if ( LOAD  = '1') then
        COUNT_VAL <= DATAIN;
```

```
            elseif ( UPDOWN = '1') then
            if ( COUT >= 255 ) then
                COUNT_VAL <= 0;
                else
                COUNT_VAL <= COUNT_VAL + 1;
            end if;
                else
            if ( COUT <= 0 ) then
                COUNT_VAL <= 255;
                else
                COUNT_VAL <= COUNT_VAL -1;
            end if;
        end if;
      end process;
        process
      begin
            wait until  CLOCK' event  and  CLOCK = '1';
        if ( CLOCKEN  = '1' )  then
            COUT <= COUNT_VAL;
        end if;
      end process;
    end COUNT_ARCH;
```

Example 34:

Write a stimulus only test bench for Example 33.

Solution:

The stimulus only test bench consists of the stimulus driver and design under test (DUT). The verification process is eliminated.

```
entity COUNT8TEST is
end COUNT8TEST;

library IEEE;
use IEEE. STD_LOGIC_1164 .all;
use STD. TEXTIO. all;
use IEEE .STD_LOGIC_TEXTIO. all;
```

```vhdl
architecture STIMULUS  of  COUNT8TEST is
component COUNT8
      port (CLOCK, UPDOWN, LOAD, CLOCKEN: in std_logic;
                  DATAIN: in integer range 0 to 255;
                  COUT: inout integer range 0 to 255);
end component;
signal CLK, LD, UP_DOWN, CLOCK_EN: std logic;
signal DIN, QOUT: integer range 0 to 255;
begin.
   DUT: COUNT8 port map (CLOCK => CLK, LOAD =>LD,
                              UPDOWN => UP_DOWN,
                              CLOCKEN => CLOCK_EN,
                              DATAIN =>DIN, COUT => QOUT);

   process                          -- reads the stimulus and applied to DUT
     variable TCLK, TLD, TUP_DOWN, TCLOCK _EN : std_ logic ;
     variable TDIN: integer;
     file   VECTOR_FILE : text is in "counter.txt.";
     variable L: line;
     variable VECTOR_TIME: time;
     variable R: real;
     variable GOOD_NUMBER, GOOD_VAL: Boolean;
     variable SPACE: character;
   begin
     while not endfile (VECTOR_FILE) loop
        readline (VECTOR_FILE, L);

          -- read the time from the beginning of the line.
        -- skip the line if it doesn't start with a number.
        read (L, R, GOOD => GOOD_NUMBER);
        next when not GOOD _NUMBER;

        VECTOR _TIME: = R * 1 ns;               --convert real number to time

           if (now < VECTOR_TIME) then        -- wait until the vector_time
          wait for VECTOR_TIME - now;
        end if;


        read (L, SPACE);                         -- skip a space
```

```vhdl
        -- read CLOCK value
        read (L, TCLK, GOOD_VAL);
        assert (GOOD_VAL)
          report "Bad clock value";

        -- read LOAD value
        read (L, TLD, GOOD_VAL);
        assert (GOOD_VAL)
          report "Bad load value";

          -- read UPDOWN value
          read (L, TUP_DOWN, GOOD_VAL);
          assert (GOOD_VAL)
            report "Bad up-down value";

          --read CLOCKEN value
          read (L, TCLOCKEN, GOOD_VAL);
          assert (GOOD_VAL)
            report "Bad clocken value";

          read (L, SPACE);                          -- skip a space
          read (L, TDIN, GOOD_VAL);
          assert (GOOD_ VAL)
            report "Bad datain value";
        CLK <= TCLK;
        LD <= TLD;
        UP_DOWN <= TUP_DOWN;
        CLOCK_EN <= TCLOCK_EN
        DIN <= TDIN;
    end loop;
    assert (false)
      report "Test complete";
    wait;
    end process;
    end STIMULUS;
```

TEXTIO is predefined package. It contains procedures and functions to read from and write to text files. There are procedures to read a line, write a line and a function that checks for end of file.

At the beginning of test bench, entity with no ports is declared.

Next in architecture, DUT (COUNT8) is declared as component. The ports and types of this component should match the DUT. Next the local interconnect signals are declared. After this DUT component is instantiated and connected to the local interconnect signals.

A process, which contains the stimulus generation capability, is declared.

Local variables are declared that receive the data from the TEXTIO procedures to read the stimulus information from the file. TEXTIO can only assign to variables and not signals; therefore local variables are assigned by the TEXTIO procedures, and these variables are assigned to the internal interconnect signals.

Inside the process there is a while loop which reads line by line data from stimulus file until an end-of-file condition is reached.

The first data read from the line is the time that this vector is to be applied. The process checks the value read is a valid number. If not, the line is discarded and the process skips this iteration through the loop and goes to the next iteration using the next clause. If the values read are a good number, then the vector is assumed to be valid. The process reads each data value from the vector and applies the values to the locally declared variables.

The first value read is the CLK signal. The TEXTIO statement (read) reads a std_logic value from line 1 and assigns the value read to variables TCLK. Later (.) TCLK variables are assigned to the signal CLK.

The process continues to read a line, read a time value, wait until that time value occurs, read all vector values, and apply vector values until the end-of-file is reached. When the end-of-file is reached, the loop terminates, an assertion message is written to standard output and process waits forever (stops execution of process).

Following is example of vector file (counter.text) which is read by TEXTIO readline statement.

```
-- vector file for counter
-- TIME, CLK, LD, UP_DOWN, CLOCK_EN, DIN.
            10      0001    0
            20      1101    50
            30      0001    0
            40      1001    0
            50      0001    0
            60      1001    0
            70      0001    0
            80      1001    0
            90      0001    0
           100      1101    10
           110      0001    0
           120      1001    0
           130      0001    0
           140      1001    0
           150      0001    0
           160      1001    0
```

The first two lines are treated as comment line. Each vector line starts with a value and then contains a string of values to be assigned to the DUT at that time.

The process reads a vector from the file and applies the stimulus to the DUT. This stimulus only test bench does not check output results of the DUT in reaction to the applied stimulus.

The results can be verified by the designer.

Example 35:

Write a full test bench for Example 33.

Solution:

```
entity FULLTEST is
end FULLTEST;

library IEEE;
use IEEE .STD_LOGIC_1164. all;
use STD . TEXTIO. all;
use IEEE. STD_LOGIC_TEXTIO. all;
```

```vhdl
architecture FULLTEST_ARCH of FULLTEST is
component COUNT8
    port (CLOCK, UPDOWN, LOAD, CLOCKEN: in std_logic;
                DATAIN: in integer range 0 to 255;
                COUT: inout integer range 0 to 255);
end component;
signal CLK, LD, UP_DOWN, CLOCK_EN: std_ logic;
signal DIN, QOUT: integer range 0 to 255;
begin.
DUT: COUNT8 port map (CLOCK => CLK, LOAD =>LD,
                            UPDOWN => UP_DOWN,
                            CLOCKEN => CLOCK_EN,
                            DATAIN => DIN, COUT => QUOT);
    -- provides stimulus and check the result
        process
            variable TCLK, TLD, TUP_DOWN, TCLOCK _EN: std_ logic;
            variable TDIN, TQOUT: integer  range 0 to 255;
            file VECTOR_FILE:  text is in  "counter.txt ";
            variable L:  line;
            variable R: real;
            variable GOOD_NUMBER, GOOD_VAL:  Boolean;
            variable SPACE: character;
        begin
            while not endfile (VECTOR_FILE) loop
                readline (VECTOR_FILE, L);
                -- read the time from the beginning of the line.
                -- skip the line if it doesn't start with a NUMBER.
                next when not GOOD_NUMBER;

                VECTOR_TIME: = r * 1 ns;        -- convert real number to time

                if (now < VECTOR_TIME) then      -- wait until the vector_time
                    wait for VECTOR_TIME - now;
                end if;

                read (L, SPACE) ;                    -- skip a space
```

```vhdl
        -- read CLOCK value
        read (L, TCLK, GOOD_VAL);
        assert (GOOD_VAL)
          report "Bad clock value";

      --read LOAD value
       read (L, TLD, GOOD_VAL);
         assert (GOOD_VAL)
              report "Bad load value";

     -- read UPDOWN value
     read  ( L, TUP_DOWN, GOOD_VAL ) ;
     assert (GOOD_VAL)
       report "Bad updown value";
    --read CLOCKEN value
read (L, TCLOCKEN, GOOD_VAL);
assert (GOOD_VAL)
  report "Bad clocken value";

read (L, SPACE);                              -- skip a space

  -- read datain value
read (L, TDIN, GOOD_VAL);
assert (GOOD_VAL)
  report "Bad datain value";

read (L, SPACE);                              -- skip a space

 --read the output value
read (L, TQOUT, GOOD_VAL);
assert (GOOD_VAL)
   report "Bad cout value";

-- compare outputs
assert (TQOUT = QOUT)
  report "Output mismatch";

CLK <= TCLK;
LD <= TLD;
UP_DOWN <= TUP_DOWN;
```

```
        CLOCK_EN <= TCLOCK_EN;
        DIN <= TDIN;
    end loop ;
    assert ( false)
        report "Test complete";
    wait;                               -- waits forever (stops execution)
    end process;
    end FULLTEST_ARCH;
```

The full test bench reads the input values as well as reads the output values and then performs a compare operation between the output values from the DUT versus the values read from the file. If mismatch is found, an assertion message is generated to acknowledge the designer that the output results did not match the known good results.

The full test bench also reads from a vector file to get the stimulus for the design and the expected results. The vector file contains a time value, the input values and the expected output values.

Following is the full test bench vector file.
-- vector file for counter
-- TIME, CLOCK, LOAD, UPDOWN, CLOCKEN, DATAIN, COUT.

TIME	CLOCK	LOAD/UPDOWN/CLOCKEN	DATAIN/COUT
0	0001	0	0
10	1001	0	255
20	0101	10	255
30	1001	0	10
40	0001	0	10
50	1001	0	8
60	0001	0	8
70	1001	0	7
80	0001	0	7
90	1001	0	6
100	0101	100	100
110	1001	0	100
120	0001	0	100
130	1001	0	98
140	0001	0	98
150	1001	0	97
160	0001	0	97

Example 36:

Write a VHDL code for Tri-state Bus.

Solution:

```
library IEEE;
use IEEE. STD_LOGIC_1164.all;

entity TRIBUS is
    port (BUS0, BUS1:  in  std_logic_vector (3 downto 0);
          ENABLE, SELECT: in std_logic ;
          DATABUS: out std_logic_vector (3 downto 0));
end TRIBUS;

architecture TRIBUS_ARCH  of  TRIBUS is
begin
process (ENABLE, SELECT, BUS0, BUS1)
begin
    if (ENABLE = '1') then
      case SELECT is
        when '0'=> DATABUS <= BUS0;
        when '1'=> DATABUS <= BUS1;
        when others => DATABUS <= "zzzz";
      end case;
    else
            DATABUS <= "zzzz";
    end if ;
  end process;
end TRIBUS_ARCH;
```

Example 37:

Write a VHDL code for mod 6 counter.

Solution:

```
library IEEE;
use IEEE. STD_LOGIC_1164. all;
entity COUNT6 is
    port (RESET: in  std_logic;
```

```
              CLOCK: in std_logic;
              COUT: buffer integer range 0 to 5);
end COUNT6;

architecture COUNT6_ARCH of COUNT6  is
begin
  process (CLOCK)
  begin
    if (CLOCK' event and CLOCK = '1') then
     if (RESET = '1' or COUT >= 5)
        COUT <= '0';
     else
        COUT <= COUT + 1;
     end if;
    end if;
  end process;
end COUNT6_ARCH;
```

Example 38:

Write a VHDL code for generation of the hardware shown in Fig. 4.48.

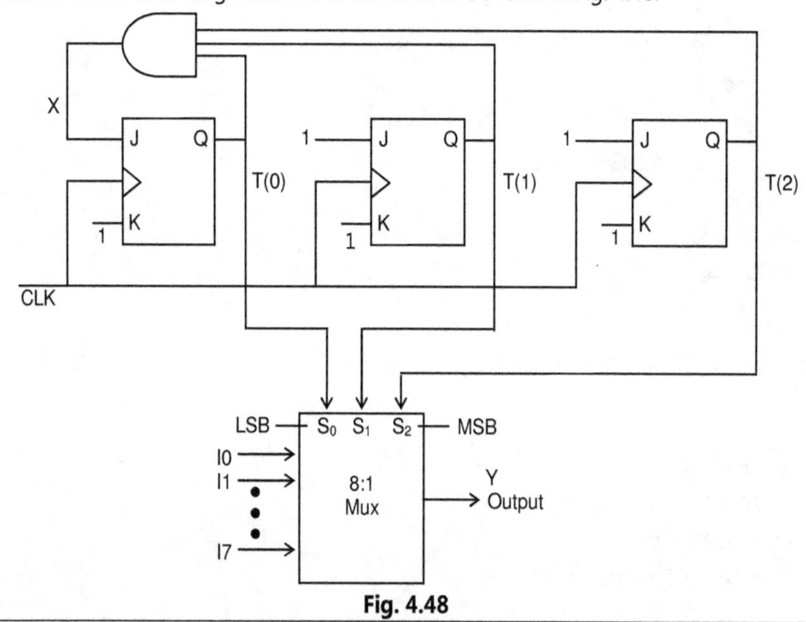

Fig. 4.48

Solution:

Consider, VHDL code for JK flip-flop, AND gate and 8:1 multiplexer are already written and analyzed. Hence these can be used as component in following code.

```
library IEEE;
use IEEE . STD_LOGIC_1164. all;

entity HARD  is
    port ( CLK: in  std_logic;
           I:  in  std_logic_vector (7  downto 0);
           Y:  out  std_ logic );
end HARD;

architecture HARD_ARCH  of  HARD  is
    component JKFF
        port (J, K, CLK:  in  std_logic;
                              Q: out  std_logic);
    end component;
    component AND1
        port( A, B, C: in  std_ logic;
                       Z: out  std_ logic );
    end component;
    component  MUX81
        port ( D: in std_ logic_vector (7 downto 0);
               SEL : in std_ logic_vector (2 downto 0);
               Y: out std_ logic) ;
    end component ;
    signal  TEMP : std_ logic_vector (2 downto 0);
    signal  X : std_logic;
begin
    FF1: JKFF  port  map ( J =>X,   K=>'1',  CLK => CLK, Q => TEMP( 0 ) );
    FF2: JKFF  port  map ( J => '1', K=> '1', CLK =>CLK,  Q => TEMP( 1 ) );
    FF3: JKFF  port  map ( J => '1', K=> '1', CLK=>CLK,   Q => TEMP( 2 ) );
    A: AND1  port  map ( A =>TEMP(0), B =>TEMP(1), C =>TEMP(2), Z =>X );
        M: MUX81  port  map ( D => I, SEL =>TEMP, Y=>Y );
end HARD_ARCH;
```

Example 39:

Write a VHDL code to design 32:1 multiplexer by using 16:1 multiplexer.

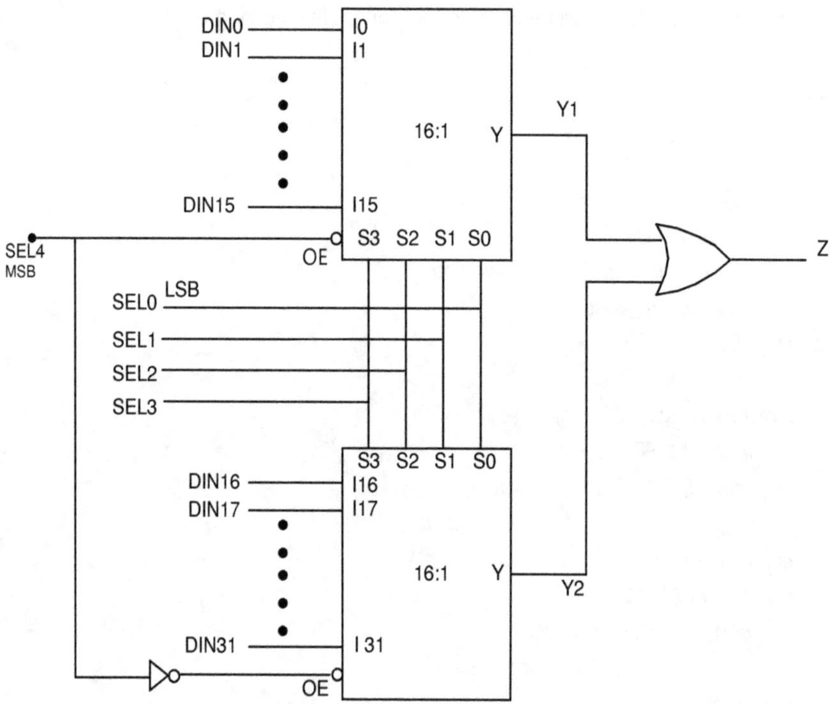

Fig. 4.49: 32:1 multiplexer

Solution:

Assume that VHDL code for 16:1 multiplexer is written and analyzed and kept in working directory. Hence, it can be used as component.

library IEEE;

use IEEE. STD_LOGIC_1164 . *all;*

entity MUX32 *is*

 port (DIN: *in std_ logic_vector* (31 *downto* 0);

   SEL: *out std_ logic_vector* (4 *downto* 0);

   Y: *out std_logic*);

end MUX32;

```
architecture  MUX32_ARCH  of   MUX32  is
      component MUX16
            port      (I:  in std_logic_vector (15 downto 0);
                        S:  in std_ logic_vector (3 downto 0);
                        OE:  in std_logic ;
                       Y:  out std_logic);
      end component;
        signal X, Y1, Y2: std_logic;

        alias DM1:  std_logic_vector ( 15 downto 0 )  is  DIN ( 15  downto 0 );
        alias DM2:  std_logic_vector ( 15 downto 0 )  is  DIN (31  downto 16 );
        alias MSEL12:  std_logic_vector ( 3 downto 0 )  is SEL (3  downto 0 );
    begin
        X <= not  SEL( 4 );
        M1: MUX16 port map (I =>DM1, S => MSEL12, OE => SEL(4),  Y => Y1);
        M2:  MUX16  port  map ( I =>DM2, S => MSEL12, OE => X, Y  => Y2 );
        Y <= Y1  or  Y2;
    end MUX32_ARCH;
```

Example 40:

Write simulator specific test bench for 4-bit adder (refer Example 10).

Solution:

In preparation for simulation, we can place the entity and architecture for the FULLADDR and for ADDR4 together in one while and compile. Alternatively, we could compile FULLADDR separately and place the resulting code in a library that is linked in when we compile ADDR4.

For this simulation example, simulator from Model Tech is used.

We use the following simulator commands to test ADDR4:

```
list A B Cin S Cout  -- put these signals on the output list
force A 1111                -- set the A inputs to 1111
force B 0001                -- set the B inputs to 0001
force Cin 1          -- set Cin to 1
run 50                     -- run the simulation for 50 ns
force Cin 0
force A 0101
force B 1110
run 50
```

We have chosen to run the simulation for 50 ns, since this is long enough for the *carry* to propagate through all the full adders. The simulation results for the above command list are:

Ns	Delta	A	B	cin	s	Cout
0	+0	0000	0000	0	0000	0
0	+1	1111	0001	1	0000	0
10	+0	1111	0001	1	1111	0
20	+0	1111	0001	1	1101	0
30	+0	1111	0001	1	1001	0
40	+0	1111	0001	1	0001	1
50	+0	0101	1110	0	0001	1
60	+0	0101	1110	0	0101	1
70	+0	0101	1110	0	0111	1
80	+0	0101	1110	0	0011	1

The final simulation results are

1111 + 0001 + 1 = 0001 with a carry of 1 (at time = 40 ns) and

0101 + 1110 + 0 = 0011 with a carry of 1 (at time = 80 ns)

The simulation stops at 80 ns, since no further changes occur after that time.

Example 41:

Write a test bench to verify design of half adder (refer Example 4).

Solution:

library IEEE;
use IEEE. STD_LOGIC_1164. *all;*

entity HALFADDR_TEST *is*   -- As test bench does not include interface ports,
                        -- empty entity is declared.
entity HALFADDR _TEST;

architecture HALFADDR _TEST_ARCH   *of* HALFADDR _TEST   *is*
    component HALFADDR -- declared design under test as component.
        port (IN1, IN2: *in bit;*
                SUM, CARRY: *out bit*);
    end component ;
    signal IN1S, IN2S, S,C: *bit;* -- declared the signals required for verification.
begin
        -- creates an instance of the AND gate.
            I1: HALFADDR *port map* (IN1=>IN1S, IN2 =>IN2S, SUM =>S, CARRY =>C);

```
    process                    -- process is defined to apply stimulus.
    constant  PERIOD: time: = 40 ns;
        begin
         IN1S <= '1';
                IN2S <= '1';
         wait for PERIOD;
         assert ( S = '0' and C = '1')
                report  "Test failed" severity error ;


                IN1S <= '1';
                IN2S <= '0';
         wait for PERIOD;
         assert (S = '1' and  C = '0')
                report  "Test failed" severity error,


                IN1S <= '0';
                IN2S <= '1';
         wait for PERIOD;
         assert (S = '1' and C = '0')
                report "Test failed" severity error,


                IN1S <= '0';
                IN2S <= '0';
         wait for PERIOD;
         assert (S = '0' and C = '0')
                report "Test failed" severity error,
    end process;
  end HALFADDR_TEST_ARCH;
```

QUESTIONS

1. Compare data flow, behavioral and structural modeling.
2. Explain the following statements with example:
   (a) Entity   (b) Array type   (c) Generic
3. Write code in VHDL for 4:1 multiplexer in three different modeling types.
4. Explain different classes of data objects in VHDL with example for each.
5. Explain operator overloading in VHDL.

6. Write short note on shift operators.

7. Explain the following shift operators with example:
   (a) SLL   (b) SLA   (c) SRA   (d) ROR

8. Write short note on operators in VHDL

9. What are the object types involved in VHDL? Explain with example.

10. Explain block statement with an example.

11. Explain guarded signal assignment with an example.

12. Explain the transport delay and inertia delay used in VHDL.

13. What is configuration specification and configuration declaration? Explain each of them with suitable example.

14. What is test bench? Write a test bench for half adder.

15. Write short notes on:
    (a) Design libraries   (b) Component instantiation (c) Library and Use clause
    (d) Level of abstraction in VLSI   (e) Data types in VHDL

16. Explain the following terms with example:
    (a) Signal   (b) Variable (c) Packages (d) Process

17. Explain "wait" statement in VHDL.

18. What is assert statement in VHDL?

19. Write VHDL code for 16:1 mux using 4:1 mux using generate statement.

20. Write VHDL code for JK FF with set and reset terminal.

21. Write VHDL code for 4-bit adder using 1-bit full adder as component using generate statement.

22. Design 3:8 decoder using VHDL.

23. Write VHDL code for BCD to seven segment decoder

24. Write VHDL code for 3-bit up-down counter.

25. Explain the following signal attributes with example of each:
    (a) 'last event   (b) 'delayed   (c) 'last-value   (d) 'stable

26. Write VHDL code for 4 bit comparator.

27. What are the three object classes in VHDL?   **(2 Marks, May 2001)**

28. Explain different classes of data objects in VHDL with example for each.
                                                                 (6 Marks, Nov. 2001)

29. What is the difference between signal/variable?
                                              (2 Marks, May 2001) (4 Marks, Dec. 2004)

30. What are the data types other than bit and bit vector which two data types are IEEE defined and what is the difference between them in VHDL?
                                              (8 Marks, Nov. 2000) (6 Marks, May 2001)

31. Explain array type with example.   **(3 Marks, May 2002)**

32. List various arithmetic operators used in VHDL.

33. Write a note on shift operators. **(6 Marks, May 2003)**

34. Compare dataflow, behavior and structural modeling. **(4 Marks, Nov. 2001)**

35. Write a VHDL model for a multiplexer having four inputs and one output in three different styles. **(12 Marks, May 2001)**

36. Explain Block Statement with example.

     (2 Marks, May 2001) (4, Marks, Dec. 2004)

37. Write VHDL code to design D-latch. **(4 Marks, Nov. 2000)**

38. What are the advantages and requirements of component instantiation? Declaring Half Adder as a component, write a VHDL code for constructing a Full Adder.

     (8 Marks, Nov. 2000)

39. Explain with example the GENERATE statement. Explain GENERATE statement with suitable example. **(4 Marks, May 2005)**

40. In an architecture for entity, all statements are concurrent. So, when do sequential statements exist in VHDL? What do you mean by sensitivity list of a process? What are its alternatives? **(8 Marks, Nov. 2000)**

41. Explain "Wait on" with example. **(2 Marks, May 2001)**

42. Write a note on multiple wait conditions. **(6 Marks, May 2002)**

43. Which severity levels exist in Assert statement and which is the default level?

     (2 Marks, May 2001)

44. Explain report statement with example. **(2 Marks, May 2001)**

45. What is need of configuration? Explain the configuration binding with example.

     (8 Marks, Nov. 2001)

46. Explain configuration and its utility with an example. **(8 Marks, Dec. 2003)**

47. Differentiate between function and procedure with respect to following points:
    (i) Return values   (ii) Preferred application
    (iii) Calling methods   (iv) Simulation time **(12 Marks, Dec. 2003)**

48. What is need of attributes in VHDL? Explain any two attributes with example. Mention whether they are synthesizable or not? **(8 Marks, May 2005)**

49. Explain the following signal attributes with example for each:
    (i) Last-event   (ii) Last-value
    (iii) Delayed   (iv) Stable **(8 Marks, Nov. 2001)**

50. Explain the role of different attributes used in VHDL. **(4 Marks, Dec. 2003)**

51. Write a note on Operator Overloading.

     (6 Marks, Nov. 2000, Nov. 2001, May 2002)

52. What is subprogram overloading? How does it help designer? Explain different types.

     (8 Marks, Dec. 2003)

53. What is meant by multiple drivers? Explain Resolution function.

(6 Marks, Nov. 2001)

54. Which two delay modes are defined in VHDL standard? Explain with example. What is the concept of Delta Delay? Draw timing diagrams.

(8 Marks, Nov. 2000) (6 Marks, May 2001), (4 Marks, Dec. 2004)

55. Write a VHDL code to design a BCD to seven segment decoder for a single digit LED display. **(8 Marks, Nov. 2000)**

56. Write a VHDL code for a rising edge triggered D flip flop with asynchronous set and reset inputs and two outputs. Develop a test bench for testing this flip flop.

(14 Marks, Dec. 2004)

57. Write a VHDL code for synchronous and asynchronous reset D flip-flop.

(4 Marks, Nov. 2000) (2 Marks, Dec. 2003)

58. Write a VHDL code for 1-bit comparator. By instantiating this component, write a code for 4-bit comparator. **(8 Marks, May 2001)**

59. Write a note on test benches. **(6 Marks, Nov. 2000) (6 Marks, May 2001)**

60. Necessity of test benches and its type. **(6 Marks, Nov. 2001)**

61. Write VHDL code for up-down counter and also write test bench for it.

(12 Marks, Dec. 2003)

62. Write a VHDL code for 8-bit up-down counter. **(8 Marks, May 2001)**

Topics discussed: Simulation, Simulation at different levels, Simulation types, Simulation process, Execution of sequential and concurrent statement, Simulator types.

5.1 What is Simulation?

Simulation is a functional evaluation of design by using a software program called simulator to check for its performance in terms of timing and results.

Simulation is the process of applying stimuli (test input) to design under test over time and producing corresponding responses from the design under test.

Motivation for Simulation comes from

- The need to test designs prior to implementation and usage
- Reduce the time for development
- Decrease the time to market.

The software which is used for Simulation is called Simulator.

5.2 Simulation at Different Levels

Simulation can be performed during all stages of design.

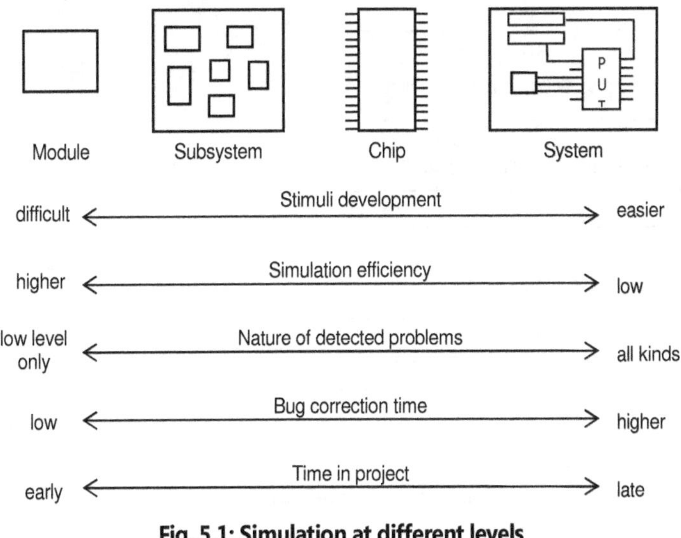

Fig. 5.1: Simulation at different levels

As verification is needed on all levels, the designer can simulate module, subsystem (part of project-group of modules), chip and system (application of project) of the project.

Fig. 5.1 shows comparison between simulations at different levels. The development of stimuli is difficult at module level while easier at system level. Simulation of module comes early while system simulation comes late in the project design. All kinds of problems will be detected at system simulation. Error correction time is less at module level simulation.

In VLSI design also, simulation can be performed during all stages as shown in Fig. 5.2.

Simulation can be done after HDL capture, after synthesis and after place and route as shown in Fig. 5.2.

After the completion of design specification, the design is described by using VHDL. The design description may be either behavioral or RTL (Register Transfer Level) description. Then behavioral description is converted to RTL description that describes the clock by clock behavior of the design.

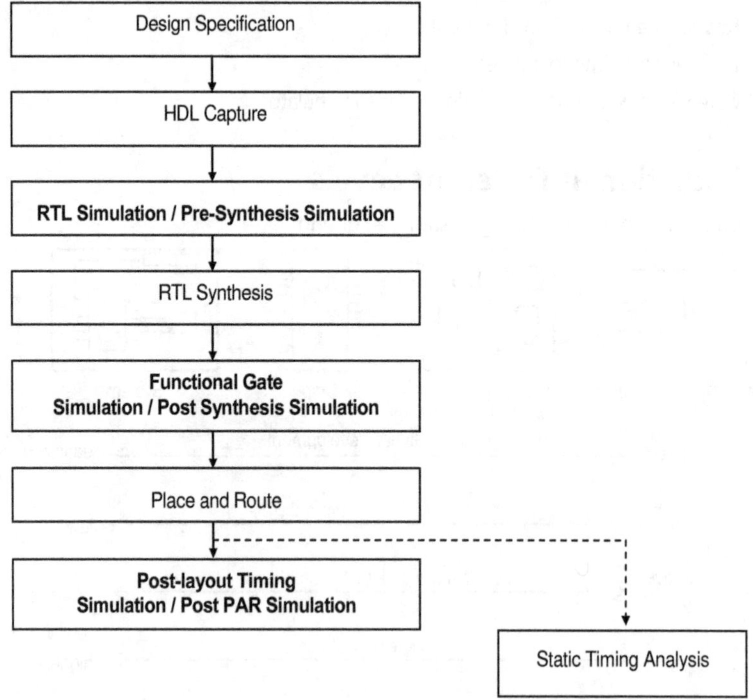

Fig. 5.2: High level design flow

RTL Simulation / Pre-Synthesis Simulation

The RTL simulation step is used to verify the correctness of the RTL VHDL description. The designer uses stimulus that represents the design environment to drive the design and check to make sure that the results are correct. Simulator can be used to read the RTL description and verify the correctness of the design.

The RTL simulation flow is shown in Fig. 5.3. After creation of VHDL description, it is compiled to remove any syntax errors. After the syntax errors have been removed, the design is simulated to verify correctness of the design. The designer loads the compiled VHDL description into the simulator and applies stimulus to the design. After the stimulus has been entered, the designer runs the simulation for as long as needed to generate enough output data to determine if the design is correct. After the simulation has been run, the simulator will have generated output data that can be analyzed. If the design is not correct, the designer must fix the VHDL code, compile and simulate the design again. This process continues until all errors are removed.

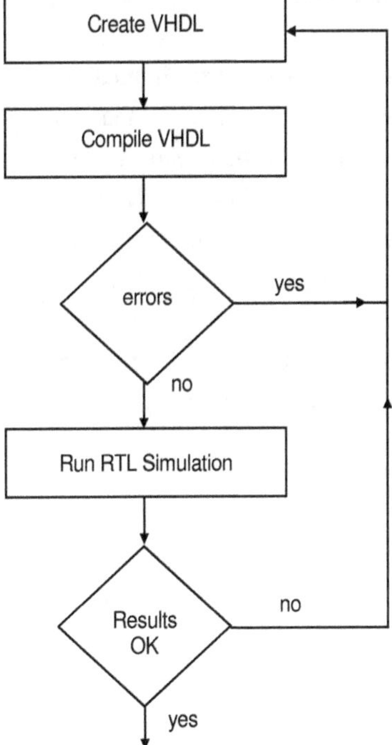

Fig. 5.3 : RTL simulation flow

Functional Gate Level Simulation / Post-Synthesis Simulation

Functional gate level simulation is used to verify whether synthesis tool is produced a correct design or not, i.e. it is used to verify output of the synthesis tool.

The simulator reads the VHDL net list (output of synthesis tool) plus a library of the synthesis primitives and stimuli when the designer runs the simulation. In this level of simulation, the functionality of the design is verified.

After the design has been functionally verified, it is passed to the place and route tools to implement the design. Place and route tools are used to take the design net list and implement the design in the target technology device.

RTL and functional gate level simulation are called as **Pre-layout Simulation**. (Simulation before place and route). Pre-layout Simulation is a functional verification of the design including logic cell delays. No timing is back annotated.

Post Layout Simulation / Post (Place and Route) Simulation

Post layout simulation verifies the results of place and route PAR process. This simulation combines the net list used by place and route with the timing file from the place and route process into a simulation that checks both functionality and timing of the design. The designer can run the simulation and generate accurate output waveforms that show whether or not the design is operating properly and if the timing is being met.

Post-layout simulation is performed after physical place and route (PAR) where interconnect delays are taken into account. (Back Annotated net list).

5.3 Types of Simulation

Simulation is divided into following categories or simulation modes:

- Behavioral simulation
- Functional simulation
- Static-timing analysis
- Gate-level simulation
- Switch-level simulation
- Transistor-level or circuit-level simulation

Behavioral simulation

Behavioral simulation models large pieces of a system as black boxes with inputs and outputs. It only represents behavior of system in terms of its input to output relationship. The functionality of design is modeled using HDL. Timing aspects are considered while simulating behavioral model.

> e.g.   C <= A *and B after* 5 *ns* ;

Functional simulation

Functional simulation verifies only the functionality of the design. Functional simulation ignores timing aspects. Simulator tests the logic in the design using unit delays. Functional simulation is usually performed at the early stages of the design process. No timing information is available.

Vector-based simulation (or dynamic simulation) can show that the design functions correctly, hence the name functional simulation. However, functional simulation does not work well if we wish to find the critical path. For this we turn to a static simulation or static timing analysis.

Static timing analysis

Once a behavioral or function simulation predicts that a system works correctly, the next step is to check the timing performance. At this point, a system is partitioned and a timing simulation is performed for each unit separately. Simulator is having built-in timing analysis tool which computes, delay for each timing path and analyzes logic in a static manner. This is called static-timing analysis because it does not require the creation of set of test (or stimulus) vectors for verifying design functionality.

Timing analysis works best with synchronous systems whose maximum operating frequency is determined by the longest path delay between successive flip-flops. The path with the longest delay is the critical path.

Timing simulation is performed after synthesis and place and route, using back annotation information. The back annotation processes generate a net list of library components annotated in a Standard Delay Format (SDF) file. Timing simulation verifies that the design runs at the desired speed or not. Timing simulation describes the circuit behavior more accurately than functional simulation.

Gate-level simulation

Gate-level simulation is used to check the timing performance of a design. Delay parameters of logic cells are used to verify timings. Gate-level simulation or logic simulation can also be used to check the timing performance of an ASIC. In a gate-level simulator, a logic gate or logic cell

(NAND, NOR and so on) is treated as black box modeled by a function whose variables are the input signals. The function may also model the delay through the logic cell.

If the timing simulation provided by a black-box model of a logic gate is not accurate enough, the next, more detailed, level of simulation i.e. switch-level simulation is to be used.

Switch-level simulation

Switch-level simulation models transistor as switches (on or off). Switch-level simulation can provide more accurate timing predictions than gate-level simulation, but without the ability to use logic-cell delays as parameters of the models.

Transistor-level or Circuit-level simulation

Transistor-level simulation is the most accurate, but also the most complex and time consuming. A transistor-level simulation requires models of transistor (Transistor used in gates), describing their non-linear and current characteristics.

Circuit is described in terms of resistances, capacitances and voltage and current sources. A set of mathematical equations relating current and voltage is set up and solved by numerical technique. Transistor-level simulation requires vast data structures and large amounts of computing resources. It gives analog results and frequency responses can be computed.

The above list is ordered from high-level to low-level simulation. High level is being more abstract and low level being more detailed. Proceeding from high-level to low-level simulation, the simulations become more accurate, but more complex and take longer time to run.

5.4 Software Languages VS HDLs
(Why is Concurrency Required?)

In a software language, all assignments are sequential. That means the order in which the statements appear is significant because they are executed in this way.

On the other hand, the events (change in value) in hardware are concurrent, and they must be represented that way. A software language cannot be used to describe hardware and so a hardware description language is required.

To illustrate this fact, consider the following circuit.

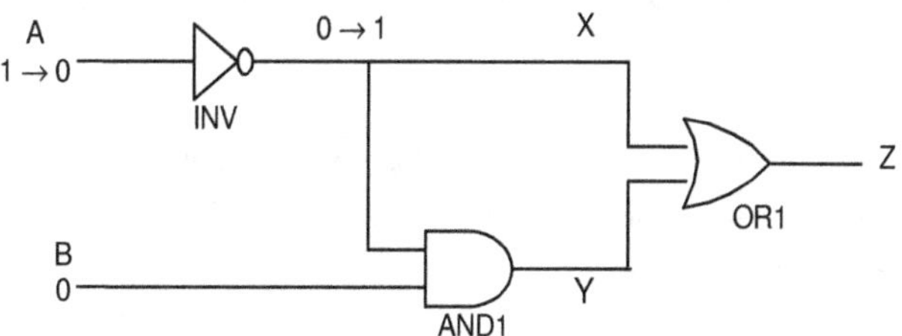

The required output is

 Z <= (not A) or (not A and B).

We can write code for this in two different styles.

 Style 1

  X <= not A;
  Y <= X and B;
  Z <= X or Y;

 Style 2

  Y <= X and B;
  Z <= X or Y;
  X <= not A;

Suppose A changes from 1 to 0 and B remains to 0, then output with style 1 is Z = 1 and with style 2 is Z = 0

This means that, if the statements are evaluated sequentially like software, we get different results when the order is changed. This is because of the fact that the hardware is always concurrent.

In VHDL language, concurrent statements are defined to take care of concurrency in hardware. The simulation engine (simulator) that runs on sequential computers also has to take care of concurrency in the simulation results.

5.5 How is Concurrency Achieved?

Concurrency is achieved by means of scheduling an event and by concept of delta delays.

Scheduling

When the simulator tags the signal for an update, it does not provide the update immediately, but rather remembers the value to be updated. The value is actually updated when the simulator has finished processing of the complete description once.

Event

Event is nothing but change on target signal which is to be updated.

Sensitivity list

Every concurrent statement has a sensitivity list. Statements are executed only when there is an event on signals in the sensitivity list, otherwise they are suspended.

    e.g.   Z <= X *and* Y

In this statement, X and Y signals are in the sensitivity list of Z. This statement will execute only if one of these (X or Y) changes.

Delta delays

The concept of delta delay is introduced to achieve concurrency and order independence. The simulator freezes simulation time until all scheduled assignments on current simulation time is finished and there are no more events on the sensitivity list. Thus, real time and simulation time is different.

Several logic changes occur simultaneously in a circuit. But a simulator cannot process events concurrently. Therefore, time is frozen within the simulator. Events are processed and logic values are updated one after the other till no more events take place. This is called one simulation cycle.

The real time that the simulator takes to execute one simulation cycle is called as delta delay (or simulation delta with zero simulation time).

Simulation with delta (δ)

Now let us see how delta achieve concurrency.

Let us take style1 of previous example

    Z <= (*not* A) *or* (*not* A *and* B).

    Style 1

        X <= *not* A;

        Y <= X *and* B;

        Z <= X *or* Y;

In the above example, A changes from 1 to 0 and B remains at 0.

In the first pass (time = N + 0δ), A changes from 1 to 0. Current value of X is calculated using the old value of A and an event on X is scheduled in the next delta.

Values of Y and Z do not change.

At time = N + 1δ, X changes from 0 to 1. Events are scheduled on Y and Z.

At time = N + 2δ, Y and Z values are updated. Since there are no events scheduled for N + 3δ, the simulation time will be incremented by one unit and Z = 1.

Now, consider style 2

       Y <= X *and* B;

       Z <= X *or* Y;

       X <= *not* A;

In the first pass (time = N + 0δ), A changes from 1 to 0. Current value of X is calculated using the old value of A and event on X is scheduled in the next delta. Values of Y and Z do not change.

At time = N + 1δ, X changes from 0 to 1. Events are scheduled on Y and Z.

At time = N + 2δ, Y and Z values are updated. Since there are no events scheduled for N + 3δ, the simulation time will be incremented by one unit and Z = 1.

So we can conclude that the result is same irrespective of order of statements.

This is how concurrency is achieved using the concept of delta.

5.6 How Logic Simulator Works?

5.6.1 Steps in Simulation

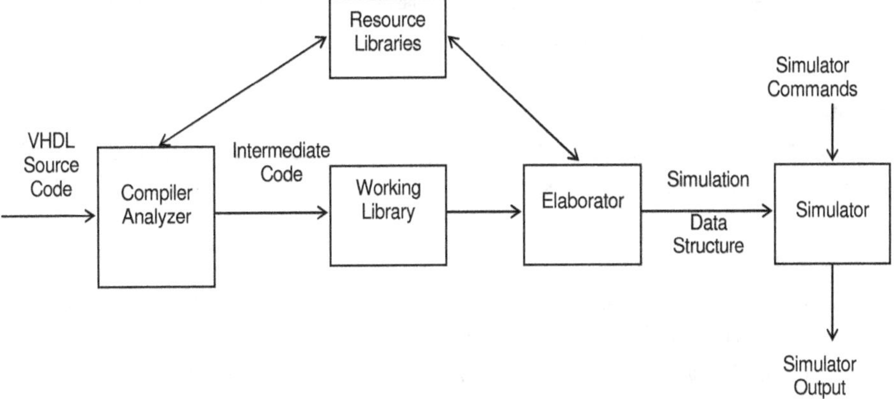

Fig. 5.4: Compilation, Elaboration and Simulation of VHDL code

After describing a design in a VHDL, simulation of VHDL code is important for two reasons. First, need to verify the VHDL code correctly implements the intended design; second need to verify that the design meets its specification.

Before simulation, the VHDL code must be complied (see Fig. 5.4).

(1) Compilation

The VHDL compiler (Analyzer) checks VHDL source code to check syntax or semantic rules of VHDL. If a syntax or semantic error occurs, then the compiler gives error message, else, the compiler generates an intermediate code. The compiler also checks to see that references to libraries are correct. This intermediate code can be used by a simulator or by a synthesizer.

Sequence of compilation – Main components are analyzed before sub-components i.e. entity before architecture, package before package body. Components which are instantiated are analyzed first.

VHDL units are analyzed in a specific manner, package before entity/architecture, configuration after entity/architecture.

(2) Elaboration

VHDL intermediate code must be converted to form that can be used by the simulator. This step is referred to as elaboration. During elaboration, ports are created for each instance of a component, memory storage is allocated for the required signals, the interconnection among the port signals are specified and a mechanism is established for executing the VHDL processes in the proper sequence. The data structure resulted after elaboration is being simulated.

(3) Initialization

After elaboration, initial values present in the declaration's statements are assigned to signals, variables etc. This process is called Initialization.

(4) Execution

After an initialization phase, the simulator enters the execution phase. The simulator accepts simulation commands, which control the simulation of the design and specify the desired simulator output. Simulation ends when all signals have been updated and new values have been assigned to signals.

5.6.2 Simulation Process

Simulation Process executes as shown in Fig. 5.5

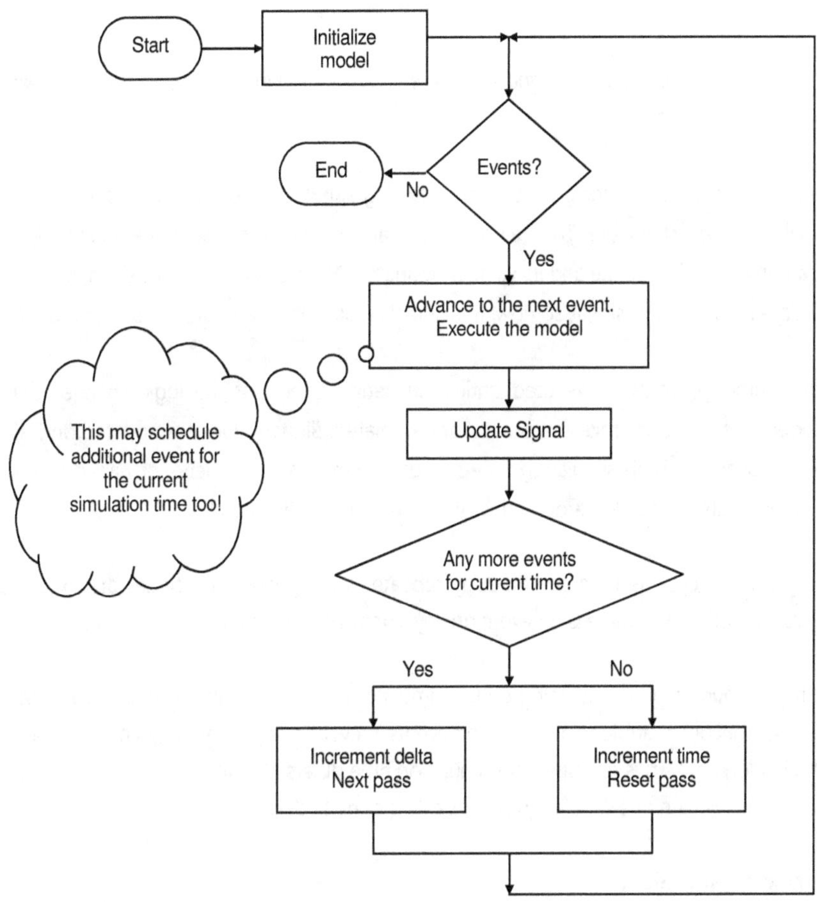

Fig. 5.5: Simulation process

At time zero, all gate outputs are set to an unknown value. The logic simulator prepares two queues, evaluation and event.

The evaluation queue keeps tracks of logic cells whose outputs are changing and the new values for each output, i.e. all the signals on the left hand side (target signal) of assignments are stored in evaluation queue. Also processes to be executed are stored in evaluation queue.

The event queue keeps tracks of logic cells whose inputs have changed, i.e. all the right hand side signals of the assignment are stored in the event queue. Signals to be updated are stored in the event list.

e.g. While simulating Z <= X *and* Y statement, Z is stored in evaluation queue whereas X and Y are stored in event queue.

When simulation time is incremented, on receiving simulation commands, a signal is updated. (Signals from event queue). Then all target signals and processes sensitive to that signals are placed on evaluation queue and its value is evaluated. Now, this updating of signal may be in the event queue of another signal, so now, that signal is called from evaluation queue for updating.

Each resumed process is executed until it suspends. Effects of the logic changes that have occurred as a result of process execution are evaluated. Signal values are updated only after the process suspends. Then simulation time set to the next event in queue, or halted if simulation time is exhausted. One loop around this cycle is known as a delta cycle.

The simulation cycle is then continuously repeated during which processes are executed and signals are updated till there is no event on any signal in the event queue.

Till this, although real time is going on but simulator keeps its simulating time frozen. When the simulation becomes stable i.e. there are no events in event queue, then only simulator increments its simulation time. Thus real time and simulation time differs. Whatever real time required for the simulator to execute one simulation cycle is called as delta delay.

Example of simulation:
As an example of simulation, execution of the following VHDL code is traced:

```
entity SIM_EXAMP is
end SIM_EXAMP;

architecture SIM_ARCH of SIM_EXAMP is
signal A, B : bit ;
begin
    P1: process (B)
```

```
        begin
            A <= '1';
            A <= transport '0' after 5 ns ;
        end process P1;
        P2: process (A)
        begin
            if ( A = '1') then
                 B < = not B after 10 ns ;
            end if ;
            end process P2 ;
    end SIM_ARCH ;
```

During elaboration, a driver is created for each signal. Each driver holds the current value of a signal and a queue of future signal values. Each time a signal is scheduled to change in the future, the new value is placed in the queue along with the time at which the change is scheduled.

Fig. 5.6 shows the drivers for the signals A and B as the simulation progresses.

After elaboration is finished, each driver holds '0', since this is the default initial value for a bit. When simulation begins, initialization takes place. Both processes are executed simultaneously one time through, and then the processes wait until a signal on the sensitivity list changes.

When process P1 executes in zero time, the two changes in A are scheduled, i.e. A changes to '1' at time δ (delta delay) and back to '0' at time = 5 ns. Meanwhile, process P2 executes, but no change in B occurs, since A is still '0' during execution at time 0 ns.

Time advances to δ, and A changes to '1'. The change in A causes process P2 to execute, and since A = '1', B is scheduled to change to '1' at time 10 ns.

The next scheduled change occurs at time = 5 ns, when A changes to '0'. This change causes P2 to execute, but B does not change. B changes to '1' at time = 10 ns. The change in B causes P1 to execute, and two changes in A are scheduled. When A changes to '1' at time 10 + δ, process P2 executes, and B is scheduled to change at time 20 ns. Then A changes at time 15 ns, and the simulation continues in this manner until the run time limit is reached.

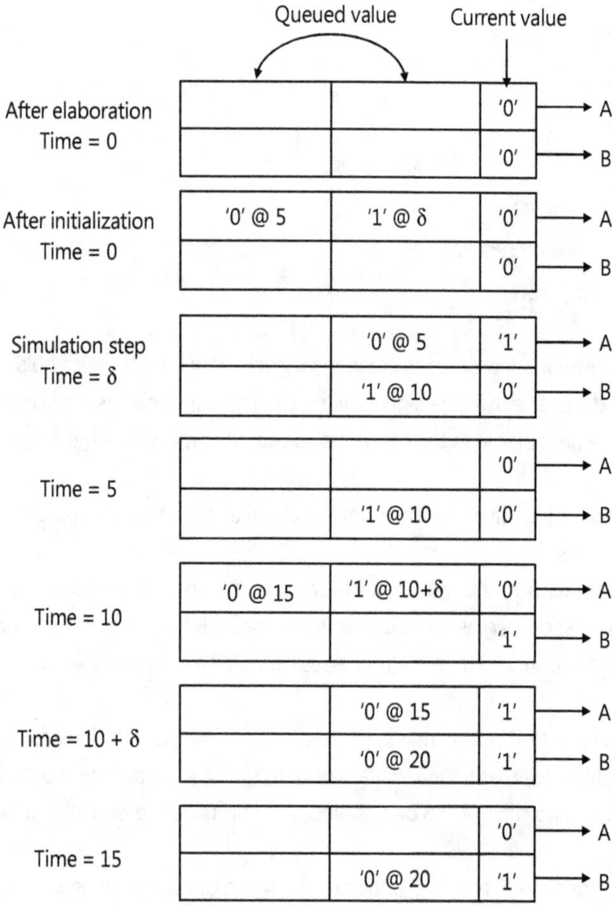

Fig. 5.6: Signal drivers for simulation example

5.7 Difference in Execution of Sequential and Concurrent Statement

The following example illustrates the difference in the way sequential and concurrent statements are executed.

A VHDL program has signals A, B, C and D of type integer. Signals are initialized to A = 1, B = 2, C = 3, and D = 0. The program contains the following concurrent statements:

    A <= B; -- statement 1

    B <= C; -- statement 2

    C <= D; -- statement 3

Assume that D changes to 4 at time =10. The following sequence of events then occurs. Since D has changed, statement 3 executes, and C is changed to 4 at time 10 + δ. Next, since C has changed, statement 2 executes, and B is updated at time 10 + 2δ. Then the change in B triggers execution of statement 1, and A is updated at time 10 + 3δ. Since A does not appear on the right hand side of any statement, no further execution is triggered.

Time	delta	A	B	C	D
0	+0	1	2	3	0
10	+0	1	2	3	4 (statement 3 executes first)
10	+1	1	2	4	4 (then statement 2 executes)
10	+2	1	4	4	4 (then statement 1 executes)
10	+3	4	4	4	4 (no further execution occurs).

Now, consider a program with same statements placed in a process (sequential statements).

    process (B, C, D)

    begin

        A <= B; -- statement 1

        B <= C; -- statement 2

        C <= D; -- statement 3

    end process

Assume that A, B, C and D are initialized as before and D changes to 4 at time = 10. Since D has changed, and D is on the sensitivity list, the process begins execution. Statements 1, 2 and 3 are executed in sequence; then the process goes back to the top and waits until signal on the sensitivity list changes. Execution of three statements takes place instantaneously at time = 10; not even delta time is required to execute the statements. However, since A, B and C are signals, their values are not updated until time 10 + δ. Therefore, the old values of B, C and D are used when the statements are executed. Signals A, B and C will change value at time 10 + δ, so the process will execute again. As a result, A and B will change at time 10 + 2δ, and the process will execute a third time. The sequence of events is summarized as follows:

Time	delta	A	B	C	D	
0	+0	1	2	3	0	
10	+0	1	2	3	4	(statements 1, 2, 3 execute; then update A, B, C)
10	+1	2	3	4	4	(statements 1, 2, 3 execute; then update A, B, C)
10	+2	3	4	4	4	(statements 1, 2, 3 execute; then update A, B, C)
10	+3	4	4	4	4	(no further execution occurs).

5.8 Types of Simulator

Event-driven simulator

Event-driven signal keeps track of any change in the signal in the event queue. The simulator starts simulation as soon as any signal in event list changes its value. For this the simulator has to keep record of all the scheduled events in future. This causes a large memory overhead but gives high accuracy for asynchronous design. It simulates events only. Gates whose inputs have events are called active and are placed in activity list. The simulation proceeds by removing a gate from the activity list. The process of evaluation stops when the activity list becomes empty.

Cycle-based simulator

Cycle-based simulation ignores intra-cycle state transitions, i.e. they check the status of target signals periodically irrespective of any events. This can boost performance by 10-50 times compared to traditional event-driven simulators. Cycle-based technology offers greater memory efficiency and faster simulation run-time than traditional pure event-based simulators. Cycle-based simulators work best with synchronous design but give less timing accuracy with asynchronous design.

Signals are treated as variables. Functions such as AND, OR etc. are directly converted to program statements. Sign-level functions such as memory blocks, adders, multipliers, etc. are modeled as subroutines. For every input vector, the code is repeatedly executed until all variables have attained steady value.

Compiled code simulator is efficient when used for high-level design verification. Inefficiency is incurred by the evaluation of the design when only few inputs are changing.

Comparison between Event-driven and Cycle-based simulator

Event-driven Simulator	**Cycle-based Simulator**
• Evaluates input looking for state change.	• Evaluates entire design every clock cycle.
• Schedule events in time.	• No event scheduling.
• Calculates time delay.	• No delay calculation or timing checks.
• Store state values and time information.	• No such storage, very fast, very efficient memory usage.
• Identifies timing violations.	• Does not identify timing violations. Requires a static timing analysis tool.

QUESTIONS

1. What is the difference between pre-synthesis simulation, post-synthesis simulation and post PAR simulation?   **(8 Marks, May 2005)**

2. What is the need of simulation? Explain simulation process.

3. Write short note on event simulation.

4. Explain different types of simulation.

5. Explain Register Transfer Level (RTL).

6. What are different types of simulator? Explain each.

7. Explain steps in simulation.

8. Compare pre synthesis, post synthesis and post PAR simulations. What are the constraints in synthesis and PAR?   **(9 Marks, May 2007)**

9. What is static timing analysis ? Explain with suitable examples.   **(8 Marks, May 2007)**

◊◊◊

Topics discussed: Synthesis process, Synthesis flow, Advantages of using synthesis, Expectations from synthesis tool, Hardware modeling examples, Synthesis guidelines, Place and Route

6.1 What is Synthesis?

Synthesis is an automatic method of converting a higher level abstraction such as a behavioral description to a lower level abstraction i.e. a gate level description. Synthesis process converts user's hardware description into structural logic description. Synthesis provides a means to convert schematics or HDL into real-world hardware. Synthesis tool converts the described hardware into a net list that a vendor may use to create the chip or board. The aim of synthesis is to produce a gate-level net list for target technology.

6.2 Synthesis Process

The synthesis process is shown in Fig. 6.1.

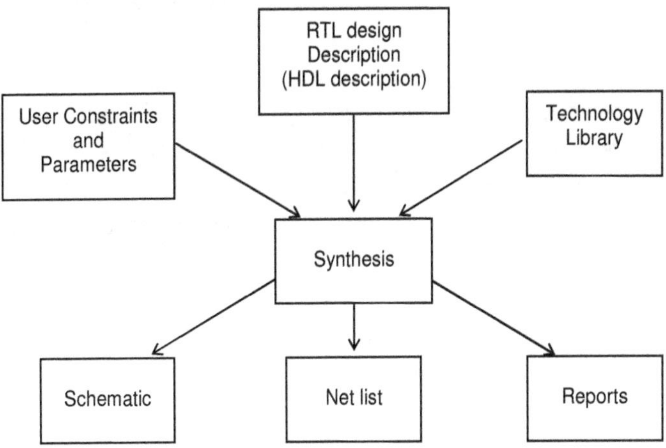

Fig. 6.1: Synthesis process

The inputs to the synthesis process are RTL VHDL description, circuit constraints and attributes for the design and a technology library. The synthesis process produces an optimized gate level net list from all of these inputs and schematic of the design.

Register Transfer Level Description:

Register transfer level description specifies all of the registers in a design, and the combinational logic in between them. This is shown by Fig. 6.2.

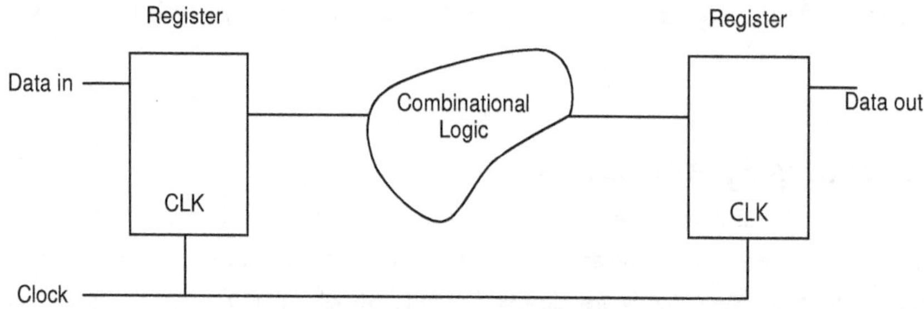

Fig. 6.2: Register and cloud diagram

The registers are shown as the rectangular objects connected to the clock signal. The combinational logic is described by logical equations, sequential control statements, subprograms or through concurrent statements which are represented by the cloud object between registers.

RTL descriptions are used for synchronous designs and describe the clock by clock behavior of the design.

VHDL description is technology independent, but synthesis can be used to create technology-specific implementations.

The registers are described either explicitly through component instantiation or implicitly through inference.

Following is an example of RTL description that uses component instantiation.

```
    entity DIF_RTL  is
        port (CLK, EN: in bit;
       DOUT: out bit);
     end DFF_RTL;


 architecture RTL_ARCH  of  DFF_RTL is
     component DFF
```

```
        port (CLK, DIN: in bit;
            Q, QB: out bit);
    end component;
    signal Q1, Q2, QB1, QB2: bit ;
begin
        D1: DFF port map (CLK, DIN, Q1, QB1);
        D2: DFF port map (CLK Q1, Q2, QB2);
        DOUT <= Q1 when EN = '1'
            else
                Q2;
end RTL_ARCH;
```

Example is the circuit for a selectable data delay circuit. The circuit delays the input signal DIN by 1 or 2 clocks depending on the value of EN. [EN = '1', DIN is delayed by 1 clock and if EN = '0', DIN is delayed by 2 clocks].

This example could be rewritten as following using register inference.

```
    entity DFF_RTL  is
        port (CLK, DIN, EN: in bit;
        DOWN: out bit);
    end DFF_RTL;


    architecture INFERENCE  of  DFF_RTL  is
        signal Q1, Q2: bit;
    begin
      process
      begin
            wait until  CLK'event and CLK = '1' ;
        Q1 <= DIN;
        Q2 <= Q1;
      end process;
      DOUT  <= Q1 when EN = '1' else Q2 ;
    end INFERENCE;
```

In this model, the DFF components are not instantiated, but are inferred through the synthesis process. The advantage of this description is that it is technology independent. In the first description, actual flip-flop elements from the technology library were instantiated which makes the description technology dependent.

After synthesis, both of these descriptions produce a gate level description (schematic and net list). The schematic is as shown in Fig. 6.3.

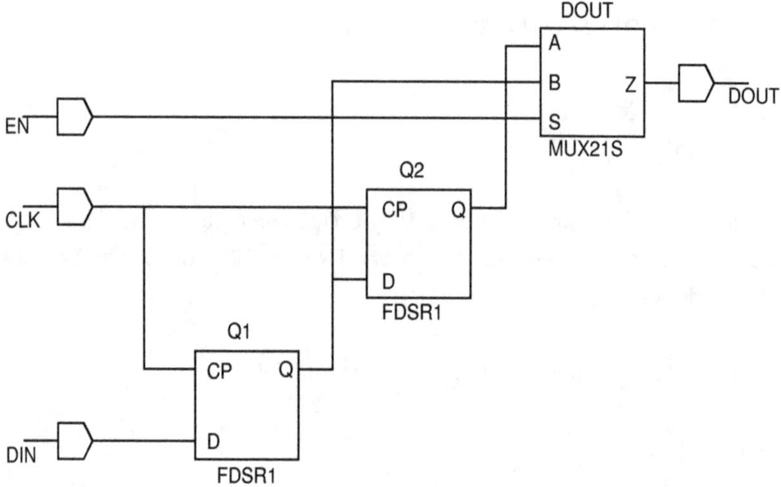

Fig. 6.3: A Gate level description

Gate level description has two registers (FDSR1) with MUX (MUX21S) logic controlling the output signal from each register.

This example shows how RTL synthesis can be used to create technology specific implementation from technology independent VHDL descriptions.

Constraints

Constraints are used to control the output of the optimization and mapping process. Constraints represent part of the physical environment that the design has to interface with. The constraints available in synthesis tools include area, timing, power and testability constraints.

Timing constraints

Timing constraints are used to specify maximum delays for a particular path in a design. A typical delay constraint in Leonardo synthesis tool format is as shown below:

set_attribute - port DATA_OUT - NAME *require_time - value25*

This constraint specifies that the maximum delay for signal DATA_OUT should be less than or equal to 25 library units. A library unit can be whatever the library designer used when describing the technology from a synthesis point of view. Typically, it is in nanoseconds.

Clock constraints

Clock constraints are used to specify timing of one clock cycle.

set_attribute - port CLK *-name clock_cycle - value 25*

This example sets a clock cycle constraint on port CLK with a value of 25 library units.

Attributes

Attributes are used to specify the design environment. Attributes specify the loading that output devices have to drive, the drive capability of devices driving the design, and timing of input signals. All of this information is taken into account by the static timing analyzer to calculate the timing through the circuit's path.

Load attributes

The load attribute specifies how much capacitive load exists on a particular output signal.

set_attribute - port XBUS - *name input_load - value 5*

This attribute specifies that signal XBUS will load the driver of this signal with 5 library units of load.

Drive attributes

The Drive attribute specifies the resistance of the driver, which controls how much current it can source. The larger a driver is the faster a particular path will be, but larger driver takes more area, so need to trade off speed and area for best possible implementation.

set_attribute - port YBUS - *name output_drive - value 2.7*

This attribute specifies that signal YBUS has 2.7 library units of drive capability.

Arrival time attributes

Some synthesis tools use a static timing analyzer during synthesis process to check that the logic being created matches the timing constraints that user has specified. Setting the arrival time on a particular node specifies to the static timing analyzer when a particular signal will occur at a node. This is important for late arriving signals.

Technology libraries

Technology libraries hold all of the information necessary for a synthesis tool to create a net list for a design based on the desired logical behavior, and constraints on the design. Technology Libraries contain the logical functions of a target device (ASIC, CPLD, FPGA) cell, the area of the cell, the input to output timing of the cell, any constraints on fan-out of the cell, and timing checks that are required for the cell. Also graphical symbol of the cell for use in schematic is stored in the Technology Library.

Technology libraries can also contain data about how to scale delay information with respect to process parameters and operating conditions. Operating conditions are the device operating temperature and power supply voltage applied to the device.

Technology libraries are created by silicon vendor (or PLD vendor), not by the synthesis tool. Most libraries are compiled before delivery. They can be understood by the tools, but are unreadable to users.

The outputs from synthesis process are schematic and gate level net list. Synthesis process produces the schematic by using graphical symbols of cells from technology library and interconnection between the cells.

Another output from synthesis is net list. The net list is nothing but textual information of schematic. It is a textual format of interconnections between logic cells used. Net list is produced in standard EDIF (Electronic Design Interchange Format) form. EDIF is industry standard net list format for exchange of graphical and electronic data between EDA (Electronic Design Automation) tools from various vendors.

6.3 Synthesis Flow (Steps in Synthesis Process)

The synthesis flow or steps in synthesis are as shown in Fig. 6.4.

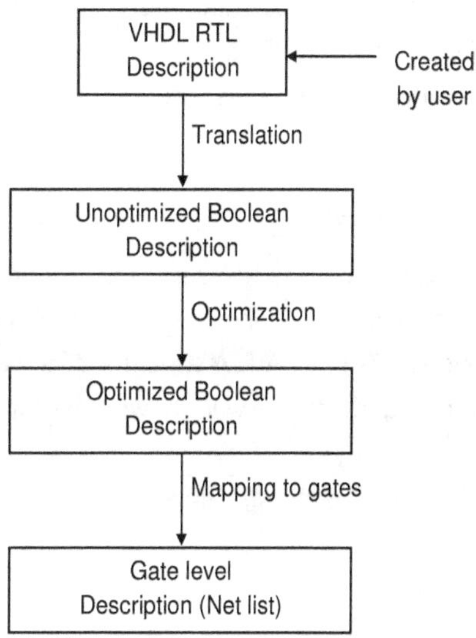

Fig. 6.4: Steps in synthesis

Synthesis process includes three steps to convert the RTL description to gates. First, the RTL description is translated to an unoptimized Boolean description which consists of gates such as AND gates and OR gates, flip-flops and latches. This is functionally correct by unoptimized description. Second, unoptimized Boolean descriptions are optimized by executing Boolean optimization algorithms. Third, the optimized Boolean equivalent description is mapped to actual logic gates by using technology library of the target process.

Translation

Conversion of RTL description to Boolean unoptimized description is called translation. Translation is usually not user controllable. This intermediate form is not viewable to the user.

All *if, case* and *loop* statements, conditional signal assignments, and selected signal assignment statements are converted to their Boolean equivalent in this intermediate form. Flip-flops and latches can either be instantiated or inferred; both cases produce the same flip-flop or latch entry in the intermediate description.

Optimization

Conversion of an unoptimized Boolean description to optimized Boolean description is called optimization. The optimization process uses a number of algorithms and rules for this conversion. One technique is to convert the unoptimized Boolean description to a very low-level description i.e. a PLA format, optimize that description using PLA optimization technique, and then try to reduce the logic generated. Optimization is done by flattening and factoring process.

Flattening

The process of converting the unoptimized Boolean description to a PLA format (sum of product forms) is known as flattening. Flattening creates a flat signal representation of only two levels: an AND level and an OR level. A PLA structure is very easy description because it has a simple structure and the algorithms are well known, hence it can optimize easily.

An example of a Boolean description is shown below:

$$A = B \text{ and } C;$$
$$B = X \text{ or } (Y \text{ and } Z); \quad \text{original equations}$$
$$C = Q \text{ or } W;$$

This description shows an output A that has three equations describing its functions. B and C are two intermediate variables that hold temporary values which are then used to calculate the final value for A.

The flattening process removes these intermediate nodes (signals or variables B and C), to produce a completely flat design, with no intermediate nodes. For example, after removing intermediate variables:

A = (X *and* Q) *or* (Q *and* Y *and* Z) *or* (W *and* X) *or* (W *and* Y *and* Z); which is Boolean equivalent of the three original equations. It has no intermediate nodes. This design contains only two levels of logic gates; an AND plane and an OR plane. As there are very few logic levels from input to output, it results in very fast design. However, there are a number of problems with this type of design.

First, this type of design can have a tremendous fan-out loading on the input signals because inputs fan-out to every term (drives more number of gates). Second, this type of design can be very large, because there is no sharing between terms. Also there are a number of circuits that are difficult to flatten, because the number of terms created is extremely large.

E.g., A 16 input XOR has the terms A and (not B) or B and (not A). An N- input XOR has $2^{(N-1)}$ terms. A 16 input XOR has 32768 terms and 32 bit XOR has over 2 billion terms. Clearly, this type of functions can not be flattened.

Flattening works best with less number of logic. Minimal logic description can be generated by use of flattening in conjunction with structuring (or factoring) which reduces the fan-out of the input pins, terms are shared.

Factoring [Structuring]

Factoring is the process of adding intermediate terms to add structure to a description. It is opposite of the flattening process.

Following is a design before factoring:

     X = (A and B) or (A and D);

     Y = Z or B or D;

After factoring, a separate intermediate node is introduced (added) for a common term bord. The results are shown here:

     X = A and Q;

     Y = Z or Q;

     Q = B or D;

Adding structure adds levels of logic between the inputs and outputs. Adding levels of logic adds more delay. The net result is a smaller design, but a slower design.

Usually the designer wants a design that is nearly as fast as the flattened design, but as small as the completely factored design. The ideal case is one in which the critical path was flattened for speed and the rest of the design was factored for small area and low fan-out.

After the design has been optimized of the Boolean level, it can be mapped to the gate functions in a technology library.

Mapping to gates

The mapping process takes the optimized Boolean description, the technology library, the user constraints, and generates an optimized net list built entirely from cells in the technology library. During the mapping process, cells are inserted that implement the Boolean function from the optimized Boolean description. These cells are then locally optimized to meet speed and area requirements.

6.4 Advantages of Synthesis

The advantages of using synthesis are:

- **The designer gets free from technology dependent issues:**

  Designer does not have to worry about technology issues i.e. maximum fan-in, maximum fan-out, interconnect capacitance, maximum sinking current, and source ability of target technology. The synthesizer will take care of it.

- **Allows technology independent coding:**

  As designer is free from technology related issues, he can easily retarget his design to another technology just be selecting separate target technology and re-synthesizing the design.

- **Constraint driven synthesis:**

  The designer can guide the synthesizer to optimize his design for speed, power, or area. Depending on these constraints, synthesis will produce different net list to optimize on selected parameters.

- Forces higher level of abstraction

- Leads to ease in debugging and code portability

- Enables designer to focus on larger design goals, as it is easier to relate RTL to Hardware.

6.5 Expectations from Synthesis Tools

All synthesis tools do not perform all expectations and do not have all features. Following are some of the expectations from a good synthesis tool:

- Synthesis tool should perform technology specific optimizations.

  e.g. vendor specific FPGAs and CPLDs.

- Best optimization techniques should be available.

- Designer should have control over the synthesis process. Synthesis process can control through coding style and constraints.

- Synthesis tool should broad Language Coverage.

- Synthesis tool should provide a user-friendly debugging environment.

- Synthesis tool should have fast compile time. Compile time should be proportional to design density.

- Synthesis tool should provide a clean and seamless link to the backend tools (simulator). i.e. transition should be very easy from front to back end tools.

6.6 Hardware Modeling Examples

Synchronous reset

Flip-flops are reset on the active edge of the clock when reset is held active.

```
process (CLK)
   begin
      if (CLK'event and CLK = '1') then
         if (RST = '1') then
      Q <= '0';
         else
      Q <= D;
         end if;
      end if;
   end process;
```

The hardware generated after synthesis is as shown in Fig. 6.5. It consists of one 2:1 mux and a D flip-flop.

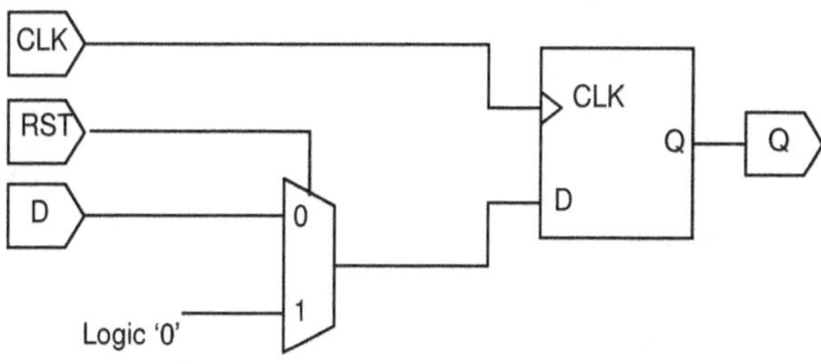

Fig. 6.5

Asynchronous reset

Flip-flops are cleared as soon as reset is asserted.

```
e.g.    process (CLK, RST)
        begin
        if (RST = '1') then
           Q <= '0';
        elsif (CLK'event and CLK = '1') then
           Q <= D;
        end if;
        end process;
```

The hardware generated is as shown in Fig. 6.6. It consists of only one D flip-flop with reset.

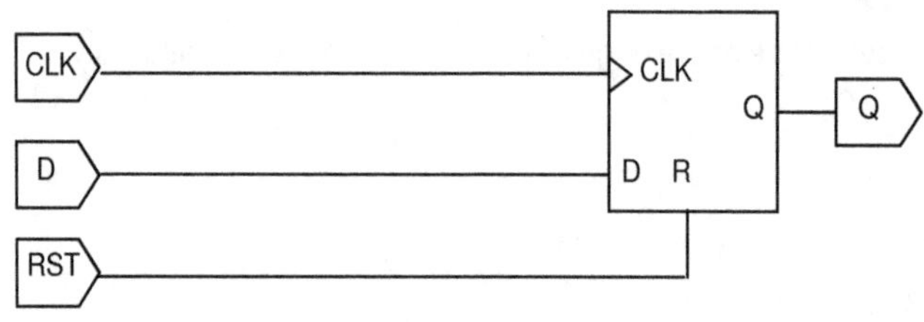

Fig. 6.6

Latch

Example *process* (CLK, IN1)

       begin

          if (CLK = '1') *then*

             OUT1 < = IN1;

          end if ;

        end process;

The hardware is shown in Fig. 6.7.

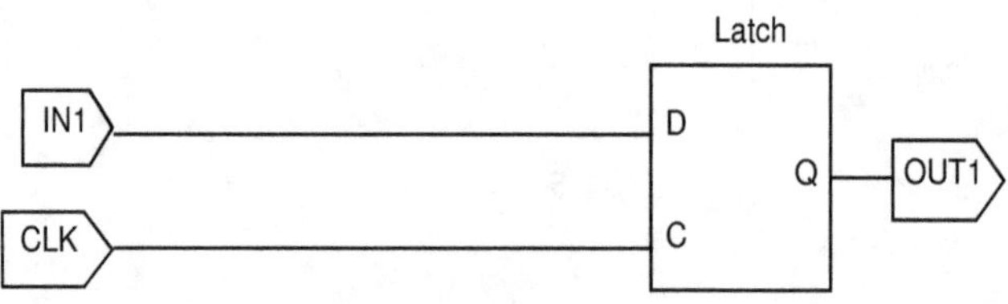

Fig. 6.7

Tri-state buffer

architecture TRI_BUF *of* TRY_STATE *is*

   begin

  OUT1 < = IN1 *when* CONTROL = '1' *else* 'z';

end TRI-BUF ;

Hardware generated after synthesis is as shown in Fig. 6.8.

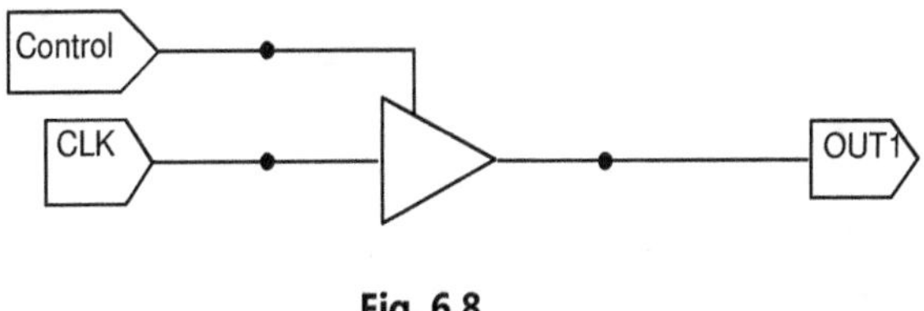

Fig. 6.8

Multiplexer

The functionality of multiplexer can be described by using *case* statement or *if-then-else* statement.

1) Case statement

```
process (SET, A, B, C, D)
    begin
        case SEL is
            when 0 => Y <= A;
            when 1 => Y <= B;
            when 2 => Y <= C;
            when others => Y <= B;
        end case;
    end process;
```

Hardware generated by synthesizer is as shown in Fig. 6.9.

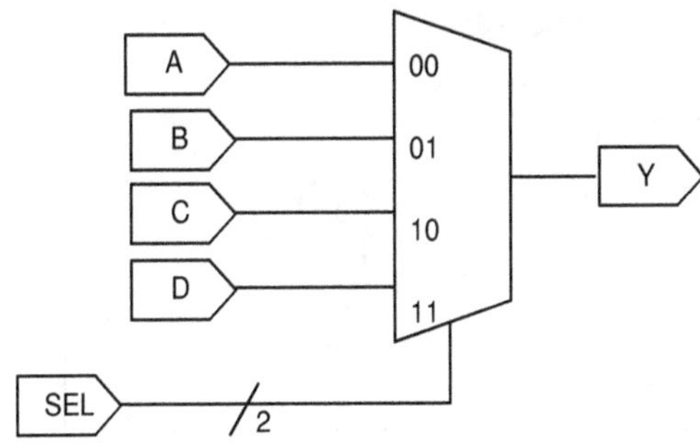

Fig. 6.9

case statement is a series of parallel checks to check a condition.

"*when others*" clause will guarantee that all conditions are covered.

"*when*" condition should not be changed, when it is being evaluated.

2) *if-then-else* statement

```
process (SEL, A, B, C, D)
    begin
        if ( SEL(2) = '1') then
        Y <= A;
        elsif ( SEL(1) = '1') then
          Y <= B;
        elsif ( SEL(0) = '1') then
           Y <= C;
        else
           Y <= D;
        end if ;
    end process;
```

Hardware obtained after synthesis is as shown in Fig. 6.10.

   "*if*" statement generates a priority encoder type structure. Do not use "*if*" statement for more than three levels. For, one "*if*" statement, synthesis will create one 2:1 mux.

Use "*case*" statement rather than "*if-then-else*" statement whenever possible.

This means that hardware generated also depends upon the VHDL statement used. It also means that, designer can control the synthesis process through coding style.

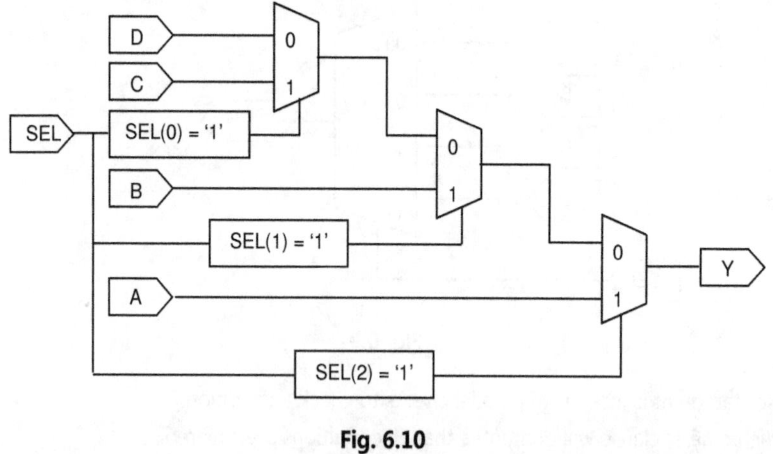

Fig. 6.10

Resource sharing

Resource sharing means sharing same hardware resources for multiple functions by rearranging the code.

Some tools have automatic resource sharing. Operations must be mutually exclusive. But sharing of operators can be forced by changing the coding style.

Consider the following code segment:

```
process (SEL, A, B, C, D)
    begin
        if (SEL = '1') then
            Y <= A + B;
        else
            Y <= C + D;
        end if ;
    end process;
```

The synthesis will generate the number of layout having same functionality for the above process.

The layout shown in Fig. 6.11 is without resource sharing.

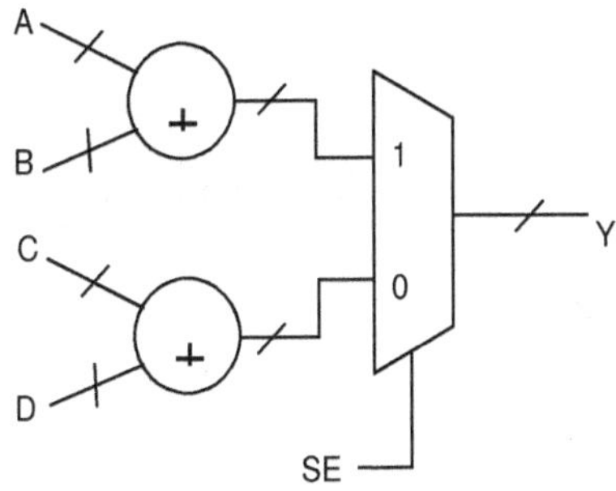

Fig. 6.11

The above layout will generate, if design is optimized for time.

The layout shown in Fig. 6.12 is with resource sharing.

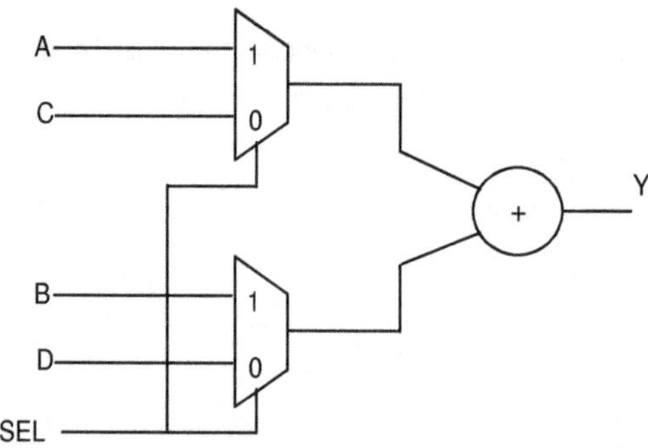

Fig. 6.12

The above layout will generate, if design is optimized for area. That means resource sharing is a technique for area optimization.

For resource sharing, operators must be of the same type and operands must be of the same width.

Forced resource sharing

Sharing of operators can be forced through coding style. It will minimize the amount of tool-specific feature.

The above functionality can be described as follows:

    NO1 <= A *when* SEL = '1' *else* C;
    NO2 <= B *when* SEL = '1' *else* D;
    Y <= NO1 + NO2;

This will generate the same type of hardware as shown above (with resource sharing).

6.7 Synthesis Guidelines

The performance of the synthesizer can be optimized by various techniques. Some of them are described here.

False paths

Synthesis tool should have control over critical path synthesis. It should remove all false paths. False paths can be removed by avoiding checking unnecessary conditions in *"if"* statements because they can create false paths.

For example, if one condition is checked in first level of *"if"*, then do not check it again in nested statements of same *"if"* as shown in following example:

> *if* (A) *then*
> *if* (C) *then*
> *if* (A) *then* -- avoid
> *if* (C) *then* -- avoid.

Unnecessary calculations in *"for"* loops

Avoid placing expressions that do not change inside *"for"* loops. Synthesizer unrolls *"for"* loops, so the structure inferred is repetitive. Moving unchanging expression outside the loop prevents synthesizer from spending time in optimizing redundant logic.

> *for* I *in* 0 *to* 4 *loop*
> NO1 <= NO2;   -- unchanging statement
> OUT1(I) <= IN1(I);
> *end loop;*

The unchanging statement should be pulled out of the loop as shown below:

> NO1 <= NO2;
> *for* I *in* 0 *to* 4 *loop*
> OUT1(I) <= IN1(I);
> *end loop;*

Restrict one clock to each module or to entire design

By restricting one clock to each module, the only need is to describe the relationship between the clock at the top level of the design hierarchy and each module clock.

Avoid complex operators

Arithmetic and relational operators are expensive. So to get better performance, they should be avoided as far as possible.

For example

> *if* (CLK'*event and* CLK = '1') *then*
> COUNT <= COUNT + 1;
> *if* (COUNT > "10011) *then*
> COUNT <= (*others* => '0');
> *end if* ;
> *end if* ;

This code can be modified slightly to get much better performance.

```
if ( CLK'event  and CLK = '1') then
    COUNT <= COUNT + 1;
    if ( COUNT > "10100") then
       COUNT <= (others => '0');
    end if;
end if;
```

Fan-out control

Larger the fan-out, greater is the delay. If the fan-out is beyond a limit, the tool will insert buffers, which will reduce the speed further.

The following example illustrates how fan-out could be controlled at design entry stage.

```
if ( CLK'event  and CLK = '1') then
        A <= C and D;
end if ;
    if ( A = "11") then - - - -
    if ( X = A ) then - - - -
    case  A  is
    when "00" =>  . . . . .
    when "01" => . . . .
        :
    end case;
    X <= A and B;
```

In the above code, the net "A" has high fan-out. In every statement "A" is used, in the case statement every assignment will have "A" associated with it.

This code can be changed to reduce the load on "A" and improve on timing.

```
if ( CLK'event  and CLK = '1') then
        A <= C and D;
        A1 <= C and D;
end if ;
    if (A = "11") then - - - -
    if (X = A) then - - - -
case A1  is
    when "00" =>  . . . . .
    when "01" => . . . .
        :
end case;
    X <= A and B;
```

Arranging expression trees for minimum delay

The designer can minimize delay through an expression tree by rearranging the sequence of the operations.

Consider the statement Z <= A + B + C + D which will generate the structure as shown in Fig. 6.13.

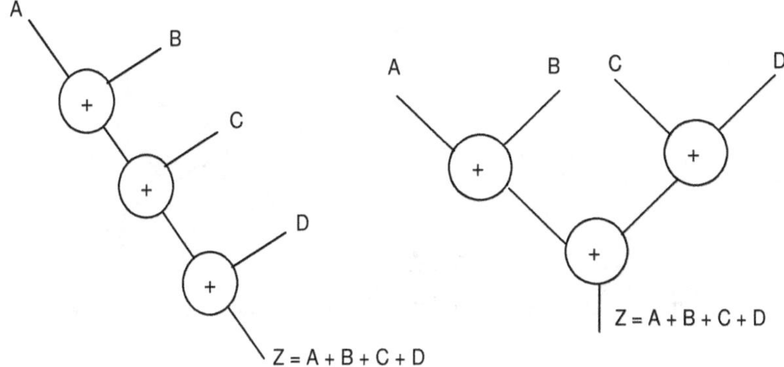

Fig. 6.13   **Fig. 6.14**

The above statement can be written as shown below to optimize the speed.

Z < = (A + B) + (C + D);

This will generate the structure as shown in Fig. 6.14.

Proper use of parentheses guides the synthesis tools in eliminating common subexpressions.

Consider the following expressions:

Z1 <= A + B + C;

Z2 <= Z1 + B + C + D;

This will generate the structure as shown in Fig. 6.15.

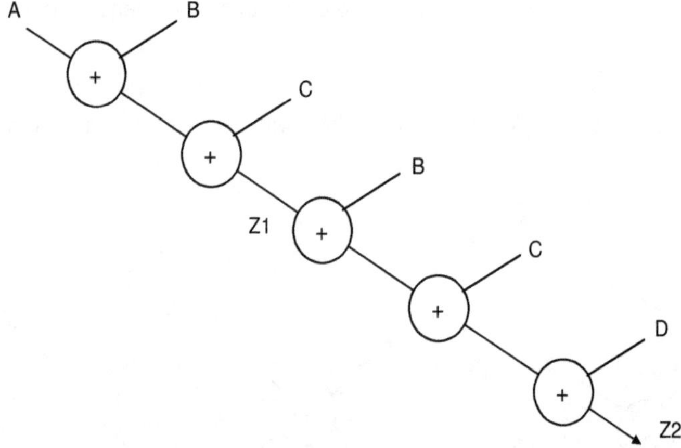

Fig. 6.15

Using parentheses, the logic can share on adder for inputs B and C, as shown below.

Z1 <= A + (B + C);

Z2 <= Z1 + (B + C) + D;

This will generate the structure as shown in Fig. 6.16.

- Separate the modules with different optimization goals (speed, power, area).

- If port is of type integer then range should be specified, otherwise it will take default range (i.e. 32 bits).

- Avoid gated clocks because it may lead to glitches and metastability.

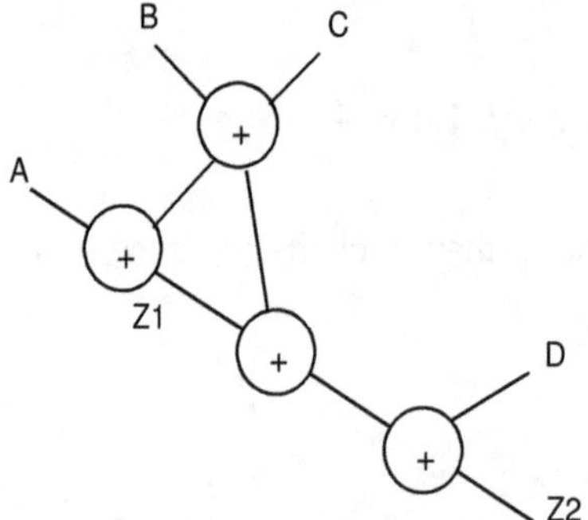

Fig. 6.16

- Do not use positive edge-triggered and negative edge-triggered flip-flops in same design. Separate out them in different units. i.e. avoid mixing clock edges.
- Avoid over constraining the design because critical path is having preference in placement. If number of critical paths increases then design will not optimize fully.
- Avoid use of mode buffer, as most ASIC vendors do not support mode buffer in their libraries.

  If a port is declared as buffer, it can only be mapped with port of buffer mode of other entities only. This can cause problem in hierarchical design (structural modeling).

6.8 Place and Route (PAR)

Place and route tools are used to implement the design in the target technology device by taking the design netlist. The place and route tools place each primitive (logic cell) from the netlist into an appropriate location on the target device and the route (lying of wires) signals between the primitives to connect the devices according to the netlist. Place and route tools are very architecture and device dependent.

Fig. 6.17 shows a dataflow diagram of the place and route tools. Input to the place and route tools are the net list and possibly timing constraints. The timing constraints give the place and route tools an indication about which signal have critical timing associated with them and to route these nets in the most timing efficient manner.

These nets are typically identified during the static timing analysis process during synthesis.

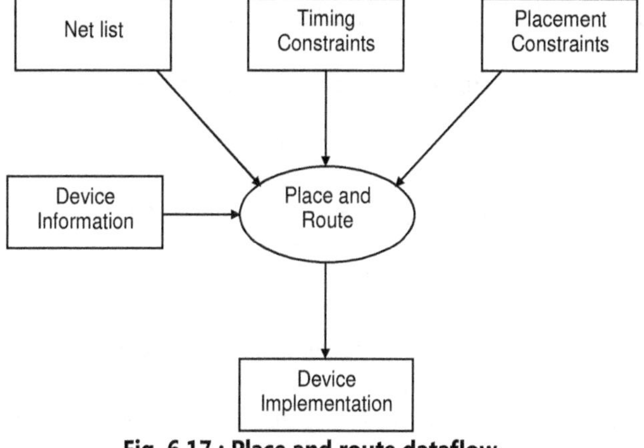

Fig. 6.17 : Place and route dataflow

These constraints tell the place and route tools to place the primitives in close proximity to one another and to use the fastest routing. The closer the cells are, the shorter the routed signals will be and the shorter time delay.

Some place and route tools allow the designer to specify the placement of large parts of the design. This process is known as **floorplanning**. Floorplanning allows the user to pick locations on the chip for large blocks of the design so that routing wires are as short as possible. The designer lays out blocks on the chip as general areas. The floorplanner feeds this information to the place and route tools so that these blocks are placed properly. After the cells are placed, the router makes the appropriate connections.

After all the cells are placed and routed, the output of the place and route tools consists of data files that can be used to implement the chip. The other output from the place and route software is a file used to generate the timing file. This file describes the actual timing of the programmed device. The most common format of this file is SDF (Standard Delay Format). SDF is used to back annotate the post route timing information from place and route tools into the post-layout timing simulation.

Place and route process

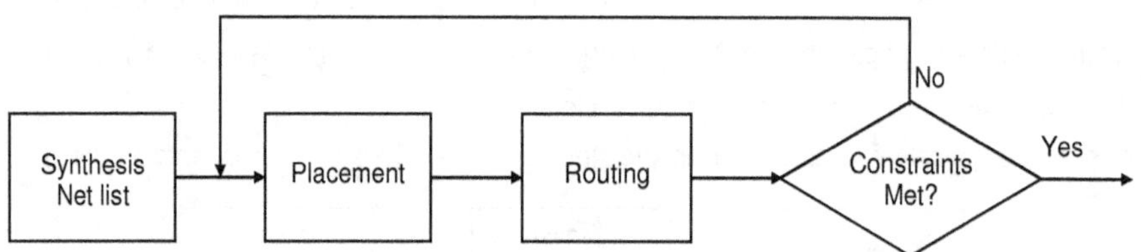

Fig. 6.18: Place and route process

The place and route process places each macro from the synthesis net list into an available location on the target silicon and connects the macros using routing resources available on the target silicon. The place and route process is shown in Fig. 6.18.

The synthesis netlist is input to the placement process. The placement process analyzes all of the macros wed in the design and their connectivity to try to determine an optimal placement for the macros. After a trial placement and signal route is attempted, the design is analyzed with respect to timing constraints. If the timing constraints are not met, the place and route software continues to try different placements and signal routing to try to meet the constraints.

Typical target devices have areas of the chip where logical functions are placed, and areas where interconnect signals are routed to connect the logical functions. This is shown in Fig. 6.19.

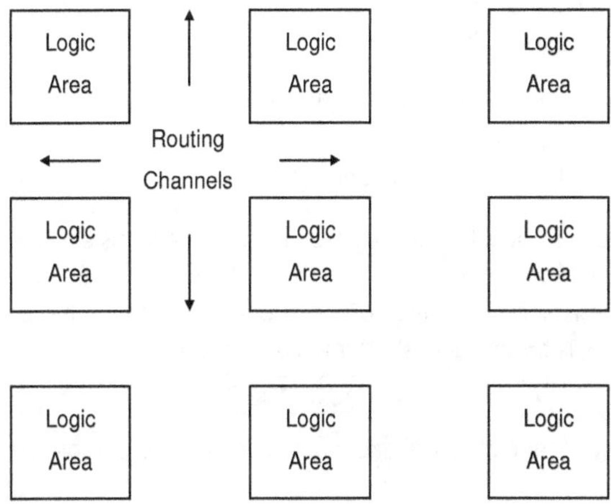

Fig. 6.19: Chip architecture

Logic areas contain the logical gates to implement the Boolean function of the design. Routing channels contain the signals that are used to connect the logical gates together. The routing channels contain programmable interconnect wires.

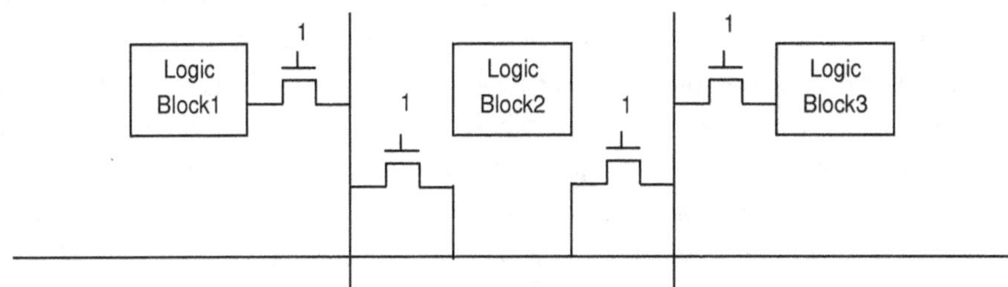

Fig. 6.20: Logic block interconnection

By enabling the proper sets of transistor gates, signal interconnection between logic gates can be formed as shown in Fig 6.20.

To make a connection from logic block 1 to logic block 3, all of the switches (transistor as switch) shown need to be enabled with logic 1 value. The control signals of the transistor are stored in a loadable RAM. The place and route generates the RAM image to be loaded into the RAM on the device.

The routing channels contain vertical and horizontal lines. The horizontal wires connect devices within a row, while the vertical lines allow connections across rows.

The job of the place and route tool is to create the programming files which will be used to specify the logic function of the logic macros in the logic areas and then switch programming of the wires used to connect the macros together.

To get the highest utilization, the place and route tools should pack as many of the logical functions into a logic area as possible and then should use as much as local routing resources as possible to connect these functions.

The place and route tool must try to minimize long connections and the number of switches for a particular signal to create designs with the highest speed. As short wires have less capacitance and resistance and, therefore, can operate at much higher speeds, and hence place and route tool is try to create short interconnections.

QUESTIONS

1.　What are the different inputs and outputs of synthesis tool? Elaborate optimization process.　　**(8 Marks, May 2001)**

2.　What is RTL? What are its advantages while writing VHDL code? Give example.　　**(9 Marks, May 2005)**

3.　List and explain the different constraints which are normally given by designer while doing synthesis and implementation.　　**(8 Marks, Dec. 2003)**

4.　What is meant by cell in technology library? What are the parameters of a standard cell?　　**(8 Marks, May 2005)**

5.　What is flattening and factoring? How does it help designer to obtain optimum performance? Explain with suitable example.　　**(8 Marks, Dec. 2003)**

6.　What are flattening and factoring in synthesis? What are merits and demerits of each and what criteria should be followed for good design?　　**(7 Marks, Dec. 2004)**

7.　What is meant by Place and Route (PAR)?　　**(3 Marks, Dec. 2004)**

8.　What do you mean by synthesis? What are inputs and outputs of synthesis? What are the constraints involved?

9.　Write a short note on synthesis issues.　　**(6 Marks, May 2002, Nov. 2001)**

10.　Explain optimization process in synthesis.

11.　Draw and explain synthesis flow.

12.　Explain floorplanning and place and route in detail.

13.　Explain the step by step process of synthesis.　　**(8 Marks, May 05)**

◊◊◊

Topics discussed: Sequential machine, Mealy and Moore machines, Designing FSM, FSM modeling using VHDL.

7.1 Introduction

Digital systems are divided into two classes:
  i.   Combinational system
  ii. Sequential system.

A **combinational system** is a digital system in which the value of the output at any time (t) depends only on the value of the input at that time (t). No feedback path can exist from output to input. No need of memory element.

A **sequential system** is a digital system in which the value of the output at any time (t) depends on the value of the input at that time (t) and on previous value of input/output. At least one feedback path exist from output to input. Memory element is needed to store previous values of input/output.

7.2 Block Diagram of a Sequential Circuit

A block diagram of a sequential circuit is shown in Fig. 7.1.

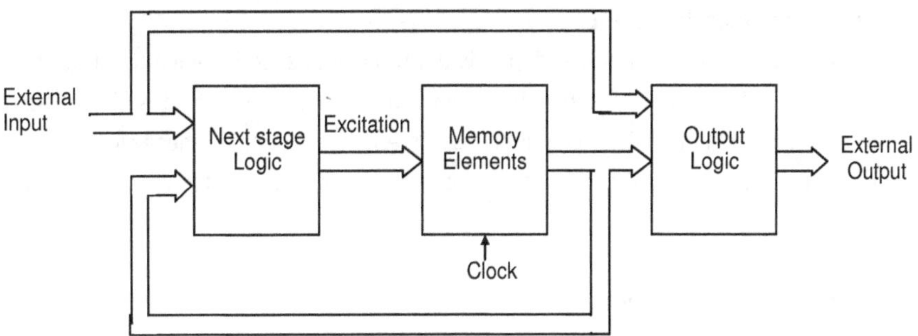

Fig. 7.1: Block diagram of a sequential circuit

Sequential circuit consists of next state logic, memory element, and output logic. Next state logic is a combinational circuit which accepts digital signal from external inputs and from outputs of memory element and generates signals for output logic and for inputs to memory element referred to as excitation.

A memory element is some medium in which one bit of information (1 or 0) can be stored or retained until necessary, and thereafter its contents can be replaced by a new value. The contents of memory element can be changed by the outputs of the combinational circuit which are connected to its input.

Output logic is a combinational circuit which performs some operation on external inputs and memory outputs to generate the external outputs.

The external output of a sequential circuit depends on the external inputs and the present contents of the memory elements. The present contents of the memory elements are referred to as the **present state** of the memory element (or system). The new contents of the memory elements are referred to as the **next state**. The next state depends on the present state and external inputs. Hence, the output of a sequential circuit is a function of the time sequence of inputs and the internal states.

Flip-flops, Registers, Counters are examples of sequential circuit.

7.3 Types of Sequential Circuits

Sequential circuits are classified into two main categories, known as asynchronous and synchronous sequential circuits depending on timing of their signals.

Asynchronous sequential circuits

A sequential circuit whose behaviour depends upon the sequence in which the input signals change is referred as an asynchronous sequential circuit. The output will be affected whenever the input changes. The commonly used memory elements in these circuits are time delay devices. These can be regarded as combinational circuits with feedback. They do not require clock pulses.

Synchronous sequential circuits

A sequential circuit whose behaviour can be defined from the knowledge of its signal at discrete instants of time is referred to as synchronous sequential circuit. In these systems, the memory elements are affected only at discrete instant of time. The synchronization is achieved by a timing device known as system clock which generates a periodic train of clock pulses as shown in Fig. 7.2. The outputs are affected only with the application of a clock pulse.

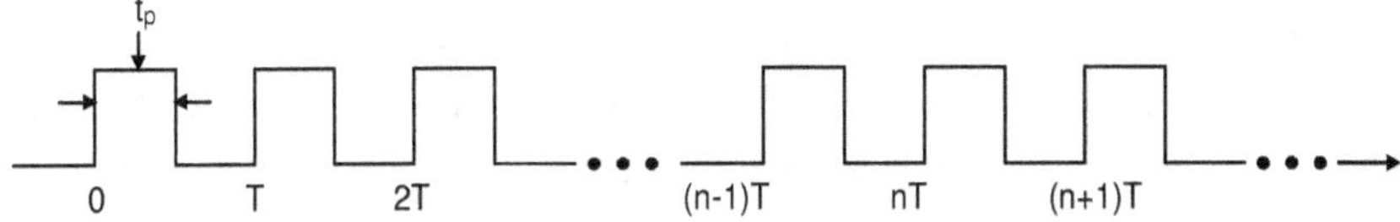

Fig. 7.2: A train of pulses

This clock signal is the "command signal" that causes the memory element (flip-flop) to READ and STORE the code at its input.

Synchronous circuits have gained considerable domination and wide popularity and are also known as clocked sequential circuits, whereas design of asynchronous circuits is more tedious and difficult for their use.

Asynchronous versus Synchronous sequential circuits

- In a clocked sequential circuit, a change of state occurs only in response to a synchronizing clock pulse. All the flip-flops are simultaneously affected by a common clock pulse. In an asynchronous sequential circuit, the state of the circuit can change immediately when an input change occurs. It does not use a clock.
- In synchronous sequential circuit, input changes are assumed to occur between clock pulses. The circuit must be in the stable state before next clock pulse arrives. In asynchronous sequential circuits, input changes should occur only when the circuit is in a stable state.
- In synchronous sequential circuits, the speed of operation depends on the maximum allowed clock frequency. Asynchronous sequential circuits do not require clock pulses and they can change the state with the input change. Therefore, in general, asynchronous sequential circuits are faster than the synchronous sequential circuit.
- In synchronous sequential circuits, the memory elements are clocked flip-flops. In asynchronous sequential circuits, the memory elements are either latches (unclocked flip-flops) or gate circuits with feedback producing the effect of latch operation.
- In synchronous sequential circuits, any number of inputs can change simultaneously during the absence of the clock. In asynchronous sequential circuits, only one input is allowed to change at a time in the case of the level inputs and only one pulse input is allowed to be present in the case of the pulse inputs. If more than one level input change simultaneously or more than one pulse input is present, the circuit makes erroneous state transitions due to different delay paths for each input variable.

7.4 Timing Considerations in Sequential Circuits

It should be noted that following three important timing constraints (specifications) are to be considered in sequential circuits: Setup time, Hold time, Propagation delay. These timing specifications determine the maximum allowable clock frequency for sequential circuits.

Setup time

The definition of setup time is the time required for the input data to settle in before the triggering edge of the clock. For example, for a D-flip-flop, the D input must be stable for a certain amount of time before the active edge of the clock. This time period is called as "setup time" (t_s).

If setup time specification is ignored, unpredictable behaviour like missed data and possible partial transient outputs can be expected.

Hold time

The definition of hold time is the time required for the data to remain stable after the triggering edge of the clock. For example, for a D-flip-flop, the D input must be stable for a certain amount of time after the active edge of the clock. This time period is called as "hold time" (t_h).

Fig. 7.3 shows the setup time and hold time for a D flip-flop that changes its state on the rising edge of the clock.

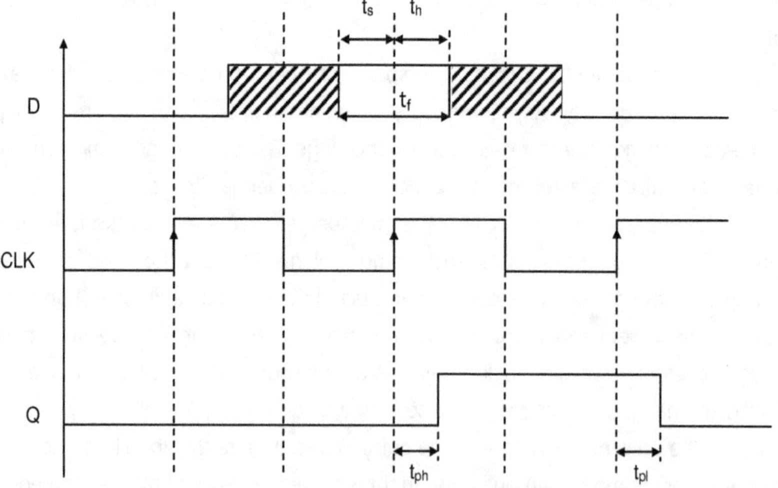

Fig. 7.3 : Setup and hold time for D flip-flop

D can change at any time during the shaded region on the diagram, but it must be stable during the interval t_s before the active clock edge and t_h after the active clock edge. If D changes during the interval t_f, flip-flop output can not be determined. Flip-flop may output a short pulse or even go into oscillation.

Propagation delay

Propagation delay is the time difference between the time the clock changes to the time output Q changes. The propagation delay for a low to high transition in Q is t_{ph} and for a high to low transition is t_{pl}.

7.5 Finite State Machines (FSM)

A finite state machine is a digital system that traverses through a predetermined sequence of states in an orderly fashion. A state is a set of values measured at different parts of the circuit. Normally, the sequential circuits are considered as state machines.

Sequential properties

1. The system must have some memory capability or memory element.
2. The system must have at least one feedback path from the memory element to the system input.

A sequential machine (state machine) can be defined in practical terms as follows.
A circuit having the two basic sequential properties described above and in addition to these properties, it must, under an input condition control, exhibit a "cyclic" nature.

A finite-state machine is defined as; a sequential circuit that has some practical bounds governing the number of different conditions (STATES) in which a sequential machine can reside.

Example: Microprocessor-based system or computer is by definition a sequential machine. But as it can reside in large number of states, for practical purpose the number of states is not finite. So it is not a finite-state machine. A 4 bit binary counter is an example of finite-state machine, as it has 16 possible states.

7.5.1 General Model of a Sequential or Finite State Machine

Fig. 7.4 shows the general model of a sequential machine or FSM.

The function of combinational block labelled Next state decoder is to decode the inputs from the outside world and present state of the machine (stored by the memory) and to generate as its output, a code called Next state code. This Next state code will become present state when the memory loads and stores it. This process is defined as a STATE CHANGE or a CHANGE OF STATE. State changing is a continual process with each new state and the present input conditions being decoded to form the new next state codes. Each new succeeding state is a function of the present inputs and the past history of these inputs.

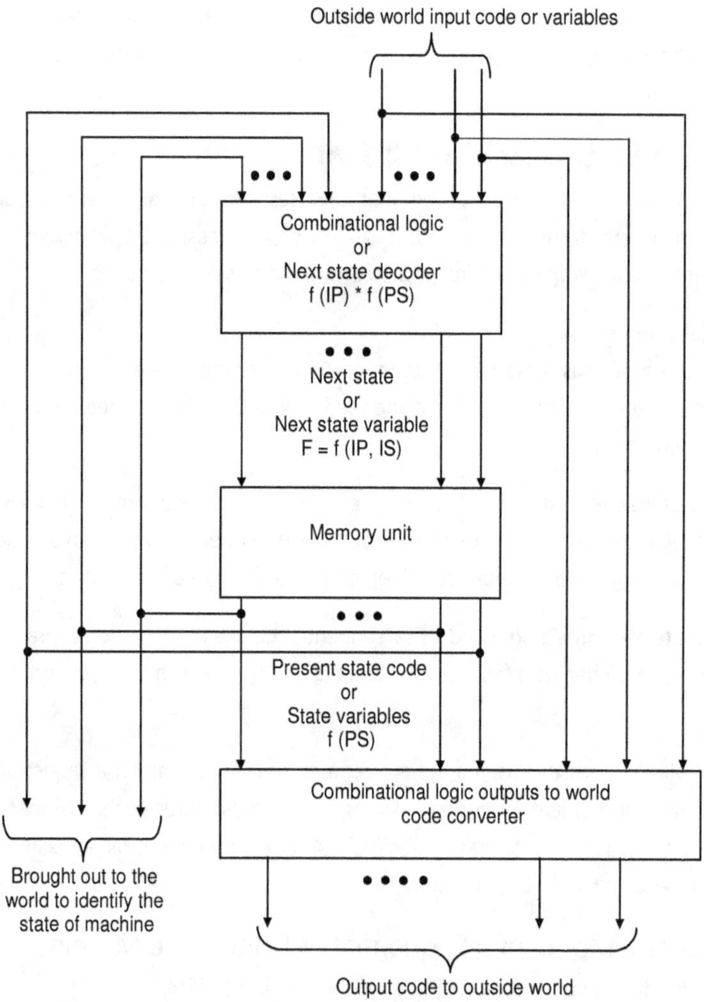

Fig. 7.4: General model of FSM

The combinational logic block in Fig. 7.4 labelled the output to world code converter has the basic function of decoding the present state of the machine and present input conditions for the purpose of generating the desired control outputs to the outside world.

7.5.2 Classification of FSM

The following models are derived from the basic model shown in Fig. 7.4 by a process of degeneration as shown in Figs 7.5 through 7.9.

For the most part these machine classes are self-explanatory; however, there are three classes worth mentioning. They are the class A, B and C. The class A machine is defined as a **MEALY machine** named after G.H. Mealy one of the pioneers of sequential design.

The basic distinction of Mealy machine is that the outputs to the outside world are function of two sets of variables:
1. The present input conditions
2. The present state of the machine.

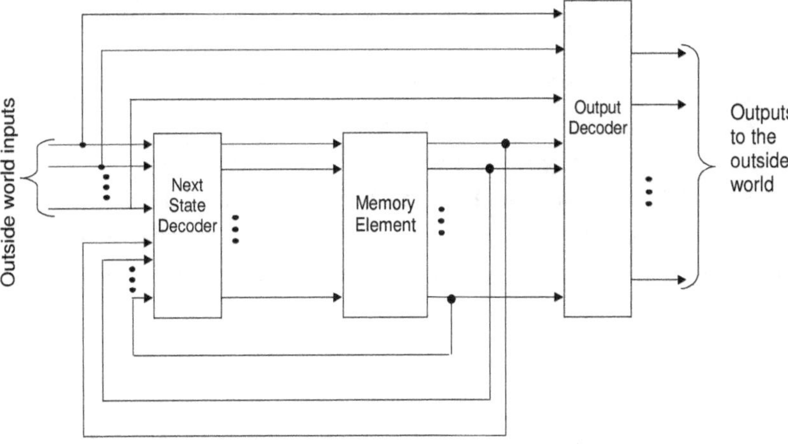

Fig. 7.5: Class A machine, referred to as Mealy machine

The class B and C machines are defined as **Moore machines**, named after E.F. Moore, another pioneer in sequential circuits. The basic distinction of a Moore machine is that its output is strictly a function of the state of the machine.

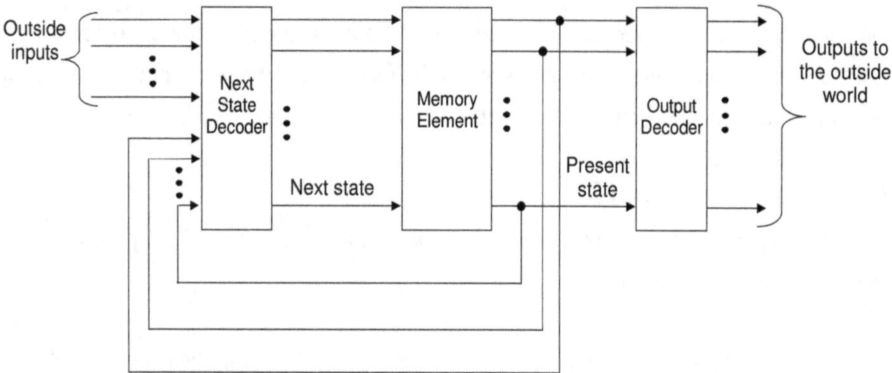

Fig. 7.6: Class B machine, referred to as Moore machine

Both the Mealy and Moore machines are widely used and it is possible to derive machines that are mixtures of both; in other words, some outputs are conditional on both the input and the state of the machine, where others are dependent only on the state of the machine.

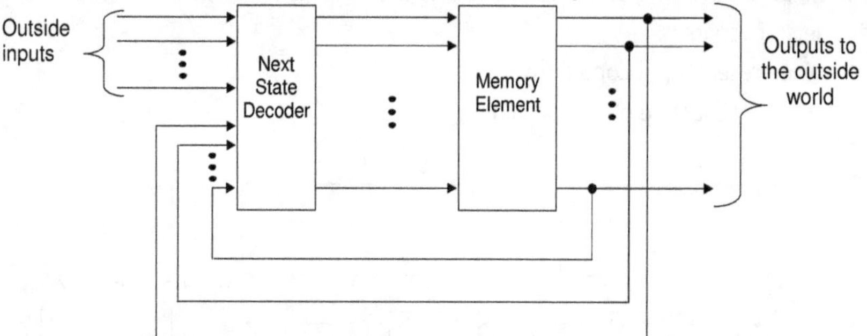

Fig. 7.7: Class C machine; Moore machine without an output decoder

The class A, B and C circuits with a single input form the general model for a counter circuit in which the events to be counted are entered directly into the memory element or through the next state decoder logic.

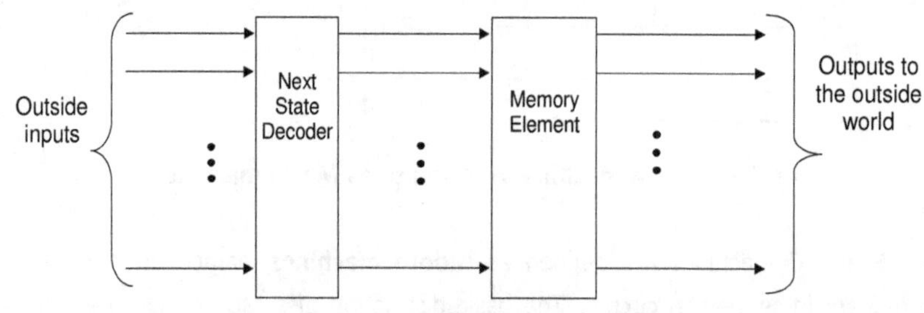

Fig. 7.8: Class D machine; look-up memory

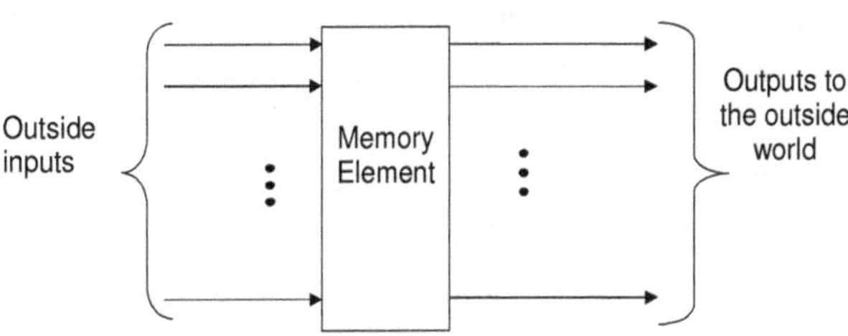

Fig. 7.9: Class E machine

The class A, B and C machines are equally applicable for both asynchronous as well as synchronous circuits, and the minimum number of inputs to any of these machines is one. For synchronous machines, that one input must be the system clock.

7.6 Design of Sequential Circuit

7.6.1 State Description and State Diagram

Sequential Circuits have the capability to retain the effect of all past inputs on present and future outputs. The memory elements retain the complete sequence of inputs at a time t_0 and able to determine the output at any time $t > t_0$. For simplification, the values of the input sequences can be grouped into a finite number of classes in such a way that all time functions having the same effect on the output at time $t \geq t_0$ are included in the same class. So the determination of output does not require the whole input sequence because knowing the class of the function is enough to determine the output. The class is kept in an auxiliary variable S called the state. Since the number of classes are finite, such systems are also called finite state machines.

The state description of a sequential circuit uses three time variables-the input, the state and the output. There are two state transition functions:
1) The state transition function which produces the next state (at time t+1) as a function of the present input X(t) and present state S(t).
2) The output function which produces the present output z(t) as a function of the present input and present state.

S(t) is known as the present state and **S(t+1) is called the next state. The transitions** and output functions are stored in a **state table**. The state table consists of first listing of all possible binary combinations of present state and inputs. The next state values are then determined from the logic diagram or from the state equations. For each present state, there are two possible next states and outputs, depending on the values of the input.

The information available in a state table can be represented **graphically** in a **state diagram**.

As combinational circuits can be described in a tabular format called truth table, similarly the behavior of sequential circuits can be described in a tabular format called **state table** and can be represented graphically on a state diagram.

State Diagram

The graphical representation of state to state transitions of a sequential circuit is called the state diagram.

An example of a state diagram is shown in Fig. 7.10 which illustrates the state-of-interest, five important and required pieces of information related to each state of the machine.

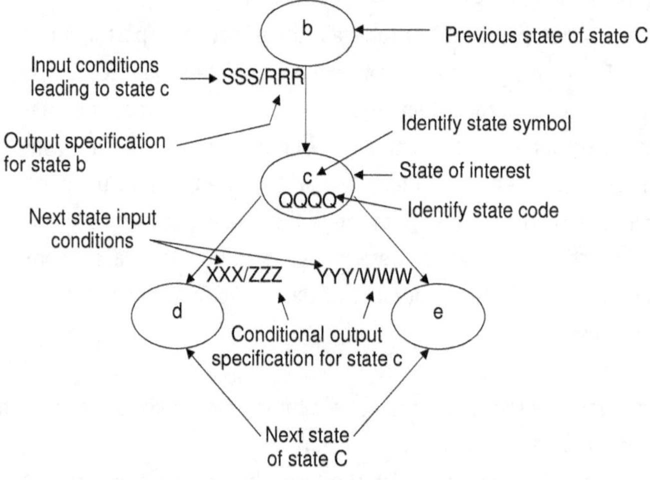

Fig. 7.10: A segment of a state diagram

As shown, the state diagram is an array of "bubbles" connected by directed line segments with arrowheads. Each bubble represents a state of the machine and the line segments are graphical indications of state changes. The five important and descriptive pieces of information for each state are given and labelled as follows:

1) Some state identifying symbol or code.
2) The previous state of the state-of-interest.
3) The input conditions leading to the state-of-interest.
4) The output specification for the state-of-interest.
5) The next states and next state branching conditions for the state-of-interest.

Moore machine

As already seen, the output signals are only dependent on the present state for the Moore machine. The output signals are usually drawn inside the state bubbles. For example, the Moore machine's state diagram is shown in Fig. 7.11 and block diagram is shown in Fig. 7.12.

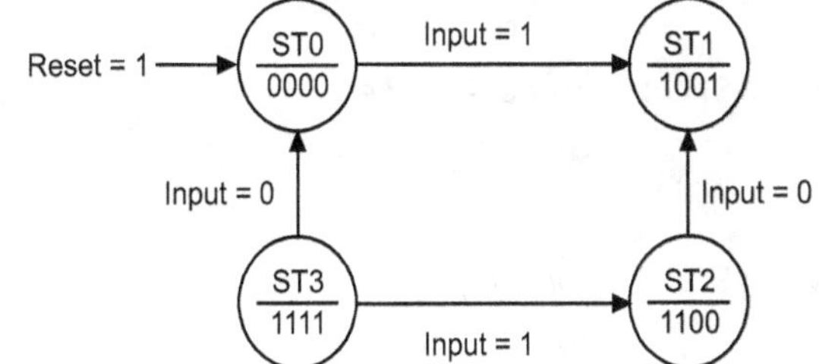

Fig. 7.11: State diagram of Moore machine

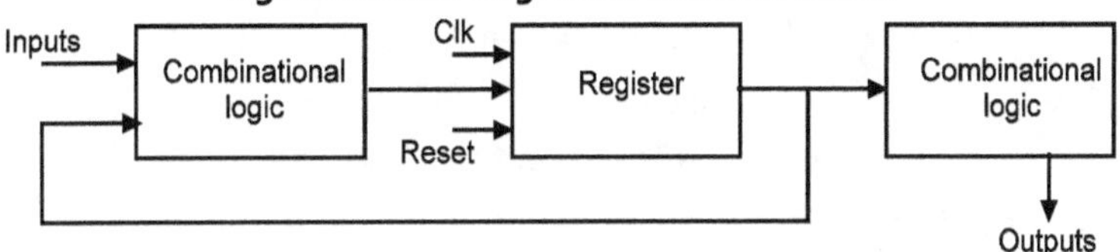

Fig. 7.12: Block diagram of Moore machine

In state ST0, the output signal has the value "0000", and in state ST1, the value "1001". Now, we will write VHDL coding for the above state machine.

```
Entity MooreSM is
        port (clk, input), reset: in std_logic;
        output: out std_logic);
end MooreSM;

    architecture Moore_arch of MooreSM is
        type state_type is (ST0, ST1, ST2, ST3);
        signal state: state_type;
```

```vhdl
begin
    P0: process (clk, reset) --- clocked process
    begin
        if reset = '1' then
            state < = ST0;
        elsif clk'event and clk = '1' then
            case state is
                when ST0 =>    if input = '1' then
                               state <= ST1;
                               end if;
                when ST1 =>    if input = '0' then
                               state < = ST2;
                               end if;
                when ST2 =>    if input = '1' then
                               state < = ST3;
                               end if;
                when ST3 =>    if input = '0' then
                               state < = ST0;
                               end if;
            end case;
        end if;
    end process P0;
P1: process (state) - - combinational process
begin
    case state is
        when ST0 => output < = "0000";
        when ST1 => output < = "1001";
        when ST2 => output < = "1100";
        when ST3 => output < = "1111";
    end case;
  end process;
end Moore_arch;
```

Above VHDL code consists of three parts:

(1) Declaration,

(2) Clocked process,

(3) Combinational process.

In declaration part, state is a signal from type state_type. Any name can be chosen for the state.

The process P0 is the clocked process. The clocked process decides when the state machine should change state. Based on the present state and the value of the input signals, the state machine can change state at every active clock edge. After that, case command is used to check which state the machine is in.

The process P1 is the combinational process, because it assigns the output signals their value depending on the present state.

Mealy machine

Mealy machine state diagram is as shown in Fig. 7.13, the output signals are dependent on both present states and all input signals. It means the output signals change immediately if the input signals change or if the state is changed.

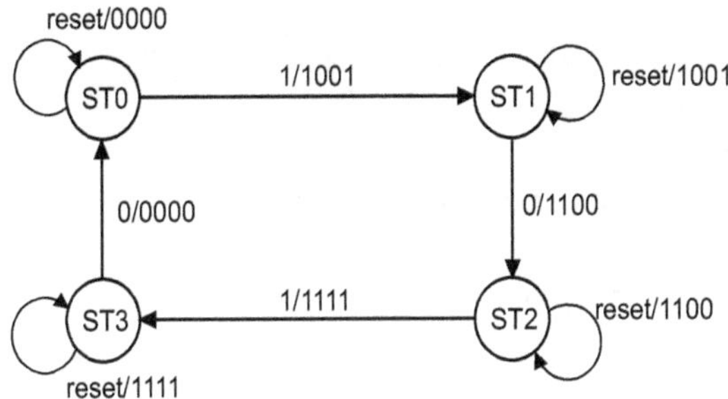

Fig. 7.13: State diagram of Mealy machine

The difference between the Moore and Mealy machines is the combinational output signal process. In Mealy machine, the output signal in combinational process should be a function of the state vector and all of the inputs. The clocked process in Mealy and Moore machines is identical.

The block diagram of Mealy machine is shown in Fig. 7.14.

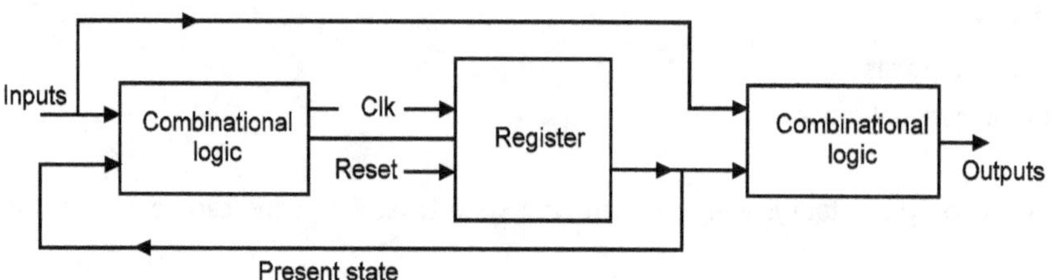

Fig. 7.14: Block diagram of Mealy machine

Next, we will write VHDL code for the above Mealy machine.

```
Entity MealySM is
    port (clock, reset, input: in std_logic;
            output: out std_logic_vector (3 downto 0));
end MealySM;

    architecture Mealy_arch of MealySM is
        type state_type is (ST0, ST1, ST2, ST3);
        signal state: state_type;
    begin
        P0: process (clock, reset)
        begin
            if reset = '1' then
                state <= ST0;
            elsif clock'event and clock = '1' then
                case state is
                    when ST0  ⇒   if input = '1' then
                                    state < = ST1;
                                  end if;
                    when ST1  ⇒   if input = '0' then
                                    state < = ST2;
                                  end if;
                    when ST2  ⇒   if input = '1' then
                                    state < = ST3;
                                  end if;
```

```vhdl
            when ST3  =>   if input = '0' then
                              state < = ST0;
                           end if;
      end case;
   end if;
end process P0;
P1: process (state, input)
begin
   case state is
      when ST0  =>   if input = '1' then
                        output < = "1001",
                     else
                        output < = "0000";
                     end if;
      when ST1  =>   if input = '0' then
                        output < = "1100",
                     else
                        output < = "1001";
                     end if;
      when ST2  =>   if input = '1' then
                        output < = "1111",
                     else
                        output < = "1100";
                     end if;
      when ST3 =>    if input = '0' then
                        output < = "0000",
                     else
                        output < = "1111";
                     end if;
      end case;
   end if;
end process p1;
end Mealy_arch;
```

The output signals for Moore and Mealy machines are from combinational logic. The state machine can have spike-free outputs at a certain temperature or supply voltage. But as temperature or supply voltage changes, it generates spike. Normally, such spikes are not important. In synchronous design, it is only at the active clock edge that the data signal must be stable.

For spike-free outputs, the following methods can be used:
1) Output - state machine
2) Moore machine with clocked outputs.
3) Mealy machine with clocked outputs.

Moore machine with clocked outputs

In this the outputs are synchronized with extra D flip-flop to obtain spike-free outputs. It means that the outputs are a clock cycle behind the ordinary Moore machine's outputs. State diagram of Moore machine with clocked outputs is shown in Fig. 7.15 and the block diagram is shown in Fig. 7.16.

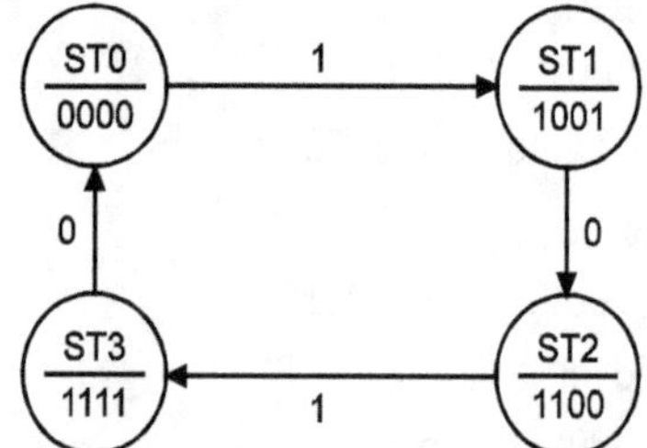

Fig. 7.15: State diagram of a Moore machine with clocked outputs

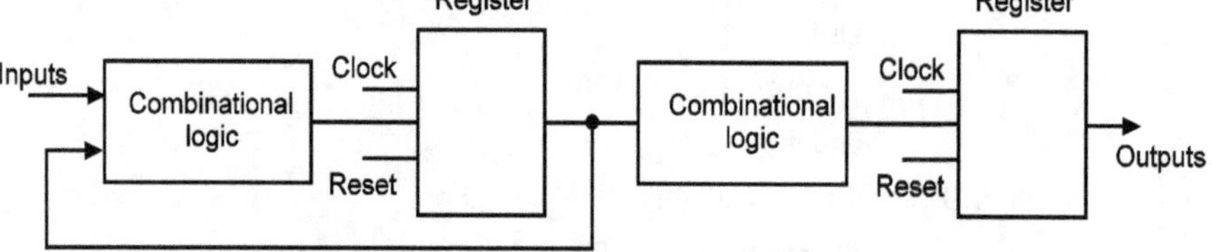

Fig. 7.16: Block diagram of a Moore machine with clocked outputs

Now, the VHDL coding is as follows:

```
Entity Mooreclk is
        port (clock, input, reset: in std_logic;
                output: out std_logic);
end Mooreclk;
```

```
architecture Moore_arch of Mooreclk is
    type state_type is (ST0, ST1, ST2, ST3);
    signal state: state_type;
begin
    P0: process (clock, reset)
    begin
        if reset = '1' then
                state <= ST0;
                output <= (others => '0');
        elsif clockevent and clock = '1' then
                case state is
                    when ST0 => if input = '1' then
                            state <= ST1;
                        end if;
                            output <= "0000";
                    when ST1 => if input = '0' then
                            state <= ST2;
                        end if;
                            output <= "1001";
                    when ST2 => if input = '1' then
                            state <= ST3;
                        end if;
                            output <= "1100";
                    when ST3 => if input = '0' then
                            state <= ST0;
                        end if;
                            output <= "1111";
                end case;
        end if;
    end process;
end Moorearch;
```

Mealy machine with clocked outputs

With clocked outputs, all the outputs are synchronized with an extra D-type flip-flop. In this also, the outputs on a clocked Mealy machine are a clock cycle behind the ordinary Mealy machine's outputs. Fig. 7.17 shows the state diagram for the Mealy machine and Fig. 7.18 shows the block diagram.

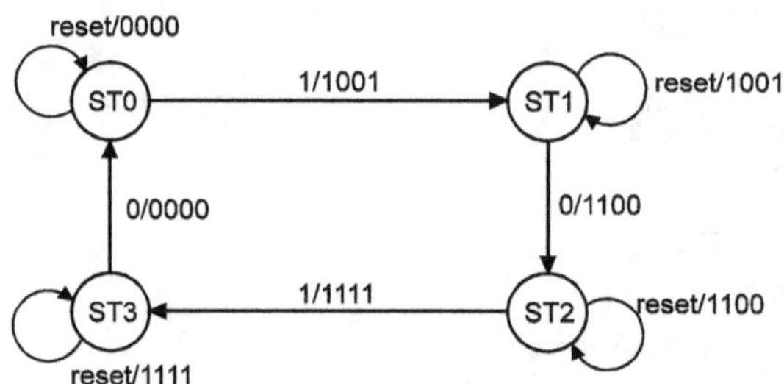

Fig. 7.17: State diagram for a Mealy machine with clocked outputs

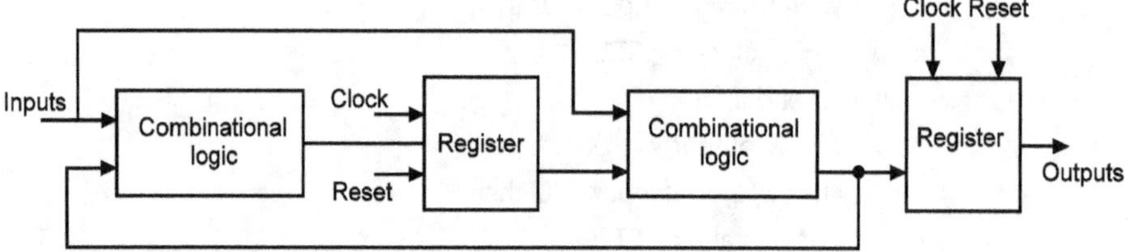

Fig. 7.18: Block diagram for a Mealy machine with clocked outputs

Now, the VHDL coding for the above state machine is,

```
Entity Mealyclk is
port (clock, reset, input: in std_logic);
    output: out std_logic_vector (3 downto 0));
end Mealy clk;

Architecture Mealy_arch of Mealyclk is
    type state_type is (ST0, ST1, ST2, ST3);
    signal state: state_type;
begin
    P0: process (clock, reset)
    begin
        if reset = '1' then
                state <= ST0;
                output <= (others => '0');
        elsif clock'event and clock = '1' then
```

```
                case state is
        when ST0 => if input = '1' then
                        state <= ST1;
                        output <= "1100";
                    else
                        output <= "1001";
                    end if;
        when ST1 => if input = '0' then
                        state <= ST2;
                        output <= "1100";
                    else
                        output <= "1001";
                    end if;
        when ST2 => if input = '1' then
                        state <= ST3;
                        output <= "1111";
                    else
                        output <= "1100";
                    end if;
        when ST3 => if input = '0' then
                        state <= ST0;
                        output <= "0000";
                    else
                        output <= "1111";
                    end if;
        end case;
        end if;
        end process;
    end Mealy_arch;
```

State Coding

For the synthesis tool, we can use any coding method, because it does not affect the function of the state machine. The different types of state coding are:

- Sequential coding
- Gray coding
- One-hot coding
- Random
- Auto

Suppose, we are using following four states for the state machine. The states are defined as follows in the VHDL code

        type state_type is (ST0, ST1, ST2, ST3);

The following state coding can be obtained for the different coding methods.

Gray coding	Sequential coding	One-hot
ST0 = "00"	ST0 = "00"	ST0 = "0001"
ST1 = "01"	ST1 = "01"	ST1 = "0010"
ST2 = "11"	ST2 = "10"	ST2 = "0100"
ST3 = "10"	ST3 = "11"	ST3 = "1000"

There are some synthesis tools available which include a state optimizer. The state optimizer makes it possible to determine the state coding when synthesizing the VHDL code. If we are optimizing a state machine without using a special state optimizer, then sequential state coding is obtained. In Gray coding, just one bit in the state vector changes value, when the state machine changes state.

One hot encoding has as many flip-flops as it has states. It means that the number of flip-flops required in one-hot encoding becomes larger. In FPGA architecture, there are lots of flip-flops. It means one hot encoding is effective when synthesizing the FPGA.

UART

Universal Asynchronous Receiver Transmitter is the serial communication interface. RxD is the received serial data signal and TxD is the transmitted data signal. Asynchronous serial data transmission is shown in Fig. 7.19. The Data is transmitted asynchronously, one byte at a time. When there is no data to transmit, Data D remains high.

At the start of transmission, Data D goes low for one bit time, which is referred to as the start bit. Then eight data bits are transmitted, LSB first Data bit at LSB is transmitted first. Eighth data bit can be used as a parity bit. When text is transmitted, ASCII code is used. After eight bits are transmitted, D must go high, for atleast one bit time, which is called as the stop bit.

Data Transmission:

As shown in Fig. 7.19, Serial Data Transmission for UART takes place on TxD pin. During transmission of data, the UART takes eight bits of parallel data and converts the data to a serial bit stream which consists of the data format as shown in Fig. 7.19, a start bit ('0'), 8 data bits (LSB first), and stop bit ('1').

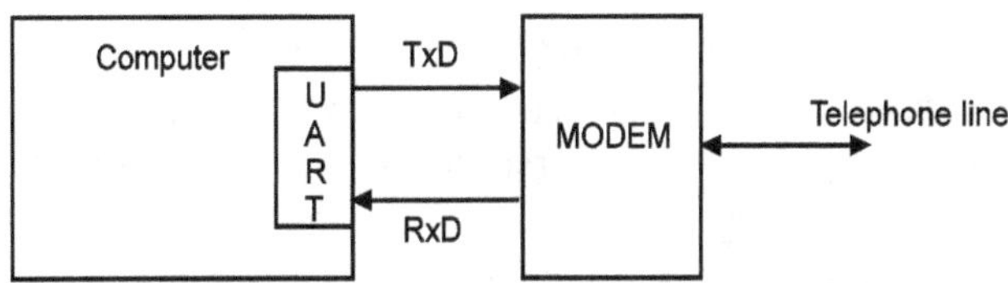

Fig. 7.19: Serial data transmission using UART

The registers used while transmission of data through UART are as follows:
1) TDR i.e. Transmit Data Register
2) TSR i.e. Transmit Shift Register
3) SCCR i.e. Serial Communication Control Register.
4) SCSR i.e. Serial Communication Status Register.

UART block diagram is shown in Fig. 7.20.

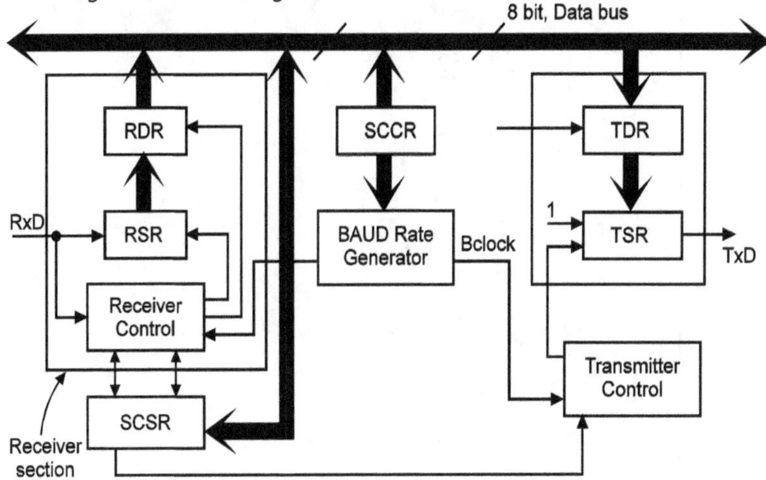

Fig. 7.20: UART block diagram

UART block diagram has three main components:
1) Baud Rate Generator
2) Transmitter Section
3) Receiver Section.

Baud Rate Generator divides the system clock to provide the Bit clock (Bclock), with a period equal to one bit time and also Bclock × 8. The Bclock × 8 has a frequency eight times the Bclock frequency.

Transmitter section has the output pin TxD, to transmit the data in serial format. The SCSR register has a bit TDRE (i.e. transmit data register empty). This bit is set when TDR is empty. When the microcontroller is ready to transmit the data, the following steps take place.

1) Microcontroller first checks the bit TDRE. If this bit is '1', then it loads a byte of data into TDR and clears TDRE.

2) The UART transfers data from TDR to TSR and then sets TDRE.

3) The UART outputs a start bit ('0') for one bit time, and then TSR register is used to transmit one bit of data at a time. The TSR bits are shifted to the right to transmit the eight data bits followed by a stop bit (logic '1').

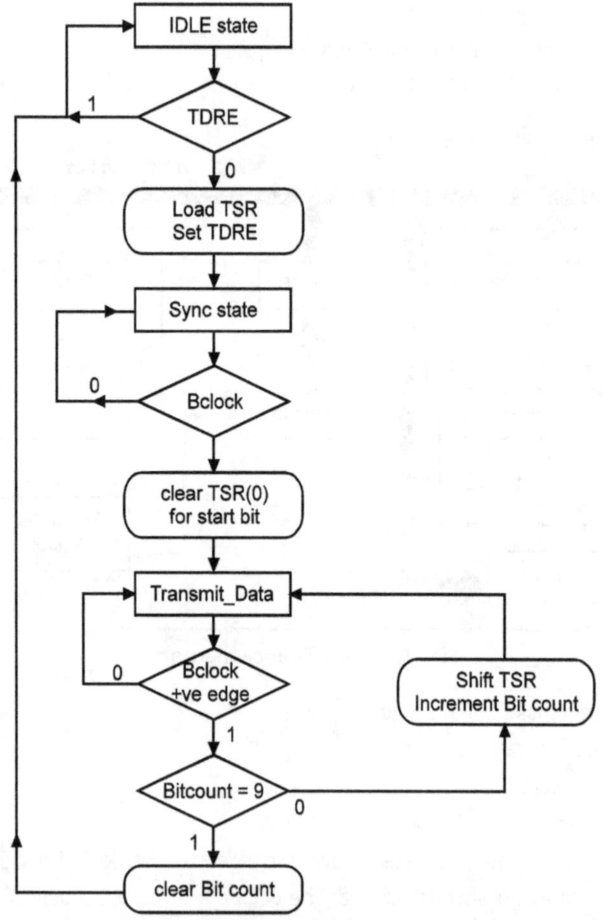

Fig. 7.21: SM chart for UART transmitter

Now, we will draw the Sequential Machine (SM) for the transmitter section of UART. This SM is clocked by the microcontroller system clock (CLK). There are three states in SM chart as discussed below:

1) **IDLE state:** In this state, the TDRE (transmit data register empty) bit of SCSR register is checked. The sequential machine waits in the IDLE state until TDR has been loaded and TDRE is cleared. When the TDRE bit is cleared, then sequential machine loads the TSR and again sets the TDRE bit.

2) **Sync state:** In this, the sequential machine waits for the rising edge of the Bit clock (Bclock), and then clears the low order bit of the TSR to transmit a logic '0' for one bit time.

3) **Transmit_Data_State:** In this state, SM checks for the positive going edge of Bclock. When positive going edge occurs on Bclock, TSR is shifted to the right to transmit the next data bit and the bit counter is incremented by one. When bit counter is 9 (means 8 data bits and a stop bit have transmitted), then Bit counter is cleared and the SM again goes back to the IDLE state to transmit the next Data byte.

UART Receiver

The Registers used in the Receiver section of UART are

1) RSR i.e. Receive Shift Register
2) RDR i.e. Receive Data Register
3) SCSR i.e. Serial Communications Status Register

Serial communications status register has a bit RDRF i.e. Receive Data Register Full. RDRF bit is set when RDR is full. The following are the steps in the UART Receiver section:

1) UART first checks for the start bit. When the start bit is detected, then it reads in the remaining bits serially and shifts them into the RSR.

2) After receiving all the data bits and the stop bit, the RSR is loaded into the RDR. When RDR register is full, the RDRF flag in SCSR register is set.

3) The microcontroller checks the RDRF flag, whether it is '0' or '1'. If it is '1', then RDR is read and the flag is cleared.

The data bit stream, coming on RxD is not synchronized with the local bit clock (Bclock). If we attempt to read the bit on RxD at the rising edge of Bclock, we would have problem, if RxD changed near the clock i.e. before the clock edge or after the clock edge. It means that setup time and hold time requirements are not satisfied. If the bit rate of the incoming signal on the RxD pin is different from Bclock by a small amount, we could end up reading some bits at the wrong time. To avoid these problems, we will sample RxD eight times during each bit time.

Fig. 7.22 shows the sampling of RxD pin on the rising edge of Bclock × 8.

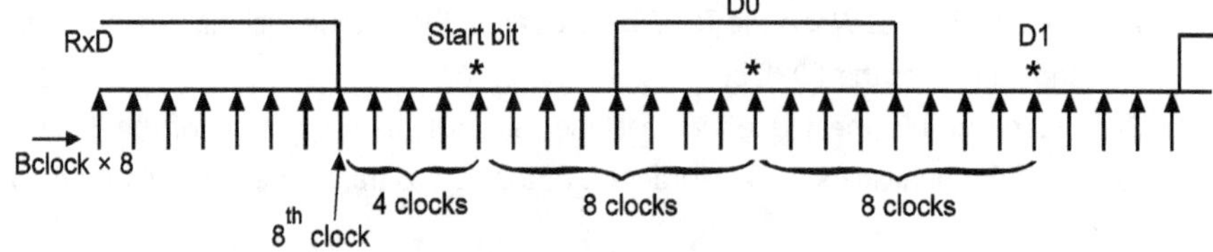

Fig. 7.22: Sampling RxD with Bclock × 8

As shown in Fig. 7.22, sampling is performed on the rising clock of Bclock × 8. For maximum reliability, we should read the bit value at the middle of each bit time. As shown, when RxD goes low, we need to wait for four clock periods, and we should be near the middle of the start bit. Then, we will wait eight more Bclock × 8 periods at that time bit D0 is sampled at the middle. Like this each data bit is sampled at the middle.

To further illustrate the use of a state diagram, consider the following example.

Example 1:

Following specifications are describing the operation of sequential machine. It has a single control input X and the CLOCK, and two outputs A and B. On consecutive rising edges of the clock, the code on A and B changes from 00 to 01 to 10 to 11 and then repeats itself if X is asserted; if at any time X is de-asserted, the machine is supposed to hold its present state. Define the state diagram for above.

Solution:

The block diagram for above sequential machine can be as shown in Fig. 7.23.

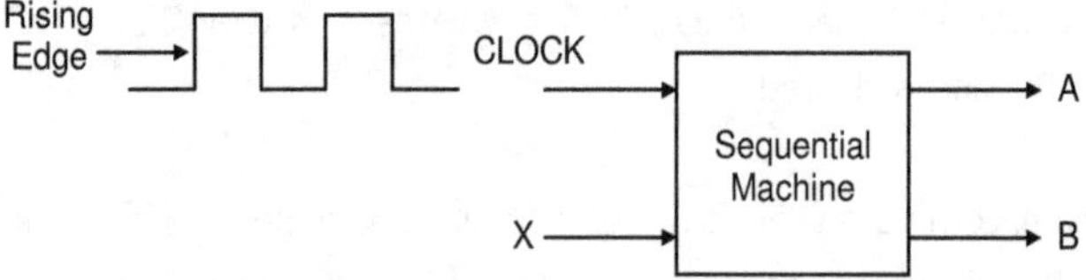

Fig. 7.23: Block diagram

The machine can be described much more clearly by the state diagram as shown in Fig. 7.24. From the state diagram, each state can be examined and the information required in determining the previous state, the conditions for the next state, and the output for each state can be obtained. State diagram is useful for defining the sequential system, analyzing sequential circuit and designing the sequential circuit.

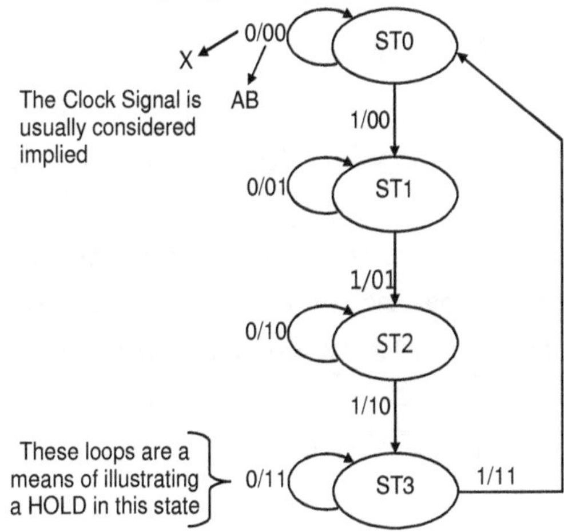

Fig. 7.24: State diagram

Example 2:

Illustrate the formation of state table and state diagram for the sequential circuit shown in Fig. 7.25.

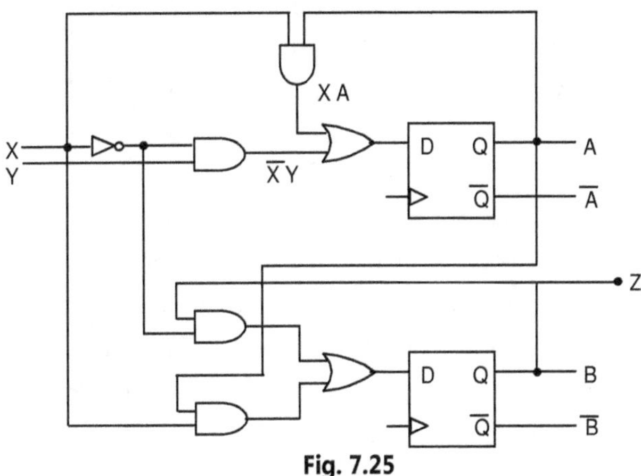

Fig. 7.25

Solution:

The circuit consists of two D flip-flops, two inputs X and Y and an output Z. The D input determines the flip-flop next state. The set of next state equations are

$$A(t+1) \;=\; A(t)\,X(t) + \overline{X}(t)\,Y(t)$$

$$B(t+1) \;=\; B(t)\,\overline{X}(t) + A(t)\,X(t)$$

$$Z(t) \;=\; B(t)$$

where A(t+1) and B(t+1) are the next states and A(t), B(t) present states. X(t), Y(t) are present inputs.

The Boolean expression for the next state can be derived directly from the gates that form the combinational part of the sequential circuit and are connected to D inputs of the flip-flop. D input values determine the next state. The present output is determined by Z = B.

The time sequence of inputs, outputs and flip-flop states are enumerated in the state table shown below.

State Table

Present state		Next State								Output
		XY = 00		XY = 01		XY = 10		XY = 11		
A	B	A	B	A	B	A	B	A	B	Z
0	0	0	0	1	0	0	0	0	0	0
0	1	0	1	1	1	0	0	0	0	1
1	0	0	0	1	0	1	1	1	1	0
1	1	0	1	1	1	1	1	1	1	1

The table has three sections, present state, next state, and output. The present state section shows the states of flip-flops A and B at any time t. The next state section shows the state of the flip-flops one clock period later at time t+1 as for the possible combinations of the two input variables X and Y. For two flip-flops, we have four combinations. The next states of the flip-flops A and B are determined from above equations for four input combinations of X and Y. The output is derived from Z=B.

The state diagram is shown in Fig. 7.26.

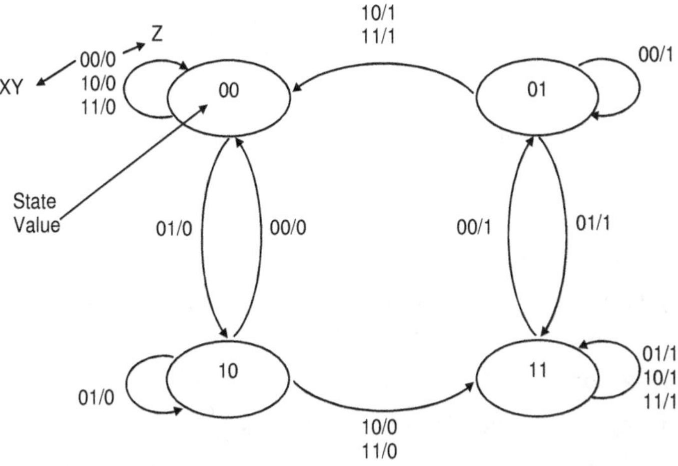

Fig. 7.26: State diagram of Fig. 7.25

7.6.2 Analysis and Design of Sequential Circuits

The sequential circuit can be analyzed in following steps:

- The transition function of the network can be obtained by determining the inputs, to the flip-flops in terms of present state and the inputs to the circuit and by using transition function of the flip-flop in determining the next state.
- The output function can be obtained by analyzing the corresponding combinational network.
- A suitable high level specification of the transition and out function should be determined.
- After performing the functional analysis mentioned above, timing analysis and size determination should be done.

The design of sequential circuit consists of following steps.

Step 1   Receive Design specification.

Step 2   Study the specifications to understand the real operational behavior of the circuit.

Step 3   Make a block model of the system. Identify all inputs and outputs.

Step 4   Design a primitive state diagram based on the information from steps 2 and 3.

Step 5   Develop a primitive state table from the primitive state diagram. Find out possible redundant states from the state table.

Step 6   If necessary; develop a simplified state diagram from the simplified primitive state table.

Step 7   Make a state assignment using rules assigned to the states in the simplified diagram.

Step 8   Develop a present state/next state table using assignment from the simplified state diagram with state assignments.

Step 9   Using this table, develop the next state maps. From these maps derive the next state decoder logic for D, T and JK flip-flops.

Step 10   Make selection of the memory element.

Step 11   Using step 3 and state diagram with state assignments, develop the output decoder logic by plotting the output maps.

Step 12   Draw the circuit schematic.

7.7 FSM Modeling using VHDL

A state machine description consists of

- A state variable, which specifies the state of the machine
- A clock
- Specification of state transitions
- Specification of outputs
- A reset condition may be synchronous or asynchronous.

The clock and reset can be specified in a PROCESS or Block statement. The output can be specified using any assignment statement.

The state variable is used to maintain the state of the circuit. All the state machine elements can be specified either in a single process or in two processes. One process to model the synchronous aspect of FSM and other to model the combinational part of the FSM.

Example 3:

Write a VHDL code to design sequential circuit described by state diagram shown in Fig. 7.27.

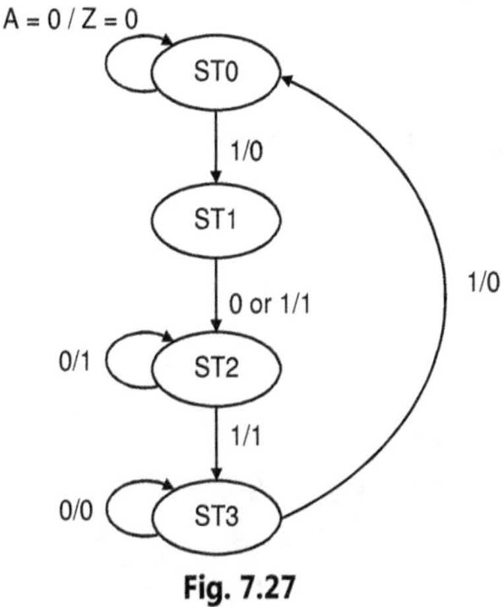

Fig. 7.27

Solution:

In above state diagram, only one input (say A) which is having a value 0 or 1, and one output (say Z) of one bit in length is specified. The four states are labelled as ST0, ST1, ST2, and ST3.

library IEEE;
use IEEE. STD_LOGIC_1164. *all;*

entity FSM1 *is*
    port (A, CLK: *in std_logic;*
      Z: *out std_logic);*
end FSM1;

architecture FSM1_ARCH *of* FSM1 *is*
    type STATE_TYPE *is* (ST0, ST1, ST2, ST3);
  signal PRESENT_STATE: STATE_TYPE;
begin
  process (CLK)
  begin
  if (CLK = '0') *then*
    case PRESENT_STATE *is*
    when ST0 => Z <= '0';
        if (A = '1') *then*

```
                    PRESENT_STATE <= ST1;
              end if;
        when ST1 => Z <= '1';
                  PRESENT_STATE <= ST2;
        when ST2 => Z < = '1';
              if (A = '1') then
                  PRESENT_STATE <= ST3;
              end if;
        when ST3 => Z < = '0';
                if (A = '1') then
                    PRESENT_STATE <= ST0;
                end if;
          end case;
        end if;
      end process;
    end FSM1_ARCH;
```

The output Z only depends upon the present state. Hence it is an example of Moore machine.

Example 4:

Write a VHDL code for the sequential circuit described in example.

Solution:

The state diagram is as shown in Fig. 7.28.

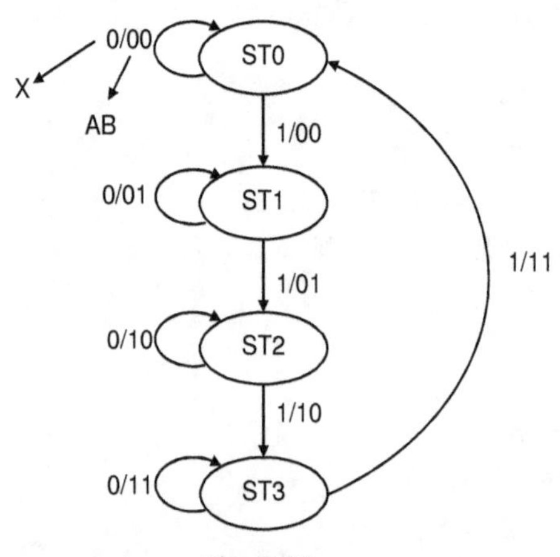

Fig. 7.28

This FSM have four states. It has one input X and two outputs A and B.

The A and B outputs depend on input X as well as the present_state (current values of A and B). Hence, it is an example of Mealy machine.

In following VHDL code, two process statements are used, one to model the synchronous aspect of FSM (i.e. at every active edge of the clock, next state is assigned to present state) and other to model the combinational part of FSM.

```vhdl
library IEEE;
use IEEE. STD_LOGIC_1164.all;


entity FSM2 is
    port (X, CLK: in STd_logic;
          A, B: out STd_logic);
end FSM2;


architecture FSM2_ARCH  of  FSM2  is
    type STATE_TYPE  is ( ST0, ST1, ST2, ST3 );
    signal P_STATE, N_STATE: STATE_TYPE;
begin
    P1: process (CLK)
        begin
         if ( CLK = '0' )  then
             P_STATE <=  N_STATE;
         end if ;
        end process P1;
    P2: process (P_STATE, X)
        begin
         case P_STATE  is
             when ST0 => if ( X = '1')  then
                         A <= '0';
                     B <= '1';
                     N_STATE <= ST1;
                 else
                     A <= '0';
                     B <= '0';
                 end if;
```

```
            when ST1 => if ( X = '1') then
                        A <= '1';
                        B <= '0';
                        N_STATE <= ST2;
                  else
                        A <= '0';
                        B <= '1';
                  end if;
            when ST2 => if ( X = '1') then
                        A <= '1';
                        B <= '1';
                        N_STATE <= ST3;
                  else
                         A <= '1';
                          B <= '0';
                  end if;
            when ST3 => if (X = '1') then
                        A <= '0';
                        B <= '0';
                        N_STATE <= ST0;
                  else
                        A <= '1';
                        B <= '1';
            end if;
          end case;
        end process P2;
      end FSM2_ARCH;
```

Example 5:

Using VHDL, design a memory controller with following features.

A memory controller is used to enable and disable the 'write enable' and 'read enable' signals of a memory buffer during read and write transactions. The signals 'ready' and 'read-write' are outputs of a microprocessor and inputs to the controller. A new transaction begins with the assertion of 'ready' signal. 'read-write' signal determines read or write transaction; and corresponding outputs 'read enable' or 'write enable' are active based upon read or write cycle respectively. Note that, both the outputs never become active at the same time.

Solution:

The block schematic can be as shown in Fig. 7.29.

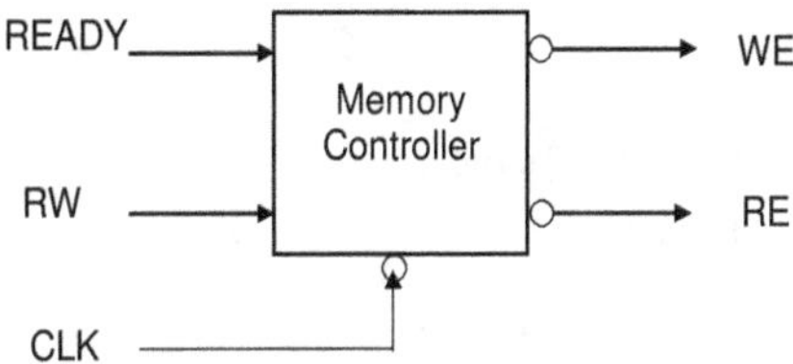

Fig. 7.29

WE and RE outputs are active low.

The given functionality can be described by state table as shown below:

Inputs		Present	Next	Outputs	
READY	**RW**	**State**	**State**	**WE**	**RE**
0	X	A	A	1	1
1	0	A	B	0	1
1	1	A	C	1	0
X	X	B	A	1	1
X	X	C	A	1	1

When RW = 0, WE output gets active and when RW = 1, RE output gets active. When ready = 0, WE and RE, both will be disabled (i.e. WE = RE = 1).

At any time, the output of memory controller will be either WE = 1, RE = 1 or WE = 0, RE = 1 or WE = 1, RE = 0. Hence it has three states, named as 'A' (WE = 1, RE = 1), 'B' (WE = 0, RE = 1), and 'C' (WE = 1, RE = 0).

The state diagram for the given functionality can be as shown in Fig. 7.30.

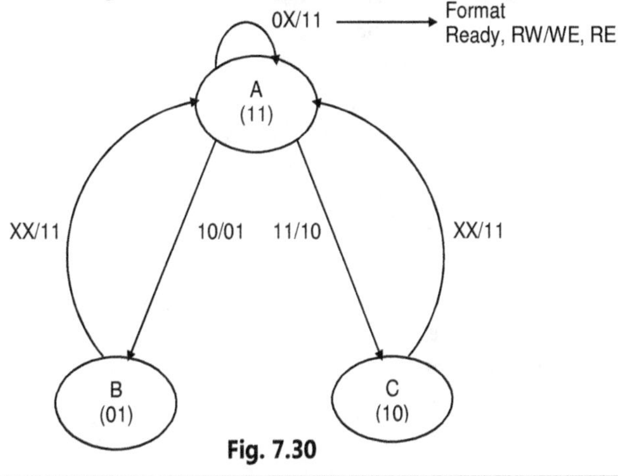

Fig. 7.30

```vhdl
library IEEE;
use IEEE. STD_LOGIC_1164.all ;

entity MEMCTRL  is
    port (READY, RW, CLK: in std_logic;
        WE, RE: out std_logic);
end MEMCTRL ;

architecture MEMCTRL_ARCH  of  MEMCTRL  is
        type STATE_TYPE  is (A, B, C);
        signal P_STATE, N_STATE: STATE_TYPE ;
begin
    P1: process (CLK)
        begin
            if (CLK'event  and  CLK = '1') then
                    P_STATE <= N_STATE;
            end if ;
            end process P1;
    P2: process (P_STATE, READY, RE)
            begin
             case P_STATE  is
             when A => if ( READY = '1') then
                            if ( RW = '0') then
                                P_STATE <= B;
                                WE <= '0';
                                RE <= '1';
                            else
                                P_STATE <= C;
                                WE <= '1';
                                RE <= '0';
                            end if;
                        else
                            WE <= '1';
                            RE < = '1';
                        end if ;
             when B => P_STATE <= A;
                        WE <= '1';
                        RE <= '1';
```

when C => P_STATE <= A ;
WE <= '1';
RE <= '1';
end case;
end process P2;
end MEMCTRL_ARCH;

Example 6:

Show the state diagram for the FSM described in following state table. Also write the VHDL code to describe the given FSM.

Present State		Next State				Output	
		X = 0		X = 1		X = 0	X = 1
A	B	A	B	A	B		
0	0	0	1	1	1	0	1
0	1	1	0	0	0	0	0
1	0	1	1	0	1	1	0
1	1	0	0	1	0	1	1

Solution:

The functionality of given FSM can be described by state diagram as shown in Fig. 7.31.

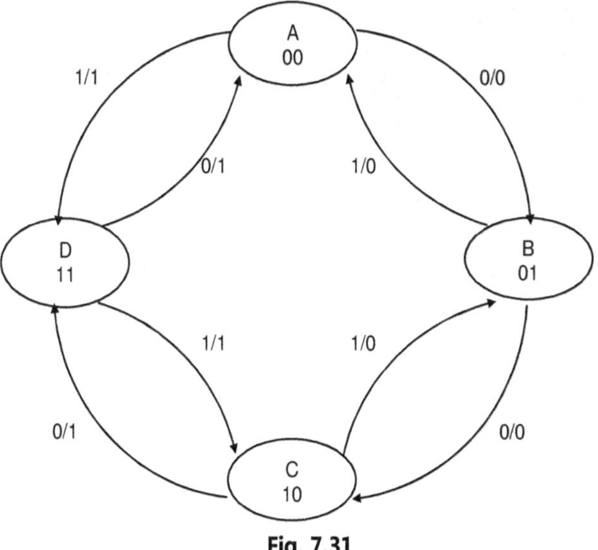

Fig. 7.31

```vhdl
library IEEE;
use IEEE. STD_LOGIC_1164. all;


entity FSM3 is
     port ( X, CLK: in std_logic;
              Z: out std_logic);
end FSM3;


architecture FSM3_ARCH of  FSM3  is
   type STATE_TYPE is (A, B, C, D);
    signal P_STATE, N_STATE: STATE_TYPE;
begin
     P1: process (CLK)
          begin
          if (CLK'event  and  CLK = '1')  then
            P_STATE <= N_STATE;
          end if;
          end process P1;
        P2: process (P_STATE, X)
          begin
          case P_STATE  is
           when A => if ( X = '0') then
                           P_STATE <= B;
                        Z <= '0';
                      else
                         P_STATE <= D;
                         Z <= '1';
                      end if ;
           when B => if ( X = '0') then
                          P_STATE <= C;
                          Z <= '0';
                      else
                          P_STATE <= A;
                          Z <= '0';
                        end if ;
```

```
                    when C => if ( X = '0') then
                                P_STATE <= D;
                                Z <= '1';
                            else
                                P_STATE <= B;
                                Z <= '0';
                            end if ;
                    when D => if ( X = '0') then
                                P_STATE <= A;
                                 Z <= '1';
                            else
                                P_STATE <= C;
                                Z <= '1';
                            end if ;
                end case;
            end process P2;
        end FSM3_ARCH;
```

Example 7:

Write a VHDL code for JK flip-flop using its state diagram.

Solution:

The block schematic of JK flip-flop is as shown in Fig. 7.32.

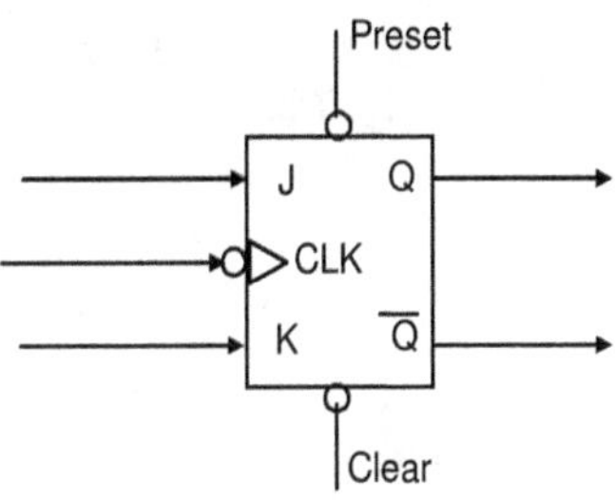

Fig. 7.32

When preset = '0' and clear = '1' then Q = 1.

When preset = '1' and clear = '0' then Q = 0.

For normal operation of JK flip-flop, preset and clear should be at logic 1.

Preset = 0 and clear = 0 are not allowed.

The operation of JK flip-flop can be described in state table shown below.

Data Inputs		Present State	Next State
J_n	K_n	Q_n	$Q_{(n+1)}$
0	0	0	$\left.\begin{array}{c}0\\1\end{array}\right] = Q_n$
0	0	1	
0	1	0	$\left.\begin{array}{c}1\\1\end{array}\right] = 1$
0	1	1	
1	0	0	$\left.\begin{array}{c}0\\0\end{array}\right] = 04$
1	0	1	
1	1	0	$\left.\begin{array}{c}1\\0\end{array}\right] = \overline{Q_n}$
1	1	1	

The state diagram can be as shown in Fig. 7.33.

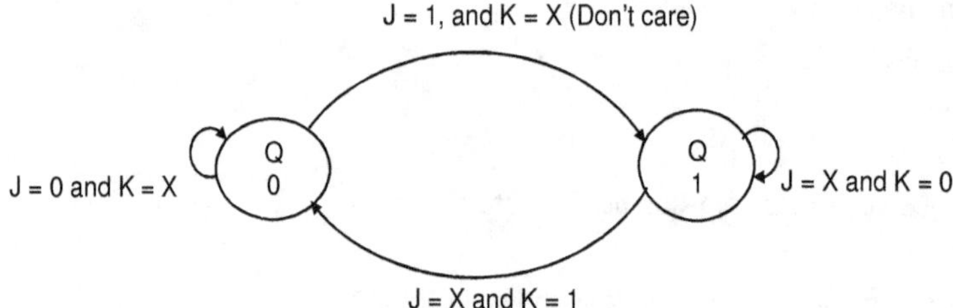

Fig. 7.33

```
library IEEE ;
use IEEE . STD_LOGIC_1164. all;


entity FSMJK  is
        port (J, K, CLK, PRESET, CLEAR: in std_logic;
                    Q, QBAR: out std_logic);
end FSMJK;


architecture FSMJK_ARCH of FSMJK is
    type STATE_TYPE  is (ST0, ST1);
    signal P_STATE, N_STATE: STATE_TYPE;
```

```vhdl
begin
    P1: process (CLK)
                begin
            if (CLK'event  and  CLK = '0') then
                P_STATE <= N_STATE;
                 end if ;
     end process P1;
     P2: process (P_STATE, J, K, PRESET, CLEAR)
     begin
         if (PRESET = '0' and CLEAR = '1') then
             Q <= '1';
             P_STATE <= ST1;
         elsif ( PRESET = '1' and CLEAR = '0') then
             Q <= '0';
             P_STATE <= ST0;
         else
             case P_STATE  is
                 when ST0 => if ( J = '1') then
                                 Q <= '1';
                                  P_STATE <= ST1;
                             else
                                 Q <= '0';
                             end if;
                 when ST1 => if ( K = '1') then
                                 Q <= '0';
                                  P_STATE < = ST0;
                             else
                                 Q < = '1';
                             end if;
             end case;
         end if ;
     end process P2 ;
    QBAR <= not Q;
end FSMJK_ARCH;
```

Example 8:

Write a VHDL code for 110 sequence detector.

Solution:

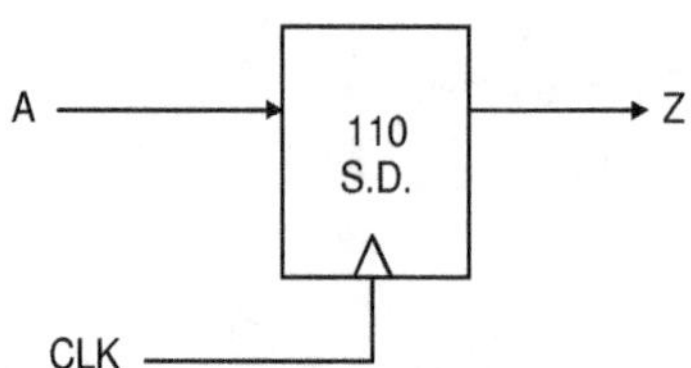

Fig. 7.34

Sequence detector accepts input A at every positive edge of clock. The output Z will be 1, only when sequence detector finds the input bit sequence 110. That means when 0 is applied at input A after applying two consecutive '1's at input A, then output Z will be 1, otherwise Z will be 0.

The state diagram is as shown in Fig. 7.35.

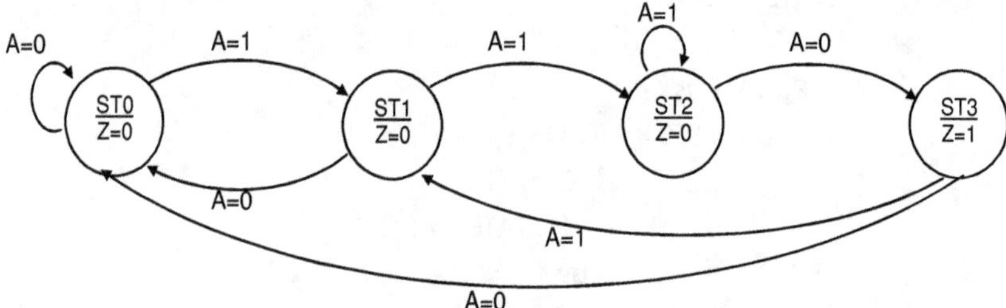

Fig. 7.35

library IEEE;

use IEEE. STD_LOGIC_1164. *all*;

entity SD *is*

　　　port (A, CLK: *in std_logic*;

　　　　　Z: *out std_logic*);

end SD;

architecture SD_ARCH of SD *is*

　　　type STATE_TYPE *is* (ST0, ST1, ST2, ST3);

　　　signal STATE: STATE_TYPE;

```vhdl
begin
     process (CLK)
   begin
      if (CLK'event and CLK = '1') then
      case STATE is
        when ST0  => Z <= '0';
                        if ( A = '0')  then
                          STATE <= ST0;
                        else
                           STATE <= ST1;
                        end if,
        when ST1  => Z <= '0';
                        if ( A = '0') then
                          STATE <= ST0;
                        else
                           STATE <= ST2;
                        end if ;
        when ST2  =>  Z <= '0';
                        if ( A = '0') then
                            STATE <= ST3;
                        else
                           STATE <= ST2;
                        end if ;
        when ST3  =>  Z <= '1';
                        if ( A = '0') then
                            STATE <= ST0;
                        else
                           STATE <= ST1;
                        end if ;
        when others => null;
      end case;
      end if ;
   end process;
 end SD_ARCH;
```

Example 9:

Realize a code converter that converts binary-coded-decimal (BCD) digit to an excess-3-coded decimal digit. Also write the VHDL code.

Solution:

The following table lists the desired inputs and outputs. After receiving four inputs, the network should reset to its initial state, ready to receive another BCD digit.

X-Input				Z-output			
at time t				at time t			
t3	t2	t1	t0	t3	t2	t1	t0
0	0	0	0	0	0	1	1
0	0	0	1	0	1	0	0
0	0	1	0	0	1	0	1
0	0	1	1	0	1	1	0
0	1	0	0	0	1	1	1
0	1	0	1	1	0	0	0
0	1	1	0	1	0	0	1
0	1	1	1	1	0	1	0
1	0	0	0	1	0	1	1
1	0	0	1	1	1	0	0

Now construct a state diagram for the code converter.

The excess-3 code is formed by adding 0011 to the BCD digit.

For example

$$
\begin{array}{ccccc}
0100 & \longrightarrow & \text{BCD I/P} & \longleftarrow & 0101 \\
+\ \underline{0011} & \longrightarrow & & & +\ \underline{0011} \\
0111 & \longrightarrow & \text{Excess 3 output} & \longleftarrow & 1000
\end{array}
$$

At t0, add 1 to the least significant bit S0, if X = 0, Z = 1 (no carry), and if X = 1, Z = 0 (carry = 1). This leads to the following partial state graph:

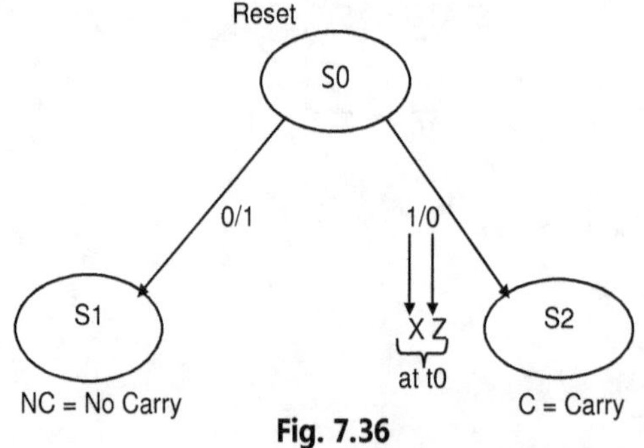

Fig. 7.36

S0 is the reset state, S1 indicates no carry after the first addition, and S2 indicates a carry of 1. At t1, add 1 to the next bit, so if there is no carry from the first addition (state S1), X = 0 gives Z = 0+1+0 = 1 and no carry (state 3), and X = 1 gives Z = 1+1+0 = 0 and a carry (state S4).

If there is a carry from the first addition (state S2), then X = 0 gives Z = 0 + 1 + 1 = 0 and a carry (state S4), and X = 1 gives Z = 1 + 1 + 1 = 1 and a carry (state S4). At t2, 0 is added to X, and transitions to S5 (no carry) and S6 are determined in a similar manner. At t3, 0 is again added to X, and the network resets to S0.

The state table and state diagram can be as shown in Fig. 7.37 (a) and (b). Since the state table has seven states, three flip-flops will be required to realize the table. The next step is to make a state assignment that will relate the flip-flops states to the states in the table.

Present State	Next State		Z	
	X = 0	X = 1	X = 0	X = 1
S0	S1	S2	1	0
S1	S3	S4	1	0
S2	S4	S4	0	1
S3	S5	S5	0	1
S4	S5	S6	1	0
S5	S0	S0	0	1
S6	S0	-	1	-

Fig. 7.37 (a): State table

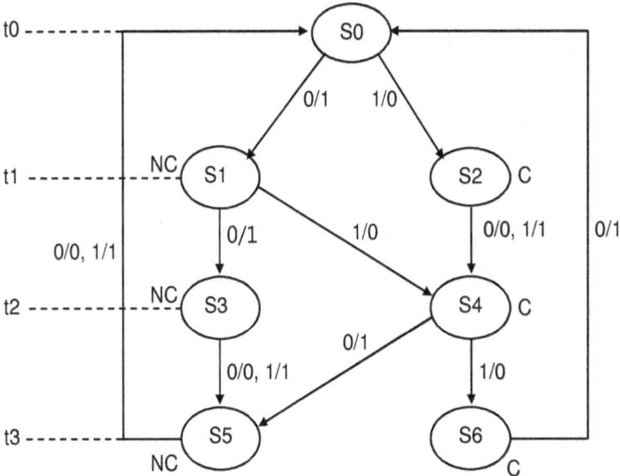

Fig. 7.37 (b): State diagram

Now consider Q1, Q2 and Q3, the outputs of three required flip-flops (say D flip-flops) as a present state of the network and $Q1^+$, $Q2^+$ and $Q3^+$ are the next states. D1, D2 and D3 are the inputs to the respective flip-flops.

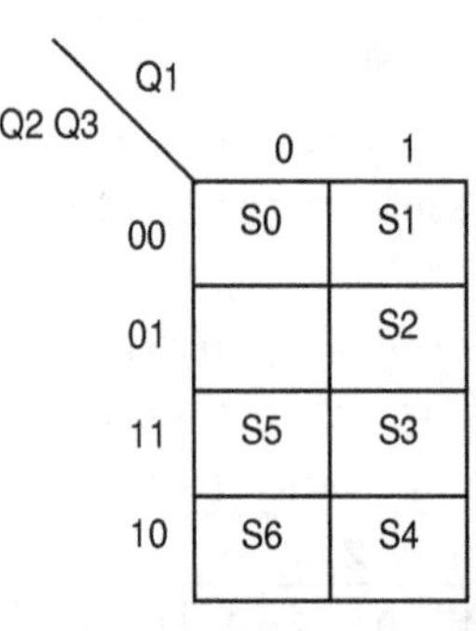

$Q_1Q_2Q_3$	$Q_1^+ Q_2^+ Q_3^+$		Z	
	X = 0	X = 1	X = 0	X = 1
0 0 0	100	101	1	0
1 0 0	111	110	1	0
1 0 1	110	110	0	1
1 1 1	011	011	0	1
1 1 0	011	010	1	0
0 1 1	000	000	0	1
0 1 0	000	XXX	1	X
0 0 1	XXX	XXX	X	X

Fig. 7.38 (a): Assignment map   **Fig. 7.38 (b): Transition table**

In order to reduce the amount of logic required, the state assignment is made using following guidelines:

1. States that have the same next state for a given input should be given adjacent assignments (look at the columns of the state table).
2. States that are the next states of the same state should be given adjacent assignments (look at the rows).
3. States that have the same outputs for a given input should be given adjacent assignments.

Using these guidelines, try to group 1s together on the K-maps for the next state and output functions.

The guidelines indicate that the following states should be given adjacent assignments:

1. (1, 2), (3, 4), (5, 6)   [in the X=1 column, S1 and S2 both have next state S4;
                                                          in the X=0 column, S3 and S4 have next state S5,
                                                          and S5 and S6 have next state S0]
2. (1, 2), (3, 4), (5, 6)   [S1 and S2 are next state of S0;
                                                          S3 and S4 are next state of S1;
                                                          and S5 and S6 are next state of S4]
3. (0, 1, 4, 6,), (2, 3, 5)

Fig. 7.38 (a) gives an assignment map, which satisfies the guidelines, and the corresponding transition table. Since state 001 is not used, next state and outputs for this state are don't cares. The next state and output equation are derived from this table in Fig. 7.39.

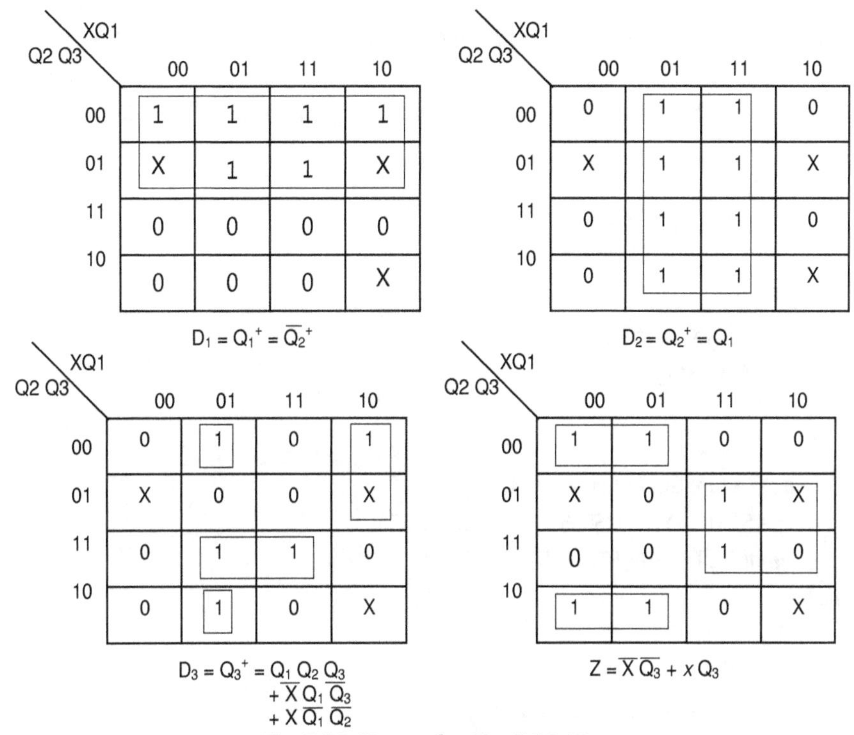

$$D_1 = Q_1{}^+ = \overline{Q_2}{}^+$$

$$D_2 = Q_2{}^+ = Q_1$$

$$D_3 = Q_3{}^+ = Q_1\,Q_2\,Q_3$$
$$+\,\overline{X}\,Q_1\,\overline{Q_3}$$
$$+\,X\,\overline{Q_1}\,\overline{Q_2}$$

$$Z = \overline{X}\,\overline{Q_3} + x\,Q_3$$

Fig. 7.39: K-map for Fig. 7.38 (a)

Fig. 7.40 shows the realization of the code converter using NAND gates and D flip-flips.

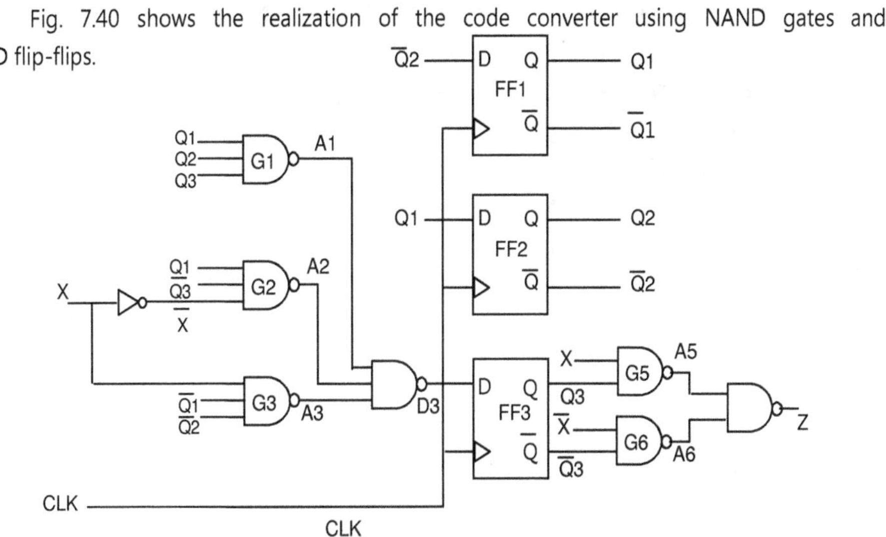

Fig. 7.40: Realization of code converter

As the output Z depends on both present state and the present input X, this is an example of Mealy FSM.

The VHDL code can be written by referring state diagram shown in Fig. 7.38 (b).

```vhdl
library IEEE
use IEEE. STD_LOGIC_1164. all;

entity CC is
    port (X, CLK: in std_logic;
        Z: out std_logic);
end CC;

    architecture CC_ARCH of CC is
    type STATE_TYPE is (S0, S1, S2, S3,S4, S5, S6);
    signal P_STATE, N_STATE: STATE_TYPE ;
begin
    P1: process (CLK)
        begin
        if (CLK'event and CLK = '1') then
                    P_STATE <= N_STATE;
                end if ;
            end process P1;
    P2: process (P_STATE, X)
        begin
        case P_STATE is
        when S0 => if (X = '0') then
                    Z <= '1';
                        P_STATE <= S1;
                    else
                    Z <= '0';
                            P_STATE <= S2;
                    end if ;
            when S1 => if (X = '0') then
                    Z <= '1';
                        P_STATE <= S3;
```

```vhdl
                    else
                    Z <= '0';
                                P_STATE <= S4;
                    end if ;
        when S2 =>  P_STATE <= S4;
                if (X = '0') then
                    Z <= '0';
                    else
                    Z <= '1';
                    end if ;
        when S3 =>  P_STATE <= S5;
                 if ( X = '0') then
                    Z <= '0';
                     else
                    Z <= '1';
                     end if ;
        when S4 => if ( X = '0') then
                        P_STATE <= S5;
                                Z <= '1';
                        else
                        P_STATE <= S6;
                                Z <= '0';
                        end if ;
        when S5 =>  P_STATE <= S0 ;
                if ( X = '0') then
                    Z <= '0';
                else
                    Z <= '1';
                end if ;
        when S6 =>  P_STATE <= S0;
                if ( X = '0') then
                    Z <= '1';
                        end if ;
        end case;
    end process P2;
end CC_ARCH;
```

7.8 Lift Controller

In this, the lift controller is designed for a two storeyed building. Fig. 7.41 shows the block diagram of lift controller and its input and output signals.

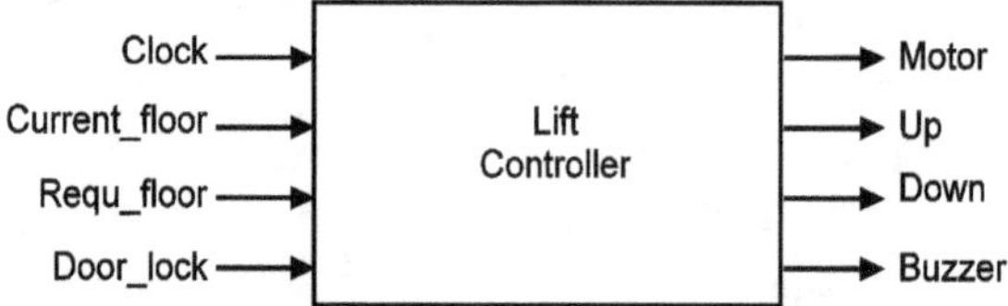

Fig. 7.41: Lift controller block diagram

Input signals are Current_floor, Requ_floor and Door_lock. Current_floor indicates the position of the lift i.e. whether the lift is on ground floor or on first floor. Requ_floor signal indicates the requested floor by a person. Door_lock indicates whether lift door is closed or open.

Current_floor:		'0' means, lift is on ground floor
		'1' means, lift is on first floor
Requ_floor :		'0' means, request from ground floor
		'1' means, request from first floor.
Door_lock	:	'0' means, lift door is open
		'1' means, lift door is closed

Output signals are motor, up, down and buzzer.

Motor	:	'0' means, motor is OFF.
	:	'1' means, motor is ON.
down	:	'1' means, lift is started in down direction
up	:	'1' means, lift is started in up direction
buzzer	:	'0' means, buzzer is OFF.
	:	'1' means, buzzer is ON.

7.8.1 Operation of the Lift Controller

First, we need to check Door_Lock signal. If the Door_lock is open, then buzzer must be ON.

Request_floor signal indicates the request for the lift. If the request is from the ground floor and the lift is on the first floor, then motor must be ON and up signal should go low and down signal should go high. If the request is from ground floor and lift is on ground floor, motor must be OFF and both up and down signals are low.

Same case for the request from the first floor.

The input and output signal conditions and state diagram is shown below:

Table: Input and output signals

State	Input signal		Output signal		
	Current_floor	Requ_floor	Motor	Up	Down
S0	0	0	0	0	0
S1	0	1	1	1	0
S2	1	0	1	0	1
S3	1	1	0	0	0

State diagram for the lift controller is shown in Fig. 7.42. In state S0, motor must be OFF and up and down signals are low. In state S1, the motor is ON and moving in the up direction, as the request is from the first floor. In state S2, motor is moving in the down direction, as the request is from ground floor. In state S3, motor is OFF.

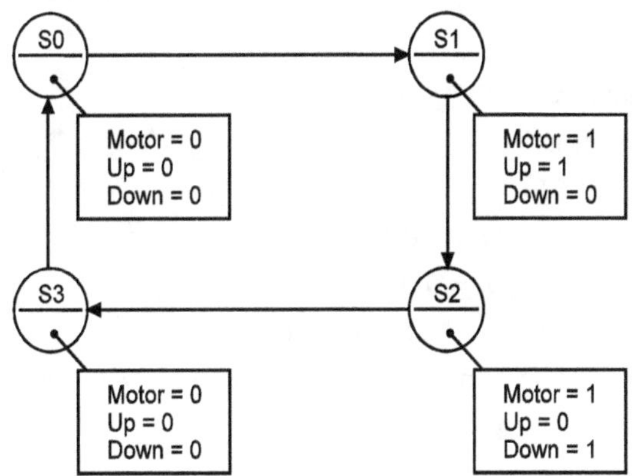

Fig. 7.42: State diagram for lift controller

VHDL code for the lift controller is as follows:

```
library ieee;
use ieee. std_logic_1164.all;
```

```vhdl
entity LC is
    port (clk; in std_logic;
          Current_floor: in std_logic;
          Requ_floor: in std_logic;
          Door_lock: in std_logic;
          Motor: out std_logic;
          up: out std_logic;
          down: out std_logic;
          buzzer: out std_logic);
end LC;

    architecture LC_arch of LC is
        type state_type is (S0, S1, S2, S3);
        signal state: state_type;
    begin
        process (clk)
        begin
            if clk'event and clk = '1' then
                case state is
                    when S0 =>
                        if Door_lock = '0' then
                            motor = '0'; up = '0';
                            down = '0'; buzzer = '1';
                        elsif (current_floor = '0' and Requ_floor = '0') then
                            motor = '0'; up = '0';
                            down = '0'; buzzer = '0';
                        end if;
                    when S1 =>
                        if Door_lock = '0' then
                            motor = '0'; up = '0';
                            down = '0'; buzzer = '1';
                        elsif (current_floor = '0' and Requ_floor = '1') then
                            motor = '1'; up = '1';
```

```
                down = '0'; buzzer = '0';
            end if;
        when S2 =>
            if Door_lock = '0' then
                motor = '0'; up = '0';
                down = '0'; buzzer = '1';
            elsif (current_floor = '1' and Requ_floor = '0') then
                motor = '1'; up = '0';
                down = '1'; buzzer = '0';
            end if;
        when S3 =>
            if Door_lock = '0' then
                motor = '0'; up = '0';
                down = '0'; buzzer = '1';
            elsif (current_floor = '1' and Requ_floor = '1') then
                motor = '0'; up = '0';
                down = '0'; buzzer = '0';
            end if;
        when others =>
            null;
    end case;
  end if;
 end process;
end LC_arch;
```

7.9 Traffic Light Controller

The input and output signals required for the traffic light controller are given in block diagram as shown in Fig. 7.43.

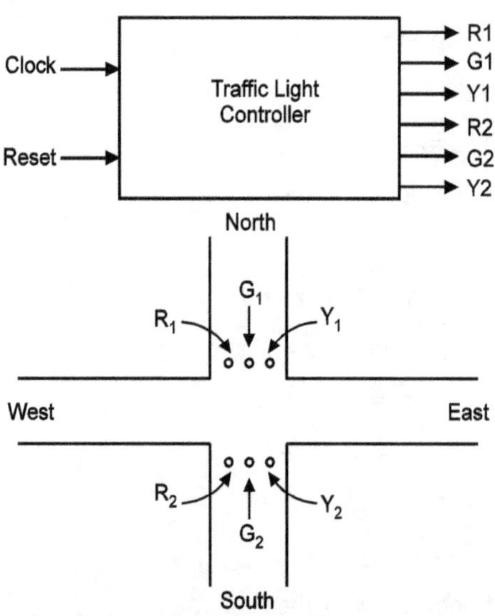

Fig. 7.43: Traffic light controller

For the understanding purpose, we have considered only North ↔ South directions. The sequence of traffic light control is as follows:

(1) Initially R1 and G2 lights are ON for 32 seconds. Remaining lights are OFF.

(2) After 32 seconds, Y2 becomes ON and R1 remains ON. Remaining lights are OFF. This condition remains for 4 seconds.

(3) After second step, R2 and G1 become ON and remaining lights are OFF for 32 seconds.

(4) After third step, Y1 becomes ON and R2 remains ON. Remaining lights are OFF. This condition remains for 4 seconds. After this repeat steps from (1) to (4).

Now, we need to generate exact timing for 32 seconds and 4 seconds. Suppose one clock period of clock is 0.25 seconds. Therefore for 4 seconds, we need total 16 clock periods as 16 × 0.25 seconds = 4 seconds.

Similarly, for 32 seconds we need 128 clock periods as 128 × 0.25 seconds = 32 seconds. For 0.25 seconds clock, f = 4 Hz. To generate 4 seconds clock period, we need to divide the clock by 16, so we need 4 bits as 2^4 = 16. Similarly, to generate 32 seconds clock period, we need to divide the clock by 128, so we need 7 bits, as 2^7 = 128.

For this, we need count1 and count2 as vectors. Count1 is a vector of 5 bits and count2 is a vector of 8 bits. Count1 and count2 are incremented, whenever there is an event on clock of 4 Hz, as given in the VHDL coding.

The state diagram for the traffic light controller is as follows:

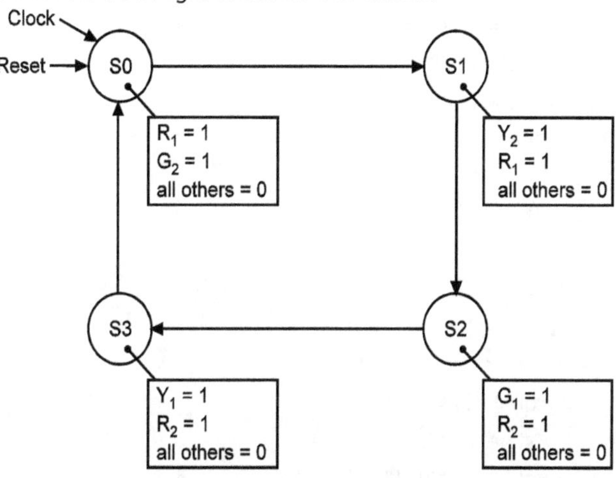

Fig. 7.44: State diagram for traffic light controller

The VHDL coding for traffic light controller is given as,

```
library ieee;
use ieee. std_logic_1164.all;
use ieee. std_logic_arith.all;
use ieee. std_logic_unsigned.all;

entity TLC is
    port (clock, reset: in std_logic;
        R1, Y1, G1, R2, Y2, G2; out std_logic);
end TLC;

architecture TLC_arch of TLC is
    signal count1: std_logic_vector (4 downto 0): = "00000";
    signal count2: std_logic_vector (7 downto 0): = "0000 0000";
    type state_type is (S0, S1, S2, S3);
    signal state: state type;
begin
    process (reset, clock)
    begin
        if (reset = '1') then
```

```vhdl
            R1 <= '0'; R2 <= '0'; Y1 <= '0';
            Y2 <= '0'; G1 <= '0'; G2 <= '0';
            count1 <= "00000";
            count2 <= "0000 0000";
        elsif (clock'event and clock = '1') then
            case state is
                when S0 =>
                    R1 <= '1';   G2 <= '1';
                    R2 <= '0'; G1 <= '0';
                    Y1 <= '0'; Y2 <= '0';
                    count2 <= count2 + 1;
                    if (count2(7) = '1') then
                        state <= S1;
                    count2 <= "0000 0000";
                    end if;
                when S1 =>
                    Y2 <= '1';   R1 <= '1';
                    Y1 <= '0';   R2 <= '0';
                    G1 <= '0';   G2 <= '0';
                    count1 <= count1 + 1;
                    if (count1(4) = '1') then
                        count1 = "00000";
                        state <= S2;
                    end if;
                when S2 =>
                    G1 <= '1'; R2 <= '1';
                    Y1 <= '0';   Y2 <= '0';
                    G2 <= '0';   R1 <= '0';
                    count2 <= count2 + 1;
                    if (count2(7) = '1') then
                        count2 <= "0000 0000";
                        state <= S3;
                    end if;
                when S3 =>
                    Y1 <= '1';   R2 <= '1';
                    Y2 <= '0';   R1 <= '0';
                    G1 <= '0';   G2 <= '0';
```

```
                count1 <= count1 + 1;
                if (count1(4) = '1') then
                     count1 <= "00000";
                     state <= S0;
                end if;
              end case;
          end if;
      end process;
  end TLC_arch;
```

QUESTIONS

1. Differentiate between Synchronous and Asynchronous design.   **(4 Marks, Dec. 2004)**
2. What are the merits and demerits of synchronous system design? **(8 Marks, Dec. 2005)**
3. Explain the difference between Moore and Mealy types of state machine, with block diagram and illustrative examples. What are the advantages and demerits of describing state machines with the state diagrams compared to ASM chart, truth table and K-map? What does word 'Finite' signify in the term Finite State Machine? **(8 Marks, Nov. 2000)**
4. Compare Mealy and Moore machines with suitable example.   **(4 Marks, May 2002)**
5. Define FSM. List various steps used to design a synchronous sequential machine.

     (8 Marks, Dec. 2003)
6. Differentiate between Mealy and Moore types of state machines. A clocked Mealy sequential network with one input (x) and one output (z) is to be designed. The output is to be zero, unless the input is 0 (zero) following a sequence of exactly two zero inputs followed by a 1 (one) input. Draw the state diagram.
   Write the output sequence for the following input sequence.
   X = 001 001 000 10   **(12 Marks, May 2001)**
7. A circuit which accepts CLK, input A and produces output Y as shown below. Draw the state diagram, state table, minimize and implement.   **(12 Marks, Nov. 2001)**

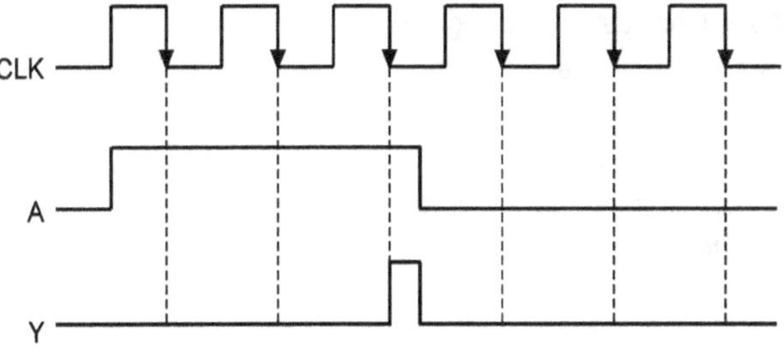

Fig. 7.45

8. Electronic hardware is to be designed for tea/coffee Vending Machine. The sequential operation of a machine is as stated below:

i)   Machine senses coin

ii) It accepts input tea/coffee as an option from customer.

iii) Pours tea/coffee for 10 sec.

iv) Gives an alarm for 2 sec.

v)   Waits for next coin.

Design the circuit, K-map minimization conventional techniques. Design the same by VHDL. Comment on the techniques.   **(12 Marks, May 2002)**

9. Draw state diagram and VHDL code for telephone answering machine controller. The machine records call for two minutes and responds to caller about non-availability of owner.   **(10 Marks, May 2002)**

10. Write a VHDL code for the Mealy machine shown in Fig. 7.46.

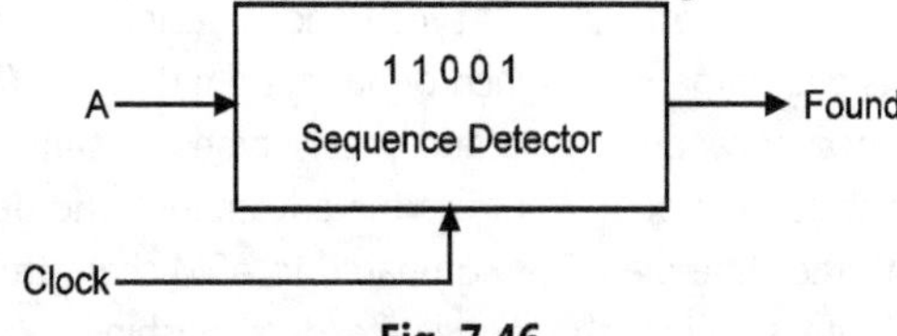

Fig. 7.46

11. Write a VHDL code for a mod 11 counter which follows the sequence shown below:
$10 - 9 - 8 - 7 - 6 - 0 - 1 - 2 - 5 - 3 - 4$ **(12 Marks, Dec. 2004)**

12. Write a VHDL code for a 4-bit Ring counter which is initialized to state "1000" at power on.   **(6 Marks, Dec. 2004)**

13. Compare Moore and Mealy machines with respect to speed, hardware, glitch, number of states.   **(8 Marks, Dec. 2005)**

14. Write a VHDL code for FSM, which detects the sequence 10110 by Moore method.

15. Write VHDL codes for
    (i) Decade synchronous counter
    (ii) Four bit asynchronous counter.   **(12 Marks, May 2005)**

16. Draw FSM and write code for T flip-flop.

17. Design 1011 sequence detector using VHDL.

18. Explain Mealy and Moore machines.

19. Explain the difference between Mealy and Moore machine.

20. Explain classification of FSM.

21. Explain timing consideration in sequential machine.

22. Write a short note on State diagram.

23. Write a short note on UART.

24. Design a Traffic Light Controller System using VHDL.

25. Design Lift Controller System using VHDL.

◊◊◊

Unit 4

Chapter 8: PROGRAMMABLE LOGIC DEVICES

Topics discussed: ASIC, Architecture of PAL, PLA, CPLD, FPGA.

8.1 Introduction

The technological growth in digital design has increased complexity of the system to a large extent. Further, size, power and speed are the major factors in the design aspect. Therefore, there is a need to study different programmable logic devices.

Need of Programmable Logic Devices:

Programmable logic provides many advantages, as listed below:

1) Programmable logic saves valuable board space or "real estate" power and debug time, which can lower the cost.

2) It also increases performance and design security. There is a security fuse, which can be used to protect proprietary intellectual property.

3) Integration increases design reliability because there are fewer dependencies on the interconnection of devices.

4) Greatest advantage of programmable logic is flexibility. If there are changes in the design, we can modify the connections inside programmable logic devices, without making and breaking connections. This will save additional NRE costs and lost time to market.

5) Programmable logic allows use of design tools that help to automate the process. The real work in programmable logic design process is in producing the design description from the design specification. The rest of the steps are automated with software. The design description can be captured in a number of languages, including VHDL/VERILOG or ABEL. The output of the software is a fuse map that is used to program a device.

8.2 Programming Technologies

Technology	Predominantly associated with
Fusible – link	Simple PLDs (SPLDs)
Antifuse	FPGAs
EPROM	SPLDs and CPLDs
EEPROM and FLASH	SPLDs and CPLDs (Some FPGAs)
SRAM	FPGAs (Some CPLDs)

EPROM, EEPROM and FLASH technologies are commonly used in PLDs and CPLDs, to establish programmable connections.

FPGAs commonly use SRAM and Antifuse technologies.

EEPROM and FLASH use electrical erasing, while EPROM requires UV erasing, which is time consuming, and therefore expensive. Clearly, electrically erasable technologies are most commonly used.

8.2.1 Fusible Link Technologies

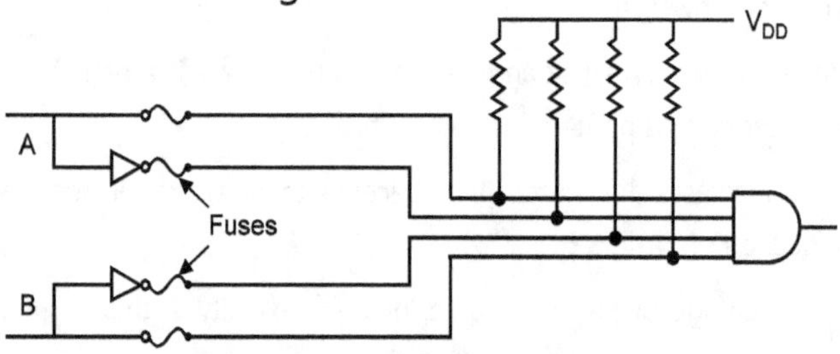

Fig. 8.1: Fusible link technology

Fig. 8.1 shows the fusible link technology. All of the fuses are initially intact (after manufacturing). Design engineers selectively remove undesired fuses by applying pulses of relatively high voltage and current to the input of the device. These devices are **one time** programmable.

8.2.2 Antifuse Technologies

In antifuse technologies, the unprogrammed device has links which are very high in resistance. It is exactly compliment of fusible link technology.

An antifuse initially provides insulation between two conductors, but a conducting path is formed when a sufficient programming voltage is applied across it.

8.2.3 PROM-based Technologies

Fusible link technology is used in PROM.

8.2.4 EPROM-based Technologies

Devices based on fusible link or antifuse can only be programmed a single time. Erasable PROM was introduced by Intel in 1971. EPROM-based technology is accomplished by introducing a floating gate to the basic structure of a MOS transistor.

Fig. 8.2 shows the structure of a FAMOS transistor (floating gate avalanche injection MOS transistor).

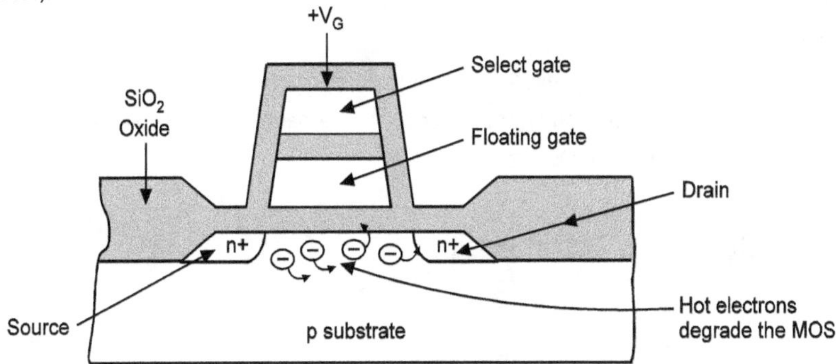

Fig. 8.2: FAMOS transistor

It has two gates, a select gate and a floating gate. When a programming voltage is applied between drain and select gate, a charge is accumulated and trapped on the floating gate. This mechanism is called as avalanche injection or hot electron injection. These hot electrons degrade the MOS parameters. In this mode, even if the voltage is applied to the select gate, the transistor will not conduct.

It means that, when there is a charge on the floating gate, the FAMOS transistor will not conduct.

Without a charge on the floating gate, the FAMOS transistor acts as a normal n-channel transistor. In this mode, when a voltage is applied to the select gate, the transistor is turned on.

Thus, when the floating gate is unprogrammable, the floating gate has no effect.

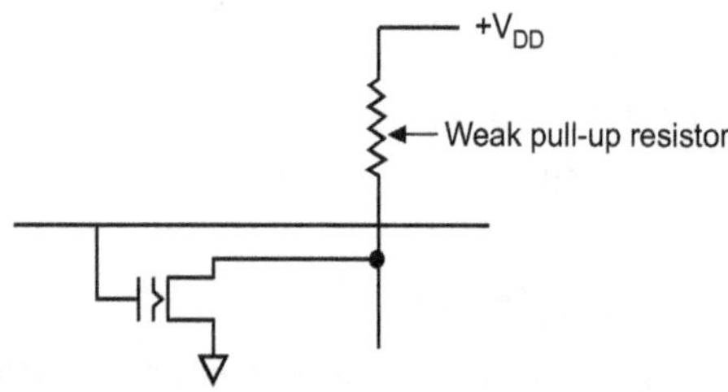

Fig. 8.3: FAMOS transistor in EPROM technology

EPROM-based programming involves placing a high voltage between gate and drain. Hot electrons accumulate on the floating gate, disabling the transistor.

Disadvantages:

To erase the cell, the device is exposed to ultraviolet light. Typical erasure time is about 20-30 minutes under high intensity ultra-violet light. The package of EPROM is also relatively expensive because it requires a Quartz window.

8.2.5 EEPROM-based Technologies

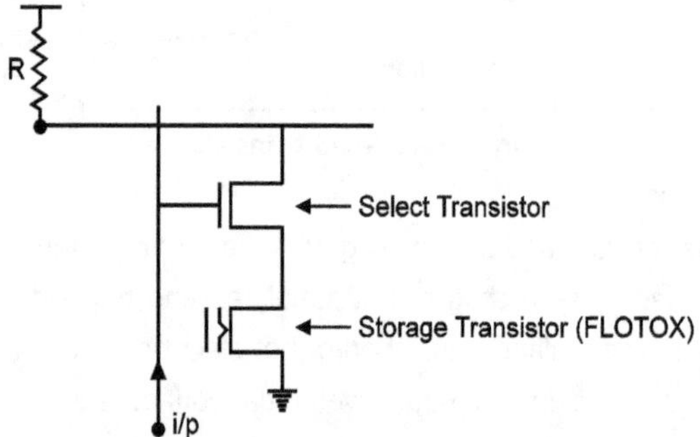

Fig. 8.4: EEPROM-based technology (one cell)

This technology requires two transistors in each cell, select transistor and storage transistor.

Storage transistor also has two gates, select gate and floating gate. When the floating gate is charged, then there is no conduction. When there is no charge on the floating gate, it means it can conduct by applying a voltage to the select gate.

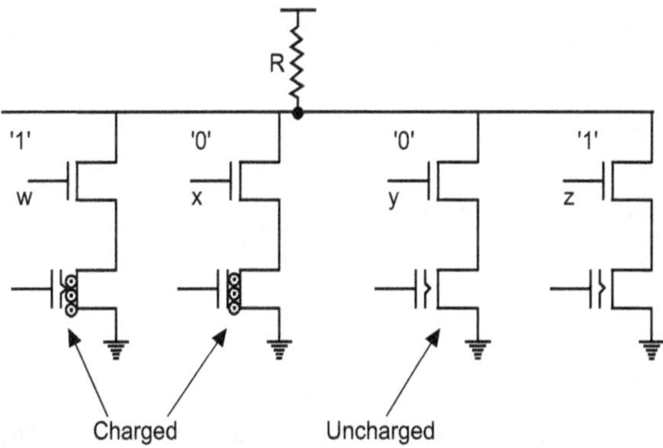

Fig. 8.5: Implementing function $\overline{y + z} = \overline{y} \cdot \overline{z}$

As shown in Fig. 8.5, w and x storage transistors are charged and y and z storage transistors are uncharged. Therefore, we can implement the function $\overline{y + z} = \overline{y} \cdot \overline{z}$.

The storage transistors in EEPROM are called as FLOTOX (floating gate tunnel oxide transistors).

The select transistor is used to remove the electrons electrically from the floating gate in a precise manner. But removing too many electrons from the floating gate leaves the gate positively charged and always on. This drawback is removed by flash technology.

8.2.6 Flash Technology

Flash term is used to reflect rapid erasure times compared to EPROM. Flash cell also has two transistors, the select and storage transistors. But in flash cell, the storage transistor is a FAMOS transistor. In this, the floating gate is shared by an erase transistor that takes charge off it via tunneling.

Comparing EPROM, EEPROM and Flash technologies, EPROM requires UV erasing, which takes more time. Therefore, EPROM is not suitable for in-system programming.

EEPROM and flash uses electrical erasing, which is suitable for in-system programming.

Various ICs, such as multiplexers, demultiplexers, adders, subtractors, code converters, shift register, counter, etc. perform a specific, fixed function. Hence, these ICs are referred to as fixed function ICs. These devices are designed by their manufacturer and manufactured in large quantities.

To design a circuit, a designer can select appropriate ICs for the circuit. The advantages of the design method using these ICs are:

1. Low development cost.
2. Fast turn around of designs.
3. Relatively easy to test the circuits.

The disadvantages are:

1. Large area (size of PCB) requirements.
2. Large power requirements.
3. Circuits can be copied by others, i.e. less security.
4. Additional cost, space, power requirements, etc. required to modify the design or to introduce more features.

To overcome the disadvantages of design using fixed function ICs, **Application Specific Integrated Circuits (ASICs)** have been developed. The ASICs are designed by the users to meet specific requirements of a circuit and are produced by an IC manufacturer as per the specifications supplied by the user.

The advantages of this method are:

1. Reduced space requirement.
2. Reduced power requirement.
3. If produced in large volumes, the cost is considerably reduced.
4. High security i.e. impossible to copy.

The disadvantages are:

1. Initial development cost may be high.
2. Need to develop testing methods, which may increase the cost and effort.

Another approach to digital design is the use of **Programmable Logic Devices** (PLDs). A PLD is an IC that is user configurable and is capable of implementing logic function. It is programmed by the user to perform a function required for his application.

PLDs have the following advantages:

1. Short design cycle.
2. Low development cost.
3. Reduction in space requirements.

4. Reduction in power requirements.
5. High design security.
6. Compact circuitry.
7. Higher switching speed.

8.3 ASIC

ASIC stands for Application Specific Integrated Circuit. It implements custom functions according to system requirements. It is useful for high volume production.

ASICs can be divided into two basic categories:
1. Full custom ASICs
2. Semi-custom ASICs

8.3.1 Full Custom ASICs

Full custom ASIC is an IC designed by using basic logic gates, circuits or layout specifically for a particulate design. In full custom ASIC, all logic cells are customized by the designer. Designer abandons the approach of using pretested and precharacterized cells for his design. In full custom ASIC, every mask is defined by the customer. The CMOS technology is used for full custom because it is easier to design analog as well as digital circuits on the same chip with better performance.

These are designed and processed like standard products with all set of masks for all fabrication layers.

e.g. Mega processor like Pentium, memory etc.

8.3.2 Semi-Custom ASICs

Semi-custom ASICs are either partly or full prefabricated, or they are structured like standard and custom ICs. Few mask patterns are predesigned.

Semi-custom ASICs can be classified as:
1. Standard cells.
2. Gate arrays.
3. Mixed signal and analogue ASICs.
4. Programmable logic devices.

8.3.2.1 Standard Cell-based ASICs

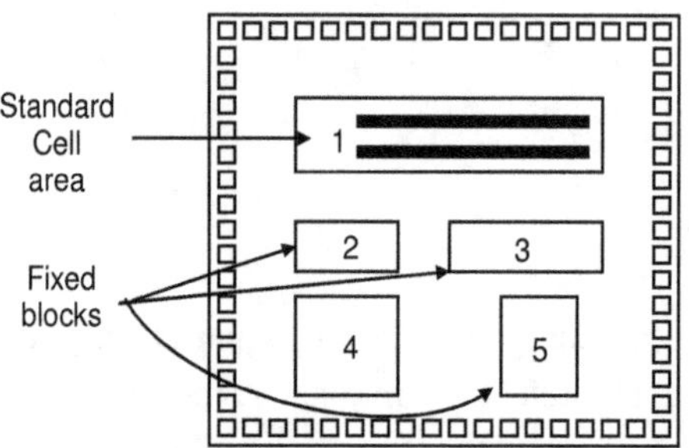

Fig. 8.6: Standard cells structure

The predesigned logic cells (gates, multipliers, flip-flop etc.) known as standard cells are used in standard cell-based ASICs. Standard cell areas in a CBIC (Cell Based IC) are built of rows of standard cells (like a wall built of bricks). Standard cell areas may be used in combination with larger predesigned cells, perhaps micro-controllers or even micro-processors, known as mega cells. All mask layers are customized this means that the standard cells can be placed anywhere on the silicon.

Standard cell is fabricated with full set of masks. The design support includes a library of macro cells. The macros contain the patterns for all the masks and the design is completed by the placement and routing which determines the location of the macros and their interconnections.

A standard cell requires less silicon for a given function as the macros are very compact.

The power and ground lines run parallel to the upper and lower boundaries of the cells, hence neighboring cells share a common power and ground bus. The input and output pins are located on the upper and lower boundaries of the cells. Fig. 8.6 shows the layout of a typical standard cell.

The features of this type of ASIC are:
- All mask layers are customized.
- Custom blocks can be embedded
- Manufacturing lead-time is about few weeks.

8.3.2.2 Gate Array-based ASICs

In gate array-based ASICs, pattern of transistors are predefined on the silicon. The predefined pattern of transistors on a gate array is the base array and the smallest element that is replicated to make the base array is the base call or primitive cell. The designer chooses from a library of logic cell. The logic cells in a gate array library are called macros.

A gate array is an IC chip on which gates are placed in matrix form without connections among the gates. By connecting gates, the logic can be realized.

Types of gate array:
1. Channeled gate array.
2. Channelless gate array or Sea of Gates array.

1. Channeled Gate Array

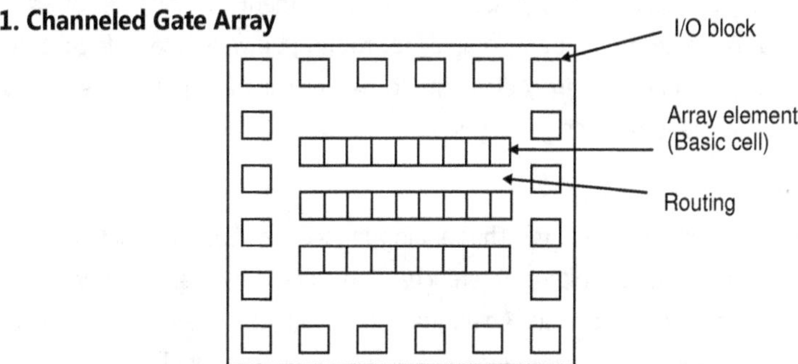

Fig. 8.7: Channeled gate array ASICs

The rows of basic cells with spaces are occupied on the silicon core. The spaces between the array element is called routing channel which is kept free for the interconnection among the basic cells. The core array is supplemented by the peripheral input/output blocks, which can be configured into input, output, or bi-directional buffer. An array element consists of two p and two n MOSFETS. The chip function is implemented by the metallization, which interconnects selected array element.

The features of channeled gate array are:
- Only the interconnect is customized.
- The interconnect uses predefined spaces between rows of base cells.
- Manufacturing time is about few days.

2. Channelless Gate Array or Sea of Gates Array

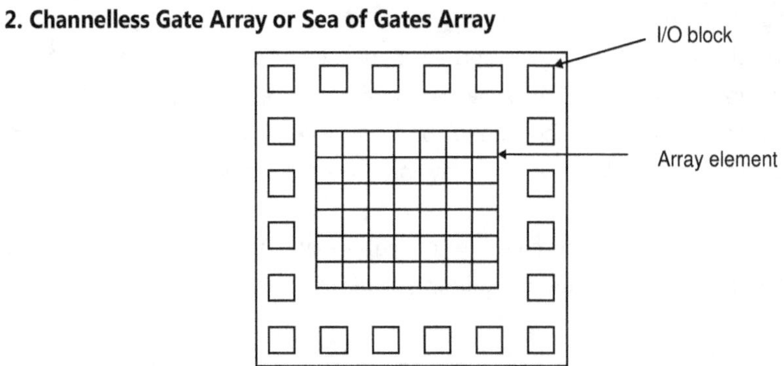

Fig. 8.8: Channelless gate array

Architecture of channelless gate array or SOG array is shown in Fig. 8.8. It occupies the entire core of the chip. All interconnects are now passed over array element. The number of array elements are increased. There are no predefined areas for routing between the cells. So SOG architecture allows a larger number of array elements to be utilized than a channeled array for the same size of die i.e. the logic density is higher.

8.3.2.3 Mixed mode and Analogue ASICs

It contains analogue and digital circuits. The analogue section covers functions like operational amplifiers, comparators, voltage references, and data converters. Standard cell format is used to construct analogue circuits. Analogue and digital macros are side by side in a mixed mode ASIC. They are formed by interconnecting a linear array which contains an assembly of bipolar transistors, resistors, and MOS capacitors. Vendor supplies the data for interconnections.

8.4 Programmable Logic Devices

Programmable Logic Devices (PLDs) are standard ICs that are available in standard configurations. PLDs are sold in very high volume to many different customers. PLDs are configured (programmed) to create a part customized to a specific application, and so they also belong to family of ASICs. PLDs use different technologies to allow programming of the device. PLDs are available as erasable or mask-programmed.

The features of PLDs are:
- No customized mask layers or logic cells.
- Fast design turn around time.
- Signal large block of programmable interconnect.

Types of PLDs

- Simple Programmable Logic Devices (SPLDs)

- Complex Programmable Logic Devices (CPLDs)

- Field Programmable Gate Arrays (FPGAs)

Simple Programmable Logic Devices

SPLDs are also known as:

- PAL (Programmable Array Logic)

- GAL (Generic Array Logic)

- PLA (Programmable Logic Array)

- PLD (Programmable Logic Device)

SPLDs are the smallest and consequently the least expensive form of programmable logic. An SPLD is typically comprised of 4 to 22 macro cells and can typically replace a few 7400 series TTL devices.

8.5 Read Only Memory (ROM) as a PLD

A ROM can store an array of binary data. Data stored in the ROM can be read out whenever required, but cannot be changed under normal operating condition. Fig. 8.9 shows a ROM that has n input lines and m output lines. It contains an array of 2^n words and each word is m bits long. The input line serves as an address to select one of the 2^n words.

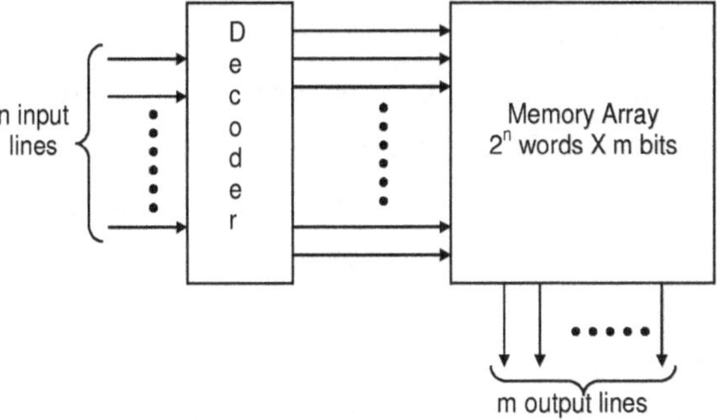

Fig. 8.9: Basic ROM structure

ROM consists of a decoder and a memory array. When binary input is applied to the decoder inputs, only one of the 2^n decoder outputs is 1, which selects one of the words in the memory array, and the binary data stored in this word is transferred to the memory output lines. A $2^n \times m$ ROM can realize m function of n variables. ROM can store a truth table with 2^n rows and m columns.

Mask-programmable ROMs and erasable programmable ROMs (called EPROMs) are the basic types of ROM.

Data is permanently stored in amask-programmable ROM at the time of manufacture. Use of Mask-programmable ROMs is economical only if large quantities are required with the same data entry. If only a small quantity of ROMs are required with a given data array, EPROMs may be used.

During the development phase, it is needed to modify the data stored in a ROM, so EPROMs are used instead of mask-programmable ROM. By using PROM programmer, data stored in EPROM can be changed. Data is erased using an ultraviolet light. The electrically erasable PROM (EEPROM) is a more recent development. EEPROM is similar to EPROM, except that, stored data is erased using electrical pulses instead of ultraviolet light.

Flash memories have built-in programming and erase capability so that data can be written to a flash memory placed in a circuit without the need of separate programmer.

8.5.1 ROM Organization

A 16 bit ROM array is shown in Fig. 8.10. To select any one of the 16 bits, a 4 bit address $(A_3\ A_2\ A_1\ A_0)$ is required. The lower order two bits $(A_1\ A_0)$ are decoded by the decoder D_L which selects one of the four rows whereas the higher order two bits $(A_3\ A_2)$ are decoded by the decoder D_H which activates one of the four column sense amplifiers.

The output is enabled by applying logic 1 at the chip select (CS) input. Programming a ROM means to selectively open and close the switches in series with the diodes.

For example, if the switch of diode D_{21} is in closed position and if the address input is 0110, row 2 is activated connecting it to column 1. Also the sense amplifier of column 1 is enabled which gives logic 1 output if the chip is selected (CS = 1). This shows that a logic 1 is stored at the address 0110. If the switch of the diode D_{21} is open, logic 0 is stored at the address 0110.

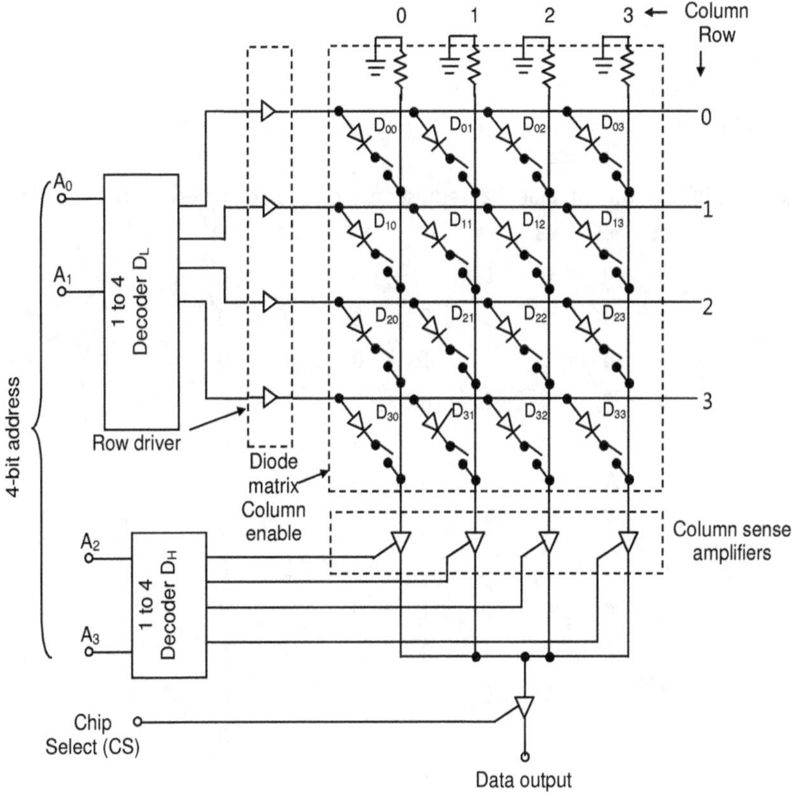

Fig. 8.10: 16 bit ROM array

A ROM consists of an array of bipolar junction transistor or field effect transistors are also available.

8.5.2 Circuit Realization using ROM

Example 1:

Using ROM, implement the circuit represented by the following conditions.

$$Y_1 = \overline{x4}$$

$$Y_2 = x1\, x3 + \overline{x2}\, x4$$

$$Y_3 = \overline{x1}\, x2 + x2\, \overline{x3}$$

$$Y_4 = x1\, x2\, x3\, x4$$

Solution:

First make the ROM program table that represents the conditions given by the equations.

x1	x2	x3	x4	Y1	Y2	Y3	Y4
0	0	0	0	1	0	0	0
0	0	0	1	0	1	0	0
0	0	1	0	1	0	0	0
0	0	1	1	0	1	1	0
0	1	0	0	1	0	1	0
0	1	0	1	0	0	1	0
0	1	1	0	1	0	1	0
0	1	1	1	0	0	1	0
1	0	0	0	1	0	0	0
1	0	0	1	0	1	0	0
1	0	1	0	1	1	0	0
1	0	1	1	0	1	0	0
1	1	0	0	1	0	1	0
1	1	0	1	0	0	1	0
1	1	1	0	1	1	0	0
1	1	1	1	0	1	0	1

The ROM implementation is shown in Fig. 8.11.

In Fig. 8.11, BL is the bit line and WL is the world line. No physical contact is there between WL and BL line. When BL line is grounded irrespective of the value on WL line, a, 0 is stored. When high voltage is applied on WL line, the diode is forward biased and 1 is considered to be stored. Thus if a diode is present, 1 is considered to be stored and if there is no diode, 0 is stored.

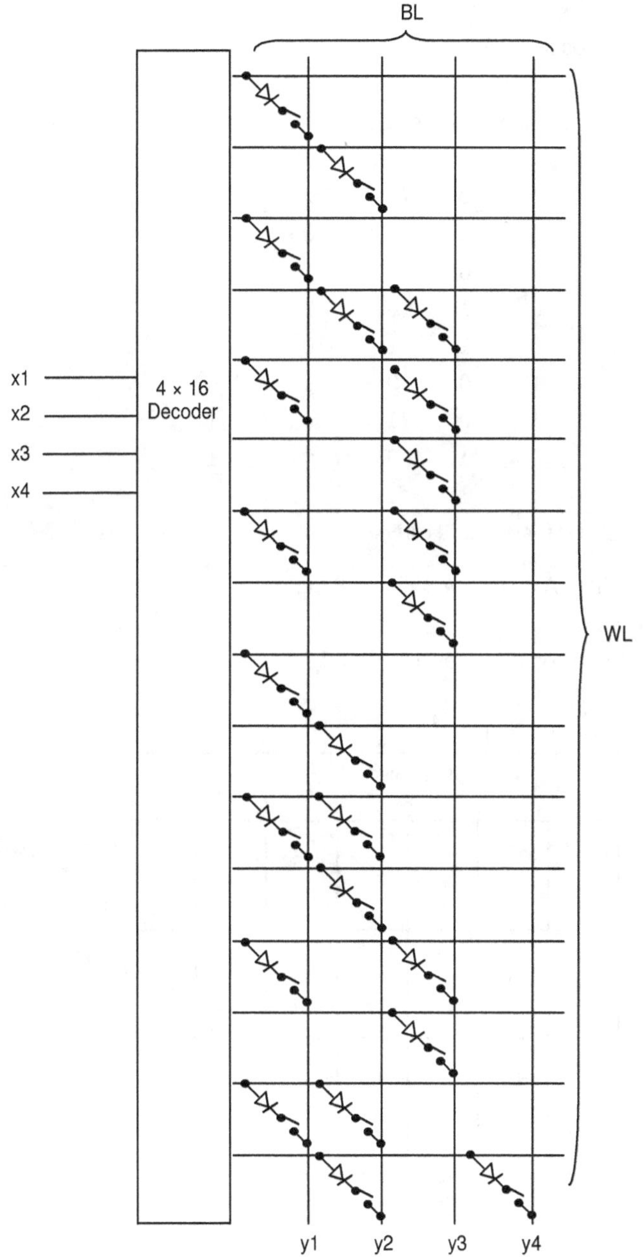

Fig. 8.11: ROM Implementation

Example 2:

Implement the full adder circuit in ROM.

Solution:

Make the ROM program table that represents the Boolean equations for sum and carry outputs from the full adder.

A	B	Cin	Sum	Carry
0	0	0	0	0
0	0	1	1	0
0	1	0	1	0
0	1	1	0	1
1	0	0	1	0
1	0	1	0	1
1	1	0	0	1
1	1	1	1	1

The Boolean equations for sum and carry are

$$\text{Sum} = \bar{A}\,\bar{B}\,\text{Cin} + \bar{A}\,B\,\overline{\text{Cin}} + A\,\bar{B}\,\overline{\text{Cin}} + AB\,\text{Cin}$$

$$\text{Carry} = A\,B + B\,\text{Cin} + A\,\text{Cin}$$

The ROM implementation is as shown in Fig. 8.12.

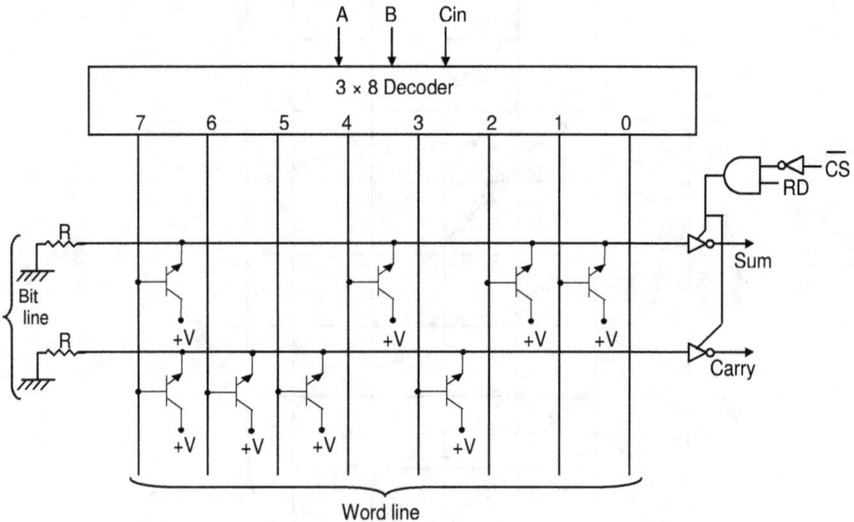

Fig. 8.12: Implementation of full adder in ROM

The ROM used contains bipolar junction transistor. Words are programmed by joining the intersections using n-p-n transistor. If a connection exists, transistor is present when the word line is addressed, the bit line goes HIGH. The tristate gates are enabled when CS is LOW and RD is HIGH.

A PROM structure includes fusible links (See Fig. 8.13) between the emitters of the npn (n-p-n) and the bit lines. To program the device, current pulses are passed through the links until the fuses are blown.

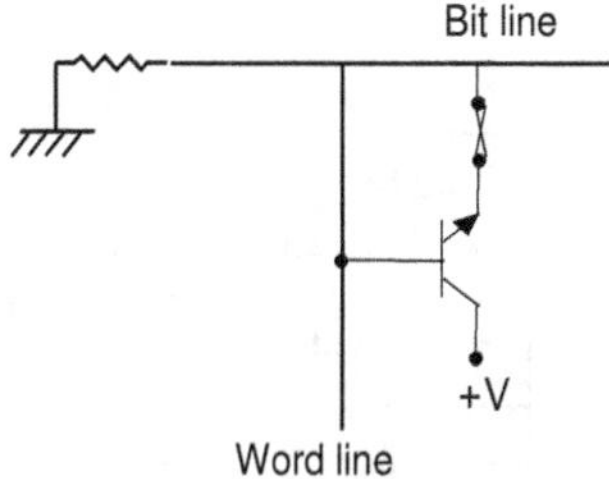

Fig. 8.13

8.6 Programmable Logic Arrays (PLAs)

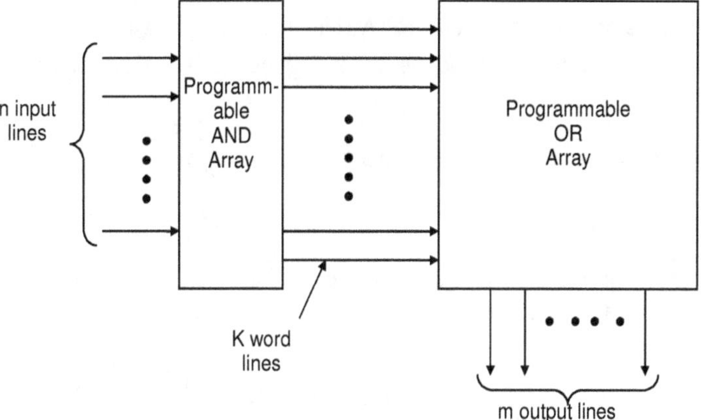

Fig. 8.14: PLA structure

Fig. 8.14 shows a PLA structure with n inputs and m outputs which can realize m functions of n variables. PLA consists of an AND array and an OR array. An AND array realizes selected product terms of the input variables. The OR array ORs together the product terms needed to form the output functions.

8.6.1 Architecture of PLA

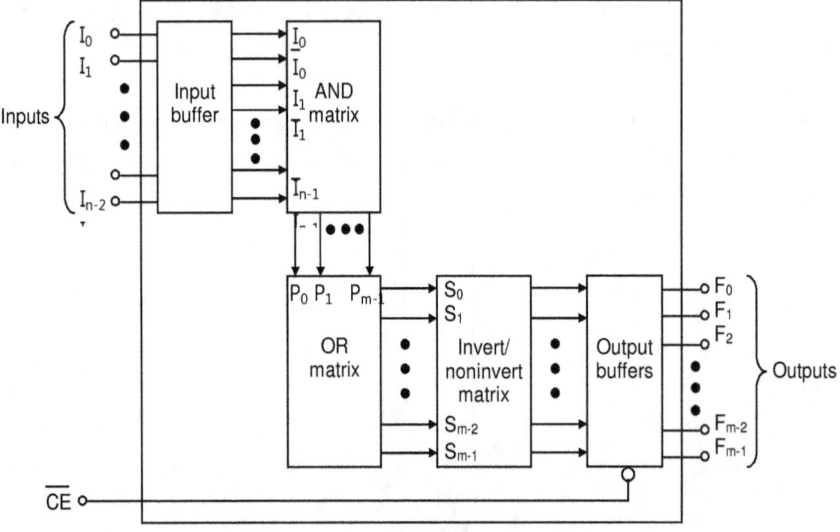

Fig. 8.15: Block diagram of PLA device

A PLA consists of two level AND - OR circuits on a single chip. The number of AND and OR gates and their inputs are fixed for a given PLA chip. The AND gates provide the product terms and OR gates ORs their product terms and generate a SOP (sum of products) expression.

The block diagram for internal architecture of PLA is shown in Fig. 8.15.

Input Buffer

Input buffer produces inverted as well as non-inverted inputs at the output as shown in Fig. 8.16 for one input. There are similar buffers for each one of the n inputs.

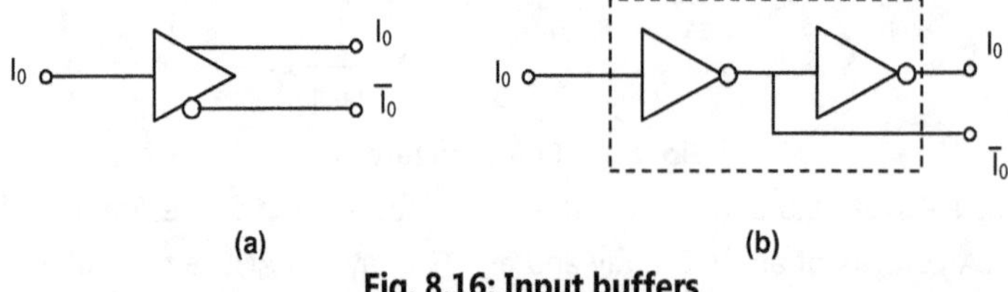

(a)   (b)

Fig. 8.16: Input buffers

Input buffers are required to limit loading of the sources that drive the inputs.

AND Matrix

An AND matrix is used to form product terms. A typical AND matrix is shown in Fig. 8.17. It has M AND gates. $2n$ (I_0 to I_{n-1} and $\overline{I_0}$ to $\overline{I_{n-1}}$) are the inputs and M (P_0 to P_{m-1}) are the outputs of AND matrix. Each AND gate has all the input variables ($2n$). Nichrome fuse link is connected in series with each diode. All the links are closed in an unprogrammed PLA device and logic 0 is stored.

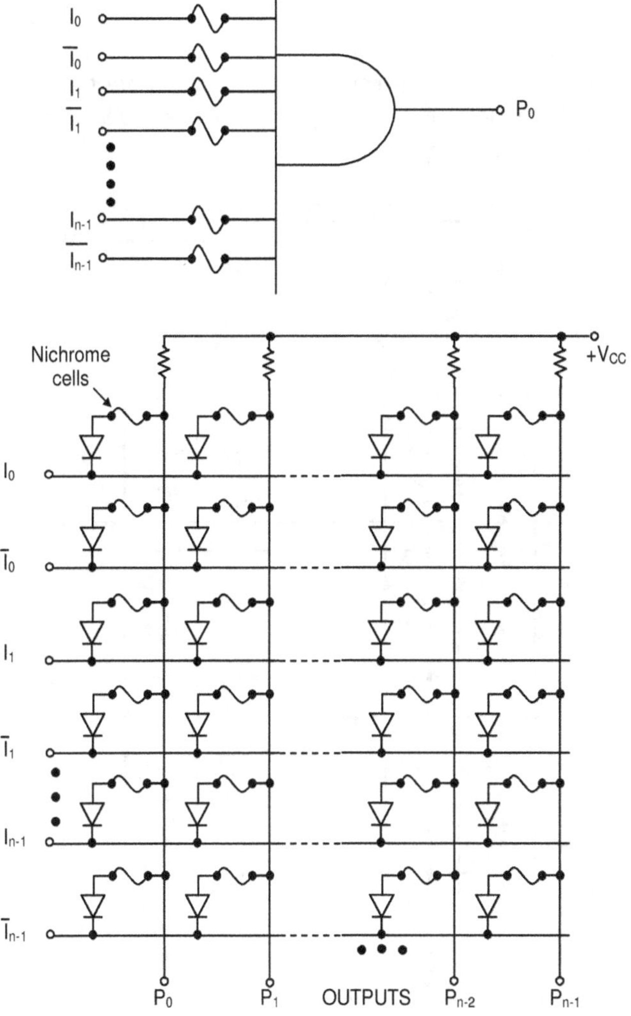

Fig. 8.17: An AND matrix

Each AND gate generates the one products term which is given by

$$P = I_0 \cdot \overline{I_0} \cdot I_1 \cdot \overline{I_1} \cdots I_{n-1} \cdot \overline{I_{n-1}}$$

By using a programmer device, unwanted links are opened, to generate required product term.

The gate representation for P_0 output is shown in Fig. 8.17.

OR Matrix

The OR matrix is used to produce the logical sum of the product terms (outputs of AND matrix). Fig. 8.18 shows an OR matrix using transistor. An OR gate consists of parallel connected transistors with a common emitter load. S_0 to S_{m-1} are the outputs of an OR matrix. All the fuse links are closed in an unprogrammed device. The S_0 output is given by,

$$S_0 = P_0 + P_1 + \cdots P_{m-1}$$

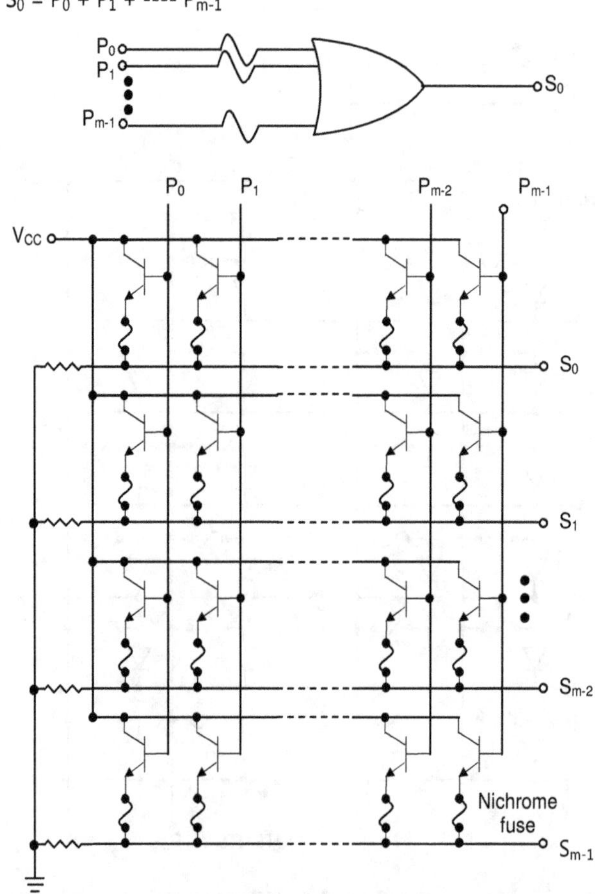

Fig. 8.18: An OR matrix

The unwanted fuse links can be opened to generate required sum terms.

For example, if P_0 and P_1 fuse links are closed and all others are blown off (opened) for the output S_0, then,

$$S_0 = P_0 + P_1$$

The logic symbol for one OR gate is shown in Fig. 8.18.

Invert/Non-Invert Matrix

This is a programmable buffer. This is used to generate active low or active high outputs. Typical circuits for this operation are shown in Fig. 8.19.

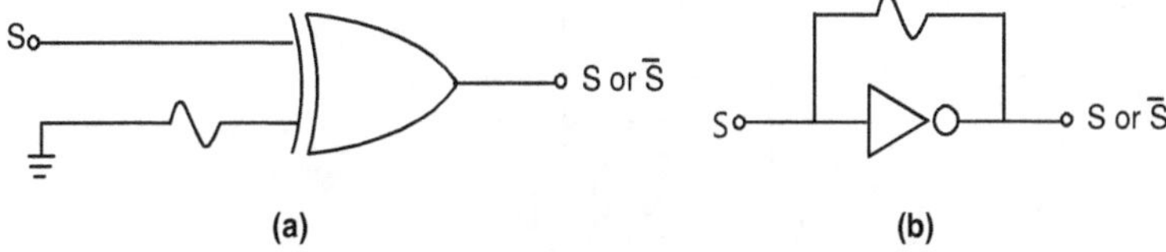

Fig. 8.19: Inverting /Non-inverting buffer

When fuse link is closed, the output is S and output is $\overline{S}$ when fuse is blown off (opened).

Output Buffer

To increase the driving capability of the PLA, output buffers are required. Usually, the outputs are TTL compatible. Fig. 8.20 shows the three-state output buffers.

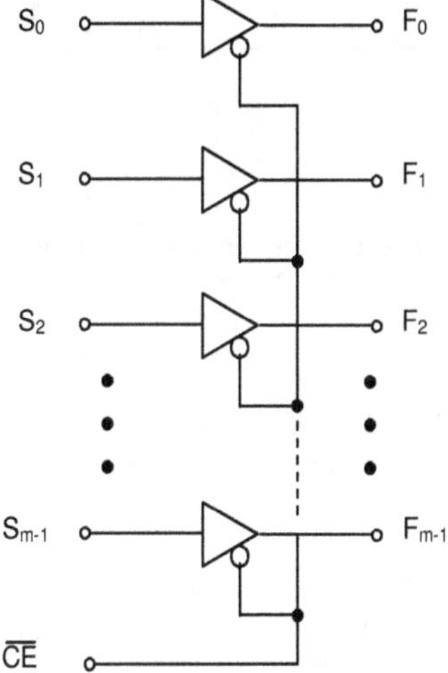

Fig. 8.20: Output buffers

Output through Flip-flop and Buffers

The output of the OR gate can be connected to the input of flip-flops. The device output can be available through tristate buffers. The PLA device with output flip-flop and buffers are suitable for state machine application.)

The PLA can be represented by AND and OR arrays as shown in Fig. 8.21.

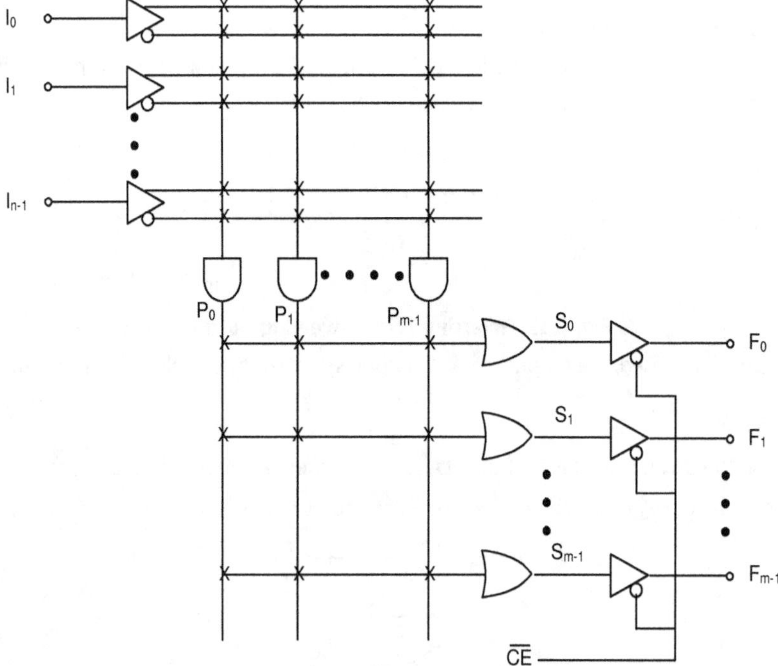

Fig. 8.21: Representation of PLA

Programming the PLA

A PLA device can be programmed similar to the programming of ROM. For a mask programmable device, the data pattern is to be specified by the customer. The appropriate masks are designed by the manufacturers and the data pattern is built in during the manufacturing process.

An FPLA (Field Programmable Logic Array) has all its nichrome links intact at the time of manufacturing. (At the time of manufacturing all the nichrome links of FPLA (Field Programmable Logic Array) are intact.) The unwanted links are electrically open circuited during programming. The links to be opened are accessed by applying voltages at the inputs and outputs of the device. The FPLAs are not reprogrammable.

8.6.2 Circuit Realization using PLA

Example 3:

Realize the following functions using PLA.

$F_0 = \Sigma\, m\,(0, 1, 4, 6)$

$F_1 = \Sigma\, m\,(2, 3, 4, 6, 7)$

$F_2 = \Sigma\, m\,(0, 1, 2, 6)$

$F_3 = \Sigma\, m\,(2, 3, 5, 6, 7)$

Solution:

If we minimize each function separately, the result is

$$F_0 = \overline{AB} + A\overline{C}$$

$$F_1 = B + A\overline{C}$$

$$F_2 = \overline{AB} + B\overline{C}$$

$$F_3 = AC + B$$

Fig. 8.22 shows an NMOS PLA that realizes the above functions.

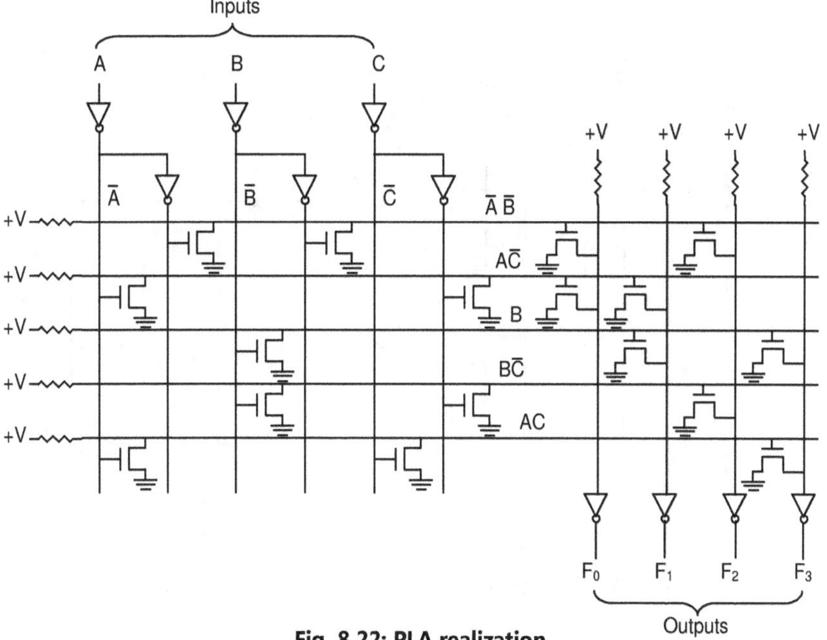

Fig. 8.22: PLA realization

Logic gates are formed in the array by connecting NMOS switching transistor between the column lines and row lines. The transistors act as switches, so if the gate input is logic 0, the transistor is off. If the gate input is logic 1, the transistor provides a conducting path to ground. Transistors connected in AND and OR array act as NOT gates.

For example, consider Fig. 8.23 (a).

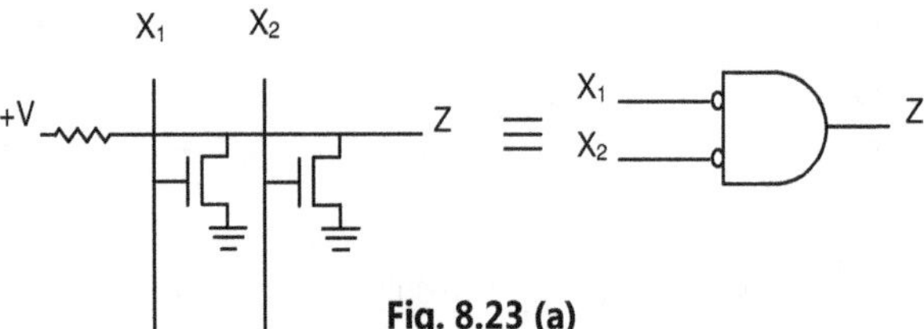

Fig. 8.23 (a)

If X1 and X2 = 0, both transistors are off, and the pull up resistor brings the Z output to a logic 1 level (+v). If either X1 or X2 is 1, the corresponding transistor is turned on, and Z = 0. Thus $\overline{X1 + X2} = \overline{X1}\,\overline{X2}$ which corresponds to a NOR gate.

The AND-OR array equivalent of Fig. 8.23 (a) is shown in Fig. 8.23 (b).

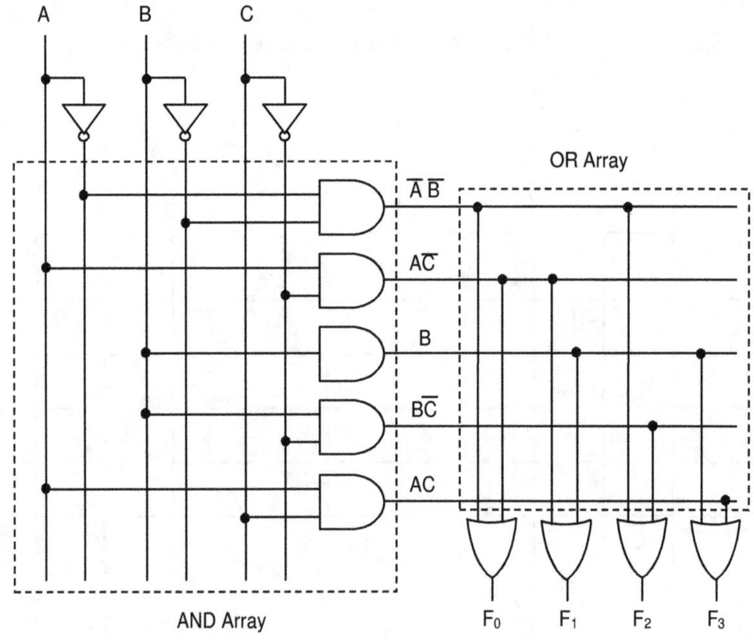

Fig. 8.23 (b): AND-OR array equivalent of Fig. 8.23 (a)

Example 4:

Implement BCD to gray code converter using PLA.

Solution:

The following table shows BCD numbers and their equivalent gray code.

BCD Code				Gray Code			
B_3	B_2	B_1	B_0	G_3	G_2	G_1	G_0
0	0	0	0	0	0	0	0
0	0	0	1	0	0	0	1
0	0	1	0	0	0	1	1
0	0	1	1	0	0	1	0
0	1	0	0	0	1	1	0
0	1	0	1	0	1	1	1
0	1	1	0	0	1	0	1
0	1	1	1	0	1	0	0
1	0	0	0	1	1	0	0
1	0	0	1	1	1	0	1

From the table, we can get

$$G_3 = B_3$$
$$G_2 = B_2 \oplus B_3 = B_2 \, \overline{B_3} + \overline{B_2} \, B_3$$
$$G_1 = B_1 \oplus B_2 = B_1 \, \overline{B_2} + \overline{B_1} \, B_2$$
$$G_0 = B_0 \oplus B_1 = B_0 \, \overline{B_1} + \overline{B_0} \, B_1$$

PLA with 4 inputs, 7 product terms and 4 outputs is shown in Fig. 8.24.

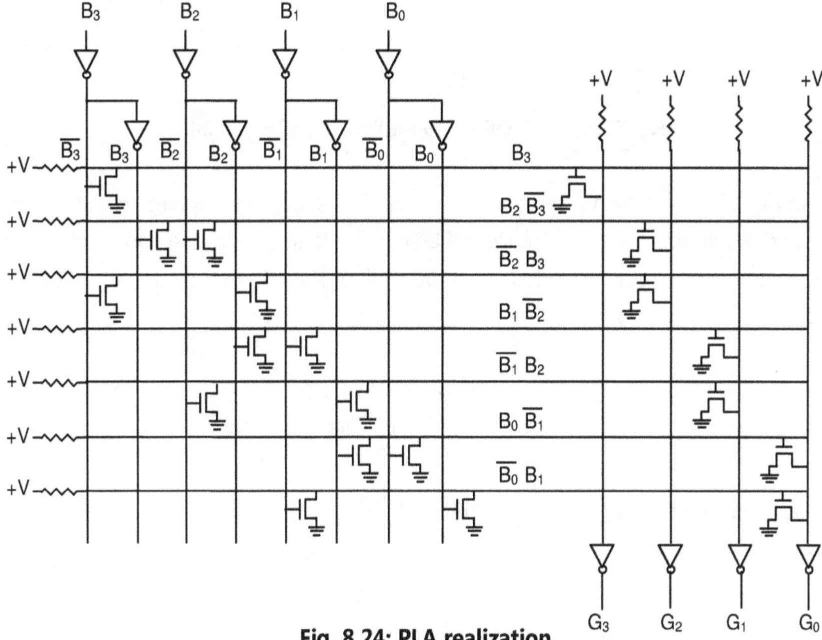

Fig. 8.24: PLA realization

The AND-OR array equivalent of Fig. 8.24 is shown in Fig. 8.25.

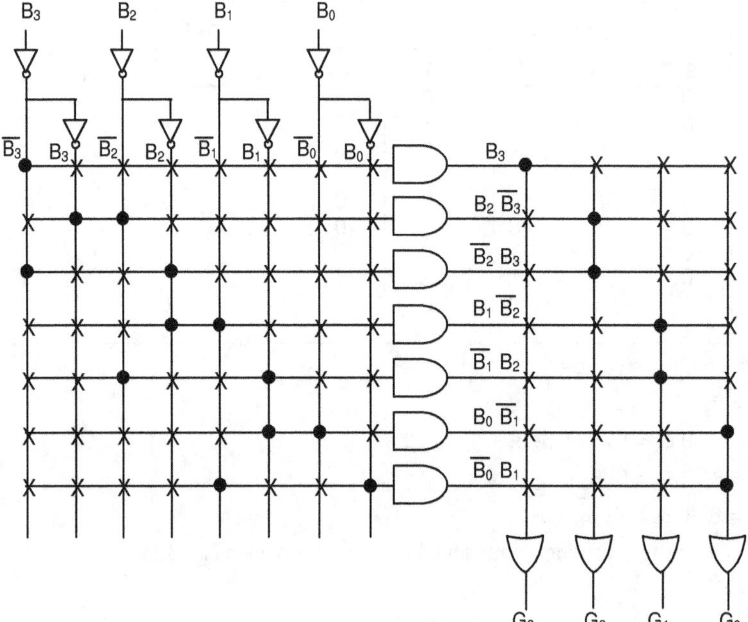

Fig. 8.25: AND-OR array equivalent of Fig. 8.24

From Fig. 8.25, it can be noticed that PLA utilizes less space as compared to ROM. A more buffer way of utilization of empty space in PLA can be done by allowing two or more input lines to share the same column or to let to product lines share the same row or by both. This sharing is known as folding.

In PLA, both AND and OR arrays are programmable. Hence PLA devices are more flexible than PAL devices. Thus the same AND output can be sent to any number of OR gates.

8.7 Programmable Array Logic (PAL)

In programmable array logic, the AND array is programmable and the OR array is fixed. The basic structure of the PAL is the same as PLA. PAL is less expensive than PLA because only the AND array is programmable.

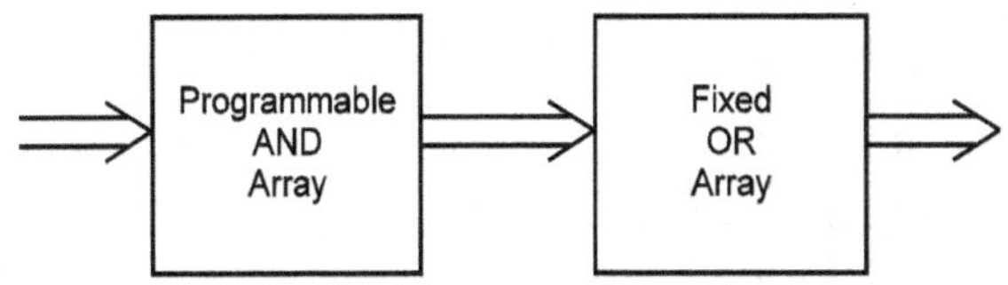

Structure of PAL

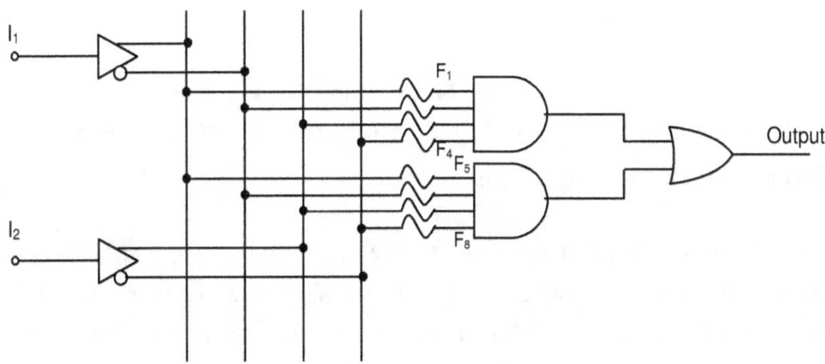

Fig. 8.26: Unprogrammed PAL segment

Fig. 8.26 represents a segment of an unprogrammed PAL.

The symbol represents an input buffer, with inverted and non-inverted outputs. A buffer is used to drive many AND gate inputs. When the PAL is programmed, the fusible links (F1, F2 - - F8) are selectively blown to leave the desired connections to the AND gate inputs. Connections to the AND gate inputs in a PAL are represented by Xs, as shown here.

Fig. 8.27 (a)

As an example, Fig. 8.27 (b) shows the realization of the function $I_1 \overline{I_2} + \overline{I_1} I_2$ by using PAL segment.

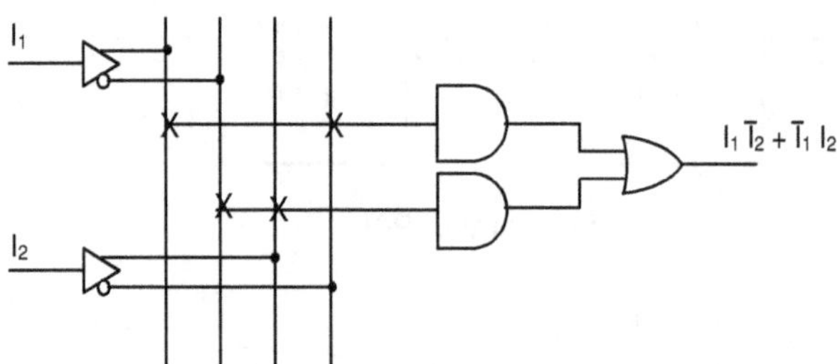

Fig. 8.27 (b): Programmed PAL segment

The Xs indicate that the I_1 and $\overline{I_2}$ lines are connected to the first AND gate, and the $\overline{I_1}$ and I_2 lines are connected to the other AND gate.

Typical PALs have from 10 to 20 inputs and from 2 to 10 outputs. 2 to 6 AND gates driving each OR gate. PALs are also available that contain D flip-flop with inputs driven from the programmable array logic. Such PALs provide a convenient way of realizing sequential networks. Fig. 8.28 shows a segment of sequential PAL. The D flip-flop is driven from an OR gate, which is fed by two AND gates. The flip-flop output is fed back to the programmable AND array through a buffer. Thus the AND gate inputs can be connected to A, $\overline{A}$, B, $\overline{B}$, Q or $\overline{Q}$. The Xs on the diagram shows the realization of the next-state equation.

$$Q^+ = D = \overline{A}B\overline{Q} + A\overline{B}Q$$

The flip-flop output is connected to an inverting tristate buffer, which is enable when EN = 1.

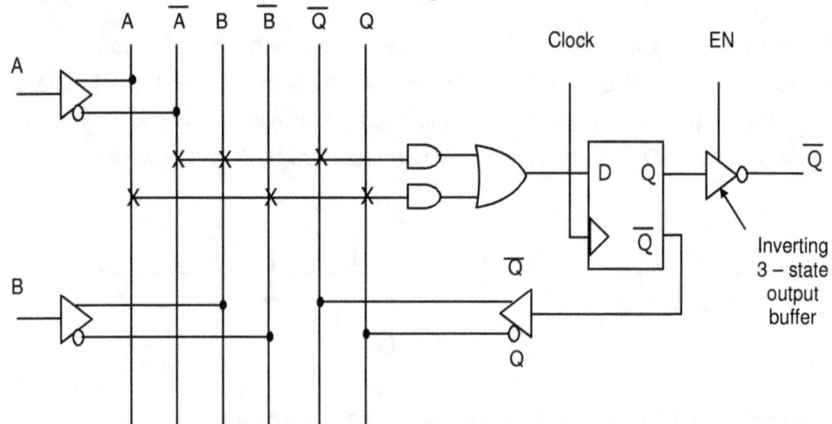

Fig. 8.28 : Sequential PAL segment

8.8 Complex Programmable Logic Devices (CPLDs)

The programmable logic devices such as PLAs and PALs have limited number of inputs, product terms, and outputs. These devices can support up to about 32 total number(s) of inputs and outputs only.

For implementation of circuits that require more input and output than that are available in a single SPLD chip, either multiple SPLD chips can be employed or more sophisticated type of chip, referred to as **complex programmable logic devices (CPLD)** can be used.

The complexity of any digital IC chip can be specified in terms of number of equivalent 2-input NAND gates. A typical PAL has 8 macrocells, if each macrocell represents about 20 equivalent gates, then the PAL can accommodate a circuit that needs up to about 160 gates. For a circuit requiring very large number of gates, CPLDs having large number of macrocells (say 512 macrocells) can implement circuits of up to about 10,000 equivalent gates, i.e. CPLDs are similar to SPLDs except that the CPLD is equivalent of 2 to 64 SPLDs. A CPLD typically contains from tens to a few hundred macrocells. CPLDs are as fast as PALs but they are more complex.

8.8.1 Block Diagram of CPLD

CPLDs are designed to appear just like a large number of PALs in a single chip connected to each other through a cross point switch. They are having same development tools and programmers, and are based on the same technologies, but they can handle much more complex logic and more of it.

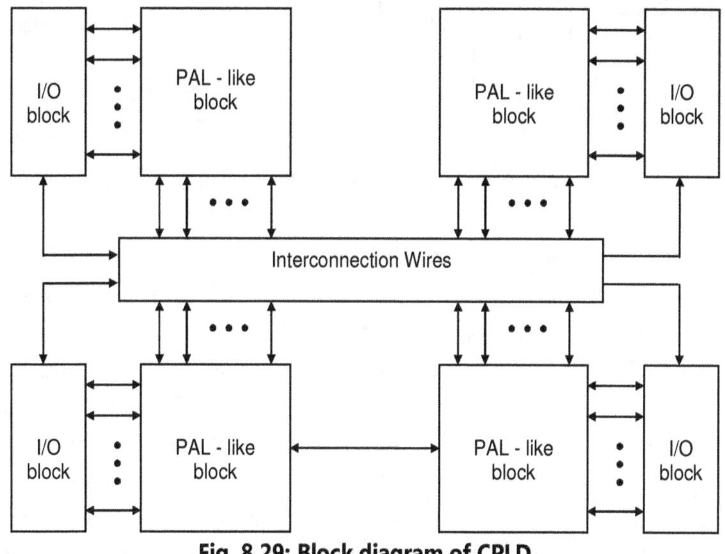

Fig. 8.29: Block diagram of CPLD

Fig. 8.29 shows block diagram of CPLD. It consists of a number of PAL-like blocks, I/O blocks and a set of interconnection wires.

The PAL-like blocks are connected to a set of interconnection wires and to an I/O block. The I/O block is used to drive signals to the pins of the CPLD device at the appropriate voltage levels with the appropriate current.

A PAL-like block (also called functional block) usually consists of 16 macrocells. Each macrocell consists of an AND-OR configuration, an EX-OR gate, a flip-flop, a multiplexer and a tristate buffer. A typical macrocell is shown in Fig. 8.30.

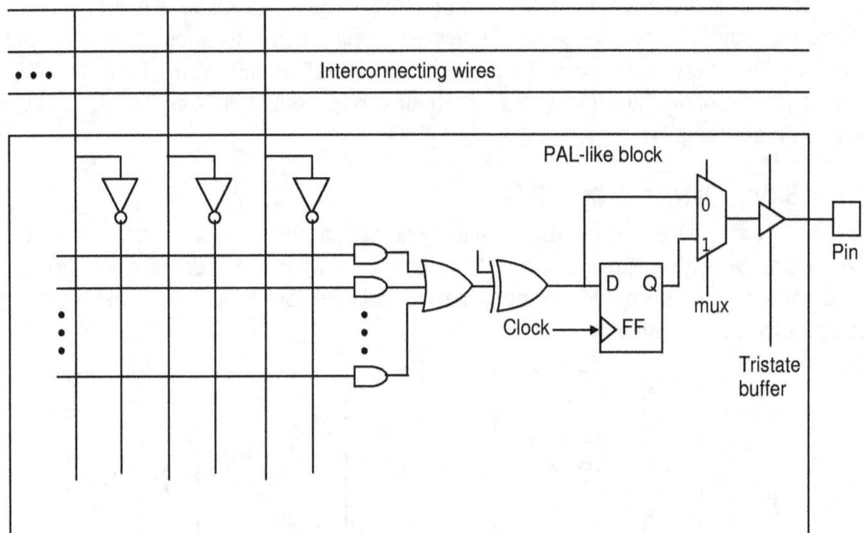

Fig. 8.30: Typical macrocell of a CPLD

Each AND-OR configuration usually consists of 5-20 AND gates and an OR gate with 5-20 inputs. An EX-OR gate is used to obtain the output of OR gate in inverted or non-inverted form depending upon its other input being 1 or 0 respectively. A D-FF stores the output of the EX-OR gate, a multiplexer selects either the output of the D flip-flop or the output of EX-OR gate depending upon its select input (1 or 0). The tristate buffer acts as a switch, which enables the chip's pin to be used as an output (tristate enabled) or as an input (tristate disabled). In case the chip's pin is used as an input pin, an external source can drive a signal on to the pin which can be connected to other macrocells using the interconnection wiring. When used as an input pin, the macrocell becomes redundant and it is wasted.

8.8.2 CPLD Programming

CPLDs are implemented using electrically erasable programmable read only memory (EEPROM) technology. One advantage of this technology is that it can be reprogrammed without external storage of configuration.

CPLD devices usually support the **In-system Programming (ISP)** (which means to perform programming with the chip remaining attached to the circuit board itself) due to the reasons mentioned below:

- CPLDs have large number of pins on the chip package and hence it is much inconvenient to take the chip out of the circuit board.

- A socket is required to hold the chip in programming unit. For large CPLDs, the packages used are very expensive than the CPLD device itself.

To program SPLDs and CPLDs, large number of programmable switches is required to be configured. It is not feasible to specify manually the desired state of each switch. For this purpose, computer-aided design (CAD) systems are employed, which specifies the state of each switch in the target PLD required to realize the desired circuit. A computer system that runs the CAD tools is connected by a cable to the programming unit. In the case of the ISP technique, a cable is used to connect the computer system and the CPLD. The programming involves transferring the programming file generated by the CAD system from the computer into the CPLD through this cable. The circuitry on the CPLD that allows in-system programming has been standardized by the IEEE and is usually called a **JTAG (Joint Test Action Group)**. Port, which uses four wires to transfer information between the computer and the device being programmed.

Features of ISP

- Hardware is flexible and easy to modify.
- Design upgrades are simple.
- ISP devices can be treated like any other device on the PCB, and no special manufacturing flow is required to program ISP devices.
- A minimum of 10,000 program/erase cycles.
- 20-year program retention is possible.
- Faster time to market.
- Superior Prototyping Solution.
- Internal Test.
- Board Reconfiguration and Field Upgrades.
- Multi-Function Hardware designs.
- Security Feature available, allowing design security. A secured device can be read back. A secured device can be reused after it has been erased.

JTAG is the commonly used acronym for the boundary scan test (BST) feature defined for integrated circuit by IEEE standard 1149.1. This standard defines input/output pins, logic control functions, and commands that facilitate both board and device level testing without the use of specialized test equipment.

JTAG pins are

TCK (clock signal)

TDI (input insertion signal)

TDO (output signal)

TMS (test mode select)

TRST (reset signal) which is not used at the time of ISP.

8.8.3 CPLD Packaging

CPLDs have a large number of pins, making it impractical to use dual-in-line packaging (DIP). Some of the commonly used packages for CPLDs are

Plastic-Leaded Chip Carrier (PLCC)

A PLCC package has pins on all four sides that 'wrap around' the edges of the chip, rather than extending straight down as in the case of a DIP. The IC socket of PLCC is soldered to the PCB, and the chip is held in the socket by friction.

Quad Flat Pack (QFP)

A QFP package also has pins on all four sides like a PLCC package, but with pins extending outward from the package and the downward-curving shape. The pins of QFPs are much thinner than those on a PLCC, making it suitable for supporting a larger number of pins. QFPs are available with more than 200 pins, whereas PLCCs are limited to fewer than 100 pins. Some of the varieties of QFPs available are: plastic quad flat pack (PQFP), power quad flat pack (RQFP), and 1.0 mm thin quad flat pack (TQFP).

Ceramic Pin Grid Array (PGA)

It has pins extending straight outwards from the bottom of the package in a grid pattern. It can accommodate a few hundred pins in total.

Ball Grid Array (BGA)

The BGA packaging is similar to the pin grid array packaging except that the pins are small round balls, instead of posts. The pins in a BGA package are very small, hence more pins can be provided on the package.

8.8.4 Xilinx's XC9500XV CPLD

Features

- Optimized for high-performance 2.5V systems
  - 3.5 ns pin-to-pin logic delays
  - Small footprint packages including VQFPs, TQFPs and CSPs (Chip Scale package)

- Lower power operation
- Multi-voltage operation
- Fast FLASH technology
- Advanced system features
  - In-system programmable
  - Output banking
  - Superior pin-locking and routability with Fast(-)CONNECT II™ switch matrix
  - Extra wide 54-input Function Blocks
  - Up to 90 product-terms per macro cell with individual product-term allocation
  - Local clock inversion with three global and one product-term clocks
  - Individual output enable per output pin with local inversion
  - Input hysteresis on all user and boundary-scan pin inputs
  - Bus-hold circuitry on all user pin inputs
  - Full IEEE Standard 1149.1 boundary-scan (JTAG) support on all devices
- Four pin-compatible device densities
  - 36 to 288 macrocells, with 800 to 6400 usable gates
- Fast concurrent programming
- Slew rate control on individual outputs
- Enhanced data security features
- Excellent quality and reliability
  - 10,000 program/erase cycles endurance rating
  - 20 year data retention
- Hot Plugging capability

Family Overview

The XC9500XV family is a 2.5V CPLD family targeted for high-performance, low-voltage applications in leading-edge communications and computing systems, where high device reliability and low power dissipation is important. Each XC9500XV device supports In-system Programming (ISP) and the full IEEE 1149.1 (JTAG) boundary-scan, allowing superior debug and design iteration capability for small form-factor packages.

The XC9500XV architectural features address the requirements of in-system programmability. Enhanced pin-locking capability avoids costly board rework. In-system programming throughout the full commercial operating range and a high programming endurance rating provide worry-free reconfigurations of system field upgrades. Extended data retention supports longer and more reliable system operating life.

Advanced system features include output slew rate control and user-programmable ground pins to help reduce system noise. Each user pin is compatible with 3.3V, 2.5V, and 1.8V inputs and the outputs may be configured for 3.3V, 2.5V, or 1.8V operation. The XC9500XV device exhibits symmetric full 2.5V output voltage swing to allow balanced rise and fall times.

Architecture Description

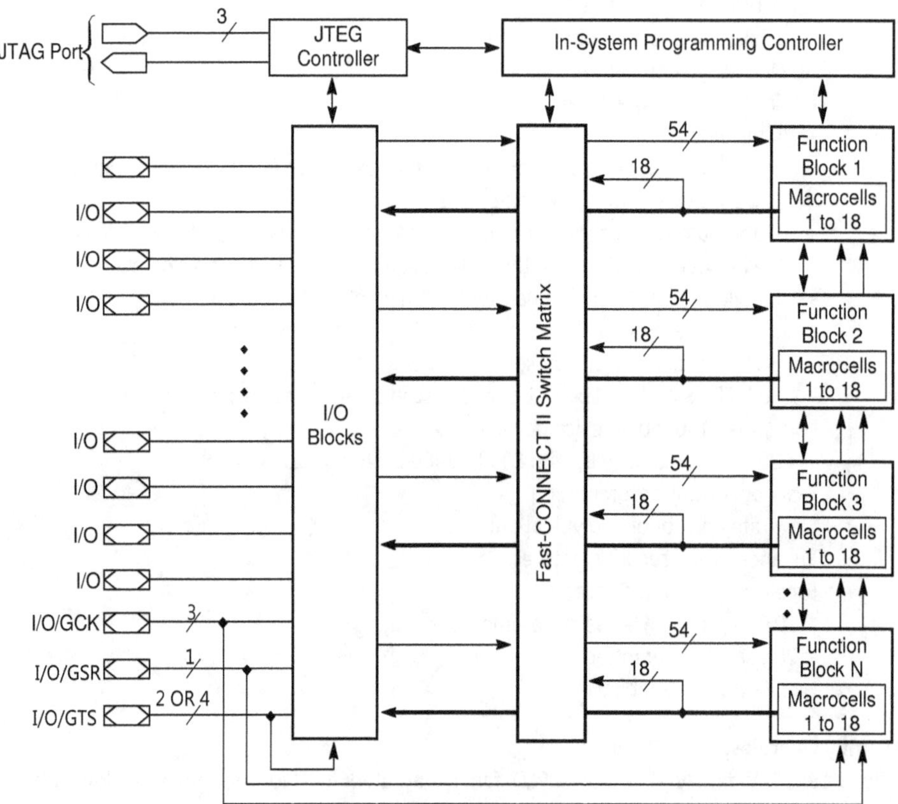

Fig. 8.31 : XC9500XV architecture

Each XC9500XV device is a subsystem consisting of multiple Function Blocks (FBs) and I/O Blocks (IOBs) fully inter-connected by the Fast-CONNECT II switch matrix. The IOB provides buffering for device inputs and outputs. Each FB provides programmable logic capability with extra wide 54 inputs and 18 outputs. The Fast-CONNECT II switch matrix connects all FB outputs and input signals to the FB inputs. For each FB, there are upto 18 outputs (depending on package pin-count) and associated output enable signals which drive directly to the IOBs. See Fig. 8.31.

Note: Function block outputs (indicated by the bold lines) drive the I/O blocks directly.

Function Block

Each Function Block, as shown in Fig. 8.32 is comprised of 18 independent macrocells, each capable of implementing a combinatorial or registered function. The FB also receives global clock, output enable, and set/reset signals.

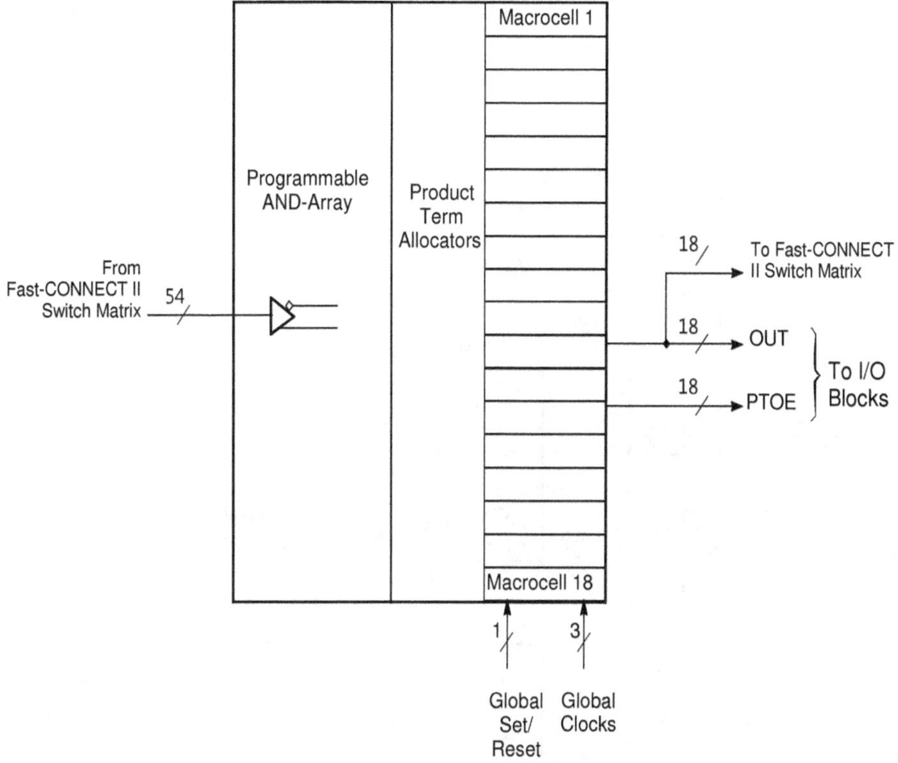

Fig. 8.32: XC9500XV function block

The FB generates 18 outputs that drive the Fast-CONNECT II switch matrix. These 18 outputs and their corresponding output enable signals also drive the IOB. Logic within the FB is implemented using a sum-of-products representation. Fifty-four inputs provide 108 true and complement signals into the programmable AND-array to form 90 product terms. Any number of these product terms, upto 90 available, can be allocated to each macrocell by the product term allocator.

Macrocell

Each XC9500XV macrocell may be individually configured for a combinatorial or registered function. The macrocell and associated FB logic is shown in Fig. 8.33. Five direct product terms from the AND-array are available for use as primary data inputs (to the OR and XOR gates) to implement combinatorial functions, or as control inputs including clock, clock enable, set/reset, and output enable. The product term allocator associated with each macrocell selects how the five direct terms are used.

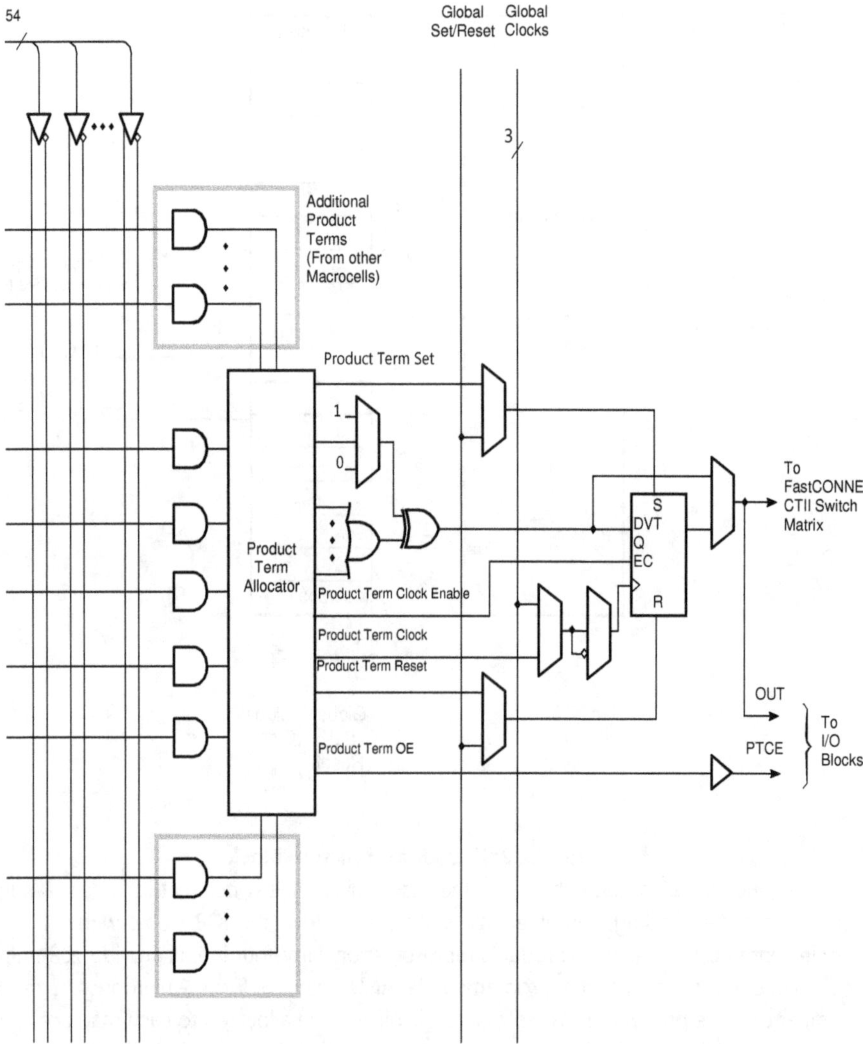

Fig. 8.33: XC9500XV macrocell within function block

The macrocell register can be configured as a D-type or T-type flip-flop, or it may be bypassed for combinatorial operation. Each register supports both asynchronous set and reset operations. During power-up, all user registers are initialized to the user-defined preload state (default to 0 if unspecified).

All global control signals are available to each individual macrocell, including clock, set/reset, and output enable signals. As shown in Fig. 8.34, the macrocell register clock originates from either of three global clocks or a product term clock. Both true and complement polarities of the selected clock source can be used within each macrocell. A GSR input is also provided to allow user registers to be set to a user-defined state.

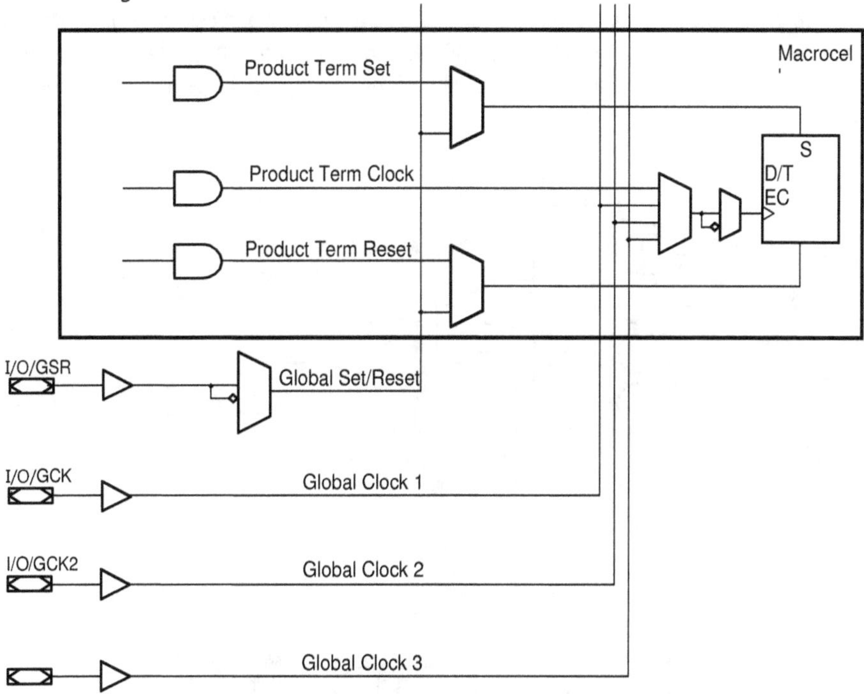

Fig. 8.34: Macrocell clock and Set/Reset capability

Product Term Allocator

The product term allocator controls how the five direct product terms are assigned to each macrocell. For example, all five direct terms can drive the OR function as shown in Fig. 8.35.

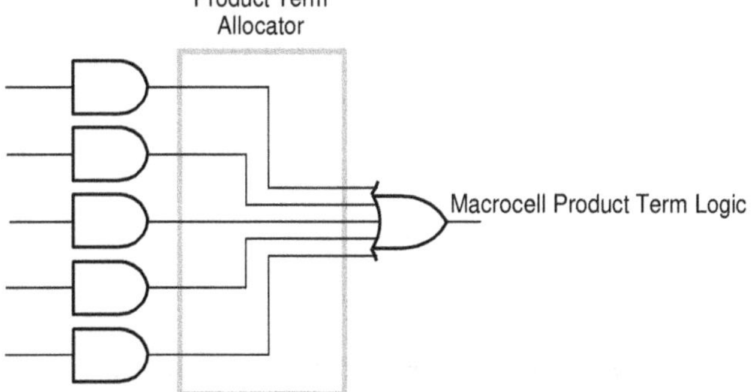

Fig. 8.35: Macrocell logic using direct product term

The product term allocator can reassign other product terms within the FB to increase the logic capacity of a macrocell beyond five direct terms. Any macrocell requiring additional product terms can access uncommitted product terms in other macrocells within the FB. Up to 15 product terms can be available to a single macrocell with only a small incremental delay of t_{PTA}, as shown in Fig. 8.36. Note that the incremental delay affects only the product terms in other macrocells. The timing of the direct product terms is not changed.

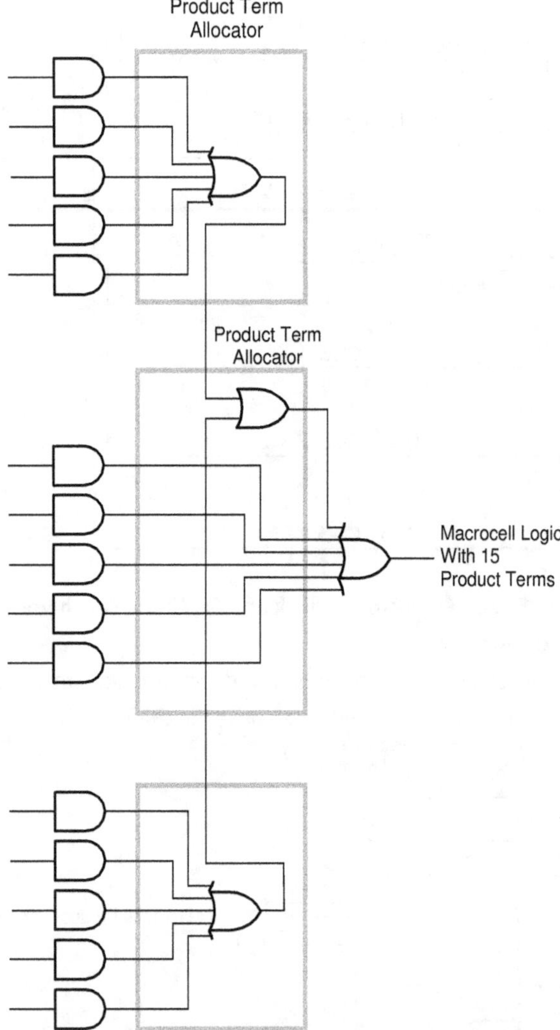

Fig. 8.36: Product term allocation with 15 product terms

The product term allocator can reassign product terms from any macrocell within the FB by combining partial sums of products over several macrocells, as shown in Fig. 8.37. In this example, the incremental delay is only $2*t_{PTA}$. All 90 product terms are available to any macrocell, with a maximum incremental delay of $8*t_{PTA}$.

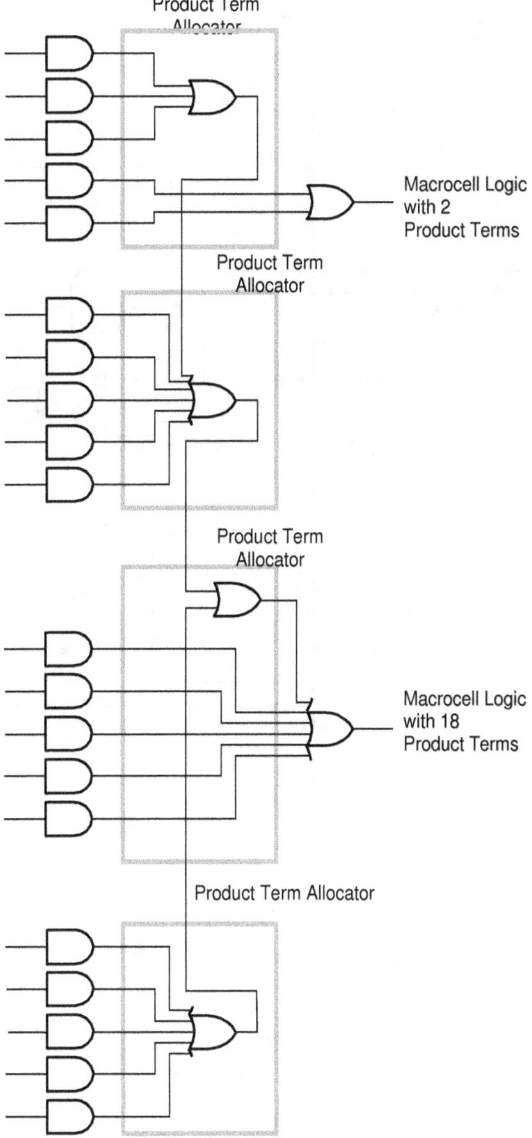

Fig. 8.37: Product term allocation over several macrocells

The internal logic of the product term allocator is shown in Fig. 8.38.

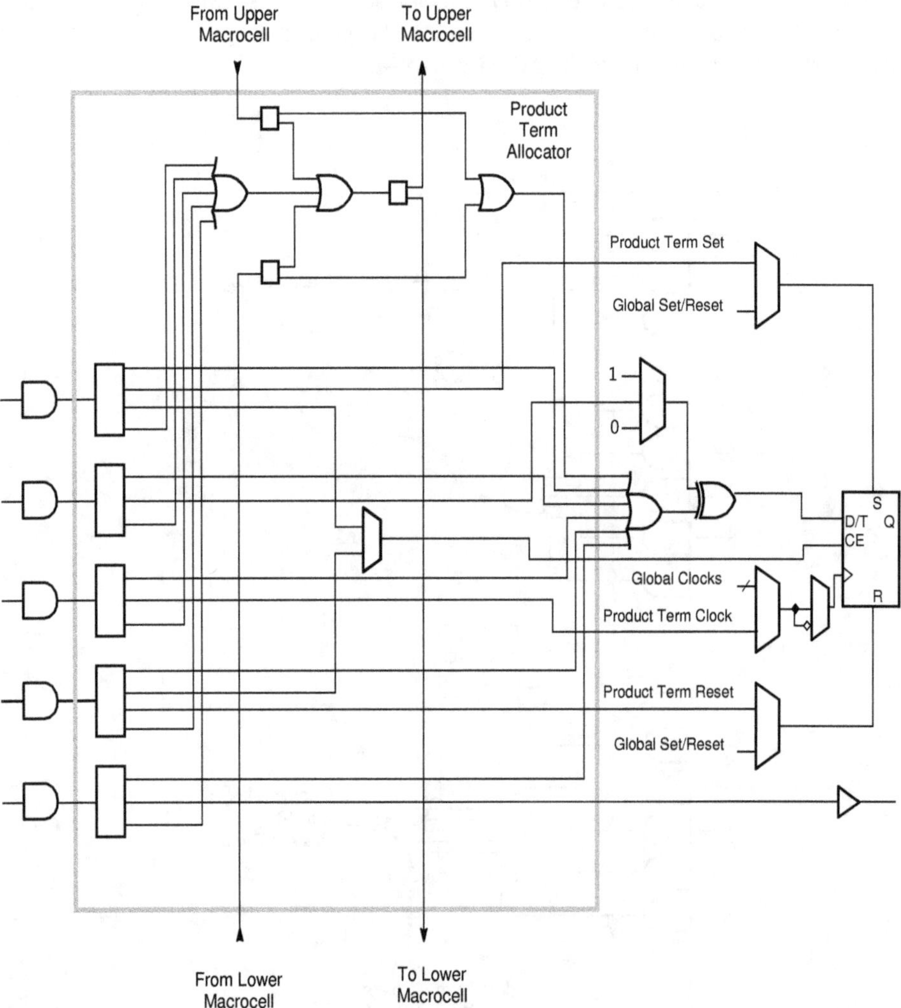

Fig. 8.38: Product term allocator logic

FastCONNECT II Switch Matrix

The FastCONNECT II Switch Matrix connects signals to the FB inputs, as shown in Fig. 8.39. All IOB outputs (corresponding to user pin inputs) and all FB outputs drive the FastCONNECT II matrix. Any of these (up to a fan-in limit of 54) may be selected to drive each FB with a uniform delay.

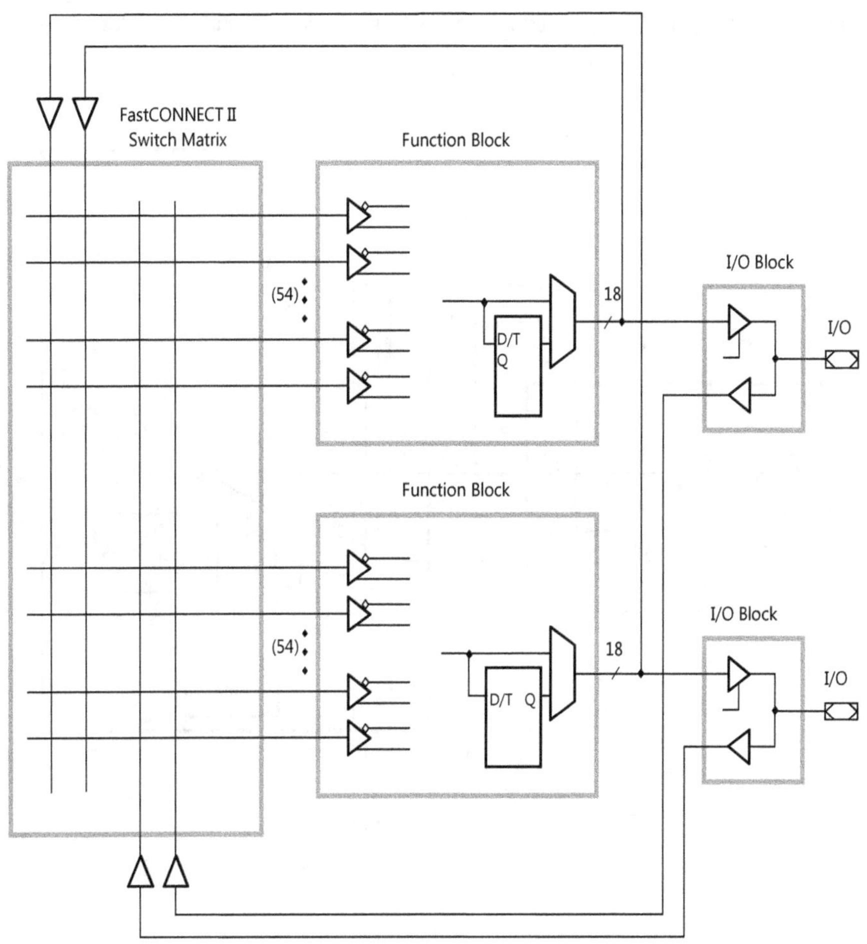

Fig. 8.39: FastCONNECT II Switch Matrix

I/O Block (IOB)

The I/O Block (IOB) interfaces between the internal logic and the device user I/O pins. Each IOB includes an input buffer, output driver, output enable selection multiplexer, and user programmable ground control. See Fig. 8.40 for details.

The input buffer is compatible with 3.3V CMOS, 2.5V CMOS, and 1.8V CMOS signals. The input buffer uses the internal 2.5V voltage supply (V_{CCINT}) to ensure that the input thresholds are constant and do not vary with V_{CCIO} voltage. Each input buffer provides input hysteresis (50 mV typical) to help reduce system noise for input signals with slow rise or fall edges.

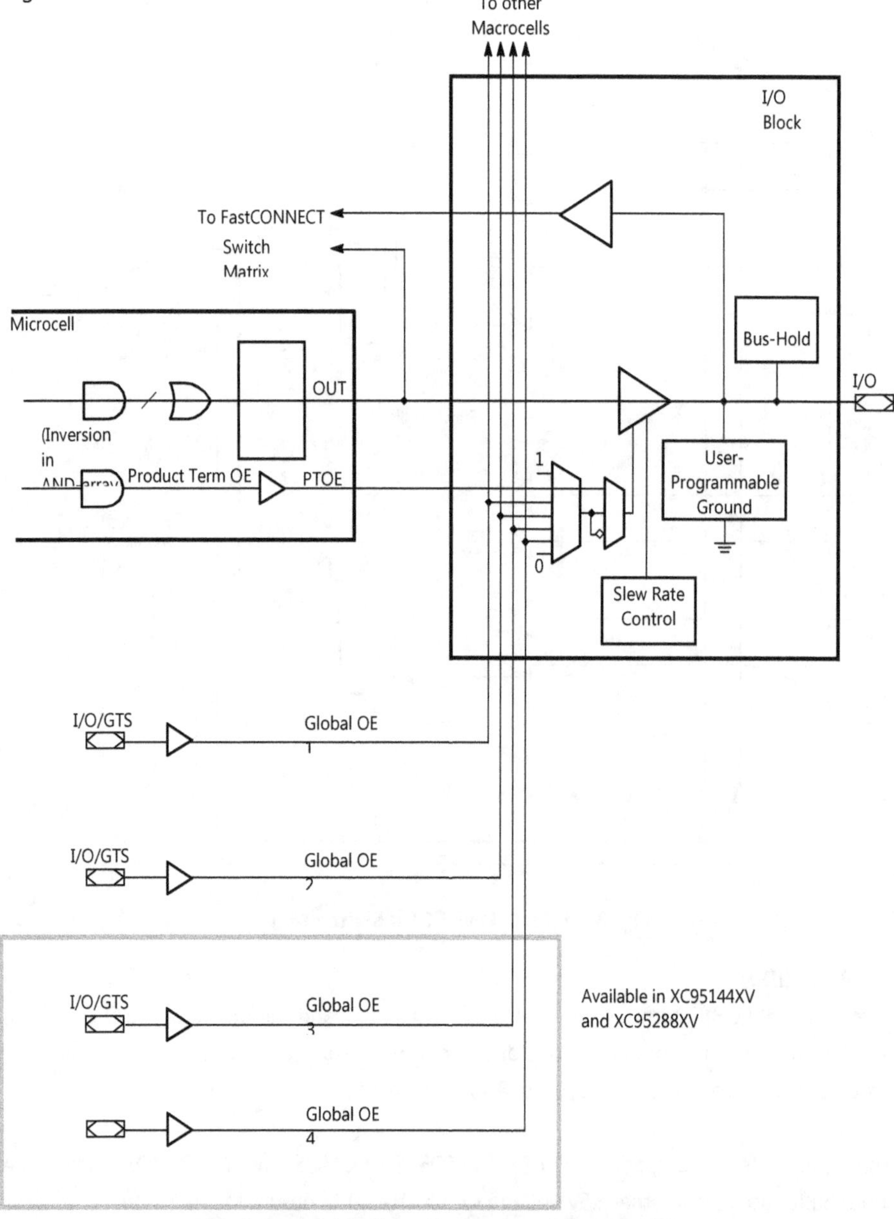

Fig. 8.40: I/O block and output enable capability

Each output driver is designed to provide fast switching with minimal power noise. All output drivers in the device may be configured for driving 3.3V, 2.5V, or 1.8V CMOS levels by connecting the device output voltage supply (V_{CCIO}) to a 3.3V, 2.5V, or 1.8V voltage supply. Fig. 8.41 shows how the XC9500XV device can be used in a 2.5V only system. Each output driver can also be configured for slew rate limited operation. Output edge rates may be slowed down to reduce system noise (with an additional time delay of TSLEW) under user control. (See Fig. 8.42)

The output enable may be generated from one of the four options: a product term signal from the macrocell, any of the global output enable signals (GTS), always "1", or always "0". There are two global output enables for devices with 72 or fewer macrocells, and four global output enables for devices with 144 or more macrocells. Any selected output enable signal may be inverted locally at each pin output to provide maximum design flexibility.

Each IOB provides user programmable ground pin capability. This allows device I/O pins to be configured as additional ground pins in order to force otherwise unused pins to a low voltage state, as well as provide for additional device grounding capability. This grounding of the pin is achieved by internal logic that forces a logic Low output regardless of the internal macrocell signal, so the internal macrocell logic is unaffected by the programmable ground pin capability. Each IOB also provides for bus-hold circuitry that is active during valid user operation. The bus-hold feature eliminates the need to tie unused pins either High or Low by holding the last known state of the input until the next input signal is present. The bus-hold circuit drives back the same state via a nominal resistance (RBH) of 50 kΩ. (See Fig. 8.43.)

Note: The bus-hold output will drive no higher than V_{CCIO} to prevent overdriving signals when interfacing to 2.5V components.

When the device is not in valid user operation, the bus-hold circuit defaults to an equivalent 50 kΩ pull-up resistor in order to provide a known repeatable device state. This occurs when the device is in the erased state, in programming mode, in JTAG INTEST mode, or during initial power-up. A pull-down resistor (1 kΩ) may be externally added to any pin to override the default RBH resistance to force a Low state during power-up or any of these other modes.

Output Banking

XC95288XV and XC95144XV devices are designed with a split-rail I/O structure. This permits the utilization of multiple output drive levels for systems able to operate best in that environment. The output partitioning is by Function Blocks (FB). With this arrangement, designers can have some sets of outputs driving to 2.5V and others set to 1.8V. Naturally, it is possible to tie all rails to a single output voltage and get all outputs driving to that level. Should designs be migrated from one density to another in the same package, care should be taken to remember the voltage assignments chosen at the outset to assure consistency.

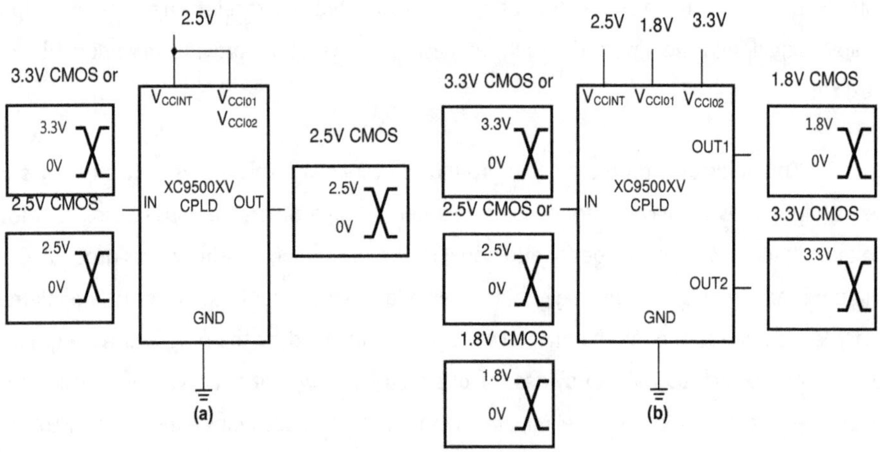

Fig. 8.41: XC9500XV devices in
(a) 2.5V only and (b) Mixed 3.3V/2.5V/1.8V systems

Mixed Voltage

The I/Os on each XC9500XV device are fully 3.3V tolerant even though the core power supply is 2.5V. This allows 3.3V CMOS signals to connect directly to the XC9500XV inputs without damage. In addition, the 2.5V V_{CCINT} power supply can be applied before or after 2.5V signals are applied to I/Os. In mixed 3.3V/2.5V/1.8V systems, the user pins, the core power supply

(V_{CCINT}), and the output power supply (V_{CCIO}) may have power applied in any order. This makes the XC9500XV devices immune to power supply sequencing problems (see Fig. 8.41).

Xilinx proprietary ESD circuitry and high impedance initial state permit hot plugging cards using XC9500XV CPLDs.

Pin-Locking Capability

The capability to lock the user defined pin assignments during design iteration depends on the ability of the architecture to adapt to unexpected changes. The XC9500XV devices incorporate architectural features that enhance the ability to accept design changes while maintaining the same pinout.

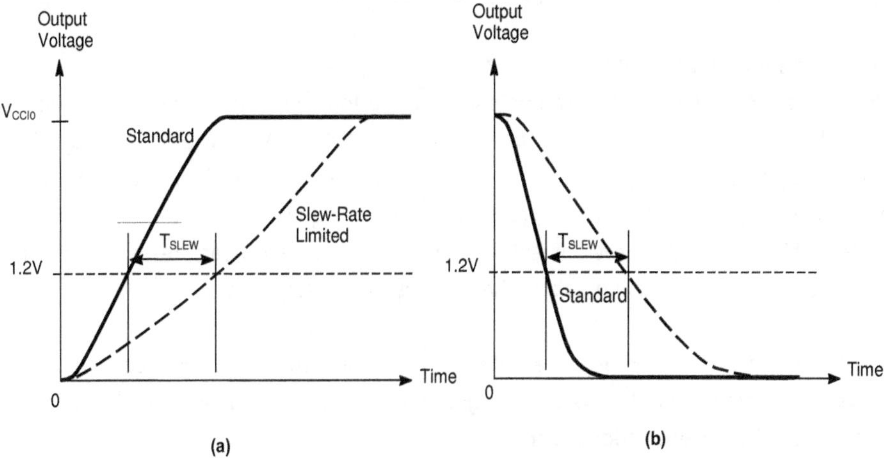

Fig. 8.42: Output slew-rate control for (a) Rising and (b) Falling outputs

The XC9500XV architecture provides for superior pin-locking characteristics with a combination of large number of routing switches in the FastCONNECT II switch matrix, a 54-wide input Function Block, and flexible, bi-directional product term allocation within each macrocell. These features address design changes that require adding or changing internal routing, including additional signals into existing equations, or increasing equation complexity, respectively. For extensive design changes requiring higher logic capacity than is available in the initially chosen device, the new design may be able to fit into a larger pin-compatible device using the same pin assignments. The same board may be used with a higher density device without the expense of board rework.

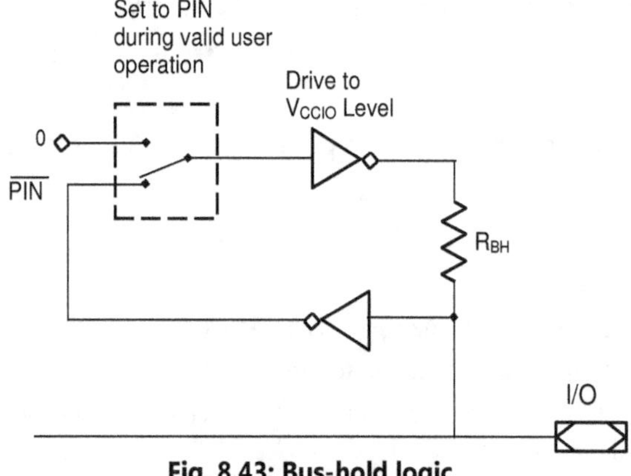

Fig. 8.43: Bus-hold logic

In-System Programming (ISP)

One or more XC9500XV devices can be daisy chained together and programmed in-system via a standard 4-pin JTAG protocol, as shown in Fig. 8.44. In-system programming offers quick and efficient design iterations and eliminates package handling. The Xilinx development system provides the programming data sequence using a Xilinx download cable, a third-party JTAG development system, JTAG-compatible board tester, or a simple microprocessor interface that emulates the JTAG instruction sequence.

All I/Os are set to a high-impedance state and pulled high by the bus-hold circuitry during in-system programming. If a particular signal must remain Low during this time, then a pull-down resistor may be added to the pin.

Reliability and Endurance

All XC9500XV CPLDs provide a minimum endurance level of 10,000 in-system program/erase cycles and a minimum data retention of 20 years. Each device meets all functional, performance, and data retention specifications within this endurance limit.

IEEE 1149.1 Boundary-Scan (JTAG)

XC9500XV devices fully support IEEE 1149.1 boundary-scan (JTAG). EXTEST, SAMPLE/ PRELOAD, BYPASS, USERCODE, INTEST, IDCODE, HIGHZ and CLAMP instructions are supported in each device. Additional instructions are included for in-system programming operations.

Design Security

XC9500XV devices incorporate advanced data security features which fully protect the programming data against unauthorized reading or inadvertent device erasure/ reprogramming. Table 8.1 shows the four different security settings available.

The read security bits can be set by the user to prevent the internal programming pattern from being read or copied. When set, they also inhibit further program operations but allow device erase. Erasing the entire device is the only way to reset the read security bit.

The write security bits provide added protection against accidental device erasure or reprogramming when the JTAG pins are subject to noise, such as during system power-up. Once set, the write-protection may be deactivated when the device needs to be reprogrammed with a valid pattern with a specific sequence of JTAG instructions.

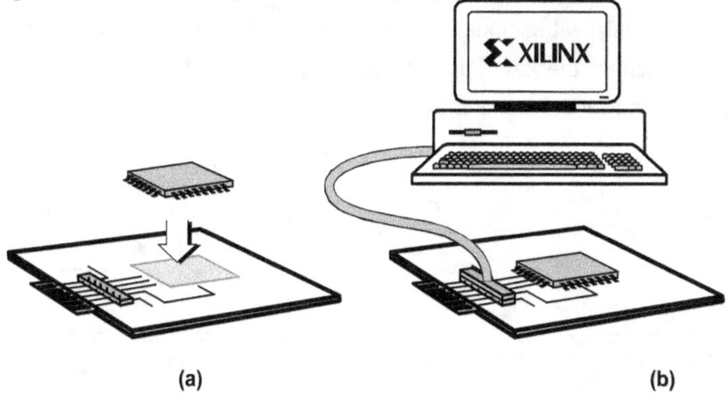

(a)   (b)

Fig. 8.44: In-System Programming operation (a) Solder device to PCB and (b) Program using download cable

Table 8.1: Data Security Options

		Read Security	
		Default	Set
Write Security	Default	Read Allowed Program/Erase Allowed	Read Inhibited Program/Erase Inhibited
	Set	Read Allowed Program/Erase Allowed	Read Inhibited Program/Erase Inhibited

Low Power Mode

All XC9500XV devices offer a low-power mode for individual macrocells or across all macrocells. This feature allows the device power to be significantly reduced.

Each individual macrocell may be programmed in low-power mode by the user. Performance-critical parts of the application can remain in standard power mode, while other parts of the application may be programmed for low-power operation to reduce the overall power dissipation. Macrocells programmed for low-power mode incur additional delay (TLP) in pin-to-pin combinatorial delay as well as register setup time. Product term clock to output and product term output enable delays are unaffected by the macro-cell power-setting.

Timing Model

The uniformity of the XC9500XV architecture allows a simplified timing model for the entire device. The basic timing model, shown in Fig. 8.45, is valid for macrocell functions that use the direct product terms only, with standard power setting, and standard slew rate setting. Table 8.2 shows how each of the key timing parameters is affected by the product term allocator (if needed), low-power setting, and slew-limited setting.

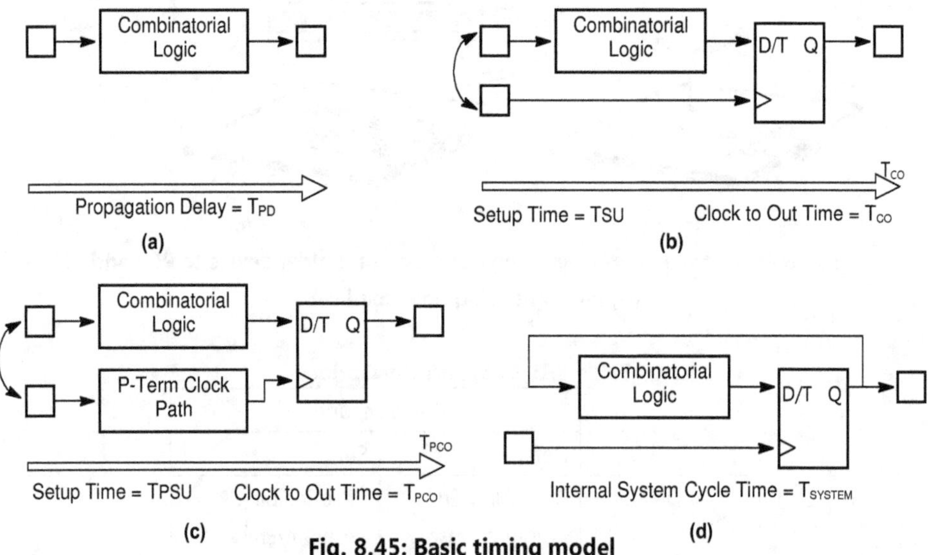

Fig. 8.45: Basic timing model

The product term allocation time depends on the logic span of the macrocell function, which is defined as one less than the maximum number of allocators in the product term path. If only direct product terms are used, then the logic span is "0". The example in Fig. 8.45 shows that up to 15 product terms are available with a span of "1". In the case of Fig. 8.45, the 18 product term function has a span of "2". Detailed timing information may be derived from the full timing model shown in Fig. 8.45. The values and explanations for each parameter are given in the individual device data sheets.

Table 8.2: Timing Model Parameters

Description	Parameter	Product Term Allocator[1]	Macrocell Low-Power Setting	Output Slew-Limited Setting
Propagation Delay	T_{PD}	+ T_{PTA} * S	+ T_{LP}	+ T_{SLEW}
Global Clock Setup Time	T_{SU}	+ T_{PTA} * S	+ T_{LP}	-
Global Clock-to-output	T_{CO}	-	-	+ T_{SLEW}
Product Term Clock Setup Time	T_{PSU}	+ T_{PTA} * S	+ T_{LP}	-
Product Term Clock-to-Output	T_{PCO}	-	-	+ T_{SLEW}
Internal System Cycle Period	T_{SYSTEM}	+ T_{PTA} * S	+ T_{LP}	-

Note:

S = the logic span of the function, as defined in the text.

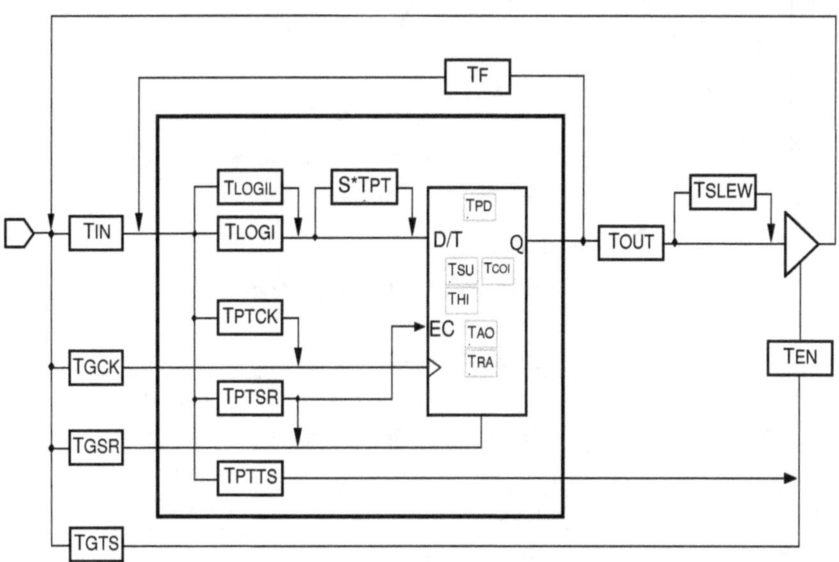

Fig. 8.46: Detailed timing model

Power-Up Characteristics

The XC9500XV devices are well behaved under all operating conditions. During power-up each XC9500XV device employs internal circuitry which keeps the device in the quiescent state until the V_{CCINT} supply voltage is at a safe level (approximately 1.9V). During this time, all device pins and JTAG pins are disabled and all device outputs are disabled with the pins weakly pulled High, as shown in Table 8.3. When the supply voltage reaches a safe level, all user registers become initialized (typically within 300 µs), and the device is immediately available for operation, as shown in Fig. 8.47. If the device is in the erased state (before any user pattern is programmed), the device outputs remain disabled with weak pull-up. The JTAG pins are enabled to allow the device to be programmed at any time. All devices are shipped in the erased state from the factory.

If the device is programmed, the device inputs and outputs take on their configured states for normal operation. The JTAG pins are enabled to allow device erasure or boundary-scan tests at any time.

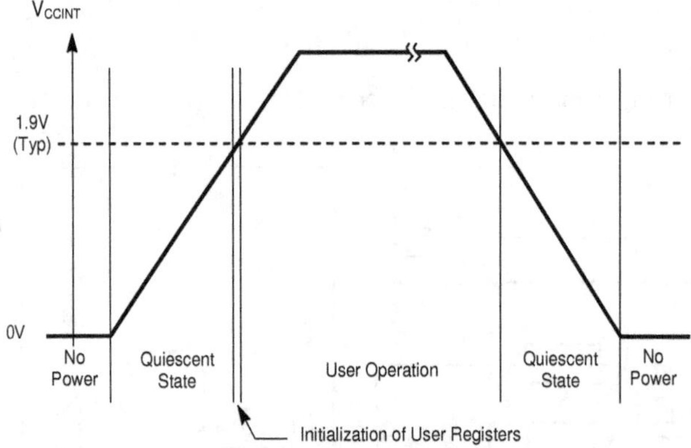

Fig. 8.47: Device behavior during power-up

Table 8.3: XC9500XV Device Characteristics

Device Circuitry	Quiescent State	Erased Device Operation	Valid User Operation
IOB Bus-Hold	Pull-up	Pull-up	Bus-Hold
Device Outputs	Disabled	Disabled	As Configured
Device Inputs and Clocks	Disabled	Disabled	As Configured
Function Block	Disabled	Disabled	As Configured
JTAG Controller	Disabled	Enabled	Enabled

Power-Up Guidelines

Fig. 8.48 shows a block diagram of the internal configuration controller, which transfers the EPROM bits to the latches. Some important things to note are:

- The V_{CCINT} is sensed to determine when to begin the loading.

- An internal clock source drives a state machine that controls the overall process.

- The bit loading process takes about 100 microseconds.

- Internal configuration latches are automatically reset at the beginning of the process.

- The state machines, counters and strobes are built from CMOS transistors, so they need voltage, setup time, hold time, and propagation delay time to work properly.

When V_{CCINT} passes a threshold, it automatically enables. The state machine cycles through addresses, delivers load strobes to internal latches and completes the process by enabling the I/O pins.

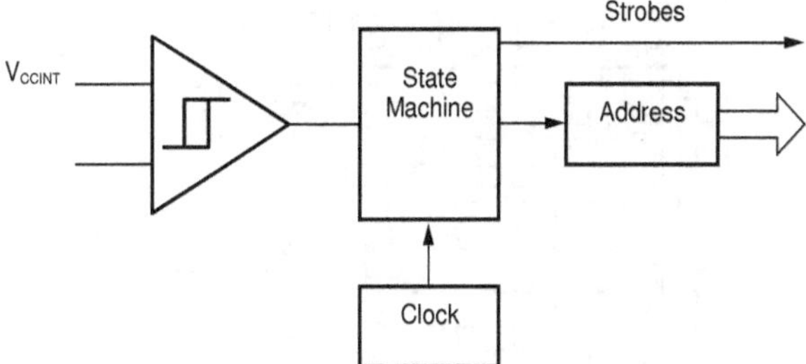

Fig. 8.48: Configuration controller

Fig. 8.49 describes what happens inside the chip as the supply rises to its final value. At low voltage, the transistors do not behave like transistors. As V_{CC} passes about a volt, the transistors begin to wake up, but are not yet fully functional. Above 1V, they can amplify and form basic gates. Near 1.8V, they work correctly and can make reliable latches. Above 2V, they can be reliably loaded with EPROM bits. It is in this voltage neighborhood the POR circuits begin transferring EPROM bits to the latches. XC9500XV POR begins about 1.8V.

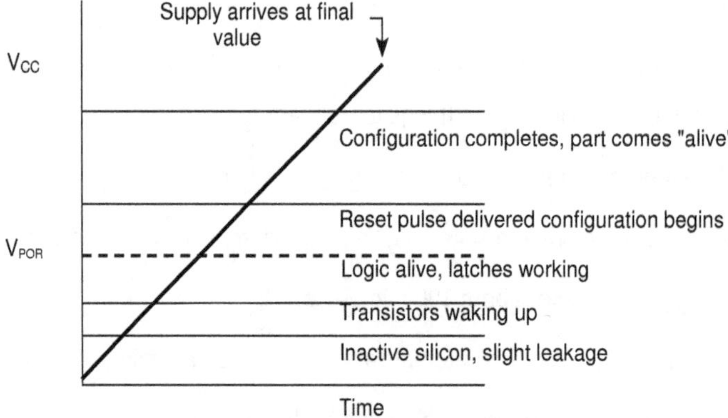

Fig. 8.49: Power-up activity

8.9 Field Programmable Gate Array (FPGA)

8.9.1 FPGA

Each FPGA vendor has its own FPGA architecture. But in general term they all are variations of that as shown in Fig. 8.50.

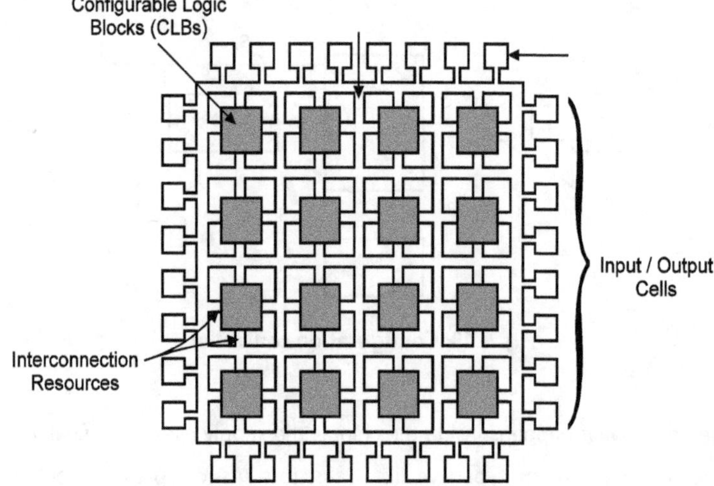

Fig. 8.50: General Architecture of an FPGA

The architecture consists of configurable logic blocks, configurable I/O blocks and programmable interconnects. Also, there will be clock circuitry for driving the clock signals to each logic block, and additional logic resources.

The two basic types of programmable elements for an FPGA are static RAM and Anti-fuses.

8.9.2 Comparison of SRAM and Antifuse FPGA

Comparison of SRAM and Antifuse FPGA is given below:

SRAM FPGA	Antifuse FPGA
1) The physical dimensions of an SRAM cell are of the order of magnitude larger than those of an antifuse element.	1) Antifuse elements take less space compared to SRAM cells. Antifuse elements can be placed very densely.
2) SRAM FPGAs can be reprogrammed.	2) Once programmed, an antifuse element cannot be erased or reprogrammed.
3) SRAM cells are volatile.	3) They are non-volatile.
4) SRAM based FPGAs typically use larger logic cells with fewer inputs and outputs.	4) They have more inputs and outputs with small number of gates in logic cells.
5) Standard fabrication process.	5) A complex fabrication process.

Antifuse Element: The opposite of a fuse. An antifuse initially provides insulation between two conductors, but when a sufficient programming voltage is applied across it, conducting path forms.

Fig. 8.51 shows an unprogrammed antifuse element and Fig. 8.52 shows a programmed antifuse element.

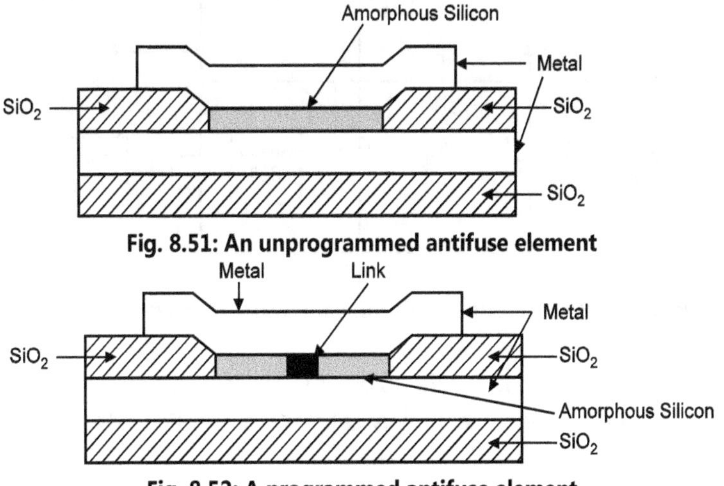

Fig. 8.51: An unprogrammed antifuse element

Fig. 8.52: A programmed antifuse element

As shown in Fig. 8.52, in an amorphous-silicon-based FPGA, the two layers of metal are separated by amorphous silicon, it provides electrical insulation. A programming pulse of 10 V to 12 V and of necessary duration can be applied across the via. It creates a bidirectional conductive link between two metals.

The programmable elements can be placed very densely. Once programmed, an antifuse element cannot be erased or reprogrammed.

FPGAs that use this technology have flexible routing architectures, which allow the electrical connection of wires at nearly every intersection.

SRAM

Fig. 8.53 shows six pass transistors that allow any combination of connections of the four wires. SRAM cells may be used to control the state of these pass transistors, which can establish connections between horizontal and vertical wires (N, S, E, W). When T_1 is ON, it makes connection between N and W wires.

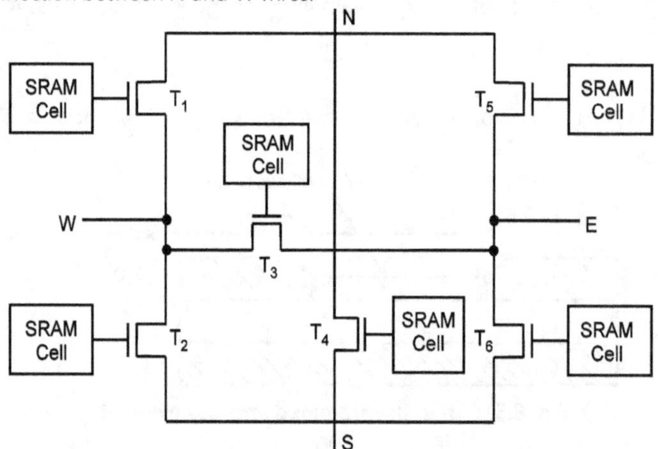

Fig. 8.53: SRAM cells used to connect horizontal and vertical wires

An SRAM memory cell consists of five transistors as shown in Fig. 8.54. One transistor is used for addressing i.e. used to select the memory cell for programming, and four transistors are used to form two inverters.

An SRAM cell is reprogrammable and volatile.

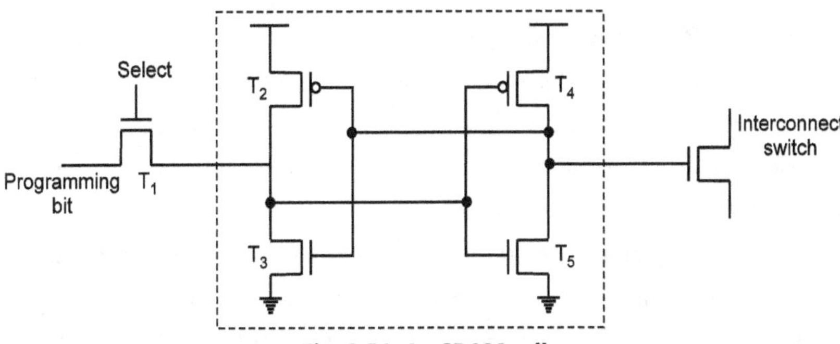

Fig. 8.54: An SRAM cell

The programming circuitry for SRAM elements must include the addressing and data registers.

SRAM FPGAs do not have routing architectures for which there is a programmable element at nearly intersection.

SRAM FPGAs typically use every **larger logic cells** with fewer inputs and outputs. These logic cells can implement larger functions without incurring routing delays.

But, because they have fewer outputs as a ratio of the number of gates in the logic cell, they are less efficient for implementing small functions.

Following factors are considered to make a choice in between SRAM or Antifuse technology:

   1) Performance of the technology: Antifuse FPGAs offer the **highest performance** for most design; due to the smaller resistance in programmable link (50Ω) as well as the flexibility in routing. However, some SRAM FPGAs have dedicated carry logic to provide better performance for some applications.

   2) Density and capacity of that device: The size of an antifuse FPGA logic cell is typically smaller and the number of outputs as a ratio of the number of logic cell gates is greater than those for its SRAM counterpart, which allows these logic cells to implement more user logic per available gate (greater capacity). But now-a-days, SRAM FPGAs are presently available at higher densities.

   3) Easy to use software: To develop a design quickly and easily, we require the availability of easy to use software and friendly device architecture.

Antifuse based FPGAs have advantage in this area. Routing Architectures make it easy for software to be developed so that placing and routing can be done automatically and design changes can still fit in the same device by rerouting. The routing limitations of some SRAM FPGAs make it impossible or difficult for a design to fit with the same device since placing and routing may have to be done by hand.

4) In-System Programmability (ISP) and In-System Reprogrammability (ISR): SRAM FPGAs give ISP for all and ISR for some. ISR is the need, which is used to reconfigure the FPGA in its system, to make design changes or field upgrades. While antifuse FPGAs are One Time Programmable (OTP).

The advantage of SRAM-based FPGAs is that they use a standard fabrication process that chip fabrication plants are familiar with and they are optimized for better performance. The SRAMs are reprogrammable, the FPGAs can be reprogrammed any number of times, just like writing to a normal SRAM. The disadvantages are that they are volatile, which means a power glitch could potentially change it. Also, SRAM-based devices have long routing delays.

The advantages of antifuse based FPGAs are that they are **non-volatile** and the **delays** due to routing are **very small**, so they tend to be **faster**. The disadvantages are that they require a complex fabrication process, they require an external programmer to program them and once they are programmed, they cannot be changed.

8.9.3 Example-FPGA Families

SRAM-based FPGA families include the following:

1) Altera FLEX family

2) Atmel AT6000 and AT 40K families.

3) Lucent Technologies ORCA family

4) Xilinx XC4000, XC5200, Virtex and Spartan families.

Antifuse-based FPGA families include the following:

1) Actel ProASIC PLUS families, SX and MX families.

2) Quicklogic pASIC family.

8.9.4 Details of FPGA Architecture

Configurable Logic Blocks

Configurable Logic Blocks contain the logic for the FPGA. In a large grain architecture, these CLBs will contain enough logic to create a small state machine. In a fine grain architecture, more like a true gate array ASIC, the CLB will contain only very basic logic. The diagram in Fig. 8.55 would be considered a large grain block. It contains RAM for creating arbitrary combinational logic functions. It also contains flip-flops for clocked storage elements, multiplexers in order to route the logic within the block and to and from external resources. The multiplexers also allow polarity selection and reset and clear input selection.

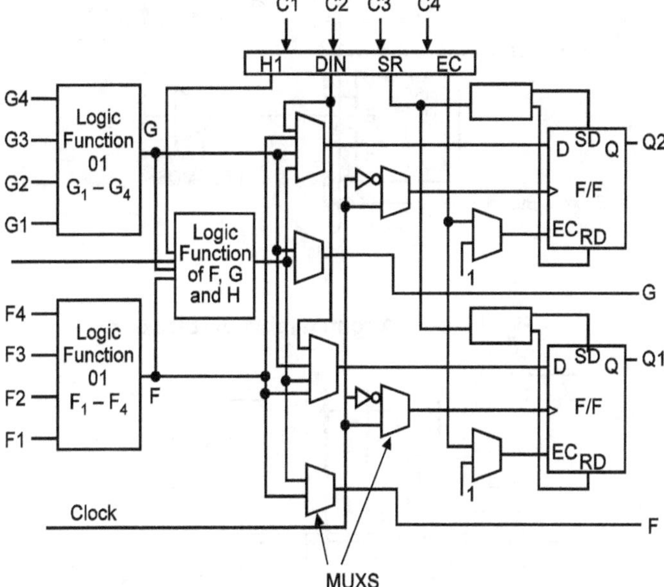

Fig. 8.55: FPGA configurable logic block

8.9.5 Configurable I/O Blocks

A configurable I/O block, shown in Fig. 8.56 is used to bring signals onto the chip and send them back off again. It consists of an input buffer and an output buffer with three states and open collector output controls. Typically, there are pull-up resistors on the outputs and sometimes pull-down resistors. The polarity of the output can usually be programmed for fast or slow rise and fall times. In addition, there is often a flip-flop on outputs so that clocked signals can be output directly to the pins without encountering significant delay. It is done for inputs so that there is not much delay on a signal before reaching a flip-flop which would increase the device hold time requirement.

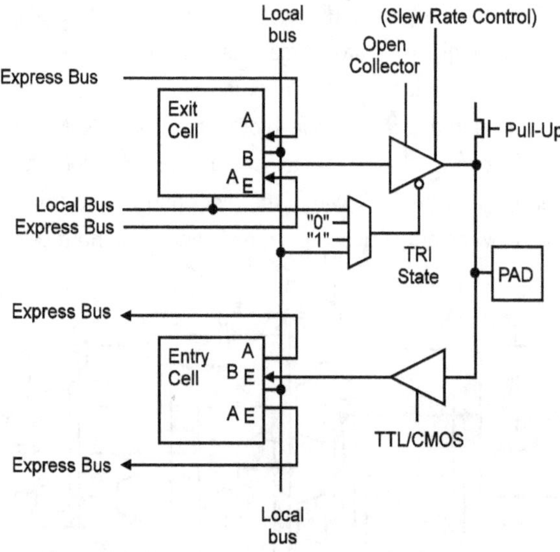

Fig. 8.56: FPGA configurable I/O block

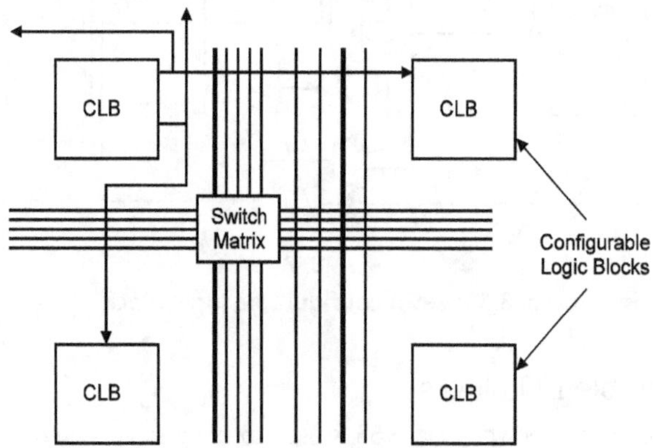

Fig. 8.57: FPGA programmable interconnect

The interconnect of an FPGA is very different than that of a CPLD, but is rather similar to that of a gate array ASIC. In Fig. 8.57, a hierarchy of interconnect resources can be seen. There are long lines which can be used to connect critical CLBs that are physically far from each other on the chip without inducing much delay. They can also be used as buses within the chip. There are also short lines which are used to connect individual CLBs which are located physically close to each other. There are often one or several switch matrices, like that in a CPLD, to connect these long and short lines together in specific ways. Programmable switches inside the chip allow the connection of CLBs to interconnect lines and interconnect lines to each other and to the switch matrix. Three-state buffers are used to connect many CLBs to a long line, creating a bus. Special long lines, called global clock lines, are specially designed for low impedance and thus fast propagation times. These are connected to the clock buffers and to each clocked element in each CLB. This is how the clocks are distributed throughout the FPGA.

8.9.6 Clock Circuitry

Special I/O blocks with special high drive clock buffers, known as clock drivers, are distributed around the chip. These buffers are connected to clock input pads and drive the clock signals onto the global clock lines described above. These clock lines are designed for low skew times and fast propagation times. As we will discuss later, synchronous design is a must with FPGAs, since absolute skew and delay cannot be guaranteed. Only when using clock signals from clock buffers can the relative delays and skew times be guaranteed.

8.9.7 Small versus Large Granularity

Small grain FPGAs resemble ASIC gate arrays in that the CLBs contain only small, very basic elements such as NAND gates, NOR gates, etc. The philosophy is that small elements can be connected to make larger functions without wasting too much logic. In a large grain FPGA, where the CLB can contain two or more flip-flops, a design which does not need many flip-flops will leave many of them unused. Unfortunately, small grain architectures require much more routing resources, which take up space and insert a large amount of delay.

Table 8.4: Small versus Large Grain FPGAs

Small Granularity	Large Granularity
1. Better utilization	1. Fewer levels of logic
2. Direct conversion to ASIC	2. Less interconnect delay

A comparison of advantages of each type of architecture is shown in Table 8.4 above. The choice of which architecture to use is dependent on your specific application.

8.10 Xilinx, XC5200 Series FPGA

Features

1. Low cost, SRAM-based, register/latch rich.

2. Reprogrammable architecture, 256 to 1936 logic cells (3000 to 23,000 gates).

3. System performance beyond 50 MHz.

4. 6 levels of interconnect hierarchy.

5. VersaRing I/O interface for pin locking.

6. Dedicated carry logic for high speed arithmetic functions.

7. Cascade chain for wide input functions.

8. Built-in IEEE 1149.1 JTAG Boundary scan test circuitry on all I/O pins.

9. Innovative VersaRing I/O interface provides a high logic cell to I/O ratio, with upto 244 I/O signals.

10. Fully supported by Xilinx Development System.

XC5200 FPGA family members

Device	XC5202	XC5204	XC5206	XC5210	XC5215
* logic cells	256	480	784	1,296	1,936
* Max logic gates	3,000	6,000	10,000	16,000	23,000
* Typical gate Range	2000 to 3000	4000 to 6000	6000 to 10,000	10000 to 16,000	15000 to 23000
* VersaBlock Array	8 × 8	10 × 12	14 × 14	18 × 18	22 × 22
* CLBs	64	120	196	324	484
* Flip Flops	256	480	784	1,296	1936
* I/Os	84	124	148	196	244
* TBUFs per Longline	10	14	16	20	24

Fig. 8.58 shows the architecture of XC5200. The XC5200 family consists of programmable IOBs, programmable logic blocks and programmable interconnect.

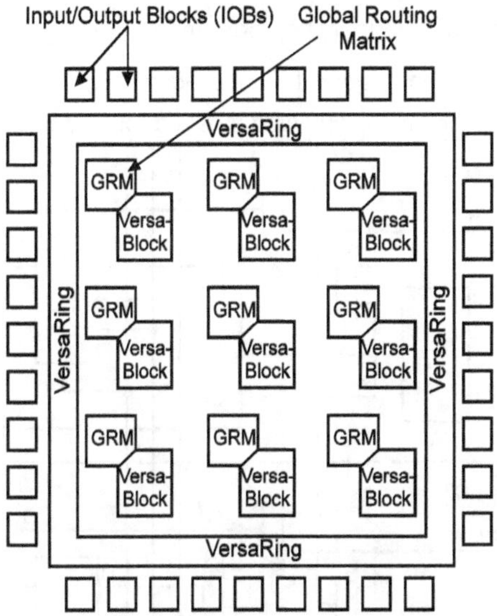

Fig. 8.58: Architecture of XC5200

8.11 XC5200

XC5200 include the following:

1) GRM – General Routing Matrix
2) VersaBlock
3) VersaRing I/O interface
4) Input / Output Blocks.

8.11.1 GRM

The GRM is functionally similar to the switch matrices found in other architectures. It contains six levels of interconnect hierarchy. It contains a series of single length lines, double length lines and long lines all routed through the GRM.

8.11.2 VersaBlock

Fig. 8.59 shows the VersaBlock. It includes CLBs (Configuration Logic Blocks) and two interconnect resources.

Two interconnect resources are :

a) LIM – Local Interconnect Matrix
b) Direct Matrix

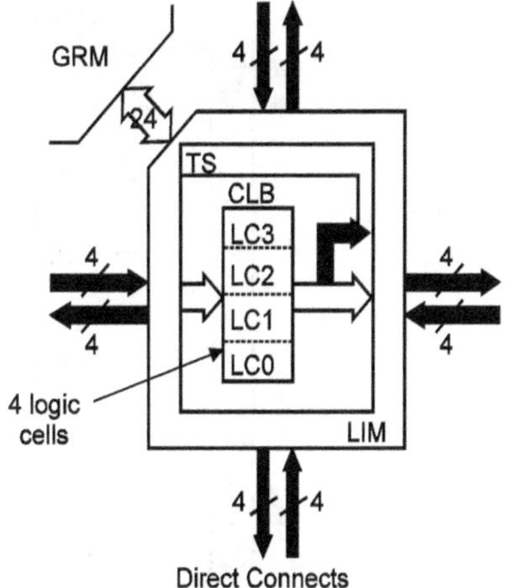

Fig. 8.59 : VersaBlock of XC5200

CLBs – The XC5200 CLBs consist of four LCs (Logic Cells).

Each CLB has 20 independent inputs and 12 independent outputs. Fig. 8.60 shows the CLB of XC5200. 5 input functions can be implemented by using top and bottom pairs of logic cells.

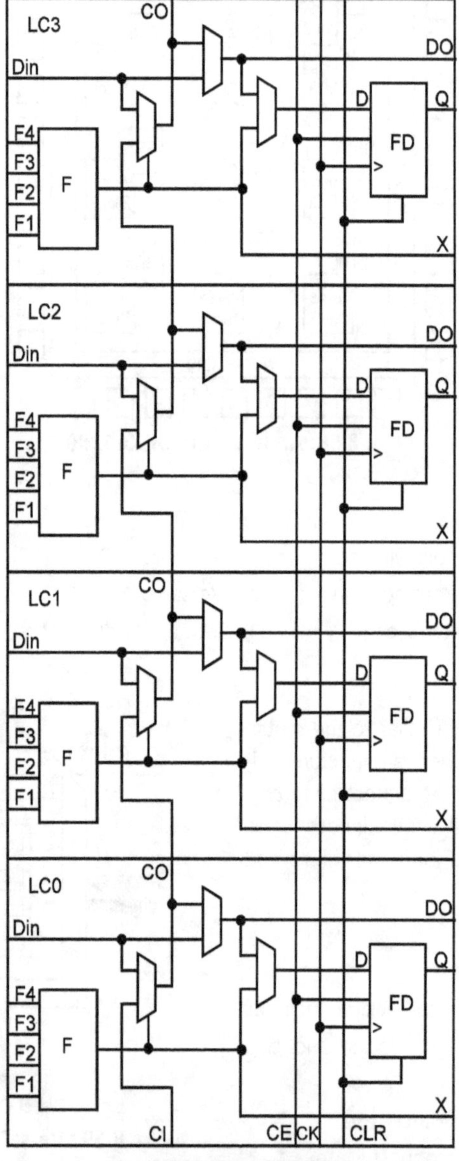

Fig. 8.60: CLB of XC5200

8.11.3 Logic Cell of XC5200

Logic Cells (LCs) are included in CLB. One CLB consists of 4 logic cells. Fig. 8.61 shows the logic cell. Each LC contains (:)

1) 4 input, function generator (F)

2) A storage device (FD).

3) Control logic.

There are five independent inputs and three outputs to each LC. The independence of the inputs and outputs allows the software to maximize the resource utilization within each LC. The storage device can be used as a D flip flop or as a latch. The control logic is used to implement fast arithmetic functions.

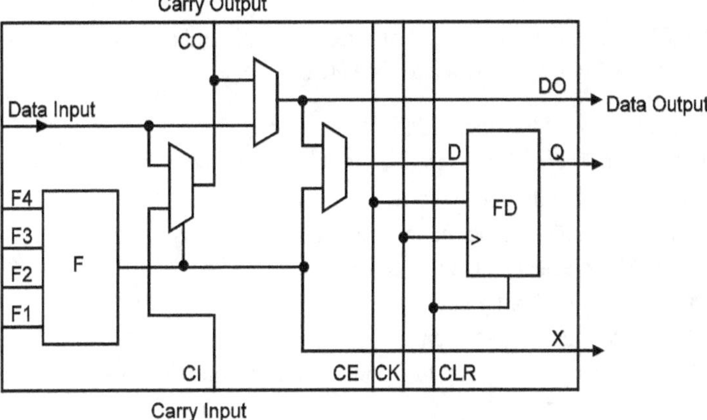

Fig. 8.61: XC5200 logic cell

8.11.4 VersaRing I/O Interface

The XC5200 IOBs contain dedicated boundary scan logic for added board level testability but do not include input or output registers. This approach allows a maximum number of IOBs to be placed around the device, improving the I/O to gate ratio and decreasing the cost per I/O. A free way of interconnect cells surrounding the device forms the VersaRing which provides connections from the IOBs to the internal logic.

8.11.5 IOB

To minimize cost and maximize the number of I/O per logic cell, the XC5200 I/O does not include flip-flops or latches. Each I/O pin provides a programmable delay element to control input set-up time. This element can be used to avoid potential hold time problems. IEEE 1149.1 type boundary scan is supported in each XC5200 I/O.

8.11.6 Pin Descriptions

There are 3 types of pins in XC5200 series:
- Permanently dedicated pins.
- User I/O pins that can have special functions.
- Unrestricted user programmable I/O pins.
  These pins are:

1) VCC → + 5V
2) GND
3) **CCLK (**Configuration clock): It is an output in master mode and input in slave mode.
4) **DONE:** As an output indicates the completion of the configuration process.
5) $\overline{\textbf{PROGRAM}}$ **:** It is an active low input that forces the FPGA to clear its configuration memory.
6) **RDY /$\overline{\textbf{BUSY}}$:** During configuration mode, this pin indicates when it is appropriate to write another byte of data into the FPGA.
7) $\overline{\textbf{RCLK}}$**:** It is useful for clocked PROMs.
8) **M0, M1, M2:** These pins determine the configuration mode to be used.
9) **TDO:** During boundary scan mode, this pin is the Test Data Output.
10) **TDI, TCK, TMS:** During boundary scan mode, these pins are Test Data In, Test Clock and Test Mode Select inputs respectively.
11) **HDC:** High During Configuration.
12) **LDC:** Low During Configuration.
13) **INIT:** It is held low during the power stabilization and internal clearing of the configuration memory.
14) **GCK1-GCK4:** These pins provide a shortest path to the four Global Buffers.
15) **A0-A17:** These 18 output pins address the configuration EPROM during configuration mode.
16) **D0-D7:** These 8 pins receive configuration data during configuration mode.
17) **DIN:** During configuration mode, DIN is the serial configuration data input receiving data on the rising edge of CCLK.
18) **DOUT:** It is the serial configuration data output that can drive the DIN of daisy-chained slave FPGAs.
19) **I/O:** These pins can be configured to be input and/or output after configuration is completed.

8.11.7 Configuration

Configuration is the process of loading design-specific programming data into one or more FPGAs to define the functional operation of the internal blocks and their interconnections.

Configuration modes

XC5200 devices have seven configuration modes. These modes are three self loading master modes, two peripherial modes and a slave serial mode.

Difference between Configuration and Programming

FPGA Configuration	Programming
1. Bits stay at the device they program.	1. Instructions are fetched from memory.
2. A configuration bit controls a switch or a logic bit.	2. Instructions select complex operations.

8.12 Spartan - II 2.5 V FPGA Family

Introduction: The Spartan-II family of FPGAs have a regular, flexible, programmable architecture of configurable logic blocks (CLBs), surrounded by a perimeter of programmable input/output blocks (IOBs). There are four Delay Locked Loops (DLLs). These DLLs are located, one at each corner of the die. Fig. 8.62 shows the Basic Spartan II family FPGA block diagram. Block RAMs lie on opposite sides of the die, between the CLBs and the IOB columns. These functional elements are interconnected by a powerful hierarchy of versatile routing channels.

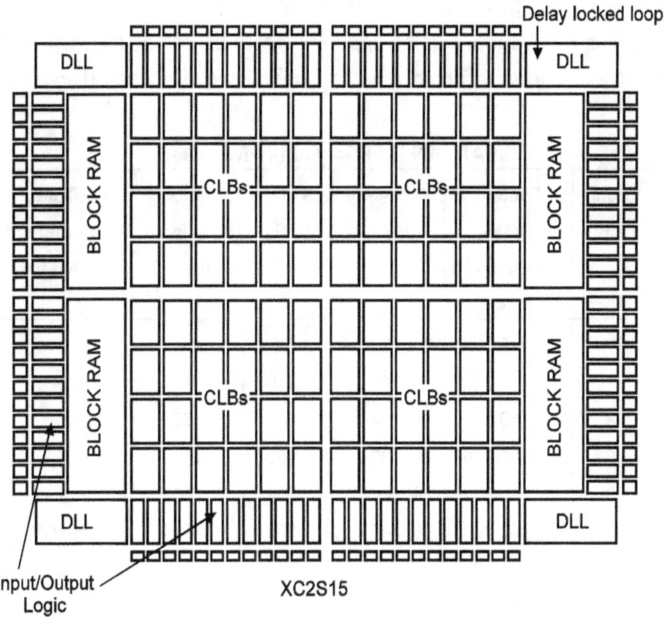

Fig. 8.62: Basic Spartan-II Family FPGA block diagram

Features

1) Densities as high as 5,294 logic cells with upto 200,000 system gates.
2) Advanced 0.18 micron process.
3) System performance supported upto 200 MHz.
4) Streamlined features based on Virtex architecture.
5) Select RAM + hierarchical memory 16 bits / LUT distributed RAM.
   Configurable 4K bit block RAM.
   Fast interfaces to external RAM.
6) Fully PCI compliant.
7) Low power segmented routing architecture.
8) Dedicated carry logic for high speed arithmetic.
9) Full readback ability for verification/observability.
10) Efficient multiplier support.
11) Four dedicated DLLs for advanced clock control.
12) Four primary low-skew global clock distribution nets.
13) IEEE 1149.1 compatible boundary scan logic.
14) Versatile I/O and packaging.
15) Fully supported by powerful Xilinx development system.

SPARTAN II devices deliver more gates, I/Os and features per dollar than other FPGAs by combining advanced process technology with a streamlined virtex based architecture.

SPARTAN II FPGA Family Members

Device	Logic cells	System Gates (logic and RAM)	CLB Array (R × C)	Total CLBs	Max. available User I/O	Total Distributed RAM bits	Total Block RAM Bits
XC 2S15	432	15,000	8 × 12	96	86	6,144	16K
XC 2S30	972	30,000	12 × 18	216	92	13,824	24K
XC 2S50	1728	50,000	16 × 24	384	176	24,576	32K
XC 2S100	2700	100,000	20 × 30	600	176	38,400	40K
XC 2S150	3888	150,000	24 × 36	864	260	55,296	48K
XC 2S200	5292	200,000	28 × 42	1176	284	75,264	56K

SPARTAN II family is a superior alternative to mask-programmed ASICs. The FPGA avoids the initial cost, lengthy development cycles and inherent risk of conventional ASICs. Also FPGA programmability permits design upgrades in the field with no hardware replacement necessary. This is impossible with ASICs.

SPARTAN II FPGAs achieve high performance, low-cost operation through advanced architecture and semiconductor technology. It offers the most cost-effective solution while maintaining leading edge performance. They also offer on-chip synchronous single port and dual port RAM (block and distributed form), DLL clock drivers, programmable set and reset on all flip flops, fast carry logic and many other features.

8.13 Spartan - 3 FPGA Family

Introduction: The Spartan-3 family of FPGAs is specially designed to meet the needs of high volume, cost-sensitive consumer electronic applications.

The eight member family offers densities ranging from 50,000 to five million system gates.

Because of their exceptionally low cost, SPARTAN 3 FPGAs are ideally suited to a wide range of consumer electronics applications; including broadband access, home networking, display/projection and digital television equipment.

Features

1) Densities as high as 74,880 logic cells.

2) Three power rails: for core (1.2V), I/Os (1.2V to 3.3V) and auxiliary purposes (2.5V).

3) Up to 784 I/O pins.

4) 622 Mb/s data transfer rate per I/O.

5) 18 single ended signal standards.

6) Double Data Rate support.

7) Abundant logic cells with shift register capability.

8) Wide multiplexers.

9) Fast look ahead carry logic.

10) Dedicated 18 × 18 multipliers.

11) JTAG logic compatible with IEEE 1149.1/1532.

12) Up to 1872 Kbits of total block RAM.

13) Up to 520 Kbits of total distributed RAM.

14) Digital Clock Manager (up to 4 DCMs).

15) Eight global clock lines and abundant routing.

16) Fully supported by Xilinx ISE development system-synthesis, mapping, placement and routing.

17) MicroBlaze processor, PCI and other cores.

18) Low-Power Spartan – 3L Family and Automotive Spartan – 3 XA Family options.

Spartan 3 family members are shown in Table 8.5.

Table 8.5: Summary of Spartan-3 FPGA Attributes

Device	System Gates	Equivalent Logic Cells	CLB Array (One CLB = Four Slices)			Distributed RAM {bits[1]}	Block RAM {bits[-1])	Dedicated Multipliers	DCMs	Maximum User I/O	Maximum Differential I/O Pairs
			Rows	Columns	Total CLBs						
XC3S60[2]	60K	1,728	16	12	192	12K	72K	4	2	124	56
XC3S200[2]	200K	4,320	24	20	480	30K	216K	12	4	173	76
XC3S400[2]	400K	8,064	32	28	896	56K	288K	16	4	264	116
XC3S1000[2,3]	1M	17,280	48	40	1,920	120K	432K	24	4	391	175
XC3S1500[3]	1.5M	29,952	64	52	3,328	208K	567K	32	4	487	221
XC3S2000	2M	46,080	80	64	5,120	320K	720K	40	4	566	270
XC3S4000[3]	4M	62,208	96	72	6,912	432K	1,728K	96	4	712	312
XC3S5000	5M	74,880	104	80	8,320	520K	1,872	104	4	784	344

8.13.1 Spartan-3 Family Architecture

The Spartan-3 family Architecture is given in Table 8.5. It consists of five fundamental programmable functional elements. These elements are:

1) CLBs (Configurable Logic Blocks)

2) IOBs (Input Output Blocks)

3) Block RAM

4) Multiplier Blocks

5) Digital Clock Manager (DCM).

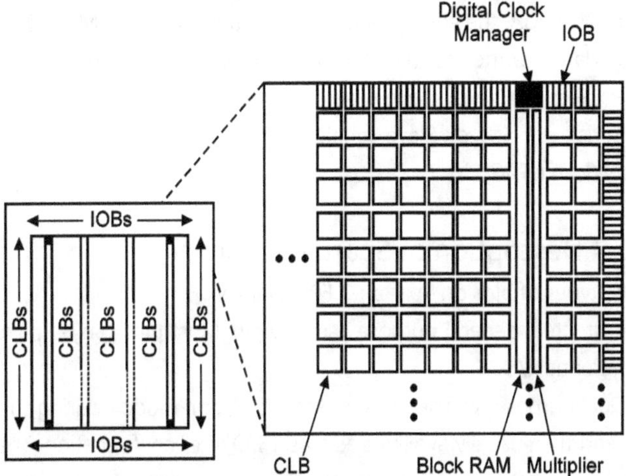

Fig. 8.63: Spartan-3 family architecture

1) **CLBs:** It contains RAM-based Look-Up Tables (LUTs) to implement logic and storage elements that can be used as flip flops or latches. CLBs can be programmed to perform a wide variety of logical functions as well as to store data.

2) **IOBs:** They control the flow of data between the I/O pins and the internal logic of the device. Double Data Rate (DDR) registers are included. The Digitally Controlled Impedance (DCI) feature provides automatic on-chip terminations, simplifying board designs.

3) Block RAM provides data storage in the form of 18-K bits dual port blocks.

4) Multiplier blocks accept two 18 bit binary numbers as inputs and calculate the product.

5) **Digital clock manager:** Digital clock manager blocks provide self calibrating, fully digital solutions for distributing, delaying, multiplying, dividing and phase shifting clock signals.

The Spartan-3 family features a rich network of traces and switches that interconnect all five functional elements, transmitting signals among them. Each functional element has an associated switch matrix that permits multiple connections to the routing.

8.13.2 Configuration

These FPGAs are programmed by loading configuration data into robust static memory cells that collectively control all functional elements and routing resources.

Before powering-ON FPGA, the configuration data is stored in a PROM. After applying power the configuration data is written to the FPGA using any of the five different modes:

a) Master Parallel   b) Slave Parallel

c) Master Serial   d) Slave Serial

e) Boundary Scan (JTAG)

8.13.3 Pin Out Description of Spartan-3 Family

Following are the types of pins on Spartan-3 FPGA family.

1) **I/O:** Unrestricted, general purpose user I/O pin. Most pins can be paired together to form differential I/Os.

2) **DUAL:** Dual purpose pin used in some configuration models during the configuration process and then usually available as a user I/O after configuration. There are 12 dual purpose configuration pins on every package.

3) **CONFIG:** Dedicated configuration pin. Not available as a user I/O pin. Every package has 7 dedicated configuration pins. These pins are powered by VCCAUX.

4) **JTAG:** Dedicated JTAG (Joint Test Action Group) pin. Not available as a user I/O pin. The JTAG pins are:

a) *TDI (Test Data Input):* It is the serial data input for all JTAG instruction and data registers. This pin is sampled on the rising edge of TCK.

b) *TCK (Test Clock):* This signal synchronizes all boundary scan operations on its rising edge.

c) *TMS (Test Mode Select):* The TMS input controls the sequence of states through which the JTAG TAP state machine passes. This input is sampled on the rising edge of TCK.

d) *IDO (Test Data Output)* The TDO pin is the data output for all JTAG instruction and data registers. This output is sampled on the rising edge of TCK.

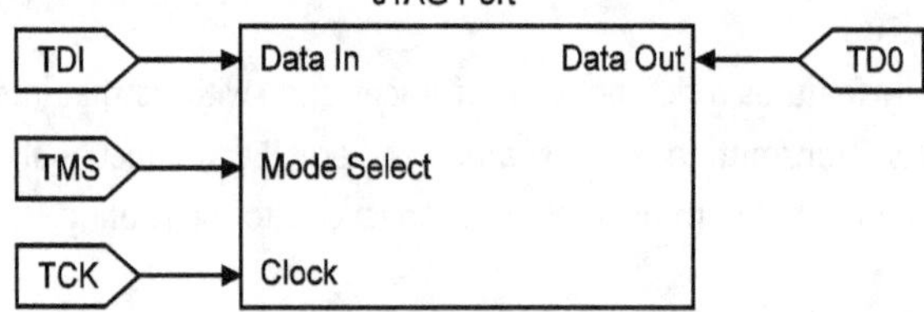

Fig. 8.64: JTAG port

JTAG port is shown in Fig. 8.64. It is used for boundary scan testing, device configuration, application debugging and possibly an additional serial port for the application.

8.14 ProASIC Plus Flash Family FPGAs

Features:

1) 75,000 to 1 million System Gates.

2) 27K to 198 Kbits of Two Port SRAM.

3) 66 to 712 user I/Os.

4) Reprogrammable Flash Technology.

5) Retains programmed design during power down/up cycles.

6) 0.22 µm LM Flash based CMOS process.

7) 3.3V, 32-bit PCI, up to 50 MHz.

8) Two integrated PLLs.

9) External system performance up to 150 MHz.

10) Secure Programming: The industry's most effective security key (FlashLock^{TM}).

11) Low Impedance Flash Switches.

12) Segmented Hierarchical Routing Structure.

13) Small, Efficient, Configurable (Combinational or Sequential) Logic Cells.

14) High Performance Routing Hierarchy.

15) Schmitt – Trigger Option on every input.

16) 2.5V/3.3V support for I/O, with individually Selectable Voltage and Slew Rate.

17) Bidirectional Global I/Os.

18) Boundary Scan Test IEEE Std. 1149.1 (JTAG) Compliant.

19) Pin Compatible Packages across the proASIC^{PLUS} family.

20) Unique clock conditioning circuitry. It includes PLL (phase locked loop) with Flexible phase, Multiply/Divide and Delay capabilities, Two LVPECL Differential Pairs for Clock or Data Inputs.

21) In-System Programming (ISP) via. JTAG Port.

22) ACTgen Net-list Generation Ensures Optimal Usage of Embedded Memory Blocks.

23) 24 SRAM and FIFO configurations with Synchronous and Asynchronous operation up to 150 MHz.

Table 8.6: ProASIC Product Family

Device	APA075	APA150	APA300	APA450	APA600	APA750	APA1000
Maximum System Gates	75,000	150,000	300,000	450,000	600,000	750,000	1,000,000
Tiles (Registers)	3,072	6,144	8,192	12,288	21,504	32,768	56,320
Embedded RAM bits (K = 1,024 bits)	27K	36K	72K	108K	126K	144K	198K
Embedded RAM Blocks (256 × 9)	12	16	32	48	56	64	88
LVPECL	2	2	2	2	2	2	2
PLL	2	2	2	2	2	2	2
Global Networks	4	4	4	4	4	4	4
Maximum Clocks	24	32	32	48	56	64	88
Maximum User I/Os	158	242	290	344	454	562	712
JTAG ISP	Yes	Yes	Yes	Yes	Yes	Yes	Yes
PCL	Yes	Yes	Yes	Yes	Yes	Yes	Yes
Package (by pin count)							
TQFP	199,	100	–	–	–	–	–
PQFP	144	208	208	208	208	208	208
PBGA	208	456	456	456	456	456	456
FBGA	–	144,	144, 256	144,	256,	676,	893, 1152
CQFP2	144	256	208, 352	256,	484, 676	896	208, 352
CCGA2				484	208, 352		624
					624		

8.14.1 ProASIC^{PLUS} Architecture

This architecture provides granularity comparable to gate arrays. Fig. 8.65 shows the ProASIC^{PLUS} Device Architecture. The ProASIC^{PLUS} device consists of a Sea-of-Tiles. Each tile can be configured as a three input logic functions such as NAND gate, D-Flip-Flop etc. by programming the appropriate FLASH switch interconnections.

Tiles and larger functions are connected with any of the levels of routing hierarchy.

Flash switches are used to provide non-volatile, reconfigurable interconnect programming. Flash switches are distributed throughout the device.

ProASIC^{PLUS} devices also contain embedded, two-port SRAM blocks with built-in FIFO/RAM control logic.

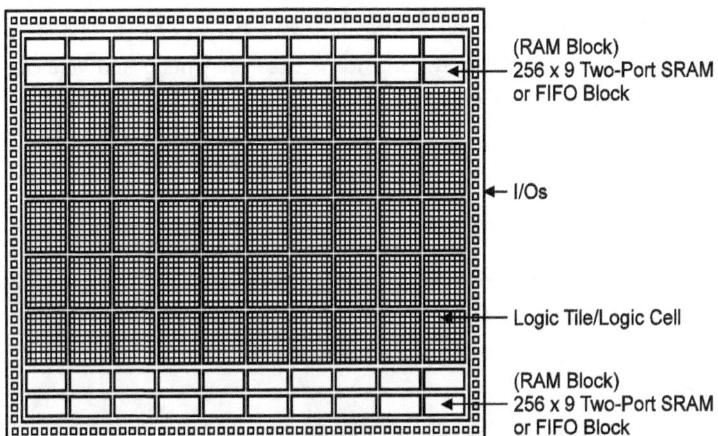

Fig. 8.65: The ProASIC^{PLUS} device architecture

The ProASIC^{PLUS} family achieves its non-volatility and reprogrammability through an advanced flash-based 0.22 µm LVCMOS process with four layers of metal. Standard CMOS design techniques are used to implement logic and control functions, including the PLLs and LVPECL inputs. This results in predictable performance compatible with gate arrays.

The unique clock conditioning circuitry in each device includes two clock conditioning blocks. Each block provides a PLL core, delay lines, phase shifts (0°, 90°, 180°, 270°), and clock multipliers/dividers, as well as the circuitry needed to provide bidirectional access to the PLL. The PLL block contains four programmable frequency dividers which allow the incoming clock signal to be divided by a wide range from 1 to 64.

ProASIC devices are fully compatible with standard 1149.1 for test access port and boundary scan test architecture.

ProASIC^{PLUS} combines the advantages of ASICs with the benefits of programmable devices through non-volatile Flash Technology. This enables engineers to create high density systems using existing ASIC or FPGA design flows and tools.

8.14.2 Flash Switch

ProASIC^{PLUS} uses a live on power-up ISP Flash switch as its programming element. Fig. 8.66 shows the Flash switch of ProASIC^{PLUS} family. As shown, two transistors share the floating gate, which stores the programming information. Two transistors, sensing transistor and switching transistor are used. Sensing transistor is used for writing and verification of the floating gate voltage. Switching transistor is used to connect/separate routing nets or to configure logic. Switching transistor is also used to erase the floating gate.

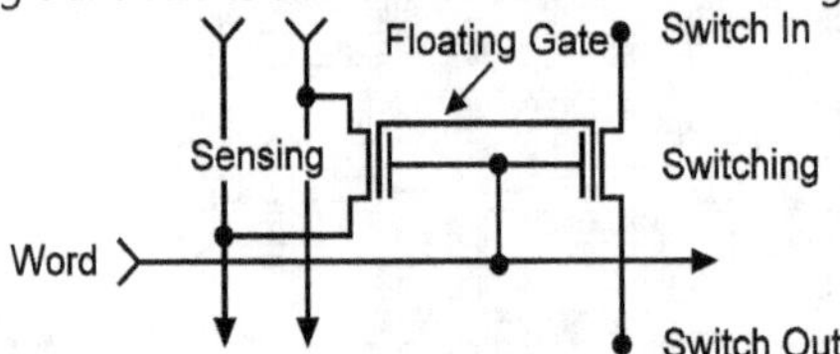

Fig. 8.66: Flash switch

8.14.3 Logic Tile

It has three inputs and one output. All three inputs can be inverted. The output can connect to both ultra-fast local and efficient long line routing resources. Fig. 8.67 shows logic tile.

Any three inputs, one output logic function can be configured as one **tile**. This tile can be configured as a latch flip-flop with clear or set. Thus, the tiles can be flexibly map logic and sequential gates of a design.

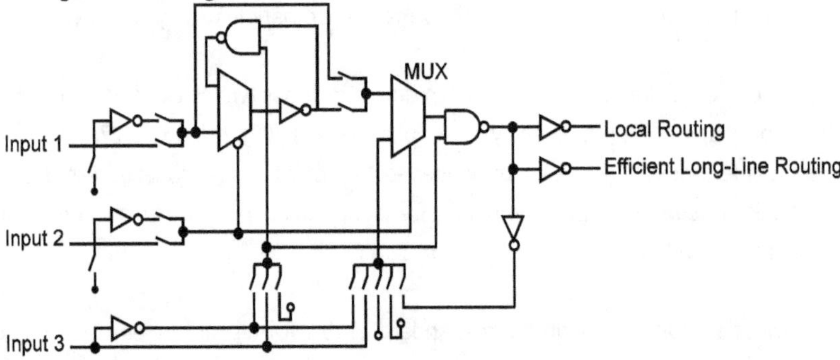

Fig. 8.67: Core logic tile

8.14.4 Routing Resources

The Routing structure is designed to provide high performance through a flexible four-level hierarchy of routing resources. These four levels of routing resources are as follows:

1) Ultra-fast local resources.
2) Efficient long-line resources.
3) High speed, very long-line resources.
4) High performance global networks.

Ultra-fast local resources:

They are shown in Fig. 8.68. These are dedicated lines that allow the output of each tile to connect directly to every input of the eight surrounding tiles.

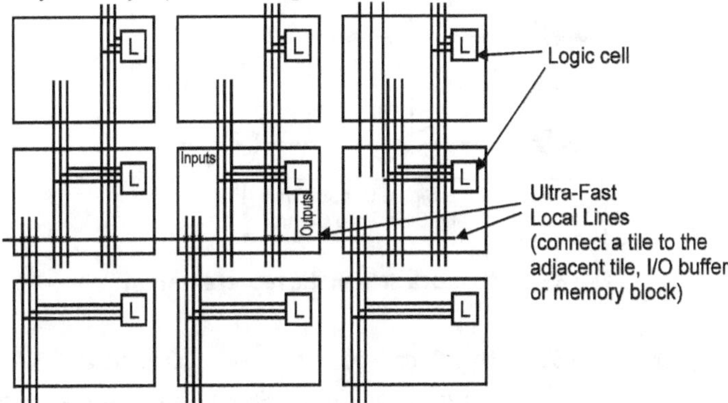

Fig. 8.68: Ultra-fast local resources

Efficient long-line resources:

They provide routing for longer distances and higher fan-out connections. These resources vary in length, run both vertically and horizontally and cover the entire ProASIC^{PLUS} device.

High-speed, very long-line resources:

They span the entire device with minimal delay, are used to route very long or very high fan out nets.

High performance global networks:

They are low-skew, high fan-out nets that are accessible from external pins or from internal logic. These nets are typically used to distribute clocks, resets and other high fan-out nets requiring a minimum skew.

8.14.5 Clock Resources

ProASIC^{PLUS} offers powerful and flexible control of circuit timing through the use of analog circuitry. Each chip has two clock conditioning blocks containing a phase-looked loop core. PLL block can drive inputs and/or outputs via the two global lines on each side of the chip (four total lines).

8.14.6 Input/Output Blocks

To meet complex system demands, large number of user I/O pins are provided, up to 712 on the APA1000.

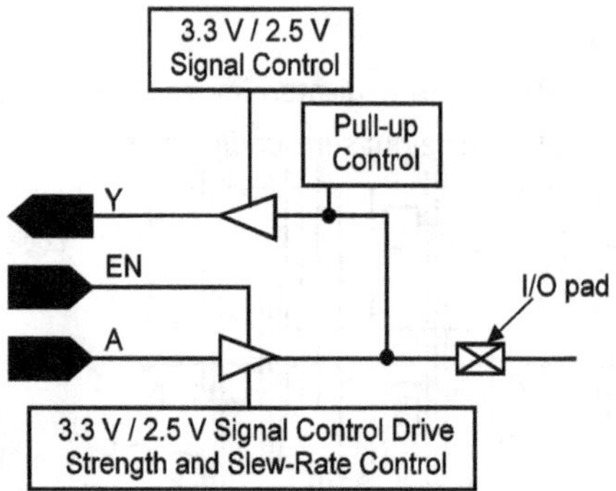

Fig. 8.69: I/O block schematic representation

If the I/O pad power is 3.3V, each I/O can be selectively configured at 2.5 V and 3.3 V threshold levels. All I/Os include ESP protection circuits. Each I/O has been tested to 2000V to the human body model. Six or seven standard I/O pads are grouped with a GND pad and either V_{DD} (core power) or V_{DDP} (I/O power) pad. I/O pads fully configurable to provide the maximum flexibility and speed. Each pad can be used as an input, an output, a tristate driver or a bidirectional buffer.

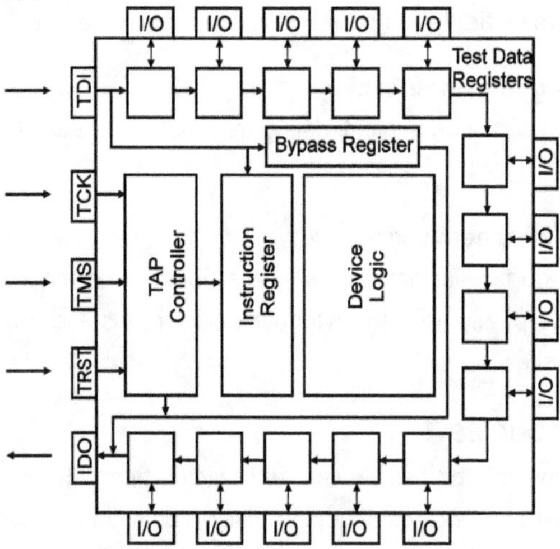

Fig. 8.70: ProASIC^{PLUS} JTAG boundary scan test logic circuit

8.14.7 Boundary Scan (JTAG)

These devices are compatible with IEEE standard 1149.1, which defines a set of hardware architecture and mechanisms for cost-effective, board level testing. The basic boundary scan logic is composed of TAP (Test Access Port), TAP controller, test data registers and instruction register. Fig. 8.70 shows the JTAG boundary scan test logic circuit. This circuit supports all mandatory IEEE 1149.1 instructions (EXTEST, SAMPLE/PRELOAD, and BYPASS) and the optimal IDCODE instruction.

It has total five associated pins. These pins are TCK (Test Clock Input), TDI and TDO (Test Data Input and Output), TMS (Test Mode Selector) and TRST (Test Reset input). The TAP controller is a 4 bit state machine.

ProASIC^{PLUS} devices have to be programmed at least once for complete boundary scan functionality to be available. The TAP controller receives two control inputs (TMS and TCK) and generates control and clock signals for the rest of the test logic architecture.

ProASIC^{PLUS} devices support three types of test data registers.
   1) Bypass Register
   2) Device Identification Register (32 bit)
   3) Boundary Scan Register

Bypass Register: It is selected when no other register needs to be accessed in a device. This speeds up test data transfer to other devices in a test data path.

Device Identification Register: It is a 32 bit shift register with four fields. These fields are lowest significant byte (LSB), ID number, part number and version.

Boundary Scan Register: It observes and controls the state of each I/O pin. Each I/O cell has three boundary-scan register cells, each with a serial-in, serial-out, parallel-in and parallel-out pin. The serial pins are used to serially connect all the boundary scan register cells in a device into a boundary scan register chain, which starts at the TDI pin and ends at the TDO pin.

The parallel ports are connected to the internal core logic tile and the input, output and control ports of an I/O buffer to capture and load data into the register to control or observe the logic state of each I/O.

8.14.8 ProASIC^{PLUS} Clock Management System

This family contains two phase locked loop (PLL) blocks which perform the following functions.

Each PLL has the following key features:

1) Input frequency range (F_{IN}) = 1.5 to 180 MHz

2) Feedback frequency range (F_{VCO}) = 1.5 to 180 MHz

3) Output frequency range (F_{OUT}) = 6 to 180 MHz.

4) Output phase shift = 0°, 90°, 180° and 270°.

5) Output duty cycle = 50 %.

Each side of the chip contains a clock conditioning circuit based on a 180 MHz PLL block. Each PLL contains four programmable dividers.

8.14.9 User Security

These devices have FlashLock protection bits that once programmed; block the entire programmed contents from being read externally. If locked, the user can only reprogram the device employing the user-defined security key. This protects the device from being read back and duplicated.

8.14.10 Embedded Memory

The embedded memory is located across the top and bottom of the device. Depending on the device, up to 88 blocks are available to support a variety of memory configurations. (For APA300, 32 Embedded RAM Blocks are available).

Each embedded RAM block comprised of 256, 9 bit words. Therefore number of bits in one block = 256 × 9 bits. Each block can be programmed as an independent memory array or combined to form larger, more complex memory configurations. Each ProASIC^{PLUS} block is designed and optimized as a two port memory (one read, one write).

Each memory block can be configured as FIFO or SRAM, with independent selection of synchronous or asynchronous read and write ports. Additional characteristics include programmable flags as well as parity checking and generation.

Fig. 8.71 shows the basic SRAM block diagram. A single memory block is designed to operate up to 150 MHz. The memory blocks may be cascaded in width and or depth to create the desired memory organization.

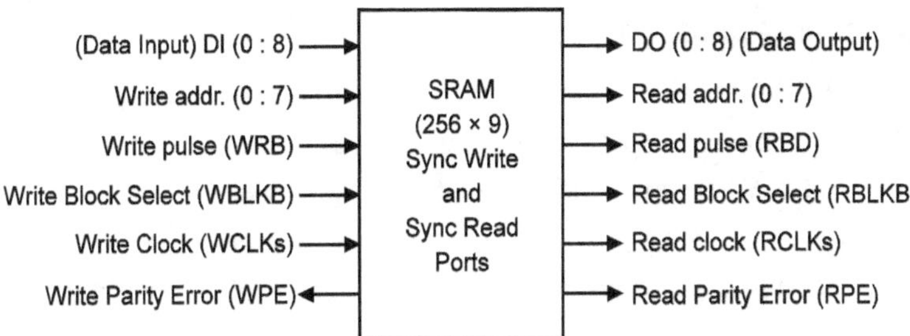

Fig. 8.71: Basic SRAM block diagram

8.14.11 Pin Description

User Pins

1) **I/O:** User Input/Output

   The I/O pin functions as an input, output, tristate or bidirectional buffer.

2) **GL:** Global pin

   Low skew input pin for clock or other global signals.

3) **GLMX:** Global multiplexing pin

   Low skew input pin for clock or other global signals. When the external feedback option is selected from the PLL block, this pin is routed as the external feedback source to the clock conditioning circuit.

4) **GND:** Ground

5) **V_{DD}:** Logic Array power supply pin.

   2.5 V supply voltage.

6) **V_{DDP}:** I/O Pad Power Supply pin.

   2.5 V or 3.3V supply voltage.

7) **TMS:** Test Mode Select – This pin controls the use of boundary-scan circuitry.

8) **TCK:** Test Clock-Clock input pin for boundary scan (Maximum 10 MHz).

9) **TDI:** Test Data In – Serial output for boundary scan.

10) **TDO:** Test Data Out – Serial output for boundary scan.

11) **TRST:** Test Reset input – Asynchronous, active low input pin for resetting boundary scan circuitry.

12) **RCK:** Running clock – A free running clock is needed during programming, if the programmer cannot guarantee that TCK will be uninterrupted.

13) **NPECL:** User negative input – Provides high speed clock or data signals to the PLL block.

14) **PPECL:** User positive input

15) **AVDD:** PLL Power Supply – 2.5 V

16) **A GND:** PLL Power Ground

17) **V_{PP}:** Programming Supply Pin – This pin may be connected to any voltage between GND and 16.5V during normal operation or left unconnected.

18) **V_{PN}:** Programming supply pin – This pin may be connected to any voltage between 0.5V and –13.8 V during normal operation, or it can be left unconnected.

To increase the effective size and to add more functionality in a SPLD and CPLD, the architecture known as FPGA have been developed. The logic densities of FPGAs are much higher than those of CPLDs. They range in size from 10,000 to a few hundreds of thousands equivalent gates. FPGA devices support implementation of relatively very large logic circuits.

The FPGA do not contain AND, OR planes, instead they provide logic blocks for implementation of the required digital functions.

An FPGA is composed of a number of relatively independent **configurable logic** modules, configurable I/O cells, and programmable inter connection paths (known as routing channels). All the resources of the device are uncommitted and that these must be selected, configured and interconnected by a user to form a logic circuit for his application.

8.15 Comparison of CPLD and FPGA

- The FPGA chips have much greater functionality and can be used to implement rather large logic networks compared to CPLD.
- FPGAs have large number of registers compared to CPLD.
- FPGAs have significantly longer propogation (propagation) delays, because of longer data paths by cascading multiple logic cells.
- FPGAs have a finer grained architecture, they perform well in pipelined designs, while CPLD's resources are partitioned into logic blocks, imposed restrictions on how they may be used.

8.16 Comparison of PLDs, ASICs and FPGAs

1) PLDs vs. ASICs

PLDs have a limited number of logic gates (in comparison to FPGAs) and can implement only simpler logic functions.

ASICs offer the ultimate in size, number of transistors, complexity and performance. But, the ASICs are extremely time consuming and expensive to design.

FPGAs occupy the **middle** ground between PLDs and ASICs, FPGAs are programmable and they contain millions of logic gates, allowing large and complex functions to be implemented.

2) FPGAs vs. ASICs

The cost of an FPGA design is much lower than that of an ASIC, given the ASIC is not produced in large numbers.

Changes in the design are also much easier with an FPGA, and the time to market much shorter than an ASIC.

8.17 Functions of FPGAs Today

- Prototype ASIC designs or verifies the physical implementation of a new algorithm.
- FPGAs include embedded microprocessor cores, high speed I/O interfaces and other features.
- FPGAs are used to implement communication devices and software defined radios, radar, image and other DSP applications up to (SoC) System-on Chip components.

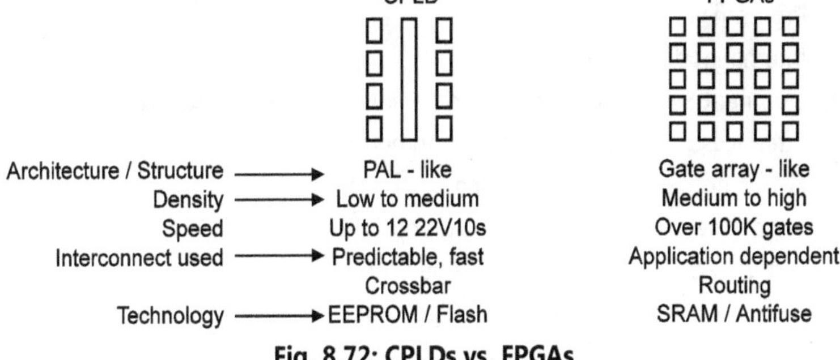

Fig. 8.72: CPLDs vs. FPGAs

8.18 XC4000 Series FPGA

Features

- System featured Field-Programmable Gate Arrays
  - Select-RAM memory: on-chip ultra-fast RAM with
    - Synchronous write option
    - Dual-port RAM option

- Fully PCI compliant (speed grades-2 and faster)
- Abundant flip-flops
- Flexible function generators
- Dedicated high-speed carry logic
- Wide edge decoders on each edge
- Hierarchy of interconnect lines
- Internal 3-state bus capability
- Eight global low-skew clock or signal distribution networks
- System Performance (is) beyond 80 MHz
- Flexible Array Architecture
- Low Power Segmented Routing Architecture
- Systems-Oriented Features
  - IEEE 1149.1-compatible boundary scan logic support
  - Individually programmable output slew rate
  - Programmable input pull-up or pull-down resistors
  - 12 mA sink current per output
- Configured by Loading Binary File
  - Unlimited re-programmability
- Read Back Capability
  - Program verification
  - Internal node observability
- Development System runs on most common computer platforms
  - Interfaces to popular design environments
  - Fully automatic mapping, placement and routing
  - Interactive design editor for design optimization
- Highest Capacity - Over 180,000 Usable Gates
- Buffered Interconnect for Maximum Speed Blocks
- Flexible New High-Speed Clock Network
- Optional Multiplexer or 2-input Function Generator on Device Outputs
- Four Additional Address Bits in Master Parallel Configuration Mode
- Highest density with 0.25 μm 2.5 V technology

Introduction

XC4000 Series high-performance, high-capacity Field Programmable Gate Arrays (FPGAs) provide the benefits of custom CMOS VLSI, while avoiding the initial cost, long development cycle, and inherent risk of a conventional masked gate array. These FPGAs combine architectural versatility, on-chip Select-RAM memory with edge-triggered and dual-port modes, increased speed, abundant routing resources, and new, sophisticated software to achieve fully automated implementation of complex, high-density, high-performance designs.

Description

XC4000 Series devices are implemented with a regular, flexible, programmable architecture of Configurable Logic Blocks (CLBs), interconnected by a powerful hierarchy of versatile routing resources, and surrounded by a perimeter of programmable Input/Output Blocks (IOBs). They have generous routing resources to accommodate the most complex interconnect patterns. The devices are customized by loading configuration data into internal memory cells. The FPGA can either actively read its configuration data from an external serial or byte-parallel PROM (master modes), or the configuration data can be written into the FPGA from an external device (slave and peripheral modes).

XC4000 Series FPGAs are supported by powerful and sophisticated software, covering every aspect of design from schematic or behavioral entry, floor planning, simulation, automatic block placement and routing of interconnects, to the creation, downloading, and readback of the configuration bit stream. Because FPGAs can be reprogrammed an unlimited number of times, they can be used in innovative designs where hardware is changed dynamically, or where hardware must be adapted to different user applications. FPGAs are ideal for shortening design and development cycles, and also offer a cost-effective solution for production rates. FPGA devices can be re-configured to change logic function while resident in the system. This capability gives the system designer a new degree of freedom. Hardware can be changed as easily as software. Design updates or modifications are easy, and can be made to products already in the field. An FPGA can even be re-configured dynamically to perform different functions at different times. Re-configurable logic can be used to implement system self-diagnostics, create systems capable of being re-configured for different environments or operations, or implement multi-purpose hardware for a given application. As an added benefit, using re-configurable FPGA devices simplifies hardware design and debugging and shortens product time-to-market. XC4000E and XC4000X devices can run at synchronous system clock rates of up to 80 MHz, and internal performance can exceed 150 MHz. XC4000 Series devices use a sub-micron multi-layer metal process.

Detailed Functional Description

XC4000 Series devices achieve high speed through advanced semiconductor technology and improved architecture. They offer on-chip edge-triggered and dual-port RAM, clock enables on I/O flip-flops, and wide-input decoders. They are more versatile in many applications, especially those involving RAM. Design cycles are faster due to a combination of increased routing resources and more sophisticated software.

Basic Building Blocks

Field programmable gate arrays include two major configurable elements: configurable logic blocks (CLBs) and input/output blocks (IOBs).

- CLBs provide the functional elements for constructing the user's logic.
- IOBs provide the interface between the package pins and internal signal lines.

Three other types of circuits are also available:

- 3-State buffers (TBUFs) driving horizontal long lines are associated with each CLB.
- Wide edge decoders are available around the periphery of each device.
- An on-chip oscillator is provided.

Programmable interconnect resources provide routing paths to connect the inputs and outputs of these configurable elements to the appropriate networks. The functionality of each circuit block is customized during configuration by programming internal static memory cells. The values stored in these memory cells determine the logic functions and interconnections implemented in the FPGA.

Configurable Logic Blocks (CLBs)

Configurable Logic Blocks implement most of the logic in an FPGA. The principal CLB elements are shown in Fig. 8.73. Two 4-input function generators (F and G) offer unrestricted versatility. Most combinatorial logic functions need four or fewer inputs. However, a third function generator (H) is provided. The H function generator has three inputs. Either zero, one, or two of these inputs can be the outputs of F and G; the other input(s) are from outside the CLB. The CLB can, therefore, implement certain functions of up to nine variables, like parity check or expandable-identity comparison of two sets of four inputs. Each CLB contains two storage elements that can be used to store the function generator outputs. However, the storage elements and function generators can also be used independently. These storage elements can be configured as flip-flops in both XC4000E and XC4000X devices; in the XC4000X they can optionally be configured as latches. DIN can be used as a direct input to either of the two storage elements. H1 can drive the other through the H function generator. Function generator outputs can also drive two outputs independent of the storage element outputs. This versatility increases logic capacity and simplifies routing. Thirteen CLB inputs and four CLB outputs provide access to the function generators and storage elements. These inputs and outputs connect to the programmable interconnect resources outside the block.

Function Generators

Four independent inputs are provided to each of two function generators (F1 - F4 and G1 - G4). These function generators, with outputs labelled 'F' and 'G', are each capable of implementing any arbitrarily defined Boolean function of four inputs. The function generators are implemented as memory look-up tables. The propagation delay is therefore independent of the function implemented. A third function generator, labelled 'H', can implement any Boolean function of its three inputs. Two of these inputs can optionally be the 'F' and 'G' functional generator outputs. Alternatively, one or both of these inputs can come from outside the CLB (H2, H0). The third input must come from outside the block (H1). Signals from the function generators can exit the CLB on two outputs. 'F' or 'H' can be connected to the X output. 'G' or H' can be connected to the Y output.

A CLB can be used to implement any of the following functions:
- Any function of up to four variables, plus any second function of up to four unrelated variables, plus any third function of up to three unrelated variables.
- Any single function of five variables.
- Any function of four variables together with some functions of six variables.
- Some functions of up to nine variables.

Implementing wide functions in a single block reduces both the number of blocks required and the delay in the signal path, achieving both increased capacity and speed. The versatility of the CLB function generators significantly improves system speed. In addition, the design-software tools can deal with each function generator independently.

Flip-Flops

The CLB can pass the combinatorial output(s) to the interconnect network, but can also store the combinatorial results or other incoming data in one or two flip-flops, and connect their outputs to the interconnect network as well. The two edge-triggered D-type flip-flops have common clock (K) and clock enable (EC) inputs. Either or both clock inputs can also be permanently enabled. Storage element functionality is described in Table 8.7.

Clock Input

Each flip-flop can be triggered on either the rising or falling clock edge. The clock pin is shared by both storage elements. However, the clock is individually invertible for each storage element. Any inverter placed on the clock input is automatically absorbed into the CLB.

Clock Enable

The clock enable signal (EC) is active high. The EC pin is shared by both storage elements. If left unconnected for either, the clock enable for that storage element defaults to the active state. EC is not invertible within the CLB.

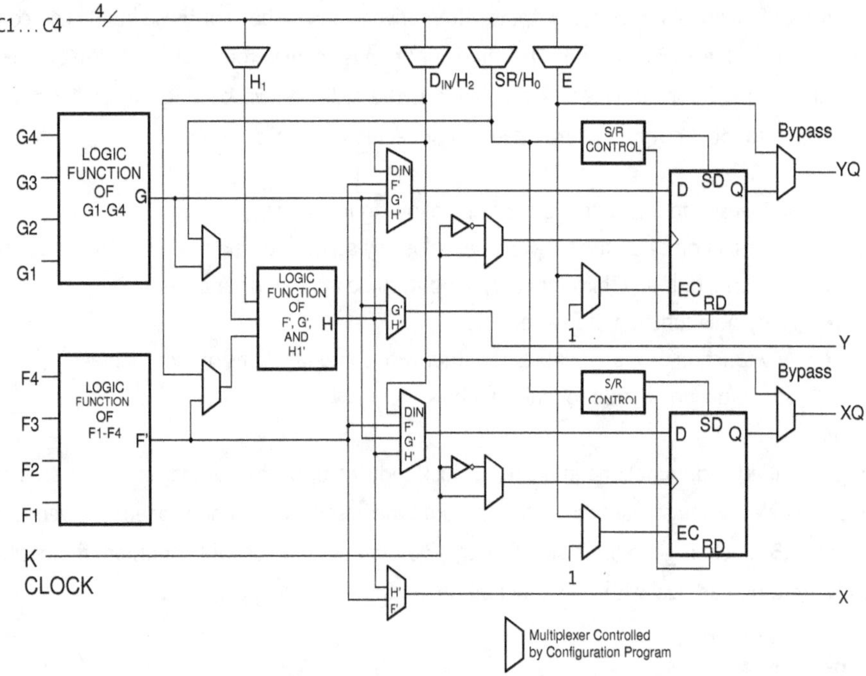

Fig. 8.73: Simplified block diagram of XC4000 Series CLB
(RAM and Carry logic functions not shown)

Table 8.7: CLB Storage Element Functionality

Mode	K	EC	SR	D	Q
Power-Up or GSR	X	X	X	X	SR
Flip-Flop	X	X	1	X	SR
	$\int$	1*	0*	D	D
	0	X	0*	X	Q
Latch	1	1*	0*	X	Q
	0	1*	0*	D	D
Both	X	0	0*	X	Q

Set/Reset

An asynchronous storage element input (SR) can be configured as either set or reset. This configuration option determines the state in which each flip-flop becomes operational after configuration. It also determines the effect of a Global Set/Reset pulse during normal operation, and the effect of a pulse on the SR pin of the CLB. All three set/reset functions for any single flip-flop are controlled by the same configuration data bit. The set/reset state can be independently specified for each flip-flop. This input can also be independently disabled for either flip-flop. The set/reset state is specified by using the INIT attribute, or by placing the appropriate set or reset flip-flop library symbol. SR is active High. It is not invertible within the CLB.

Global Set/Reset

A separate Global Set/Reset line (not shown in Fig. 8.73) sets or clears each storage element during power-up, re-configuration, or when a dedicated Reset net is driven active. This global net (GSR) does not compete with other routing resources; it uses a dedicated distribution network. Each flip-flop is configured as either globally set or reset in the same way that the local set/reset (SR) is specified. Therefore, if a flip-flop is set by SR, it is also set by GSR. Similarly, a reset flip-flop is reset by both SR and GSR. GSR can be driven from any user-programmable pin as a global reset input. To use this global net, place an input pad and input buffer in the schematic or HDL code, driving the GSR pin of the STARTUP symbol (See Fig. 8.74). A specific pin location can be assigned to this input using a LOC attribute or property, just as with any other user-programmable pad. An inverter can optionally be inserted after the input buffer to invert the sense of the Global Set/Reset signal. Alternatively, GSR can be driven from any internal node.

Data Inputs and Outputs

The source of a storage element data input is programmable. It is driven by any of the functions 'F', 'G', and 'H', or by the Direct IN (DIN) block input. The flip-flops or latches drive the XQ and YQ CLB outputs. Two fast feed-through paths are available, as shown in Fig. 8.73. A two-to-one multiplexer on each of the XQ and YQ outputs selects between a storage element output and any of the control inputs. This bypass is sometimes used by the automated router to repower internal signals.

Control Signals

Multiplexers in the CLB map the four control inputs (C1 - C4 in Fig. 8.73) into the four internal control signals (H1, DIN/H2, SR/H0, and EC). Any of these inputs can drive any of the four internal control signals.

When the logic function is enabled, the four inputs are:
- EC - Enable Clock
- SR/H0 - Asynchronous Set/Reset or H function generator Input 0
- DIN/H2 - Direct In or H function generator Input 2
- H1 - H function generator Input 1.

When the memory function is enabled, the four inputs are:
- EC - Enable Clock
- WE - Write Enable
- D0 - Data Input to F and/or G function generator
- D1 - Data input to G function generator (16 × 1 and 16 × 2 modes) or 5th Address bit (32 × 1 mode).

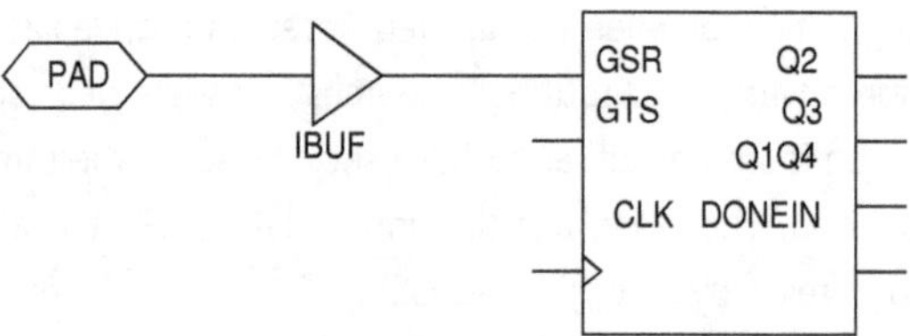

Fig. 8.74: Schematic symbols for global Set/Reset

Advantages of On-Chip and Edge-Triggered RAM

The on-chip RAM is extremely fast. The read access time is the same as the logic delay. The write access time is slightly slower. Both access times are much faster than any off-chip solution, because they avoid I/O delays.

Edge-triggered RAM, also called synchronous RAM, is a feature never before available in a Field Programmable Gate Array. The simplicity of designing with edge-triggered RAM, and the markedly higher achievable performance, adds up to a significant improvement over existing devices with on-chip RAM.

RAM Configuration Options

The function generators in any CLB can be configured as RAM arrays in the following sizes:

- Two 16 × 1 RAMs: two data inputs and two data outputs with identical or, if preferred, different addressing for each RAM

- One 32 × 1 RAM: one data input and one data output. One F or G function generator can be configured as a 16 × 1 RAM while the other function generators are used to implement any function of up to 5 inputs.

  Additionally, the XC4000 Series RAM may have either of two timing modes:

- Edge-Triggered (Synchronous): data written by the designated edge of the CLB clock. WE acts as a true clock enable.

- Level-Sensitive (Asynchronous): an external WE signal acts as the write strobe.

  The selected timing mode applies to both function generators within a CLB when both are configured as RAM.

The number of read ports is also programmable:
- Single Port: each function generator has a common read and write port
- Dual Port: both function generators are configured together as a single 16 × 1 dual-port RAM with one write port and two read ports. Simultaneous read and write operations to the same or different addresses are supported. RAM configuration options are selected by placing the appropriate library symbol.

Supported CLB memory configuration and timing modes for single- and dual-port modes are shown in Table 8.8.

Table 8.8: Supported RAM Modes

	16 x 1	16 x 2	32 x 1	Edge-Triggered Timing	Level-Sensitive Timing
Single Port	√	√	√	√	√
Dual Port	√			√	

Fast Carry Logic

Each CLB F and G function generator contains dedicated arithmetic logic for the fast generation of carry and borrow signals. This extra output is passed on to the function generator in the adjacent CLB. The carry chain is independent of normal routing resources.

Dedicated fast carry logic greatly increases the efficiency and performance of adders, subtractors, accumulators, comparators and counters. High-speed address offset calculations in microprocessor or graphics systems, and high-speed additions in digital signal processing are two typical applications. The two 4-input function generators can be configured as a 2-bit adder with built-in hidden carry that can be expanded to any length. This dedicated carry circuitry is so fast and efficient that conventional speed-up methods like carry generate/propagate are meaningless even at the 16-bit level, and of marginal benefit at the 32-bit level. This fast carry logic is one of the more significant features of the XC4000 Series, speeding up arithmetic and counting into the 70 MHz range. The carry chain in XC4000E devices can run either up or down. At the top and bottom of the columns where there are no CLBs above or below, the carry is propagated to the right. (See Fig. 8.75) Additionally, standard interconnect can be used to route a carry signal in the downward direction. Fig. 8.76 shows an XC4000E CLB with dedicated fast carry logic. As shown in Fig. 8.76, the carry logic shares operand and control inputs with the function generators. The carry outputs connect to the function generators, where they are combined with the operands to form the sums. Fig. 8.77 shows the details of the carry logic for the XC4000E. This diagram shows the contents of the box labeled "CARRY LOGIC" in Fig. 8.76. The fast carry logic can be accessed by placing special library symbols, or by using Xilinx Relationally Placed Macros (RPMs) that already include these symbols.

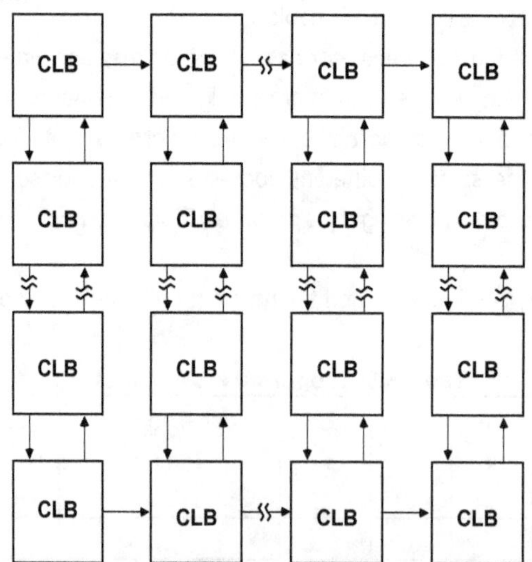

Fig. 8.75: Available XC4000E carry propagation paths

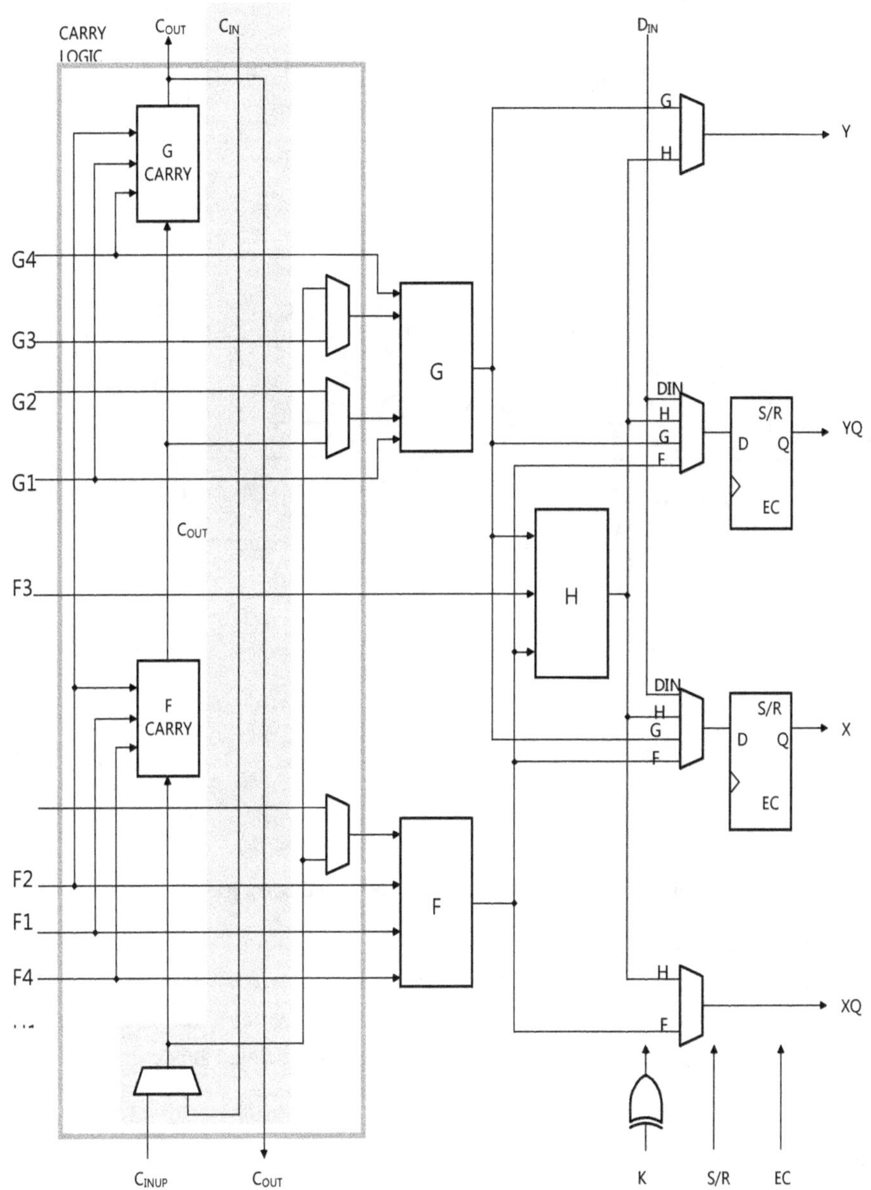

Fig. 8.76: Fast carry logic in XC4000E CLB

(shaded area not present in XC4000X)

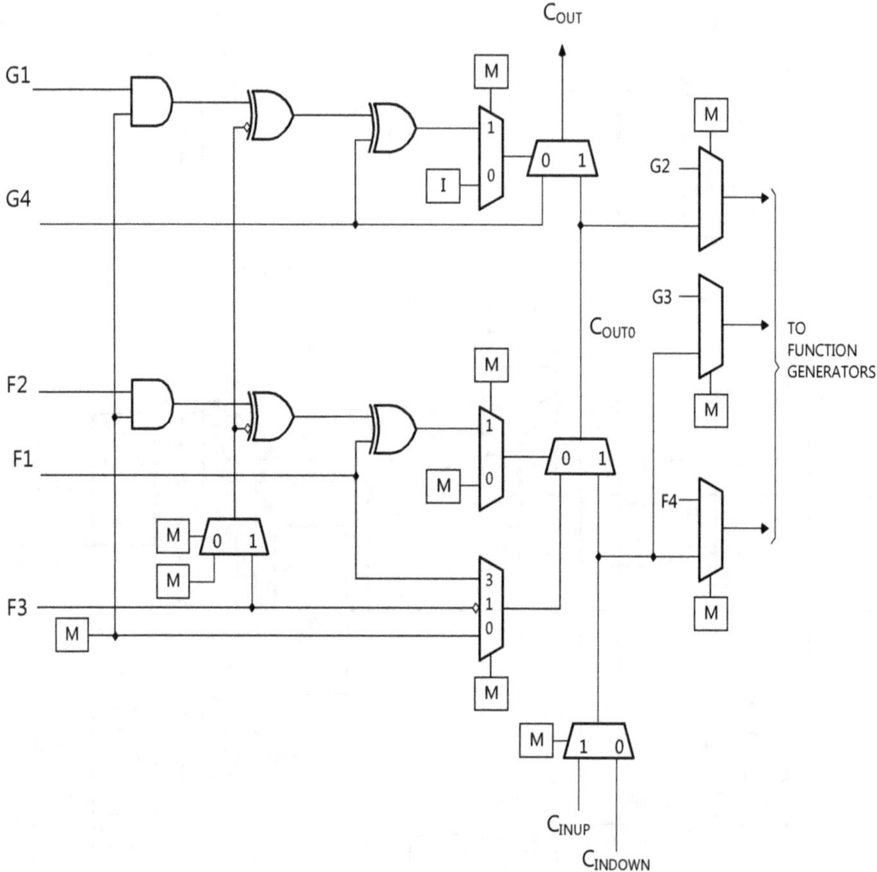

Fig. 8.77: Detail of XC4000E dedicated carry logic

Input/Output Blocks (IOBs)

User-configurable input/output blocks (IOBs) provide the interface between external package pins and the internal logic. Each IOB controls one package pin and can be configured for input, output, or bidirectional signals. Fig. 8.78 shows a simplified block diagram of the XC4000E IOB.

IOB Input Signals

Two paths, labelled I1 and I2 in Fig. 8.78, bring input signals into the array. Inputs also connect to an input register that can be programmed as either an edge-triggered flip-flop or a level-sensitive latch.

The choice is made by placing the appropriate library symbol.

For example, IFD is the basic input flip-flop (rising edge triggered), and ILD is the basic input latch (transparent-High). Variations with inverted clocks are available, and some combinations of latches and flip-flops can be implemented in a single IOB.

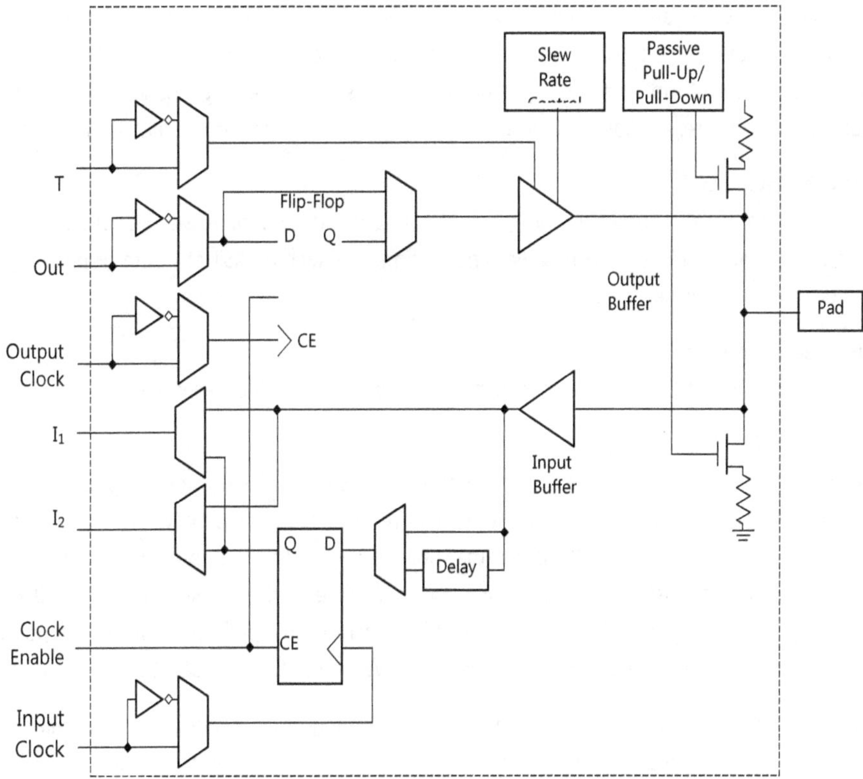

Fig. 8.78: Simplified block diagram of XC4000E IOB

IOB Output Signals

Output signals can be optionally inverted within the IOB, and can pass directly to the pad or be stored in an edge-triggered flip-flop. An active-High 3-state signal can be used to place the output buffer in a high-impedance state, implementing 3-state outputs or bidirectional I/O. Under configuration control, the output (OUT) and output 3-state (T) signals can be inverted. The polarity of these signals is independently configured for each IOB. The 4-mA maximum output current specification of many FPGAs often forces the user to add external buffers, which are especially cumbersome on bidirectional I/O lines. The XC4000E and XC4000EX/XL devices solve many of these problems by providing a guaranteed output sink current of 12 mA. Two adjacent outputs can be interconnected externally to sink up to 24 mA. The XC4000E and XC4000EX/XL FPGAs can thus directly drive buses on a printed circuit board. By default, the output pull-up structure is configured as a TTL-like totem-pole. The High driver is an n-channel pull-up transistor, pulling to a voltage one transistor threshold below V_{CC}. Alternatively, the outputs can be globally configured as CMOS drivers, with p-channel pull-up transistors pulling to V_{CC}. This option, applied using the bit stream generation software, applies to all outputs on the device. It is not individually programmable.

Output Slew Rate

The slew rate of each output buffer is, by default, reduced, to minimize power bus transients when switching non-critical signals. For critical signals, attach a FAST attribute or property to the output buffer or flip-flop.

Other IOB Options

There are a number of other programmable options in the XC4000 Series IOB.

Pull-up and Pull-down Resistors

Programmable pull-up and pull-down resistors are useful for tying unused pins to V_{CC} or Ground to minimize power consumption and reduce noise sensitivity. The configurable pull-up resistor is a p-channel transistor that pulls to V_{CC}. The configurable pull-down resistor is an n-channel transistor that pulls to Ground. The value of these resistors is from 50 kΩ – 100 kΩ. This high value makes them unsuitable as wired-AND pull-up resistors. The pull-up resistors for most user-programmable IOBs are active during the configuration process.

After configuration, voltage levels of unused pads, bonded or un-bonded, must be valid logic levels, to reduce noise sensitivity and avoid excess current. Therefore, by default, unused pads are configured with the internal pull-up resistor active. Alternatively, they can be individually configured with the pull-down resistor, or as a driven output, or to be driven by an external source. To activate the internal pull-up, attach the PULLUP library component to the net attached to the pad. To activate the internal pull-down, attach the PULLDOWN library component to the net attached to the pad.

Independent Clocks

Separate clock signals are provided for the input and output flip-flops. The clock can be independently inverted for each flip-flop within the IOB; generating either falling-edge or rising- edge triggered flip-flops. The clock inputs for each IOB are independent.

Global Set/Reset

As with the CLB registers, the Global Set/Reset signal (GSR) can be used to set or clear the input and output registers, depending on the value of the INIT attribute or property. The two flip-flops can be individually configured to set or clear on reset and after configuration. Other than the global GSR net, no user-controlled set/reset signal is available to the I/O flip-flops. The choice of set or clear applies to both the initial state of the flip-flop and the response to the Global Set/Reset pulse.

JTAG Support

Embedded logic attached to the IOBs contains test structures compatible with IEEE Standard 1149.1 for boundary scan testing, permitting easy chip and board-level testing.

Three-State Buffers

A pair of 3-state buffers is associated with each CLB in the array. These 3-state buffers can be used to drive signals onto the nearest horizontal longlines above and below the CLB. They can therefore be used to implement multiplexed or bidirectional buses on the horizontal longlines, saving logic resources. Programmable pull-up resistors attached to these longlines help to implement a wide wired-AND function.

The buffer enable is an active-High 3-state (i.e. an active-Low enable).

Another 3-state buffer with similar access is located near each I/O block along the right and left edges of the array.   The horizontal longlines driven by the 3-state buffers have a weak keeper at each end. This circuit prevents undefined floating levels. However, it is overridden by any driver, even a pull-up resistor.

Special longlines running along the perimeter of the array can be used to wire-AND signals coming from nearby IOBs or from internal longlines.

Three-State Buffer Modes

The 3-state buffers can be configured in three modes:
- Standard 3-state buffer
- Wired-AND with input on the I pin
- Wired OR-AND

Standard 3-State Buffer

All three pins are used. Place the library element BUFT. Connect the input to the I pin and the output to the O pin. The T pin is an active-High 3-state (i.e. an active-Low enable). Tie the T pin to Ground to implement a standard buffer.

Wired-AND with Input on the I Pin

The buffer can be used as a Wired-AND. Use the WAND1 library symbol, which is essentially an open-drain buffer. WAND4, WAND8, and WAND16 are also available. The T pin is internally tied to the I pin. Connect the input to the I pin and the output to the O pin. Connect the outputs of all the WAND1s together and attach a PULLUP symbol.

Wired OR-AND

The buffer can be configured as a Wired OR-AND. A High level on either input turns off the output. Use the WOR2AND library symbol, which is essentially an open-drain 2-input OR gate. The two input pins are functionally equivalent. Attach the two inputs to the I0 and I1 pins and tie the output to the O pin. Tie the outputs of all the WOR2ANDs together and attach a PULLUP symbol.

Wide Edge Decoders

Dedicated decoder circuitry boosts the performance of wide decoding functions. When the address or data field is wider than the function generator inputs, FPGAs need multi-level decoding. XC4000 Series CLBs have nine inputs. Any decoder of up to nine inputs is, therefore, compact and fast. However, there is also a need for much wider decoders, especially for address decoding in large microprocessor systems. An XC4000 Series FPGA has four programmable decoders located on each edge of the device. The inputs to each decoder are any of the IOB I1 signals on that edge plus one local interconnect per CLB row or column. Each row or column of CLBs provides up to three variables or their compliments. Each decoder generates a High output (resistor pull-up) when the AND condition of the selected inputs, or their complements, is true. This is analogous to a product term in typical PAL devices.

The decoder outputs can drive CLB inputs, so they can be combined with other logic to form a PAL-like AND/OR structure. The decoder outputs can also be routed directly to the chip outputs. For fastest speed, the output should be on the same chip edge as the decoder. Very large PALs can be emulated by ORing the decoder outputs in a CLB. Users often resorted to external PALs for simple but fast decoding functions. Now, the dedicated decoders in the XC4000 Series device can implement these functions fast and efficiently.

On-Chip Oscillator

XC4000 Series devices include an internal oscillator. This oscillator is used to clock the power-on time-out, for configuration memory clearing, and as the source of CCLK in Master configuration modes. The oscillator runs at a nominal 8 MHz frequency that varies with process, V_{CC}, and temperature. The output frequency falls between 4 and 10 MHz.

The oscillator output is optionally available after configuration. Any two of four resynchronized taps of a built-in divider are also available. These taps are at the fourth, ninth, fourteenth and nineteenth bits of the divider. Therefore, if the primary oscillator output is running at the nominal 8 MHz, the user has access to an 8 MHz clock, plus any two of 500 kHz, 16 kHz, 490 Hz and 15 Hz (up to 10% lower for low-voltage devices). These frequencies can vary by as much as -50% or +25%. These signals can be accessed by placing the OSC4 library element in a schematic or in HDL code. The oscillator is automatically disabled after configuration if the OSC4 symbol is not used in the design.

Programmable Interconnect

All internal connections are composed of metal segments with programmable switching points and switching matrices to implement the desired routing. A structured, hierarchical matrix of routing resources is provided to achieve efficient automated routing.

The implementation software automatically assigns the appropriate resources based on the density and timing requirements of the design.

Interconnect Overview

There are several types of interconnect.
- CLB routing is associated with each row and column of the CLB array.
- IOB routing forms a ring (called a VersaRing) around the outside of the CLB array. It connects the I/O with the internal logic blocks.

- Global routing consists of dedicated networks primarily designed to distribute clocks throughout the device with minimum delay and skew. Global routing can also be used for other high-fan-out signals.

Five interconnect types are distinguished by the relative length of their segments: single-length lines, double-length lines, quad and octal lines, and longlines. Direct connects allow fast data flow between adjacent CLBs, and between IOBs and CLBs. Extra routing is included in the IOB pad ring.

CLB Routing Connections

A high-level diagram of the routing resources associated with one CLB is shown in Fig. 8.79. The shaded square is the programmable switch matrix. In general, the entire architecture is symmetrical and regular. It is well suited to established placement and routing algorithms. Inputs, outputs, and function generators can freely swap positions within a CLB to avoid routing congestion during the placement and routing operation.

Programmable Switch Matrices

The horizontal and vertical single- and double-length lines intersect at a box called a Programmable Switch Matrix (PSM). Each switch matrix consists of programmable pass transistors used to establish connections between the lines (See Fig. 8.80).

For example, a single-length signal entering on the right side of the switch matrix can be routed to a single-length line on the top, left, or bottom sides, or any combination thereof, if multiple branches are required. Similarly, a double-length signal can be routed to a double-length line on any or all of the other three edges of the programmable switch matrix.

Single-Length Lines

Single-length lines provide the greatest interconnect flexibility and offer fast routing between adjacent blocks. There are eight vertical and eight horizontal single-length lines associated with each CLB. These lines connect the switching matrices that are located in every row and a column of CLBs. Single-length lines are connected by way of the programmable switch matrices, as shown in Fig. 8.81. Single-length lines incur a delay whenever they go through a switching matrix. Therefore, they are not suitable for routing signals for long distances. They are normally used to conduct signals within a localized area and to provide the branching for nets with fan-out greater than one.

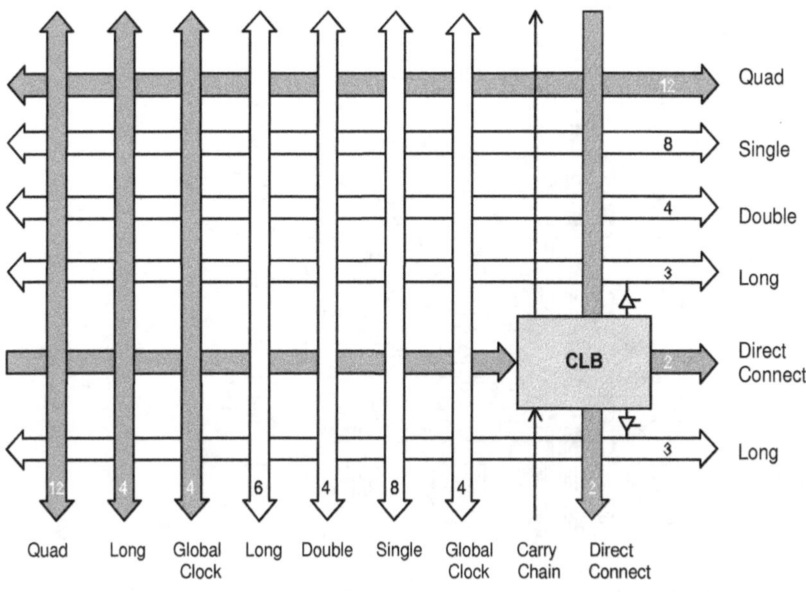

**Fig. 8.79: High-level routing diagram of XC4000 series CLB
(shaded arrows indicate XC4000X only)**

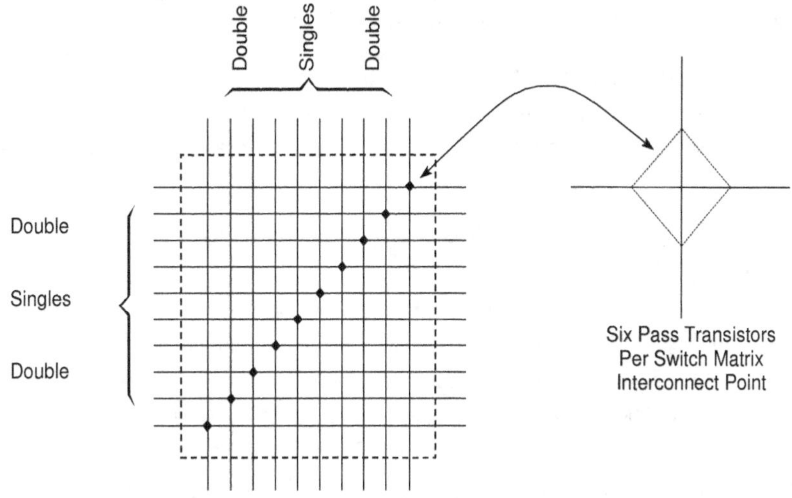

Fig. 8.80: Programmable Switch Matrix (PSM)

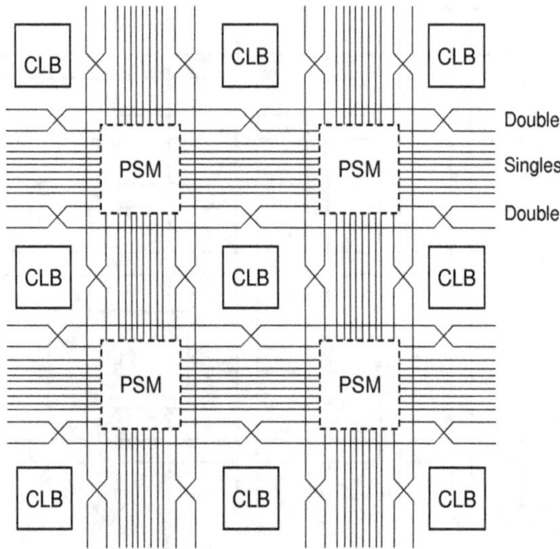

Fig. 8.81: Single- and double-length lines, with Programmable Switch Matrices (PSMs)

Double-Length Lines

The double-length lines consist of a grid of metal segments, each twice as long as the single-length lines: they run past two CLBs before entering a switch matrix. Double-length lines are grouped in pairs with the switch matrices staggered, so that each line goes through a switch matrix at every other row or column of CLBs (see Fig. 8.81).

There are four vertical and four horizontal double-length lines associated with each CLB. These lines provide faster signal routing over intermediate distances, while retaining routing flexibility. Double-length lines are connected by way of the programmable switch matrices.

Longlines

Longlines form a grid of metal interconnect segments that run the entire length or width of the array. Longlines are intended for high fan-out, time-critical signal nets, or nets that are distributed over long distances. Two horizontal longlines per CLB can be driven by 3-state or open-drain drivers (TBUFs). They can therefore implement unidirectional or bidirectional buses, wide multiplexers, or wired-AND functions. Each horizontal longline driven by TBUFs has either two (XC4000E) or eight (XC4000X) pull-up resistors. To activate these resistors, attach a PULLUP symbol to the long-line net. The software automatically activates the appropriate number of pull-ups. There is also a weak keeper at each end of these two horizontal longlines. This circuit prevents undefined floating levels. However, it is overridden by any driver, even a pull-up resistor. Each longline has a programmable splitter switch at its center. This switch can separate the line into two independent routing channels, each running half the width or height of the array.

I/O Routing

XC4000 Series devices have additional routing around the IOB ring. This routing is called a VersaRing. The VersaRing facilitates pin-swapping and redesign without affecting board layout. Eight double-length lines spanning two CLBs (four IOBs), and four longlines are included. Global lines and Wide Edge Decoder lines are provided. There are two IOBs per CLB row or column.

Global Nets and Buffers

The XC4000 have dedicated global networks. These networks are designed to distribute clocks and other high fan-out control signals throughout the devices with minimal skew.

Four vertical longlines in each CLB column are driven exclusively by special global buffers. These longlines are in addition to the vertical longlines used for standard interconnect. The four global lines can be driven by either of two types of global buffers. The clock pins of every CLB and IOB can also be sourced from local interconnect. Two different types of clock buffers are available in the XC4000E:

- Primary Global Buffers (BUFGP)
- Secondary Global Buffers (BUFGS)

Four Primary Global buffers offer the shortest delay and negligible skew. Four Secondary Global buffers have slightly longer delay and slightly more skew due to potentially heavier loading, but offer greater flexibility when used to drive non-clock CLB inputs.

The Primary Global buffers must be driven by the semi-dedicated pads. The Secondary Global buffers can be sourced by either semi-dedicated pads or internal nets. Each CLB column has four dedicated vertical global lines. Each of these lines can be accessed by one particular Primary Global buffer, or by any of the Secondary Global buffers. Each corner of the device has one Primary buffer and one Secondary buffer. IOBs along the left and right edges have four vertical global longlines. Top and bottom IOBs can be clocked from the global lines in the adjacent CLB column. A global buffer should be specified for all timing-sensitive global signal distribution. To use a global buffer, place a BUFGP (primary buffer), BUFGS (secondary buffer), or BUFG (either primary or secondary buffer) element in a schematic or in HDL code. If desired, attach a LOC attribute or property to direct placement to the designated location. For example, attach a LOC=L attribute or property to a BUFGS symbol to direct that a buffer be placed in one of the two Secondary Global buffers on the left edge of the device, or a LOC=BL to indicate the Secondary Global buffer on the bottom edge of the device, on the left. L = Left, R = Right, T = Top, B = Bottom.

Power Distribution

Power for the FPGA is distributed through a grid to achieve high noise immunity and isolation between logic and I/O. Inside the FPGA, a dedicated V_{CC} and Ground ring surrounding the logic array provides power to the I/O drivers, as shown in Fig. 8.82. An independent matrix of V_{CC} and Ground lines supplies the interior logic of the device. This power distribution grid provides a stable supply and ground for all internal logic, providing the external package power pins are all connected and appropriately decoupled. Typically, a 0.1 µF capacitor connected between each V_{CC} pin and the board's Ground plane will provide adequate decoupling.

Output buffers capable of driving/sinking the specified 12 mA loads under specified worst-case conditions may be capable of driving/sinking up to 10 times as much current under best case conditions. Noise can be reduced by minimizing external load capacitance and reducing simultaneous output transitions in the same direction. It may also be beneficial to locate heavily loaded output buffers near the Ground pads. The I/O Block output buffers have a slew-rate limited mode (default) which should be used where output rise and fall times are not speed-critical.

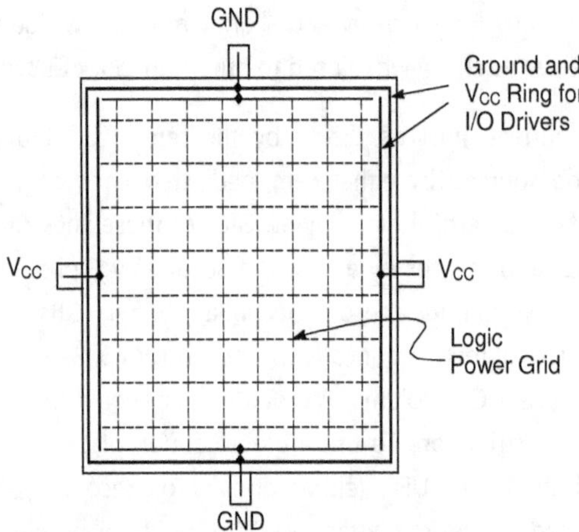

Fig. 8.82: XC4000 Series power distribution

Pin Descriptions

There are three types of pins in the XC4000 Series devices:

- Permanently dedicated pins
- User I/O pins that can have special functions
- Unrestricted user-programmable I/O pins.

  Device pins for XC4000 series devices are described in Table 8.9.

Table 8.9: Pin description for XC4000

Pin Name	I/O During Confi-guration	I/O After Confi-guration	Pin Description
Permanently Dedicated Pins			
V_{CC}	I	I	Eight or more (depending on package) connections to the nominal +5 V supply voltage (+3.3 V for low-voltage devices). All must be connected, and each must be decoupled with a 0.01 - 0.1 µF capacitor to Ground.
GND	I	I	Eight or more (depending on package type) connections to Ground. All must be connected.
CCLK	I or O	I	During configuration, Configuration Clock (CCLK) is an output in Master modes or Asynchronous Peripheral mode, but is an input in Slave mode and Synchronous Peripheral mode. After configuration, CCLK has a weak pull-up resistor and can be selected as the Readback Clock. There is no CCLK High or Low time restriction on XC4000 Series devices, except during Readback. See "Violating the Maximum High and Low Time Specification for the Readback Clock".
DONE	I/O	O	DONE is a bidirectional signal with an optional internal pull-up resistor. As an output, it indicates the completion of the configuration process. As an input, a Low level on DONE can be configured to delay the global logic initialization and the enabling of outputs. The optional pull-up resistor is selected as an option in the XACT stepprogram that creates the configuration bitstream. The resistor is included by default.

contd...

PROG -RAM	I	I	PROGRAM is an active Low input that forces the FPGA to clear its configuration memory. It is used to initiate a configuration cycle. When PROGRAM goes High, the FPGA finishes the current clear cycle and executes another complete clear cycle, before it goes into a WAIT state and releases INIT. The PROGRAM pin has a permanent weak pull-up, so it need not be externally pulled up to V_{CC}.
User I/O Pins That Can Have Special Functions			
RDY/ BUSY	O	I/O	During Peripheral mode configuration, this pin indicates when it is appropriate to write another byte of data into the FPGA. The same status is also available on D7 in Asynchronous Peripheral mode, if a read operation is performed when the device is selected. After configuration, RDY/BUSY is a user-programmable I/O pin. RDY/BUSY is pulled High with a high-impedance pull-up prior to INIT going High.
RCLK	O	I/O	During Master Parallel configuration, each change on the A0-A17 outputs (A0 - A21 for XC4000X) is preceded by a rising edge on RCLK, a redundant output signal. RCLK is useful for clocked PROMs. It is rarely used during configuration. After configuration, RCLK is a user-programmable I/O pin.
M0, M1, M2	I	I (M0), O (M1), I (M2)	As Mode inputs, these pins are sampled after INIT goes High to determine the configuration mode to be used. After configuration, M0 and M2 can be used as inputs, and M1 can be used as a 3-state output. These three pins have no associated input or output registers. During configuration, these pins have weak pull-up resistors. For the most popular configuration mode, Slave Serial, the mode pins can thus be left unconnected. The three mode inputs can be individually configured with or without weak pull-up or pull-down resistors. A pull-down resistor value of 4.7 kΩ is recommended. These pins can only be used as inputs or outputs when called out by special schematic definitions. To use these pins, place the library components MD0, MD1, and MD2 instead of the usual pad symbols. Input or output buffers must still be used.

... Contd.

TDO	O	O	If boundary scan is used, this pin is the Test Data Output. If boundary scan is not used, this pin is a 3-state output without a register, after configuration is completed. This pin can be user output only when called out by special schematic definitions. To use this pin, place the library component TDO instead of the usual pad symbol. An output buffer must still be used.
TDI, TCK, TMS	I	I/O or I JTAG	If boundary scan is used, these pins are Test Data In, Test Clock, and Test Mode Select inputs respectively. They come directly from the pads, bypassing the IOBs. These pins can also be used as inputs to the CLB logic after configuration is completed. If the BSCAN symbol is not placed in the design, all boundary scan functions are inhibited once configuration is completed, and these pins become user-programmable I/O. In this case, they must be called out by special schematic definitions. To use these pins, place the library components TDI, TCK, and TMS instead of the usual pad symbols. Input or output buffers must still be used.
HDC	O	I/O	High During Configuration (HDC) is driven High until the I/O go active. It is available as a control output indicating that configuration is not yet completed. After configuration, HDC is a user- programmable I/O pin.
LDC	O	I/O	Low During Configuration (LDC) is driven Low until the I/O go active. It is available as a control output indicating that configuration is not yet completed. After configuration, LDC is a user-programmable I/O pin.
INIT	I/O	I/O	Before and during configuration, INIT is a bidirectional signal. A 1 kΩ – 10 kΩ external pull-up resistor is recommended. As an active-low open-drain output, INIT is held Low during the power stabilization and internal clearing of the configuration memory. As an active-Low input, it can be used to hold the FPGA in the internal WAIT state before the start of configuration. Master mode devices stay in a WAIT state an additional 30 to 300 μs after INIT has gone High. During configuration, a Low on this output indicates that a configuration data error has occurred. After the I/O go active, INIT is a user-programmable I/O pin.

contd...

PGCK1 - PGCK4 (XC4000E only)	Weak Pull-up	I or I/O	Four Primary Global inputs each drive a dedicated internal global net with short delay and minimal skew. If not used to drive a global buffer, any of these pins is a user-programmable I/O. The PGCK1-PGCK4 pins drive the four Primary Global Buffers. Any input pad symbol connected directly to the input of a BUFGP symbol is automatically placed on one of these pins.
SGCK1 – SGCK4 (XC4000E only)	Weak Pull-up	I or I/O	Four Secondary Global inputs each drive a dedicated internal global net with short delay and minimal skew. These internal global nets can also be driven from internal logic. If not used to drive a global net, any of these pins is a user-programmable I/O pin. The SGCK1-SGCK4 pins provide the shortest path to the four Secondary Global Buffers. Any input pad symbol connected directly to the input of a BUFGS symbol is automatically placed on one of these pins.
GCK1 - GCK8 (XC4000X only)	Weak Pull-up	I or I/O	Eight inputs can each drive a Global Low-Skew buffer. In addition, each can drive a Global Early buffer. Each pair of global buffers can also be driven from internal logic, but must share an input signal. If not used to drive a global buffer, any of these pins is a user-programmable I/O. Any input pad symbol connected directly to the input of a BUFGLS or BUFGE symbol is automatically placed on one of these pins.
FCLK1 - FCLK4 XC4000X LA and XC4000X V only)	Weak Pull-up	I or I/O	Four inputs can each drive a Fast Clock (FCLK) buffer which can deliver a clock signal to any IOB clock input in the octant of the die served by the Fast Clock buffer. Two Fast Clock buffers serve the two IOB octants on the left side of the die and the other two Fast Clock buffers serve the two IOB octants on the right side of the die. On each side of the die, one Fast Clock buffer serves the upper octant and the other serves the lower octant. If not used to drive a Fast Clock buffer, any of these pins is a user-programmable I/O.

contd...

CS0, CS1, WS, RS	I	I/O	These four inputs are used in Asynchronous Peripheral mode. The chip is selected when CS0 is Low and CS1 is High. While the chip is selected, a Low on Write Strobe (WS) loads the data present on the D0 - D7 inputs into the internal data buffer. A Low on Read Strobe (RS) changes D7 into a status output — High if Ready, Low if Busy — and drives D0 - D6 High. In Express mode, CS1 is used as a serial-enable signal for daisy-chaining. WS and RS should be mutually exclusive, but if both are Low simultaneously, the Write Strobe overrides. After configuration, these are user-programmable I/O pins.
A0 - A17	O	I/O	During Master Parallel configuration, these 18 output pins address the configuration EPROM. After configuration, they are user-programmable I/O pins.
A18 - A21 (XC4003XL to XC4085XL)	O	I/O	During Master Parallel configuration with an XC4000X master, these 4 output pins add 4 more bits to address the configuration EPROM. After configuration, they are user-programmable I/O pins. (See Master Parallel Configuration section for additional details.)
D0 - D7	I	I/O	During Master Parallel and Peripheral configuration, these eight input pins receive configuration data. After configuration, they are user-programmable I/O pins.
DIN	I	I/O	During Slave Serial or Master Serial configuration, DIN is the serial configuration data input receiving data on the rising edge of CCLK. During Parallel configuration, DIN is the D0 input. After configuration, DIN is a user-programmable I/O pin.
DOUT	O	I/O	During configuration in any mode but Express mode, DOUT is the serial configuration data output that can drive the DIN of daisy-chained slave FPGAs. DOUT data changes on the falling edge of CCLK, one-and-a-half CCLK periods after it was received at the DIN input. In Express mode for XC4000E and XC4000X only, DOUT is the status output that can drive the CS1 of daisy-chained FPGAs, to enable and disable downstream devices. After configuration, DOUT is a user-programmable I/O pin.
Unrestricted User-Programmable I/O Pins			
I/O	Weak Pull-up	I/O	These pins can be configured to be input and/or output after configuration is completed. Before configuration is completed, these pins have an internal high-value pull-up resistor (25 kW - 100 kW) that defines the logic level as High.

Configuration

Configuration is the process of loading design-specific programming data into one or more FPGAs to define the functional operation of the internal blocks and their interconnections. This is somewhat like loading the command registers of a programmable peripheral chip. XC4000 Series devices use several hundred bits of configuration data per CLB and its associated interconnects. Each configuration bit defines the state of a static memory cell that controls either a function look-up table bit, a multiplexer input, or an interconnect pass transistor.

Configuration Modes

XC4000E devices have six configuration modes. XC4000X devices have the same six modes, plus an additional configuration mode. These modes are selected by a 3-bit input code applied to the M2, M1, and M0 inputs. There are three self-loading Master modes, two Peripheral modes, and a Serial Slave mode, which is used primarily for daisy-chained devices. The coding for mode selection is shown in Table 8.10. During configuration, some of the I/O pins are used temporarily for the configuration process.

Table 8.10: Configuration Modes

Mode	M2	M1	M0	CCLK	Data
Master Serial	0	0	0	output	Bit-Serial
Slave Serial	1	1	1	input	Bit-Serial
Master Parallel Up	1	0	0	output	Byte-Wide, increment from 00000
Master Parallel Down	1	1	0	output	Byte-Wide, decrement from 3FFFF
Peripheral Synchronous	0	1	1	input	Byte-Wide
Peripheral Asynchronous	1	0	1	output	Byte-Wide
Reserved	0	1	0	—	—
Reserved	0	0	1	—	—

Master Modes

The three Master modes use an internal oscillator to generate a Configuration Clock (CCLK) for driving potential slave devices. They also generate address and timing for external PROM(s) containing the configuration data. Master Parallel (Up or Down) modes generate the CCLK signal and PROM addresses and receive(s) byte parallel data. The data is internally serialized into the FPGA data-frame format.

Peripheral Modes

The two peripheral modes accept byte-wide data from a bus. A RDY/BUSY status is available as a handshake signal. In Asynchronous Peripheral mode, the internal oscillator generates a CCLK burst signal that serializes the byte-wide data. CCLK can also drive slave devices. In the synchronous mode, an externally supplied clock input to CCLK serializes the data.

Slave Serial Mode

In Slave Serial mode, the FPGA receives serial configuration data on the rising edge of CCLK and, after loading its configuration, passes additional data out, resynchronized on the next falling edge of CCLK. Multiple slave devices with identical configurations can be wired with parallel DIN inputs. In this way, multiple devices can be configured simultaneously.

Ordering information

Example

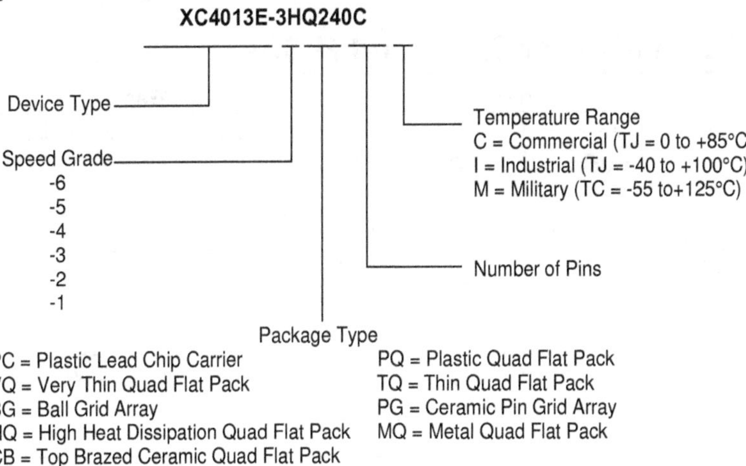

8.18.1 Designing with FPGAs

Sophisticated CAD tools are available to assist with the design of systems using programmable gate arrays. Following steps are used in designing a digital system with FPGA:

1. Draw a block diagram of the digital system. Define condition and control signals and construct state graphs that describe the required sequence of operations.
2. Write a VHDL description of the system. Simulated and debug the VHDL code, and make any necessary corrections to the design that was developed in step 1.
3. Work out the detailed logic design of the system using gates, flip-flops, registers, adders etc.
4. Enter a logic diagram of the system into the computer using a schematic capture program. Simulate and debug the logic diagram, and make any necessary corrections to the design of step 3.
5. Run a partitioning program. This program will break the logic diagram into pieces that will fit into the configurable logic blocks.
6. Run automatic place and route program. This will place the logic blocks in appropriate places in the FPGA and then route the interconnections between the logic blocks.
7. Run a program that will generate the bit pattern necessary to program the FPGA.
8. Download the bit pattern into the internal configuration memory cells in the FPGA and test the operation of the FPGA.

    When the final system is bits, the bit pattern for programming the FPGA is normally stored in an EPROM and automatically loaded into the FPGA when the power is turned ON.

8.19 Comparison of CPLDs and FPGAs

	CPLDs	**FPGAs**
Architecture	Large, wide fan-in blocks of AND-OR logic	Array of small logic blocks surrounded by I/O.
Gate Capacity	300-6000 gates	800-100,000 gates
Number of I/Os	30-200	50-400
Number of flip-flops	30-200	100-5,500
Design Timing	Fixed, like PAL very fast pin-to-pin performance	Application dependent very high shift frequencies
In-system programmable	Some EEPROM-and FLASH-based devices	SRAM-based devices and some EEPROM-based devices
Power consumption	0.5 - 2.0W static 0.5 – 4.0W dynamic	Very low static Dynamic consumption is application dependent, 0.1 – 2W typical

contd...

Key Attributes	Fast pin-to-pin performance predictable timing. Easy to use	Very high density Lots of I/Os and flip-flop generally lower power SRAM devices are reprogrammable.
Application	Bus Interfaces complex state machines fast memory interfaces wide decoders PAL-device integration	Logic consolidation board integration Replaced obsolete devices simple state machines complex controllers/interfaces.

QUESTIONS

1. Explain construction of basic memory cell. Give detailed architecture of PLA and FPLA.

2. Draw and explain architecture of XC9500.

3. Explain architecture of FPGA.

4. Explain PAL and PLA architecture.

5. Write short note on CPLD architecture.

6. Draw Block schematic of 9500 family. Explain features and give specifications.

7. What is function of PTOE in CPLD?

8. What is meant by hot plugging capability of 9500?

9. List the features of 9500 family.

10. Compare EPROM, PLA, PAL, CPLD, and FPGA.

11. Compare CPLD and FPGA.

12. What do you mean by field programmable?

13. Explain with block schematic the architecture of Xilinx 4000 FPGA.

14. What is need of optional additional delay provided after input buffer in I/O block of FPGA?

15. Write short notes on: (a) ASIC,   (b) ASIC design flow.

16. Differentiate among CPLD, FPGA and ASIC. How are these devices different from PAL, PLA and EPROM?   **(8 Marks, Nov. 2000)**

17. What is meant by configuration as referred to PLD?   **(3 Marks, Dec. 2004)**

18. What are the different methods of configuring CPLD and FPGA?   **(3 Marks, Dec. 2004)**

19. What are the constraints as referred to FPGA Design flow?   **(4 Marks, Dec. 2004)**

20. Describe following in not more than five words (Any 16)
    GRM, LIM, EDIF, Suprim, JED, HDL, HDL, XNF, ASIP, SRAM, DPLD, DRC, LVS, SRC, IRSIM,
    FPGA – Advantage, Ledit, Magic, Antifuse.

(8 Marks, May 2005)

21. State True or False with reasons.
    (i)   FPGA acts as glue logic for processors in embedded system.
    (ii)   The interconnect delays are more complex and unpredictable in FPGA as compared
           to CPLD.
    (iii) Presently the design density is greater than device complexity.
    (iv)   LUT in FPGA acts as arithmetic and logic generator.
    (v)   CPLD is rich in latches as compared to FPGA.
    (vi)   FPGA is a fine grained structure.   **(12 Marks, May 2005)**

22. What is the role of CPLD and FPGA in embedded system developments?

(9 Marks, May 2005)

23. Describe following in not more than five words:
    CLB, IOB, JTAG, LUT, IP, ISP, STA, UCF, DLL, Xiliax, Altera, Virtex, Spartan, Stratix, ASIC,
    PLA.   **(8 Marks, Dec. 2004)**

24. What is the criteria for selection of CPLD or FPGA in an embedded system?

(8 Marks, Dec. 2005)

25. What is the difference between logic implemented in CPLD and implemented in FPGA?

(8 Marks, Dec. 2005)

26. "SRAM-based FPGA can be configured only once". State (whether) this statement is
    True/False and explain.   **(3 Marks, Dec. 2005)**

27. State True or False and Explain. "Use of PLD in an embedded system increases NRE cost
    and time to market".   **(3 Marks, Dec. 2005)**

Chapter 9: FAULT TOLERANCE AND TESTABILITY

Topics discussed: Testing combinational logic, Testing sequential logic, Scan testing, Boundary scan test, Built-in self test, Fault simulation.

Introduction

In this chapter, digital system testing and design methods that make the systems easier to test are introduced. We know that, VHDL test benches can be written to verify that the overall design and algorithms used are correct. We can also use simulation at the logic level to verify that design is logically correct and it meets required specifications. After the design of an IC is completed, additional testing can be done by simulating it at the circuit level to verify that the design has been correctly implemented and that the timing is correct.

When a digital system is manufactured, further testing is required to verify that it functions correctly. When multiple copies of an IC are manufactured, each copy must be tested to verify that it is free from manufacturing defects. This testing process can become very expensive and time consuming. The cost of testing is a major component of the manufacturing cost. Therefore, it is very important to develop efficient methods of testing digital systems and to design the systems so that they are easy to test.

In this chapter, first, methods of testing combinational logic for the basic types of faults are discussed. Then methods for determining test sequences for sequential logic are described. Then concepts of scan design and built-in self test are introduced.

9.1 Testability

Testability is actually a **manufacturing test**. The chip must be exercised to demonstrate that no manufacturing defects render the chip useless.

Now-a-days, large number of unlimited variety of chips are manufactured. But, it introduces the problem of checking those chips, whether they have been manufactured correctly or not. Chip designers accept the need to **verify** or **validate** their designs to make sure that the circuits perform the specified function. Verification or validation is different than testing. Verification or validation is the initial step to check the functionality and testing of a chip is the final step, to check the functionality of the chip.

Verification word is used for formal proofs of correctness.

Validation word is used for any technique which increases confidence in correctness, such as simulation.

Design for testability is used to indicate that we need to build fault models to test the chip, which comes off the manufacturing line, called as the manufacturing test.

9.2 Need of Design for Testability

There are various types of defects introduced during manufacturing. These defects can be catastrophic i.e. contamination that destroys every transistor on the wafer. Also, the defect may be a single misfired wire or a crystalline defect that kills only one transistor.

Some bad chips can be found very easily. While in some cases, we need to test each chip thoroughly to find even subtle flaws that produce erroneous results only occasionally. Therefore, the task of determining whether the fabricated chips are fully functional or not is highly complex. Also it is very time consuming. If the faulty chip passes an improperly designed test, they can cause system failures and due to this enormous difficulties can arise in system debugging.

The debugging cost increases around tenfold from chip level to board level and also from board level to system level. Therefore, it is very important to detect faults as early as possible. As the transistor density (number of transistors in unit area) increases, the task of testing to ensure correct functionality becomes increasingly more difficult. But, still we need to test the chip within a short time for timely delivery to customers. Therefore, to overcome such difficult issues, **Design for Testability (DFT)** has become **even more critical.**

All the chips which are designed are not equally testable. Some faults may require long input sequences as test vectors, other faults may not be testable at all, because they cause chip malfunctions that are not covered by the fault model. Testability problems are often fixed easily, early in the design process at relatively little cost in area and performance. Traditionally, chip design engineers have ignored design problems, leaving them to a separate **test engineer**, whose job is to find a set of inputs to adequately test the chip. But, the job of test engineer becomes both difficult and unpleasant. Therefore, the modern chip designers must understand testability requirements, analysis techniques must be designed to identify hard to test sections of the design.

9.3 Defects or Faults on a Chip

There are different faults caused by manufacturing defects. The faults caused by physical defects include:

- Process variations and abnormalities. There may be excessive variations in the fabrication process.
- Defects in silicon substrate: size or area of the silicon substrate may be different for PMOS or NMOS.
- Photolithographic defects.
- Mask contamination and scratches.
- Oxide defects.

Due to the above mentioned physical defects, electrical faults and logical faults are generated.

The electrical faults include:

- Excessive change in the threshold voltage of the MOS device.
- Shorts (which form the close path).
- Opens (one of the terminals of MOS may always remain unconnected).
- Transistor stuck-on, stuck-open.
- Resistive shorts and opens.
- Excessive steady-state currents.

Due to the above mentioned electrical faults, logical faults are generated. The logical faults include:

- Logical stuck-at-0 or stuck-at-1 (s-a-0 or s-a-1).
- Delay faults (slower transition).
- Bridging faults such as AND bridging, OR bridging.

Now, we will see the relationships between physical defects, electrical faults and logical faults by using a 2 input NOR gate as shown in Fig. 9.1. As shown, a metallic blob is there, between the common drain terminal in the n diffusion region and the ground bus line in Fig. 9.1 (a).

This fault can be modelled as a **resistive short** between the output node Z and the common ground as shown in Fig. 9.1 (b). This resistive short acts as a stuck at zero logical fault, as shown in Fig. 9.1 (c).

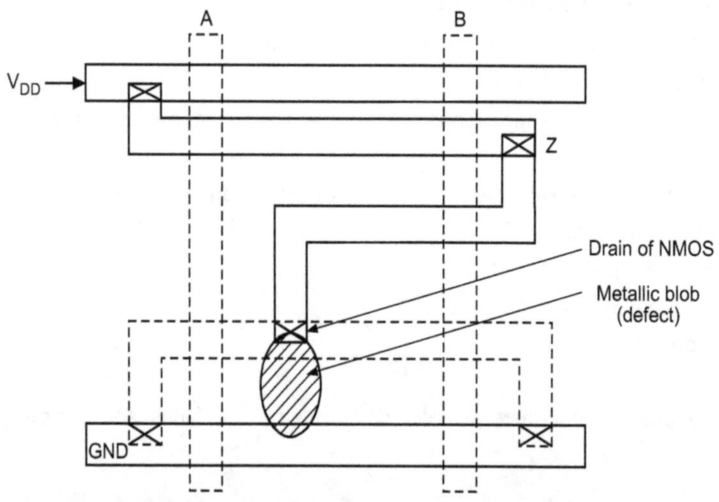

(a) Physical defect in 2 input NOR gate fabrication

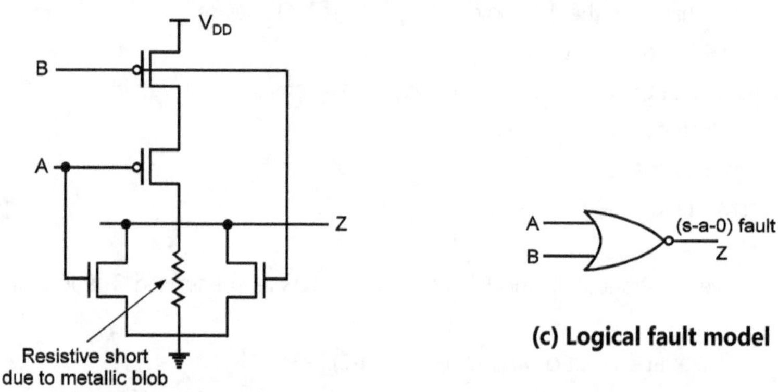

(c) Logical fault model

(b) Electrical fault model

**Fig. 9.1: Relationship between physical defect, logical fault
and electrical fault**

In case of stuck-at-1 fault, the input A of the MOS gate is shorted to V_{DD} as shown in Fig. 9.2, since some part of the input line is shorted to the power rail.

Similarly, the PMOS transistor at the B input is stuck-on due to process fabrication problem that causes a short between its source and drain terminals as shown in Fig. 9.2.

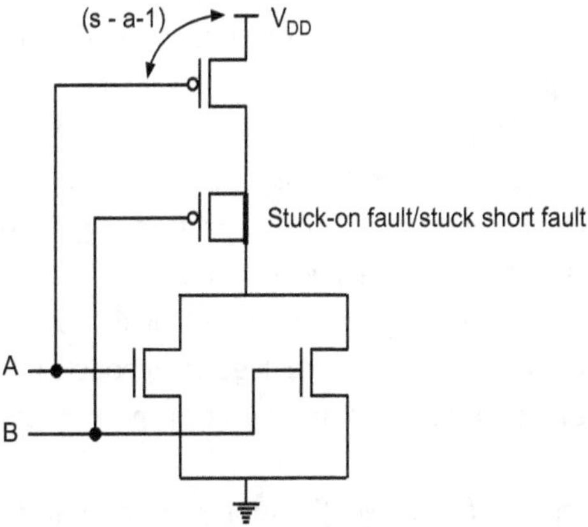

Fig. 9.2: Stuck-at-1 and stuck-on fault

Stuck open (off) fault and stuck-on (short) fault are shown in Fig. 9.3.

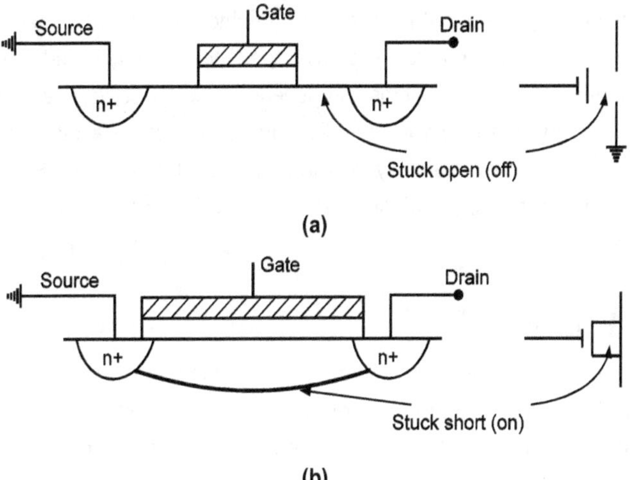

(a)

(b)

Fig. 9.3: (a) Stuck open (off) fault, (b) Stuck short (on) fault

Stuck open (off) fault is due to:

    (1) Either an incomplete contact (open) of the source to drain node.

    (2) Due to a large separation of drain or source diffusion from the gate. This fault causes permanent turn off of the transistor regardless of the input value.

In the layout, two lines can be close to each other; these two lines can be shorted due to under-etching in the line patterning process.

We can use **single** stuck at fault models. But as compared to **multiple** stucks at fault model, the single stuck at fault models cannot be mapped to the DUT. In other words, multiple stuck-at-fault models are preferred for DUT; due to the following reasons:

1) Single stuck-at fault model is independent of technology, design style.
2) Single stuck-at tests cover a large percentage of multiple stuck-at faults.
3) Single stuck-at tests cover a large percentage of unmodeled physical defects.
4) Complexity of test generation is greatly reduced in multiple stuck-at fault models.

Multiple stuck-at fault models find applications for fuse or anti-fuse based programmable design such as programmable gate arrays, FPGAs and RAMs.

As the clock frequency of the chips goes on increasing, the at-speed test becomes a difficult problem. While sending the test signals from the tester to DUT, there is a signal integrity problem. Signal integrity relates with the transient ringing problem. Also there are problems, while detecting the signals from DUT such as impedance mismatch and transmission line problems. In addition to these problems, the generation of correct test vectors to detect all modelled faults and design errors in complex chips has become a difficult task. We can generate test patterns either manually or through an Automatic Test Pattern Generator (ATPG), but due to complexity and number of physical defects, it becomes difficult to generate test vectors.

9.4 Delay Faults

Delay faults cause timing failure in the chip. There are number of timing parameters, which need to be satisfied, such as setup and hold time etc. But, when we are testing a chip at target speed, it causes timing failures due to the delay faults. Delay faults occur due to the following reasons:

1) Variations in the fabrication process which cause variations in circuit delays and clock skews.
2) Improper estimation of on-chip interconnect and routing delays and other timing considerations.
3) There may be opens in metal lines connecting parallel transistors which make the effective transistor size much smaller.
4) Aging effects, for example hot carrier induced delay increase.

Detection of delay faults is more difficult than detecting functional faults at steady state, because delay faults can be observed only at system clock frequency. The functional test is usually done at speeds lower than the target speed due to the limitations of the testers. So, we need to apply **special clocking** for delay tests on a slow tester.

Delay fault is due to the accumulation of delay errors along the entire path.

9.5 Controllability and Observability

Testing a logic gate in a network is harder than testing it in isolation. When the gate is in a combinational network, its inputs and outputs are not directly accessible. Therefore, testing a gate inside a combinational network requires applying inputs and checking outputs from the gate, in place, with direct access to its inputs and outputs. This problem can be split into two parts.

Controlling the inputs of the gate by applying values to the networks primary inputs.

Observing the outputs of the gate by inferring its value from the values at the networks primary outputs.

For example, suppose for the circuit shown in Fig. 9.4, we need to test gate "C".

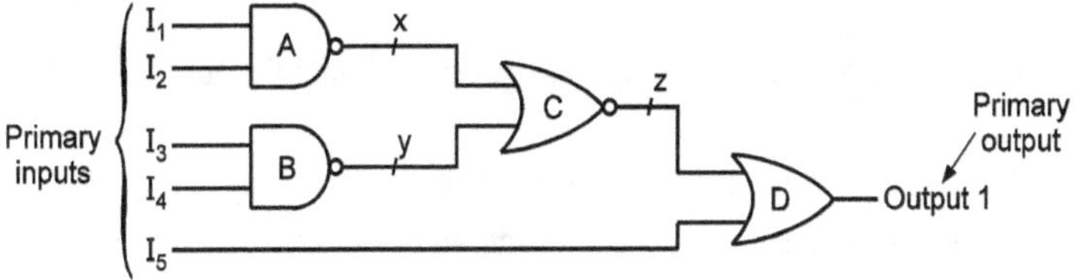

Fig. 9.4: Testing for combinational fault

As shown, gate C, is inside the combinational network. Inputs and outputs of gate C are not directly accessible. So, we need to control the inputs of gate 'C', by applying values to the networks primary inputs i.e. I_1, I_2, I_3 and I_4. At the same time, we need to observe the outputs of the gate C, by inferring its value from the values at the networks primary outputs i.e. output 1. So, we need to control the nodes x, y and z for the gate C.

The testability will be defined in terms of observability and controllability.

9.5.1 Controllability

Definition: The controllability of an internal circuit node within a chip is a measure of the ease of setting the node to a logic 1 or 0 state.

Controllability measure has importance when accessing the degree of difficulty of testing a particular signal within a circuit. Easily controllable node is the node, which is directly available as an input pad. It means it has a high value of controllability. A node with little controllability takes many hundreds or thousands of cycles to get it to the right state.

It is very difficult to generate a test sequence; to set a number of poorly controllable nodes into the right state. Our aim for a well designed circuit is to have all nodes easily controllable.

9.5.2 Observability

Definition: The observability of a particular internal circuit node is the degree to which, one can observe that node at the outputs of an integrated circuit (i.e. the output pin).

Observability measure has importance, when a designer or tester desires to measure the output of a gate within a larger circuit to check that it operates correctly. High observability means less number of cycles are required to measure the output node value. Low observability takes more number of cycles to observe the value of output node.

For well-designed chips, the aim is to have easily observed gate outputs.

The degree of testability of a circuit (i.e., controllability and observability) can be measured with respect to whether test vectors are generated deterministically or randomly. For example, if a logic node is set to either logic 0 or 1, only through a very long sequence of random test vectors, the node is said to have very low random controllability, since the probability of generating such a vector in random test generation is very low.

The deterministic procedures for test generation of combinational circuits are available such as D-algorithm, PODEM (Path Oriented Decision Making) and FAN-out-oriented test generation (FAN).

D-algorithm uses a recursive search procedure advancing one gate at a time and backtracking, if necessary until all the faults are detected. This algorithm requires large amount of computer time. To overcome this drawback, many improved algorithms are developed such as PODEM and FAN out-oriented test generation.

Sequential circuit test generation is more difficult than the above mentioned algorithms.

If a large number of input vectors are required to set a particular node value to logic 1 or logic 0 (i.e., applying input to the node) and to propagate an error at the node to an output (propagation of fault to the output pin), then the testability is low. Poor controllability includes those circuits with feedbacks, decoders and clock generators. Similarly, the circuit with poor observability includes sequential circuits with long feedback loops and circuits with reconvergent fan-outs, redundant nodes and embedded memories such as Random Access Memories, Read Only Memories and Programmable Logic Arrays.

9.6 Fault Coverage

Fault coverage gives a measure of goodness of a test program. It means, for the test vectors applied, what percentage of the chip's internal nodes were checked.

The following method can be used to find the fault coverage in a circuit. The steps are:
1) Each circuit node is taken in sequence and held to logic '0', (S-A-0).
2) Then the circuit is simulated, comparison of chip output is done with a known "good machine".
3) When there is a discrepancy between a "faulty machine" and a "good machine', the fault is marked as detected and the simulation is stopped.
4) The same process is repeated by setting the node to logic '1' (S-A-1).
5) In turn, every node is stuck at logic '1' and '0' sequentially.
6) Then the percentage fault coverage is calculated as total number of nodes that result in the detection of the fault, divided by the number of nodes in the circuit.

$$\% \text{ Fault Coverage} = \frac{\text{Total number of nodes (when set to 0 or 1) result in the detection of the fault}}{\text{The total number of nodes in the circuit}}$$

The above method of fault analysis is called as the fault grading. The time taken by fault grading may be very long. The time is calculated as follows:

Suppose N/2 cycles are needed to detect each fault.

    K = number of nodes in the circuit

    N = length of the test sequence

We need,

Total number of cycles to be simulated = K × N cycles.

For example,

1) When K = 1000,   N = 12,000

∴ K × N = 12 million cycles are required.

Suppose 1 ms is required for one cycle for f = 1 kHz

∴   Total time taken for simulation = 1.2 million cycles × 1ms

= 12,000 seconds

= 3 Hrs and 20 minutes.

2) When K = 1,00,000 and N = 3,60,000

∴ Total cycles required = K × N = 36,00,00,00,000

Assuming 1 sec per cycle, we need 1040 years to do sequential fault grading.

9.7 Comparison of Verification and Testability

Verification	Testability
1. It verifies correctness of design.	1. It verifies correctness of manufactured hardware.
2. Performed by simulation, hardware emulation, or formal methods.	2. Two-part process: - (a) Test generation: software process executed once during design. - (b) Test application: electrical tests applied to hardware.
3. Performed once prior to manufacturing.	3. Test application performed on every manufactured device.
4. Responsible for quality of design.	4. Responsible for quality of devices.

9.8 Test Methodology

In 1980s, test vectors were usually created manually. A subset of test vectors used for verification (simulation) of the circuit was reused. Separate test vectors are also written to achieve maximum fault coverage. Generally, only 70-75 percent fault coverage was achieved relatively easily. If the ASIC has 15,000 gates, it usually took four to five weeks to create test vectors which satisfied all the requirements of the specific circuit tester at the chosen ASIC supplier. Fault coverage seldom exceeded 85 percent.

In 1990's, writing test benches also started to be automated. Automatic Test Pattern Generator (ATPG) is used to machine - generate test vectors. By using ATPG, fault coverage of more than 99 per cent can be achieved in one or two days work.

9.9 Testing Combinational Logic

Two common types of faults occurring are:

- **Short circuit:** If the input to a gate is shorted to ground, modeled as stuck-at-0 (s-a-0). To test a gate input for s-a-0, the gate input must be 1, so a change to 0 can be detected. If the input to a gate is shorted to a positive power supply voltage, modeled as stuck-at-1 (s-a-1). To test a gate input for s-a-1, the gate input must be 0, so a change to 1 can be detected.

- **Open circuit:** If the input to a gate is an open circuit, the input may act as if it is stuck at 0 or stuck at 1, depending on the type of logic being used.

We can test AND gate for s-a-0 by applying 1s to all inputs as shown in Fig. 9.5 (a). The normal gate output is then 1, but if any input is s-a-0, the output becomes 0. The notation $1 \rightarrow 0$ means that normal value is 1, but the value has changed to 0 because of s-a-0 fault. We can test AND gate for s-a-1 by applying 0 to the input being tested and 1s to the other inputs. As shown in Fig. 9.5 (b) the normal gate output then is 0, but if the input being tested is s-a-1, the output becomes 1.

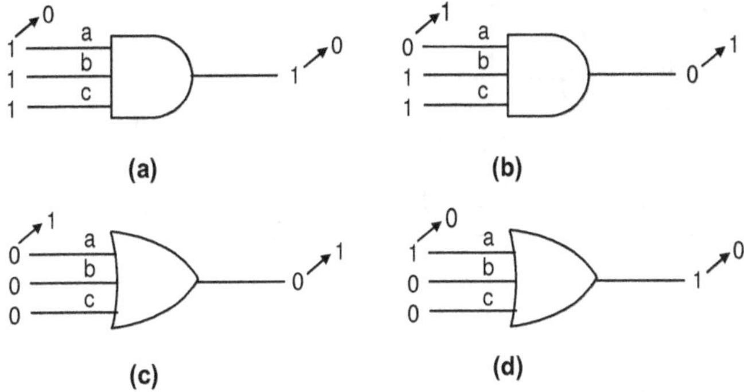

Fig. 9.5: Testing AND-OR gates for stuck-at-faults

To test OR gate input for s-a-1, apply 0s to all inputs, and if any input is s-a-1, the output will change to 1 as shown in Fig. 9.5 (c).

To test an OR gate input for s-a-0, apply a 1 to the input under test and 0s to the other inputs. If the input under test is s-a-0, the output will change to 0 as shown in Fig. 9.5 (d). In the process of testing the inputs to a gate for s-a-0 and s-a-1, we can also detect s-a-0 and s-a-1 faults at the gate output.

9.9.1 Testing AND-OR Network

The two level AND-OR network is shown in Fig. 9.6.

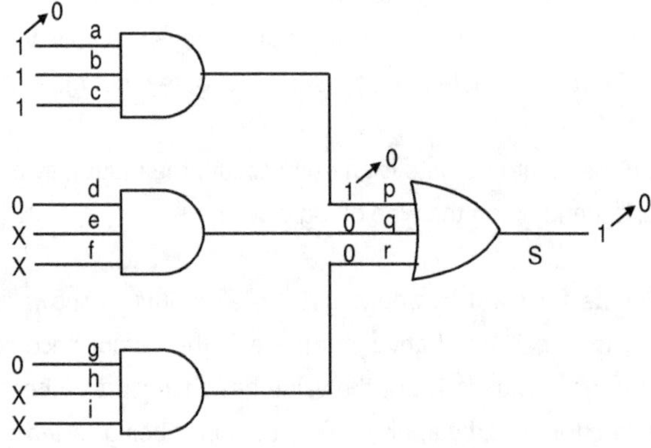

(a) Stuck-at-0 test

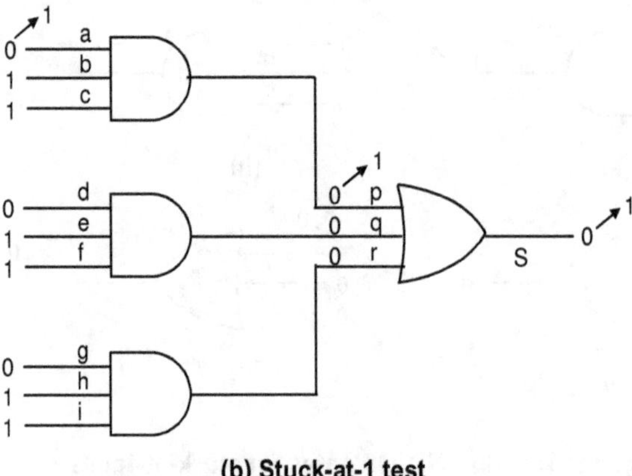

(b) Stuck-at-1 test

Fig. 9.6: Testing AND-OR network

Assume that the OR gate inputs p, q and r are not accessible, so the gates can not be tested individually. One approach to test the network would be to apply all different input conditions (2^9 = 512, as 9 inputs) and observe the output. A more efficient approach is based on testing for all s-a-0 and s-a-1 faults as shown in Fig. 9.6.

To test AND gate inputs a, b, c for s-a-0, apply 1s to a, b and c. Then if any gate input is s-a-0, the gate output p will become 0. In order to transmit the change to the OR gate output, the other OR gate inputs must be 0. To achieve this, set d = 0 and g = 0 whereas e, f, h and i are then don't cares. This test vector will detect p0 (p stuck-at-0) as well as a0, b0, and c0. In a similar manner, we can test for d0, e0, f0, and q0 by setting d = e = f = 1 and a = g = 0. A third test with g=h=i=1 and a = d = 0 will test the remaining s-a-0 faults.

To test 'a' for s-a-1 (a1), we must set a = 0 and b = c = 1 as shown in Fig. 9.6 (b). Then if 'a' is s-a-1, p will become 1. In order to transmit this change to the output s, we must have q = r = 0. If we set d = g = 0 and e = f = h = i = 1, we can test for d1 and g1 at the same time as a1.

The following table 9.1 shows test vectors for Fig. 9.6.

Table 9.1

Inputs									Fault Tested
a	b	c	d	e	f	g	h	i	
1	1	1	0	×	×	0	×	×	a0, b0, c0, p0
0	×	×	1	1	1	0	×	×	d0, e0, f0, q0
0	×	×	0	×	×	1	1	1	g0, h0, i0, r0
0	1	1	0	1	1	0	1	1	a1, d1, g1, p1, q1, r1
1	0	1	1	0	1	1	0	1	b1, e1, h1, p1, q1, r1
1	1	0	1	1	0	1	1	0	c1, f1, i1, p1, q1, r1

When we apply the six tests, we can determine whether or not a fault is present, but we can not determine the exact location of the fault. In the analysis, we have assumed that only one fault occurs at a time. In many cases, the presence of multiple faults will also be detected.

Testing multilevel network is more complex than testing two-level networks. To test an internal fault in a network, we must choose a set of inputs that will excite that fault and then propagate the effect of that fault to network output.

Consider Fig. 9.7, where a, b, c, d and e are network inputs and F is output.

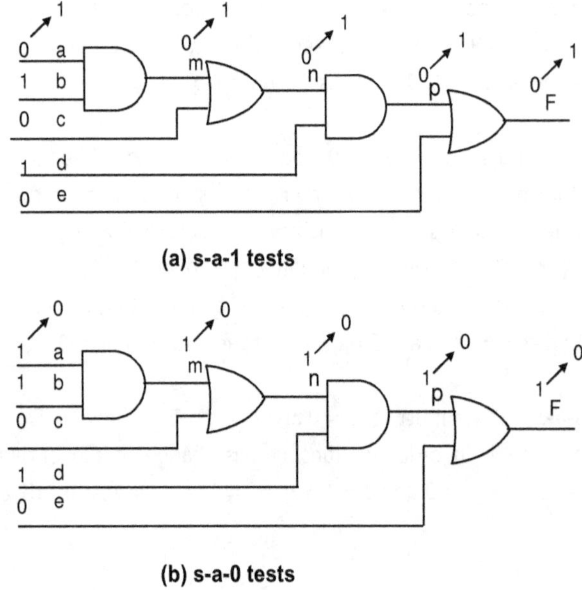

(a) s-a-1 tests

(b) s-a-0 tests

Fig. 9.7: Fault detection using path sensitization

If we want to test for gate input n for s-a-1, n must be 0. To achieve this, make c = 0, a = 0, and b = 1 as shown in Fig. 9.7 (a). To propagate the fault n s-a-1 to the output F, we must make d = 1 and e = 0. With this set of inputs, if a, m, n or p is s-a-1, the output F will have the incorrect value and the fault can be detected. Furthermore, if we change 'a' to 1 and gate input a, m, n or p is s-a-0, the output F will change from 1 to 0. We say that the path through a, m, n and p has been sensitized, since any fault along the path can be detected. This method of path sensitization allows us to test for a number of different stuck-at faults using one set of network inputs.

When two unconnected signal lines are shorted together, the fault occurred is called **bridging fault**. For a large combinational network, finding a minimum set of test vectors that will test for all possible faults is very difficult and time consuming. Many algorithms and corresponding computer programs have been developed to generate such sets of test vectors. Computer programs have been developed to simulate faulty networks.

Example 1: Determine a minimum set of test vectors to test the network shown in Fig. 9.8.

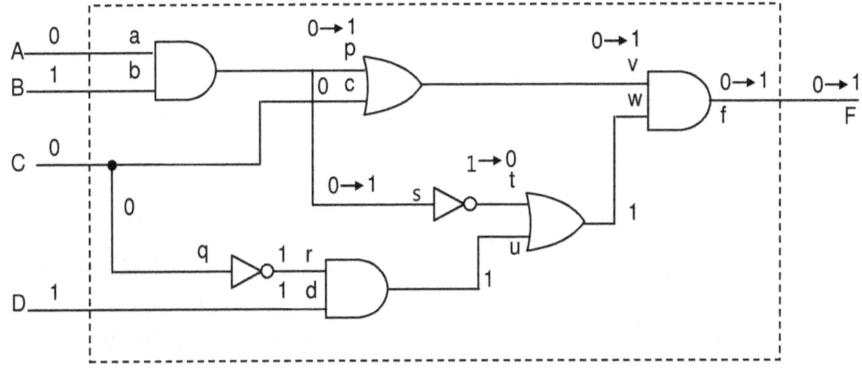

Fig. 9.8: Example network for stuck-at fault testing

Solution:

We assume that we can apply inputs to A, B, C and D and observe the output F and the internal gate inputs and outputs can not be accessed.

Suppose that, we want to test input p for s-a-1. To do this, we must choose inputs A, B, C and D such that p = 0, and if p is s-a-1, we must propagate this fault to the output F so that it can be observed.

In order to propagate the fault, we must make C = 0 and w = 1. We can make w = 1 by making t = 1 or u = 1. To make u = 1, we must have both D and r = 1, our choice of C = 0 makes r = 1. To make p = 0, we choose A = 0. By choosing B = 1, we can sensitize the path A-a-p-v-f-F so that the set of inputs ABCD = 0101 will test for faults a1, p1, v1, and f1. This set of inputs also tests for C s-a-1. We assume that C s-a-1 is a fault internal to the gate, so it is still possible to have q = 0 and r = 1 if C s-a-1 occurs.

To test for s-a-0 inputs along the path A-a-p-v-f-F, we can use the inputs ABCD = 1101. In addition to testing for faults a0, p0, v0 and f0, this input vector also tests the following faults: b0, w0, u0, r0, q1, and d0. To determine tests for remaining stuck-at faults, we can select an untested fault, determine the required ABCD inputs, and then determine the additional faults that are tested. Then we can repeat this procedure until tests are found for all of the faults. Table 9.2 lists a set of five test vectors that will test for all single stuck-at faults in Fig. 9.8.

Table 9.2

A	B	C	D	a	b	p	c	q	r	d	s	t	u	v	w	Normal Gate Inputs	Fault Tested
0	1	0	1	0	1	0	0	0	1	1	0	1	1	0	1		a1, p1, c1, v1, f1
1	1	0	1	1	1	1	0	0	1	1	1	0	1	1	1		a0, b0, p0, q1, r0, d0, u0, v0, w0, f0
1	0	1	1	1	0	0	1	1	0	1	0	1	0	1	1		b1, c0, s1, t0, v0, w0, f0,
1	1	0	0	1	1	1	0	0	1	0	1	0	0	1	0		a0, b0, d1, s0, t1, u1, w1, f1
1	1	1	1	1	1	1	1	1	0	1	1	0	0	1	0		a0, b0, q0, r1, s0, t1, u1, w1, f1

9.10 Boundary Scan

The boundary scan provides a standardized serial scan path through the I/O pins of an IC. The Boundary scan is an IEEE 1149 standard. The architecture of IEEE 1149 Boundary scan is shown in Fig. 9.9.

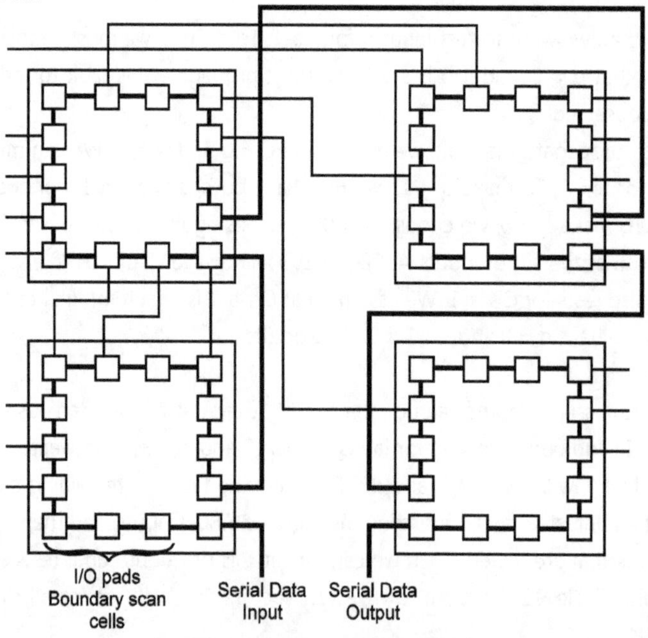

Fig. 9.9: Boundary scan architecture

The ICs to be tested may be connected in a variety of series and parallel connections to enable the testing of a complete board. We can also test collection of boards by connecting them in series or parallel form.

The different tests which are carried out by this standard can be of

1) Sampling and setting chip Input/Outputs.
2) Connectivity tests between components.
3) Distribution and collection of self test or built-in-test results.

9.11 Test Access Port (TAP)

The TAP is included in an IC. It is an interface, which is used during boundary-scan logic. The TAP port has four or five connections. These connections are:

1) TCK i.e. The Test Clock Input:
   It is used to clock tests into and out of chips.
2) TMS i.e. The Test Mode Select:
   It is used to control test operations.
3) TDI i.e. The Test Data Input:
   It is used to input test data to a chip.
4) TDO i.e. The Test Data Output:
   It is used to output test data from a chip.
5) TRST i.e. The Test Reset Signal: It is used to asynchronously reset the TAP controller. If the power-up reset signal is not available in the chip being tested, then this pin is used for the reset purpose. This signal is optional.

The TDO signal is a tristate signal, and it is only driven when the TAP controller is outputting test data.

9.11.1 Test Access Port Architecture

Fig. 9.10 shows the TAP architecture. This TAP architecture is implemented on a chip. It consists of:

- A TAP controller, which interprets test instructions, and according to those test instructions, they control the flow of data into and out of the TAP.
- Test Data Registers are included to collect data from the chip.
- An Instruction Register is included to enable test inputs to be applied to the chip.
- TAP interface pins such as TDI, TDO, TCK, TMS and TRST.

The Data from the TDI port may be fed to the instruction register or to one or more test data registers. As shown in Fig. 9.10, the MUX selects between the instruction register and the data registers to be output to the tristate TDO pin.

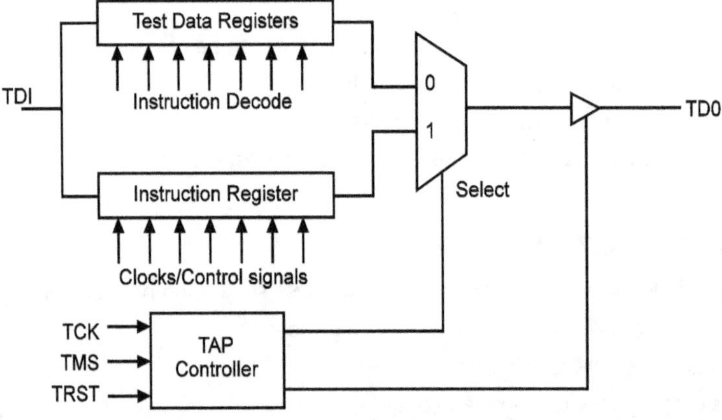

Fig. 9.10: TAP architecture

Next, we will see the details of each block, which are included in the TAP architecture.

9.11.1.1 TAP Controller

TAP controller is actually a 16 state Finite State Machine, and it proceeds from state to state based on the TCK and TMS signals. The TAP controller provides signals that control the Test Data Registers and the Instruction Register. The signals include serial-shift clocks and update clocks.

9.11.1.2 Instruction Register (IR)

The instruction register must be at least two bits long. The logic detecting the state of the instruction register has to decode at least three instructions. These instructions are BYPASS, EXTEST, SAMPLE/PRELOAD, INTEST and RUNBIST which are discussed later.

Fig. 9.11 shows the diagram of Instruction register bit implementation.

As shown, instruction register has at least 2 bits. Select bit 'S' selects the data from the multiplexer, it is then given to the 1-bit register on clock IR signal. When signal from update IR is activated, it updates the data of the next 1-bit register.

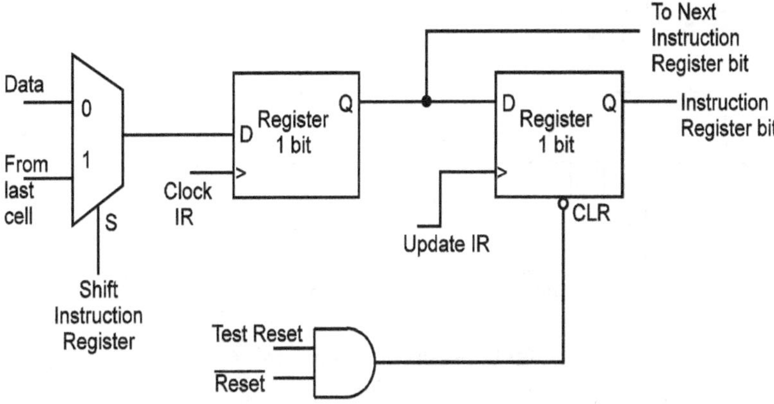

Fig. 9.11: Instruction register bit implementation

The Test Reset signal is used to clear the output of second register.

9.11.1.3 Test Data Registers (DRs)

These registers are used to set the inputs of modules to be tested and to collect the results of running tests. The generalized structure of the data register is shown in Fig. 9.12. It contains Boundary Scan Registers, Bypass Registers and Internal Data Registers. As shown, a multiplexer is used to select which particular data register is routed to the Test Data Output pin.

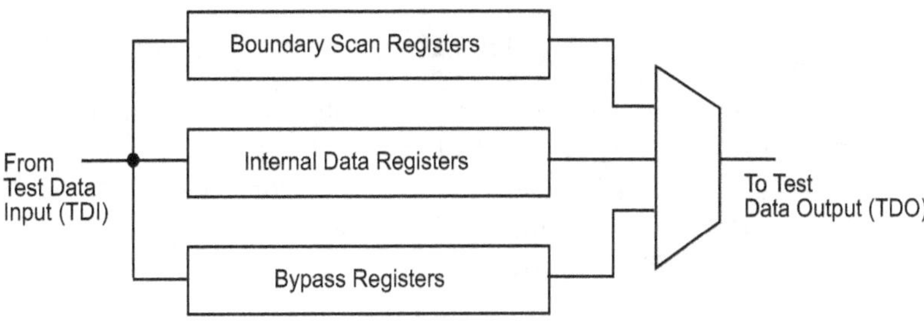

Fig. 9.12: TAP data registers

9.11.1.4 Boundary Scan Registers

It is a special case of a data register. It is used to test circuit-board interconnections, external components and the state of the chip digital I/Os to be sampled. Fig. 9.13 (a) gives the boundary scan input cell and Fig. 9.13 (b) shows the boundary scan output cell.

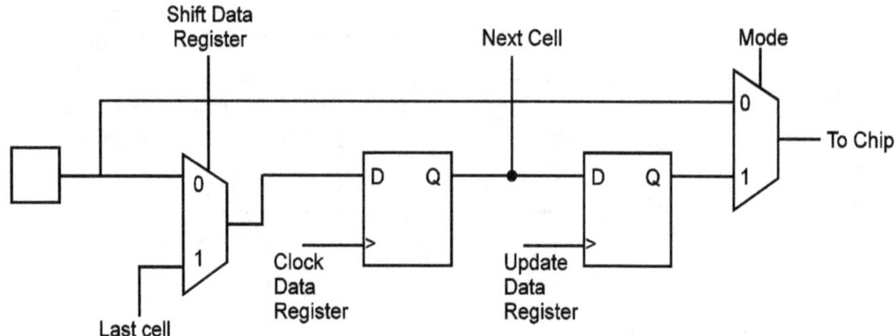

(a) Boundary scan input cell

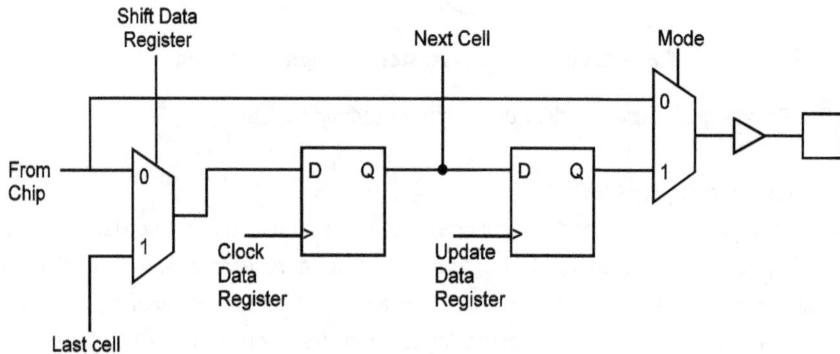

(b) Boundary scan output cell

Fig. 9.13

As shown, boundary scan registers consist of two multiplexers and two edge-triggered registers. As shown in Fig. 9.13 (a), two register bits allow the serial shifting of data through the boundary scan chain and the local storage of a data bit. When mode = 1, this data bit may be directed to internal circuitry in the INTEST or RUNBIST modes. When mode = 0, the cell is in EXTEST or SAMPLE/PRELOAD mode.

A multiplexer, under the control of Shift Data Register controls the serial/ parallel nature of the cell.

The signal Clock Data Register is used to load the serial register. Similarly, the signal Update Data Register is used to load parallel register.

For output cell of Fig. 9.13 (b), when mode = 1, the cell is in EXTEST, INTEST or RUNBIST modes, used to communicate the internal data to the output pad. When mode = 0, the cell is used in SAMPLE/PRELOAD mode.

9.12 Testing Sequential Logic

Sequences of inputs are used to test the sequential logic network. If we can observe only the input and output sequences and not the state of the flip-flop in a sequential network, a very large number of test sequences may be required. If we are attempting to test the network using the brute-force approach, we should reset the network to the initial state, apply a test sequence, and observe the output sequence. If the output sequence is correct, then we should repeat the test for another sequence. We have to try all possible input sequences. For the network having N states, we have to apply input sequences of length equal to 2N-1.

As an example, consider a sequential network that has five inputs, one output and four states. If we use the brute-force approach, we have to apply, all input sequences of length seven (2 × 4-1). At time = 1, we can apply any one of the 2^5 input combinations, and similarly at times 2 to 7. Thus the total number of test sequences required is,

$$(2^5)\ (2^5)\ (2^5)\ (2^5)\ (2^5)\ (2^5)\ (2^5) = 2^{35}$$

The number of test sequences is very very large.

To derive relatively small set of test sequences for a sequential network, one way is to convert sequential network to an iterative network. Iterative network is a combinational network. Hence, we can derive test vectors for the iterative network using one of the standard methods for combinational network.

Fig. 9.14 shows a standard Mealy sequential and the corresponding iterative network.

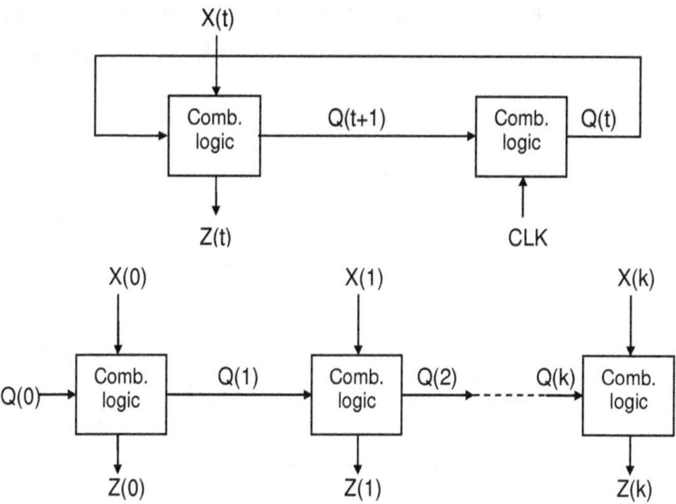

Fig. 9.14 : Sequential and iterative network

In Fig. 9.14, X, Z, and Q can either be single variable or vectors. The iterative network has k identical copies of the combinational network used in the sequential network, where k is the length of the sequence used to test the sequential network, $X(t)$ represents a sequence of input in time. In the iterative network, $X(0)$, $X(1)$ - $X(k)$ represents same sequence in space. Each cell of the iterative network computes $Z(t)$ and $Q(t + 1)$ in terms of $Q(t)$ and $X(t)$. The leftmost cell computes the value for $t = 0$, the next cell for $t = 1$, etc. After the test vectors have been derived for the iterative network, these vectors then become the input sequences used to test the original sequential network. The number of cells in the iterative network depends on the length of the sequences required to test the sequential network.

9.13 Scan Testing

If we can observe the state of all the flip-flops instead of observing the network outputs, then the problem of testing a sequential network is greatly simplified. For each state of the flip-flops and for each input combination, we need to verify that the network outputs are correct and that the network goes to the correct next state. One approach is to connect the output of each flip-flop within the IC being tested to one of the IC pins. This increases the number of IC pins, hence this approach is not very practical. Another approach is to arrange the flip-flops to form a shift register, so that, we can shift out the state of the flip-flops bit by bit using a single serial output pin on the IC. This approach leads to the concept of scan path testing.

Fig. 9.15 shows a method of scan path testing nested on two port flip-flops. The sequential network is separated into a combinational logic part and a state register composed of flip-flops. Each of the flip-flops has two D inputs and two clock inputs. When C1 is pulsed, the D1 input is stored in the flip-flop. When C2 is pulsed, D2 is stored in the flip-flop. The Q output of each flip-flop is connected to the D input of the next flip-flop to form a shift register. The next state ($Q1^+$, $Q2^+$,- - Qk^+) generated by the combinational logic is loaded into the flip-flop when C1 is pulsed, and the new state ($Q1$, $Q2$, - - Qk) feeds back into the combinational logic. When the network is not being tested, the system clock (SCK = C1) is used. A set of inputs ($X1$, $X2$ ---, Xn) is applied, the output ($Z1$, $Z2$, -- Zm) are generated, SCK is pulsed, and the network goes to the next state.

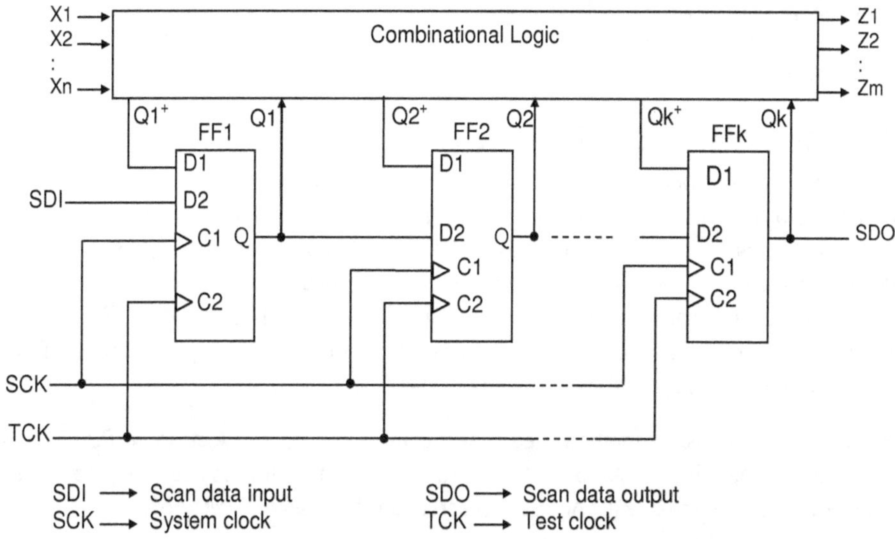

Fig. 9.15: Scan path test circuit using two port flip-flops

When the network is being tested, the flip-flops are set to a specified state by shifting the state code into the register using the SDI and the TCK. A test input vector (X1, X2, -- Xn) is applied, the outputs (Z1, Z2, -- Zm) are verified, and SCK is pulsed to take the network to the next state. The next state is then verified by pulsing TCK to shift the state code out of the scan data register via the scan data output (SDO). This method reduces the problem of testing a sequential network to that of testing combinational network. Any of the standard methods can be used to generate a set of test vectors for the combinational logic. Each test vector contains (n + k) bits, since there are n, X inputs and k state inputs to the combinational logic. The X part of the test vector is applied directly, and the Q part is shifted in via the SDI.

The test procedure is summarized as follows:
1. Scan in the test Vector Qi values via SDI using the TCK.
2. Apply the corresponding test values to the Xi inputs.
3. After sufficient time for the signals to propagate through the combinational network, verify the output Zi values.
4. Apply one clock pulse to the SCK to store the new values of Q_i^+ into the corresponding flip-flops.
5. Scan out and verify the Qi values by pulsing the TCK.

6. Repeat steps 1 through 5 for each test vector.
    Steps 5 and 1 can overlap, since it is possible to scan in one test vector while scanning out the previous test result.

9.14 Boundary Scan Test (BST)

ICs have become more complex, when number of pins becomes more. Similarly, printed circuit boards have become denser, with multiple layers and very fine traces. When these PC boards loaded with complex ICs, then testing of such PC boards become very difficult. When PC boards are less dense and wider traces, testing is done using a bed-of-nails test fixture. This method uses sharp probes to contest the traces on the board so test date can be applied to and read from various ICs on the board. Bed-of-nails testing is not practical for high density PC boards with fine traces and complex ICs.

Boundary scan test is the method used to test complex PC boards. A standard for BST was developed by the Joint Test Action Group (JTAG), and this standard has been adopted as IEEE standard 1149.1, "Standard Test Access Port and Boundary Scan Architecture."

Fig. 9.16 shows as IC with added boundary scan logic.

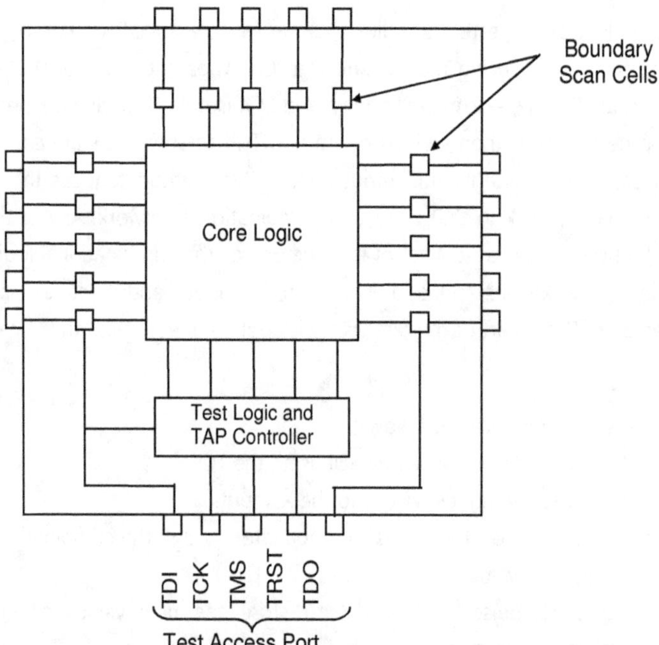

Fig. 9.16: IC boundary scan register and Test access port

One cell of the boundary scan register (BSR) is placed between each input or output pin and the internal core logic. Four or five pins of the IC are devoted to the Test Access Port (TAP). The TAP controller and additional test logic are also added of the core logic on the IC. The functions of the TAP pins are as follows:

TDI –   Test data input. This data is shifted serially into the BSR

TCK –   Test clock

TMS –   Test mode select

TDO –   Test data output. This data is serial output from the BSR.

TRST – Test reset. It is optional pin which resets the TAP controller and test logic.

Fig. 9.17 shows a typical boundary scan cell.

In the normal mode, data from the input pin is routed to the internal core logic in the IC, or data from the core logic is routed to the output pin.

In the shift mode, serial data from the previous cell is clocked into flip-flop Q1, at the same time as the data stored in Q1 is clocked into the next boundary scan cell. After Q2 is updated, test data can be supplied to the internal logic or to the output pin.

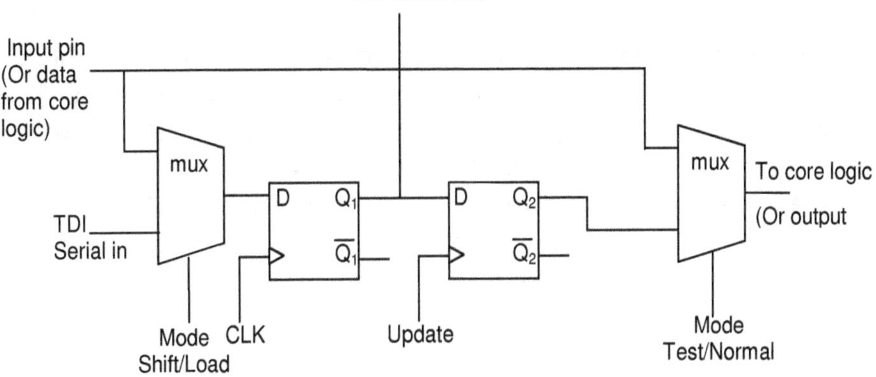

Fig. 9.17: Typical boundary scan cell

Fig. 9.18 shows the basic boundary scan architecture that is implemented on each boundary scan IC.

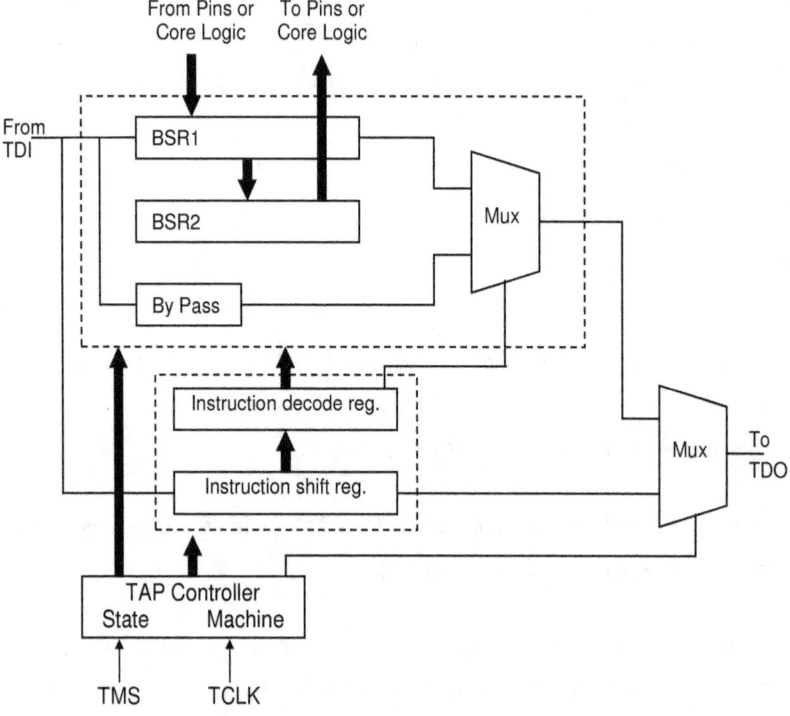

Fig. 9.18: Boundary scan architecture

BSR1 and BSR2 are the two parts of boundary scan register (BSR). BSR1 represents the shift register. BSR1 consists of Q1 flip-flops in the boundary scan cells. BSR2 represents the Q2 flip-flops, which can be parallel-loaded from BSR1 when an update signal is received. The serial input data (TDI) can be shifted into the boundary scan register (BSR1), through a bypass register, or into the instruction register. The TAP controller on each IC contains a state machine (See Fig. 9.19). The input to the state machine is TMS, and the sequence of 0s and 1s applied to TMS determines whether the TDI data is shifted into the instruction register or through the boundary scan cell. The TAP controller and the instruction register control the operation of boundary scan cells.

Fig. 9.19 shows the TAP controller finite state machine. States with suffix '_DR' operate on the data register and states with suffix '_IR' apply to the instruction register. All transitions between states are determined by the TMS signal and occur at the rising edge of TCK.

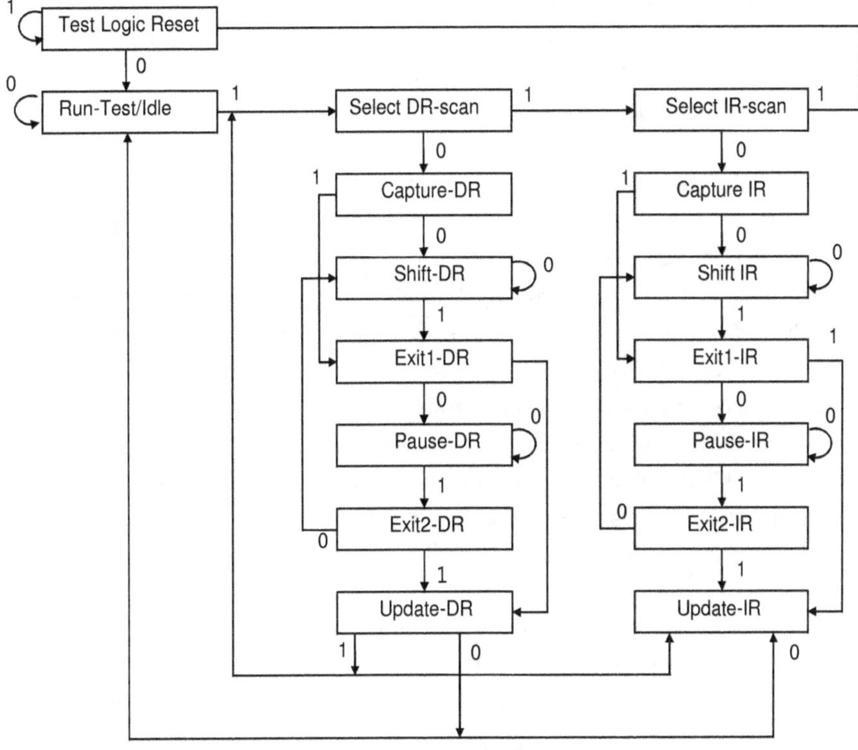

Fig. 9.19: State machine for TAP controller

The following instructions are defined in the IEEE standard for instruction register:

- **BYPASS:** This instruction is represented by an IR having all zeros in it. It is used to bypass any serial-data registers in a chip. This allows specific chips to be tested. This instruction allows the TDI serial data to go through a 1-bit bypass register on the IC instead of through the boundary scan register. In this way, one or more ICs on the PC board may be bypassed while other ICs are being tested.

- **SAMPLE/PRELOAD:** This instruction places the boundary scan registers in the Data Register chain. It means at the chips I/O pins. This instruction is used to scan the boundary scan register without interfering with the normal operation of the core logic. Data is transferred to or from the core logic from or to the IC pins without interference. Samples of this data can be taken and scanned out through the boundary scan register. Test data can be shifted into the BSR.

- **EXTEST:** This instruction allows for the testing of off-chip circuitry. It is represented by all ones in the Instruction Register. It also allows testing of clusters of components that do not incorporate the boundary scan test features. Test data is shifted into the BSR and then it goes to the output pins. Data from the input pins is captured by the BSR.
- **INTEST:** This instruction is used for single-step testing of internal circuitry via the boundary scan registers. This instruction allows testing of the core logic by shifting test data into the boundary scan register. Data shifted into the BSR takes the place of data from the input pins, and output data from the core logic is loaded into the BSR.
- **RUNBIST:** This instruction causes special built-in-self-test (BIST) logic within the IC to execute. It is used to run internal self-testing procedures within a chip.

The test sequence for state machine is as follows:

- A low on TMS transitions the FSM to the Run-Test Idle mode.
- When TMS is high for the next three TCK cycles, the FSM is placed in the select DR scan, select IR scan and finally Capture - IR mode.
- In this mode, two bits are input to the TDI port and shifted into the instruction register.
- Asserting TMS for a cycle allows the instruction register to pause, while serially loading to allow tests to be carried out.
- When TMS is asserted for two cycles, it allows the FSM to enter the Exit2 - IR mode, on exit from the Pause - IR state and then to enter the update - IR mode.
- In the update IR mode, the instruction register is updated with the new IR value.
- Similarly, to load the data registers, same sequencing is used as mentioned above.

9.15 Built-In-Self-Test

The trend to add test logic to the IC is referred to as Built-In-Self-Test (BIST). BIST is a set of structured-test techniques for combinational and sequential logic, memories, multipliers and other embedded logic block. In each case, principle is to generate test vectors, apply them to the Circuit Under Test (CUT) or Device Under Test (DUT), and then check the response.

We need to add logic to the IC so that, it can test itself. This is called as Built-In-Self-Test.

Fig. 9.20 illustrates the general method for using BIST. When the test mode is selected by the test-select signal, an on-chip test generator applies test patterns to the circuit under test. The resulting output is observed by the response monitor, which produces an error signal if an incorrect output pattern is detected.

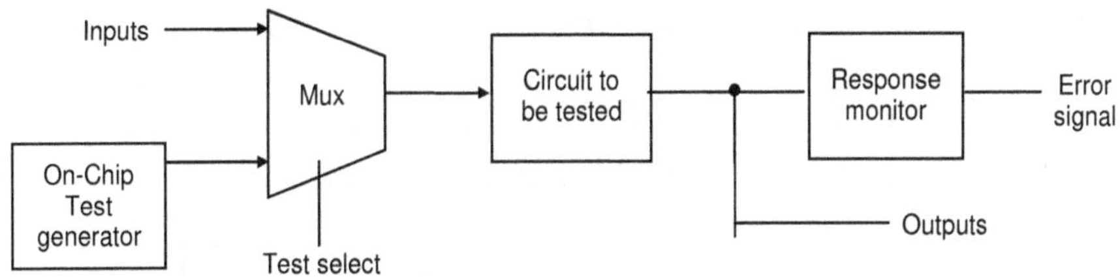

Fig. 9.20: Generic BIST scheme

BIST is often used for **testing memory**. Fig. 9.21 shows a block diagram of a self-test circuit for a RAM. The BIST controller enables the write-data generator and address counter so that data is written to each location in the RAM. Then the address counter and read-data generator are enabled, and the data read from each RAM location is compared with the output of the read-data generator to verify that it is correct.

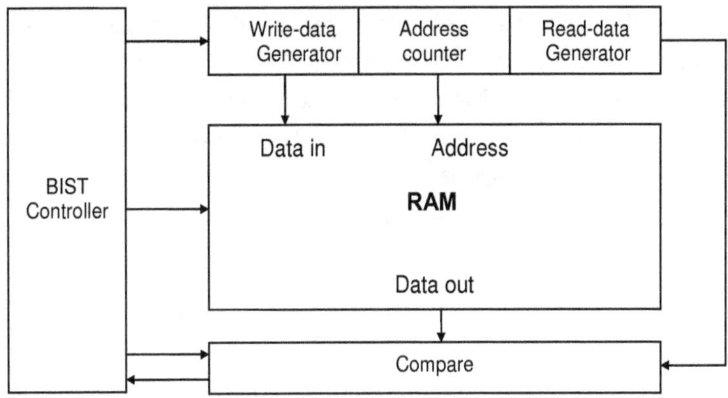

Fig. 9.21: Self-test circuit for RAM

The test circuit can be simplified by using a **signature register**. The signature register compresses the output data into a short string of bits called a signature, and this signature is compared with the signature for a correctly functioning component. A multiple-input signature register (MISR) combines and compresses several output streams into a single signature. Fig. 9.22 shows a simplified version of the RAM self-test circuit. The **read-data generator** and **comparator** have been eliminated and replaced with a MISR. One type of MISR simply forms a check sum by adding up all the data types stored in the RAM. When testing a ROM, Fig. 9.22 can be simplified further, since no write-data generator is needed.

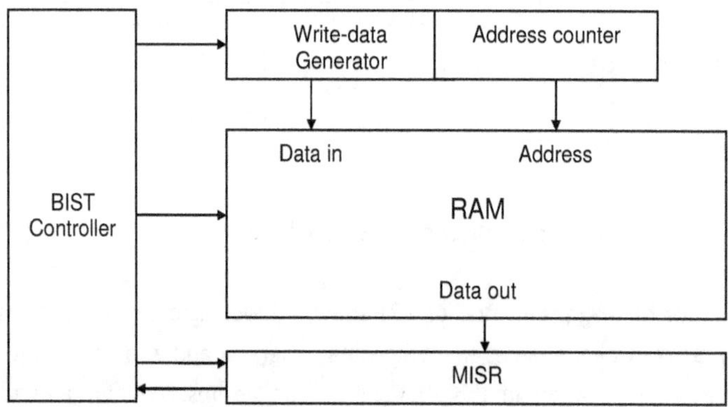

Fig. 9.22: Self-test circuit for RAM with signature register

Linear Feedback Shift Registers (LFSRs) are often used to generate test patterns. Fig. 9.23 shows an example of a LFSR. The outputs from the first and fourth flip-flops are XORed together and fed back into the D input of the first flip-flop. The general form of a LFSR is a shift register with two or more flip-flop outputs XORed together and fed back into the first flip-flop. The name linear comes from the fact that exclusive OR is equivalent to modulo-2 addition and addition is a linear operation.

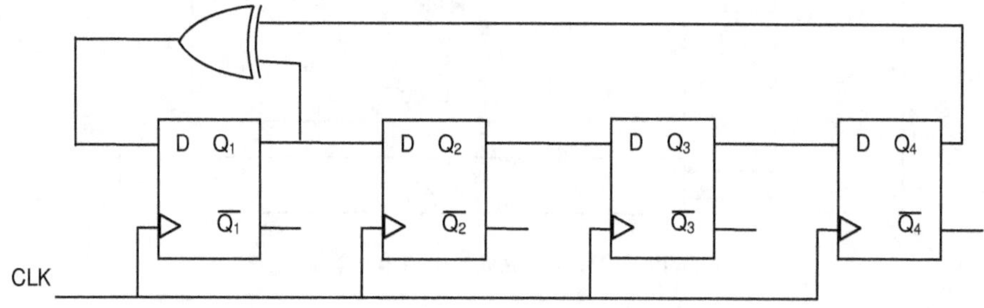

Fig. 9.23: 4-bit LFSR

By correctly choosing the outputs that are fed back through the XOR gate, it is possible to produce 2^n-1 different bit patterns using n-bit shift register. All possible patterns can be generated except for all 0s. The patterns generated by 4-bit LFSR (See Fig. 9.23) are: 1000, 1100, 1110, 1111, 0111, 1011, 0101, 1010, 1101, 0011, 1001, 0100, 0010, 0001, 1000...These patterns have no obvious order, and they have certain randomness properties. Such a LFSR is often referred to as a pseudo-random pattern generator (PRPG). PRPGs are very useful for BIST, since they can generate a large number of test patterns with a small amount of logic circuitry.

MISR (Multiple Input Shift Register)

A MISR can be constructed by modifying a LFSR by adding XOR gates, as shown in Fig. 9.24. The test data (Z_1 Z_2 Z_3 Z_4) is XORed into the register with each clock, and the final result represents a signature that can be compared with the signature for a known correctly functioning component.

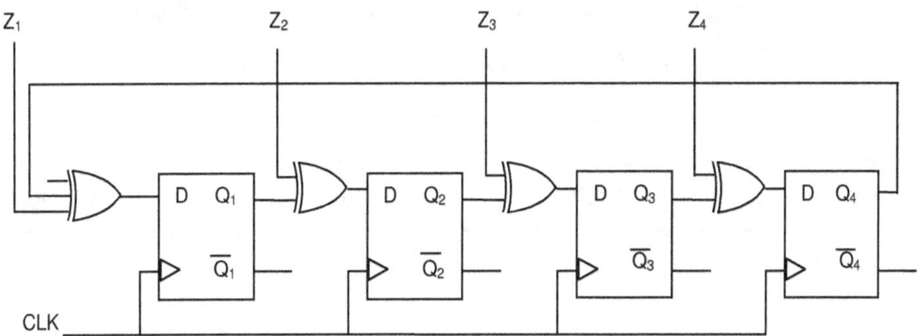

Fig. 9.24: MISR

An n-bit signature register maps all possible input streams into one of the 2^n possible signatures. One of these is the correct signature, and the others indicate that errors have occurred.

9.16 Joint Test Access Group (JTAG)

JTAG is a IEEE 1149.1 standard. It is normally used to verify that the circuit has been mounted on the circuit board correctly. So, the JTAG specification defines a method to test device functionality and connections to other devices on the board through a test access port and boundary scan.

The JTAG used to test internal circuitry is shown in Fig. 9.25.

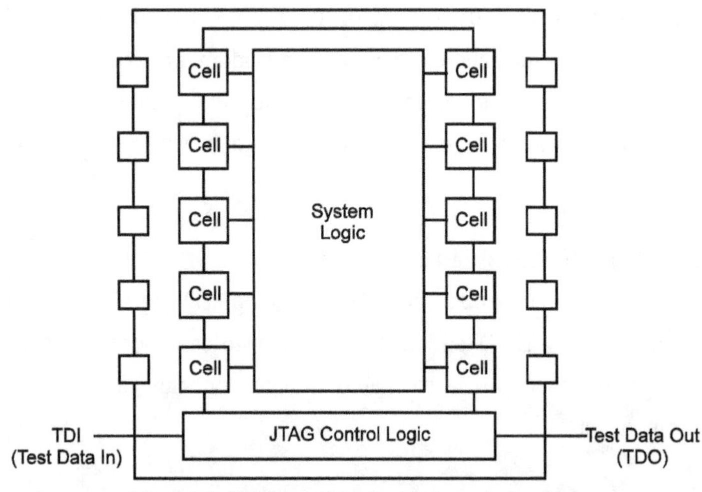

Fig. 9.25: JTAG used to test internal circuitry

JTAG is a methodology used for testing and quality assurance or for debugging. JTAG also specifies a mode called as BIST (Built-in-self-test). BIST is used to limit the number of vectors that need to be clocked through the scan path. A device placed in the BIST mode generates pseudo-random test-vectors as stimuli, compares internal outputs against expected results and indicates success or failures.

JTAG used for external testing of connections to other JTAG devices are shown in Fig. 9.26. As shown, Test Data Input is applied to the TDI of first JTAG. The Test Data Output of first JTAG is connected to the next JTAG Test Data Input and so on.

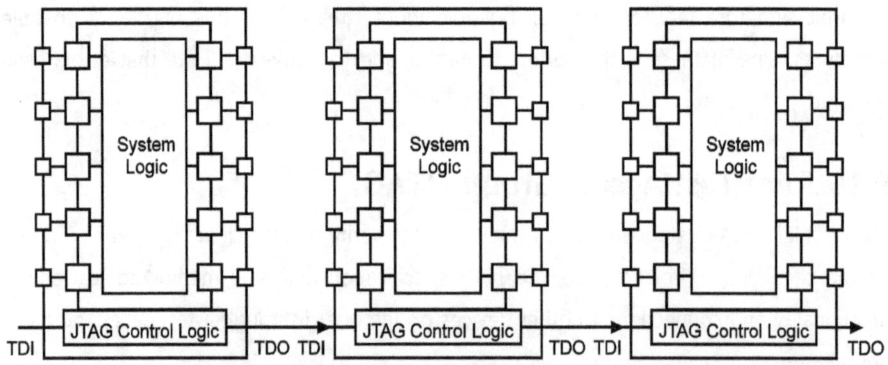

Fig. 9.26: External testing of connections to other JTAG devices

9.17 Full Scan and Partial Scan

Full scan means, all the flip flops in the circuit are connected to a scan chain. While, in case of partial scan, only a subset of the flip-flops are connected in the scan chains. The percentage of gates in the overhead required for the two scan methods would be

Full scan:	10 to 20 per cent extra gates.
Partial scan:	5 to 15 per cent extra gates.

By using these extra gates and an ATPG tool, the fault coverage is around 99 per cent for full scan and slightly lower for partial scan. In partial scan not all the flip flops have been connected to scan chain, they cannot be checked. Partial scan is used instead of full scan, if the area or in some cases, timing constraints for the design are particularly stringent. A scan-flip-flop is normally slightly slower than a normal flip-flop. Full scan or partial scan choice is based on whatever has the greatest priority: area or fault coverage.

9.18 Fault Simulation

Fault simulation is used after completion of logic simulation. Fault simulation is used to see what happens in a design when faults are deliberately introduced. As each fault is inserted, the fault simulator runs the test program. If the fault simulation shows that the outputs of the fault circuit are different than the inputs of the good circuit at any strobe time, then we have detected a fault; otherwise we have undetected fault. The list of fault origins is collected in a file and as the fault is inserted and simulated, the results are recorded and the faults are marked according to the result. At the end of fault simulation, we can find the fault coverage.

Fault coverage = detected fault / detectable faults.

There are several algorithms for fault simulation: serial fault simulation, parallel fault simulation, and concurrent fault simulation.

Serial Fault Simulation

Serial Fault Simulation is the simplest fault simulation algorithm. We simulate two copies of the circuit; the first copy is a good circuit. We then pick a fault and insert it into the faulty circuit. Two copies are good circuit and faulty circuit. We then repeat the process, simulating one faulty circuit at a time. Serial simulation is slow and is impractical for large ICs.

Parallel Fault Simulation

Parallel Fault Simulation takes advantage of multiple bits of the words in computer memory. In a computer that uses 32-bit word memory, we can simulate a set of 32 copies of the circuit at the same time, as only one bit is needed to represent either a '1' or '0' for each node in the circuit. One copy is the good circuit, and we insert different fault into the other copies.

The number of bits per node that we need in order to simulate each circuit depends on the number of states in the logic system we are using. Thus, if we use a four-state system with '1', '0', 'x' and 'z' states, we need two bits per node.

Parallel Fault Simulation is not as fast as simple prediction because we have to simulate all the circuits in parallel until the last fault in the current set is detected. If we use serial simulation, we can stop as soon as a fault is detected and then start another fault simulation. Parallel fault simulation is faster than serial simulation but not as fast as concurrent fault simulation. It is also difficult to include behavioral models using parallel fault simulation.

Concurrent Fault Simulation

It is the most widely used fault simulation algorithm and takes advantage of the fact that a fault does not affect the whole circuit. Thus, we do not need to simulate the whole circuit for each new fault. In concurrent simulation, we first completely simulate the good circuit. We then inject a fault and simulate a copy of only that part of the circuit that behaves differently.

QUESTIONS

1. What is JTAG? List the different signals involved. Explain the need of boundary scan.
[8 Marks, Dec. 2003]
2. Describe the following: (a) BSDF (b) JTAG **[4 Marks, Dec. 2005]**
3. Explain the functions of JTAG pins. **[7 Marks, May 2005]**
4. Explain the need of Design for Testability.
5. Compare Testability and Verification.
6. What are the different manufacturing faults on a chip?
7. Explain stuck-at-0 and stuck-at-1 fault.
8. Explain the faults caused by manufacturing defects.
9. Explain controllability and observability.
10. Explain the concept of fault coverage.
11. What is boundary scan? Explain in detail.
12. Write a note on TAP controller.
13. Explain Instruction Registers and Test Data Registers.
14. Write a note on BIST.
15. What is boundary scan? What is JTAG? Explain the function of TDI, TCK, TMS, TDO, and TRST
16. What is mean by boundary scan.
17. What is JTAG?
18. What is JTAG? List the different signals involved. Explain the need of boundary scan.
19. With suitable schematic, explain the operation of TAP controller. **(8 Marks, May 2007)**
20 What is full and partial scan ? Explain in detail. **(8 Marks, May 2007)**
21. Write short notes on:
    (a) Fault coverage and its significance. (b) Testability. **(16 Marks, May 2007)**

◊◊◊

Chapter 10: SIGNAL INTEGRITY AND SYSTEM-ON-CHIP

Topics discussed: SoC, Important issues in SoC design, Clocked systems and strategies, Power optimization, Power distribution, Wire and vias, Design validation, Floorplanning, I/O architecture, Layout design rules and analysis tools in CMOS, Memory elements

10.1 Introduction

System-on-Chip (SoC) is a major revolution taking place in the design of integrated circuits due to the unprecedented levels of integration possible. As a result, new methodologies and tools are demanded to address design, verification and test problems presented by SoC's in this rapid evolving area.

System-on-Chip allows systems to be made at much lower cost than the equivalent board-level system. On-chip connections are more efficient than chip-to-chip connection, which also increases the performance; it also reduces the power consumption.

10.2 What is Soc?

System-on-Chip (SoC) technology is the packaging of all necessary electronic circuits and components for a "system" on a single Integrated Circuit (IC), for example, cell phone or a digital camera, generally known as a microchip.

SoC for a sound-detecting device might include an audio receiver, an analog to digital converter (ADC), a microprocessor, memory and the input / output control logic - all on a single microchip.

Fig. 10.1 shows an example of a SoC. It includes different electronic components such as microprocessor, DMA, SRAM and display. Also the DSP functionality is provided with the help of DSP processor. Separate bus is provided for DSP code and data bus.

SoC and IP: Due to VLSI technology, we can put tens of millions of chips on a single die at reasonable cost. System-on-Chip design teams make use of Intellectual Property (IP) blocks in order to improve their productivity. An IP block is actually a pre-defined component that can be used in a larger design. The IP blocks are basically divided into two types:

1) **Hard IP:** As the name indicates, it is a pre-designed layout. The advantage of using hard IP is that, as the full layout is available, the block's size, performance and power consumption can be accurately measured.

2) **Soft IP:** It is a synthesizable module in a hardware description language such as VHDL or Verilog or ABEL. The advantage of using soft IP is that, it can be easily targeted to new technologies. But the drawback of soft IP is that it is difficult to characterize and it may not be as fast as or as small as hard IP.

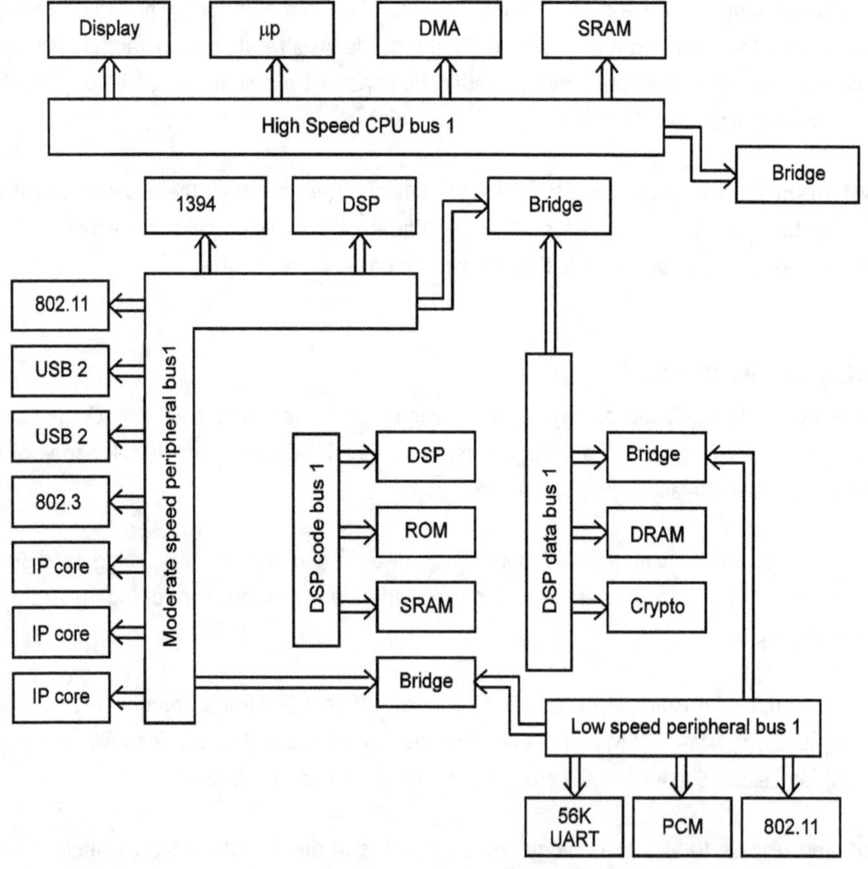

Fig. 10.1: System-on-Chip

IP-based design has several challenges.

i)   To ensure that, the designed IP block must work properly in SoC, all types of functions, such as arithmetic, logical functions, performance, power consumption and testability of the IP block must all be verified in the context of the system.

ii) We need to design the IP blocks that are generally useful. It takes a lot of efforts to fully test an IP block and document it so that it can be used by another designer.

iii) Designing an interface standard for the IP block is also a challenge. IP blocks must clearly be able to communicate with each other, but unfortunately no one interface standard is best for all types of systems.

Embedded CPUs are designed by using intellectual property for SoC. Embedded CPUs can be programmed to perform certain functions on the chip. 8 bits CPUs were used for basic sequencing. Now-a-days, powerful 32 bit CPUs can be embedded on a System-on-chip. Embedded CPUs are most popular on SoCs for the following reasons:

(a) Applications such as MP3 audio and MPEG video are difficult to implement without some amount of embedded software.
(b) For many complex systems, embedded software is required to implement their applications. Many SoCs also use windows CE, Linux, the palm OS etc. to provide file management and networking.
(c) Less design time is needed for embedded CPUs.

10.3 Important Issues in SoC Design

(1) Analog and Digital Signal Processing

VLSI manufacturing processes are not especially good at analog components. System-on-chip requires interface with the outside signals and therefore SoC needs mixed-signal elements i.e. analog as well as digital processing. In such cases, we may need to put some types of analog interfaces on a largely digital chip and for some parts; we need mixed-signal processing on a separate chip manufactured with a different process.

(2) SoCs require input and output devices

I/O devices may be available as IP blocks; others may not be available from outside sources.

(3) Memory system requirement

Many SoCs are designed towards memory intensive applications. On chip memory includes the main memory or the caches for the embedded CPUs. The on-chip memory may be the flash memory, SRAM or DRAM. In some cases, SoCs also need off-chip memory. Care must be taken while designing the memory system, to meet performance and power requirements, as well as to make best use of silicon area.

(4) Hardware/Software Co-design on SoC

Hardware/Software Co-design requires careful measurement and design judgement. SoCs require sophisticated architectures, number of CPUs, I/O devices and on-chip memory systems. These architectures must be carefully designed to meet strict power requirement and real-time deadlines.

We need to take care of the above issues while designing the system on chip.

10.4 Clocked Systems and Clocking Strategies

In every VLSI system, we must store some state, it means, some form of storage elements are required (Access to the internal memory is controlled by the clock input). In finite state machine we are using registers and combinational logic to produce the set of logic outputs, as shown in Fig. 10.2. The outputs from the storage elements are fed back to the combinational logic block. The storage elements are operated by a clock.

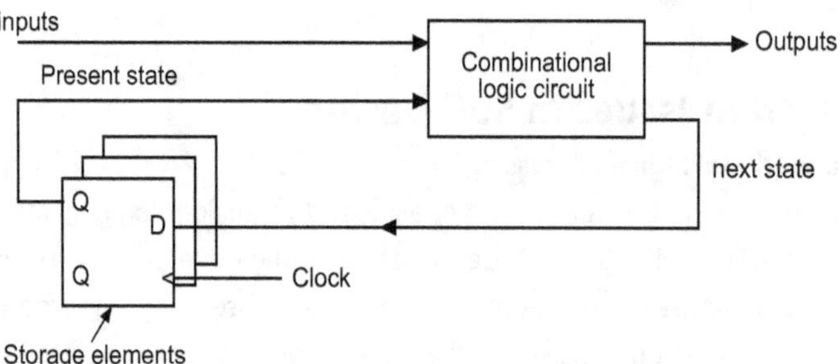

Fig. 10.2: A simple finite state machine

When the clock changes from low to high, the next state bits are transferred to the present state, through the storage element. After that, the present state and inputs trickle through the combinational logic to the outputs and the next state bits. All this takes some time. After the outputs are stable, again the system is clocked.

The minimum time required to settle the output and next state bits, determines the maximum frequency of the clock. Therefore, to decide the maximum frequency of the clock we need to consider suitable memory elements and logic elements.

The clocking strategy plays a very important role before the commencement of the design, because of the following reasons:

1) The clocking strategy decides how many clock signals need to be routed throughout the chip.
2) The clocking strategy also decides how many transistors are used per storage element.
3) The above decisions impact the power dissipated by the chip and also the size of the chip.

The clocking discipline ensures that the system will work at some clock frequency. Making the system work at the required clock frequency requires additional analysis and optimization. Now, we will see the use of a single phase clock and two phase clock.

10.4.1 Single Phase Clock

A single phase clock is shown in Fig. 10.3. Also, the different timing parameters of interest are shown. Suppose, this single phase clock is applied to a flip-flop.

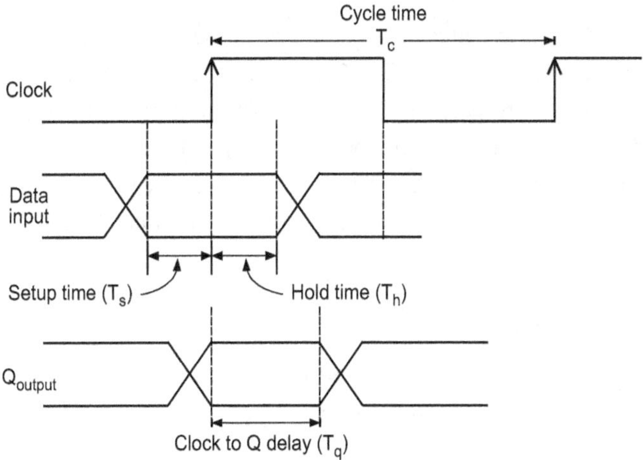

Fig. 10.3: A single phase clock with different timing parameters

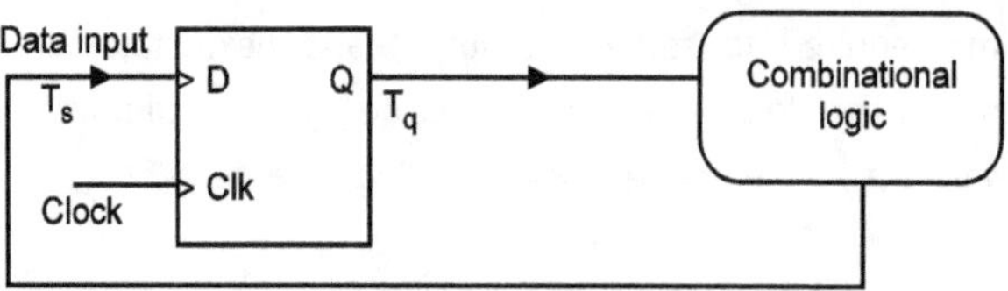

Fig. 10.4: Flip-flop with a combinational logic

If the data input remains stable within a window around the positive transition of the clock, then after some time later the data input value will propagate to the output of the register. The timing parameters are defined below.

Setup time (T_s): The time before the clock edge that the data input has to be stable is called the setup time (T_s).

Hold time (T_h): The time after the clock edge that the data input has to remain stable is called the hold time (T_h).

Clock to Q delay (T_q): The delay from the positive clock input to the new value of the Q output is called the clock to Q delay (T_q).

We have defined the timing parameters that the clock and data signals must satisfy, which are conservative but safe. As shown in Fig. 10.4, the flip flops read their inputs on the positive clock edge. The data inputs must have reached stable values at the flip flop inputs on the rising clock edge. The length of the clock period is adjusted to allow all signals to propagate from the data inputs to the flip flops. If all the data inputs satisfy these conditions, then only flip flop will latch the proper next state value. The signals generated by the flop flops satisfy the clocking discipline requirements.

10.4.2 Two Phase System

In single phase clock systems, we need to generate near-perfectly overlapping clocks. It is not always possible to generate perfectly overlapping clocks.

Now, we will take an example of a single latch system. As shown in Fig. 10.5, when the latch's clock is high, the latch will be transparent. If the clock signal is held high long enough, the signal can make more than one loop around the system and next state value can go through the latch and changes the output of the system.

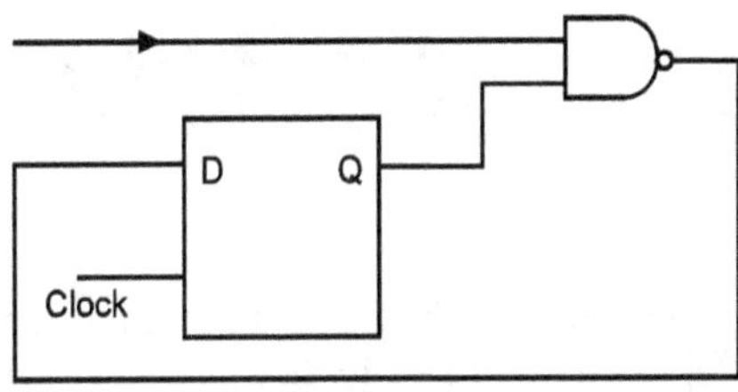

Fig. 10.5: Single latch system

In such cases, there are two requirements.

1) The clock must be high long enough to securely latch the new value, but
2) The clock should not be so long that erroneous values can be stored.

It means, a two-sided constraint, on the relative lengths of the clock period and the combinational logic delays are required.

It is possible to meet these two-sided constraints, but again the problem is that, it is very difficult to make such a circuit work properly.

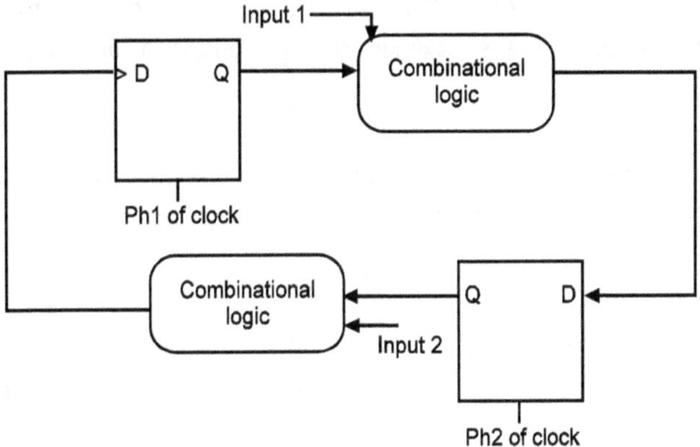

Fig. 10.6: Two-phase clocking system

To avoid this problem of the single phase clock, a safer architecture is to use, the two-phase clocking system. Fig. 10.6 shows the strict two-phase clocking system.

As shown, the latches are controlled by the **non-overlapping** clock phases. Non-overlapping clocks are as shown in Fig. 10.7. The Ph1-high, then Ph2-high, sequence forms a complete clock cycle.

Due to the use of non-overlapping clock, it is ensured that no signal can propagate all the way from a latch's output back to the same latch's output.

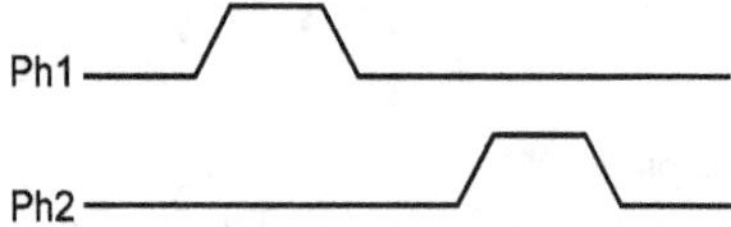

Fig. 10.7: A two-phase, non-overlapping clock

When Ph1 is high, the Ph2-controlled latches are disabled. Similarly, when Ph2 is high, the Ph1 latches are off. Due to this, the clock and the delays through the combinational logic need to satisfy only a **one-sided** timing constraint.

The only timing constraint that needs to satisfy is that, each phase must be longer than the longest combinational delay through that phase's logic. If the clocks are run slow enough, the phases will be longer than the maximum combinational delay and then the system will work properly.

We can stretch the clock phases and inter-phase gaps to ensure that the strict two-phase system works. If the clock cycle is properly designed, the system will work properly.

When mostly static logic is used, the single-phase clocking scheme is preferable using fully self-contained static registers. For gate array design and standard cell, single phase clock is the only option permitted. The clock routing problem is minimal in data-path designs.

For RAMs, ROMs and PLAs, a two phase clocking strategy is easier to work. For small dynamic latches, the two-phase clocking system was popular because it guaranteed latch behavior.

But, in today's complex, high speed CMOS circuits, cycle times are so short that guaranteeing the non-overlap time for a two phase clocking scheme is difficult. Also the CMOS processes are extremely dense, thus obviating the need for the smallest latch possible.

10.4.3 System Timing

Fig. 10.8 shows a typical pipelined system with input and output registers separated by combinational logic.

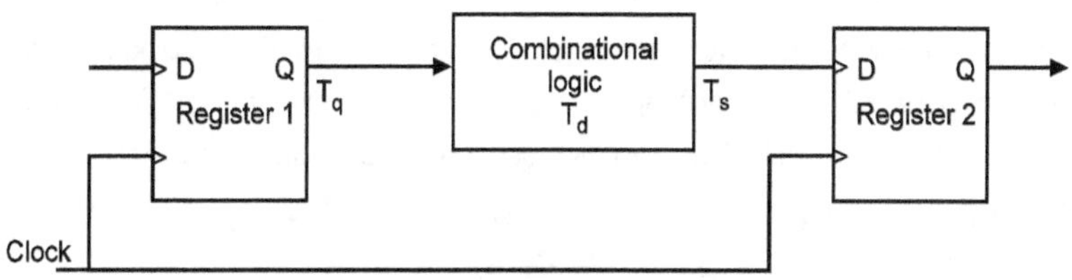

Fig. 10.8: A register based pipeline system

The cycle time is given by,

$$T_c = T_q + T_d + T_s$$

where, T_c = one cycle time

T_q = clock to q output

T_d = worst-case delay through the combinational logic block

T_s = setup time.

The register pipeline strategy is the simplest, because it is edge based.

10.4.4 Clock Distribution

Clock distribution is challenging due to the large capacitive load that must be driven to produce a very sharp transition. In large CMOS design, if we count up all the capacitances it may well add up to over a **1000 pF.** If this large value of capacitance is driven in a small time and at a high repetition rate, the peak transient current and average dynamic current can be in the ampere range.

We will take an example, suppose

V_{DD} = 5 V,

$C_{register}$ = 1000 pF (i.e. 10 K register bits @ 0.1 pF).

T_{clock} = 10 ns, F_{clock} = 100 MHz

$$T_{rise/fall} = 1 \text{ ns}$$

$$\therefore \quad I_{peak} = C\frac{dv}{dt} = \frac{1000 \times 10^{-12} \times 5}{1.0 \times 10^{-9}} = 5 \text{ A}$$

$$P_d = C.V_{DD}^2.f = 1000 \times 10^{-12} \times 25 \times 100 \times 10^6$$

$$P_d = 2.5 \text{ watts}$$

As seen from above example, peak current is 5A and power dissipation is 2.5 watts.

Clock distribution actually comes under floor planning because clock delay varies with the position on the chip. While placing the logic blocks in the design of the clocking network, the clock delay must be taken into account. Fig. 10.9 shows an example of clock delay versus position. At position A, the clock delay is almost zero, and at position B, the clock delay is maximum.

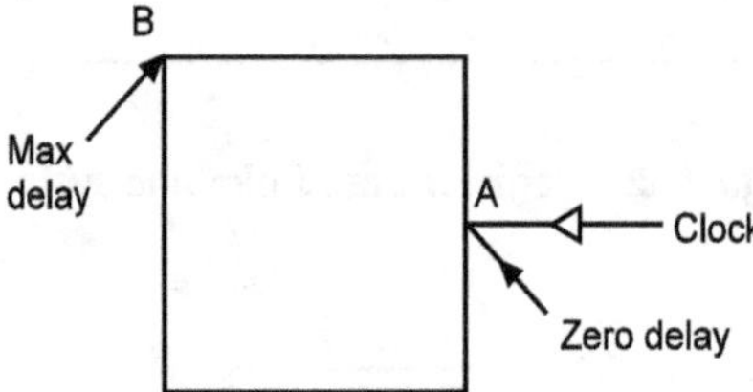

Fig. 10.9: Clock delay versus position

There are two main techniques to improve clock distribution:
(1) A distributed **clock tree** approach i.e. **physical design**.
(2) Using several stages of driver to drive the clock distribution network, to minimize delays i.e. circuit design for drivers.

Physical design of clock distribution networks

In this the layout is designed to make clock delays more even, or at least more predictable. The two most commonly used methods for physical clocking networks are:

(a) H tree

(b) Balanced tree

(a) H tree: H tree allows predictable delays. It is shown in Fig. 10.10. It is a recursive structure. For main H structure, four smaller H structures can be added at the four endpoints of the H bars. The width of the wires in the H tree is adjusted to account for variations in load capacitance to equalize skew in the H tree. We can also add buffers into the H tree network to increase drive capability. H tree is a top down clock distribution methodology, because the floor plan of the H tree determines the floor plan of the logic to which H is connected. As the physical distance in the H tree increases, the skew also increases. So, memory elements must be grouped together to make use of nearby distribution points or the same distribution points in the H tree network.

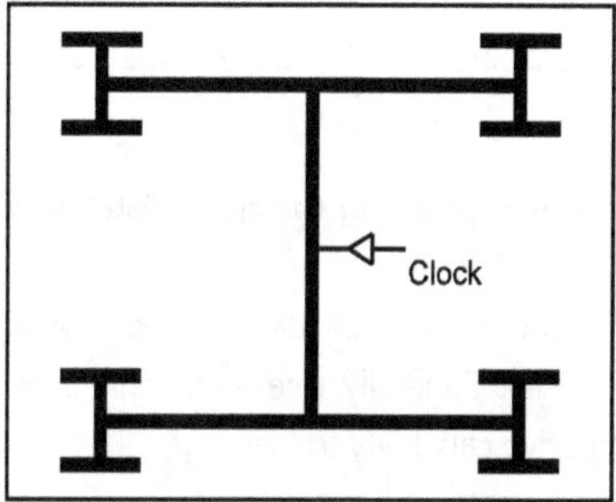

Fig. 10.10: H tree approach

(b) Balanced tree clock network: It is generated by placement and routing as shown in Fig. 10.11. In this approach, the memory elements are clustered (clustering means combining of memory elements which has same characteristics or properties) and grouped together.

The clustering method is used to guide placement. After that the clocking tree is synthesized based on the skew information generated during clustering. The tree generated can be irregular in shape. The tree has been balanced during design to minimize skew.

Several tools are available for generating balanced clock trees, during balancing wire widths can be varied in the tree and buffers can be added.

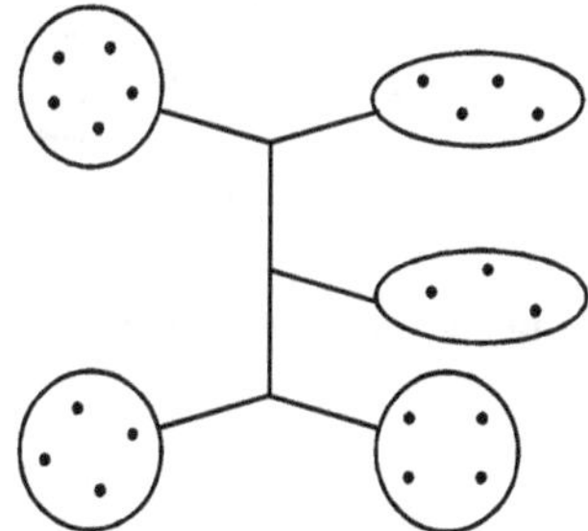

Fig. 10.11: A balanced clock tree approach

Two methods are used to distribute the clock:

(1) Using a driver chain.

(2) A hierarchical clock distribution system.

In a driver chain method as shown in Fig. 10.12, several inverters are connected in a chain.

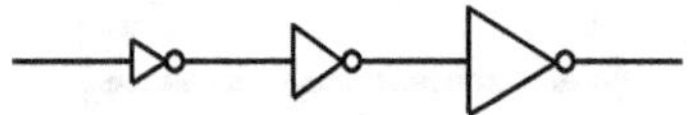

Fig. 10.12: A driver chain for the clock distribution network

But the problem with this method is that, logic delay increases as the capacitance attached to the logic's output becomes larger. Generally, one small logic gate is driving an equally small logic gate, roughly matching drive capability to load.

To drive large capacitive loads is to increase current by making wider transistors. Therefore, in a driver chain, a sequence of successively larger drivers is used as shown in Fig. 10.12. In the chain of inverters, each inverter can produce α times more current than the previous stage.

The hierarchical clock distribution system is shown in Fig. 10.13. The distributed clock tree method constructs a tree of clock buffers. The delay to each data path can be carefully simulated and matched. The distribution of clock is arranged to adjust the resistance and capacitance delay in a safe slew direction.

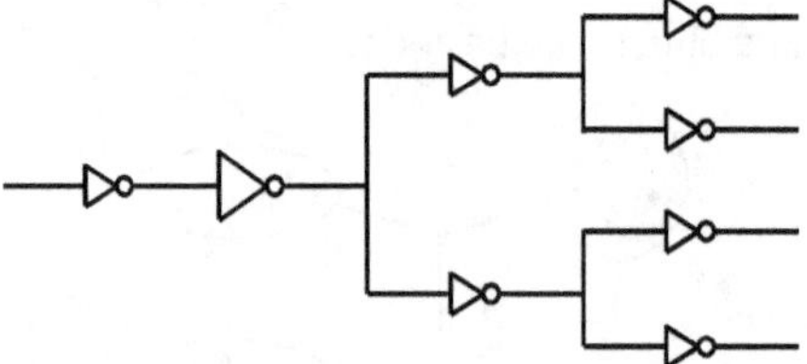

Fig. 10.13: The hierarchical clock distribution tree

We will see an example of the design of a clocking network which uses a regular physical design.

Clock distribution in the DEC Alpha 21164

DEC Alpha 21164 contains 16.5 million transistors on a 16.5 mm × 18.1 mm die. The basic floor plan of the clock distribution system is shown below.

As shown in Fig. 10.14, the first stage of the clock driver is the pre-clock driver. The pre-clock driver is located at the centre of the chip. The clock generator drives this pre-clock driver. This network consists of a six-level inverter tree and generates 24 outputs on the pre-clock signal. The pre-clock signal is fed to two final clock driver systems, one on each side of the chip. Each final clock driver contains 44 drivers. The system also includes a set of 12 conditional clock drivers on each side.

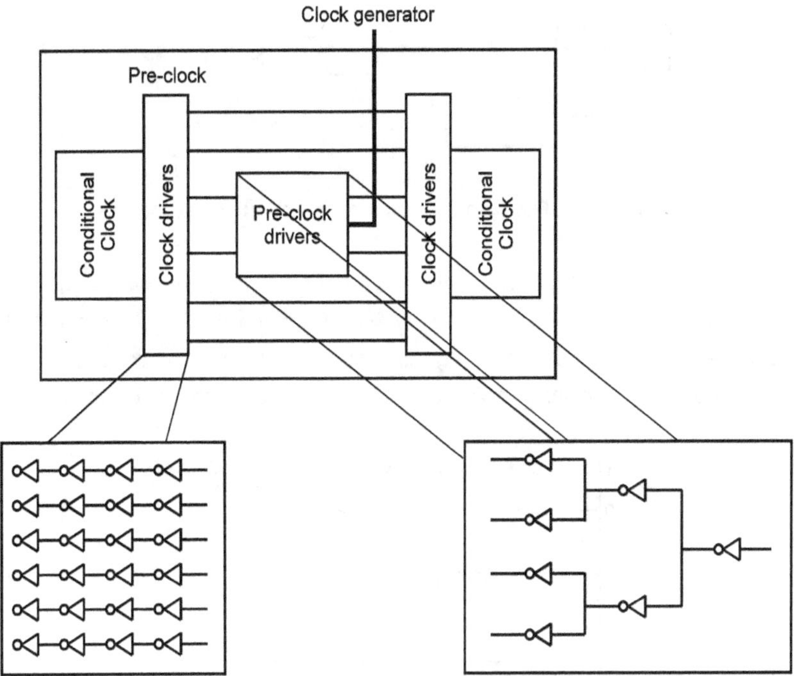

Fig. 10.14: DEC Alpha 21164, clock distribution

10.5 Power Optimization

The consumption power of gate is reduced if its output changes few times. We need to design the logic network to reduce the number of unnecessary changes to a gate's output.

Also we can reduce the power consumption by eliminating the glitches in CMOS logic. Glitch reduction is applied more effectively in sequential logic as compared to combinational logic.

To stop the propagation of glitches in sequential machines, we use registers, independent of the logic function to be implemented. Fig. 10.15 shows how the flip flops are used to stop glitch propagation.

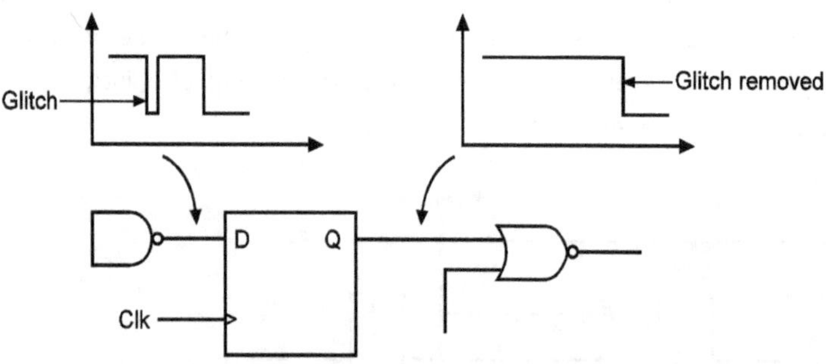

Fig. 10.15: Flip flop used to stop glitch propagation

As shown in Fig. 10.16, the D flip flop changes its output only for positive-edge trigger of the clock. Therefore, after positive edge of the clock, even though the D input has a glitch, it is not reflected at the output. But adding registers will change the number of cycles required to compute the output of machine and also it must be compatible with the rest of the system.

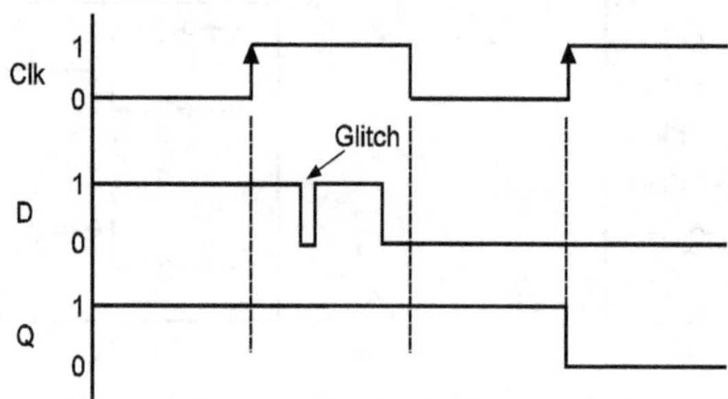

Fig. 10.16: Flip flop used to stop glitch propagation

The other way to reduce power consumption is by proper state assignment. One-hot encoding requires only two signal transitions per cycle. These transitions are on the old state and new state signals. But, one-hot encoding requires a large number of memory elements. We also need to consider the power consumption of the logic that computes the required current state and next state functions.

In multi-level logic network, glitches are more likely to occur. In multi-level logic network, the signal arrives at the input of the gates at different times. Therefore, the differences in arrival time at the gate input cause the glitch.

There is also probability of glitches in the long chain of gates. Suppose we need to compute the sum output as w + x + y + z. There are two ways to get the sum output as shown in Fig. 10.17 (a) i.e., long chain. In long chain when any one of the input (w, x, y or z) changes, that change propagates through the successive stages. Due to this, the output of each adder assumes multiple values.

On the other hand, the circuit shown in Fig. 10.17 (b) is more balanced. Intermediate results from the various sub-networks reach the next level of the adder around the same time. Due to this, the possibility of glitch in balanced tree is less, while settling to their final values.

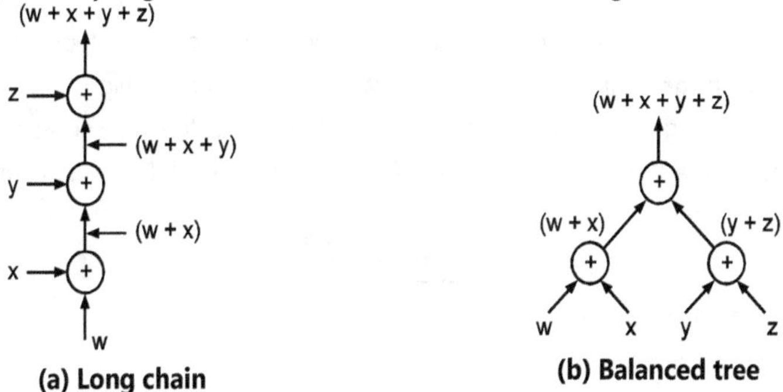

Fig. 10.17: Long chain and balanced tree

10.6 Power Distribution

Power distribution comes under floor planning. While distributing the power on the chip, there are two approaches.

(1) Proper sizing of wires to ensure that they can deliver the required power without being destroyed.

(2) We need to design a global power distribution network that runs both V_{DD} and V_{SS} entirely in metal.

Fig. 10.18 shows the power and ground trees usually routed as trees. The power supply i.e. V_{DD} is at the route and the different logic gates are connected to the **twigs**. The main requirement is that, each branch must be wide enough to carry the current in all of its branches. If the logic gates use only a few transistor sizes, then computing the power line width is easy.

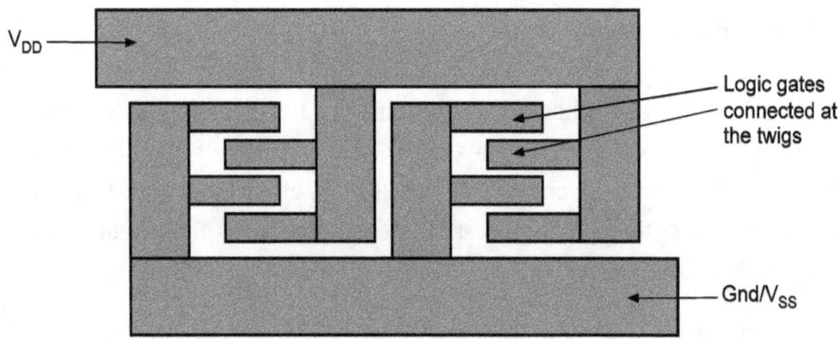

Fig. 10.18: Power and ground trees

If too much current is carried through a wire, then the wire quickly disintegrates. This is also called as **metal migration limit**. **Metal migration** means under high currents, electron collisions with metal grains cause the metal to move. Also the **Mean Time to Failure** (MTF) for metal wires is the time it takes for 50% of testing sites to fail. It is a function of current density.

$$\text{MTF} \ \alpha \ j^{-n} \ e^{Q/KT}$$

where, j = current density

         n = a constant between 1 and 3.

        Q = diffusion activation energy.

A metal wire can handle 1.5 mA of current per micron of wire width under the SCMOS rule. A width of the wire is measured perpendicular to the current flow. Therefore, 4.5 mA of current can be handled by a 3 µm wire. Generally 4.5 mA is a enough current to supply a large number of logic gates. So, in small design, the metal migration problem is not a major problem. But, in case of large designs, sizing power supply lines is critical to ensure that the chip does not fail once it is installed.

In case of large designs, metal migration is not the only problem; large current may still cause **power supply noise**. The power supply noise is due to IR drops in the power supply network. So, we need to analyze the power network, using circuit simulations with the high level models for major components, to model their current requirements over time.

Decoupling capacitors across the power supply pins are traditionally used in PCB design to reduce power supply noise. In large chips, decoupling capacitors may be used on-chip. For example, DEC Alpha microprocessor uses 250 nF of on-chip capacitance to decouple the power supply. We can also minimize the noise by modifying the sequential design of the machine.

Next, we will see an example of the BELLMAC-32A, 32 bit single chip microprocessor. The basic layout of the BELLMAC power bus is shown below.

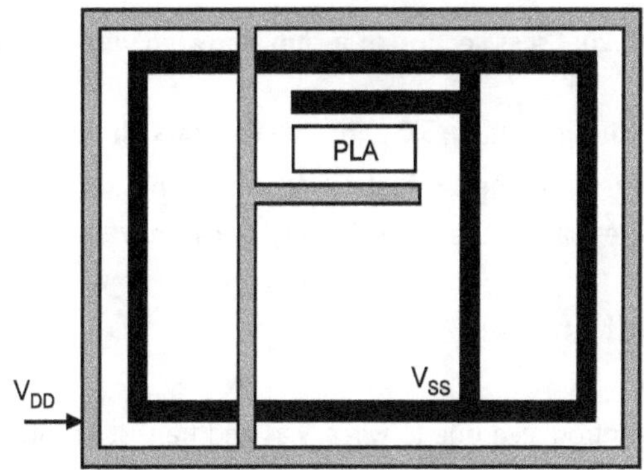

Fig. 10.19: BELLMAC-32A power bus

As shown in Fig. 10.19, the layout is designed with power pads at both ends. Due to this, the power bus noise is reduced by a factor of 4, as the impedance and switching current are cut in half.

10.7 Wire and Vias

In transistor manufacturing using CMOS logic, N diffusion and P diffusion wires are created by doping regions of the substrate. Polysilicon and metal wires are laid over the substrate (SiO_2). Silicon dioxide is used to insulate them from the substrate and each other. Wires are added in layers on the chip.

A layer of wires is added on the top of the existing SiO_2 and then the assembly is covered with an additional layer of SiO_2, to insulate the new wires from the next layer.

Fig. 10.20 shows the cross section of the nest of wires and vias.

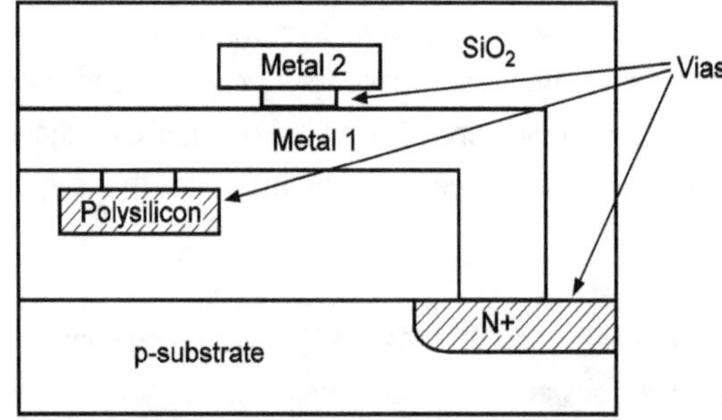

Fig. 10.20: Cross section of a chip, showing wires and vias

Vias are the cuts in the insulating SiO_2. The metal flows through the cut to make the connection on the desired layer below. Metal wires are used to supply power throughout the chip. On-chip metal wires have limited current carrying capacity.

10.7.1 Wire Parasitics

Parasitic elements are introduced due to wires, vias and transistors into the circuits. The two main parasitic components are resistance and capacitance. Fig. 10.21 shows the side wall and bottom wall capacitances of a diffusion region.

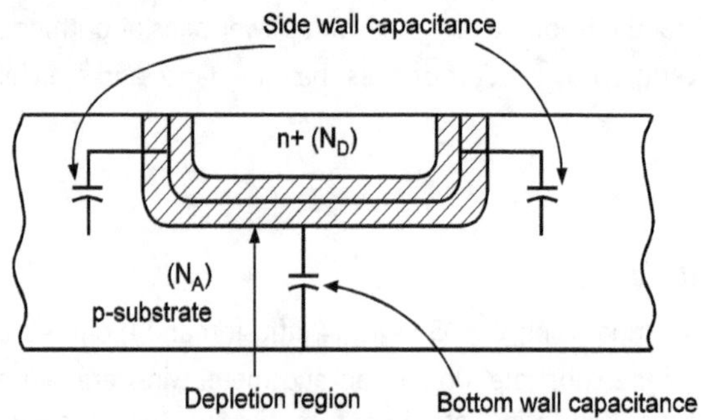

Fig. 10.21: Diffusion wire capacitances in diffusion region

Diffusion wire capacitances are introduced by the p-n junctions at the boundaries between the diffusion and underlying substrate. These capacitances change with the voltage across the junction, which varies with the circuit operation. As shown in Fig. 10.21, there are two capacitances in the depletion region.

(1) Bottom wall capacitance – it depends on the diffusion area.

(2) Side wall capacitance – it depends on the perimeter.

The depletion region capacitance value is given by,

$$C_{jo} = \frac{\varepsilon_{si}}{x_d} \qquad \text{... (1)}$$

where, C_{jo} = depletion capacitance at zero bias

       ε_{si} = permittivity of Si = $11.9\varepsilon_0$

       ε_o = permittivity of free space = 8.854×10^{-14} F/cm^2

       x_d = depletion region width

       x_{do} = depletion region width with zero bias, it is given by,

$$x_{do} = \sqrt{\left(\frac{1}{N_A} + \frac{1}{N_D}\right) \frac{2\varepsilon_{si} V_{bi}}{q}} \qquad \text{... (2)}$$

The V_{bi} is the built-in voltage and it is given by,

$$V_{bi} = \frac{KT}{q} \ln \frac{N_A N_D}{x_i^2} \qquad \text{... (3)}$$

Now, as already mentioned the junction capacitance is a function of applied voltage across the junction i.e. V_r. So, the junction capacitance at voltage V_r is given by,

$$C_j (V_r) = \frac{C_{jo}}{\sqrt{1 + \dfrac{V_r}{V_{bi}}}} \qquad \text{... (4)}$$

From above equation, the junction capacitance decreases as reverse voltage increases.

Capacitance due to poly and metal wire

Capacitance is also formed due to poly and metal wires; these are called as the plate capacitance and fringe capacitance.

The plate capacitance per unit area assumes infinite parallel plates. The fringe capacitance is due to the changes in the electrical fields at the edges of the plates. These capacitances are shown in Fig. 10.22.

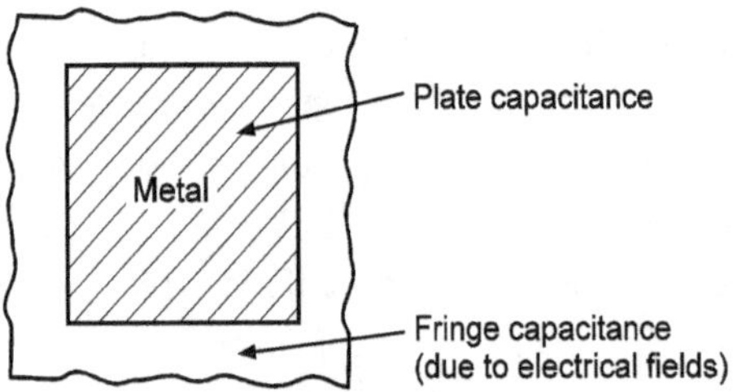

Fig. 10.22: Plate and fringe capacitances

Capacitances between different layers and wires

As the number of metal layers increases and the capacitance of the substrate decreases, wire to wire capacitance becoming more important.

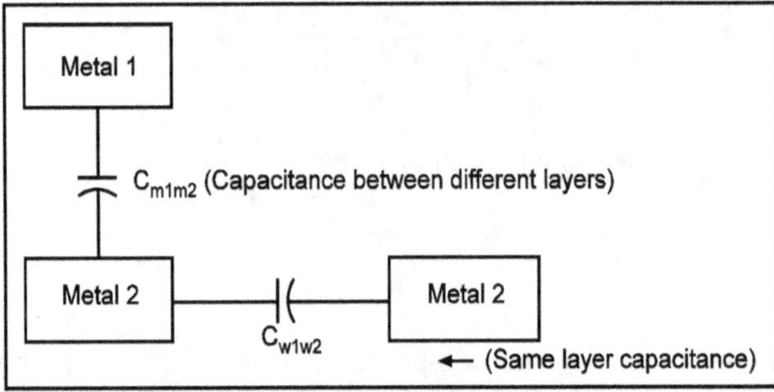

Fig. 10.23: Capacitance between same and different layers

As shown in Fig. 10.23, C_{m1m2} is the capacitance between two different layers of metal. This capacitance depends on the area of overlap between the two wires. When two wires from the different metals, run together for a long distance, with one staying over the other, the layer to layer capacitance can be very large.

C_{w1w2} is the capacitance between two wires on the same layer. This capacitance is formed by the vertical sides of the metal wires. Metal wires are very tall in relation to their width. When two wires from the same layer run in parallel for a long distance, the coupling capacitance can become very large.

10.7.2 Wire Resistance

There are also wire resistances in the circuit design. The wire resistances are computed by measuring the size of the wire in the layout. The unit of resistivity is given by ohms per square ($\Omega /\square$).

The resistance of a square unit of material is the same for a square of any size. For example, suppose, a unit square of material has a resistance of 2 Ω. When we connect two squares of material in parallel, we will get a total resistance of,

$$\frac{1}{R_{equ}} = \frac{1}{2} + \frac{1}{2}$$
$$\therefore R_{equ} = 1\Omega.$$

Now, connecting two such rectangles in series creates a 2 × 2 square with a resistance of $1\Omega + 1\Omega = 2\Omega$.

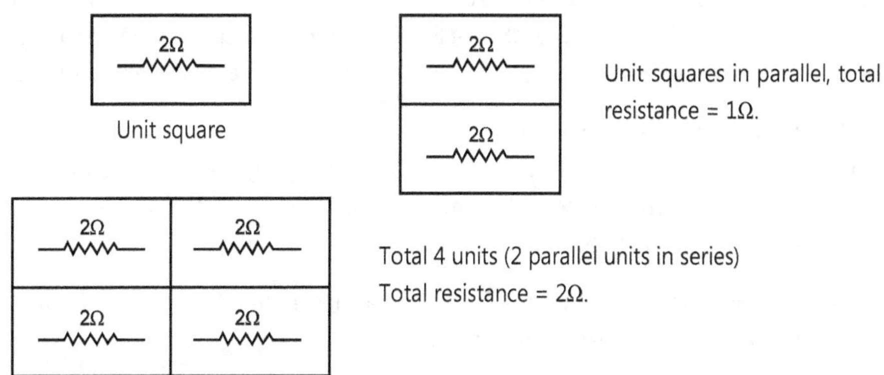

We can therefore measure the resistance of a wire by measuring its aspect ratio.

10.8 Design Validation

We are generally using simulation to validate the design. We can use different verification tools, which can automatically compare a combinational logic description or sequential machine description against the implementation. We can simulate a single description of the design, such as the register-transfer description to make sure, we designed what we wanted.

We can also compare the results of two different simulations, such as the logic and register transfer designs, to make sure that the two are equivalent. Depending on the available tool, we can use several simulators to verify the design.

We must simulate our design, before implementing it. If the specified function is wrong and do not discover the error before implementation, we will waste a lot of logic and layout design before we discover our mistake.

Following are the simulators generally used to validate the design:

(1) Register-transfer simulator

It gives the correct cycle by cycle behavior at its inputs and outputs. It is actually a functional simulation. In this, the internal implementation of the simulator has nothing to do with the logic implementation. Several specialized languages for hardware description and simulation are available, such as VHDL and VERILOG.

(2) Logic simulator

This simulator accepts net-list whose components are logic gates. This simulator evaluates the output of each logic gate based on the values presented at the gates inputs. In this, we can trace through the network to find logic bugs. We can also compare the actual value of a wire, to what we think the value should be. A library provides simulation models for the logic gates. A net-list tells the simulation system how the components are connected together.

(3) Switch simulator (Layout simulation)

It models the entire system. It includes both combinational logic gates and memory elements as a network of switches. In this, the simulator evaluates the individual nets, but the simulation is performed at a lower level of abstraction.

The switch simulation is most suitable for a circuit extracted from a complete layout. The circuit extractor generates a net-list of transistors.

Catching any errors before layout saves time and efforts. Switch simulation checks the correctness of the layout and also identifies charge sharing bugs which can be found only in a switch-level design.

A net-list comparison program can check the layout against the net-list of the logic before layout. The net-list extracted from the layout will use n-type and p-type transistors as its components.

Performance verification: In this, timing analysis algorithms are used to ensure that the chip runs at the required rate. Timing or circuit simulation can be used to optimize paths which are expected to be critical. Timing analysis ensures that the paths which are optimized, are in fact the critical paths.

Floor planning is used to estimate the size and set the initial relative locations of the various blocks in our ASIC. It is also used to allocate the space for clock and power wiring. Also decides the location of the I/O and power pads.

10.9 Floorplanning

Floorplanning is actually a chip-level layout design. Floorplanning uses adders, registers and FSMs as the building blocks. The layout program must place the components on the chip by position and orientation, leaving sufficient space between the components for the necessary wires. To improve the floorplan, blocks must be redesigned. **Floorplanning**, **Placement** and **Routing** are the **back end tools**.

Floorplanning has three phases: Block Placement, Global Routing and Detailed Routing.

Block Placement: As the name indicates, places the blocks on the chip.

Global Routing: Assigns wires to routing channels between the blocks.

Detailed Routing: Designs the layouts for the wiring.

Comparison of Placement and Routing

Placement

- Defines the location of logic cells.
- Sets space for the interconnection between each logic cells.
- Assigns each logic cell to a position in a row.

Routing

- Makes the connections between logic cells.
- Global routing: Determines where the interconnections between the placed logic cells and blocks will be placed. (Please check?)
- Local routing: Joins the logic cells with interconnects.

Floorplanning

Goals: Calculate the sizes of all the blocks and assign them locations.

Objective: Keep the highly connected blocks close.

- **Placement:**

Goals: Assign the interconnect areas and location of the logic cells.

Objectives: Minimize the ASIC area and the interconnect density.

- **Global Routing:**

Goals: Determine the location of all the interconnects.

Objectives: Minimize the total interconnect area used.

- **Detailed Routing:**
  Goals: Completely route all the interconnects on the chip.
  Objectives: Minimize the total interconnect length used.

Interactive floorplan editors and global placement and routing tools are used mostly in floorplan design. Floorplanning tools allow us to enter blocks with pinouts, plot the rat's nests to evaluate routability, define routing channels and also perform global routing. Global layout tools perform the job of detailed block placement, global routing and detailed routing.

Power, ground nets and clocks have specialized requirements for routing to the blocks. Power (V_{DD}) and ground (V_{SS}) nets must be supplied to the logic gates with minimal voltage drop and must be adequately wide to carry the required current. Clocks must be distributed to minimize the skew. We need to take special care on both power / ground and clock nets in large chips.

Fig. 10.24 shows the floorplan sketch. The first step in floorplanning is to arrange the blocks to minimize wasted space.

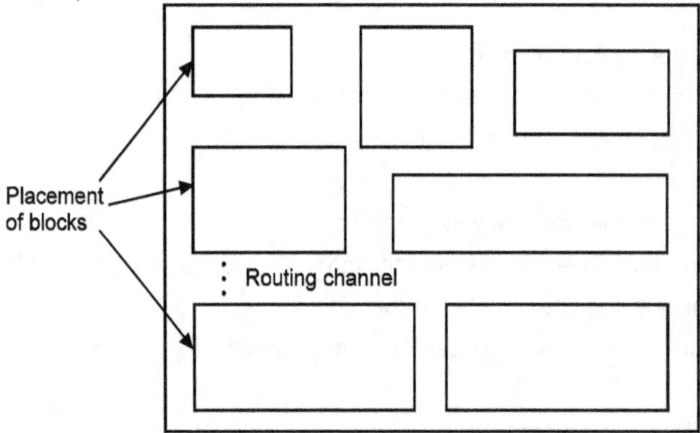

Fig. 10.24: Floorplan sketch

To experiment the floorplan, is to draw the blocks on graph paper, cut them out, and arrange them on another block of graph paper. The wiring between the blocks can be used to adjust the positions of the blocks. We need to try different rotations and reflections of the blocks. If the blocks are similar, they are easier to change. Interchangeability makes wiring optimization easier.

Floorplanning and block design should go hand in hand to get best results. If area is important, floorplanning before block design help guide the design of blocks.

Most placement decisions are determined by the space needed for wires, not block shape. Therefore, floorplanning without consideration of routing is dangerous. A **switchbox** is a routing area with connections anywhere along its four sides; we must define routing channels and switchboxes, during placement of boxes.

Channel Definition: We need to break up the space between the blocks into rectangular regions for simplicity during detailed routing, this is known as channel definition. Fig. 10.25 shows that by changing the block spacing, we can form the rectangular routing channel. We know the space required between two blocks only after we know the number of wires routed through the channel.

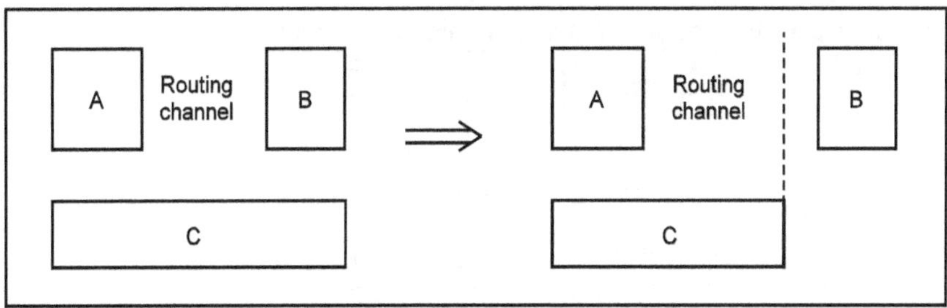

Fig. 10.25: Block spacing changes the channel definition

There are several ways to route the channels as shown in Figs. 10.26, 10.27 and 10.28.

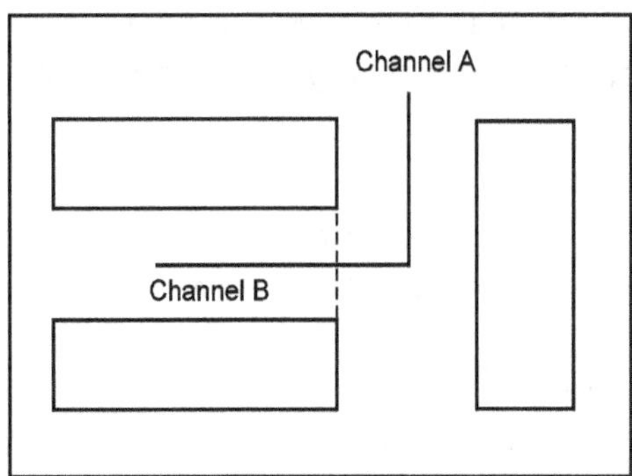

Fig. 10.26: Channels must be routed in order

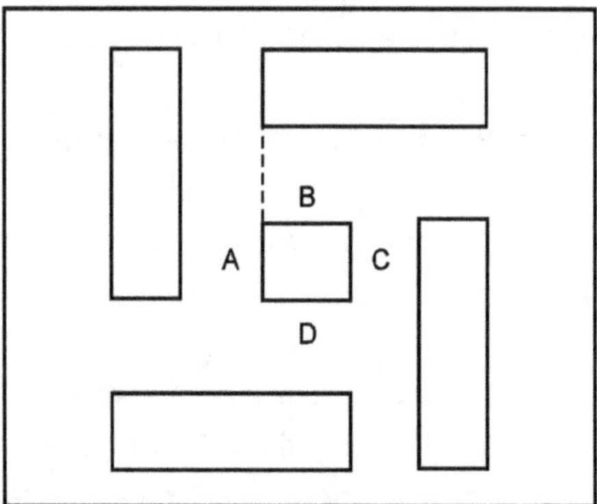

Fig. 10.27: Windmill structure

Windmill structure introduces irresolvable constraints on the routing order.

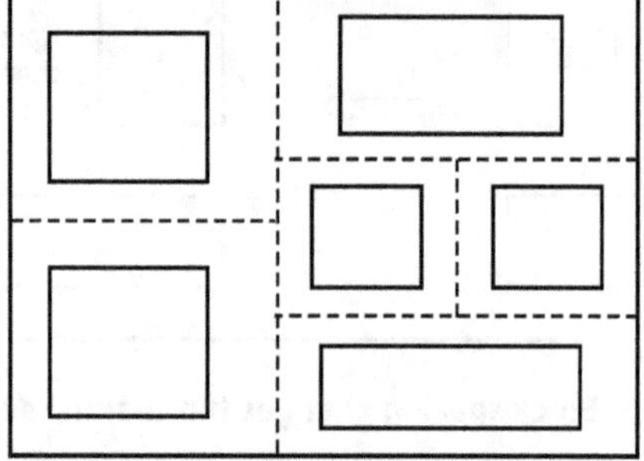

Fig. 10.28: A slicable floorplan

A slicable structure can be recursively sliced down to different blocks.

Now, we will study the details of Global Routing and Switchbox Routing.

10.9.1 Global Routing

The global routing is used to assign each net a route through a set of areas (net means a wire). Global routing uses available routing channels to avoid wasting chip area.

Optimal routing for a single net is much easier than optimal routing of a sequence of nets. Generally, most layout systems work by routing nets one wire at a time, choosing the order of nets to route by some method which gives good results.

There are various algorithms for global routing. Maze routing also called as Lee / Moore algorithm, finds the shortest path for a single wire between a set of points, if any path exists. The maze algorithm is as follows:

The algorithm works in two phases.

    (1) Points on the grid are iteratively labelled with their distance from a source point. All points at distance 1 from the source are labelled with 1, as shown in Fig. 10.29.

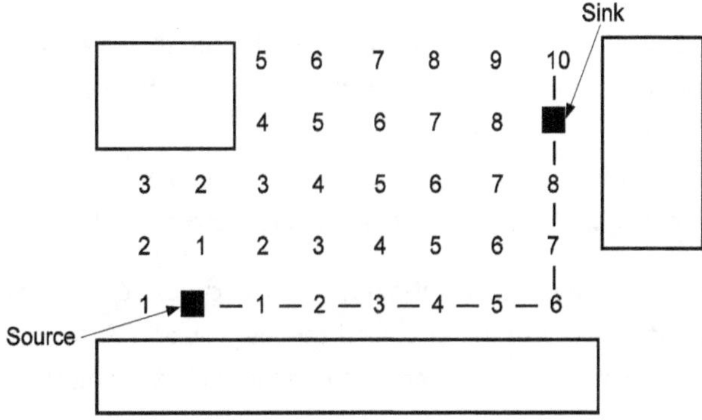

Fig. 10.29: Maze routing algorithm

    (2) In second iteration, all unlabelled points adjacent to the 1 point are labelled with 2 and so on.

    (3) The labelling stops when the sink of the net to be routed is found.

    (4) After that, a route is traced back from the sink to the source.

There are many possible paths back to the source, but only one is shown in Fig. 10.29. From Fig. 10.29, we can observe that, the traced path is the shortest path. This algorithm has a high cost in both memory and CPU time. The grid map takes more memory. If the distances are stored in chip units, then an n × m chip requires a map of n × m integers. To avoid this memory problem, it is possible to reduce each grid point to two bits, the algorithm does not need to know the exact distance from the source, only the direction to travel more close to the source, but even with this, the array is large.

The second algorithm for hand routing is the **line-probe method**, introduced by Mikami, Tubuchi and Hightower. This algorithm can work on arbitrary-shaped routing regions. As shown in Fig. 10.29, this algorithm starts at one pin on the net and constructs a series of line along which the other pin may lie. This algorithm may not find the shortest route for the wire; it also may not find an existing path. But, it often works in practice and the advantage is that it is **very fast**.

Global routing should be such that, it should give the best detailed routing for all the channels and switchboxes. Our goal is to assign wires to paths such that all channels are about equally full. The following are the rules:

(1) We need to route those nets whose delays are critical. These wires need to be as short as possible, so they should get priority for the channels and give the shortest path.

(2) Sometimes, we need to reroute the wires. We must route the wires in some order. If the earlier decision was bad, remove the wires that are in the way, route the new wires, then reroute the ripped-up wires.

(3) Sometimes, some wires are accommodated within one channel or require a short trip between few channels. We need to route these wires early to get them out of the way.

We need to go through the placement-global routing cycles several times. If necessary, we need to change the floorplan to get around serious problems. Floorplans are complex a change in one wire's route may make another important wire's route much worse.

10.9.2 Switchbox Routing

As already mentioned, a switchbox is a routing area with connections anywhere along its four sides. Switchbox routing is actually harder than channel routing, because we cannot expand switchbox to make room for more wires.

As shown in Fig. 10.30, a switchbox is used to route wires between two intersecting channels.

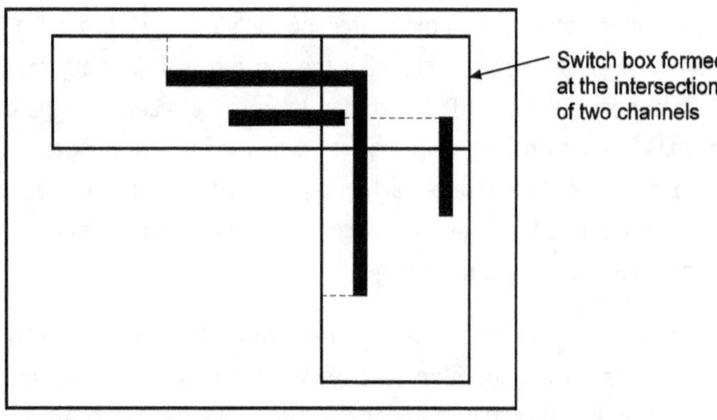

Fig. 10.30: Switchbox routing

The track assignment at the ends of the channels defines the pins for the switchbox. Net ordering can be critical when routing switchboxes as shown in Fig. 10.31.

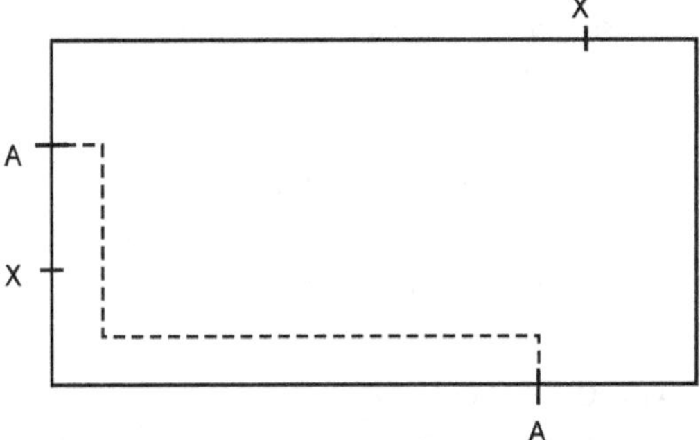

Fig. 10.31: Switchbox attempting to use same layer

While routing both horizontal and vertical segments of a wire, it is tempting to use the same layer, but there may be a problem as shown in Fig. 10.31. If A and X pins are on the same layer, routing A as shown completely blocks X. It means there is no space to insert a via for the net, as it is from the same layer.

So, we avoid such problems, for switchbox routing, is to arbitrarily pick layers for vertical and horizontal segments, than to treat the switchbox as a routing problem with fixed pins at the ends of the channel. Switchbox routing algorithm may sometimes fail due to the added constraints. Channel routing algorithms can often give reasonably good results in such circumstances.

Some simple rules of thumb for floorplanning:
(1) Combine small components into larger blocks:
The block diagram has isolated gates or slightly larger components. The small component creates lots of problems during floorplanning. For the placement of small components, we require extra efforts, and they disrupt the flow of wires across the chip. We can combine these small components into an existing larger block or create a glue logic block to contain all the miscellaneous elements.

(2) Develop a wiring plan:
Use different layers for different directions or for different types of nets. Sketch a plan on a graph paper to think about rational regular schemes for assigning layers to wires.

(3) Design a simple wiring plan:
It will be harder to change the design, when you need to make larger changes, move blocks then move pin locations to simplify routing topology.

(4) Design planar wiring:

A planar wiring means, all the nets are routed in the plane without crossing. First design a floorplan on which the most important signals have a planar routing, and then add the less critical signals later.

(5) Power and clock signals require separate wiring plans:

We need a separate chart of power and clock routing that helps us to convince that our design is good for signals, power and clock.

10.9.3 Off-Chip-Connections

Chips are encased in packages. Through the packages the connections are made to the outside world. So, we need to study the details of the packages.

Packages

The main functions of the packages are:

(1) It gives the chip mechanical support.

(2) It conducts heat away from the chip to the environment.

(3) To protect the chip from chemical damage. Ceramic package is most commonly used to protect the chip from chemical damage.

(4) The pins of packages provide manageable solder connection.

The structure of a typical package is shown in Fig. 10.32. As shown, the chip fits in a cavity of the package. The circuit board connects the pins at the edge of the package. Wiring built into the package goes from the pins to the edge of the cavity. Very fine bonding wires are connected to the packages lead by robot machine to the chip's pads.

Pads: Pads are actually the metal rectangles large enough to be soldered to the leads. Pads used to connect the chip's internals to the package and surrounding circuitry. The cavity, on which the chip sits, is gold plated to provide a connection to the chips substrates for application of a bias voltage. Bonding pads, which are used to connect to the package's pins, surround the four sides of the cavity. Ceramic packages offer better heat conductivity and environmental protection.

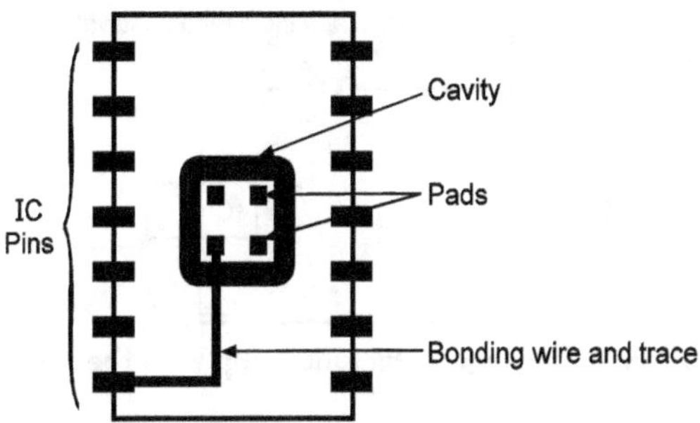

Fig. 10.32: A package structure

There are different types of packages. These packages have different pins and they vary in cost. As the number of pins of the packages increase, the cost will also increase. Examples of packages are as follows:

(1) DIP (Dual in-Line Package): It is the cheapest and has the fewest number of pads.

(2) PGA (Pin Grid Array): It has pins all over its bottom and can accommodate about 256 pins.

(3) BGA (Ball Grid Array) : It uses solder balls to connect to the package across the entire bottom of the package.

(4) PLCC (Plastic Leadless Chip Carrier) : It has pins around its four edges. These leads are designed to be connected to PCBs without through-board holes.

(5) PQFP (Plastic Quad Flat Pack) : It is similar to the PLCC but has a different pin geometry.

Because of the limited pinout of the packages, they introduce system complications. Generally, 256 are the lot of pins. Off-chip bandwidth is one of the important commodities in high performance designs.

There are some electrical problems in the packages. The most common problems are due to the inductance of the pins and the PCB attached to them. The inductance of the on-chip wire has negligible value, but the inductance due to the package can introduce significant voltage fluctuations.

The package inductance causes the most problems on the power line because the largest current swing occurs on power line pin. Inductance can also cause problem in very high frequency parts. Now, we will see how this inductance causes the problem on power line. The system's complete power circuit looks like as shown in Fig. 10.33.

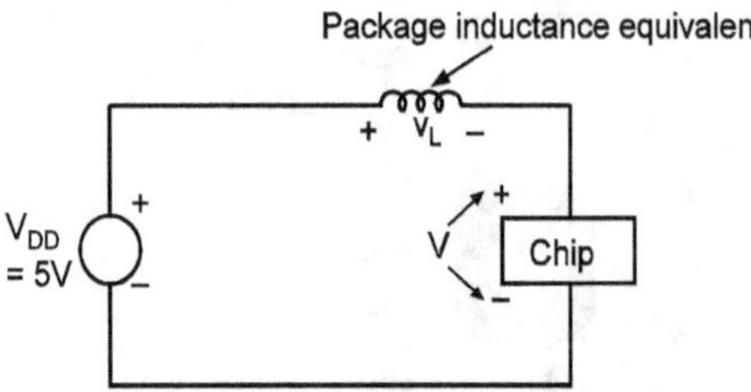

Fig. 10.33: Package inductance chip with the supply

As shown, the power supply is connected externally to the chip. The package inductance comes in series with the power supply and chip. The voltage across the inductance is given by,

$$v_L = L\frac{di_L}{dt}$$

In steady-state condition, the voltage drop across the inductance is almost zero. But, if the current supplied by the power supply changes abruptly, then voltage drop across inductance increases suddenly (i.e. v_L). Due to this, the voltage which actually appears across the chip decreases by the same amount. Suppose power supply current changes by 0.8 A in 1 ns and value of package and PCB inductance is 0.5 nH. This gives a peak voltage drop of,

$$v_L = 0.5 \times 10^{-9}\,H \times 0.8A/1 \times 10^{-9}\,s = 0.4\,V$$
$$\therefore \quad v_L = 0.4\,V$$

This v_L, voltage drop across inductance is large enough to cause dynamic circuits to malfunction.

To remove such type of problem, we need to add multiple power and ground pins. By adding multiple power and ground pins in parallel, we can distribute the current to reduce di/dt in each pin, which reduces the total voltage drop. For example, the first generation of Intel Pentium package has total 497 V_{CC} pins and 497 V_{SS} pins.

10.10 I/O Architecture

Pads are used to connect the chip's internal circuitry to the package and surrounding circuitry i.e. inputs/outputs. Pads are distributed around the edge of the chip. In advanced, high density packaging schemes devote a layer of metal to pads and this metal is distributed across the entire chip face. The pad must be large enough to have a wire soldered to it. Each pad has its standard width and height for simplicity. A typical pad structure frame is shown in Fig. 10.34.

As shown in Fig. 10.34, the pad has large V_{DD} and V_{SS} lines running through it. As shown a pad includes a large piece of metal to which the external wire is soldered. In the middle of the pad ring, there is a **chip core**. The pads must be arranged in certain order, to get the required connections.

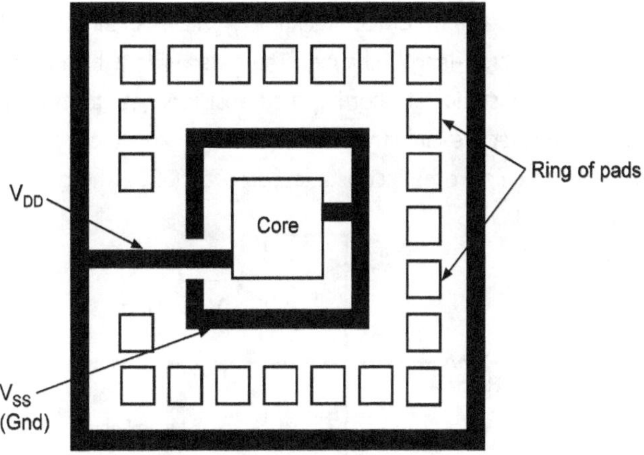

Fig. 10.34: Structure of a pad frame

If all the pad pins are not used, spacers are added to keep the power lines connected. The wires connected to the package should not be crossed without the danger of shorting.

Routability of the board and electrical noise are generally determined by the order of the pins on the package. The order of pins is very important, as it determines which manufacturer wins a design contest. V_{DD} and V_{SS} pads are much larger than other pads, as these pads need to carry large amount of current. So, the design of V_{SS} and V_{DD} are simple as compared to other pads. Generally, multiple power pins are used to limit inductive voltage drop.

10.10.1 Pad Design in a Chip

We need to design the pad very carefully to protect the chip from static electricity. Therefore, pads which are used for input and output signals require different supporting circuitry. The pads which are used as bidirectional (both input and output) sometimes called as Tri-state pin, combines elements of both input and output pads.

10.10.1.1 Input Pad Design

The main job of input pad is to protect the chip's internal circuitry from static electricity. During handling of the chip, large static voltage may be developed in a pin, which may cause damage to the chip. We are using CMOS technology for manufacturing the chip. CMOS circuits are very sensitive to static discharge because of the thin oxide used in the CMOS design. We have already seen in CMOS technology, how small the gate oxide is in comparison with the submicron-length channel. The gate oxide, which is very thin, can be totally destroyed by a single static jolt, shorting the transistors gate to its channel. Therefore, we need to add some protective circuitry between the pad and the transistor gates in the chip core. To protect the chip from Electrostatic discharge (ESD), the protection circuitry is added as shown in Fig. 10.35.

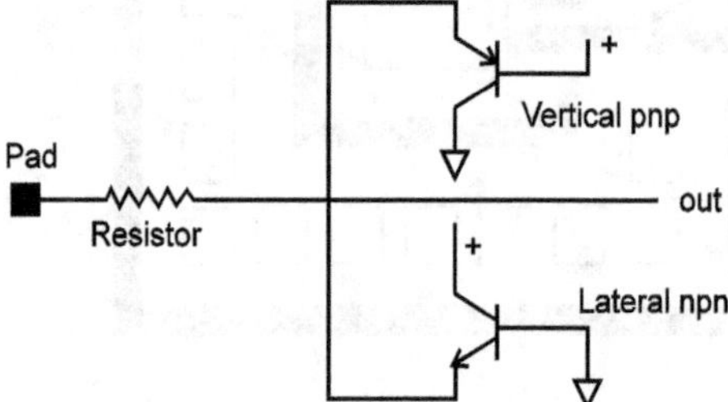

Fig. 10.35: Input pad protection circuitry

Electrostatic discharge can cause two types of problems. These problems are dielectric rupture and charge injection. The charge injected by an electrostatic discharge event can be sufficient to damage the internal circuitry of the chip. When the dielectric ruptures, chip structures can short together, causing damage. As shown in Fig. 10.36, the resistor which is usually made of a long diffusion run between the pad and the protection circuitry. The resistor is used to limit the current caused by a voltage spike. As shown, parasitic bipolar transistors are used as diodes to draw excess current from the output node.

The pnp transistor is used to protect the chip from high positive voltage which appears to the input pad. When input pad voltage goes above V_{DD} by 0.7V, the pnp transistor turns on and limits the positive going voltage. Similarly npn transistor is used to protect the chip from negative going voltage, 0.7V below V_{SS}. The standard mask is used to design both npn and pnp transistors as shown in Fig. 10.36. The layout must be carefully designed to minimize the chance of latch-up.

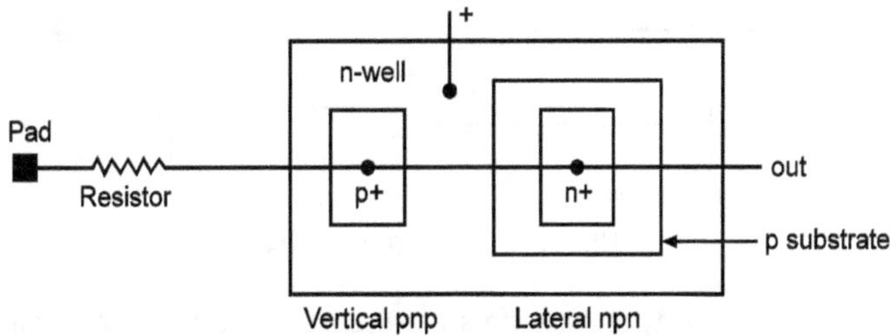

Fig. 10.36: Layout of protection circuitry at input pad

10.10.1.2 Output Pad Design

The output pad should be able to drive the large capacitance seen on the output pin. The output pad circuitry includes a chain of inverters to drive the large off-chip load. The final stages use very large transistors as shown in Fig. 10.37. Therefore creative layout techniques are used to reduce the pad's size. The transistors near the output pad are often folded to reduce pad's height. The transistors may also be wrapped around the extra space surrounding the pad.

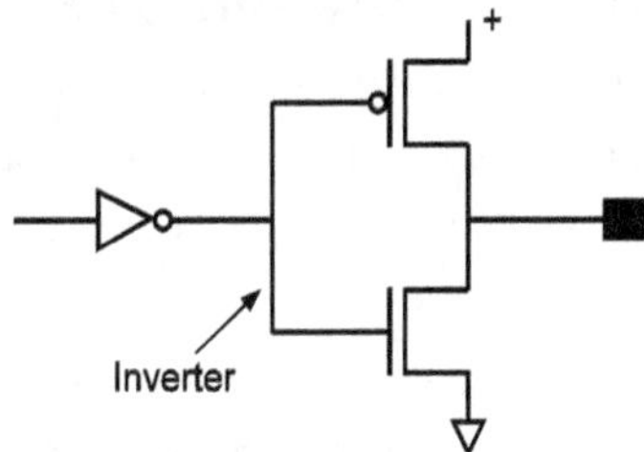

Fig. 10.37: An output pad circuit

10.10.1.3 Three State Pad Design

This pad is used for both input and output. These pads are used to solve the problem of pin count. We cannot use the same pad simultaneously as input or output. The chip core is responsible for switching between input or output mode. As already mentioned, electrostatic protection is required, when the pad is used as an input pad and output driver is required, when it is used as an output pad. We also need circuitry to switch the pad between input and output modes. Fig. 10.38 shows the circuit which is used for mode switching.

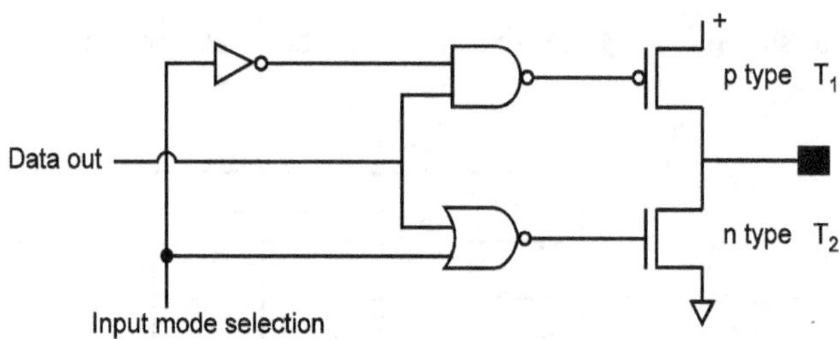

Fig. 10.38: Three state pad circuit

As shown, the n type and p type transistors are used to drive the three state pad in the output mode. When the input mode selection is '0', the logic gates are arranged so that the output signal turns on exactly one of the two transistors. When the input mode selection is '1' the NOR gate emits a '0', turning off the pull-down (T_2) and the NAND gate emits a '1', turning off the pull-up (T_1). In this case, when both driver transistors are disabled, the pad can be used as an input.

We need to add circuitry to the pad to support boundary scan. Chips which are supporting boundary scan can be chained to form a single scan path for all the chips on a printed circuit board.

10.11 Layout Design Rules and Analysis Tools in CMOS

A variety of tools are available that help us to design and verify outputs. The most important tools are layout editors, design rule checkers and circuit extractors.

10.11.1 A Layout Editor

It is actually an interactive graphic program that lets you create and delete layout elements. Magic is a layout editor, which works on symbolic layouts. Magic includes detail than do stick diagrams but are still more abstract than par layouts. Symbolic layout has many advantages, such as the layout is easier to specify because it is composed of fewer elements. In this the same symbolic layout can be used to generate several variations such as n-tub, p-tub and twin-tub versions of a symbolic design.

10.11.2 Design Rule Checker (DRC) Program

DRC looks for design rule violations in the layout. DRC program checks the CMOS rules while laying out different layers on the grid, such as minimum size of the layer, minimum spacing between two layers, DRC ensures that combinations of layers form legal components. After laying out layers, design rule checker program is executed and it shows the results in the form of highlights, on top of the layout. Microwind uses DRC, which provides on-line design rule checking.

10.11.3 Circuit Extraction

This program is an extension of the design rule checking. A circuit extractor performs a job of component and wire extraction. Circuit extractor produces a net list. This net list contains the transistors in the layout and the electrical nets which connect their terminals. The circuit extractor is generally used to measure parasitic resistance and capacitance on the wires.

For the semiconductor manufacturer and the chip designer, we need to provide mask database. The mask database is actually the interface between the semiconductor manufacturers and chip designer. For this mask database, **two basic checks** have to be completed, to ensure that this database turned into a working chip. The first check is based on the **specified geometric** design rules. This program checks the geometrical rules of the mask database. Second check is for interrelationship of the masks. To check these two requirements, two basic CAD tools are required, namely a Design Rule Check (DRC) program and a mask circuit-extraction program. To implement these tools, is to provide a set of subprograms that perform general geometry operations.

So, there are set of DRC rules and extraction rules for a given CMOS process. These rules are provided by a specification of the operation that must be performed on each mask.

10.12 Memory Elements

A circuit that can hold a binary value as required by the system is called as memory cell. It is basically a data storage device. Memories are required for different functions such as:

1) To store monitor programs.

2) To store user programs.

3) To store data.

Each memory cell is capable of storing one bit of data. General memory cell is shown in Fig. 10.39. There are basically three operations to characterize the memory cell: **write, hold** and **read**.

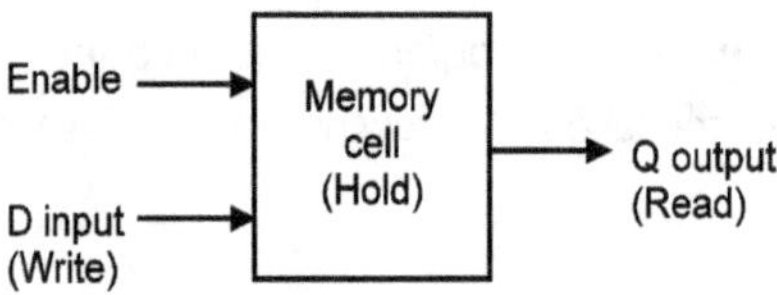

Fig. 10.39: General memory cell

10.12.1 High Density Memories

By using analog design methods, we can build memories that are both smaller and faster. Now-a-days, on-chip memories are becoming increasingly important. As the levels of integration increase, we can build both processors and useful amounts of memory on a single chip. On-chip memories can be engineered to be very fast and to have unique access paths.

Memory elements are basically divided into following categories:

1) Random Access Memory

2) Serial Access Memory

3) Content Access Memory

In random access memory, the physical location of data is not important, while accessing the data. Due to this the access time is reduced, which increases the speed. But, in case of serial access memories, the physical location of data is important, there is some latency associated with the reading or writing of a particular datum.

Random access memory is again classified into different types, RAM and ROM as shown in Fig. 10.40.

ROM as the name implies can be read but not written. ROM is generally used to store data or program, values that will not change. ROMs generally have a write time much greater than their read time. ROM memory classification is also shown in Fig. 10.40. In masked ROM data is permanently stored at the time of manufacturing as per requirement. The data cannot be altered in masked ROM. In Programmable Read Only Memory (PROM), user can load his program only once.

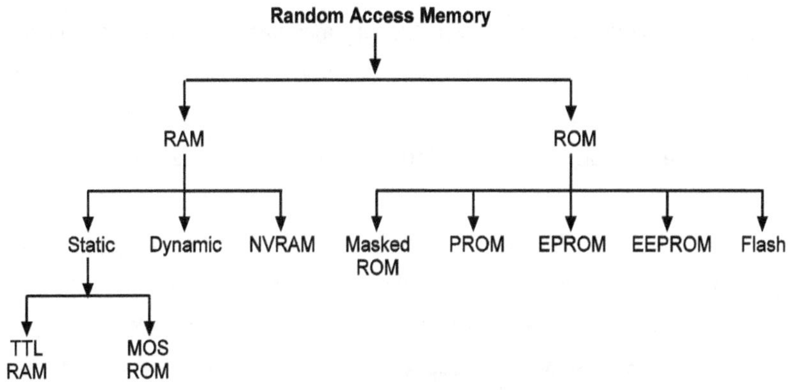

Fig. 10.40: Classification of Random Access Memory

EPROM (Erasable Programmable Read Only Memory) is programmable by user. It uses MOS circuitry to store data. They store 1's and 0's in the form of charge. The data stored can be erased by exposing the memory to ultraviolet light. After erasing it can be reprogrammed by EPROM programmer. The advantage of EPROM is that it can be programmed, erased and reprogrammed. The disadvantage of this is that, all the data get erased even if you want to change single bit of data. Also the erasure time is more, around 20-30 minutes.

EEPROM (Electrically Erasable Programmable Read Only Memory) is similar to EPROM, except that the erasing is done by electrical signals instead of ultraviolet light. The main advantage of EEPROM is the memory location can be selectively erased and reprogrammed. But, the drawback is that, the manufacturing process is complex and expensive, so not commonly used.

Flash Memory is the dominant form of EEPROM. The main advantage of flash memory is that it takes very short time to erase the data.

10.12.2 RAM

RAM memories have very similar read and write times. RAM memories are also classified according to the mode of operation as:

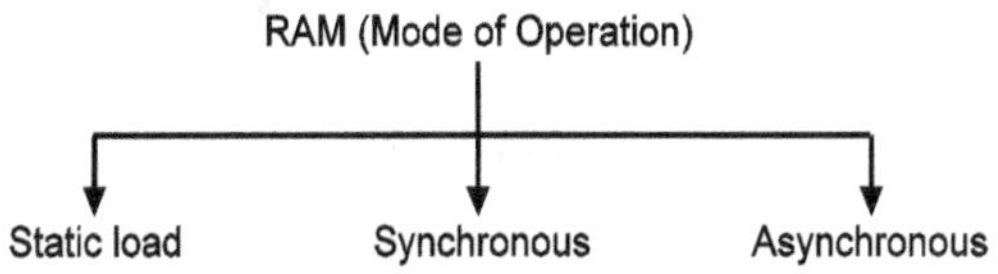

Static load memories require no clock. Synchronous memories require a clock to enable the operation. It operates on clock edge or clock level. Asynchronous RAM recognizes address changes and output new data after any such address change. Static load and synchronous memories are easier to design as compared to asynchronous memories.

The memory cells used in RAMs are also divided into static SRAMs and dynamic DRAMs. SRAM and DRAM use different circuits, each of which has its own advantages. SRAM is faster, but it uses more power and is larger. DRAM takes less space and uses less power. But, the DRAM cells are somewhat slower and require refreshing of memory. Static RAMs are easier to design and less troublesome than Dynamic RAMs.

10.12.3 Memory-Chip Architecture

Large memories often divide the address into row and column sections. These row and column addresses are sent to the memory separately. A typical memory chip architecture is shown in Fig. 10.41. A row (or word) decoder addresses one word and the column decoder (or bit decoder) addresses bits of the accessed row. The column decoder accesses a multiplexer, which routes the addressed data to and from interfaces to the external world.

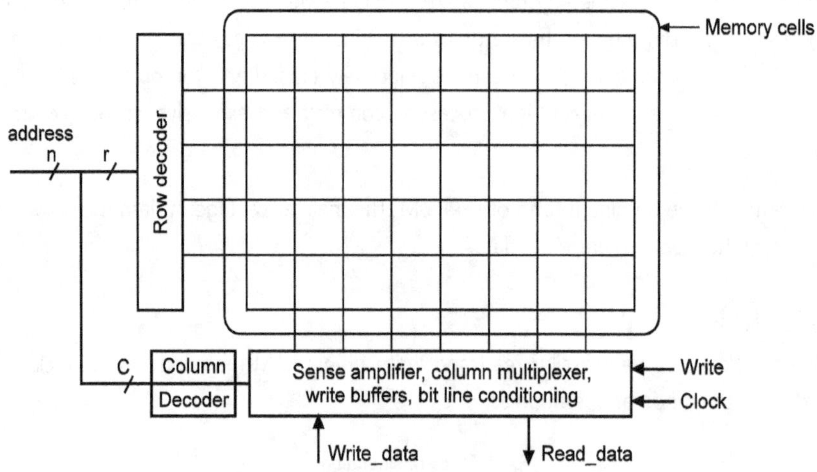

Fig. 10.41: Architecture of memory-chip

The sense amplifiers, column multiplexer, write buffers and bit-line conditioning circuitry form a tightly coupled circuit that provide for the hazard-free reading and writing of the memory cell. The bit line conditioning circuitry provides bit lines, which run as complementary signals. There are many variations for these circuits to achieve varying density/speed/noise-margin requirements. In many cases, the column decoder may be merged with the column multiplexer.

10.12.4 Static RAM

Static RAM is capable of holding the stored data as long as the power is connected to the electronic circuit. It is based on the characteristic of a closed loop containing two inverters connected as shown in Fig. 10.42.

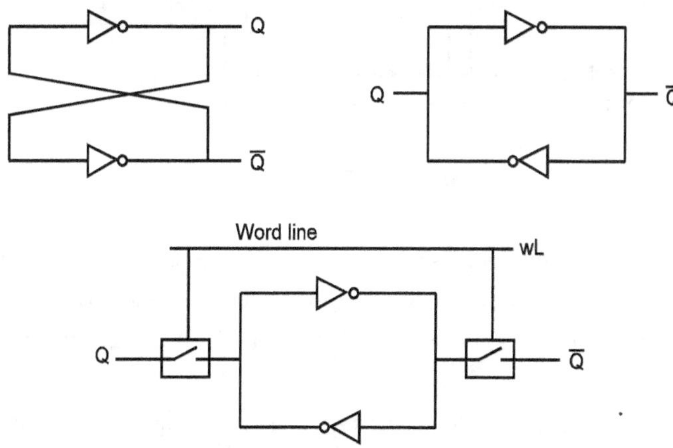

Fig. 10.42: Basic Static RAM cell

Depending on the components used to build up flip flop, the static RAM is classified into two types, TTL RAM cell and MOS RAM cell.

10.12.4.1 TTL RAM Cell

As shown in Fig. 10.43, two transistors Q_1 and Q_2 form cross coupled inverter, in which one transistor is always ON and the other transistor is OFF. X and Y select lines are connected to the Row and Column select lines. Both X and Y select lines are normally low, so a current will pass through Q_1 and Q_2 transistors to ground.

When both X and Y select lines are made high, the current will start flowing through one of the sense amplifier emitters. The sense amplifier detects the current passing through emitter and knows the data stored whether it is zero or one.

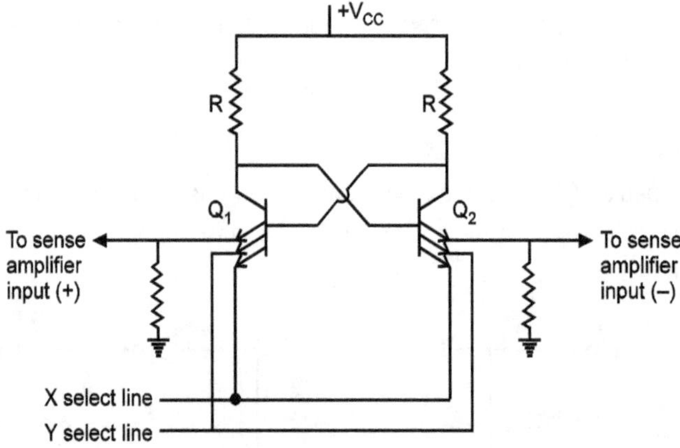

Fig. 10.43: TTL RAM cell

Read Operation: Sense amplifier is used to detect the current passing through the emitter of Q_1 and Q_2 transistors. As shown, emitter of Q_1 is connected to the positive input of sense amplifier. Therefore logic '1' is stored in cell if Q_1 transistor is ON and Q_2 transistor is OFF.

Write Operation: To store logic '0' in the cell, Q_1 must be turned OFF. Since Q_1 is OFF, transistor Q_2 will become ON.

10.12.4.2 MOS RAM Cell

It consists of two cross coupled MOS inverters T_1 and T_3 as shown in Fig. 10.44.

Transistors T_2 and T_4 are connected as load instead of resistors. X and Y select lines are used to address and select the memory cell. When X select line is at logic '1', transistors T_5 and T_6 will become ON and Data and $\overline{Data}$ line are connected to the cell. Similarly, when Y select line is at logic '1' transistors T_7 and T_8 will become ON and we can perform Read and Write operation. It means to perform any operation with the memory cell, we need to keep X and Y select lines at logic '1'.

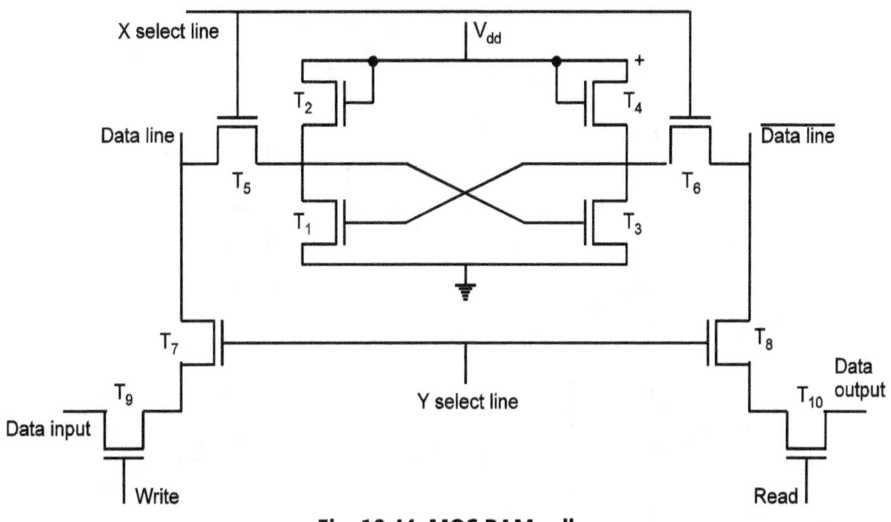

Fig. 10.44: MOS RAM cell

Read Operation: When the Read signal goes high, transistor T_{10} will become ON and the status of $\overline{\text{Data line}}$ will be available at the Data output line.

Write Operation: To write into the cell, write signal must be active (logic '1'). When write signal goes high, T_9 will become ON. If Data input = '1', the voltage on Data line will be logic '1', making T_3 ON and $\overline{\text{Data line}}$ goes low. Similarly, if Data input = '0' then T_3 will become OFF and $\overline{\text{Data line}}$ goes high.

10.12.5 Dynamic RAM

Basically, in Dynamic RAM cells, the data is stored in the form of charge on capacitors. There are various ways to implement dynamic RAM as shown in Fig. 10.45.

A three transistor Dynamic RAM cell is shown in Fig. 10.45 (a). The cell stores data on the gate of the storage transistor. Separate Read and Write control signals are used. To perform write operation, when write line goes high, transistor T_1 will become ON and if write data is at logic '1', capacitor C gets charged to logic '1'.

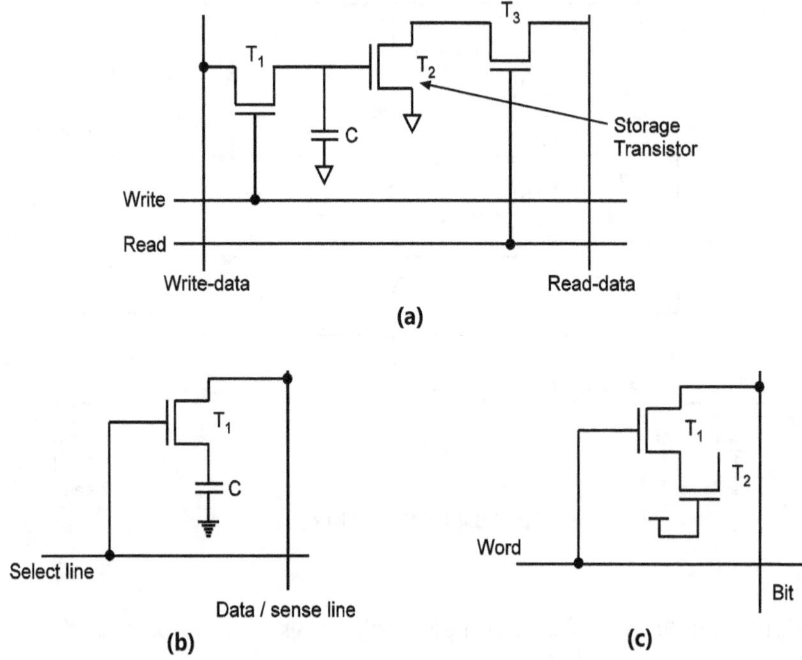

Fig. 10.45: Dynamic RAM circuit

Similarly Fig. 10.45 (b) shows one transistor and a capacitor. Transistor T_1 is used simply as a switch; it connects data/sense line to the storage capacitor 'C', when its select line is active.

To write data into cell: When data = '1' and select line is active, T_1 transistor is ON and storage capacitor gets charged to logic '1'. When select line goes low, T_1 transistor is OFF and storage capacitor retains its charge.

To read the cell: Select line is made active and voltage of storage capacitor is sensed by using sense line. If capacitor is charged, logic '1' will be available at sense line.

Fig. 10.45 (c) shows that, capacitor can be implemented as a transistor. As shown in Fig. 10.45 (c), transistor T_1 acts as the select transistor and transistor T_2 acts as the capacitor.

The two major techniques for DRAM fabrication are the stacked capacitor and the trench capacitor. Fig. 10.46 shows the trench capacitor cell cross section. As shown, a trench is etched into the chip, then oxide is formed and the trench is filled with the polysilicon. In this structure, bottom plate of the capacitor is automatically connected to the grounded substrate. A contact is used to directly connect the polysilicon plate to the access transistor.

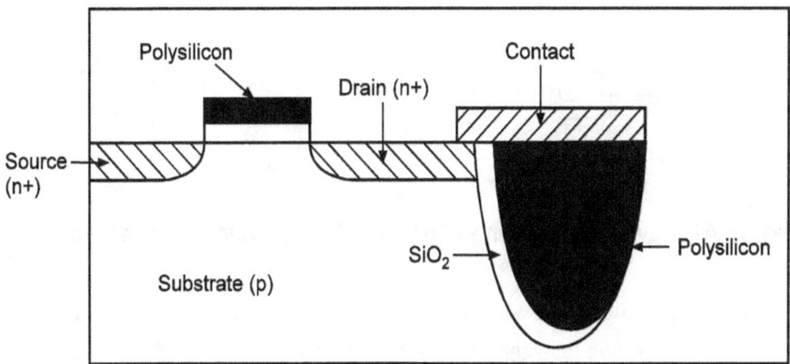

Fig. 10.46: One transistor DRAM cell using trench capacitor

For most high density DRAM cells, one transistor DRAM cell with one capacitor is most commonly used. The main drawback of Dynamic RAM cell is the loss of the stored charge due to leakage or stray substrate currents created by surrounding digital logic.

10.12.6 Non Volatile RAM (NVRAM)

It is a combination of RAM and EEPROM. By combining static RAM / EEPROM, one can save contents of RAM into EEPROM in case of power failure. Special signals are required and are available to transfer the contents of RAM in parallel to EEPROM within very less time. The main advantage of NVRAM is that no battery backup is required to convert volatile to non-volatile memory. But, NVRAM is complex in nature and are costly.

10.12.7 Row Decoders in RAM Cells

Fig. 10.47 shows a row decoder using an AND gate. It is actually a static complementary NAND gate followed by an inverter. The NAND transistors are generally made of small size to reduce the load on the buffered address lines. This row decoder is the simplest form of row decoder.

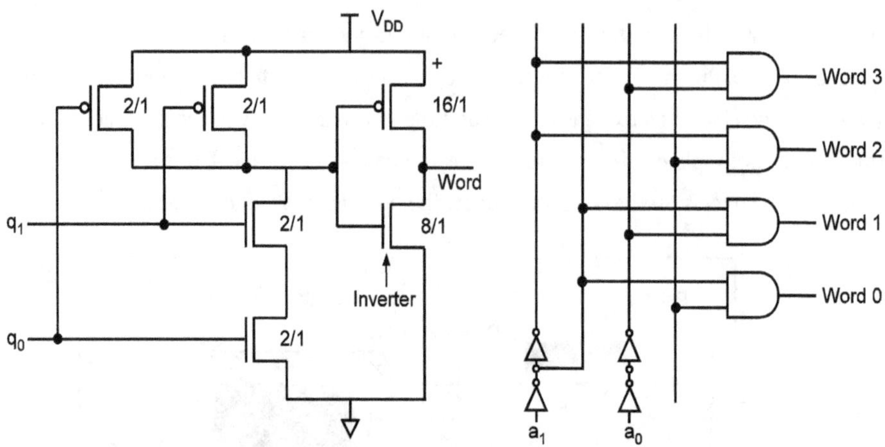

Fig. 10.47: Row decoder using AND (NAND gate followed by an inverter)

The second implementation of row decoder is shown in Fig. 10.48. It uses a pseudo n-MOS NOR gate buffered with two inverters. The NOR transistor can be made of minimum size and the inverters can be scaled to drive the word line as shown in Fig. 10.48.

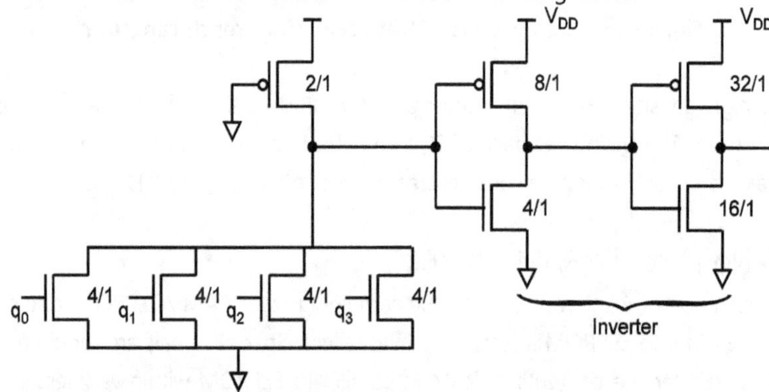

Fig. 10.48: Pseudo n-MOS gate for row decoder

We can also use smaller NAND and NOR gates to construct large fan-in AND gates as shown in Fig. 10.49.

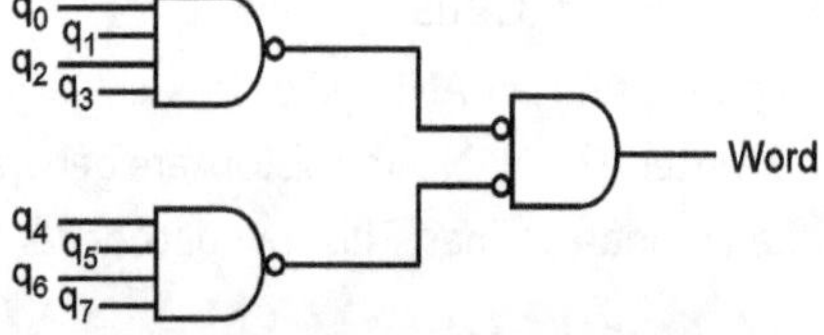

Fig. 10.49: Cascaded NAND-NOR gates

Column Decoder

It is also called as the bit decoder. It is used to select data bits from the accessed row. A tree decoder is shown below in Fig. 10.50.

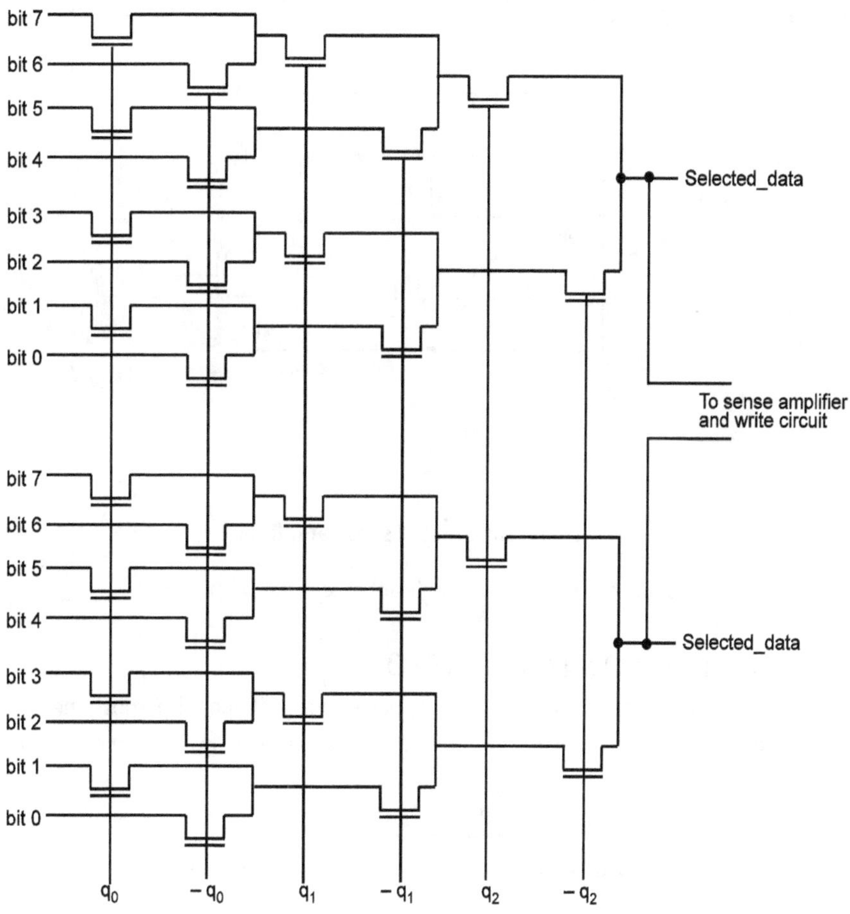

Fig. 10.50: Column decoder (Tree style)

In this the data is routed via the pass gates, which are enabled by the column address lines. Decoders for bit and bit lines are shown.

10.12.8 Sense Amplifiers

These amplifiers are used to sense the output bits. Different sense amplifiers have been invented to provide faster sensing, smaller layout and low power-dissipation sensing. The simple inverter sense amplifier provides for low power sensing at the expense of speed. The differential sense amplifier is shown in Fig. 10.51.

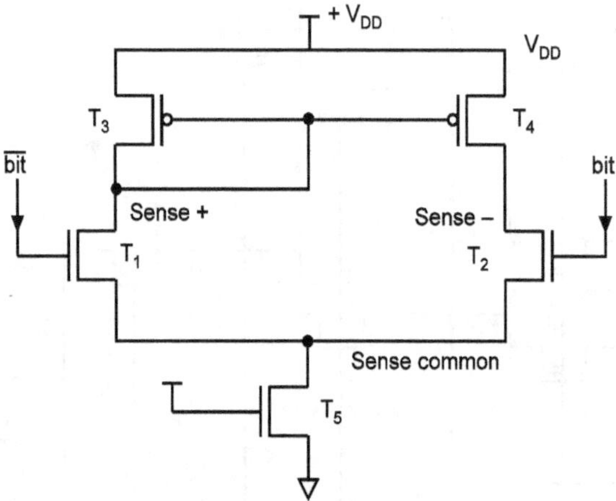

Fig. 10.51: Differential sense amplifier

Differential sense amplifier can consume a significant amount of DC power.

10.12.9 First In First Out Memory (FIFO)

By using basic RAM memory cell, we can construct a variety of special purpose memories. A FIFO memory is generally useful for buffering data between two asynchronous data streams.

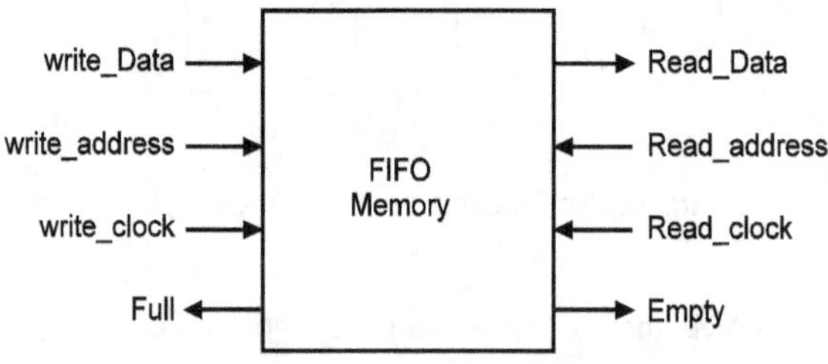

Fig. 10.52: FIFO memory interface signals

Fig. 10.52 shows the interface diagram of the FIFO memory. When write_clock goes high, the data available at the write-data is stored in the specified write_address. Full flag signal is asserted when the FIFO cannot accept input data (FIFO is full).

When Read_clock is active, FIFO can read the data from the Read_data line, from the specified Read_address. Empty flag is used to indicate that there is no data available in the FIFO memory.

10.12.10 Read Only Memory (ROM)

ROM memory can be implemented with only one transistor per bit of storage. ROM retains the state indefinitely, even without power. Basic ROM architecture is shown in Fig. 10.53.

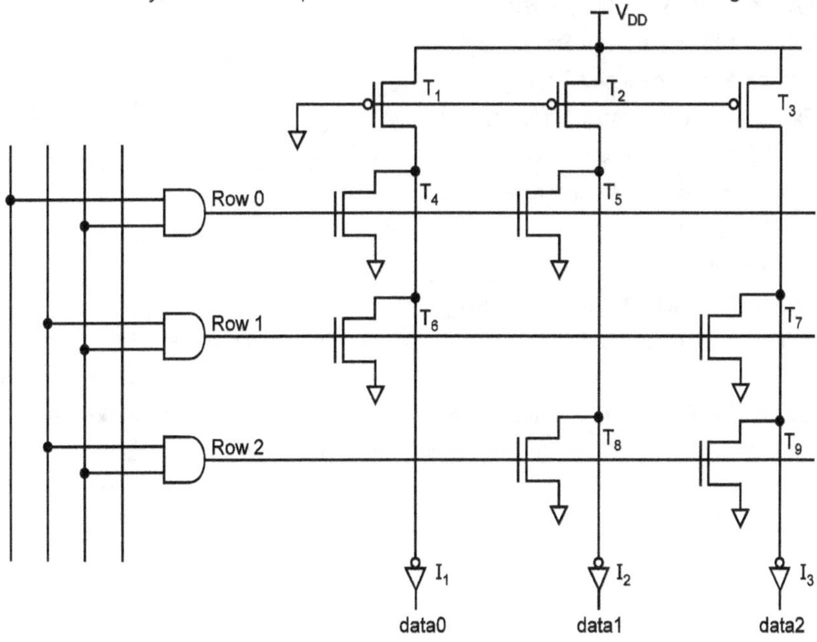

Fig. 10.53: Basic Read Only Memory Architecture

A ROM array is generally implemented as a NOR array. If we require ultra-small ROMs, then NAND array may be used. As shown, T_1, T_2 and T_3 are PMOS transistors, therefore they are always ON (gates are connected to ground). When Row 0 is selected, transistors T_4 and T_5 will turn ON and pulls their drain low. Inverters I_1 and I_2 give high output for Row 0.

QUESTIONS

1. What is SoC? Explain with the help of example.
2. Explain the concept of Soft IP and Hard IP?
3. Explain the concept of single phase clock and two phase clock.
4. What is Clock Distribution? Explain H tree and Balanced tree for Clock Distribution.
5. Write a note on Power Optimization.
6. Explain the concept of Power Distribution.
7. What is Via in CMOS fabrication?
8. What are the different parasitic elements introduced due to wires and vias?
9. What are the different parasitic capacitances associated in CMOS fabrication?
10. Explain Design validation in detail.
11. What is a Floorplanning? Explain in detail.
12. Compare Placement and Routing.
13. Explain Global Routing and Switchbox Routing.
14. What are the functions of Packages? Draw a typical package structure.
15. Write a note on I/O Architecture.
16. Explain input pad design, output pad design and three state pad design.
17. Write a note on DRC.
18. Explain the different memory elements.
19. What is power optimization? Explain the methods of optimization at various levels.

(9 Marks, May 2007)

20. Explain the on-chip I/O architecture in detail.   **(9 Marks, May 2007)**
21. With the help of suitable schematic, explain the architecture of DRAM cell.

(9 Marks, May 2007)

22. What is wire parasitic ? How do parasitics affect the performance of chip?

Appendix - A

VHDL LANGUAGE SUMMARY

Reserved words are in Italic and boldface style. Square brackets enclose optional items. Curly brackets enclose items that are repeated zero or more times. A vertical bar (|) indicates or.

Disclaimer : This VHDL summary is not complete and contains some special cases.

Signal assignment statement : (sequential or concurrent statement)

signal <= [***reject*** pulse-width I ***transport***] expression [***after*** delay-time];

Note : If concurrent, signal value is recomputed every time a change occurs on the right-hand side. If after time-specification is omitted, signal is updated after delta time.

Variable assignment statement : (sequential statement only)

variable := expression;

Note : This can be used only within a process, function, or procedure. The variable is always updated immediately.

Conditional assignment statement: (concurrent statement only)

signal <= expression1 ***when*** condition1

      else expression2 ***when*** condition2

     ....

   [***else*** expression];

Selected signal assignment statement: (concurrent statement only)

with expression ***select***

    signal <= expression1 [***after*** delay_timel ***when*** choice1,

         expression2 [***after*** delay_time] ***when*** choice2,

        ....

       [expressionN [***after*** delay_time]***when others***] ;

entity declaration:

entity entity-name ***is***

    [***generic*** (list-of-generics-and-their-types);]

    [***port*** (interface-signal-declaration);]

    [declarations]

end entity-name ;

Interface-signal declaration :
    list-of-interface-signals: mode type [:= initial-value] ;
    { ; list-of-interface-signals: mode type [:= initial-value] }
    Note : An interface signal can be of mode in, out, inout, or buffer.

Architecture declaration:
architecture architecture-name **of** entity-name **is**
    [declarations]   -- variable declarations not allowed
begin
      architecture-body
end architecture-name ;
Note : The architecture body may contain component-instantiation statements, processes, blocks, assignment statements, procedure calls, etc.

Integer type declaration:
type type-name **is range** integer-range ;

Enumeration type declaration:
type type_name **is** (list-of-names-or-characters) ;

Subtype declaration:
subtype subtype-name **is** type_name [index-or-range-constraint] ;

Variable declaration:
variable list-of-variable-names : type_name [:= initial_value] ;

Signal declaration:
signal list-of-signal-names : type_name [:= initial_value] ;

Constant declaration:
constant constant_name : type_name := constant_value ;

Alias declaration:
alias identifier [:identifier-type] **is** item_name ;
Note : Item-name can be a constant, signal, variable, file, function name, type name etc.

Array type and object declaration:

type array_type_name **is array** index_range **of** element_type ;

signal | **variable** | **constant** array_name : array_type_name[:= initial_value] ;

Process statement (with sensitivity list):

[process-label :] **process** (sensitivity-list)

      [declarations]   -- signal declarations not allowed

        begin

          sequential statements

       end process [process-label];

Note : This form of Process is executed initially and thereafter only when an item on the sensitivity list changes value. The sensitivity list is a list of signals. No wait statements are allowed.

process statement (without sensitivity list):

[process_label :] **process**

        [declarations]   -- signal declarations not allowed

        begin

        sequential statements

       end process [process-label] ;

 Note : This form of Process must contain one or more wait statements. It starts execution immediately and continues until a wait statement is encountered.

wait statements can be of the form:

wait on sensitivity-list ;

wait until boolean-expression ;

wait for time-expression ;

If statement: (sequential statement only)

   if condition **then**

     sequential statements

   { **elsif** condition **then**

      sequential statements }   -- 0 or more elsif clauses may be included

   [**else** sequential statements]

   end if ;

Case statement: (sequential statement only)
case expression **is**
  when choice1 => sequential statements
  when choice2 => sequential statements
  ... ...
  [**when others** => sequential statements]
end case ;

 For loop statement: (sequential statement only)
[loop-label :] **for** identifier **in** range **loop**
      sequential statements
      end loop [loop-label];
Note : you may use **exit** to exit the current loop.

While loop statement: (sequential statement only)
[loop-label :]**while** boolean-expression **loop**
      sequential statements
      end loop [loop-label] ;

Exit statement: (sequential statement only)
exit [loop-label] [**when** condition] ;

Assert statement: (sequential or concurrent statement)
assert boolean-expression
  [**report** string-expression]
  [**severity** severity-level] ;

Report statement: (sequential statement only)
report string-expression
[**severity** severity-level] ;

Procedure declaration:
procedure procedure-name (parameter list) **is**
    [declarations]
begin
    sequential statements
 end procedure-name;
Note : Parameters may be signals, variables, or constants.

Procedure call :

procedure-name (actual-parameter-list) ;

Note : An expression may be used for an actual parameter of mode in; types of the actual parameters must match the types of the formal parameters; open cannot be used.

Function declaration:

function function-name (parameter-list) **return** return-type **is**

      [declarations]

begin

        sequential statements   -- must include **return** return-value ;

end function-name ;

Note : Parameters may be signals or constants.

Function call:

function-name (actual-parameter list)

Note : A function call is used within (or in place of) an expression.

Library declaration:

library list-of-library-names ;

Use statement:

use library_name . package_name . item ;   -- (.item may be .all)

Package declaration:

package package-name **is**

      package declarations

end [**package**] [package-name] ;

Package body:

package body package-name **is**

      package body declarations

end [**package body**] [package name] ;

Component declaration:

component component-name

      [**generic** (list-of-generics-and-their-types);]

port (list-of-interface-signals-and-their-types);

end component;

component instantiation:
label: component-name
[generic map (generic-association-list);) **port map** (list-of-actual-signals);
Note : Use **open** if a component output has no connection.

generate statements:
generate-label: **for** identifier **in** range **generate [begin]**
concurrent statement(s) **end generate** [generate-label];

generate-label: **if** condition **generate [begin]**
concurrent statement(s) **end generate** [generate_label];

file type declaration:
type file-name **is file of** typename;
file declaration: **file** file-name: file_type **[open** mode] **is** "file_pathname";
Note : Mode may be read-mode, write-mode, or append-mode.

INTRODUCTION TO XILINX ISE 6.3i AND MODELSIM TOOLS

DESIGN IMPLEMENTAION

As an example, we will see the different steps to be performed to design FPGA for particular application. The software used for this are XILINX ISE 6.3i (for synthesis and implementation) and MODELSIM (for simulation). The device XC2s50 (FPGA) from xilinx spartan2 family is used as target device.

FPGA Design Flow Overview

The steps for FPGA design are outlined below:

Design Entry

1. Create a new project, or open a current project.
2. Create and add files to your project.
3. Create an implementation constraints (UCF) file (optional).
4. Assign constraints such as timing constraints, pin assignments, and area constraints.

Design Synthesis

1. Set synthesis and/or implementation properties.
2. Simulate the behavior of your design.

   Simulation is commonly run after translate or synthesis (behavioral), after implementation (functional) and after place and route (timing). Other simulation points are after the mapping process.

3. Run the Synthesis Process.
4. Simulate the function of your design.

Design Implementation

1. Implement your design.

   Your design will be synthesized (if it's not already) and implemented (Translate, Map, Place and Route).

2. Review reports for translate, map, place & route, and timing results.
3. Change properties, constraints, and source as necessary, then re-synthesize and re-implement your design. Repeat until design requirements are met.

4. View the placed design in Floorplanner. You can manually place and group logic prior to Mapping with Floorplanner (optional).

5. View the placed and routed design in FPGA Editor. You can manually route sections of the design in FPGA Editor (optional).

6. Set up multiple place and route runs on your design. The tools will identify the best results and keep as many as you specify (optional).

Design Verification

1. Create a programming file (.BIT) to program your FPGA.

2. Generate a PROM, ACE, or JTAG file for debugging or to download to your device.

3. Use IMPACT to program the device with a programming cable.

Starting the ISE Software

For PC users, start ISE from the Start menu by selecting **Start >Programs >Xilinx ISE**

Xilinx>Project Navigator

The window displayed is as shown below.

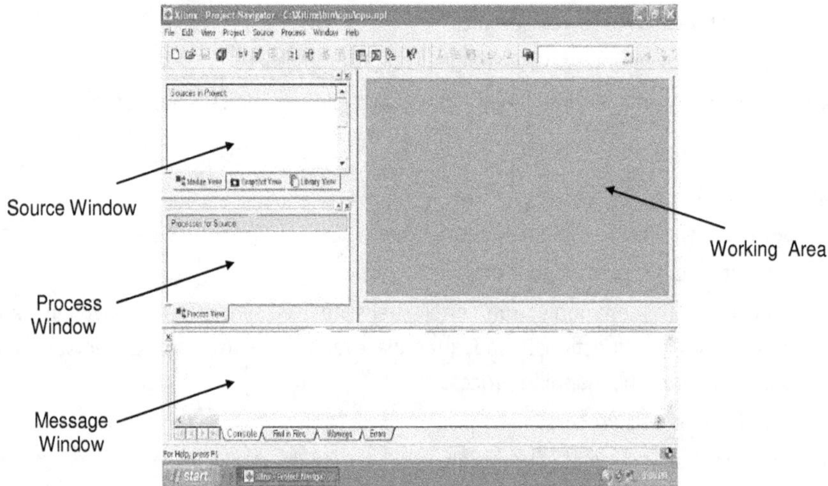

Design Entry (VHDL)

Creating a New Project

A project in ISE is a collection of all files necessary to create and download a design to the selected device. To create a new project:

1. Select **File > New Project**.

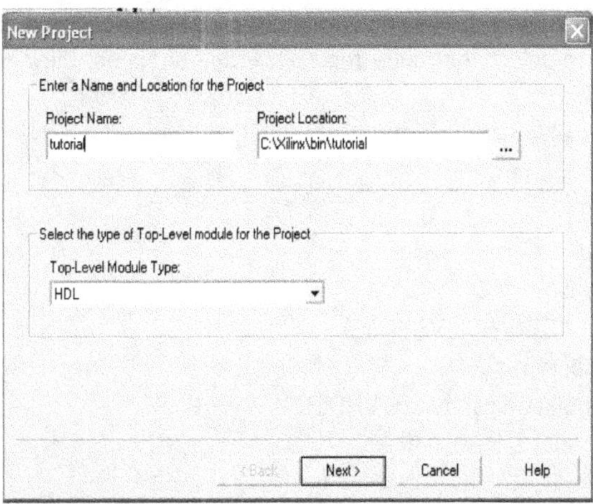

2. In the New Project Wizard dialog box shown above, type the desired location in the Project Location field, or browse to the directory under which you want to create your new project directory using the browse button next to the Project Location field.

3. Enter 'Tutorial' in the Project Name field.

   When you enter 'Tutorial' in the Project Name field, a Tutorial subdirectory is automatically created in the directory path in the Project Location field. For example, for the directory path C:\xilinx\bin, entering the Project Name 'Tutorial' modifies the path as C:\xilinx\bin\Tutorial.

4. Use the pull-down arrow to select HDL from the Top-Level Module Type field. Click in the field to access the pull-down list.

5. Click **Next**

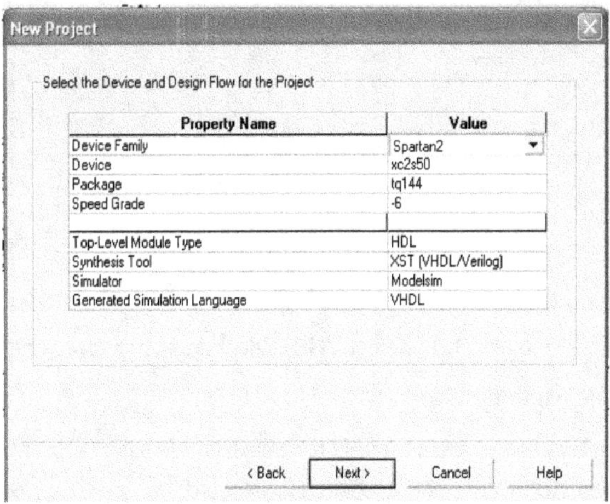

6. In the New Project Wizard Device and Design Flow dialog box, shown above, use the pull-down arrow to select the Value for each Property Name. Click in the field to access the pulldown list.

    Change the values as follows :

    *   Device Family: spartan2
    *   Device: xc2s50
    *   Package: tq144
    *   Speed Grade: -6
    *   Synthesis Tool: XST (VHDL/VERILOG)
    *   Simulator: Modelsim
    *   Generated Simulation Language: VHDL

7. Click **Next**.

8. Click next

9. Click Finish.

10. Next, create a VHDL module for a half adder. To create a half adder module:

    Select **project** > **new source** to add one new source to your project.

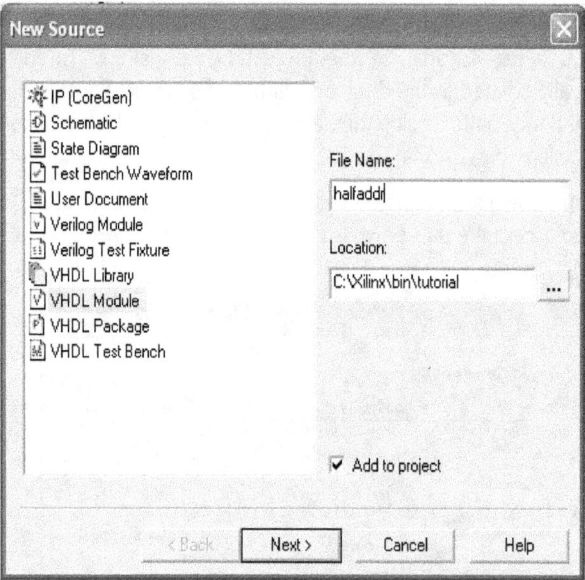

11. In the New Source dialog box, select **VHDL Module** as the source type.

12. Type in the file name 'halfaddr'.

13. Select proper location in location field for this example select c:\xilinx\bin\tutorial
    Verify that the "Add to Project" checkbox is selected.

14. Click **Next**.

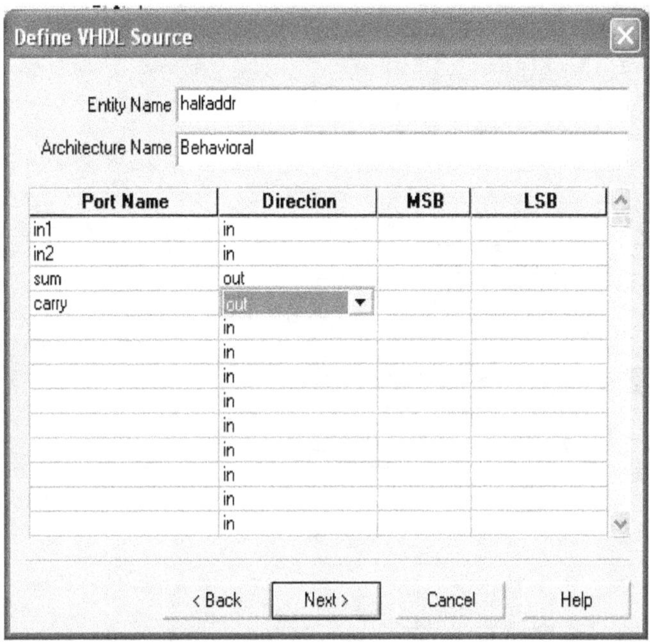

15. Enter entity name and architecture name for VHDL module. Normally the same name is used for entity as that of VHDL file name.

16. In the port name field, enter the names of required ports. For the half adder module, two input ports in1, in2 and two output ports sum, carry can be entered.

17. In the direction field choose proper direction of respective port. To choose the direction, click in the respective field.

18. The MSB and LSB fields are used to enter the width of the port. For example, for the port of type (3 downto 0), enter 3 in the MSB field and 0 in the LSB field.

19. Click Next.

20. Click Finish.

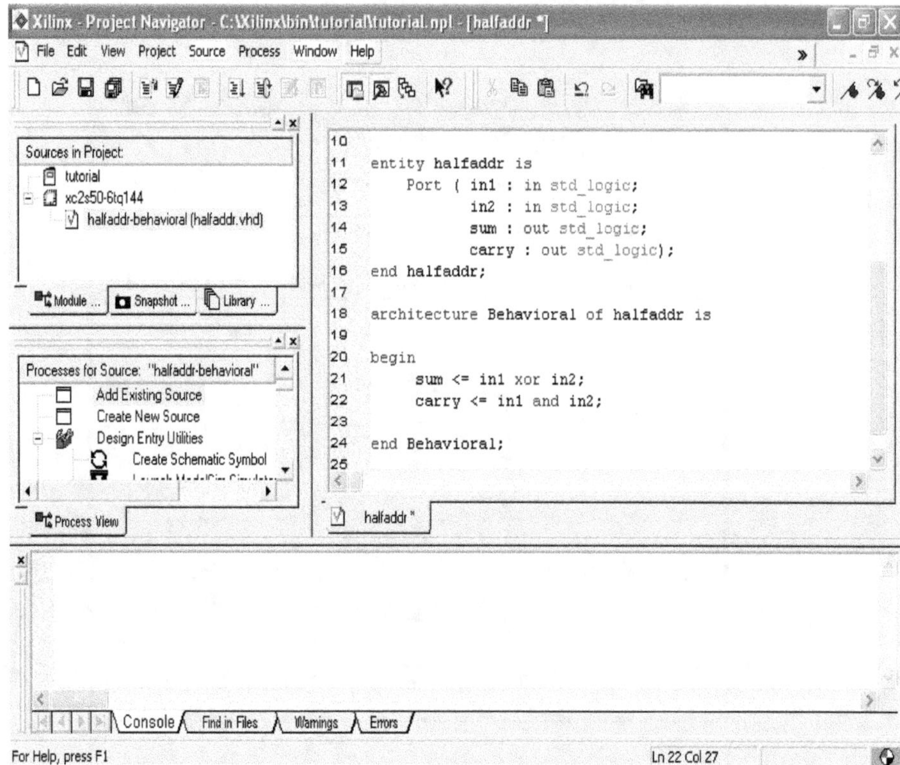

21. In working area, describe the functionality of the design. For the half adder design, enter the following statements after the begin of architecture.

    Sum <= in1 xor in2;

    Carry <= in1 and in2;

22. Save the vhdl file. To save select **file > save**.

Design Constraints

You can use constraints in a design to control or modify the behavior of the timing within a design. Constraints will allow for specific placement of elements defined within a design. You can also control the synthesis process through the use of constraints in the synthesis constraints file.

Creating User constraints file (.UCF)

The constraints entered by the designer are stored in .UCF file

1. To create .UCF file select **Project > new source**

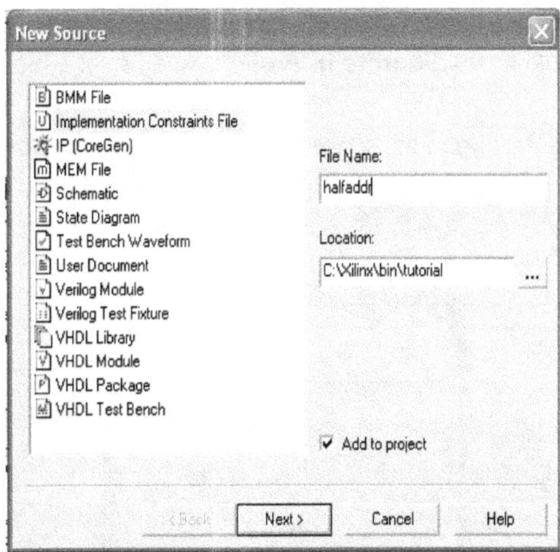

2. Select Implementation Constraint file
3. Enter the file name in the file name field. For example, halfaddr
4. Browse the proper location in the location field. For example, c:\xilinx\bin\tutorial
   Verify that the "Add to Project" checkbox is selected.
5. Click **Next**.
6. Select proper source file. For example select halfaddr.

Double-click on the appropriate process under the **User Constraints** toolbox in the Processes for Source window to enter the desired constraints.

Creating Timing Constraints

You can specify precise timing constraints for your Xilinx designs. You can specify the timing constraints for any nets or paths in your design or you can specify them globally. Constraints such as ALLCLOCKNETS, PERIOD, OFFSET_IN_BEFORE, TIG, MAX_DELAY, OFFSET_OUT_AFTER, CLOCK_SIGNAL and others can be set in Project Navigator using the Xilinx Constraints Editor program.

Timing constraints improve the performance of your design by placing logic closer together so shorter routing resources can be used.

To Create Timing Constraints Using Xilinx Constraints Editor

Double-click on the **Create Timing Constraints** in the **Processes for Source** window to display the Xilinx Constraints Editor.

Assigning Package Pins

You can assign input signals and output signals to package pins in a design module. You can also assign certain IO properties like IO Standards. Project Navigator uses Xilinx PACE to make these assignments.

To Assign Package Pins

1. Select the design module in the **Sources in Project** window for which you want to assign a pin package.
2. Double-click the **Assign Package Pins** process in the **Processes for Source** window.
3. The Xilinx PACE program launches with the file_name.ucf file loaded.

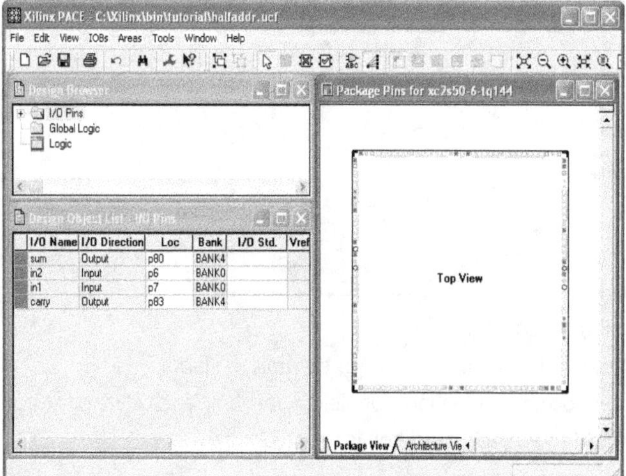

I/O Name	I/O Direction	Loc	Bank	I/O Std.	Vref
sum	Output	p80	BANK4		
in2	Input	p6	BANK0		
in1	Input	p7	BANK0		
carry	Output	p83	BANK4		

4. Enter the pin no. for corresponding I/O ports in respective Loc field in Design Object-I/O Pin window. For half adder example, for input in1 and in2 pin no. 7 and 6 are assigned respectively by entering p7 and p6 in respective Loc field. For output sum and carry, pin no. 80 and 83 are assigned respectively.
5. Save the UCF file.

Creating Area Constraints

You can create area constraints that apply to the placement of logic on your device. You can create area constraints for each type of logic element, such as flip-flops, ROMs and RAMs, FMAPs, F5MAPs, and HMAPs, CLBMAPs, BUFTs, CLBs, IOBs, I/Os, edge decoders, and global buffers in FPGA designs.

To Create Area Constraints Using Xilinx PACE

Double-click on the **Create Area Constraints** process under the **User Constraints** toolbox in the Processes for Source window.

Note Area constraints can also be added to the UCF using the text editor.

Running the Synthesis Process

You can synthesize your design once design files have been created. The synthesis process will check code syntax, and analyze the hierarchy of your design. These processes will ensure your design is optimized for the design architecture you have selected.

Select the source file in the **Sources in Project** window you want to synthesize. To synthesize halfadder design select halfaddr.vhdl in source window.

To Run the Synthesize Process

Double-click on the **Synthesize** process in the **Processes for Source** window.

- All processes necessary to successfully complete the Synthesis process run automatically.
- XST will create an NGC   file and place it in your project directory.
- LeonardoSpectrum or Symplify synthesis tools will create an EDIF   file and place it in your project directory.
- You can view a schematic version of the synthesis results in the View RTL.

Schematic process.

You can perform any of the following :

- View synthesis reports.
- Run the implement design process.
- Generate a post-translate simulation model.
- Perform post-translate (functional) simulation.
- Run the Implementation Design process.

Running the Implement Design Process for FPGA

After you create a design source, the Implement Design process converts the logical design represented in that source (and all sources in the hierarchy from that source down) into a physical file format that can be implemented in the selected target device.

You can use the Implement Design process to run the full ISE suite of implementation tools on your design. You can set properties for running the implementation tools for CPLD and FPGA devices.

Select the design top level module in the **Sources in Project** window.

To Run the Implement Design Process

Double-click on **Implement Design** in the **Processes for Current Source** window.

What to Expect

- The Translate process merges all of the input netlists and design constraint information and outputs a Xilinx NGD (Native Generic Database) file. The output NGD file can then be mapped to the targeted device family.

- The Map process first performs a logical DRC (Design Rule Check) on the design in the NGD file produced by the Translate process. Map then maps the logic to the components (logic cells, I/O cells, and other components) in the target Xilinx FPGA. The output design is an NCD (Native Circuit Description) file physically representing the design mapped to the components in the Xilinx FPGA. The NCD file can then be placed and routed.

- The Place and Route process (PAR) takes a mapped NCD file, places and routes the design, and produces an NCD file to be used by the programming file generator (BitGen).

Properties

Default property values are used for the implementation process unless you modify them. You can set several types of implementation properties. Properties can be set from the Implement Design properties dialog box or from individual processes within the Implement Design process.

The following are the property types that can be set for the Implement Design process :
- Translate Properties
- Map Properties
- Place and Route Properties
- Incremental Design Properties
- Simulation Model Properties
- Post-Place and Route Static Timing Report Properties
- Post-Map Static Timing Report Properties

What to do Next

- Check the Map and PAR report files.
- Analyze power consumption (optional).
- Run **Generate Programming File** process to create a bitstream, module_name.bit and place it in your project directory.

Implementation

- Translate - The Translate process runs NGDBuild to merge all of the input netlists as well as design constraint information into a Xilinx database file.
- Map - The Map program maps a logical design to a Xilinx FPGA.
- Place and Route (PAR) - The PAR program accepts the mapped design, places and routes the FPGA, and produces output for the bitstream generator.
- Floorplanner - The Floorplanner allows you to view a graphical representation of the FPGA, and to view and modify the placed design.
- FPGA Editor - The FPGA Editor allows you view and modify the physical implementation, including routing.
- Timing Analyzer - The Timing Analyzer provides a way to perform static timing analysis on FPGA and CPLD designs. With Timing Analyzer, analysis can be performed immediately after mapping, placing or routing an FPGA design, and after fitting and routing a CPLD design.
- Fit (CPLD only) - The CPLD Fit process maps a netlist(s) into specified devices and creates the JEDEC programming file.
- ChipViewer (CPLD only) - The ChipViewer tool provides a graphical view of the inputs and outputs, macrocell details, equations, and pin assignments.

Device Download and Program File Formatting

- BitGen - The BitGen program receives the placed and routed design and produces a bitstream for Xilinx device configuration.
- iMPACT - The iMPACT tool generates various programming file formats, and subsequently allows you to configure your device.
- XPower - XPower enables you to interactively and automatically analyze power consumption for Xilinx FPGA and CPLD devices.

Launching ModelSim Simulator

You can launch the ModelSim Xilinx Edition (MXE) to simulate your design. Integration with ModelSim XE is provided in ISE. Once you have installed and licensed ModelSim you can use it to simulate your Xilinx design.

ModelSim XE comes with built-in language templates to create VHDL and Verilog code, a test bench wizard to generate common test bench functions and supports the latest Xilinx devices.

Select the top-level module to simulate your entire design, or select a single module to simulate in the **Sources in Project** window.

Double-click on the **Launch ModelSim Simulator** process under the Design Entry toolbox in the **Processes for Source** window.

Default property values are used for this process unless you modify them. You can set the Simulation Properties, Display Properties in the Process Properties dialog box.

ModelSim opens with your design loaded.

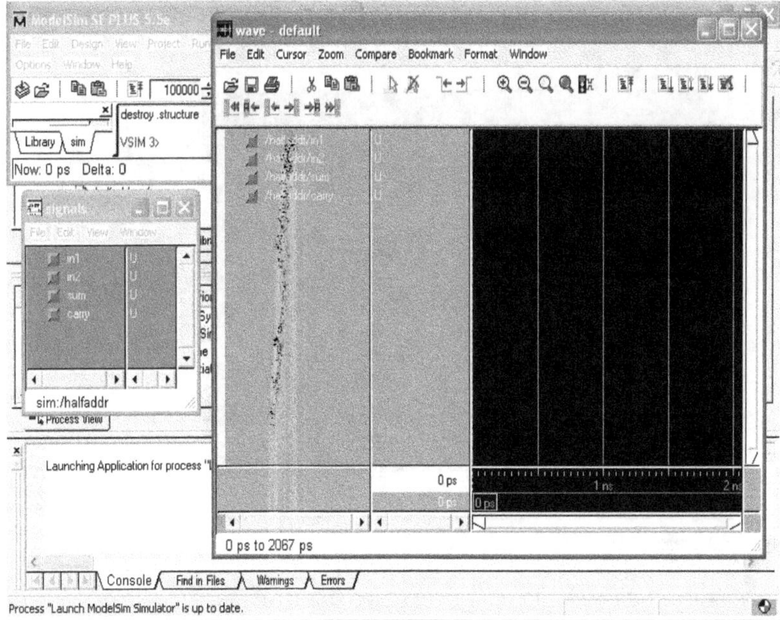

1. Select the input signal (in1) and then select **Edit > Clock** from signal window to create waveform for input signal (in1). Repeat the same for all input signals required to verify the designs.   OR

   Select the input signal (in1) and then select **Edit > Force** from signal window to assign value '1' or '0' for input signal (in1). Repeat the same for all input signals required to verify the designs.

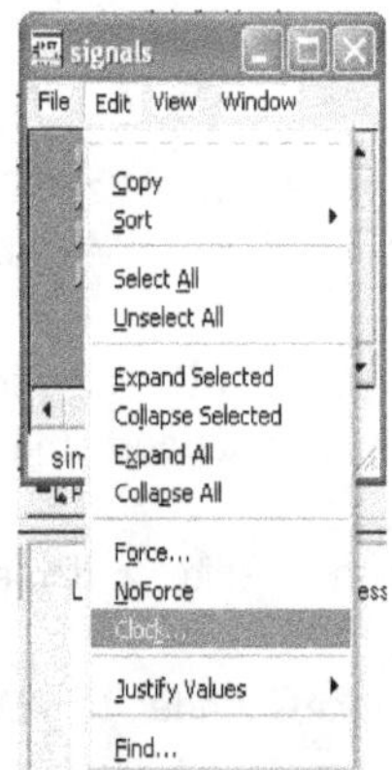

2. Run the simulation selecting **Run** menu from ModelSim window. Simulation process will execute and output results will be displayed in wave window.

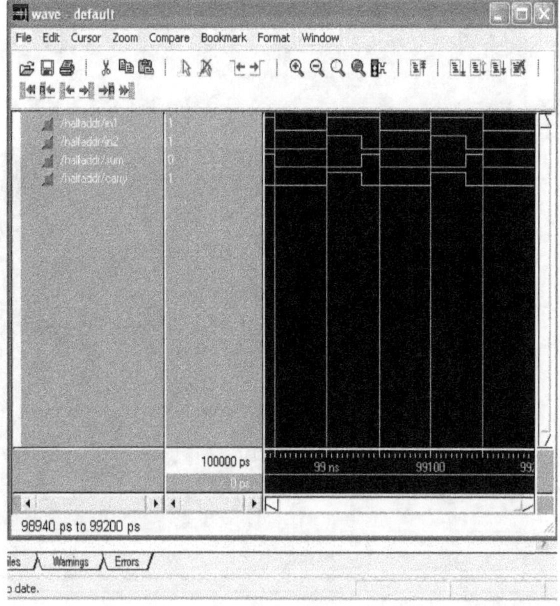

SAMPLE SYNTHESIS REPORT

This report is generated for the VHDL code for the half adder (refer Example 4) by the tool Xilinx ISE 6.3i. The target device used for this is xc2s50-6-tq144.

Release 6.3i - xst G.35
Copyright (c) 1995-2004 Xilinx, Inc. All rights reserved.
--> Parameter TMPDIR set to_projnav
CPU : 0.00 / 1.45 s | Elapsed : 0.00 / 2.00 s

--> Parameter xsthdpdir set to ./xst
CPU : 0.00 / 1.45 s | Elapsed : 0.00 / 2.00 s

--> Reading design: halfaddr.prj

TABLE OF CONTENTS
1) Synthesis Options Summary
2) HDL Compilation
3) HDL Analysis
4) HDL Synthesis
5) Advanced HDL Synthesis
    5.1)   HDL Synthesis Report
6) Low Level Synthesis
7) Final Report
    7.1)   Device utilization summary
    7.2)   TIMING REPORT

```
===============================================================
         *            Synthesis Options Summary            *
===============================================================
---- Source Parameters
Input File Name                   : halfaddr.prj
Input Format                      : mixed
Ignore Synthesis Constraint File  : NO
Verilog Include Directory         :
```

---- Target Parameters

Output File Name	:	halfaddr
Output Format	:	NGC
Target Device	:	xc2s50-6-tq144

---- Source Options

Top Module Name	:	halfaddr
Automatic FSM Extraction	:	YES
FSM Encoding Algorithm	:	Auto
FSM Style	:	lut
RAM Extraction	:	Yes
RAM Style	:	Auto
ROM Extraction	:	Yes
ROM Style	:	Auto
Mux Extraction	:	YES
Mux Style	:	Auto
Decoder Extraction	:	YES
Priority Encoder Extraction	:	YES
Shift Register Extraction	:	YES
Logical Shifter Extraction	:	YES
XOR Collapsing	:	YES
Resource Sharing	:	YES
Multiplier Style	:	lut
Automatic Register Balancing	:	No

---- Target Options

Add IO Buffers	:	YES
Global Maximum Fanout	:	100
Add Generic Clock Buffer(BUFG)	:	4
Register Duplication	:	YES
Equivalent register Removal	:	YES
Slice Packing	:	YES
Pack IO Registers into IOBs	:	auto

```
---- General Options
Optimization Goal               :  Speed
Optimization Effort             :  1
Keep Hierarchy                  :  NO
Global Optimization             :  AllClockNets
RTL Output                      :  Yes
Write Timing Constraints        :  NO
Hierarchy Separator             :  _
Bus Delimiter                   :  <>
Case Specifier                  :  maintain
Slice Utilization Ratio         :  100
Slice Utilization Ratio Delta   :  5

---- Other Options
lso                             :  halfaddr.lso
Read Cores                      :  YES
cross_clock_analysis            :  NO
verilog2001                     :  YES
Optimize Instantiated Primitives :  NO
tristate2logic                  :  NO
```

==

==
              *   HDL Compilation   *
==

Compiling vhdl file C:/Xilinx/bin/tutorial/halfaddr.vhd in Library work.
Entity <halfaddr> (Architecture <Behavioral>) compiled.

==
              *   HDL Analysis   *
==

Analyzing Entity <halfaddr> (Architecture <Behavioral>).
Entity <halfaddr> analyzed.Unit <halfaddr> generated.

==
              *   HDL Synthesis   *
==

Synthesizing Unit <halfaddr>.
    Related source file is C:\Xilinx\bin\tutorial/halfaddr.vhd.
    Found 1-bit xor2 for signal <sum>.
Unit <halfaddr> synthesized.

```
==========================================================================
            *            Advanced HDL Synthesis            *
==========================================================================
```

Advanced RAM inference ...
Advanced multiplier inference ...
Advanced Registered AddSub inference ...
Dynamic shift register inference ...

```
==========================================================================
```

HDL Synthesis Report

Macro Statistics
XORs   : 1
 1-bit xor2   : 1

```
==========================================================================


==========================================================================
            *            Low Level Synthesis            *
==========================================================================
```

Optimizing unit <halfaddr> ...
Loading device for application Xst from file 'v50.nph' in environment C:/Xilinx.

Mapping all equations...
Building and optimizing final netlist ...
Found area constraint ratio of 100 (+ 5) on block halfaddr, actual ratio is 0.

```
==========================================================================
            *            Final Report            *
==========================================================================
```

Final Results
RTL Top Level Output File Name   :   halfaddr.ngr
Top Level Output File Name   :   halfaddr
Output Format   :   NGC
Optimization Goal   :   Speed
Keep Hierarchy   :   NO

Design Statistics
IOs   :   4

Cell Usage :
BELS   :   2
LUT2   :   2
IO Buffers   :   4
IBUF   :   2
OBUF :   2
==

Device Utilization Summary :

    Selected Device : 2s50tq144-6

    Number of Slices: 1 out of   768   0%
    Number of 4 input LUTs: 2 out of 1536   0%
    Number of bonded IOBs: 4 out of   96   4%

==
                          TIMING REPORT

NOTE : THESE TIMING NUMBERS ARE ONLY A SYNTHESIS ESTIMATE.
FOR ACCURATE TIMING INFORMATION PLEASE REFER TO THE TRACE REPORT
GENERATED AFTER PLACE-and-ROUTE.

Clock Information:

No clock signals found in this design

Timing Summary:

Speed Grade: -6

Minimum period: No path found
Minimum input arrival time before clock: No path found
Maximum output required time after clock: No path found
Maximum combinational path delay: 8.234ns

Timing Detail:

All values displayed in nanoseconds (ns)

Timing constraint: Default path analysis
  Delay: 8.234ns (Levels of Logic = 3)
  Source: in1 (PAD)
  Destination: carry (PAD)

  Data Path: in1 to carry
                        Gate   Net
    Cell:in->out   fanout Delay Delay Logical Name (Net Name)
    -- -------------

    IBUF:I->O   2   0.776   1.206   in1_IBUF (in1_IBUF)
    LUT2:I0->O   1   0.549   1.035   carry1 (carry_OBUF)
    OBUF:I->O   4.668   carry_OBUF (carry)

        Total   8.234ns (5.993ns logic, 2.241ns route)
                         (72.8% logic, 27.2% route)

==
  CPU : 4.76 / 7.39 s | Elapsed : 5.00 / 8.00 s

-->

Total memory usage is 54556 kilobytes

VLSI DESIGN & TECHNOLOGY
B.E. (E & T/C)

Time : 3 Hrs.   **May 2008**   **Max. Marks : 100**

Section - I

1. (a) What do you mean by configuration ? Explain with suitable example. (8)
    (b) Write VHDL code for 4 bit shift register for SISO and SIPO operation. (8)

OR

2. (a) What is the need of attributes ? Explain any two attributes in detail. (8)
    (b) Write VHDL code for 4 bit counter. Write separate function to check clock. (8)
3. (a) What is metastability ? How to avoid ? (8)
    (b) Write VHDL code for traffic light controller. (8)

OR

4. (a) Explain with suitable examples Static and Dynamic Timing Analysis. (8)
    (b) Write VHDL code for lift controller. (8)
5. (a) With suitable schematic explain Antifuse, SRAM and flash technologies for PLD. (9)
    (b) Explain the architecture of CPLD in detail. (9)

OR

6. (a) What is the selection criterion of CPLD/FPGA in an application. (9)
    (b) With suitable schematic explain the architecture of EPGA in detail. (9)

Section - II

7. (a) What is the need of power optimization ? Explain the techniques. (8)
    (b) Explain SCR and DRC rules in brief. (8)

OR

8. (a) Draw the schematic and explain I/O architecture. (8)
    (b) What are techniques of DRAM cell architecture ? (8)
9. (a) Draw the low frequency and high frequency equivalent model of MOSFET. Explain body effect. (8)
    (b) What is technology scaling ? What are the effects of it ? (8)
10. (a) Design CMOS logic for Y = ABC + D. Calculate area needed on chip. (8)
    (b) Explain power dissipations in brief. Derive an expression for power delay product. (8)
11. (a) Why is DFT needed ? Explain in brief with suitable example. (9)
    (b) What are the types of fault ? Explain with schematic. (9)

OR

12. (a) With the help of suitable schematic explain the architecture of TAP controller. (9)
    (b) What is BIST ? Why is it needed ? Design BIST for 4 bit synchronous counter. (9)

❖❖❖

VLSI DESIGN & TECHNOLOGY
B.E. (Electronics)

Time : 3 Hrs.   **May 2008**   **Max. Marks : 100**

Section - I

1. (a) Write VHDL code for 4 : 1 mux. Also write test bench for it. (10)
   (b) List synthesizable and non-synthesizable VHDL statements. (6)

OR

2. (a) Explain complete VLSI design flow of a EDA tools. (10)
   (b) Write VHDL code of 4 bit shift registers. (6)
3. (a) Draw SM chart for UART transmitter and write VHDL code for it. (13)
   (b) Write a note on "metastability". (5)

OR

4. (a) Draw state diagram and write VHDL code for traffic light controller. (13)
   (b) Write in short state minimization. (5)
5. (a) Draw block diagram and explain the architecture of CPLD. (12)
   (b) Write in short four specification of CPLD. (4)

OR

6. (a) Differentiate PLD, CPLD and EPGA. (8)
   (b) Draw only the block diagram of EPGA. (8)

Section - II

7. (a) Explain Global and switch box routing. (8)
   (b) Write short note on SDRAM and FIFO. (8)

OR

8. (a) Explain SRC and DRC. (8)
   (b) Explain off chip connection and I/O Architecture. (8)
9. (a) Explain in detail VI characteristics of CMOS inverter. (10)
   (b) Explain power dissipation and power delay product. (8)

OR

10. (a) Derive $(W/L)_P = 2 (W/L)_N$. (10)
    (b) Draw CMOS NAND2 and NOR2 gates. (8)
11. (a) Explain full and partial scan. (8)
    (b) Explain stuck at fault model. (8)
12. Write short notes on : (16)
    (a) DFT.
    (b) JTAG.
    (c) BIST.
    (d) TAP controller.

❖❖❖

VLSI DESIGN & TECHNOLOGY
B.E. (E & T/C)

Time : 3 Hrs.　　　　　　**May 2009**　　　　　　**Max. Marks : 100**

Section - I

1. (a) Design, write VHDL code and test bench for realization of EX-NOR gate functionality using 2 : 1 multiplexer.　　(9)

   (b) Differentiate :　　(9)

   (i) Synchronous reset Vs Asynchronous reset.

   (ii) Signal Vs Variable.

   (iii) Inertial delay Vs Transport delay.

OR

2. (a) Write VHDL code and test bench to perform tabulate operation for mode M and output Y and Z, where A is 3-bit binary input data.　　(12)

M	Function
0	$Y = Y^2 + 16$
1	$Z = A * 03$

   (b) Explain with example : (i) Delta delay, (ii) Transport delay, (iii) Interial delay.　　(6)

3. For following RTL shown in Fig. 3 (a) design FSM and write VHDL code and test bench.　　(16)

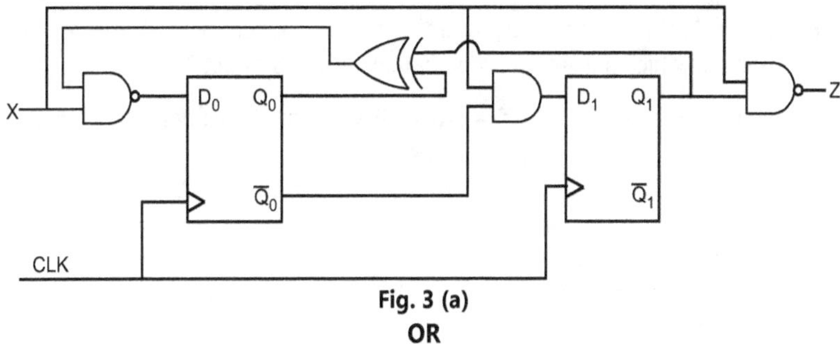

Fig. 3 (a)

OR

4. Draw FSM for　　(16)

   (a) JK Flip Flop.

   (b) SR Flip Flop.

   Write VHDL code for both FSM along with their test bench which will cover all conditions.

5. (a) Expalin antifusable FPGA architecture ?　　(8)

   (b) Differentiate FPGA Vs ASIC.　　(8)

OR

6. (a) Explain selection criteria for FPGA design.　　(8)

   (b) Explain with neat schematic generic CPLD architecture.　　(8)

Section - II

7. (a) Draw neat schematic diagram for SRAM layout showing placement of SRAM cell, row decoder, column decoder, read circuit, write circuit and buffers.   (9)

   (b) Explain the terms :   (9)
   - (i) Global routing.
   - (ii) Switch box routing.
   - (iii) Power distribution.

OR

8. (a) Explain with waveform that how much clock skew between CLK1 and CLK2 can be tolerated in following circuit shown in Fig. 8 (a) when
   - (i) CLK1 delayed after CLK2.
   - (ii) CLK2 delayed after CLK1.   (9)

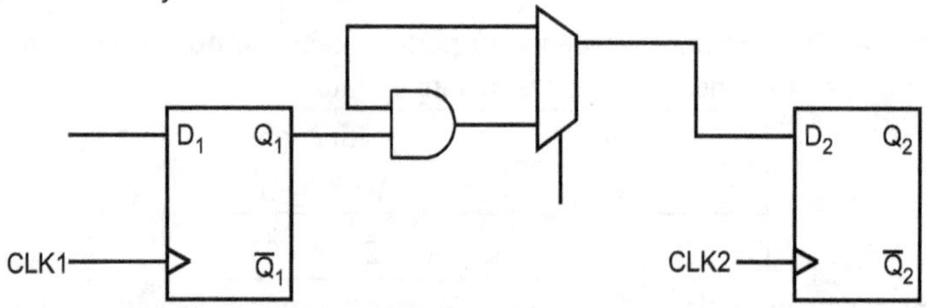

Fig. 8 (a)

   (b) What are the problems in one phase clock ? Explain the concept of two phase clock with example.   (9)

9. (a) Explain in detail static and dynamic power dissipation. What are the main components which make power dissipation in CMOS circuit ?   (8)

   (b) Design CMOS logic gates for $Y = \bar{A}B + A\bar{B}$. Calculated area needed on chip.   (8)

OR

10. (a) Explain :
   - (i) Body effect.
   - (ii) Transmission gate.

   (b) Why NAND is preferred over NOR ? Why pull up is designed from PMOS and pull down network from NMOS ?   (8)

11. (a) Differentiate :   (8)
   - (i) White Box Vs Black Box testing.
   - (ii) Partial scan Vs Full scan.

   (b) What are objectives of boundary scan technique ? Draw state diagram for TAP controller.   (8)

OR

12. (a) Explain why model faults ? Explain different fault model with schematics ?   (8)

   (b) Explain DFT in detail. How it can be categorized ? Where it is useful ?   (8)

❖❖❖

VLSI DESIGN & TECHNOLOGY
B.E. (Electronics)

Time : 3 Hrs.   **May 2009**   **Max. Marks : 100**

Section - I

1. (a) What is the necessity of test benches ? State types of test benches and explain any one with suitable example. (8)

   (b) Explain the following delays and write VHDL code for the following with an example :

   (i) Transport delay modeling.

   (ii) Inertial delay modeling. (8)

OR

2. (a) Explain the VLSI design flow from design entry to downloading. (8)

   (b) Write sequential and concurrent VHDL descriptions, to describe a 2 : 4 decoder. (8)

3. (a) Draw state diagram and write VHDL code for traffic light controller controlling traffic for two lane intersection. (10)

   (b) What are the effects of synchronous clock on power dissipation, noise in FSM with examples. (8)

OR

4. (a) Draw state machine chart of UART transmitter and write VHDL code for UART Baud rate generator for baud rate of 9600 assuming system clock of 8 MHz. (10)

   (b) What is metastability ? State the solutions. Explain any one solution in detail. (8)

5. (a) What size lookup table (LUT) is required, if we want to implement two independent logic functions of 5 variables. (2)

   (b) When implementing an 8 bit counter in an FPGA. How many CLBs are required ? (2)

   (c) Explain (with diagram) how is a 2 : 1 mux implemented in an FPGA. (4)

   (d) What are the merits of FPGA/CPLD over other logic implementing devices ? (8)

OR

6. (a) On FPGAs that use LUTs, we can built larger SRAMs out of individual LUTs. However, most FPGAs include monolithic blocks of SRAMs. What are the advantages of a monolithic SRAM block over a SRAM built from LUTs ? (4)

(b) A PLL, DLL on an FPGA accomplishes two functions. What are these functions ?   (4)

(c) What is the difference between logic implemented in CPLD and logic implemented in FPGA ?   (8)

Section - II

7. (a) Explain the two methods of clock distribution.   (8)

(b) Explain the parasitics involved in routing matrix. How to achieve EMI immune design ?   (8)

OR

8. (a) Explain SRC and DRC.   (8)

(b) Explain power distribution and how to achieve power optimization ?   (8)

9. (a) Derive the relationship between width of n and p channel MOSFET in an inverter. Why sizing is so important ?   (8)

(b) Why is the Pull up of size 2W and Pull Down of size W in an inverter considered in design ?   (4)

(c) Draw 3 input CMOS NOR gate. Evaluate the sizing of transistors ?   (6)

OR

10. (a) If all transistors were of the same size in a gate, how would it affect the performance ?   (4)

(b) Draw 3 input CMOS NAND gate. Evaluate the sizing of transistors ?   (6)

(c) Write short note on CMOS layout.   (8)

11. (a) Explain stuck at fault methods.   (8)

(b) Explain TAP controller with its state diagram.   (8)

OR

12. (a) What is the need of design for testability ? Explain in short different types of faults.(8)

(b) What is need of boundary scan ? Give suitable examples.   (8)

◆◆◆

DECEMBER 2009

3 Hours   **100 Marks**

Section - I

1. Write VHDI code for mux 8 : 1 using any two modelings and also write test bench for it.   (16)

OR

2. (a) Explain VLSI design flow.   (8)

(b) Write VHDL Code for Decoder 2 : 4.   (8)

3.   Draw SM chart and write VHDL code for VART transmitter.   (16)

OR

4.   By considering suitable examples, explain different techniques of state minimization.

(16)

5.   Draw block diagram and explain detail architecture of CPLD.   (18)

OR

6.   Draw block diagram and explain detail architecture of FPGA.   (18)

| Section - II |

7.   Explain different types of memory.   (16)

OR

8.   Explain different types of power distribution and optimization techniques in CMOS VLSI circuits.   (16)

9.   What is scaling? What are different scaling parameters? Explain constant field and constant voltage scaling.   (16)

OR

10. With respect to VTC explain the operation of CMOS inverter. Also derive, for CMOS inverter, $[W/L]_P = 2\ [W/L]_N$ (16)

11. (a) What is fault coverage? Explain with examples different stuck faults.   (9)

     (b) Explain with block diagram full and partial scan.   (9)

OR

12. Write short notes on :   (18)
     (a) TAP controller.
     (b) DFT.
     (c) BIST

◈◈◈

MAY 2010

3 Hours   **100 Marks**

| Section - I |

1.   Using structural modeling draw schematic and write VHDL code of 16:1 Mux by 4 : 1 Mux (as a component).   (16)

OR

2.   (a) List different synthesizable VHDL statements.   (4)

     (b) Explain function and procedure with VHDL examples.   (12)

3.   Draw state diagram and write VHDL code for Traffic light control.   (16)

OR

4. (a) What is metastability and synchronization? (6)

    (b) Write VHDL code for Lift control. (10)

5. Draw detail block diagram and explain different sub-blocks of CPLD. (18)

OR

6. (a) Draw only the block diagram FPGA and explain difference between CPLD and FPGA. (12)

    (b) Write specifications of CPLD and FPGA. (6)

Section - II

7. (a) What is clock skew and jitter? Explain different techniques of clock distribution. (12)

    (b) Define global and switch box routing. (4)

OR

8. (a) Explain the classification of memory. (12)

    (b) Define off chip connection. (4)

9. (a) What is technology scaling? Explain different scaling techniques. (12)

    (b) Explain what is body effect in MOSFET. (4)

OR

10. (a) Explain different power dissipation in CMOS inverter, also define power delay product. (12)

    (b) Draw schematic and explain Transmission Gate. (4)

11. (a) What is the need of DFT? With schematic explain different faults. (12)

    (b) Define controllability and observability. (16)

OR

12. Write short notes on : (18)

    (a) TAP Controller.

    (b) BIST.

    (c) JTAG.

◊◊◊

MAY 2011
B.E. (E & T/C)

3 Hours **100 Marks**

Section - I

1. (a) What do you mean by multiple drivers ? Give suitable example and explain how to solve it by resolution function. (9)

   (b) Write VHDL code for 4 bit latch. Write test bench for it. (9)

OR

2. (a) Explain high level design flow in detail. What constraints can user give ? At what levels ? (9)

   (b) Write optimum VHDL code for 4 bit adder and test bench for it. (9)

3. (a) Draw state diagram for 11100 Moore sequence detector and write VHDL code for it. (8)

   (b) What are the methods of encoding FSM ? Compare these methods. (8)

OR

4. (a) What are the advantages of asynchronous over synchronous machine ? Explain each in brief. (8)

   (b) Draw state diagram of lift controller for ground plus two floors. Write optimum VHDL code for it. (8)

5. (a) How does half adder logic get implement in CPLD and FPGA differently ? Explain with suitable schematic. (8)

   (b) Draw the generic block diagram of FPGA and explain in brief. Explore I/O block in detail. (8)

OR

6. (a) What are the merits and limitations of CPLD ? Explain each in brief. (8)

   (b) Draw the internal details of Macrocell and explain in brief. (8)

Section - II

7. (a) Draw DRAM cells made up of different number of MOSFET. Explain Write and Read operation of any one of them. (9)

   (b) What are global and switch box routing ? Explain each in brief. What are the challenges involved? (9)

OR

8. (a) Why are power distribution and power optimization so important ? Explain the techniques of each in brief. (9)

   (b) Compare CMOS based SRAM, DRAM, SDRAM and FLASH architectures in detail. (9)

9. (a) Draw high frequency equivalent circuit of MOSFET. Mention body effect and device parasitic parameters. Comment on these parasitics. How do they affect on performance ?   (8)

    (b) Certain CMOS logic has static power dissipation of 100 μW. What is the total power dissipation of the same circuit if operates at 10 MHz, V_{DD} = 1 V, load of 100 pF ?   (8)

OR

10. (a) Design CMOS logic for output Y = AB + CDE. Calculate width of each device. Comment on this transistor sizing.   (8)

    (b) What are the advantages of Transmission Gate ? Draw 8:1 MUX using transmission gates and compare with conventional method.   (8)

11. (a) What is the need of boundary scan ? Explain boundary scan technique in detail.   (8)

    (b) What is the necessity of DFT ? What is BIST ? Explain with suitable example.   (8)

OR

12. (a) Explain stuck at faults in detail.   (8)

    (b) Draw the state diagram of TAP controller.   (8)

◈◈◈